the hands pulling the strings

More by Brooke Shaffer

The Timekeeper Chronicles

The Chivalrous Welshman
Time to Kill
Tick Tock
Windup
Stopwatch
Free Time
Leap Second
Imminence (Summer 2022)

The Hands of Time
In the Hands of the Enemy
The Hands Pulling the Strings
The Hand Holding the Knife (Winter 2022)

The Lone Wolf
Wolf Pack
Alpha Wolf (Spring 2022)

Singles
Of Saints and Sinners

the hands pulling the strings

Book Two of The Hands of Time
The Timekeeper Chronicles

Brooke Shaffer

Black Bear Publishing

Published in Michigan by Black Bear Publishing.

This novel is a work of fiction. Names, characters, places, and incidents are either products of the author's imagination or used fictitiously. All characters are fictional and any similarity to persons living or dead is purely coincidental.

ISBN:
Hardcover: 978-1-953113-14-6
Softcover: 978-1-953113-15-3
eBook: 978-1-953113-16-0
Audiobook: 978-1-953113-17-7

For Probie Taylor

1 | Fifanarahana ny Fifampiraharahana

The Caves of Meroian, 1964

Contracts and Negotiations

Rifun hadn't been around when Julianna made up the fake invitations, nor when Cassius sent them out. He hadn't been there to see the Auctionhouse as it was filling up with all the Tacagan leaders and their hired Gentleman Killers. He had not witnessed Cassius setting up the charges, Disguising them as ordinary objects. He had not been present for Cassius' speech, Disguised as Julianna and promising to show those gathered something they had never seen before.

He hadn't been there when Cassius dropped the Disguise and set off the charges. He hadn't seen the few survivors of the initial explosions get skewered and picked off by any number of other booby traps rigged up around the room. Nor had he seen Cassius fend off a particularly brutal Gentleman Killer who had evidently forgotten, momentarily, how to be a gentleman. He also hadn't seen Cassius threaten the Auctioneer and send him to warn everyone of the might of the Cult of the Akari.

He had seen none of it, but he'd heard all about it.

Cassius had returned to the abandoned temple in the ancient ruins that the Cult of the Akari used as their base camp. The dark-skinned man had been covered in ash and blood and other bodily fluids, looking no worse for wear except maybe he'd gone out for a jog. That was all death and killing was to him: an exercise. A game, even. He relished it, savored it. He became sexually excited at the prospect of death. Assassinating five hundred Tacagan elites and a good handful of the higher-ranked Gentleman Killers was nothing to him. It did not register in any way on his moral compass, assuming he even had one or consulted it from time to time.

Rifun hadn't really been paying attention at the time and had no idea what Cassius had been up to, though he'd been the one in charge of shaking things up. Rifun had simply found Cassius in his room, cleaning his knives the same way a normal man might clean his tools after working on some project or other.

That was when Cassius had detailed everything that had gone on, with no prompting from Rifun. It was unclear whether he was just recounting events, or if he'd hoped to provoke some sort of response; the man's words and posture had been very matter-of-fact, which was perhaps the most frightening part.

As he'd detailed the carnage, Rifun was transported back to his fighting days, his time in the Malagasy army, but especially his days as a nationalist freedom fighter, hoping to win independence for his home country of Madagascar. He recalled how the French had rounded up entire villages, innocent men, women, and children, locked them in wagons and set them on fire, or machine gunned them until everything simply collapsed in on itself. He remembered the sights, and he remembered the smells. The memories haunted him at night, and sometimes during the day. Listening to Cassius had made him wonder whether the mercenary haunted his own nightmares.

He'd been saved from having to react or engage in conversation by the appearance of Julianna. She wanted to know how things went, so Rifun just left the two of them to it and returned to his own room. It wasn't that he disapproved of what had happened necessarily—he had no qualms about deposing tyrants and dictators—but it was the lack of reaction and emotion from Cassius that spooked him. Sometimes it seemed as though he just did not feel, and then when he did feel, it was for all the wrong things.

Rifun had been brought into the Cult of the Akari to kill Cassius, and he'd had the opportunity on several occasions. And while he wouldn't have a problem with seeing the madman disappear, he'd learned long ago that madness also occasionally served a purpose. They were trying to overthrow a corrupt industry. That was not going to be a clean endeavor. If extreme measures had to be taken, why not use someone whose mind was already twisted and warped, rather than sacrifice countless others to achieve the same ends? Work smarter, not harder.

This wasn't to say they could rely only on Cassius. The man was still human and had no shortage of enemies. That was where Rifun came in. While Rifun considered himself a formidable opponent in Time, Akari, and hand-to-hand combat, he preferred to win his battles through manipulation and negotiation. When using force, people tended to blame the one with the heavy hand. In negotiations, people had only themselves to blame if things went wrong. Maybe it was a mean, deceitful way of doing business, but he preferred to think of it as the forced evolution of getting people to think for themselves and consider logic on a little higher plane. It was usually trial by fire.

It had certainly been trial by fire for him as he resisted the urge to touch the bald spot on the back of his head, covered by his otherwise long hair. The bald spot was twisted scar tissue from where he'd taken a pickax to the head, the result of being a hotheaded young man easily provoked to anger. It had blinded him for a time, but it had only served to introduce him to the Time industry, and the spirits had been kind enough to partially restore his vision through blindsight. He did not physically see anything, but because his eyes still functioned normally, he saw everything as an imprint on his mind, like how a man might close his eyes and picture something familiar.

He'd learned from that incident. He'd trained to be stronger, faster, but he'd also trained his mind. He had to, lest the horrors of watching his people burn alive and being tortured in prison for a decade overwhelm him.

He pulled his shirt on, covering the scars he bore from that time, most of them burn wounds. Used to be that he wore long sleeves because he was ashamed of his body and the criss-crossing scars. Now he did so for more practical reasons. The Caves of Meroian where the ruins were located were deep underground and could get rather chilly. Furthermore, he was preparing to meet with Korin leaders on Irig to discuss alliance potential, and the place where they would be meeting was rumored to be rather cold also.

He turned as the door opened and Julianna, one of the original founders of the Cult of the Akari, stepped inside. She was a prim and proper woman, very practical in the way she walked and dressed herself, as if she'd just walked out of a photograph of a schoolteacher whose use of the ruler was very well known. The scars on her face—perfect squares, as if a hot wire mesh had been burned into her skin—made her both menacing and pitiable at the same time. Those scars had been delivered to her personally by Cassius.

But for all that, Julianna was an emotional woman, as all women tended to be. It was part of the reason she had convinced her husband to leave the Akarin—the Cult's parent group—and start the Cult. It was part of the reason she had those scars in the first place, because she had loved her husband to death, almost literally, and underestimated Cassius' bloodlust. Even now as she tried to be calm and logical, there was still the unmistakable current of emotion in her gaze, and her scars did not allow for small facial movements to go unnoticed.

"Off to meet our allies?" she inquired pleasantly enough.

"And hope to keep them as allies and not enemies, yes," Rifun replied steadily. "The Korin today, the Turitians tomorrow."

"Any word from the Borelians?"

"No, but I expect it won't be long before we do."

"Let's just hope Cassius' little stunt impressed them enough to want to be allies rather than slavers."

He gave her a sideways glance. "Borelians are always slavers. They always look out for themselves first, and pay us inferior species no mind. The glory of Brelix or nothing. It's just a matter of convincing them that allying with us is in their best interests, better than simply enslaving us all."

Julianna nodded slowly. "Well, we could all say many things about Cassius, few of them pretty or gentle, but he has made it abundantly clear that he will be no one's slave ever again. I expect he would be, or try to be, a one-man army if the Borelians ever came looking for our blood."

Rifun could only agree, though he did it grudgingly. He was trying to solve a puzzle to disarm a nuclear weapon, but the only pieces he had to work with were ignition sources. Somehow, he had to arrange them in such a way that they canceled each other out or else killed each other without taking him with them. But he was confident that he could do it, as long as he didn't try to rush anything, and as long as he allowed himself to be a little flexible in his plans.

"You expect the rest to ally with us, then?" Julianna questioned.

He looked at her. "We're about to find out."

With that, he departed, leaving his room and the ancient temple now used as an officers building. The ruins were coming back to life, the recruits dividing their time between Akari training and restoring the old stone. It almost looked like some sort of reenactment model or maybe a movie set, but it was all very real and really being used.

He headed out, away from the city and its glow by torchlight, glittering from the many jewels inlaid into the rock, and into one of the connecting tunnels. The darkness would help to conceal the exact location of the portal to the ruins and the base. It was a tumultuous time in the Time industry, and not a good time to be an Akari-bearer either. At best, anyone who did manage to trace the portal's origin would only find the Region and District and assume that it was some part of the city that lay aboveground.

There were two ways to open a portal, by exact coordinates and by feel. It was the difference between following the directions on a map to a place, and getting there by memory or landmark directions. They trained their recruits to go by feel, so that only they, the leaders and trusted officers, actually knew where the base was located.

Rifun headed to Irig based on coordinates, locating the correct Region and District, then homing in on planetary GPS so that he ended up right where he needed to be.

It was indeed cold when he arrived at the fortress, though its regular occupants seemed not to notice. The residents of Irig were like humanoid rhinos with large horns and three-fingered hands covered in a keratin-like pseudo-hoof. Theirs was a system where a peace house ruled for eighty-one years, followed by a war house for eighty-one years, intended to be a system of perfect balance so as to please their primary god, whose name also happened to be Irig. The residents of the planet Irig were called by the name of the current ruling house. In this case, Korin.

The Korin were eight years into their current war dynasty, so all the palaces and peacetime finery had been converted into war fortresses and entrenched battlements. Fine china and linens were replaced with disposable wood, stone, and coarse leather and furs. Paintings and other arts were replaced with weapons and memorabilia of past war glories. They conducted skirmishes against each other, neighboring provinces and so forth, in order to practice for the times they fought against other races. Because of their approach to government, the Korin were not conquerors, else they would lose all their conquests every eighty-one years when the peace houses took over. Rather, they were primarily raiders, taking what they needed but otherwise leaving the general populace alone.

It was a bit of a double-edged sword, really. If the Cult could get everything done in the next seventy-three years and secure their reign in the Time industry, then they were golden. If, for some reason, they couldn't get everything settled in eighty-one years, or else they remained severely undertrained in the Akari and still relied heavily upon the Korin themselves, well, there were probably other problems at play, say it that way.

But Rifun was optimistic that in seventy-three years, even if they weren't in control of the Time industry, then they would at least have more allies to rely on.

Hopefully these allies would be found in warmer climates, he thought ruefully, making his way through the cold castle whose only protections came from blocking the wind. He was led into an open chamber that, in peacetime, may have been a grand display of opulence and culture. Now it was all about war and proclaiming one's might. Korin soldiers lined the walls, armed with both knives and space weapons of varying styles. A Korin general approached to meet him at a spot halfway from all points of the room, proclaiming equality and so respect for their guest.

"We heard what you did," the general began, not even bothering with formalities. "We heard about the bombing in the Auctionhouse, the war you have declared on the Tacagan humans and the Gentleman Killers."

"We've nothing against them," Rifun told him. "Our war is with the Time industry. The Akari is for all peoples."

"But it is only the early opportunists who receive the benefits of governing."

"They get the privilege of knowing that they were right from the beginning, that they were around when all others laughed and scorned. Once the Time industry has been dismantled, all are free to govern themselves, answering only to the Author, not bureaucrats."

"Is there a place for both war and peace?"

"In perfect balance. A time for everything."

The general studied him. Then, "The initial talks you had, with Commander Kerloff, he indicated that you promised the Korin a role in the new industry, whatever form it may take, in a yet-to-be-devised court system. If all are free to govern themselves, what need is there for courts or judgments?"

"How shall an Araxi and a Refari make peace? What should happen when a Tuvak and a Tolin get into a fight? We may not have courts, but having mediators would be invaluable, those who are skilled in both peaceful negotiation as well as fair retribution. We may have the skill of the Akari and the blessing of the Author, but we are yet imperfect mortals, are we not?"

He had him. The Korin operated on a system of balance, and when making offers or deals or negotiating in any way, one had to appeal to that idea of balance. Every Korin had a mental scale. If that scale wasn't balanced, he wasn't happy. It was a bit like obsessive compulsive disorder, the near-irrational drive to do something a certain way in order to ward off perceived ill fortune. But once that thing was done, whatever it was—clicking a pen a certain number of times before putting it down, having to walk an even number of steps before stopping, providing a means of balancing mental scales—all was well with the universe once more.

Rifun wondered if the general was even aware of this. Did he simply see it as part of his own culture that Rifun was careful to respect? Did he never once question whether this obsession with balance could be used against him and his people? Or did they leave that kind of philosophy for the peacetime scholars? And what did he do during peacetime? Any grunt could turn from soldier to civilian, but a general? What did he do? Was he an artist? A baker? A high-level mediator of some form?

"I cannot promise you all the Korin at this time," he said finally. "It would be imprudent as we have our own battles to fight. However, if the men I send you return with great power such as you are promising, I would be inclined to send more. I have heard rumors that some of the mercenary defectors, who were in direct competition with the Gentleman Killers, may be coming to you anyway, of their own free will."

"How would you like me to deal with them?" Rifun inquired politely. "I understand the Korin view such defection as an imbalance, to be punished rather harshly."

"It is my understanding that you are running your training in military fashion. Incorporate the defectors with the proper soldiers. Perhaps they will remember where their loyalties ought to lie. If they do not, we will deal with them in our own way."

"Of course. We will not interfere, if you deem such a thing necessary. I only ask that you give us a heads up so we know what is going on, what to expect."

The general agreed and promised to send a fair group of soldiers to train with the Cult. Rifun agreed to return in a few days to collect his new crew, then departed, grateful to be leaving the chilly castle. Even the ruins and the officers building in the ancient temple felt warmer.

He was not well-suited to cold environments, hailing from a tropical island. Even when he'd lived in France and England, he had merely tolerated the cold and occasional snow, but with little love for the frozen flakes that turned into a conglomerative mess.

So it was that he built a roaring fire in the hearth in his chambers that evening, taking wood from here and there as needed. He experimented a bit with Energy as it pertained to fire and burning and the whole pyrolysis process, trying to get his fire to burn hotter and use less fuel in the process. Simple Time could not constrain fire, but manipulating the Energy of the burning process, well, that was little more productive, and the ancient stone carvings all around the room came to life in dancing shadow theater that had not had an audience in generations.

He unintentionally fell asleep in front of the fire, and when he woke, it had reduced to glowing red coals. He studied the carving of the hearth and decided that he could build a nice shrine there to his ancestors, something better than his measly offerings he'd conjured up in his days in Europe.

He'd developed a sort of meditative yoga for himself over the last few weeks, something to bring his mind back to the present when memories of war and other abuses threatened to tear him apart, and he spent a good hour or so focusing on his forms. He did these things blindfolded, telling himself not to take his unusual blindsight for granted, nor neglect his other senses. Once he felt calm and steady, he removed the blindfold and went about his day.

As he was freshening himself up a bit, Julianna paid a visit. He updated her on his meeting with the Korin.

"Visiting the Turitians, now, then?" she wondered.

"Yes," he replied simply. "Did you know, the Turitian language has only twelve conjugated verbs? Every single idea that they wish to convey is built around these twelve verbs. Their poetry and songs are legendary. Their legal contracts are...notoriously open to interpretation."

"Loopholes are wonderful things."

"Aren't they? Speaking of loopholes, any word from the Borelians?"

"Not yet."

"Well, don't resign us to slavery until I get back. If anyone is going to chop my head off, I'd rather be present for it."

Julianna nodded uncertainly, but Rifun was already moving away, and the next thing he knew, he was on Turit. The Turitian sun had gone nova long ago and fried the planet, and the populace lived primarily in large, domed cities, moving from here to there by way of small, automatic vehicles, much like a streetcar system.

Turitians themselves were rather top-heavy, extremely muscular, and had a rigid and complex system of turns and gestures, denoting all manner of rank, respect, moods, and other non-verbal conversational cues. Where their spoken and written words left much to the imagination, their body language did not, and an incorrect turn could mean the end of all negotiations both present and future. True, they were a patient people who understood that an outsider might not fully grasp every nuance, but Rifun liked to give himself every advantage, and if he could make a good impression by using the correct turns, thus securing their alliance, he would certainly make the effort to learn.

As he went to meet with the royal family, he learned that King Srori was in ill health and would not be attending any meetings for the foreseeable future. He still held all the authority as befitted his rank and station, but Princess Aronet, his denoted successor, would, as the Turitians said, have the goblet during negotiations.

Being considered an official foreign species ambassador, Rifun was considered of inferior station only to the royal family and the Commander General. All others he encountered — be they civilians, servants, guards, or other Turitian diplomats — were considered inferior to him. He had every right to use the "superior" turns with these folk, but when he walked in the meeting room, he was obligated to use the "inferior" turns.

Prince Alron, twin dukes Erit and Eldor, and Commander General Dira were also present for the meeting, and much ado was made over the formalities and his apparent mastery of the turns and gestures — or well enough for a foreigner, he supposed.

"Ambassador Rifun Ndolo, we welcome your return," Princess Aronet began cordially, and Rifun might have even said there was a little eagerness in there as well.

"I am happy to be back," Rifun replied. "It gives me hope that we can come to an agreement, if not a full alliance."

"We heard of the incident in the Auctionhouse. While it was perhaps more violent than we would have preferred, it has allowed us the opportunity to reestablish ourselves and our Merchant allies within the Time industry."

"I'm glad we could be of assistance."

As it came down, Turit would not stand at the forefront of their alliance, announcing it for all the universe to see just yet. They would, however, gladly support the effort from behind. This included a trickle of supplies and finances. It wouldn't be a lot, mostly out of some surplus that could afford to disappear, but it was better than nothing.

The Turitians would also put in a good word for the Cult among their allies and other races they came in contact with, try to gradually expand the influence and interest. There was power in the word of a royal, no matter the species or race.

"We do, however, ask for something in return," Aronet was saying.

"Of course. That's why we're here." Rifun dipped his head.

"Any and all business you do with the Turitians regarding this matter of our alliance, you will do with us and no other royal family. If victory is within sight, they will try to take power for themselves in this. The Bordir will offer you weapons and arms and other military advantages. The Durn will attempt to bribe you with vast wealth. The Yurl will promise land and other agricultural means. Smaller duchies and provinces may try to turn your ear also. You will do no business with them. If you do, not only will you lose our alliance, but we, the royal family Jalar, will work against you, fracturing Turit and damaging your own reputation. And you will also find that the other royal families are not so accommodating, nor trustworthy."

"I will keep it in mind. As of this moment, I've no inclination of betrayal, and you have been wonderful to work with."

"Good. You will recall that the royal family Jalar is a dynasty built on invention and merchantry. We have vast influence among both royalty and commoners, to say nothing of our extensive trade market. As we return to the stars and the distant systems who have been starved of the Time Capsules we have long provided them, we will also bring them word of the Akari and its Cult."

"Of course." Rifun made a gesture of acquiescence. "How, then, shall I deal with the other royal families?"

"It is expected that you will be polite and submissive and show all appropriate turns and gestures. But you will not negotiate with them in these matters. At least, not without consulting with us first to perhaps find an alternative to whatever needs you find you may have."

Rifun really didn't have any plans of betraying the royal family Jalar at this time, and he could see why they were being less patient and "Good Samaritan-ish" with their own people. This was a power play for them. The royal family Jalar had always been the odd man out among the Turitian royals. In securing this alliance—especially if the Cult remained prominent, powerful, and victorious, with the added bonus of liberating slaves and bringing freedom—they would have leverage over the other families. Rifun respected them for it, and found that he was eager to have them as an ally.

He wasn't keen on the thought of betrayal, actually. It left a bad taste in his mouth. He wanted to try and do things carefully, thoughtfully, to minimize the political problems later on. But in trying to build an empire, it was inevitable that not everyone would get along and someone would eventually cry foul. But if he could entrench some of these allies, then they would have the benefit of long-standing alliances, making future foul-criers look less credible in their assertions that the Cult betrayed them.

Arrangements were made to form the supply line, and Rifun promised to uphold their agreement and even help spread the word that the Turitians were the ones in charge of the marketplaces now. This pleased the Turitians greatly, and they separated on friendly terms.

He was well-received by the Turitians, and for a while, he could pretend that he was the one solely in charge of the whole endeavor, the sole leader of the Cult, second only to the Author.

But then he had to return to Sadurnon and update the others on his progress, all the while hoping and praying that the Borelians weren't waiting at the gate, ready to storm and enslave them all.

Irig had been cold, Turit quite warm, and now he returned to a cold cave where he made for the cold temple to his cold room where he got a fire going in no time, trying to get warm. Was it really too much to ask for a little consistency? He was tired of dragging layers around to accommodate the different weather, and manipulating Thermodynamics was great until it fizzled out after a while. Damn laws of physics anyway.

With the fire underway, he surveyed the northeast corner of his room. Northeast was the most favorable direction for all things. He wasn't sure that the ancestors and spirits could hear him, halfway across the universe, but he constructed a small shrine to which he dutifully bowed and prayed.

He had no offering to give, but he'd already pledged his life, so it would have to do for the time being. Guilt gnawed at him for it, and even he felt as though he were snubbing the ancestors.

He broke off his prayer and spent a good hour searching for and preparing a meal to set before his shrine. Only then did he feel any sort of relief and a lightening of the spirit to be able to pray again.

"And you call us villains."

Isthim's voice sounded behind him, making his heart jump though he remained where he was. Without moving, he asked, "Have you never heard of privacy?"

She did not leave the room, and he could hear her sit down in one of the chairs.

"You call us monsters for worshiping Tujor, the god of death. Yet here you are, worshiping the dead."

"I pray to my ancestors for guidance and wisdom and strength," Rifun said, still not moving. "I do not pray for death, torture, and slavery upon my enemies."

She did not reply. After a moment of consideration, Rifun got his limbs moving and reluctantly stood. He faced her. "What do you want?"

Isthim appeared completely at ease in the chair as she replied, "Councilman Midikijor has contacted me."

"Seeing how we're not being assailed at the moment, I would guess that suggests good will?"

"We may take it as such. He wants to meet to discuss more detailed terms." Now she rose. "Julianna and Cassius are already assembled. Just waiting on you."

It was difficult to read her tone. Only a few weeks ago, she'd gone to her people to propose this alliance, but ended up being thrown in prison. She'd been beaten and her vocal chords cut so she could not scream. Since one of the commanders stood up for her and appeared to agree to this endeavor, at least entertain the thought, she'd been using an electronic voice assist that made it sound as though she spoke through fan blades.

So it was not only tough to tell how she felt about the whole thing, but how she felt about him, or them. Rifun still couldn't decide how guilty he felt about sleeping with her.

Nevertheless, he followed her out of the room and down the corridor to a room they'd repurposed as a meeting room. It, too, had once been dedicated to one of the old Elif goddesses. In this case, Wibani. Rifun could glean little about the goddess as many of the carvings had weathered away or been intentionally removed, leaving just enough to know her name and that she had some relation to Fif, the primary Elif god, and was involved in some war. All the rest was lost to history or mythology.

The hearth was aglow with grand flames, and in the center of the room was a stone table, though judging by the ancient stains that were now reduced to little more than slight discoloration, it had probably once been used as an altar of sacrifice at one time. Rifun tried to put it out of his mind as he faced the others.

Julianna Brown, one of the founders of the Cult of the Akari, alongside her husband Richard. While the Akarin went through a tumultuous time both socially and politically, some had broken away, and the Browns had reformed them into their own sect.

Enter Cassius, the former slave who had made contact with the spirits and so gone to the Browns to dictate the writing of the three journals and formally establish the Cult. When Julianna tried to set him up and take him down, however, he'd turned on them, had Richard executed, cut up Julianna's face, and jumped ahead from the mid-nineteenth century to the early twentieth century. Upon seeing all the chaos that had happened because of their reckless schemes, they'd declared a truce, not helped in small part by Rifun and Isthim.

Isthim, the Borelian, walked in the room behind him, a dangerous place for her to be. Borelians were raised on the premise of glory to Brelix or nothing, and everything was done for the Borelian home world. Being an exile for over a century, some days it was hard to tell where her loyalties lay, especially since she had reconnected with her people on a tentative basis. On the one hand, she was finally achieving her mission of bringing the Akari to her people. On the other hand, they'd maimed her for it.

"The Korin and the Turitians are in," Rifun reported. "Both peoples can only spare so many recruits at this time, until we prove the Akari a worthwhile pursuit. Furthermore, all communication with the Turitians is to go through the royal family Jalar. I expect that I will be the one to run politics and logistics, but I don't want ignorance to be an excuse."

"Fair enough," Julianna said calmly. "Isthim was just telling us that the Borelians are ready to come to the table and talk terms."

"Sounds like a job for our liaisons," Rifun said, looking at Isthim and Cassius. Isthim was a liaison for obvious reasons. Cassius was a liaison because both Rifun and Julianna wanted him dead. Using the Borelians to kill him meant their hands were clean and they got warning if the Borelians intended to turn on them.

"Indeed," Isthim agreed. "I was just about go and get them, but wanted to make sure all of us were here and on the same page."

"Go and get them? As in, bring them here?" Cassius questioned. "Is that a good idea? If things don't go well, they'll know where we are."

"If things don't go well, then we'll have a fantastic opportunity to demonstrate the superiority of the Akari," Rifun said, though he couldn't deny his own fear at the prospect of the most dangerous and feared species in the universe coming to stand in the heart of their camp. "If they do go well, I can't come up with any good reasons not to extend the same offer of training to them that I've given to every other ally, other than we don't like them and don't trust them. But then Isthim has the advantage."

He could see Julianna wanted to speak, but she said nothing. Probably it was the same protest they all knew and were hiding away in the back of their minds. It was a bad idea to bring Isthim into this in the first place and they shouldn't be here. But they were here, and this was what they had to deal with.

"It will only be four," Isthim went on. "A priest of the Ul Ik Zol, Councilman

Midikijor, Admiral Jetindar — " She said this with a mix of sorrow and hope. "—and Commander Misik."

"Four here, but they'll tell everyone," Julianna stated.

"They've agreed to be kept in the dark about the precise location, using the darkness and tunnels, so long as they can see our operation. But once we reach an agreement, they will want to know coordinates."

"Well, we'll go over that in negotiations," Rifun said, staring at a stain on the table which he thought looked a bit like a butterfly or a moth, an unknown soul. He looked around at the other three. "Might as well get this over with."

Cassius grunted and Julianna made a motion. Isthim left them.

"Do not speak," Rifun said sharply, cutting off the others, "unless you can improve upon the silence."

It was two minutes before Julianna decided that she could, saying, "Do we have a backup base in the event we need to quietly evacuate?"

Rifun, who had gone back to staring at the butterfly stain, sighed and said, "Yes, it's called stand and fight followed by a retreat strategy of scatter and don't let them catch us all in one spot for a while." He met her gaze. "The Borelians are fearsome, but so is any army, any battle. War is terrifying. It is absolutely petrifying. I don't know that you have ever been on the frontlines, but I have. It's not a place I have enjoyed being, but it is necessary in order to advance the theater of war and battle.

"We can't expect the Time industry to just roll over. The Tacagans will come back swinging, and the Gentleman Killers may not be so gentlemanly the second time around. Eventually we will reach a point where we cannot rely on guerrilla tactics and must take things to the field, army to army, Akari to Time."

He went on before she could protest. "You are in charge of humanitarian aid and logistics as they apply to morale and ensuring everyone understands what we're fighting for, spiritually. You are the undercurrent, we are the wave. If you have nothing constructive to offer, something other than complaints, criticisms, and fretful feminine worrying, then you don't have to be part of these negotiations."

For a moment, Julianna looked stunned that she'd been spoken to in such a way. She opened her mouth but no words came out. Finally she closed her mouth and looked away at Cassius who just shrugged as if agreeing.

Before any of them could say or do more, Isthim returned with four Borelians in tow.

Admiral Nici Jetindar, a *vodrak* Borelian who had been Isthim's idol and considered one of, if not the most dangerous person they would be dealing with.

Commander Misik, the yellow and gray Borelian who had advocated for Isthim and made the negotiations possible from the Borelian side. It was still unclear what his motives were concerning his advocacy, though Rifun got the impression that it had more to do with their personal relationship, whatever it was, than anything political.

Councilman Ridik Midikijor, a purple Borelian who was well-versed in outside politics, whatever his title and job description said.

And the priest of the Ul Ik Zol, the Holy Men of War, the secretive organization known only to outsiders by name and fearsome reputation. It was nearly impossible to tell whether the priest was male or female, or what toxin he pushed as he was covered horn to toe in bones interwoven with jewels and other adornments. Rifun wasn't even sure this was the same priest they'd met with in the Wheel the first time. Only a careful study said that the priest might actually be an orange female, though he wouldn't be willing to bet his life on it.

"Welcome," Rifun greeted cordially, "to our humble abode."

"A deceptive description," Councilman Midikijor said, "considering your actions in the Auction were loud and anything but humble on your part."

"You're welcome," Cassius told him.

"Our people have wrangled in the chaos for the time being in limited measure," Admiral Jetindar cut in. "What offer do you have for us that makes it worth our while to close in and keep a hold on it?"

"That depends," Rifun said. "How many of your men do you want to train with us?"

"What is that supposed to mean?"

"We expect a bit of give and take here. This is a mutual alliance, is it not? If you have no interest in training with us and being associated with us in some way, having a little skin in the game, then these negotiations can end right now and you are free to go. No need to get involved in anything or keep hold of anything. No need to flex your muscles beyond whatever cute little display you've made of yourselves. You can just retreat back into the shadows, the black depths of space which you crawled out of, and let us take over entirely."

The look on the Borelians' faces was utterly priceless.

"This is blackmail!" Midikijor sputtered in protest.

"That's exactly what this is," Rifun told him. "And now we want hostages.

Good hostages. Not just your exiles you leave by the wayside, beaten and maimed, because you lack vision."

While he would say he was rather pleased with himself, something about the priest's gaze made the hair on the back of his neck stand up, and he felt cold all over.

"I'll volunteer," Commander Misik said, his tone impossible to judge. "I advocated for Isthim and so it is only right that I should add stones to my words."

Rifun did not miss the look that passed between the two of them, but he kept a straight face, dipped his head in acknowledgment, and glanced at the other three Borelian leaders. "It's a good start, but I want more than just him."

"How many do you want?" Jetindar asked. There seemed to be a hint of disdain as well as a bit of admiration in his voice.

"How long do you think you can carry a soft hand in the Wheel?" Cassius countered. "Because the mercenaries won't wait forever."

The Borelians murmured among themselves for a few minutes, their expressions clearly unhappy about the situation. Rifun tried to tell himself not to get cocky, but this was a damn good feeling, to think he'd backed the Borelians into a corner. As long as they didn't lash out and enslave them all, things could turn out all right.

Finally they came back to the present discussion.

"We will attempt to locate five more volunteers," Midikijor said grudgingly. "We will be doing our own tests and monitoring of their progress."

"I would expect nothing less," Rifun said coolly. "New and untested things must be observed to the fullest extent possible."

"Shall we perhaps continue these negotiations at a later date?" Julianna inquired politely, if mockingly. "That way you have time to locate these volunteers and we can inform them more fully of what is going on, what is expected of them?"

If looks could kill, any one of them should have dropped dead on the spot. For a moment, Rifun wondered if this altar to Wibani was going to see its first sacrifice in a very long time. They were toeing a line here, and that line was only half a step away from a cliff. Fall off the cliff and into Borelian slavery. Not a prospect any of them wanted to entertain. And Isthim, who was a Borelian, would not be enslaved, but imprisoned, which couldn't be much better.

The Borelians took the out, and Isthim escorted them out of the room. The remaining Cult leaders breathed a collective sigh of relief. Julianna was the first to break into a laugh, half humor, half anxiety. She shook her head and looked at Rifun.

"I can't believe you actually pulled that off," she said, grinning. "I didn't even realize what you did until they realized it. And that was...that was almost beautiful to behold, except for that fear of being enslaved."

"They don't have the high ground here," Rifun told her, "and I made sure they know it. It doesn't mean we're in the clear, but we're in a better position than we were."

He met Cassius' gaze across the altar. The dark-skinned man held himself well, but there was a certain rigidity to his posture that bespoke a jealous hatred. Rifun didn't even have to guess at the reasons. Cassius was supposed to be the liaison with the Borelians, alongside Isthim. But the Borelians wanted to deal with Rifun instead. Furthermore, Rifun had slept with Isthim, something the boorish sexual predator did not take kindly to.

They were supposed to be working together to find the Book of Abilities and be rid of the Borelians. Rifun was doing well to corner the Borelians. Julianna had even confided in him the location of the journal. He needed to work things slowly, calmly. Finesse, not force.

Unfortunately, force was glaring at him from the other side of the altar.

It took four days for the Borelians to return to the table.

"We have sealed our hold on the Wheel, inasmuch as we are now the acting policing force," Midikijor informed them. "The Tacagan humans and other interested parties are quite displeased with this arrangement and also highly suspicious that this is where we have ceased operation. As you have said, it is typically intended to be all or nothing in such a coup. We are the policing force but not the ones making the laws that must be policed. We hope you are ready to seize control before the enemy can regroup and retaliate."

"Who do we have from your people besides Commander Misik?" Rifun asked.

The only volunteer Isthim did not approve of was her cousin Medik, and even Rifun questioned the wisdom of the decision.

"Two lethri cannot well co-exist," he recited. "Isthim is the head of our training for new recruits. Dissent in the ranks is not good discipline, I should think."

"Borelians are capable of appropriate discipline within the ranks," Medik Makijor informed him. "We simply cannot command together."

Isthim held rank within the Cult, but Medik held the social and military rank on the home world, to say nothing of their familial relation. Was this a test of Isthim's resolve and commitment? Were they hoping to sow discord, to fracture the Cult in order to take it over, cart them off to slavery? Were they hoping to turn Isthim back to them, the Borelians, and have her sell out the Cult willingly?

Rifun didn't like it. There were too many things that could go wrong.

"No," he told them. "We won't take her. Send another or none at all."

"Very well," Midikijor assented, too easily. "I will go in her stead at training. Medik Makijor will be our assessor of our own choosing to ensure we are learning something of value to bring back to our people."

They'd slipped in a sixth man and still managed to keep the one Rifun didn't want. And having Medik as the assessor meant she was not bound by the same rules as the rank-and-file. She didn't have to swallow her pride or her attitude when she grilled Isthim on the training.

What else had they planned over the last four days?

Rifun could see what the Borelians had done. Julianna and the others could piece it together as well. The Borelians knew very well what they had done, and they were clearly pleased with themselves.

It was to be expected, he supposed. The poisonous, horned bastards hadn't gotten where they were by brute force alone. But Rifun had gotten where he was only by his mind, so he considered his the sharper sword of wit. Two could play this game.

"I'm glad we could come to an arrangement," he said politely. "Are they quite ready to begin?"

It was a rhetorical question as they had come packed and ready for an extended stay. He glanced at Cassius. "Would you care to show our guests around town and send our temporary visitors back to where they came from?"

The Borelians looked a mix of smug amusement and certain confusion that Isthim was not going to be their guide. But they said nothing as the whole posse left the room.

"I see what they did," Rifun said before Isthim could speak.

"There was no good answer, but you chose the better option," she replied. "Then I need no excuse to beat her when she annoys me."

"Just keep your menstrual spats between yourselves, hm? We don't all need to know what's going on if it's just you girls."

Her expression was impossible to read, though "irritated" was most definitely one of the top contenders. She left the room, leaving only Rifun and Julianna.

"So, what's our next move?" Julianna wondered, sighing.

"I don't know," Rifun admitted. "I know what needs to be done, but it requires more resources in less time with a certain level of secrecy that I don't know I can pull off, considering we're actively trying to put ourselves out there. I feel as though everything is happening in the wrong order."

"At least there is an order in your mind. I'm rather overwhelmed by the whole thing. I'd really like to step back and merely assume my role as the humanitarian, but I don't dare leave Cassius or Isthim alone for very long."

Rifun wondered what she would do if she did catch them in treachery, but he did not say this aloud. Instead he opted for, "Well, I think it will take a few days or so for everyone to come to terms with Borelians in our midst. Perhaps we ought to see how things will pan out on the homefront before turning our gaze outward too distantly."

Julianna agreed and said nothing further.

Rifun left the room, glad to get away from the bloodstained altar. He could return to his chambers, but he would accomplish nothing. Going out into the reviving city might be good, but he was sending Cassius for a reason and did not want to interfere. Well, when in doubt, there was no place like home. So home he went.

The Wheel of Time, 1964

kokumbo

Cassius brooded over a hot drink in the Food Court in the Wheel. He was alone at the table, but the place itself was rather sparse. Must have something to do with the sudden, stunning presence of the Borelians about, he figured. He took a drink.

He didn't care for the situation, and he wasn't sure how far he wanted to trust that Rifun — or any of the others, for that matter — knew what he was doing and was able to weasel them out of this. All right, fine, he accepted responsibility that most or all of this was his doing. Now how did they undo it? He didn't know. He didn't know that Rifun really knew either.

He did not flinch or give any immediate acknowledgement to the person who sat down across from him, setting down a tray of food. Instead he took another drink, stared at it a moment, then looked up.

She was Tibidi, a humanoid race with birdesque features, including skin growths on the lower arms and legs that were almost like pseudo-feathers, with feather-like hair on top of their heads, and large, insect-like wings which they could use to hover for short distances, much like a bee. Their skin had a yellowish tint to it, and feathers came in a variety of colors, much the same as human hair. This particular Tibidi had pink and orange feathers. Cassius silently wondered whether it was natural.

"Pilory," he stated.

"Close enough," she replied, shrugging and taking a large bite of food. Her forehead sloped down so that she had a terrible blind spot between her eyes, and it continued down to a point, like a pseudo-beak that nevertheless appeared quite solid and sharp at the end. Two antennae on the top of her head wiggled whenever she moved her head.

The Tibidi had no grace or etiquette when it came to table manners, and she happily continued speaking even as she ate. "I don't recall Calis Cutthroat ever asking for help from another mercenary. But then, I've never heard of Calis

Cutthroat being a team player and co-leading a religious cult, either."

"We live in strange times, don't we?" he mused. "What a time to be alive."

"Oh, no doubt." She swallowed, took another large bite of food, and kept right on talking. "So then, what can I do for you? Or rather, what can my captain do for you? I'm guessing that's really why you wanted to see me. No one really cares about a meager lieutenant." She shook her head and took more food in her mouth though she did not appear to have finished what she already had. "Middle management gets no respect."

"Indeed not." Cassius shifted in his seat. "How did Titik know about the Tacagans' link to the Gentleman Killers?"

Pilory laughed, a small spray of food shooting out of her mouth. She shook her head again, swallowed what food remained in her oral cavity, and gave him a look. "Oh, that's easy. 'Money is the only pleasure in the world.' Gods, the number of times I hear that in a day from Titik..." She grinned and chuckled. "Ah... Captain Morain leRou Titik has a nose for money like elchior have a nose for blood. Once he's on the scent, there's no calling him back unless you have a greater prize. Believe me, none of us who work for him ever want for currency.

"When the Gentleman Killers came on the scene, his leads within the Time industry dried up, same as yours, and he wanted to know why. The only thing more unpredictable than Titik when he's on the scent of money is Titik when he's on the scent of a thief. He doesn't like to see his funds dry up, so he went looking for the cause. The scent trail didn't stop at the Gentleman Killers; he followed it all the way to the top."

"Why didn't he do anything about it? Why stand on a soapbox and complain?"

"What did you expect him to do about it?" Pilory shifted uncomfortably. "We're space pirates, Calis. We commit crimes of opportunity, but rarely engage in prolonged warfare. And we have no interest or skill to pull off a coup d'etat. Pretending that we did expose and overthrow the Tacagan humans as you did, what would we have replaced it with? There would have been another group after them. And another and another. In the immediate aftermath, it looked like you were going to sit in the captain's chair, and now the Borelians have swooped in for some unknown, sinister purpose. Money is well and fine, but we're not stupid."

Cassius grunted and said nothing. Pilory went back to her food, and he took a drink.

"Can Titik sniff out more than just money?" he asked.

She gave him a look. "If he's got his heart and mind set on it, he can sniff out anything." She went on before he could speak. "But he's not some petty thug. He's no treasure hunter gone to look for trinkets and heirlooms for minor fees or good will. He's hard-pressed to do such niceties for even his crew. Whatever you're looking for, you couldn't afford what he would ask for such a venture."

"How about training and power that could last a lifetime?"

The Tibidi appeared unimpressed. "Captain Titik, and most of his crew, is Psiaco. If you don't know, Psia is home to some of the most prestigious Time Academies in their sector of space. He was once one of their most promising students, and he could have had a lavish career in Time. He hates politics more than he loves money, which is why he decided to do things his own way, and, again, why he didn't do anything about the Tacagans once he sniffed them out."

Cassius frowned and Pilory shifted again. She tilted her head. "What exactly are you looking for, anyway?"

"A journal," Cassius answered absently. "An 'heirloom trinket' as you call it. Actually, I'm looking for two journals."

"What's in these journals?"

He stood, abandoning his drink which had cooled to lukewarm. "Nothing that matters to someone who isn't going to look for it."

With that, he turned and walked away. About ten steps later, he heard a rumbling humming behind him, and Pilory fell in step beside him.

"What kind of training and power are we talking about here?" she asked.

"What's it to you?" Cassius wondered casually, almost mockingly.

"I don't know yet. But I can guarantee that my fees are lower than Titik's."

"You're just going to up and leave him? I don't know too many good captains who would take kindly to that."

"Of course not. I still have my pride and loyalty, after all. But maybe I can learn a few things, find a few leads, persuade him to look into it. If the prize is big enough."

"Oh, it's big enough. If it's not, then he's a fool."

She flitted in front of him and he stopped. "All right. What's in this journal of yours?"

"It is the Book of Abilities, written by Richard, the founder of the Cult of the Akari. It details everything the Akari can do, teaches a diligent student how to perform them. I read it and memorized it and I'm teaching the rest, but there is power in physical presence."

Even for her alien physiology, Cassius could see her unbridled interest. She tried to hide it as she asked, "True. What can the Akari do? No one doubts that the Auction assassination was you, but you've always been a bloodthirsty son of a bitch, or so I hear. Where's the rest of it?"

He altered Gravity, then, forcing it to be so heavy that she could not overcome it and was grounded. Then he tweaked the Thermodynamics a little, making the air around him much warmer, and around her much cooler. He could see the panic setting in just moments before she appeared to become sluggish and lethargic, her wings becoming brittle.

Finally he released it all, and things quickly went back to normal. It took a minute for her to perk up, but when she did, she took a noticeable step back, eyes huge, expression evidently unsure what to do with whatever just occurred.

"And that's just a taste," Cassius told her. "Imagine all the forces at work in the universe, yours to command. Is that a big enough prize?"

Pilory blinked and finally composed herself, though not without a shiver of fear and curiosity.

"All right," she said at last. "That...it's...you've convinced me."

"Now you should convince your captain."

"I'll definitely do my best. But I'll warn you of something: he wasn't happy about the Tacagan humans and the Gentleman Killers running the show. He's far more leery of the Borelians. It's unlikely he would want to come back to the Wheel for any instruction. You would have to go to him or meet somewhere else."

"You think our army is staged here, in the Wheel? Hardly. There is a place for him."

The Tibidi bid him a hasty farewell and departed. Cassius watched her go, mildly pleased with himself. Rifun was too slow, and too entangled in his web with the Borelians and figuring out army logistics. It would take years to find the Book of Abilities. Entice a famous treasure hunter on the other hand, and maybe things would get done.

Delegation, that's what this was. He was delegating responsibility. He was being a good, responsible team player. He was considering and using the resources he had available.

He smiled smugly to himself as he made his way through the Wheel. It had become quiet lately, with the Gentleman Killers gone or scattered and the Borelians a notable presence, even if only in the Judgment Wing. Cassius recalled that the Korin were supposed to have taken over part of the Judgment Wing, too. How did they feel about this, then? Did they know it was related? Did they feel betrayed by the Cult, or perhaps they placed all the blame on the Borelians and their mighty presence. If that was the case, then, did that spark any doubts about the power of the Akari?

He shook his head. Politics and logistics. Leave that to Rifun. Cassius was here to be the trainer, the strong arm, the one working with the Borelians alongside Isthim. He wasn't here to make sure everyone got along and played nice in the sandbox.

The portal room was largely empty and it was no trouble to find his portal. It was completely black, leading to an unknown cave. Not one of the Caves of Meroian, but a cave on Earth. From there, he would open a portal to Sadurnon. All recruits were also instructed to go to the Wheel via portals based on their home world or other location. While not utterly foolproof, as some species like the Lixon were capable of tracking closed portals, it made it more difficult to trace them, anyway.

Cassius jumped from the Wheel to Earth, and from Earth to Sadurnon, still ending up in one of the caves, surrounded by darkness. Light did not work well in total cave darkness, but he'd learned to use Sound, building an image using echolocation to find his way back to the ruins. It wasn't a long trek, up a rise to the left, around the corner, and light began filtering in, enough for a skilled Light user to manipulate and illuminate his way. Continue upwards and around a long bend to the right, keeping close to the wall to avoid a death drop, and by the time one made the crest, even a beginning student of Light could better illuminate the rest of the path, assuming he needed to. For Cassius, arriving in the middle of the day when the sun shone directly through the crevasse in the rock ceiling, there was plenty of light to see by. He descended the slope toward the ruins.

The city was alive and well, life breathed into sterile ruins. From a distance, it was like watching an ant colony, tiny shapes moving here to there. As he drew near, the shapes got bigger, and sound came into focus. This was a city once more, with daily life happening all around. Rifun was more sentimental about history and culture, sometimes imagining what the place had been like when primitive Elif still made their migration to this spot. Cassius was less concerned.

As he approached, Cassius nearly hit the deck when he saw a shadow overhead and felt the breeze of something huge and heavy coming toward him. But when he Banded, he saw it was only a group of Shatai, large creatures that appeared to be the result of a bat and a dragon mating, then meeting the front end of a large truck. They were large and bony, almost like flying shadowy skeletons, with an ear-piercing screech that could echo forever in these caves. It hadn't been difficult to convince the Shatai to join them. If anything, they had been ready and willing a long time ago and just waiting for the invitation. Cassius didn't understand the story behind it, but there seemed to be a feud betwen the Shatai and the Iuri, and the Iuri were sided with the Akarin.

Cassius wondered how that feud would factor in with Rifun's plan of reuniting the Cult and the Akarin. Well, that wasn't his problem.

Hoping that no one saw his startle, Cassius let out a breath and kept moving. He made his way down to the old wall around the city, the gates twisted and marred and forever propped open. Not a few times, Cassius wondered why the Elif thought it necessary to build a wall around an underground city. He sometimes wondered how the gates had become as twisted as they were.

Once inside the city, the activity was even greater. Originally, anyone living in the city had just claimed whatever abandoned building they wanted. Since Isthim had gone through and tested most of the recruits, dividing them into ranks based on their skill level, the recruits were now being assigned buildings, like barracks. It was a little difficult, seeing how not everyone could stay in the city full time. Some were from Unengaged worlds and had other chores and duties to tend to. They couldn't just disappear, or tell their families they were leaving to join a cult army halfway across the universe.

Well, they could, Cassius supposed. Personally, he'd rather mandate it, that they stay in the city and train. No more half-ass conviction. But as Rifun liked to point out, they couldn't be seen solely as an army. It had to be seen as a way of life, and they had to allow recruits loyalty to their families and their people. Whatever.

Cassius had lost his sense of loyalty and belonging a long time ago. Every so often, he could call up memories of freeing slaves from their masters and returning to Africa on a stolen ship. Sometimes he could almost remember the solidarity they'd had, the comradery as they made the journey home. But that was centuries gone now. He no longer recalled their names, and they were but faceless phantoms in his mind's eye anymore. Dreams, but for the stark reality that it was how he'd gotten where he was.

Ever since, he'd lived only for himself. Titik may have had the mantra of money being the only pleasure in the world, but for Cassius, it was about his satisfaction. As it was, he would not deny the bitterness he felt when he considered that he seemed to owe something to some dark spirit, obedience just to be kept alive. There must be something he could do to remove the bullet from his face and cut that thread, but how did one outwit a spirit?

He remained in a grim mood as he approached the officers building. Once, it had been a temple, with the main chamber dedicated to the worship of the main pagan god of the primitive Elif, which had apparently included sacrifice at some point in history. A large altar was set up at one end of the chamber, directly in front of a massive hearth that was nearly a room in itself. Fif, the sky god, had been worshipped here for generations, abandoned when the Elif found reason and technology and could move to the surface permanently in their domed cities, safe from the elements Fif once controlled.

Smaller antechambers were littered about here and there, each one dedicated to other minor gods and goddesses who had not seen service in years but were, apparently, powerless to scold their disloyal subjects with godly wrath.

There were seventeen antechambers in all, fourteen for the gods and goddesses, two for the ancient priests and priestesses, and one whose purpose was unknown, or the Elif were unwilling to tell. Given its location and the air of despair that clung to it, Cassius might have guessed that it was where the sacrifices had been kept prior to being taken to their respective altars. This was the only room the others were unwilling to touch—even the Borelians were leery of it, with exception of the Ul Ik Zol—and Cassius used it for his own private purposes.

Cassius had never really had his own religion, though he'd been duped into Christianity for a short period. He did not have what Rifun had, a doctrine inundated within him since birth, with rites and rituals, gods and ancestors and power to call his own. He did not have any kind of structure or old memories to use as a guide. The best he could do was kneel in the middle of the room that was no more than a stone box perhaps twenty by twenty feet and hope someone or something heard his rambling.

Reverence had never been his forte. Giving thanks and honor and glory to anything, especially something he could not see or converse with at will yet seemed to have total power over him, was antithetical to his own personal, selfish ambitions. So it was that he did not really pray, that is, show respect and deference in hopes of getting scraps from the heavenly table, so much as start talking, make demands, maybe try to strike up a bargain, and wait to see if anything answered.

Every so often, something did.

He wasn't sure if it was a vision or if the shadows did in fact coalesce into the shape of something resembling a dragon, but whatever the case, the spirit emerged from the gloom.

"Why are the Borelians here?" Cassius demanded. He'd wanted to know ever since the possibility had existed. "And why did it take until after their alliance for you to answer?"

"I do things in my time, my way, small one," the spirit said, its voice rumbling like distant thunder. "Each of you has a purpose to accomplish my goals."

"Seeing how we've been talking for a few centuries now, I'd like to think that means I'm entitled to a little gratitude. And a few answers."

The spirit rumbled something like a laugh. "You believe a few centuries is significant to me? Mere moments. I chose the Borelians long ago, gifted them power, made them mine. You are nothing."

"Most of them don't even believe in you anymore. And here I am, desiring to communicate."

"I don't need them to believe. They are easy enough to control. As for you—" The dragon lowered its head and breathed hot, sulfurous, smoky breath in Cassius' face. "You desire power, elevation for yourself."

"And so far all I get is disdain and mistrust. You have the power to kill me. The switch is lodged in my face. Barring that, I know you raised up Rifun against me, a polite, political way to mask it for the world. So there must be a reason you're keeping me alive."

Another rumble, almost like an amused "hm." Then, "You will get your power." The spirit lifted its head. "You will walk among shadows and one day command them."

Cassius nodded. "That's more like it."

The shadowy dragon moved, as if trying to stand but was frustratingly constrained by the small room. "Do not be so arrogant."

"I haven't even reached arrogance yet. Right now, I'm just happy with a little appreciation and a little promise of favor."

It was impossible to read the body language and expressions of a smoky, ethereal being, but Cassius got the impression that the spirit was annoyed.

"As a show of good faith," he added, "I'll even say thank you. If you want, I might even be willing to do a small favor for you. We're in a temple with a lot of old sacrificial altars, after all."

Truth be told, he was kind of hoping the spirit would ask for Rifun or Julianna to be sacrificed. Instead, the dragon replied, "The blood already spilled is sufficient for now. There will be more later that I will ask of you."

"I'll be here."

The darkness swallowed the dragon and Cassius was left alone in the stone room. He still couldn't decide whether that had physically happened, or if it had been mere spiritual vision, but regardless, it had happened on some level.

Frustrated, he left the room. As he walked, he passed all the other antechambers. He, Julianna, Isthim, and Rifun had each claimed one as their own private quarters while they stayed in the ruins, and one had been converted into a private meeting room. Now that the Borelians were official allies, a couple of them had also claimed private quarters in the old temple. Misik, the gray and yellow military commander, was adjacent to Rifun's room. Medik Makijor, an orange *tevak*, was Isthim's cousin and the "independent assessor" of the Akari for the Borelians. The two women did not get along in any form, and likely Medik had chosen her particular room next to her cousin's just to spite Isthim and try to provoke a fight.

The door to Misik's room was open and the commander was inside. He spotted Cassius and called to him, motioned for him to approach. Cassius did so, hoping he didn't seem too apprehensive. Gray toxins caused brain problems, and yellow was for the heart and circulatory system. A well-trained Borelian could not only haphazardly kill someone with their toxins, but they could manipulate a victim's body in indescribable and heinous ways.

"Close the door," the commander, presently gray, ordered as Cassius walked in.

He did so cautiously and went to stand across from Misik at the altar which he used as a common table. Papers and maps were laid out, meticulously arranged in some spots, strewn about in others.

"I have a question for you," Misik said before Cassius could speak. He looked up from his papers. "How far do you trust Rifun? How far should I trust him?"

"His strength does not come from his body, but his mind," Cassius told him. "He negotiates by deception and trickery."

The commander nodded slowly for a second or two. Finally, "Then it appears he has tricked us all." He returned to his papers. "That will be all."

"You asked me in here and told me to close the door just for that?"

Misik looked up. "Yes. It seems I did. That's all." And back down.

His frustration mounting, Cassius stormed out of the room. What kind of question or conversation was that? It was nothing. It meant nothing, explained nothing, advanced nothing!

He paused just outside the temple, standing on the steps leading down to the revived city. Taking a breath, he forced himself to calm down some and look at least a little presentable. He would not say he had the calm and poise of the others, nor did he want it, but he couldn't stomp around like a raging bull.

He wasn't the only one leery of the Borelian presence, but it was more widely accepted than he would have initially expected. Maybe it was because Isthim had taken over for almost a century and hadn't enslaved them. Maybe it was the hope that if they played nice, they wouldn't be enslaved. Or maybe it was as Rifun had once suggested, simple interaction and taking the taboo out of the untouchable people.

That didn't necessarily mean that the proverbial blacks and whites were freely intermingling. It was still very easy to tell where the Borelians were at any given moment: just look for the parting of the Red Sea around them. But there did not appear to be any cause for alarm, and tight, hesitant respect was exchanged between parties. Well, the Cult managed some hesitant respect. The Borelians were just as stuck up as they ever were.

The Borelians were the policing force in the Wheel, and the Korin were supposed to have some part in it as well. The Turitians had been promised a share in the marketplaces. Logically, they, the Cult leaders, would assume control of the Seat of the Hands. So why weren't they assuming control of the Seat? If they didn't do something soon, the Tacagans and the Gentleman Killers would return in greater force. With no backup, the Korin, the Turitians, other allies would melt away. The Borelians, disdainful of politics, would turn on them.

Cassius wanted to know, but he knew that if he asked, he would only be drowned in a sea of boring politics. Why did politics require such confusing nuance? Why was every political arrangement automatically a harrowing endeavor, a web of lies to ensnare everyone involved? Why could things not be simple? What happened to the days when if one man wanted something another man had, he took it? When did villages stop raiding other villages for goods and women? When did wars move from the battlefield to the meeting room?

The Gentleman Killers had risen to power, not only from their backing from the Tacagans, but because of a shift in the way things were done. When people hired a mercenary, they no longer looked for the biggest, toughest candidate covered in the most blood. These days, they wanted a clean kill, something quiet that they could forget about and soothe their conscience so they could sleep at night.

Cassius had been left out in the cold because of the Gentleman Killers and their smoother methods of killing, and that was how he'd ended up with the Cult. Again.

He toured the city, watched some of the training, observed some of the restoration. It bored him. He thought about the massacre at the auction. That had been exciting. That had gotten things moving again. That had motivated certain allies to accept their proposals, take them seriously. Rifun was all talk, but Cassius put the fist behind his words.

"You look bored."

He turned from where he was watching a bunch of green recruits try to repair a partially collapsed roof in one of the abandoned buildings. Isthim approached and stood near him. Her current color could not be determined, for it lay beyond the spectrum perceptible to humans.

"I massacred hundreds of people at the auction," he said, folding his arms and returning his gaze to the recruits. "I thought something was going to happen. Alliances were secured with the Korin and the Turitians, the Borelians are...here. Why, then, do we sit here? The Tacagans and Gentleman Killers will not wait forever. They will return, and they will not be duped in such a way a second time. Next time, they will be much harder to kill."

Isthim gave him a look. "I am curious. Tacaga is a colony planet of Earth, yet there is great animosity. How did this come to be?"

Cassius opened his mouth to speak but could only shrug. "I don't know."

"I do."

Julianna was the one who had spoken, and she had been the one generally supervising the restoration. She joined their group. Her demeanor said she was trying to be pleasant, but there was a great deal of fear in her posture.

"The first Tacagans were scholars from Ancient Greece, thousands of years ago. Their introduction and early involvement in Time is unknown—at least to the rest of us humans—but they founded a colony on Tacaga. Later on, refugees from a collapsing Roman empire joined them. Tacaga was intended as a purely humanistic colony. Everything that is said or done must be proven by science, fact, and logic. To that end, they have advanced far beyond Earth's technology so they may even be considered Scientifically Advanced. But they hold terrible disdain for religion and anyone who even considers such a thing. They are also rather disgusted by even Earth atheists for their inability to convert inhabitants to atheism."

"In that sense, is not their atheism also a religion?" Isthim inquired.

Julianna shrugged. "You might call it that. The Tacagans have also discovered how to technologically alter themselves, and they are quite determined to genetically engineer themselves away from the rest of us. One day they hope to file a petition to be recognized as their own species and so their own planet, so they will no longer be a colony planet of Earth."

"So I guess this means that recruiting them to the Cult is out of the question," Cassius sighed.

Julianna gave him a look. "Yes, quite."

"The Tacagans, maybe, but what about the Gentleman Killers?" Isthim wondered. "Cassius has proven himself cunning and deadly in many ways in the past, and now he can add a demonstration of the Akari to his killing repertoire. What would it take to perhaps win some converts from the Gentleman Killers?"

"We already have a group of Korin mercenaries training with us, and a few of the Gentleman Killers have made inquiries. But we can't be seen solely as an army, or a horde of mercenaries. People fear armies. We have to have some semblance of...kindness to us, too, a bit of humanitarian effort so we are not so easily vilified."

"That is a nice sentiment," Cassius told her, "but restoring antiques and feeding orphans isn't going to win us the Time industry."

"He's right," Isthim agreed, her stance turning cold and militaristic. "We must train well and give our enemies cause to fear us."

Julianna huffed and looked at Cassius. "Well, I think he's done quite enough of that."

She turned then and went back to overseeing the restoration of the building, moving the debris out of the way so the building could be used. If Cassius remembered correctly, this was to be a storage building.

"She is right, though," Isthim said before he could also leave. "You have done well to perpetuate our name and reputation. It has brought my people into the fold, though it is still tentative at this point." She looked at him. "What is the next step?"

Cassius gave her a look. "You tell me, master of the army. I got their attention, and that is all I was supposed to do. Rifun is doing his work in politics, and Julianna is clearly enthralled with her humanitarian efforts. Seems to me that the ball is in your court."

Isthim frowned and studied the recruits still struggling to move the boulders and debris from the building. She shook her head. "They're not ready yet. We're not ready for a full invasion and hostile takeover." She gave him a look and cut him off before he could speak, her voice low and almost garbled in the electronic assist. "If we had the Book of Abilities, things would move much faster. Where is it?"

"I'm working on it."

She made a noise that sounded wretched coming from the assist, and her expression was displeased. "We've shown our hand too early, and all we have is a flimsy wall, a charade, with nothing to back it up. Someone—the Tacagans, the Gentleman Killers—will strike and find nothing."

Cassius shifted his stance. "Maybe that's a good thing." At her look, he went on, "You chastised me many times for being too loud, too obvious. Maybe we can use it to our advantage. Use my loud noise as a sleight of hand. Divert the attention of the Tacagans and the Gentleman Killers and string them along until they don't know which way is up."

"Strike the shadows," Isthim stated. "Wear them out, expose them, and keep them guessing until we are ready."

"Yes, something like that."

"I expect it will involve more killing."

"Do you have a problem with that?"

"No, but it must be strategic. With my people as the policing force in the Wheel, we may be able to set up a cooperative effort. With Rifun negotiating alliances, we may be able to shift things in our favor." She nodded. "You will be the dog snapping at the heels of the sheep, and we will merely be the guides to get them to go where we want."

"I like how you think," Cassius told her.

Isthim shifted her stance, thoughtful yet stoic. "I will see where our numbers are and what positions are held. We will also have to check in on Rifun's latest political negotiations; it may be that we have to persuade a few reluctant allies to join us."

Cassius grinned and nodded. "I'll start sharpening my knives."

He walked away, heading for the officers building. Finally, it felt as though they were getting somewhere. Something was being done. They weren't going to squander his heady efforts to massacre a bunch of hoity-toity Tacagan bastards and their mercenary horde. Gentleman Killers anyway. Stinking sons of bitches, the lot of them. Killing was killing, no matter how clean. Lipstick on a pig, Cassius heard it said once.

He strode into the officers building with renewed purpose and made for Rifun's chambers. His first thought was to walk in without announcing his presence. Then he considered several things that he had no desire to walk in on, and came up just short of the door. Three seconds, he told himself. Knock and give three seconds for a reply.

He knocked. More to the point, because of how heavy the doors were, he had to pound on them pretty hard to be noticed.

"Enter," came the reply.

Cassius did so without ceremony, letting himself in and making himself right at home, taking a seat in one of the chairs near the hearth which was full of fire. Rifun was at a table, looking over some papers. More diplomatic stuff, Cassius mused silently.

"I'm surprised at you," Cassius said rather loudly.

"Shall I take this as a straight compliment or inquire as to your meaning?" Rifun wondered, still looking over his papers.

"Tortured for ten years, more scar tissue than flesh over most of your body, and yet you still keep a fire going, still practice Energy skills upon it."

"You may have noticed, it tends to get rather chilly in here. As for your remarks, you speak as though I should be fearful of fire. I assure you, I am deathly terrified of it. But I refuse to allow myself to be controlled by such fear. I can either die of exposure resulting from said fear, or I can keep myself warm and suffer only a bout of anxiety."

"Yes, Isthim mentioned something about your experimenting with yoga or tai chi or something." When he got no reaction, Cassius sighed. "Don't you know how to have fun once in a while? Why must you be so serious all of the time?"

"I wouldn't know what fun was if it introduced itself," Rifun sighed. "Did you come here for a reason, or are you simply looking for someone to patronize? If it is a reaction you are looking for, might I suggest Commander Misik?"

Cassius stood, still casual and carefree. "And have him burst my heart? I don't think so." He went to the table and leaned against it, across from Rifun. He grinned. "We have a plan."

Now Rifun looked at him without moving his head, raising a brow. "I believe this is one of the rare occasions when you have used the plural pronoun 'we' rather than your customary selfish 'I.' Pray tell, who else is in on this plan? I admit, I am more interested in that than the plan itself."

"Isthim and I came up with this plan, and it involves a bit of cooperation with the Borelians as well."

Rifun leaned back in his seat. "Well now, this is truly astounding. The slave and the slavers, working together." Cassius straightened stiffly and Rifun grinned. "You're not the only one who can stick a knife in old wounds." He made a gesture. "What is this plan of yours? Yours and Isthim's and the Borelians'?"

Cassius glowered at him for a long moment. Then, "The massacre was a good launching point, and it brought us some allies. But we are not ready for a full takeover. But we can't just sit here and wait to be ready. The Tacagans will regroup, the Gentleman Killers will be better prepared, and our advantage will be lost."

"This is known," Rifun stated. "I assume this plan resolves that issue?"

"I was already out killing candidates before you brought me back. Send me back out to do the same. Candidates, Tacagans, and I'll even do the Gentleman Killers for free. The people will be afraid, and if their leaders are brought low, they will have nowhere to turn. With the Borelians backing us as the policing force, we can squeeze the Time industry from all sides. On top of that, I have a lead on the journals; I just have to buy them enough time to go out searching and come back, and provide a little cover for their activities."

The last bit was a lie, but Rifun didn't need to know that. In fact, the man looked genuinely curious about the whole thing.

"Come on," Cassius pressed. "The massacre was our declaration of war against the Tacagans and the Gentleman Killers, maybe against the Time industry itself. We are powerful, and we are coming. And we will not be stopped. In fact, we already have more power than people realize, with the Akari and the Borelians. We can't waste this opportunity!"

"And how will this round of killing be seen differently from your first round of killing?" Rifun asked. "You have come and gone from the Cult several times. How will you distinguish yourself as being allied and working on behalf of the Cult rather than simply for yourself or your latest contract?"

"Because the Borelians will proclaim it so. They are the policing force. They are supposed to stop me. But they won't. They will declare the Akari and their alliance to it, or at least to us. When the people see that the Borelians will not touch us, touch me, that they are in fact working with us, then the people will know. Then they will see."

Rifun frowned but nodded. "I'm impressed. Do the Borelians know of their part in this yet?"

"Isthim will speak to them."

"Hm...that does not inspire the most confidence, but it is a logical start." He paused and drummed his fingers on the table. "I see no reason to bring this up to Julianna. She will most assuredly be aghast at the whole thing, say something about how we should not do this, should not be in this situation. Likely she will say something about being more humanitarian."

"Julianna was there for this conversation, and she said all of those things," Cassius grumbled.

"So we already know her point of view. But I would say three votes out of four is good enough, assuming the Borelians agree." Rifun nodded again. "Let me know before you leave. I will see what I can learn through diplomatic channels. There may be some recommendations on whom to assassinate to achieve the desired effects."

Cassius raised a brow. "I'm surprised you're willing to go along with this."

"Cassius, there is a difference between butchering the innocent for the sheer joy of bloodlust, and targeting certain political individuals in order to effect a desired change. I will never forgive the French for what they did to me and my people, but I will not cry over the removal of Hitler. And I am sorry if you are unable to differentiate the two."

Well, it wasn't the undying support Cassius had wanted, but then, he hadn't been expecting that much. He was, truly, surprised that Rifun was willing to go along with the idea. He was always so caught up in the diplomacy and politics of the arrangement that it was sometimes difficult to believe that he was once a soldier.

All the same, Cassius judged it best to quit while he was ahead. He had the man's support; better to leave now while he had it, rather than say something that might see that support revoked. Now he just had to wait for word from Isthim.

In truth, he had hoped for a little speedier response than what he got. He had envisioned Isthim taking the offer and plan to her people and dangling it in front of them like a steak before a starving dog. The Borelians would slobber for it, clamber for the right to rip into their new power and assert their status.

Instead, when he grew impatient after two days of no news and cornered Isthim about it, she merely said that the Great Admirals of the Fleet, the Council of

Ancrath, and the Ul Ik Zol were debating the issue.

"What do you mean, they're debating the issue?" he demanded hotly. "What is there to debate? Don't they want power and status and access to slaves?" He spat the last word with venom.

Isthim sighed and gave him a look. "My people are already incredibly powerful. But we did not get to be this way by being foolish and short-sighted. The power we gain, we always intend to keep, and we work out strategies to ensure this is so. Less time is wasted in planning ahead thoughtfully than attempting to patchwork plans and counter-plans as foolishness falls apart." She went on before he could speak. "You have spent too many years going here and there, having no plan, no purpose, and therefore no power. You wander aimlessly, make foolish, short-sighted, loud actions and so are unable to be taken seriously. If the Cult had remained under your leadership on Earth, there would be no Cult left today. But I took charge, and I ensured that we held onto what we had. If a strategy works, why change it, especially to a strategy that has proven disastrous in the past?"

Cassius glowered at her, if only because he knew she was right. Finally, "How long do you expect them to take? Are you part of the debates?"

She huffed a sigh. "No."

"Don't your people trust you?"

"Their debates are for the glory of Brelix. They believe that I am still too...tainted by outside influence and ideas. They wish for a more objective approach."

"Hm. So much for the collective."

She gave him a look. "I still work for the glory of Brelix. I always have. But even in a collective, there are different roles to be played. I am playing my role by leading the Cult and being a bridge between it and my people. It is not my duty to do everything."

With that, she turned and left. Cassius watched her go and was unprepared for Julianna to speak behind him.

"What do you make of that?" the woman wondered quietly. She moved to stand beside Cassius. "What do you suppose her intentions are?"

"To cart us off to slavery no doubt," Cassius growled.

"Well, besides that."

"I don't know."

"I might have an idea. Teach her people the Akari. Then, when they are sufficiently powerful, then enslave us and assert themselves with power greater than the Time industry."

Cassius rolled his eyes and turned to face her. "And you're going to give me another lecture on how this is my fault?"

Julianna shook her head. "No. To do so now would serve no purpose, for here we are now. All that remains is how to deal with it."

"And I suppose you have a plan?"

She shrugged. "Only a foolish one. I'm no strategist like her or Rifun."

He studied her, wondering if he shouldn't just cut her throat and save them all the trouble of having to listen to her worry and nag and fret about humanitarian things. He decided against it; she was still the only one with true knowledge of the location of the other journals.

"Fine," he sighed. "I may not be as intuitive about people as Rifun, but even I can see that you're dying to tell me this plan of yours."

"We need to get rid of her. And all the Borelians."

"I like ambitious women. How did you expect me to do this? You think I haven't considered the same thing?"

"Then why haven't you?" Julianna shifted her stance. "You are arguably the most powerful one here when it comes to the Akari, and your physical prowess is well-known. No one can deny your distaste for their slave trade. What is it that is stopping you?"

For a long moment, he did not answer, simply ground his teeth and chewed on his words. Then, "Because I can't stop them all. If I had killed Isthim at first approach, no harm would have been done. If I had killed her before she went to her people, this could have been avoided. But now there are more involved. Bring one, bring them all, even if they aren't all here. With Rifun negotiating with them, a broken contract would bring the slavers here faster than we could blink."

Julianna nodded slowly. "Well, you're not wrong there. At the same time, I have thought a bit about this plan of yours. Have you spoken to Rifun yet about the particular political assassinations?"

"He gave me a few names."

"You know, once you make us known—again—then there will be resistance, especially if the Borelians do own up to their involvement with us. There may be counterattacks from the Tacagans and the Gentleman Killers."

"Yes, of course there will be. It's what we want, what we're trying to direct. What are you getting at?"

"Why not kill two birds with one stone?" She sighed when he did not understand and lowered her voice. "Controlled opposition, Cassius. Kill the targets that we need gone, then go after some of the Borelians and make it look like the Tacagans or the Gentleman Killers. The people do not yet understand or fear the Akari, but they fear you and they fear the Borelians. Those will be their targets for counterattack. Others may not be able to get very close to the Borelians, but you can."

Gradually, Cassius began piecing things together in his mind. He grinned. "I like ambitious women." He gave her a look. "At least this sounds like a more sensible plan than hanging your husband."

He did not react as she slapped him.

"You know I will never forgive you for that," she hissed.

"I don't need your forgiveness," was all he said as he stalked off.

Yes, he was liking this more and more. And to think, this time, it had been his idea that they were rallying behind. He had finally done something right and taken his place as leader of the Cult. This was his idea and the others were following his lead. He rather liked the sound of that. Well, Julianna and Rifun were following him and realizing his idea. Now he just needed Isthim and the Borelians to agree to it.

His enthusiasm began to wane as the debates went on for another four days. Time was slipping by and nothing was happening. He debated himself whether he shouldn't just go out and start killing anyway, force the Borelians to make a decision. He was just about to do so when he spotted Commander Misik and Isthim in the officers building. Misik had been at the debates, and he hadn't been seen around the camp at all during that time.

Cassius intercepted the pair.

"And?" he demanded shortly.

Misik raised a brow, apparently annoyed that his conversation with Isthim had been interrupted. Finally he sighed. "I assume you wish to know what we have decided in regards to your plan?"

"Have we had other conversations of mutual interest that I've missed out on?" Cassius asked sarcastically.

"Indeed not. But..." Misik sighed. "The short answer is that we will support your efforts."

Cassius pushed past them, coming dangerously close to skin-to-skin contact, whispering, "It's about time."

3 | Zava-Misy sy Tantara Foronina

Fact and Fiction

The Caves of Meroian, 1964

Rifun did not care to know the details of Cassius' engagements, though he knew well that he would hear about them, if not through general gossip from the Wheel and Time industry at large, then certainly from the man himself. Cassius seemed to have it in his head that he needed to recount his murderous tales upon his return, perhaps in order to solidify the idea that he was someone to be feared. As if there had ever been any doubt.

At the same time, if that was his motivation, then that meant that he was afraid that they were unafraid of him, which meant that he feared them. Perhaps not Julianna, but Isthim and Rifun, and Rifun decided that he would not dissuade this thinking, if indeed it were true.

He maintained his relaxation routine, with his tai chi-like forms and a bit of meditative prayer before his shrine each morning. He did not react as the door to his chambers opened and Julianna's light steps entered. She was the only one who maintained some semblance of respect for his beliefs and did not immediately launch into some diatribe, thereby interrupting his meditation. Though she did clear her throat after a minute or two.

Well, the day had to start at some point, he supposed.

He straightened and faced her.

"Yes?" he inquired, removing his blindfold.

"I have an idea I would like to run by you," she began meekly, slowly closing the door. "Seeing how you seem to be the most sensible one. Isthim will overrule me and Cassius will berate me, but I hope you would at least listen first."

"What is this idea about?"

He motioned for her to sit at the table, which she did politely, like a proper Englishwoman. He sat across from her, moving papers and notes aside. He had no worries about her seeing them, for they were all in Malagasy.

"I may have a way to clean up this mess," Julianna said, her tone changing to one of pure business and planning.

"To which mess are you referring?" Rifun inquired, raising a brow.

"All of them. Cassius, Isthim, the Borelians, all of it."

"So you were just being polite a moment ago, about them overruling and berating you."

"Isthim was just down the way as I spoke. I wish to be discreet."

"When considering the assassination of your business partners, discretion is certainly warranted, I think. What is this plan of yours?"

"Has Cassius approached you with his plans to go out on another killing spree, proclaiming the Akari and having the backing of the Borelians?"

"Of course he has. I would be surprised if half the recruits didn't know about it."

She nodded. "Well, I added a bit of sweetener to his tea, and I'd like to think that this sweetener is poisonous."

"Truly the weapon of a woman. Do elaborate."

"I gave him a secondary plan, to become the controlled opposition. As he is killing the Tacagans and proclaiming the Akari, the people will come to fear it. They will be powerless against it, but they will want to strike back at something. Anything. Anything to make themselves feel less powerless and more in control. The face of this evil will be Cassius and the Borelians. So I figure—"

"Send Cassius after the Borelians, make it look like retaliation from the Tacagans or the Gentleman Killers," Rifun finished. "Have him kill Isthim, Commander Misik, and other key players, hope that one of his missions goes sideways and he is killed, or send another assassin after him."

"Exactly." She shifted in her seat. "With Cassius and Isthim gone, you and I are free to retrieve the journals, study them well, and learn everything about the Akari, enough to overthrow any Borelians foolish enough to remain in our ranks and think they have control. We defeat the Borelians, earn the fear and respect of the Time industry for it, and take over."

Rifun mulled this over, trying to decide whether the plan was incredible or incredibly stupid. It sounded simple enough, and yet things felt so complicated that it couldn't possibly work.

"And what happens if Cassius is everything he touts himself to be and is not haphazardly killed?" he inquired. "Or what if he is killed before he can take out Isthim or the other Borelians?"

Julianna huffed a sigh. "Then we'll be no better or worse than if this plan hadn't been conceived. We already expect him to be the buffer between us and them; I'm just trying to keep him occupied."

Well, there was that.

He shifted in his seat. "Although, I am curious to know, how many assassination attempts do you have planned for my life?"

She blinked. "Why would you say that?"

"If they'll do it with you, they'll do it to you."

She coughed a nervous laugh. "I understand that mistrust is high and we're all struggling to work together, but wouldn't you agree that Cassius and Isthim are rather dangerous and need to be eliminated?"

"I'm not saying they aren't, but let me put it this way. You are one of the founders of the Cult. You intended to be its leader, or one of them beside your husband. You're using me to try and erase your past errors of bringing in Cassius who brought in Isthim. What happens when I am no longer useful or needed? Shall I be discarded as well?"

"Of course not! Please, do not misunderstand. I made a poor decision with whom I did business. You are the one I wished I could have met initially, not Cassius. I am simply trying to be rid of a terrible mistake!"

Rifun frowned and considered her words, tried to judge her sincerity. He could not expect someone to hang onto past mistakes forever without attempting to correct them. Cassius was volatile while he was with the Cult, but also when he was running free. At least when the man was working for the Cult, he had his uses and could be better controlled, or at least kept under surveillance. The only way to erase that mistake, short of the man having a Saul on the road to Damascus encounter, would be to kill him. Isthim and the Borelians, the same.

So why did it feel as though he were missing something sinister? Could it be that she was telling the truth? He could not allow himself to be ruled by paranoia, but caution was rarely unrewarded.

"You don't believe me," Julianna stated after a minute of silence.

"I'm debating," he mused. He shifted in his seat. "Although, just because a man is sinister does not mean he is a liar. He simply may not be disclosing the whole truth. Half-truths may cause another man to act foolishly compared to what he may have done had he been given the whole truth. However, it is not a half-truth to say that Cassius and Isthim are dangerous, both to us personally as well as our operation. But they are also useful. To an extent. We ought to see that they are utilized to their maximum capabilities and then disposed of appropriately."

"You're a thoughtful man. I like that."

"Thoughtful does not mean gullible."

"Am I not allowed to dispense even the mildest of compliments with you?"

Rifun sighed. "Very well. Thank you."

After a moment, she cleared her throat.

"Was there more?" he wondered.

"Often it is appropriate to return one compliment for another?"

He gave her a look. "Don't push your luck. Trust is not something that can be forced."

"Do you need to trust someone to compliment them? Have you never told a woman that she looks nice or that she's pretty?"

"Unfortunately for you, you're not my type."

"Indulge me." He gave her another look and she sighed. "Honestly, I'm not trying to kill you, nor do I have any inclination to sleep with you. All I want is a simple compliment. I get very few of those these days, either because of the nature of this place or because of my looks."

"I have little sympathy for your looks, given the ability to Disguise yourself."

"Yes, but then it is only a compliment to a mirage, not who I really am."

"Fair enough. But I also happen to know that the grunts out there adore you, and they do compliment you. I think what you're looking for is some sort of romantic interest, someone to take notice of you, befriend you with no pretext, accept you, and perhaps desire some manner of intimacy."

"Is that wrong?" Julianna asked, suddenly defensive.

Rifun shrugged. "I didn't say it was. But it does contradict your earlier statements. As I have mentioned before, the difference between half-truths and whole truths. All this to say that the compliment you are fishing for will not be found from me. Either you will have to go out and find yourself the romance you seek in the regular world, or else discard such notions."

She huffed. "Well, given Cassius' propensity for violence and Isthim's tragic cunning, I don't know that I would want to seek out a relationship in the regular world."

"Which is why you came to me."

She glared at him. "Damn you."

"I will take that as another compliment, thank you."

The Hands Pulling the Strings

In a manner most unbecoming of a woman as prim and proper as she, Julianna stood suddenly and stormed out of the room. Rifun watched her go, saying nothing. Honestly, he didn't know what she expected. She probably didn't know what she expected. He would admit to feeling some sympathy for her over the loss of her husband, but didn't she know that it was bad form to begin a relationship with one's coworkers? Hadn't she already chastised him and Isthim for that very thing?

Well, no matter, he supposed. He stood, stretched, and gathered a few things. He had stuff he needed to do. Might as well get started on it. For those of a more action-oriented persuasion, the slow drudgery of politics and waiting for things to happen did not go over well. He had to be out and about and looking busy.

He did a tour of the city first, to see how things were progressing. There seemed to be a sense of order now, a rather militaristic air in some places where recruits were out actively training. Isthim was certainly whipping them into shape. Despite his misgivings about having the Borelians around, they were quite useful when it came to organization and discipline. There were few problems when punishment could range from something as minor as having one's senses dulled to something as severe as having one's clock broken.

Just the thought of clock breaking was enough to give even Rifun pause. Even the basest creatures had a concept of time. It may have been as simple as day and night, before and after, but it did exist. A green Borelian's toxin, when used to its fullest extent, could break a man of even that, so that he had no concept of the passage of time. He could be a young man of twenty years and live to be a hundred, but he would know virtually nothing of the time in between inasmuch as being able to construct a timeline and look back on events. All that mattered was the literal, present moment.

Feeling his skin crawl, Rifun made for the tunnels and prepared to open a portal to the Wheel. Things were dangerous enough without allowing phantoms to terrorize his thoughts as well. To an extent, he had to focus on the here and now and what he could accomplish. What he needed to accomplish.

He'd sent out a few more messages to various peoples and rulers, trying to get a feel for the situation, assessing prospects and likelihood of alliance. Some did not reply, others were uncertain. Most did not want to proclaim new alliances so soon after such a dramatic political upheaval. They wanted to be secure in the alliances they already had—of which there was no guarantee, not always—before forging new ones, especially with the ones responsible for said upheaval.

It was a process, Rifun mused. He kept one eye and ear out for nearby ne'er-do-wells, but for the moment, things appeared peaceful in the Message House.

Sending and receiving messages between races — or even just between places on the same planet — varied from civilization to civilization depending on their available technology. Those who could communicate through space did so, but they were far more advanced than Earth. Other civilizations had their own technological interfaces, where they could link up to the Wheel and use it as a relay for their messages. Earth was just tipping into this point with the advent of the computer, but most humans and other technologically-impaired species were forced to do things the old-fashioned way: the post office. Some got home delivery, others rented a post office box.

Rifun had no doubt that each piece of mail was scanned and cataloged in some fashion. He might have thought that the secretaries read through it, but for as many secretaries as there were, there was just too much mail coming and going for mere mortals to be so efficient and effective at such a task. All the same, he was careful about how he worded things he sent. And if there was something truly pressing that he just couldn't hide, sugarcoat, or mince words, he could always just hand-deliver the message if he had to.

But with nothing of particular importance coming through today, he left the Message House and made for the Archives. Knowledge was power, and it was one place he wouldn't be disturbed, at least by the likes of Cassius. The man might burst into flames if he ever touched a book, at least a book that wasn't the journals. Rifun paused and briefly wondered if there was a way to make it happen.

He spent several hours in the Archives, reading up on politics, war, religion, and a number of other subjects from a variety of cultures and time periods.

At some point, he found himself staring at a tablet, but not reading the words. Something had struck him, a feeling or an idea. It had started out simply as being numb and feeling disconnected from his own body, but once he became aware of it, it quickly turned into something of a panic attack. His chest tightened; he could not breathe and his heart raced. He broke out in a terrible sweat. He saw no images before his eyes for he could not see what was not there, nor could he say that he found any intrusive memories flooding his mind. Rather, his blindsight vision seemed to fade, and he was left as a disembodied spirit of fear.

He tried to think of something, couldn't seem to remember how to think. He wanted to feel, get his spatial bearings, but his skin had gone numb and was no longer sending that information to his brain. He wanted to move his eyes, shift his focus point, try to see, but his eyes would not obey his commands.

In the distance, he heard something. It sounded familiar, and for a moment, he couldn't tell whether it was friendly or unfriendly. He was still rigid with terror, and something told him that it was unfriendly. Unfriendly and potentially dangerous. Either he had to run away, or he was going to be in for the fight of his life.

Still he could not bring any specific memory into focus to say what was going on, and still he could not see around him. There was an element of fear that stemmed from this, too, that perhaps his blindsight had failed him. True, he went through his prayers and meditative forms each morning with a blindfold on in order to train his other senses, but the thought of actually losing what little sight he had was terrifying.

He had to do something. He couldn't just sit here like a prey animal and wait to be picked off. He had to make a decision. Fight or flight.

Initially he was going to flee, but then he was lashing out as something touched his shoulder. He hit it away and struck out with a sharp hand. As soon as flesh met flesh, his flight instinct deserted him in favor of the need to fight.

Still blind, he could only rely on his other senses as he swung and lashed out, striking flesh more often than not. Fear drove him on, though he was uncertain whether he was actually trying to best his opponent, or simply buy himself a chance to escape.

Whoever or whatever his opponent was, they were well-matched. As Rifun's mind shifted into military instinct, he realized that while his opponent was well defending himself, he wasn't doing much more than that. Any strikes he made against Rifun were in places that were not exactly lethal, though it would provide more tactical advantage. Attempting to subdue, but not necessarily kill.

Not an assassination attempt, then, but taking him away to be tortured.

No. Not this time. Not today.

Now he heard something, and it took a minute for him to realize that the furious snarling was coming from him. He was defiant. He was not going to be taken away. He was not going to be tortured. Not today. This time, he was going to fight back. He was going to be the victor.

His heart pounded so hard in his chest he was surprised it didn't burst out of his ribcage. He was dizzy with fear and rage, and also from lack of oxygen as his lungs refused to take in air. Even so, he could feel his opponent wearing down, giving in. He was weakening. He wasn't going to last much longer.

His opponent went down—for a humanoid, he might have gone to a knee. As he struck again, his blow hardly threatening, Rifun grabbed his wrist, pushed him back, yanked him forward, then spun him around so his legs were tangled and he could not escape the sleeper hold that Rifun forced on him.

Something heavy hit Rifun in the side of the head and he released his opponent.

For a long minute, all of his senses were terribly fuzzy, but whatever had hit him, it seemed to have knocked some sense into him. At the very least, it seemed to have knocked the irrational fear out of him. His senses slowly returned, including his blindsight.

He found himself sitting against a bookshelf in the Archives, looking up at Micaiah, one of the Akarin.

"What...?" he began, then trailed off and shook his head. "What happened? What did I do?"

"Quite frankly, you kicked my ass," Micaiah said. He offered a hand, but Rifun veered away from it as he got to his feet.

"Did I hurt you?"

"Only my pride. Question is, are you all right?"

Rifun let out a breath. "I don't know. I'm not even sure what happened."

Micaiah nodded. "You had that look that some guys get when they return from the war. Their body is present, but their mind is still far away. Guess it's my own fault for interrupting you, given your aversion to touch."

"I suppose I should be grateful it was you, someone who knew that. I don't know that I would have fared so well against other, larger aliens who may not have understood." Rifun brushed himself off self-consciously. "But now the question becomes, was this a happy chance, or were you seeking me out intentionally?"

The Irishman seemed to remember himself then as he answered, "Actually, I was coming here on my own errands. I happened to see you and notice that something didn't look right."

Rifun nodded. "Well, I thank you, then. Although, I am not one to believe in such coincidence, not with the thousands of aliens populating this location, nor the timing of the incident."

Micaiah frowned thoughtfully. "You think I'm stalking you, then?"

"No, not at all. I believe this most fortuitous turn of events has been scripted by the Author."

"Ah. Then, being an insightful, well-spoken individual, you know also why she brought us together?"

"In a show of friendship, comradery. Had you simply been walking by and we saw each other, we may have exchanged pleasantries, maybe not, but nothing of significance would have occurred. However, in you helping me—by dint of being another human being who recognizes when one is not in his right mind—then it shows that we can still care about one another, despite any of our other disagreements."

"Other disagreements," Micaiah echoed. "You are still part of the Cult, then?"

"Indeed."

"How can you be? After what Cassius did to the Tacagans? And now there are rumors circulating about an alliance with the Borelians?"

"Did anyone protest the removal of Hitler and his top advisers? Did not the United States and Soviet Union put aside their differences for a time and unite against a common foe?"

Micaiah raised a brow. "You may have a point about the Nazis, but the common foe alliance does not hold up when you consider that the Borelians do not need your alliance; you need theirs."

Rifun lowered his voice. "And believe me when I say that I am working on every available solution and opportunity to be rid of them; it was not my idea."

"Fair enough, but here you are, still working for them."

"I'm trying to help them, believe me. Their leadership is dreadful, and if I do manage to get rid of the Borelians, they'll need more stable minds than Cassius and Julianna to lead them."

"And what will you do then? If you manage to succeed in your goal, what will you do? Where will you lead them?"

"I will lead them to a glorious future, one without the Time industry dictating its will upon the universe."

"How will you be any different than the Tacagans whom Cassius just slaughtered?"

"Because we do not demand undying fealty. It is not about the collective, but the individual and the Author. Once the Time industry is reformed, then all Akari-bearers may live in peace."

Micaiah frowned. "There are a number of things I could say to that, but I don't know that I want to."

"Try me."

The man hesitated a moment longer before saying, "Do you think that killing all of the French residents in your occupied country would have brought peace to your people? Or do you think it would have only made things worse?"

Rage flared in Rifun's heart, but he kept a stony expression. "I did not seek to kill civilians, only evict them. The only way to get them to leave was by forcing the hand of their leaders." He continued before Micaiah could speak. "It was the French who slaughtered my people, burned them alive and pushed them out of airplanes. Now tell me, could you have just stood by and watched such a thing?"

Micaiah sighed. "No, of course not."

"Then you understand that I have only the best of intentions, but the worst of circumstances."

The Irishman gave him a look. "And once the Time industry is gone, what then? When you have reformed it in the image you desire, what then? And what do you do when someone else decides they don't like this new system?"

"That is why I am taking my time, being cautious, and being diligent with whom I choose to ally us. Borelians notwithstanding, of course, for that was not a willful decision."

"And when one of your allies gets into a fight with another one of your allies?"

"We will be united in the Akari."

"And if you aren't? If they aren't? Are you going to force them to like each other?"

Rifun shifted his stance. "All right. I can acknowledge flaws. I also get the sense that you are trying to say something. Tell me, how do the Akarin deal with such matters? What happens when warring species meet in your fortress?"

"Then they are united in the Akari, for we stick to our doctrine. That does not mean we do not have disputes, but we have something uniting us. You expect to rule many peoples while they have nothing in common, certainly no common moral code. And you simply expect them to adapt, adhere, and accept it as is because you say so. I can tell you now, that will not work."

"Then I expect that we shall need your help. You boast success in such matters with the Akarin. If the Cult and the Akarin can be reunited once more, how much better shall we demonstrate the Author's power and rule effectively?"

Micaiah shook his head. "I fear your mind is twisted and your logic unsound, though it will not appear so to your own mind. I'm sorry, but I can't debate someone whose reason has fled."

He started to walk away, but Rifun spoke again. "You were happy enough before, when we spoke in my apartment, or in the fortress."

Micaiah turned. "Because your mind was still open, still curious, still thirsty for knowledge and wise enough to analyze everything, every argument and every detail. You saw things from an outside perspective and desired to make a good decision. But now you've stepped into a place where you either cannot see these things, or you choose not to. For your sake, I hope it is the former."

Wary of listening ears, Rifun went after Micaiah, stopping him and lowering his voice. "Would it make a difference if Cassius, Isthim, and the Borelians were removed from the picture, and things could be seen as they were originally meant to be?" He went on before Micaiah could protest. "No doubt you are wondering how I would justify this removal, since it can only happen one way, but again I ask, did anyone mourn for Hitler? Sometimes you can only put such evil to rest through death. But once the cancer is removed, the body is free to breathe once more. Let me get rid of the cancer. Then perhaps we can speak."

The Irishman looked terribly uncertain, almost comically so. He hesitated for a long moment. Finally, "I would be willing to consider it, yes. Richard and Julianna departed the Akarin at a time of great turmoil, and I've little doubt that Cassius took advantage of them in their confusion and weakness. The Cult has been operating under these principles born of desperation, compounded by treachery and fractured leadership."

"Please, spare no words on your opinion," Rifun said.

"If Cassius and the Borelians were removed from the Cult, I would be open to the idea of talking," Micaiah repeated. "But it would have to be done fairly soon; the more Cassius kills and the more the Borelians sink their claws in, the harder it will be to be rid of them and clear your name."

"You do not need to warn me of the dangers of the lion. I know them well, for I sleep with them."

"Good. Then I trust you will take care of yourself, and your business with Cassius and the Borelians."

This time when Micaiah walked away, Rifun let him go.

He was unsure what to make of the exchange. It sounded like a step in the right direction, almost a vote of confidence. At the same time, if Micaiah really was interested in opening up talks and helping the Cult, he might have offered some sort of, well, help. Maybe an army of Akarin wouldn't come to their aid to storm the castle and dispose of Cassius, Isthim, and the Borelians, but give him something to work with as a show of good faith on their part.

Well, in the end, he was left with the same options and the same plans as before. He just had a little more confidence in a reconciliation following success. If he got to that point, he would count himself lucky.

He returned to his work, pleased that it was undisturbed from the fight or any curious passersby afterwards. All the same, his heart wasn't in it anymore. His mind was elsewhere, though thankfully not in the dark place it had been only minutes before. It felt like a lifetime ago already, but it really couldn't have been much more than five minutes since he'd fought Micaiah. Fought, and very nearly beaten, except for some final maneuver that both freed Micaiah and knocked some sense back into Rifun.

Uncertainty nipped at him, like a mosquito. He didn't like the memories and the panic attacks, how they slunk around in his shadow, waiting for him to sit down, relax, and let his guard down. They'd improved some with time, distance, work, and his meditation, but still they were there. Was there nothing more he could do to stop them from overtaking him? Who knew what might have happened if anyone but Micaiah had found him? What if Cassius had found him? A sudden, otherwise unprovoked, very public attack would be just the excuse Cassius would need to kill him and be able to justify it. It wasn't as though the man didn't already suspect that the rest of them might be trying to get rid of him.

After a few minutes of no productivity, and no ability to concentrate and prove otherwise, Rifun packed up and left the Archives. He told himself that he needed time to think over what he'd studied and make out a schedule of appointments to meet with leaders and other potential allies. It was something he did need to do, but it wasn't the primary reason for his departure, whatever he lied to himself.

The tunnels and caves were exactly how he had left them, and the revived ruins did not appear in any distress. It was almost as though he had never left. He was uncertain how to feel about this. Grateful, yes, that things were running smoothly, but was any of it credited to him? Was he actually making a difference here, or just lauding himself as a glorified lackey? Did anyone miss him while he was away, for reasons unrelated to business?

He skittered through the ruins like a mouse and slipped into the officers building just as quietly. No one appeared to have noticed him, nor his absence.

While he was also grateful for the peace and quiet...did no one miss him?

He went and bowed before his shrine, murmuring a prayer. He knew the spirits had led him here, knew that this was part of Nibe's prophecy, but he could not deny that some days he questioned himself, wondered why he insisted on walking this road, this tightrope. What was it that he was supposed to do exactly?

After a minute or two, he got up and was ready to go about his business when something caught his attention. There, on the table. He approached cautiously, then chastised himself when he saw it was only a book.

At the same time, it was not a book he recognized, thus, he could not have left it there. He picked it up.

In the Hands of the Enemy, Book One of The Hands of Time.

Brooke Shaffer.

The Author.

The same as the ones in the Akarin Archives.

Rifun could not decide whether his blindsight cut out, or his memory, because it was a long moment before he could move from his stunned state.

He had received a Book. His Book, his story, written by the Author.

His amazement gave way to sheer joy. Ah ha! He was right! This was proof that the Author was on his side! He was doing the right thing after all! This was all the confirmation he needed! He was doing exactly as the Author intended, exactly what she wanted. There was no way Micaiah or the other Akarin could deny him now! He had the proof right here!

He sat down, got comfortable, opened the book, and read the inside cover.

His joy tempered a bit as he saw that he was not the only one being written about. It seemed as though Cassius had a say in this as well. Opening to the first chapter, it indeed started off from Cassius' point of view, or Kokumbo as his name had been. Being punished, no surprise there.

But then, Rifun wondered, finishing that first chapter, did that mean that Cassius was also correct? That he was, somehow, also in the right? Did that mean Rifun could be going against the will of the Author to kill Cassius? What was he supposed to make of this?

He continued to the second chapter, opening up with him on the chain gang and his fight with Ranivoa. Even as he read the words, he relived everything in his mind as though it were only yesterday. His hand instinctively went to his head wound, now many years healed, as if expecting to find blood and sundered flesh.

He finished the chapter and closed the Book, then sat back in his chair and just thought. He contemplated his existence. Did the Author foretell his every move, his every thought, or did she simply relay events as they happened? There were Books listed in the front that were not yet in existence in his current time, and yet they already existed at some undetermined point in time in the future. And perhaps there were more to come. What, then, did that say about the nature of free will? Was he in any future Books, or were they perfectly independent of one another? If he did make an appearance, could he influence those future Books by his actions here today, or was everything in the past set in stone by a future that hadn't even happened to him yet? Did the Author even notice the discontinuity, or was it all the same to her, simply jumping from here to there as needed?

Rifun frowned and stood, not wanting to stare at the Book any longer, yet not wanting to look away. He made a few laps of his chambers, then stopped to consider something.

Micaiah had said that there were always two copies of a Book, one in the Akarin Archives, and one delivered to the subject of the Book. Except this particular book focused on two people. Had Cassius also received a Book?

After a few minutes of batting the idea back and forth, Rifun headed down to Cassius' chambers and knocked.

"Enter," came a rather disagreeable voice.

Rifun knew the only way to approach Cassius was by presenting oneself as the king of the world, fearless of whatever may come. He did so now, donning his mask and attitude of general indifference with a dash of cunning and scheming.

"What do you want?" Cassius demanded. The man stood at his work bench, the tools of his preferred trade laid out before him. "I'm just making my final preparations. This kind of work is more delicate than some of you seem to realize."

"I'm sure you're more than adequately prepared," Rifun told him. "But that's not why I'm here."

"Then what is it?"

"Have you received any strange gifts lately? Packages left for you with no explanation?"

"Can't say as I've seen any. Why?"

"Because someone left a gift for me. Turned out to be nothing dangerous, but I was curious if you had received anything similar."

Cassius straightened and looked at him. "Assassination?" He relaxed his stance.

"Wouldn't surprise me. Something like that, I would suspect Julianna. Less messy for her to simply leave a gift and walk away."

"It certainly would be feminine style. But if you've not gotten anything, then I will leave you to your work."

Before Rifun could leave, Cassius spoke again. "Why would she leave something for you and not for me, if that is the case? What exactly did you receive?"

"A book. It was left on my table."

"Well, now I think we know why she didn't leave one for me."

Rifun dipped his head. "Perhaps. Or perhaps it was not malicious, but a gift."

"A gift? Why?"

"Friendship among leaders? Psychological warfare? Who can know? At any rate, at least I shall have something to entertain me this evening to take my mind off my work. Good day."

He left Cassius' chambers before the man could say anything more.

So either Cassius hadn't gotten a Book, or he was lying about it. He was pretty quick to point the finger at Julianna. But why conceal it? Was he ashamed? Angry, perhaps? Did he question himself, the spirits, the Cult, and he wasn't going to admit to it just yet? If that was the case, what did that mean for the Cult going forward? What did that mean for Cassius and his mission that he was about to carry out with bloody efficiency and no moral compass?

Or could he be telling the truth, that he hadn't gotten a Book? What were the implications of that? What did it mean if someone didn't receive his Book? Was it a sign of some form? A snub from the Author? But then, did that mean that Rifun was, in fact, in the right in his plans to kill Cassius?

He returned to his shrine where he bowed and prayed some more. He wished for a vision or some divination to tell him what to do. Where was a shaman when you needed one? His family shaman was probably long since dead, and even he knew that such divination now was not the same as it had been decades ago. There was considerably more Christian influence, and he wasn't sure how he felt about that.

So he did his best to pray on his own. He had no crystals, rocks, beads, or talismans of any sort; the most he had was his food offering as well as his soul's willingness.

He received no visions or commands, and when he went to sleep that night, he had no dreams, visions, or visitations. He woke up the following morning feeling deeply troubled about the whole thing. He didn't understand, didn't know what to expect.

He ended up seeking out Julianna, finding her in her chambers, freshening up and preparing for the day like a proper Englishwoman.

"There is much talk of the journals, and you know that the two missing ones are yet sought after," Rifun began. "But where do the Authored Books come into play?"

Julianna glanced at him as she fixed up her hair, combing it just so. Her hair was actually remarkably long, falling to the middle of her back. How she tucked it all into her customary proper bun was beyond him. "You've read the Book of Philosophy, haven't you? Interesting, threads that tie into the Beloved characters, but —"

"Yes, and that's all well and good as long as the Books remain distant and detached from us and our work. But what if they weren't?"

"What do you mean?"

"I received a Book yesterday."

Now she turned to face him. "What?"

"When I returned from the Wheel yesterday, there was a Book on my table. From the Author, signed in purple ink. Since I highly doubt that any member of the Akarin could walk into my chambers just so, there is only one logical explanation remaining."

"You believe it is from the Author."

Rifun shrugged. "Have you another explanation?" He shifted position. "Although, it is a curious thing. It's not just about me, but Cassius as well. I've not finished the Book, but our stories seemed perfectly balanced and intertwined. Yet when I roundabout questioned him about it, he denied receiving a Book also, which I find highly irregular. Quite frankly, I'm not only puzzled, I'm stumped."

Julianna huffed a sigh. "Well, it is a mystery indeed."

"Should we ask the Akarin if they have received a Book also?"

She barked a laugh. "Ha! Ask them? If a man can make one counterfeit, he can surely make two! What does it take for a man to write a book and sign it with a purple pen?"

He gave her a look. "Julianna, how would anyone but Cassius know his true name and life story from two hundred years ago, when he was flogged and then launched a revolt against his master? How would anyone but me know of my life and some of the things that happened?"

Julianna frowned. "Are you having second thoughts about joining the Cult over the Akarin?"

Rifun shook his head. "Of course not. I am simply trying to reconcile the two sides. I know Isthim blanches and Cassius scoffs, but I do wish to heal the rift. This Book presents me with theological questions that I struggle to reconcile, and yet, I am certain that if I can, then this goal can be achieved. And I would like input from all sides, all leaders, help from all to make this happen. When we are united once more, it should be of no matter and no consequence to dispose of the Time industry."

For a long minute, neither of them said anything. Then Julianna spoke.

"Well, I'm afraid I have no good answers for you except what is written in the Book of Philosophy. It is certainly a puzzle, and if you receive any divine answers, make sure to let me know."

It was not the answer he was hoping for, but it was the only one he would get. He left her chambers and returned to his own, picking up the Book once more and returning to where he'd left off.

Fascinating thing, to read about one's own life. Except this was less like a biography and more like a memoir, a memoir with intimate details that no one else should know, and he wasn't the one who'd written it. It was unnerving to say the least.

When he got to the part in his story where World War II turned into the Uprising and all the atrocities committed therein, he found himself in such a state of panic—no, greater than that, greater even than unadulterated terror—that he found himself becoming dizzy and nearly passing out because he could not breathe. His shirt was soaked with sweat and he lay on the floor, uncertain of where he was. Given that his chambers, in his delirium, looked rather like the torture chamber the French had dragged him to for countless nights over ten years, he would never have known if the world had ended.

He slept. When he woke, he felt exhausted, but at least in his right mind once more.

He found himself still on the floor, on one of the rugs he'd laid down to keep out the chill of the stone. He was facing his shrine, some fifteen feet away, and the Book lay on the floor several feet from there where he thought he may have dropped it, or flung it away like a poisonous snake. He couldn't recall.

Every part of him hurt, and all his scars felt as though they were fresh wounds, ripped open only moments ago. These things, years old, suddenly felt as real and as fresh as the rug under his body. As he sat up, the memories of imprisonment and tortured lingered in his mind like a dreadful nightmare he desperately wanted to be rid of but would not leave so easily. It clung to him like humidity in the Madagascan summer, something certainly felt, but nothing he could do about it.

He glanced at the Book, knew he should pick it up, hesitated. It seemed to him a living object, perhaps accursed. Would something terrible befall him if he touched it? If so, he reasoned, his mind slowly coming back to him, it would have done so already. The only dangerous thing in the room at the moment was him. The only thing in the room dangerous to him at the moment was his own mind, his terrible memories and the fearful desire to do whatever it took to escape those memories.

He picked up the Book. He did not burst into flames, nor did he feel the pull of a curse or ill omen upon his soul. It was a simple object. But he could not bear even the thought of continued reading, not right now.

Even so, it did not feel as simple or as inconsequential as he lied to himself. It was far more than an ordinary book. Whatever Julianna said, this was not a counterfeit, fake, or forgery. This was a Book from the Author. He just had to figure out what it meant. But not now. He would wait until he was a little more prepared to face himself.

To that end, he could not simply tuck the Book away on his shelf as any common reading material. It deserved more special treatment. He added it to his shrine and stepped away, returning to his chair to stare at it.

Nothing mystical or supernatural occurred.

Something significant had happened to him in the last couple days, and he wasn't sure what it was. That was perhaps what frustrated him the most. He needed to figure it out. If he did that, he was certain that his path going forward, the fulfillment of destiny as foretold by Nibe, would unfold perfectly, exactly as it needed to be.

4 | Rudurudu ati Itelorun

The Caves of Meroian, 1964

Chaos and Contentment

kokumbo

Cassius slung his bag over his shoulder and left the officers building. He had his first dozen names; that was all he needed. He had a list of over a hundred targets, but sometimes, things changed depending on how people reacted to the first few. This was to be expected. Thus, he only wanted to start with the first ten or twelve names on his list.

But killing was not the only thing on his mind as he left the ruins and made for the tunnels. He found himself well distracted by his conversation with Rifun. The man claimed to have received a mysterious gift, possibly an assassination attempt, possibly an innocent gesture of goodwill. The first problem was that it hadn't killed him. The second problem was that no one in the leadership was innocent. So then what was the purpose of the gift? And a book, of all things. True, Rifun was more scholarly than him, but it was an odd gesture.

It was puzzling, and not a little frustrating. Cassius didn't like intrigue and shadow games as much as the others; he preferred the more direct way of dealing with things, hence his current mission.

The Borelians still seemed a bit hesitant on their part of the deal, declaring for the Cult and allying themselves and functioning as the police force and whatnot, but Cassius wasn't going to stand around and wait for them to conduct studies and hold sessions and make up their minds. He was going to get an answer, and he was going to do it now. He was going to make them choose.

His first mission was a two-for-one deal. The political target was Dormus Regent, a Tacagan emissary who had been invited to the Auctionhouse that fateful day but had declined due to some other obligations. Naturally he'd heard of the fate of his brethren and so increased his own security drastically. This was why Cassius had picked him; he wanted to go straight for the challenge, to prove that he would not be hindered by mere bodyguards.

One of these bodyguards was his second target, a Gentleman Killer, an Obezod with an attitude, but that was a redundant statement. The Obezod were humanoid, an average of eight feet tall and five hundred pounds, using human calculations. The skin on their lips was as thick as the skin on Cassius' heels. Like humans, it was the thinnest skin on their body. They had rather large hands and feet, and they gave a new meaning to the term barrel-chested. They also didn't have hair, but unusual growths not unlike boogers in appearance and texture that grew in a manner similar to hair; however, their heads were also plated with a hard, leathery, almost stone-like substance, making head shots very difficult to pull off with conventional human weapons.

Luckily, Cassius had access to more than just conventional human weapons. Some of them made conventional human weapons look like little more than sticks and stones. And even they paled in comparison to the Akari.

He headed to the Wheel first, mostly just to get a feel for things, the state of the Time industry, the mood of the people. Of the herd. Were the sheep grazing contentedly, or were they on alert and ready to run?

Truthfully, he was also hoping to run into Pilory, or another of Titik's crew, and be told that the crude Psiaco space pirate was able and willing to seek out the journals, at least the Book of Commands. But he found none of them, not Pilory, not another of the crew, and he certainly didn't see Captain Titik himself.

This wasn't to say that there weren't other soapbox preachers out and about in the marketplaces, and their messages and loyalties ran the full political spectrum. Some remained loyal to the Hands of Time and the way things used to be. Others supported the Tacagans and condemned the attack at the Auctionhouse. Others condemned the attack, but showed no love for the Tacagans, instead calling for a variety of other systems and governing methods.

One might have expected these preachers to be at odds with one another to the point where they or their followers would come to blows. Under ordinary circumstances, this might have been the case, except the conspicuous presence of the Borelians seemed to keep the people in line for the time being.

They did not make themselves flagrantly known, strutting through the crowd like a flock of peacocks, nor did they bully or intimidate the populace looking for lunch money. Rather, they made themselves known just enough to keep the peace. They were the fence to keep the cattle in, but the Cult would have to bring the hammer down. Cassius made eye contact with a few of the Borelians, wondering how much the average grunt understood about the situation, why they had the orders they did. Did they know why they were supposed to stand guard here? Did they know who they were supporting? Did they expect to take over the industry for themselves?

No words were said, and Cassius ceased his passive observations to pursue his original mission.

Dormus Regent was sporting exceptionally tight security these days, but every man had a weakness. Despite Tacagans proclaiming themselves far superior to their terrestrial brethren—physically and mentally above the base needs of beasts—Tacagan men were still very much men. Tacaga itself did not permit whorehouses—though Cassius was willing to bet that some still existed—but being more open to the Time industry meant that the people, especially people of rank and means, could get around.

It was entirely possible that Regent wasn't going to let himself get caught in a room alone with anyone, no matter how lusty he was, at least for the time being. And his security would undoubtedly go with him anywhere he went.

But doors were only so big, and there was more than one way to utilize a bottleneck.

According to his information, Dormus Regent preferred to visit a "blue house" as they were called on Juris. Juris was, galactically speaking, in the same neighborhood as Ferul. It just so happened that Cassius' favorite black market arms dealer, Jora, was Ferulian.

"Very impressive what you did in the Auctionhouse," Jora mused as they did a bit of dealing. "I saw the aftermath." He chuckled in the wet, guttural, Ferulian way. "I know many people think you're dumb, that you don't know your jikda from your wojip, but you are smarter than people give you credit for."

"Well, at least someone acknowledges it," Cassius grumbled, picking something up off the table that he wasn't quite sure what it was, but he pretended to anyway.

"Your friends in the Cult don't? Why would they make you a leader, then?"

"I think it's to appease me somehow. Placate me." He set the object down. "I think they're going to try to kill me."

Jora grunted and shrugged. "Well, that's just business."

"In fact, I think someone may be trying to kill Rifun. And it's surprisingly not me. Or not yet."

"Again, that's just business. And I try not to concern myself with inner politics. The less I know, the less I know."

"I understand," Cassius said casually, picking up another item.

Jora approached and took the thing out of his hands, turning Cassius so they looked each other in the eye. "But understand something: I'm in this particular business for me. Now I don't know your involvement with the Borelians, whether it's you or the whole Cult, but you ought to know that if I suspect trouble—and you know the trouble I mean; I don't shy away from a good scrap—then I'm out of here, and you need to find yourself a new arms dealer. Understand me?"

Ferulians were normally very tall with huge eyes, but Jora was shorter than Cassius with very small eyes, and his general alien disposition made it difficult to take him seriously. Even so, Cassius wasn't worried as he replied, "You don't have to worry about a thing."

"Good," Jora said simply. "I am glad to have an understanding. Now maybe we can come to an understanding on these arms, and you can make your appointment on time."

Cassius traded a few of his older weapons for some new merchandise, and bought a few new things for himself just in case. But no matter where he went, what his task was, he always kept his trusty knife hidden in his belt. When all else failed, the blade never did. And about an hour after he entered the dealer's secret warehouse, he departed with his goods, slipping back into the flow of traffic as though nothing had happened. The soapbox preachers continued to prattle on, and the Borelians kept a cool eye on the crowd. As for Cassius, he let the current take him to his exit, snaking his way through the Wheel back to the portal room where he found one leading to Ferul.

Twenty minutes later, Jora joined him.

Ferul was pretty easy-going about interdimensional and standard space travel. Juris was not. They had a strict monitoring system for all portal activity, and written permission was required for all aliens to visit the planet. Cassius was ninety-nine percent certain that his abilities would have made such things moot, and he wasn't above the idea of another massacre, but he didn't want to tip off Regent to his arrival. The Auctionhouse had him on high alert; a second attempt, if not successful, would not only make it harder to find him again, but it would make Cassius look like a fool.

Besides, in diversifying his methods, it made Cassius look more resourceful. He wasn't a one-trick pony. Even for a very powerful trick as the Akari, it could become predictable. It not only ruined the mystique and the fear, but anything that could be anticipated could be defended against. He had to keep his targets guessing.

Jora had agreed to take Cassius to Juris; it would be easier for a Ferulian to get him through than trying to get through himself, even with the papers which were forged anyway. Ferulians, Jurisi, and neighboring Fedurians were all related on some genetic level, though their societies were well different. Even so, this relation would work in their favor since the Jurisi afforded certain privileges to the Ferulians and Fedurians.

Cassius had never been in a spaceship before, and looking out the small windows to the stars made him inexplicably nauseous so that he elected to spend the trip simply resting in an enclosed compartment. Jora found this rather amusing but resigned himself to his post at the pilot's seat.

The trip was thirty-four hours from Ferul to Juris, and Cassius eventually emerged from his hiding spot, trying not to think about being afloat in outer space and instead focus on his mission. He sat down in the co-pilot's seat. Jora was busy working on some 3D puzzle made of what appeared to be bamboo of some form.

"I got this from a Gigogi trader," Jora said, focusing intently on the puzzle. "He told me that if I managed to solve it, he would give me his best restafar."

"Is that a weapon?" Cassius wondered.

"Oh, goodness, no. It's a Gigogi dish. Absolutely sacred. The recipe is guarded like the most valuable thing on the planet. Even the Time industry is forbidden from producing it in the Food Court. Outsiders are not permitted to eat of it, but I managed to steal a few bites once and get myself banned from even being in the same system as Gogi. But it is the most luxurious thing you have ever tasted. Nothing you eat afterwards even comes close to its magnificence." He leaned back and sighed. "Of course, I suspect that the trader was merely baiting me. I cannot imagine that he would risk his own livelihood for such a thing. I also suspect that there is no real answer to this puzzle, and so even if the offer is real, I shall never obtain it." He set the puzzle aside and turned to face Cassius. "But that is neither here nor there, I suppose."

"How long until we reach Juris?"

Jora pointed out the window. Cassius looked long enough to see a marble in the distance. "There it is. Shouldn't be more than one Base Hour." He shifted in his seat. "But tell me something. Why would a Tacagan come all the way here for sexual pleasure? Are Tacagan women not enticing?"

Cassius shrugged. "If you want my guess, he likes big women."

"And Tacagan women are small? I have seen some human women, and while they are smaller than men, they still seem to be of a relative size."

"Extra weight is bad for humans, and Tacagans have engineered themselves to be perfect in every physical way, which means no extra weight that they don't need. So Regent has to go elsewhere for his kicks."

"But why Juris? Ferul is much easier to visit, and the Fedurians are the largest of our three related species."

Cassius grinned. "The thrill of the chase and the exclusivity of obtaining that sacred permission."

Forty-five minutes later, Jora's radio squawked and he engaged in some preliminary conversation with the Jurisi authorities, babbling back and forth in their tongues. Cassius' translator picked up on all of it. He ignored most of it, but it sounded as though Jora was giving the Jurisi the same story that Regent had probably given: he was here to visit a blue house and see big women. Yes, he appeared to have papers, but Jora wasn't the authority on that; he was just the taxi.

They were given permission to dock at the station orbiting the planet. Both of them were questioned, Jora's ship was searched, and Cassius' papers were scrutinized. As for his weapons, well, a little Disguise and a little Light bending to make some appear invisible made it a little easier to get through customs.

If any of the Jurisi knew who he was, his involvement in the Auctionhouse massacre, or his involvement with the Cult, no one said anything. He was given thirteen-hour permissions. After that, he had to be gone. Since he was a Time Agent with decent abilities, this shouldn't be a problem, right?

Jora was summarily dismissed, and he departed. Meanwhile, Cassius was taken to the planet's surface via another small spacecraft, and their descent into the atmosphere left much to be desired as far as his nausea was concerned.

Deep down, past the layer of nausea and concern for his immediate affairs, Cassius was disgusted with himself for such a weakness. The poor piloting of the Jurisi might be understandable, but the trek with Jora had been nothing if not smooth, almost perfectly nonexistent except for the mild hum of the engines. What was it that had caused him to be so ill, then? Was it merely the thought of being in outer space? How trivial! How frivolous! How embarrassing! For a man who could torture and disembowel anything with no moral conflict, why should he flinch at a simple voyage in a space ship?

When they finally landed on the planet's surface and the ship stopped shaking—or perhaps it was just him—Cassius Banded in order to buy himself time to compose himself. Regardless of his intentions, he couldn't be seen stumbling around like a drunken idiot. He had business to attend to, and that business demanded a certain level of cognitive function. He might not be as classy and regal as the Gentleman Killers, but he wasn't a slavering idiot. He wasn't an animal as the slavers and certain other morally conscious individuals thought.

After a minute or two, he was able to get himself reoriented, and he dropped the Band. His wares were inspected again, and again the Jurisi found nothing amiss. Cassius thanked them as politely as he could, then asked for directions to some blue houses.

Apparently there was enough of a demand for such things from outsiders that there was a Las Vegas-style strip full of blue houses specifically for outsiders, this way they didn't have to interrupt the rest of polite Jurisi society. Thirteen blue houses in about the space of five city blocks, ranging from cheap and dirty to rather high end.

Physically and morally superior or not, if a Tacagan was committing the sacred sin of fraternizing with outsiders, Cassius imagined that his tastes might be a little more expensive. He would indulge as much as he could while he had the time, and he had enough money to keep the girls quiet. And they would be well enough off that they wouldn't need to come after him for money if something happened.

Cassius looked around a bit, but saw no sign of the emissary. Well, he wouldn't hire a new swath of security only to ditch them when he would be most vulnerable, and the Obezod would stand out on his own.

He checked all thirteen blue houses, but couldn't find Regent. Had he been mistaken on the date and time? Could the man have other arrangements for his pleasure? Wave enough money around and anyone could be made to look the other way on just about anything. No, his source wouldn't have enough standing to know anything about something like that. Or if he did, Cassius would have expected that it would have been imparted to him.

Just as he was considering whether his source may have been lying, mistaken, or committing some other mischief against him, something caught his eye. A large group of non-Jurisi humanoids walked down the sidewalk on the other side of the street. He couldn't see who was in the middle of the group, but he knew the Obezod with them. Cassius turned his body three-quarters away from the group, pretending to be interested in something in a storefront, but always keeping one eye on the group, watching to see which alley they ducked down.

Apparently, the man had cheaper, dirtier tastes, as they entered an establishment that was not particularly high-end. It was supposed to look that way, but there was a difference between flaunting one's wealth in real leather and furs, and trying to hide one's poverty in faux leather and furs. Still, Cassius wasn't complaining. He waited a few minutes after the last of the security had entered before heading down the alley and ducking inside.

He'd debated whether he wanted to kill the man on his way in or his way out, then decided to let the man have one last pleasure before his death. He could be a kind, merciful assassin.

Cassius hadn't understood why the brothels were called blue houses. Except for some possible decor that varied from place to place, nothing about the brothels was obviously blue. Neither, apparently, were any relevant bodily fluids of the Jurisi. When he'd finally asked about it, he'd been told that the name had come about from some fad almost forty years ago where the prostitutes would rub a particular blue gel on themselves that was as stimulating as it was decorative, and that drove the market boom which drew in all the outsiders. Since then, any brothel that catered to outsiders was called a blue house.

Lipstick on a pig, Cassius thought, putting his pipe between his teeth and lighting it. Regent was far across the room, noticeable only because of his security detail. Apparently he was known well enough that the girls knew not to disturb the security, for not one of them was approached, not even a wink as far as Cassius could see.

The seating arrangements were like that of bowls scooped out of the floor, about five feet deep and twelve to fourteen feet across, faux leather seating encircling the bowl except for a break for the steps leading into and out of the bowl. A piece of furniture sat in the middle of the bowl. It may have started out as a round table, perhaps three or four feet tall and eight feet across, but the center, about six feet across, was scooped out as a bowl. The remaining two feet was flat and smooth, yet not continuous, instead being cut out at regular intervals, almost like flower petals, so that the flat surfaces were little bigger than common dinner plates.

He found the furniture curious, though no more so than simple alien carpentry, and discovered its more practical uses as he observed an adjoining bowl of about ten non-Jurisi enjoying an erotic dance upon the table and its narrow dinner plate ledges before putting the dancer in the bowl and each having his way with her, getting close by the cuts in the table.

"Haven't seen you around here before," a Jurisi prostitute said, lumbering down into the bowl. "And all alone, too." She leaned on the table across from him.

Cassius smiled around the pipe and puffed smoke. "This isn't normally my scene."

"Hm, first time for everything, isn't there?"

"And a last time. I'm here on business."

"Oh, others are coming?"

"They're already here, but I would prefer it if they didn't know. I don't want to spoil their evening just yet."

"So they're the ones playing hooky, then? I like this idea. But if they're occupied, why don't I occupy you for a little bit?"

He puffed more smoke. "As I said, this isn't my scene." He shifted position. "But since it might be a little obvious if I'm not being entertained, I suppose you could go through your routine."

She seemed uncertain how to proceed, and he could tell that she was just as uncertain about her erotic table dance seeing as he was not aroused. Nor was he really paying attention. He kept his attention well fixed on Regent who appeared to be fully enjoying himself.

While only torture and death could truly give Cassius pleasure, he could not recall that he had a "type" of woman he preferred. It made no difference to him whether a woman was big or small, or that she was even human as far as he was concerned. He derived no pleasure from watching the Jurisi dance, nor was he repulsed by Regent's incredibly lusty motions across the room. It was all the same to him. Motions to be gone through to derive a moment of pleasure.

Regent satisfied his lust, then sat down to collect himself. He spoke to his security force and a couple of them left the house.

Cassius looked up at the Jurisi prostitute still making erotic movements on the table. He saw everything a normal man might desire to see and plenty more, and yet he felt nothing until he considered a dozen different ways to bind and torture her. Did these blue houses allow such things? Considering they catered to outsiders, they probably had to accommodate a wide variety of unusual practices, but most species seemed to have a certain aversion to the things he enjoyed.

Well, that was neither here nor there. He was here on business, after all. Maybe he could return later and find out more.

Across the room, Dormus Regent stood and his security force gathered around.

"You can stop now, dear," Cassius told the prostitute.

The Jurisi did so, midway through a pose and a touch. He was no expert at alien body language, but he might have suspected that she was fully expecting to be pushed into the bowl so clients could have their way with her, and confused when he did no such thing. He tried to smile in that way that Rifun did, when he was trying to be both smug and reassuring. "It's not you, it's me. Trust me, you couldn't handle what I require of a woman." He stood and fished out some local currency. "Keep the change anyway."

He didn't know whether it was a generous tip or being a cheapskate, but he hardly cared. His target was about to be on the move, and he had to be ready.

Regent took his own sweet time getting ready, which made it easy for Cassius to slip out of the blue house unnoticed. Or it would have been unnoticed except for the two guards waiting outside.

"Wait, aren't you — ?" one began.

Cassius dispatched both of them with deft ease. No one saw it, and no alarms were raised. He took care to Imprint their last standing poses so that even after he dragged the bodies away, it still appeared as though they were at the door. Of course it was merely an illusion, trapping their image in Time. A strong gust of wind could shatter the image.

This task done, Cassius found a hiding spot and waited. He was about twenty feet from the door. The alley was remarkably clean, but the blue house had to take its trash somewhere, and he hid out near the dumpster. He used the Akari to bend Light around him, making him nearly invisible, perhaps completely invisible in the dim light.

The door opened. The Obezod walked out first, glanced at the two guards that weren't really there, looked around the alley for a moment, then gave some signal that evidently meant all clear.

More security came out, but they could only move one at a time. Cassius used a Fast Band to slow Time and make sure Regent wasn't using some sort of disguise. He hadn't going in, but Cassius couldn't be too careful. The man was a nervous rabbit; if he missed this chance, it was going to be hell trying to find another.

Then Dormus Regent walked through the door. In the Band, Cassius could count the tassels on his long coat. He could see the way the man walked, as a man clearly satisfied in more than one respect. His smug expression put Cassius in mind of Rifun, and that made him want to kill the man all the more.

He put on gloves, reached into his bag, and took out two Mishim paper sticks. The name was hardly fearsome, but they did wonders for assassinations. They were about eight inches long, flat, about half an inch thick. One end, about half the length of the stick, was sharpened to a needle point.

Cassius was no darts player, but he only needed decent aim. With a swift hand, he flung both of them at Regent, not dropping the Band until the needles were already piercing skin. Really he only needed one to kill the man, but he wasn't about to take any chances that he or one of his guards could somehow rip one out in time or provide some sort of antidote. Rifun was the conservative one, doing only what was required and no more. Cassius preferred a more liberal approach, ensuring that the deed was done so he didn't have to worry about his targets coming back for his blood later. Overkill was often a wise precaution.

Then he released the Band.

The way the paper sticks worked was that they reacted to the iron in the blood of most creatures, similar to oxidization, effectively rusting the blood and turning to, well, paper. Rust flakes might be more accurate, but seeing how the name of the weapon was a paper stick, that was what he went with.

The process was not a quick one, either. Regent stumbled as the two darts stuck in his neck, his hand instinctively going to them. Immediately the Obezod began shouting orders and looking around, scanning for a threat. Cassius simply Slow Banded the security force and walked up to Regent.

Initially, the pain was no more than being stuck with darts.

Ten seconds in and Regent was beginning to feel as though something wasn't quite right. His expression was that of pain, perhaps of a violent hornet sting in his neck.

Fifteen seconds in and the man spotted Cassius. Cassius could see that the skin on his neck was becoming weak, brittle, paper thin, and his skin was turning orange-brown, the color of the rusty blood flowing beneath.

The emissary tried to run, but his body was losing blood as it turned to rusty paper, and he couldn't keep up the pace for more than twenty feet, not even enough to reach the main street. He collapsed, his skin continuing to turn rusty and brittle, scraping off on the ground but the wounds not bleeding. Cassius walked casually behind him.

Now thirty seconds in, he began to suffocate, his blood unable to hold the oxygen in his body, his lungs not getting what they needed to function. The man began to choke, limbs flailing as he tried to still get away.

"It hurts, doesn't it?" Cassius said, reaching the man and kicking him onto his back. He could feel a large swath of skin tear away from the man's body. Looking down, Regent's gaze was wild and panicky. His pallor was sickly beyond description, his eyes like that of an idiot. His mouth hung open and it appeared as though his gums were also becoming brittle, peeling away and choking him further.

Cassius knelt beside him. "It hurts to know that all your money and power and influence cannot buy the security you truly need. But don't worry. That pain will be over in just a minute."

Mishim paper sticks normally took about three to four minutes to work, but having used two of them, Regent was on the fast track to death, relatively speaking. He still choked, but his twitching had ceased. All muscle movement had stopped, and he seemed to decay before Cassius' eyes, his body shriveling as all blood and moisture slowly withered away to rust and paper.

Cassius did not know the exact moment that Dormus Regent died, but he hoped that the man was still alive when Cassius satisfied himself on his body. Dormus Regent had done in a minute and a half with his death throes what the Jurisi prostitute had been unable to do in twenty minutes with her promiscuous gyrations.

Now he turned his attention back to the security force, suddenly unemployed. He didn't care about all of them, only the Obezod whom he released from the Slow Band.

The Gentleman Killer appeared confused for only a moment before his gaze settled on Cassius and the dead Dormus Regent beside him.

"Future prospective employers are not going to like this," Cassius said, grinning. "Assuming you live long enough to find any prospective employers."

The Obezod did not say a word as he launched himself at Cassius. The alien's skin was too tough for the average knife and would never succumb to something like the paper sticks, but that did not mean that his eyeballs were as fortified.

Cassius allowed the Obezod to grab one of his arms, creating a distracting sense of impending victory while he slid a knife from its place on his back and, using an invisible Akari Band, got close to the Gentleman Killer and stabbed at his eye.

But the Gentleman Killer was already attempting a kill strike of his own, using Time to Band and attempting to stab him with a knife also. Cassius suddenly found himself with dueling Bands and locked in the iron grip of an Obezod. While terribly annoying, it also provided a certain thrill that he had found a worthy opponent.

He knocked the knife away, his own blade glancing off the alien's thick hide and opening him up in a way that made him more vulnerable than he preferred. He contorted himself to get away from the Obezod's blade as it struck at him again, but his movement was still limited by being in the creature's stony grip.

Cassius feinted, getting close to the Obezod and baiting him to stab at him again with his blade. As the Obezod made his stab, Cassius danced away, prompting the alien to lower his head and move forward, when Cassius made his move with his own knife, driving it into the Gentleman Killer's right eye.

The Obezod howled and screamed in pain, releasing Cassius, but then doing something unexpected. He hissed and gobs of yellow phlegm began spraying from his mouth. A moment later, Cassius felt the burn on his skin. His face, his chest, his arms. As the acidic poison ate through his clothing, he felt the burn on his legs, too, and he was unable to suppress a cry of pain himself. He backed up and looked around for something, anything to stop the burning. When he finally got a moment of clarity, he reached for the Akari, reached for Matter.

Somehow he was able to neutralize the acid—for the moment—and he looked back at the alien with a knife in his eye. The poison was still spewing from the Obezod's mouth, and there was no good way to get close to him now to finish him off.

In all reality, Cassius could have just manipulated Gravity to crush the Gentleman Killer flatter than a pancake, but that just felt like cheating. He enjoyed combat, the thrill of the fight. He also enjoyed a challenging opponent, and this Obezod was proving to be a challenge. Of course, that was why Cassius had decided to kill him in addition to the emissary. Now he was torn. Did he return to finish the fight another day, or just end it right here, right now?

Whether his efforts to neutralize the poison wore off, or he was somehow struck with more of the acid floating through the air, he did not know, but his body began burning again, and he made his decision.

Cassius opened a portal to the Wheel and departed. He would come back another day to face the Obezod. For now, he had to do something about the acid.

By the time he made it back to the hideout and the officers building, the burning had become a constant pain that was only slowly subsiding. As he headed toward his chambers, he happened to pass Rifun in the corridor. The man barely acknowledged him the first time, then did a double-take and called for him as he passed by.

"What happened?" Rifun asked, looking both curious and concerned and maybe a little afraid.

"Did you know Obezod spit acid as a defense mechanism when they're wounded?" Cassius asked sarcastically. "I didn't."

"It looks like it's still burning."

"Very astute of you, O Learned One."

The man raised a brow. "The water in the cavern here is quite alkaline. You might try bathing in that."

Cassius shrugged him off, then waited until he was gone before heading down to the black sandy beach not far from the outside of the ruins. He waded into the water, pleasantly surprised to find that the water eased and even erased the burning. He washed himself several times before slogging out of the water, and he did not fully examine himself until he was back in the privacy of his own chambers.

He looked like he'd had smallpox, and the scars covered his front from head to toe. It looked wretched and he didn't feel much better. How was it that he hadn't been prepared for such a thing? He couldn't recall ever seeing an Obezod spit acid before. He couldn't recall hearing such a thing or reading about it—not that he read much. Probably the others would silently chastise him for not doing more research beforehand. They already thought him a fool. Now he'd just proven them right.

He couldn't let them see him like this. Bad enough Rifun knew about it. He had to erase it, make it as though it had never happened. It would cover up his misstep. It might also confuse the Obezod and perhaps even put a little fear in the Gentleman Killer, that his acidic response had no lasting effect on his victim. Whatever the case, he could not advertise his foolishness, nor wear it as a blanket of self-pity as Rifun did.

He spent the better part of the day Feeling himself, trying to understand the damage done to his body and how to repair it. Had he gotten to the alkaline water sooner, the scarring may have been superficial. Because he'd waited so long, however, some of it ate into muscle tissue. This was much harder to repair.

No one came to disturb him. If anyone knew he was still around in the officers building, they gave no indication of it. Perhaps the others were running their own errands. Perhaps things were just quiet for the moment.

Or perhaps he should stop worrying about the others and focus on his mission. He still had more people to kill.

He flexed his arm as he finished healing the scars. Good as new, maybe better.

As he considered his other scars, knowing that the only ones he would never heal were his flogging scars, he momentarily entertained the idea of removing the bullet from his face, the one that the shadow spirit was using as leverage to get him to do whatever it wanted. The acid had eaten away at some of the flesh around it, even into the lead ball itself. That ought to make it easier to remove, shouldn't it?

Even as he thought it, the pain in his face increased, becoming even worse than just the bullet wound itself, but all the acid as well. Cassius was suddenly consumed with pain, his only thought to make it stop. He went to all fours, one hand clutching his eye and cheek where the bullet remained buried.

Do not mock me, little one, a dark voice hissed in his mind. You are mine.

Then the pain eased up and Cassius was left on the floor like a dog, panting and drooling.

He hated himself. He hated the spirit. He hated the others. He hated everything. But there was nothing he could do about any of it.

There was only one thing left, then, and that was to keep going on his hit list. He still had a dozen names that needed to be crossed off in short order in order to drive the kind of chaos he was looking for. He got the Tacagan emissary. The Obezod had been secondary, a target only for his own personal pride. And who knew? Maybe the Obezod would yet die from his wounds. Or if not, maybe he would spread the word that Calis Cutthroat was at it again, and this time he had the backing of the Cult and the Borelians.

And then there was that matter of getting rid of the Borelians in controlled opposition. He had to pick out which Borelians to kill first and how he wanted to go about doing it. Isthim was an obvious choice, as was Misik, but that might be a little too obvious. If the assassinations were supposed to be the Tacagans or whomever lashing out at those they believed were part of the Cult, they couldn't have such dumb luck in taking out the two most influential Borelian Cult members.

He scoffed and shook his head. He couldn't get all wrapped up in such minute details so far into the future. He had to work with what he had now in front of him. Let Rifun and the others worry about the political details.

Still frustrated, he left his chambers, left the officers building, and headed out of the city. He needed to do something. He needed to kill something. He needed to succeed. He needed to gain some leverage somewhere.

Maybe later he would look for Pilory and Titik again, see if they had any information for him, see if they were even willing to work for him.

His next target was another Tacagan emissary, this one of slightly less prestige and less fear. His name was Germos Fide. He had also heard of the Auctionhouse massacre and upped his personal security, but he did not seem as skittish as Regent had, and continued to move freely about on business. Nor did he have some tragic Achilles heel as simple as an uncontrollable sex drive, or not one that took him off Tacaga to satisfy it.

He did, however, present Cassius with a tantalizing opportunity when their paths did happen to cross in the Wheel, in an intermediate marketplace, because he happened to be in the company of another target Cassius was after, another emissary by the name of Marcus Georgos.

Fide was a long-time, well-known political figure, perhaps one of the top people in the Tacagan circle of influence before the massacre. He had politely declined the invitation to the event with no reason given. Whether it had been other obligations or suspicion, it had served him well. Cassius figured that it couldn't have been paranoia, however, because the man still went about his business.

Georgos was a newcomer, and the only way he could be so well-liked by one such as Fide was either through familial relation or else he was being intentionally groomed for something. Either way, he could not be allowed to carry on Fide's mantle.

Still frustrated by the incident with the Obezod, Cassius did not waste time playing games with Fide and Georgos, and he killed them just as soon as he got his opening, crushing them with a sudden, massive change in Gravity.

Of course, changing Gravity in the Wheel was a little more disruptive than changing Gravity anywhere else, and the whole place suddenly went topsy-turvy, people and wares flying every which way, drawn in different directions. Even the room itself seemed to shift and change a bit. There were many shouts of alarm, and even more cries of pain as everything from Time Capsules to booths to small wares and even other aliens struck people in the shifting gravitational confusion. Cassius felt the same nausea that he had when in Jora's space ship as he glanced around, watching as one large alien crushed a smaller one, and a humanoid alien was struck unconscious by a flying booth. Then the room gave a violent jerk, as something moving quickly in one direction is suddenly struck and sent out of control in another direction, and he went limp as everything gradually righted itself, Gravity returning to normal. He covered his head as aliens and objects rained down around him, then remained on the floor for a moment. Several things struck him, but he was not crushed nor terribly injured. When the room and his head stopped spinning, he picked himself up and looked around.

Any cries of murder or foul play had been drowned out by the surprised cries of panic as the Gravity of the room, perhaps even the entire Wheel, suddenly changed. As everything settled down, those cries were muted as the security force debated whether the deaths of the emissaries had preceded or succeeded the gravitational anomaly. Had an incident killed the emissaries and so shifted the gravity of the Wheel, or had a gravitational anomaly thrown the Wheel off-kilter and so killed the emissaries? Three security guards were also dead after being struck by various objects in the confusion, so it was not impossible.

Either way, there wasn't quite the outrage that Cassius had been hoping for. At the same time, he was not being pursued which meant he had the luxury of sticking around to observe the aftermath of the event.

Grandfathers came to investigate the bodies, and a small legion of secretaries were summoned to ensure the safety of the Wheel and the balance of Gravity. Apparently the effects had been quite far-reaching. Some places had seen effects similar to the ones in the marketplace where everything had been turned upside down. Other places had seen only minor fluctuations, hovering for a few moments, perhaps a minor turn of the room. Few places had remained unaffected.

Whether it was because they believed it or were confused on how to make good on their agreement, the Borelian Grandfathers declared the deaths of the emissaries incidental. Whatever gravitational force had shaken the Wheel, it had resulted in their deaths as well. They had simply been in the wrong place at the wrong time.

Cassius noted how several of the secretaries looked uneasy at this explanation. They were the ones in charge of keeping the Wheel running. A misfired portal, a bad translator, incorrect mailing, these were minor incidents that could be easily corrected. The gravity of the Wheel was a little bigger issue, and people had died because of it.

Because of Cassius. He smiled smugly to himself and carried on his way, stepping carefully around the debris. Some people still lay moaning and calling for help, buried under booths or wares, but he paid them no mind. If anyone recognized him or suspected his involvement, they did not say anything. There was no alarm raised whatsoever.

He made his way back through the Wheel, observing damage to varying degrees. It was all people could talk about, and why not? It was something remarkable. Spectacular. Something potentially dangerous and deadly.

He left the Wheel.

5 | Boky sy Mpanorina   Books and Builders

The Wheel of Time, 1964

Rifun was studying quietly in the Archives when suddenly it was as though the whole room was upended and shaken like a dog mangling a rabbit. He was hardly able to process what was going on, as one moment he was sitting quietly, and the next he was in the air but seemingly going nowhere. Everything around him floated for a brief moment before suddenly being shaken about in the manner aforementioned. He hit something, something hit him, shouts of panic and pain all around.

Everything moved so quickly, his blindsight could barely keep up and he was well enough blind. His own panic set in, and yet he could perceive no obvious threat to fight against. Something struck him and he lashed out but found nothing. Still he was being tossed about as a ball in play, everything muddled and confused. He closed his eyes, tried to figure something out, tried to bring to mind his forms, letting go of his sight and focusing on his other senses. Problem was, his other senses were just as confused.

Something hit him in the head and dazed him. Then it was the feeling like going through a portal, as the air was squeezed from his lungs and his whole body was compressed. He opened his mouth but his muscles couldn't figure out how to work to take in air. Part of his mind panicked, but another part of him was still confused from being struck.

Finally, something gave way. Gravity righted itself and he hit the floor. He coughed once and gasped for breath, blinking open his eyes and trying to bring everything back into focus.

Fear surged through him again as he found his surroundings to be dark. Had he somehow lost his vision completely? No, the room itself was dark, but there was enough light that his eyes were beginning to adjust. He let out a breath, tried to breathe, closed his eyes, envisioned his forms.

His head still hurt, but the fog of confusion lifted, and he got to his feet.

Where was he? And how did he get here?

He stood in a corridor. It was dim, but he could see that it was primarily metal. Down one way, he thought he could barely make out what might have been the path to the entrance. The entrance of what, he didn't know. To his other side was a spiral staircase heading down into murky blackness.

Every part of him prickled with unease. Was this some part of the Archives he'd not discovered yet? How did he get here? Was he supposed to be here? For what purpose? Did it have anything to do with the sudden jolt and change in gravity, whatever it had been?

There did not appear to be any immediate danger, and only the two directions. He seemed to be the only one around; no one else had been transported to this place. Was it a fluke, or had he been brought here intentionally? Why? By whom?

Eventually he decided that this was some kind of direction from the Author. She had brought him here for a purpose. Given that he'd been dropped off right next to a staircase, he guessed that this was where he was meant to go. His purpose would be found at the bottom.

There was a certain sense of forboding that emanated from the staircase, and just touching the handrail made his skin crawl, scar tissue twisting in ways he was not comfortable with. Every instinct told him to flee, and for a moment, the best he could do was remain rooted where he was. This was where he was supposed to be, where he was supposed to go. He had to keep moving. He had to follow the will of the Author.

This thought got him about three steps down the staircase before he hit his next obstacle. More than just psychological unease, he began to feel as though he were standing in quicksand, or perhaps thick tar. His feet felt as though they had lead weights attached as he forced himself to take another step. When he bent to feel the ground around him, he found no evidence of tar or other hindrance, yet it felt so real when he tried to move. At least to move down. He discovered zero resistance if he tried to go back up. It seemed to be purely psychological.

While the idea comforted him enough to get him to go down a few more steps, it did not make it any easier on his psyche to feel the thick tar as it crawled up his body yet know it wasn't really there. Knowing it wasn't there didn't seem to help either. If he had any advantage it was that he had been training himself to not rely on his sight, so he was less affected by the darkness than he imagined most people would be.

Down and down he went, his next major obstacle being the progression of tar up his body to his mouth. He'd barely dared to breathe as he descended the stairs, and he instinctively raised his chin as he got deeper, certain he would suddenly swallow tar or sand when he got too far. None came, and he was soon completely enveloped.

Terror gripped him as much as the tar, but there was nothing he could do about it. He felt as bound as he had been under French torture, feeling everything yet unable to protect himself in the most basic manner. He wanted desperately to run back up the stairs. Only the thought that the Author had brought him here kept him going, but it was terribly small comfort.

He focused only on putting one foot in front of the other, a simple task that almost anyone could accomplish. Even blind, he could do that. He could navigate stairs. Just one foot in front of the other. One step at a time. Simple. Easy. He could do this. The Author had brought him here and given him this challenge; the least he could do was try.

Step. Step. Step. Each one more difficult than the last, the tar dragging his feet and constricting his body, the terror racing through his mind. He stopped several times, forcing himself to breathe, though whether the difficulty came from the fear or the tar, he could not tell. He did not allow himself to open his eyes out of an irrational fear that he might find himself back in the torture chamber. It was terribly illogical, but logic had left him at the top of the stairs.

Just how far was he going, anyway? He had to have descended several floors by now, at least seven or eight. Maybe more. It seemed like more and less at the same time, the way the darkness and the fear played tricks on him.

And where was he going? What awaited him at the end of the tunnel of terror? Did he really want to find out? If the tunnel was horrifying enough, just getting to wherever he was supposed to be going, how much worse was the prize at the end? Or, perhaps, how much greater that it had to be protected so? How much could a man bear before he gave in? How much could a weak will withstand?

He was not weak willed. He was not a sniveling fool. He was not the weakling Cassius thought he was. He was strong, defiant. He'd faced greater dangers and bigger monsters than mere darkness and psychological chains. He'd faced real danger, defeated true monsters. Even now he was playing a dangerous political game with some of the worst monsters in the universe. He could do things the average man could only dream of, and that was assuming that man had an imagination.

He could navigate a flight of stairs in the dark. This was just one more step, one more challenge, one more obstacle to overcome. If he couldn't overcome a monster that didn't exist, how did he expect to defeat the monsters that did? If he could not face his own fear, how could he hope to slay a dragon?

If the resistance of the tar was dependent upon the will of the one walking the stairs, it did not react to his mental chastising. Either he had not accumulated enough bravery, had not had enough of a spiritual or psychological breakthrough, or else the tar would remain consistent regardless. Considering the latter as the most likely possibility gave him some hope, and he pressed on.

Just one foot in front of the other, he told himself. He could do this. He could do this blind. It was nothing. Step. Step. Step. Push through the tar, pull against the weight. Step. Step. Step. He didn't have to go fast; he just had to go and get there in his own time. Step. Step. Step. Simple enough in principle, and simple enough in practice. He just had to keep going, keep his head on straight.

Suddenly there were no more steps and the tar released like a popped balloon. Rifun's force against the tar that was no longer there carried him into open air. His mind went totally blank as he fell. At the last second he wondered if he should fall forever, that perhaps it was a trap for the foolhardy.

Then he hit cold metal. His head slammed against the ground. Stars burst before his eyes and a migraine erupted in his brain almost instantly. The rest of his body didn't feel much better, and he lay there, groaning, for a long couple of seconds.

Several things he noticed as he sat up. First, the inexplicable terror that had suffocated him on the staircase had evaporated, leaving only a lingering anxiety. Second, the room was quiet and had the overall appearance of being in a cinema, the large bright screen lighting up a dark room.

After a moment of absolutely nothing happening, Rifun stood and dared to look around. He was on a platform about thirty feet wide by fifty feet long. Three sides of the platform were enclosed by walls, though they appeared more as darkness than tangible surfaces. The fourth side, where his back had been when he sat up, was completely open save for a small protective rail.

Looking out over the railing, Rifun felt more than saw what was out there, and it very nearly stopped his heart. What he did see was like the razor edge of a star, and such a description sounded both incoherent and yet insufficient. He blamed his unique eyesight for the visual rendering, but there was nothing to protect him from the feel of the thing. Whatever the thing was.

To say the thing felt "pure" would have been to ascribe something definitive to it, something that had boundaries as well as an equal and opposite. To say it felt "empty" would be to imply that it could be filled. To say it felt "powerful" would be like saying that a gorilla was strong or a cheetah was fast. To say that it felt "alive" would have implied the possibility of death.

The thing did not "feel" pure, for it itself was purity, and the razor edge of the star was the boundary of good and evil, as sharp a line as life and death. The thing did not "feel" empty, but infinite, something that could swallow entire universes and never notice. The thing did not "feel" powerful for it was in fact power unrestrained. The thing did not "feel" alive, for it was the essence of life force itself.

This thing was the razana, the culmination of all power and energy of the spirits, the life force of creation itself. The imagination of the Author. Vast and powerful, capable of conjuring literally anything. Literally. Anything. Capable of bringing life to impossible wonders through no other means than her will. And so birthed this universe. But the universe had to remain tied to her, and the only way to rectify and contain this power was by the layered dimensions of the Wheel. Just as a brain was folded and layered to contain more surface area for more intelligence and creativity and the human soul, so the Wheel was layered. And from the Wheel sprang forth everything to all parts of the universe, like the brain sending out signals to all parts of the body.

Rifun took in a sudden gasp of air and stumbled back, tripping over himself and landing on his seat. He sat there, staring at the razor edge of a star, mouth open, completely oblivious to the universe around him.

He wasn't sure how much time passed before his faculties returned to him. He stood and approached the edge of the platform again. The core of the Wheel, perhaps the core of the universe itself. How was it that he did not go insane? Should he not drop dead upon seeing God? Well, that seemed only to apply to the face of God, and it had nothing to do with the imagination, which truly seemed far more infinite and astounding. Or perhaps this was merely the Author, and this was the conduit for the spirits to travel back and forth. Who could know? Who could truly know?

He bowed before the thing as he did before his shrine, offering up babbling prayers to the ancestors, the spirits, the Author, anyone who would listen, and he remained there for what felt like several hours, though it couldn't have been more than twenty minutes. Even when he sat up, he felt as though his prayers had been wholly inadequate and his spirit just as much, a pauper going before a king.

A thought entered his mind then, perhaps a foolish one. He got to his feet, unsteady in the presence of this thing, and reached out as if to touch it.

He woke up on the floor, unsure just what had happened. All he knew was that the power and strength he had just touched was best sought by bench-pressing galaxies, and the power and strength that had flowed through him made his torture wounds feel like paper cuts in comparison. Indeed, for the first time in a very, very long time, he felt no pain in his body. Everything felt very much normal.

His first motion to attempt to sit up dissolved that illusion, and he moved with all the speed and agility of a hundred year old cripple. Sitting up was exhausting; standing was even worse.

The razor edge of a star did not appear to have changed one bit. He did not know what he expected for he did not know what happened, but it stood to reason that he was, in the eyes of this thing, unworthy. He approached gingerly, reached out as if to touch it again, then stopped. Perhaps the only thing that had saved him the first time was naivete, disciplining a child who didn't know any better. Now he did know better. Then it moved from discipline to punishment. If discipline had knocked him out like it had, punishment would probably kill him.

He needed to know more, get more information on this thing. What was it? How was it connected to the Author? How did he appease it?

Looking around, he was faced with another dilemma. How did he get out? He saw the stairs at one end of the room, yet they were easily twenty feet above his head. He saw no other stairs or doors or exits of any kind. But that didn't make much sense. Didn't the secretaries come down here? How did they leave this place?

He felt along the walls and the floors, finding no indication of hidden panels, trap doors, or doors of any kind. He went and stood under the stairs, only the last two steps visible before the whole staircase was swallowed by inexplicable darkness. He distinctly remembered falling from the last step to the ground, so it wasn't as though they were invisible, and a physical examination of the area proved that.

Gravity seemed the logical choice, then, but what sense did that make? This was the Wheel, and the Akari was resented, if not scorned or even banned. The secretaries would not have knowledge of this, would they? Did they leave by some other means? Did they learn the Akari in secret? Did they use Gravity without realizing that it stemmed from the Akari? As a Warden Timekeeper, he was aware of most all Time abilities, so why had he never been aware of this?

Or could there be more to the story? Could there be some Akari remnant slumbering within the Wheel? He knew the history of the Wheel as the Hands of Time taught it, but was it the truth?

Well, he would never find out unless he left this place and could ask questions and do research, and the only way he could see to escape was by using Gravity to lift himself up to the staircase.

He did this without incident, and from there it was a much easier trek up the stairs. The only pain or resistance he felt was from his own exertion and experience from whatever it was that was down there. He reached the top no worse for wear, and stood there at the staircase for another long minute.

He'd just had a phenomenal experience, and he wasn't sure what to do with it. It was a bit like the vision he'd had of Nibe during his review, except this time he had no course of action to follow, and he'd seen something far more powerful than a vision of his dead grandmother. What, then, was he supposed to do?

What did other people do when they had spiritual revelations or encounters? How was he supposed to interpret this? He wished for a shaman, but the only people who might be even remotely qualified for this were not people he wanted to talk to, not about this, not about what he'd seen or felt. It was too big, and, quite frankly, he didn't trust them with it. Under no circumstances could Cassius or Isthim be allowed to touch that kind of power. As for Julianna, well, he wasn't really sure about her.

The Book of Philosophy might have an answer, he figured.

He turned away from the staircase and looked down the corridor. He still had no idea where he was in the Wheel, but given that he had already explored one direction, now might be a good time to explore the other direction.

The light grew brighter as he walked until it was very nearly common lighting and he could see all around him. The corridor opened up into a large room, perhaps fifty by fifty feet. Several more corridors branched off in different directions, and there was another room across the way. In the middle of the room was another spiral staircase, this one going up. Looking around, everything appeared as though it had suffered the same fate as the Archives when it had been upheaved and overturned, and several secretaries were busy trying to put things back in order.

Trying not to disturb them, Rifun made for the staircase and started up, unsure what he would be walking into.

This staircase was not nearly as long as the other one, nor was it as spooky and forboding. He had no troubles or resistance climbing it. He did notice, however, that as he climbed, he started to see that there were tablets on the steps.

Eventually he neared the top of the stairs, but he could not go all the way as one of the shelving units of the Archives had fallen and blocked the staircase. Nudging aside a pile of tablets with his foot, he put his shoulder against the unit and pushed. Immediately he could tell that it was not the only one there; likely several had fallen on top of each other.

Given the sudden shift of Gravity in the Wheel, he was leery of using it again to move the shelves. Instead he opted for Force, gathering a mass of Energy and blasting the shelves out of the way, and he soon had the area cleared enough that he could navigate to the top of the stairs and look around.

So this was all hidden beneath the Archives? He knew where he was, and he knew that there were easily a dozen floors still beneath this one, and yet the room with the corridors, not to mention the staircase to the razor edge of a star, did not even seem to register here. Was that just part of folding the dimensions on top of one another? Well, it would make sense, considering everything else in the Wheel. But why hide it here? Anyone could go down there.

But not everyone would have the fortitude to continue, nor would they have the ability to escape.

That corridor was psychologically invisible, Rifun realized. It didn't exist as anything consequential to those who weren't called to go down there. And the only ones called to go down there were Akari-bearers chosen by the Author. But it still begged the question: why? What was that thing? Why was such a powerful Akari-related entity hidden in the heart of the Wheel?

He let out a breath and looked around. The Archives were a mess, and that was putting it nicely. Considering the number of secretaries it took to keep the place organized on a normal day when there was a system for reading and returning the tablets, it was going to be a good long time before things were sorted out. Seeing how the tablets had not only fallen off the shelves, but the shelves themselves had been tossed around like confetti, there was no way to know where to start with any kind of research.

The whole place was a disaster, and when he finally emerged from the Archives, he discovered that the whole Wheel had been affected, some places more than others.

Judging from the gossip that was flying around, it had started in one of the intermediate marketplaces. What it was, no one was quite sure, other than something had gone wrong with the gravitational balancers, the bit of technology that made it possible for anyone to walk natively on all surfaces without adverse effects. No one quite knew how such a thing could occur, and whatever had gone wrong had apparently righted itself. Secretaries were working hurriedly to determine the cause and whether any other areas in the Wheel might be susceptible to this anomaly.

Whatever the cause or outcome, it did not appear to be affecting the portal room, at least for the moment, and Rifun made sure to make his return to the ruins as quick and painless as possible.

News of the incident had apparently already reached the troops, for it was the major theme of conversation as he wound his way through. When he reached the officers building, Julianna and Isthim were just exiting, but stopped when they saw him.

"There you are!" Julianna said with a certain sigh of exasperation. "We thought something must have happened to you. Were you in the Wheel at the time?"

"I was in the Archives," he stated calmly. "It gets to be a mess when you have one-point-seven quintillion bookshelves containing up to a thousand tablets each suddenly put in a sack and shaken violently."

"Are you injured?" Isthim inquired.

"I'm fine. A few bumps and bruises is all." He looked around. "Is Cassius about?"

Julianna sighed again, this time with double the exasperation. "Oh yes. He's bragging about how he's the one who caused the incident."

In all honesty, Rifun was not surprised. "Then seeing how we four are accounted for, is there anything else I should know about it? Is anyone else missing?"

"Some of the recruits are trickling in slowly, but it does not appear that we've lost anyone."

Rifun nodded. "Good. I don't like to make those visits, especially if it's one of the officers who got someone killed."

"Agreed," Julianna said. Isthim dipped her head silently. "Well then, now that we're all back, maybe we should reel in Cassius and discuss what happened, see if it changes anything."

Cassius was still out strutting his feathers around the city and wasn't quite ready to come in for a meeting yet. Only after a good ten minutes of asking did he consider it, and it was another five minutes before he actually followed Rifun back to the officers building for said meeting. He had the demeanor of a teenager who's just had real sex for the first time and wants everyone to know it, Rifun thought. All things considered, he couldn't figure out why this incident should make him feel that way, except, perhaps, for the sheer scale of the mayhem caused.

"But does it change anything?" Julianna demanded. She looked at Isthim. "Have your people said anything about it?"

"Only the common complaints, that it greatly disrupted the order of things, tossed everything and everyone at great risk to all," Isthim reported. "Some places worse than others, but all affected to some degree. As for the Council, the Admirals, and the Ul Ik Zol, they have been silent so far. It may be a few more hours or days before they comment on the matter, if anything has changed."

"Do we expect anything to change?" Rifun inquired. "I understand that it may take some time for things to get cleaned up — I was in the Archives at the time, and it was a tragic mess — but what would change because of it? It's been ruled an accident, and the secretaries are working on it."

Cassius laughed. "No. No, things should change. Everyone should know that we — that I have done this. Show them the power of the Akari, that we can disrupt the Wheel so! Maybe then they will tremble before us. And with our alliance to the Borelians, no one would dare stand against us! We can move in any time we please."

"Agreed," Isthim stated.

"Not agreed," Rifun said. "What of the journals?"

Cassius shrugged. "I have a lead, but it's not exact yet. Dependent on our results. If we take over, the Book of Abilities may appear." Given what Julianna had told him about the Book of Abilities, Rifun was curious to know what in the world Cassius was talking about. The man continued, "Besides. What need do we have for the Book of Abilities beforehand? I have proven my mastery of the Akari. If we take over, the journals will not matter. If and when they turn up, they will only reinforce an already solid rule."

"He's right," Isthim said. "We should act while we have their attention and not squander the opportunity."

"And what of the Akarin?" Rifun wondered. "Shall we send Cassius to take them on single-handedly? We may grasp the throne, but we will not claim it for long if we have an unskilled army."

"I will gladly face them in single combat," Cassius boasted.

Rifun sighed. "Yes, I'm sure you would."

"And we have the Borelians to back us up. Surely they would only see our delay as weakness."

Isthim dipped her head. "This is true. We must seize this opportunity or risk losing more than only that."

"Fine," Rifun cut in. "Fine. But may I suggest that rather than moving in this instant and appearing as mere scavengers to something that has already been declared an accident, instead, do it again. Wait a day or two, then go back and do it again. Intentionally. And make sure that everyone knows it is intentional and who is doing it." He looked at Isthim. "And if the Borelians cause some kind of scene for it to show our alliance, so much the better."

"I can tie it in to my hit list," Cassius mused. "Show that we have power physically and politically."

"That would be most efficient of you. And if Julianna can arrange some cleanup crews for afterwards, try to show that we are after the evils and corruption of the Time industry and are not merely indiscriminate mass murderers...?"

"Of course," Julianna murmured, nodding. "I'll assemble some teams."

"And what will you be doing?" Isthim asked.

"I will be notifying our allies of our imminent ascent to power. That should also bolster us a bit and hide our poorly-trained army. And...I also have a bit of searching of my own to do. Seeing how the Archives have been shaken like a snowglobe, I fear I shall have to do my research a slightly different way."

The meeting was adjourned, each man and woman to his task.

Things were happening in all the wrong order, Rifun thought. They had the opportunities but not the army they needed to seize those opportunities. They had one man with great power, but he enjoyed playing God too much to share his knowledge of how to use that power beyond a tip or a hint here and there. And what would he do once the Book of Abilities was found? More to the point, what was he talking about having a lead on it?

Rifun caught up to Julianna outside the officers building. He used Sound to mask their conversation.

"Last time we spoke of it, you said the Book of Abilities was hidden in the cave you used to jump into the future," he began. "How certain are you that it is still there?"

"As certain as I can be without going and looking," she replied. "Believe me, I am just as confused as you by Cassius' words. It may be that he is trying to get me or us to crack and tell him where it is. It could be that he is simply trying to make himself look better than he is by pretending to have a lead. I don't know. But the honest truth is that the last I knew of the Book of Abilities, it was still hidden in that cave."

Rifun nodded. "All right. I might ask him about it later, see if I can't get him to brag a little more."

"What are you going to do now?"

"A little soul searching, I think. Let's just say that I had a spiritual encounter while I was being tossed around the Archives. I wish to explore it."

He ignored her look, released the Sound shield, and left the city, making for the tunnels so he could open a portal. He did not go to the Wheel, however, but the Akarin fortress. Their Archives were smaller, but at least they weren't scattered about over an area roughly the size of Africa, or larger.

The fortress appeared to be in a bit of a frenzy, and their gossip was the same as the Cult's gossip, all about the incident in the Wheel. What happened? What did it mean? Was it really an accident or was there some mischief involved?

Rifun elected to say nothing about it. He moved about the fortress freely, but he was rapidly becoming known as one of the leaders of the Cult. How long before he was barred from entry? He'd better get all the information he could.

He searched for information on the Wheel itself, its construction and history. He knew what the Wheel Archives said, what he'd studied for many years to advance through the Timekeeping ranks. But what did the Akarin Archives have to say about it? Was there another side to this history? What was the dirty underbelly of the heroes? Rifun thought of the horrors he'd witnessed during the Uprising, whole villages slaughtered by the French, men, women, and children burned alive. Yet the common French knew nothing about it, believing their soldiers heroes.

Seeing how the Time industry barely even pretended to have morals, what could they be trying to conceal?

The Akarin Archives were not technologically advanced like the Wheel. They did not have an ultra-precise search system, nor did they have tablets. Rather, they had paper copies, everything from ancient scrolls to more modern books. Their system of organization was unique to them, but the librarian was happy to point him in the right direction.

He picked out several volumes he thought might be useful, then retreated to a small table to peruse quietly. He'd also brought writing materials of his own to take notes. He couldn't be sure, but he didn't think he qualified for a library card to take things home.

According to the Wheel Archives, the Wheel had been built innumerable millennia ago by ultra-advanced civilizations. Their incredible technology and species evolution had allowed them to break through the space-time barrier to not only build the Wheel, but harness Time itself. Over many centuries and millennia, they refined this craft so that it was able to be spread to less-evolved species, and on down it went to present day where anyone with sufficient exposure to Time could learn to wield it.

According to the Akarin Archives, the Wheel had been constructed by the Author for the use and enjoyment of Akari-bearers. But the Akari-bearers became selfish, greedy, and divided, so much so that a civil war broke out. Disgusted with her people, the Author threw the original Akari-bearers out of the Wheel and gave it to the rest of the universe to maintain.

But that was not the end of the story, not by a long shot.

Accounts were fragmented and a bit inconsistent, but it seemed as though the Akari-bearers, over the centuries, tried several times to retake the Wheel, only to be repelled each time. But the wars they waged were so dangerous and so violent, so devastating to the Wheel and the universe at large, that they always resulted in something called a Rebuild, where the Wheel itself had to be effectively dismantled and rebuilt from scratch. Reportedly, this could only be done through the Core of the Wheel by specially-trained Akari-bearers called, creatively enough, Builders.

Could that be what he had encountered there, deep in the Archives? Had that been the Core of the Wheel? How did one get to be a Builder? None of the volumes he'd selected had anything useful on the Core. The volumes on the construction of the Wheel did little more than mention its existence, never once saying how to get there or what it was made of. They certainly didn't tell how to manipulate it. Rebuild it, to use a new term.

He went back to the many shelves and continued searching, but he could find nothing of substance. The volumes did little more than mention the existence of the

Core, if they did that much. As for Builders, he found a book of famous Builders, but no mention of what they'd learned, whom they'd learned from, what their specific abilities were, the criteria for becoming a Builder, or their relation to the Core.

He returned to his seat empty-handed, surprised to find someone else sitting at the table, looking at his notes. It would be a miracle if he could read them, seeing how they were all Malagasy.

"Can I help you?" he asked.

It was a human man, maybe thirty years old by appearance, white, black hair, black mustache and beard, glasses, pretty average in every sense of the word. He stood and held out a hand. "Drew."

"I'm sorry, I don't shake hands," Rifun told him. "Rifun."

"Ah, apologies. I had noticed that you were looking at the roster of famous Builders."

"Do you know them?"

"I've met a couple of them in my time. I thought maybe you were studying to become one."

"I wouldn't know where to start. I admit, my own abilities are a bit lacking, compared to some."

Drew grinned and shook his head. "It always seems to be that way, doesn't it? Always someone better than you? I know the feeling."

"Do you know how to become a Builder?"

The man waved a hand as though the answer were obvious. "Weeks, months spent in prayerful meditation, seeking the Author. The Author chooses her Builders, you know."

"Of course," Rifun said, trying to sound casual. "But how do you know when you've been selected?"

Drew shrugged and seemed a bit squirmy. "I guess you just know. The Builders never tell. If they never tell, then no one knows who isn't supposed to know, you know? At least, that's what I tell myself."

Rifun sat down across from him. "Do you want to be a Builder?"

"That would be a great honor, believe me. It might be needed after what happened in the Wheel."

"What happened in the Wheel?"

Drew sat up. "Oh, you didn't hear? One of the gravitational balancers went out in one of the marketplaces."

"Really? How did that happen?"

"Well, the Borelians—or the Grandfathers, but I repeat myself—ruled it an accident."

"Was it?"

"Me personally? I think it was sabotage. What with the Cult declaring war on the Tacagans. Question is, which one did it? The Tacagans have the technology to sabotage the balancers technologically. The Cult..."

"Wields the Akari and Gravity?"

Drew shook his head. "I don't think they wield the Akari. Not really. I mean, you can't have the Books and the journals and have them both be right. But whatever they do have, it's powerful enough to do something like throw the balancers off kilter."

"What happens now, you think?"

"I don't know, but I think it's going to escalate. Whoever has the power to throw off Gravity like that is going to try to take control of the situation, threaten to do it again if the other side doesn't back down."

Something in the man's expression just then as he looked at Rifun set off multiple red flags. This was not a casual social call with a bit of gossip. The man knew something. He had more knowledge, power, and rank than he was letting on. Rifun met his gaze.

"And what will the Akarin do?"

"Intervene if we must. We don't want the Akari or the Author tarnished by senseless acts of violence perpetrated by one lawless man, or a small misguided group. And if it gets too bad, if this issue with the balancers is only the beginning, well, there may be another Rebuild in the very near future, and the Builders will be needed."

By now they had both dropped the pretext. "And what if the Cult tries to Rebuild themselves with their version of the Akari?"

"Not possible," Drew told him smugly. "No one, other than a Builder, can look at the Core of the Wheel and live. Its power is too magnificent for normal mortal eyes to behold."

Rifun met his smugness with a smirk of his own. "Then I guess it's a good thing I don't have normal mortal eyes." He stood calmly and collected his notes still set out in front of Drew, if indeed that was his real name. "It has been charming chatting with you, but I really must be going. Other business to attend to, and things are very hectic in the Wheel right now."

Before he could go anywhere, Drew stood and spoke again. "Consider this a friendly warning. If you go through with this, whatever it is you're planning to do, you will be treated as an enemy. The council has humored you, your questions, your questionable actions, even your presence here. We have been very patient. We're even willing to consider that today's incident was either an accident or caused by the Tacagans. But if you take it any further, it will be seen as blatant aggression and an act of war."

"An act of war against whom, exactly?"

"Physically, the Tacagans. But we cannot allow you to tarnish the name and reputation of the Akari and the Author."

"You cannot tarnish what does not exist, and no one cares for the name and reputation of something they believe is a fairy tale. We will show the people, the universe, that the Akari is real. That the Author is real."

"Yes, Micaiah has recounted his conversations with you. It won't work."

"It has not yet been tried."

With that, Rifun turned and stalked off. No one attacked him, no one stopped or questioned him.

He didn't like where this was going with the Akarin, and he questioned both the wisdom and the feasibility of reunification. The Akarin were so...pathetic, if he had to choose a word. They were pacifist to a fault. They talked big and shook their fingers, but they never did anything. They never wanted to do anything. They squatted in their Authored Books and shouted at the universe from a fictional world. Anyone could be a hero when they wore the costume and the cape. But the real world demanded real action.

At the same time, how much longer could he humor Cassius? The longer he waited, the stronger Cassius got. What was it going to take to kill him? And if this plan succeeded, it was only going to further cement the alliance with the Borelians.

How could he cut off both his arms and still retain use of his hands? This was an impossible task that he was faced with.

Did he dare try to sabotage the plans, try to buy just a little more time? To what end? What would be the goal? He could only put things off for so long before Cassius or Isthim grew suspicious and perhaps had him killed instead. And who was to say that their usefulness had run its course? Was he not already chastising the Akarin for not wanting to play dirty? Why should he be any nobler about it, comparing himself to Cassius and Isthim? The Akarin wanted to deny the threat outright, unwilling to face the possibility of conflict. Similarly, he could not stay attached to the romantic notion of war; he had to face the realities of it. His shoulder ached at the thought as he was reminded of his wound at Antsrinana Bay.

The French and the British fighting each other. Allies fighting each other. That was exactly how this was likely to play out. One fought so the other was not annihilated, but the other was too proud to see it.

And in the middle had been the grunts, enlisted or conscripted against their will, sent to fight another man's war. Not again, he resolved. Not this time.

He found that he had reached a fork in the road. Both ways were gated, and he held a key, but the key would only work in one lock: the way he chose.

He returned to the officers building where he spent some time praying at his shrine, seeking answers.

The Core was known only to those to whom it mattered.

The Author herself chose her Builders.

It was no accident that Rifun had been flung from the Archives and landed next to the staircase that led to the Core. Supposedly he was not supposed to be able to look upon it and live, and yet he had, either thanks to his head injury or because he had been chosen.

The Core was where Builders Rebuilt the Wheel.

The Wheel only needed Rebuilding when its very existence was threatened due to the instabilities associated with war and violence.

Violence that Cassius was more than proficient in and planned to cause more of.

Rifun let out a breath and sat up, eyes still closed. He could not deny the things he had read. He could not deny the things he had seen. He could not deny the things that had been done to him to lead him here, all for a purpose. Stars and monsters. Kingship and treachery. A destiny walked on the edge of a knife. He had to make a choice.

He bowed one last time, then stood and left his chambers. He headed down the corridor to Cassius' chambers and knocked.

"What?" came a grouchy reply.

Rifun opened the door and stepped inside.

As always, Cassius looked like he was preparing to go out onto the battlefield as a one-man army.

"What is it?" the dark-skinned man asked irritably.

"This is far cry from the jovial mood you were in this morning," Rifun observed.

"I'm busy planning. That is something you know a little bit about, don't you? Maybe more than a little?"

"I'm not here to stop you if that's what you're thinking."

"Then why are you here?"

"What lead are you talking about on the Book of Abilities? Does someone have it or know where it is?"

Cassius grinned and looked up from his work. "Ah, so that's it. Julianna sent you here to get the information out of me. Where, oh where, could her husband's journal be?"

Rifun approached slowly. "Considering that it is something rather essential to the core beliefs of the Cult—something vital that is missing and should be returned with all haste in order to strengthen the validity of our claims to our very existence— it seems rather imprudent to keep such information to yourself. And seeing how you are now intent on destroying the Wheel, it would be a shame if it were to get lost in the shuffle, if it isn't already because of the first incident."

Cassius shook his head. "It is not in the Wheel, don't worry about that."

"Then where is it? Who has it? Or who has the information?"

But the man just laughed and went back to his work. "I am going to meet with my contacts in a couple of days. Once I have the information from them and have verified it, then I will go about sabotaging the 'gravitational balancers' in the Wheel."

"As I recall, we agreed to work as a team on this. I applaud your dedication to research, but if I remember correctly, I would do the research, you would do the heavy-lifting, we kill the Borelians, present their heads and the journal to Julianna as a gift."

"Then I am merely saving you the hassle of the research," Cassius said. "You prefer doing things the political way. The polite way. Keeping our noses clean and our reputation in tact. But I get things done that matter. And when I get the journal, I'm going to kill the Borelians."

"And the rest of us?" Rifun wondered nonchalantly.

"We'll see."

Rifun left Cassius' chambers, greatly disturbed. Cassius could not be allowed to get his hands on the Book of Abilities. That much was absolutely certain. Given his proximity to the rest of them, assassination was the only option.

At the same time, if he really did have information that would lead to its recovery, Rifun couldn't just go back there and cut his throat. Plus he was supposed to be doing all their heavy lifting for shaking up the Wheel—literally this time.

When the only tool you have is a hammer, every problem is a nail.

Were they perhaps relying too much on Cassius? If he were suddenly removed, could they get everything done they needed to do without him? Of course they could.

But he claimed to know someone who knew something about the journal. That could not be ignored.

Rifun might have to try and tail him for a bit, see if he couldn't find out who the contact was. If he could speak to them after they spoke to Cassius, it might level the playing field a little.

It was as good a plan as any, and if Cassius wasn't supposed to be meeting with his contacts for a couple of days, it would give Rifun time to contact all their known allies and give them a heads-up on what might be happening in the near future, let them know to be ready to make good on their promises.

He returned to his chambers to pray some more. He considered what Drew had said, about it taking weeks or even months of prayerful meditation in order to even be considered as a Builder. Was that true, or had it been a test to see how Rifun would react? What was he supposed to do with the information?

More to the point, considering all that had happened, did he want to try it? Could he do it? Could he take weeks or months out of his schedule to spend in meditation? He supposed he could Band or ask someone to Band him, but it seemed only logical that it should be done in Base Time. He had so many things to do, and so many things were going to happen, that he wasn't sure he had that kind of time. But then, was that not the nature of faith and sacrifice?

6 | Ipade ati Wiwa

The Wheel of Time, 1964

Meeting and Seeking

It took four days for the Food Court to be put to rights after it had been shaken like a martini, and it was the first majorly-disrupted area to be reopened to the public. Even a few of the marketplaces were still closed.

Many Time Agents still hadn't returned. Some feared that the whole incident had been sabotage by some group or maybe a crazed individual. Others feared that with the chaos in the Wheel, general maintenance was not being done, so any part of the Wheel could be next to succumb and have an "accident." And the next "accident" might not right itself as well as the first one had.

Cassius had considered that, briefly. What would he do if he went to sabotage some part of the Wheel, another gravitational balancer for instance, and the problem didn't correct itself? Any incident by itself could kill him, but given his gastrointestinal distaste for such circus acts, what would he do if he was unable to rein in an out-of-control incident?

Well, what was a little risk? He took a drink and another bite of steak. That was inherently what life was, wasn't it? Every day was a risk. To wake up was to risk death. To stay asleep was to guarantee it. Therefore, to wake up was to risk life. How poetic. Rifun would be proud.

Cassius smirked. Ah, Rifun. Suddenly in a panic now that Cassius had something he didn't. A plan. A lead. Contacts and information. It was a race to find the journal and Cassius was in the lead. Yes, yes, Rifun had mentioned something about being a team and whatnot, but he really didn't want to have to listen to his words of caution and everything else. If there was an opportunity, seize it. He was powerful enough to deal with whatever came his way. If Rifun wasn't strong enough or confident enough, that was his problem. Cassius was going ahead with or without him.

And, truthfully, Cassius preferred to go ahead without him. Made things a lot simpler. If not for the damn spirit, he might have wandered away from the Cult once more. Or maybe not. He couldn't decide. On the one hand, he liked the idea of having an army at his disposal. On the other hand, those in management with him left much to be desired.

But then there was the point of, what would he do with an army anyway? His interests did not lie in the realm of sheer conquest, as it seemed to be for the others. His goal was more aligned with the idea of abolishing slavery. And somehow they had become allies with the most brutal slavers in the universe.

Yes, yes, his fault. The others seemed to enjoy reminding him of that. But could they not appreciate that he was trying to fix the problem? Recover the Book of Abilities, destroy the Borelians, then take over the Time industry.

It sounded simple enough, but as recent events had proven beyond a doubt, such things would only be accomplished by one with a strong enough stomach and an empty enough conscience. Water might erode a boulder over eons, but dynamite would destroy it in the blink of an eye. One was polite, the other was effective.

He finished his steak and leaned back in his seat, feeling rather content. Well, content about the steak. His current predicament? Not so much.

He looked around the Food Court and spotted his contact just entering. She went to the buffet and began loading several plates. She wouldn't need so much food if she had any concept of table manners and could keep her food in her mouth, Cassius thought. He would admit that he wasn't the most refined dinner guest, and if she couldn't even meet his fairly low standards, well, that was saying something.

For a moment, Cassius thought about stepping out of the Food Court and just waiting ten or fifteen minutes, let her eat where he didn't have to watch, then mosey back in as if he'd just arrived.

Actually, that sounded like a very good plan. He didn't think she'd seen him, but just to be sure, he Banded to make his escape.

The Wheel was pretty empty, compared to its normal flow of people, but it still resembled a holiday sale at any retail store. He meandered his way around, not really interested in anything. A few patrons knew who he was, and most went out of their way to avoid him. He did not say or do anything, but he was simply brimming with satisfaction. He was powerful. He was in control.

Or he would be, once he got that journal.

He quickly grew bored of his wanderings. He had business to conduct. He didn't want to watch Pilory's disgusting eating habits. Eventually, he decided that he could suffer poor table manners. He killed for fun, and he was offended by a little half-masticated food product? How was that for irony?

He returned to the Food Court and spotted the Tibidi almost immediately. She looked up and spotted him as well, food falling out of her mouth haphazardly to the floor. But it appeared as though she was nearly finished. He bought himself a few more minutes by getting another plate of food for himself. He wasn't hungry, but he wanted the distraction, something to look at other than her.

By the time he sat down and began politely eating his food — it wasn't etiquette as Julianna might have demanded, but at least he wasn't a pig — Pilory was just finishing off her drink and pushing her dishes aside.

Before either of them could speak, however, they were interrupted by the sudden arrival of Rifun and Captain Titik. Rifun helped himself to the seat beside Cassius, and Titik took the chair beside Pilory. Cassius Banded himself and the Tibidi, but before he could say anything, the Band was summarily dismantled and Rifun spoke.

"No need for secrets here, I think. After all, we're all in this together. We're all partners, equally invested in this endeavor, aren't we? I was afraid I'd missed you, actually. But here we are. All together. No need to play the telephone game."

If there was any reason to be thankful for small favors, Cassius was thankful that Akari Bands were invisible, so that when he Banded himself and Rifun now, Titik and Pilory would not notice.

"Why are you here?" Cassius asked.

"You said you have a lead on the Book of Abilities," Rifun stated nonchalantly. "Seeing how we are supposed to be a team, if not a part of the larger leadership quartet, I thought it might be appropriate."

"You don't trust me."

"Diplomacy is not one of your best leadership qualities. I am here to ensure that nothing goes sideways."

"Pirates aren't known for their diplomacy either."

"No, but they are known for their greed, and Titik especially, or so I understand. It's an easy string to pull, but like any string, it has its limits."

Cassius hated the man. He considered whether anything would actually be lost if he were to kill him right there. But then, pirates were unusually loyal. One leader killing another probably wouldn't look very good in front of the captain or his lieutenant.

"Fine," he said at last. "But don't assume that these are your type of leaders and dignitaries and politicians. They're not."

"Neither were the Borelians," Rifun quipped. He continued before Cassius could speak. "Fine. These are your friends. They have been in contact with you. They work with you. I'm just an observer."

Cassius grunted. He wasn't the best at reading people, but he knew Rifun wouldn't pass up a chance to show off his negotiating skills. The problem was, negotiating only prolonged the inevitable.

After a short standoff, Cassius released the Band and turned his attention back to Titik and Pilory. He was uncertain whether Titik had intended to sit in on this meeting, or if Rifun had brought him here as uninvited as himself. Whatever the case, Pilory did not seem affected by it, other than she was in the presence of her captain. If she had any misgivings about him being at the negotiating table, if indeed that was what was about to take place, she did not give any indication of it.

"I assume we all know each other, then?" Cassius began. "At least by association?"

"If you do not know that you have been dealing with Captain Morain leRou Titik, then you are a fool," the Psiaco pirate said, grinning with a mouth like a wolf. "And Pilory would have done me a disservice."

"She has done you no disservice. In fact, she has done you a great deal of service by bringing you to us."

Titik burst into laughter, a thunderous abomination that tapered off into bestial choffing. "Ah, such whimsy! Now I must ask. Why do you think this way, that I have been brought to you?"

"Why shouldn't I think that? Captain Morain leRou Titik has no need for trinkets or heirlooms. He is not on a mission of mercy or charity. And he cannot be intimidated by petty thieves." Cassius grinned. "Money is the only pleasure in the world, is it not?"

"Life is too short to waste on unattainable dreams," Titik agreed.

"But what if some dreams could be made attainable? What if some of those prizes you've been putting off could be gained? As I understand it, the Turitians are breathing down your neck pretty hard, and your own people aren't too impressed by your antics."

The Psiaco pirate just grumbled and may have murmured something he didn't catch.

Before Cassius could continue, Rifun Banded the two of them.

"Before you go any further, just remember that the Turitians are our allies, too," he said lowly.

"It's about loyalty to one's people, isn't it?" Cassius replied simply. "Not a business."

"It's about loyalty to one's people and fealty to the Author. We can't start attacking each other."

"Titik is not our ally, nor do we know if he even wants to learn the Akari. And even so, are we not planning on attacking the Borelians? Is that not attacking each other?"

Cassius shrugged off Rifun's Band.

"My ship is powerful," Titik mused. "And fast. But even I cannot match a Turitian battleship, even with great luck and fortune."

"What if you could?" Cassius asked.

The four-eyed alien made a rumbling noise. "You promise the impossible."

He made as if to leave, but Cassius wasn't about to let him go without a fight. "Give me a task. Any task." He stood with Titik. "Any task you say is impossible."

Titik studied him for a long minute. Then, "Bring me the crown of King Srori. I wish to wear it as my own."

He made a motion. Pilory stood, and the two of them departed. Cassius watched them leave the Food Court, but it was another moment before he looked back at Rifun who was giving him a look.

"What?"

"You know what."

"I told him to name a task. He named a task."

"Suggestive thinking, already naming the Turitians."

"I didn't know what he was going to say or do."

Rifun stood. "The Turitians are our allies. They are supposed to be helping us. We can't steal something from them, especially not anything like that! As it is, we're lucky it's only his crown and not his head! What do you expect me to tell them? Shall I just ask for the crown? And what do you think they'll do if Titik does decide to join us?"

"I don't know," Cassius said irritably, "but you'll notice we still have decent recruiting numbers considering all the Borelians running around. I think a little feud between Turitian royalty and one Psiaco space pirate is pretty small, don't you?" He huffed. "Besides, Titik is only in it for the money; he couldn't care less about long-term power and prestige. He wants party tricks, something to help him fill his coffers."

"That's great and all, but what about the journal?"

"I bring him the crown of Srori. He brings us the journal."

"That's not the bargain I heard."

"It's the one that is understood. I don't expect you to understand how negotiations are done between beings lesser than yourself and your dignitaries."

Rifun looked rather taken aback by that statement, and Cassius knew a moment of smug satisfaction.

"I thank you for actually letting me handle the negotiations this time," Cassius said, swallowing the bitter pill that was his pride. "Now do me another favor and let me see it through to the end. Extending a bit of trust. Partner."

Rifun was visibly displeased, but he assented and left the Food Court. Cassius watched him go, still rather pleased with himself. For once, he'd managed to trip him up. Now he just had to keep going, keep control, and follow through.

Having already indulged in more food than his stomach was comfortable with, Cassius also left the Food Court. Maybe he could track down Titik and Pilory and further their discussion without Rifun hanging around.

As luck would have it, he found Titik in one of the marketplaces, but he was already on his soapbox, complaining about this and that. Cassius did not speak to him, but he did find Pilory a distance away, heading for a portal, perhaps going to the portal room. Cassius fell in beside her.

"So if I do manage to get this crown, will Titik help us?" he asked casually.

Pilory glanced at him, her alien expression unreadable. "There's a chance."

"How good of a chance?"

"Depends on his mood, I suppose. And how fast you're able to procure it."

Cassius stepped in front of her and they stopped. "I need some assurances, Pilory. I need this journal. I'm not one of Titik's crew to be ordered here and there looking for treasure. If he wants proof of the Akari's power, fine. I can demonstrate almost anything. I'll even go on this mission for the crown, if not for you, then for my own reasons. But I need to know if I can count on you."

"Count on Titik, you mean," Pilory retorted. "You are not his crew, and he is not yours."

"But surely he must recognize the value of what I'm offering."

"Whatever your friend said to convince him to come to the meeting today, it at least got his attention. If you want to get his interest, then you need to get that crown. But as he himself said, life is too short. He's not interested in politics, diplomacy, alliances. If he wanted that, he could have stayed on Psia, graduated the Time Academy with honors. But he didn't. The fact that he's standing there pontificating is of terrible significance. All he's interested in is what he can do now, or in the very near future. The Tacagans and the Gentleman Killers ruined things Time-side. The Turitians are only one of our problems out in space. If you want Titik on your side, you need to show him something immediate that he can use. Am I making any sense?"

Cassius huffed. "And where does the journal come in?"

"You need to give him a reason to go after it. Do you even know where it is?"

He growled a bit but finally admitted, "No."

"So there you go."

"But a book that powerful, surely he knows other treasure hunters who have heard rumors?"

Pilory studied him. "He does know other treasure hunters, other pirates, even a few ignoble dignitaries. He doesn't always share what they talk about."

"Even with his own lieutenant?"

"They're his friends, not mine. I oversee ship operations. As for Titik, if you want to get in on that circle, then I suggest you start with the crown of Srori. I can't speak for Titik or his intentions or his imagination. He can be a touch unpredictable at times."

"But—"

"If you want to talk to Titik again, bring him the crown. Otherwise, find another treasure hunter to help you."

With that, she pushed past him and continued on her way. Cassius did not go after her.

So then, it all rested on the crown of Srori, one of the Turitian kings. If not for the fact that pulling off such a theft would spite Rifun, Cassius might have indeed given up on trying to talk to Titik and instead gone to another treasure hunter. Jora probably knew of a few who might be willing to help. But what would their prices be? And how many of them would as soon steal the journal for themselves as hand it over to him? Having a short-term thinker like Titik might be his best choice.

One mercenary was as good as any other, he supposed, and it seemed to work the same way with pirates and treasure hunters.

Well, if nothing else, he was going to steal the crown just to annoy Rifun.

Alliances with dignitaries didn't seem to be doing much for them. It might bring in the recruits, but what were they going to teach the recruits without the journal? They needed the Book of Abilities, and Titik was an avenue they had to explore. Difference was, Cassius knew this territory and Rifun didn't. It was an oddly satisfying thought.

Cassius started off again, making for the portal room to return to the ruins. Titik liked things done quickly. He didn't mind a scrap as long as the rewards were worth it. Well then, Cassius was going to have to get the crown quickly, and then he was going to have to demonstrate the Akari's power just as quickly, and perhaps with some force, just to make the point that it might be smarter to be allied with them rather than fight against them. One petty feud between Turitian royalty and a Psiaco space pirate was hardly a concern, and they couldn't abandon a whole mission because they picked up a few thorns along the way.

He returned to the ruins.

This wouldn't be his first time robbing someone of prestige, but it would be the first time he'd done so for the direct benefit of another, because they wanted him to do it. Well, that wasn't quite true either, but this mission still felt different than all the rest.

From what Rifun indicated from his negotiations, King Srori was king in title only; he was very old and frail, and possibly quite ill as well. It was almost a shame Titik hadn't asked for the king's head, too; it sounded easy enough to procure believably.

On the other hand, if he was that old, frail, and sickly, with or without Titik's short attention span, Cassius would have to move quickly. There was no telling when he might die, and security was always more paranoid around a newly-installed monarch. Not that he was worried about it necessarily, but lax security did tend to make things easier.

As much as he didn't care that he was going to be stepping on diplomatic toes with this little endeavor, he figured that there might be some merit to the idea of doing this anonymously. The best way to achieve that would be to go to Turit, simply Band, rummage around the palace until he found the crown, take the crown, find a good hiding spot, send portal chasers on a chase around a few decoy landing spots, then return to the Wheel and wait for Titik.

As he reached the officers building and entered, he mentally paused. How big was Titik's mouth? Sure, he might brag about having the crown of Srori, but would he also brag about how he obtained it?

After thinking about it, Cassius determined that he probably wouldn't, or that he probably wouldn't tell the truth. What notorious pirate wanted to brag about asking someone else to go after such a treasure, especially one from one of his greatest foes? No, he would more likely come up with some other tale, one that made him the hero. Well, if it got Cassius the journal, Titik could keep his crown and his wild stories.

Since he was planning to simply Band and do his work entirely in secret, he figured he didn't need to pack much for this mission. A bag to carry the crown, a few lock picking tools, and a few knives just in case he did come across some opposition. Akari Bands were basically invisible to anyone who didn't know they existed, but that didn't mean that someone might not get some sort of intuition that something wasn't right. And if the ailing monarch was being attended in any way, well, word could spread quickly once the crown suddenly vanished.

He half-expected Rifun to come walking in the door, preaching and fretting about politics or diplomacy or any of the usual things, but he didn't. This was a relief to Cassius until he considered that maybe the man was running to the Turitians to warn them of what was about to occur. Wouldn't that be just perfect? But little more than a minor annoyance, considering how he intended to pull this off.

Annoyance pricked the back of Cassius' mind as he thought about this. Exactly what was Rifun's end goal here? What did he want out of the Akari, the Cult, any of it? What were his ambitions? It had started out with him wanting to heal his scars. Well, that hadn't happened. In fact, the man seemed to have come to terms with his scars and embraced them. Good for him, Cassius thought, so what was next? What kept him coming back? What made him go out on his diplomatic missions? If he'd wanted power, there had been no shortage of opportunities to seize it, whether for himself or the Cult as a whole, and everyone but him seemed to see that they were squandering some golden opportunities here.

So if it wasn't healing, and it wasn't power, what was it? It couldn't be for love, seeing how he appeared to be no more than commonly familiar with Julianna, and he didn't appear to be overly infatuated with Isthim in spite of their ill-conceived romp. Was the man really dumb enough to think he was going to bring peace to the universe? He was sweating over a minor feud between Turitian royalty and one Psiaco space pirate; there was no way he was going to handle any real issues.

And he claimed to be African.

Cassius scoffed and shook his head. Rifun was a fool, but he was a useful fool anyway. A scapegoat, if it ever came to that.

He finished packing his bag and slung it over his shoulder, almost stunned at how light it was compared to other missions he'd undertaken. Well, this was just a quick in and out, or that was his intent. This was a means, not an end. He didn't care much for this crown.

Although, he thought as he departed his chambers, it would be nice bragging rights, to say that he had been the one to steal the Turitian crown. Stolen it right out from under their noses. That would be quite a notch on his belt, wouldn't it?

Maybe he ought to put it out there that he and Titik were competing for this crown. Then when it came to pass that he, Cassius, emerged triumphant, it would only make the people fear him more and be more in awe of the Akari. Titik would have no excuse not to get him the journal, and then Cassius would be the one calling all the shots.

Hm...perhaps he was being a bit fanciful. He would never say he didn't have an ego, but even he knew that some things were just a little too much, even for him.

He and Titik were, by all rights, rivals, in a certain sense, though their preferred line of work differed a little. It just happened to be that their interests coincided and they needed to sort of work together this time to help each other out and achieve their goals. A bit like how the Cult leadership was supposed to work, except he was having a much harder time deciphering the terms of this contract and when it was supposed to expire. Well, that was politics for you, he supposed.

The ruins were alive and well with the sounds of life, and it was getting harder and harder to call them ruins. Aside from the number of people now living in the ruins, reconstruction efforts—aided and overseen by select Elif authorities—meant that many of the buildings that had broken down were now being rebuilt so that things looked almost as good as they might have been when the primitive Elif societies dwelt there.

They might need to do something about that, Cassius thought. They didn't need any curious interlopers snooping around because they thought they heard something.

But then, even if someone did discover them, what were they going to do? Who were they going to tell?

Well, there was that bit about the Tacagans not liking them very much, and considering that just their capital city had a population of over three billion, it wasn't going to be pretty for either side. Cassius had no doubt that the Cult would win, especially if he led the effort, but there was no telling what else might happen because of it.

Hey, Rifun and the others might think he was just a bumbling idiot who was only looking for his next victim, but that didn't mean that he was oblivious to the goings-on around him, or that he didn't understand the concept of cause and effect. Most times, he just didn't care. Well this time, he could be made to care a little. As long as the others didn't fuck things up. He was trying to give them their best shot at fully overtaking the Wheel, so they couldn't blame him if things went sideways.

He left the ruins and made for a tunnel. Traffic to and from the ruins was considerably more crowded than it used to be, which could also be a problem. Well, it would be something to bring up at the next meeting; the others did love their meetings. But for right now, he had a mission to complete.

He offered some stiff compliments to a few of the incoming recruits, but he himself left before they could reply. He'd never been very good at complimenting and inspiring others, no matter how much he told himself that there was some benefit to being likable to the underlings. Rifun wasn't very smart, but he was likable, which was why others followed him. Same went for Julianna. Isthim led through fear. How did Cassius lead? Did he lead at all? Did anyone look to him over the others for direction?

No time to worry about that now, he scolded himself, opening yet another portal, the last one before Turit, and stepping through.

Turit was not the most hospitable planet, even for its indigenous inhabitants. Had the Turitians been any less advanced scientifically, they may have been wiped out when their sun went nova. But they had the drive and ingenuity to build protective domes around their cities. A network of similarly-protected tubes, much like an aboveground subway system, connected their cities and provided an excellent view of a dead or dying landscape.

The cities themselves, however, were quite lush, as pristine as the day they were encapsulated, with thick foliage and tall trees. Construction efforts were also evidently underway, the Turitians looking to slowly build more protective shielding and so revive some of the landscape.

On any ordinary day—not that Cassius did a lot of leisure traveling—one city was very much like any other. People had places to be, things to do, errands to run, and so forth. Daily life was daily life. And for the Turitians, who were Openly Engaged, having an alien in their midst would be nothing of terrible significance. In fact, it was considered a great honor, and in Turitian society, peaceful alien visitors were considered one of the most distinguished guests, and the only ones considered "superior" were the Commander General and the royal family.

Today was not one of those days. Even to Cassius, who again did not do much vacationing, something was a little off. First and foremost, the general, dull monotony of daily life was nowhere to be found. The construction efforts on the outside of the protective wall lay dormant, and the whole area appeared to be abandoned. If it were only the abandoned construction, Cassius might have guessed it was a weekend, maybe a holiday. But if that were the case, why no civilians?

Looking around, Cassius did not perceive any immediate danger, but there was an inherent anxiety in being out in the open like he was.

Keeping his suspicions quiet for the time being, he elected to carry on as he had planned otherwise. He Banded, bringing everything to a standstill. Given the lack of people, this amounted to little more than freezing small animals, the Turitian birds and squirrels and the like.

He gave the area another quick canvas just to ensure that he truly was alone here. He found nothing terribly suspicious in the immediate vicinity. Adjusting his pack, he turned and headed toward the palace.

Turitians were a rather large species, and their cities reflected this fact. Streets were wide, buildings were enormous, and the doors would take a hefty effort to open. And while Cassius appeared to be little more than a small dog in a big city, he was also the only sentient soul to be seen. He stopped in his tracks and looked around, now more confused than suspicious. Just what was going on here?

Cautiously, he released the Band.

He startled as some small animal flew out of a tree and directly in front of him, but otherwise, nothing of significance happened. But as he calmed down and took in his surroundings, he heard a great commotion, perhaps a few blocks away.

Curiosity getting the better of him, Cassius followed the noise. It took him straight to the palace anyway, so it wasn't as though he was going out of his way. With any luck, whatever was going on would help disguise his crime.

Finally, about a block from the palace and the great commotion, he saw people. He also saw what appeared to be heavy security. And why not? It was the royal palace, and there was some major shindig going on.

He approached one of the guards.

"What's going on?" he asked, trying to sound moderately amiable. "Is something wrong?"

"Now is the time of mourning for King Srori, for he has passed on as all great kings before him."

Srori was dead? Well, it shouldn't have been so surprising, really. But how was this going to affect his mission?

"We are asking all outsiders to please return another time while we honor our king," the guard went on.

The words were pleasant enough, but his posture was far more sinister, his turns and gestures suggesting force would be used if necessary. Cassius was hardly intimidated, but he needed to buy himself five minutes to think things over. He made a pleasant sort of gesture to the guards as he backed away, turned around, and departed as if intending to leave. Once he was out of sight of security, he Banded and sat down on the curb.

All right. So, Srori was dead. Rest in peace and all that. Now how to get his crown... On the one hand, it could mean that he was now technically stealing the new monarch's crown. Garnet, wasn't it? Was that her name? Or was it another king? Didn't matter. If the crown was passed on to the new monarch, nothing really changed except the new monarch was unlikely to be lounging in bed all day.

But if it wasn't passed on for some reason, if a crown was buried with its wearer...he could be in trouble, and he would have to steal it now or never.

He mulled this over for a few minutes. He was unfamiliar with Turitian royal burial customs, and he'd be damned if he asked Rifun for any insight on it.

On the other hand, he was literally right in the middle of said customs, and it seemed to be a rather exclusive affair. He wasn't sure what kind of invitation he might need, but being Turitian seemed to be one of the most obvious requirements.

He stood and donned a Disguise. A common Turitian citizen, he hoped. Their system of turns and gestures was obscenely complex, so he would have to avoid it as much as possible. Their clothing was also reflective of one's caste. A single cloth band over the belly was standard, and a second sash over the shoulder denoted military standing. He chose a single belly band, since he had a feeling that military personnel had extra duties to perform today.

Or should he feign military rank? Maybe it would help him get closer to the dead king.

Yes, he would do that, he decided. But he couldn't pretend to be too important. The High Commander or whatever her title was would surely know her closest underlings and confidants.

The color and pattern of the sashes determined one's rank and standing. Streamers coming off the sashes were special commendations, awards, and so on. Cassius was entirely unfamiliar with the history and significance of any and all of this. As much as he only had a single mission and didn't care about the details, he also didn't want to get it wrong and cause the whole thing to go sideways. Stealing the crown was bad enough, but if he spoiled the festivities, well, he didn't need to hear it from the others.

Still in the Band, Cassius returned to the festivities in his Disguise, observing the soldiers and their garb, trying to decide who was important and who was just a body. He decided on a blue sash with a silver zigzag design, decorated with a streamer of silver, a streamer of white, and a streamer of black and white stripes. These seemed to be fairly common, safe to imitate.

The only problem, then, came from the crowd itself. Disguise worked wonders when no physical contact was made, for it was only a temporary change, and a good portion of it was a trick of the eye. The ratio of actual change to trickery depended on how great the gap was between the host and his intended Disguise target. For a human to Disguise himself as a Turitian, well, there would be far more trickery than change, highly susceptible to discovery if touched with force, and lasting only a short time.

Keeping his Band close around him, Cassius tried to navigate the crowd. This proved little challenge to him as a human, but he could not do this and hold his Disguise, too. Any time he bumped into something, that portion of his Disguise evaporated, and he couldn't afford to stop every three steps to pull himself together.

Finally he dropped the Disguise and slithered among the crowd until he broke into the open.

The procession line for the dead king was tragically long. Cassius could not see where it began or where it ended, nor did he know where the king himself would be.

He scoured the line for about a mile in either direction until he finally came upon Srori in his marvelously decorated casket.

His crown was nowhere to be found.

Frustrated, Cassius kicked the casket, regretting this decision immediately as he went down in terrible pain, his foot and ankle throbbing.

He lay there in the street, in the middle of a grand procession of a dead king, for a full fifteen seconds. He pitied himself for at least ten of those seconds, chastised himself the other five, then picked himself up. He couldn't be weak, and he couldn't be put off by this minor setback. He'd had worse setbacks, like when Julianna fled across the ocean to escape him. So why weep over a missing crown? It had to be here somewhere.

So he again walked the length of the procession, this time going to the front of the line where the first people were just arriving at a grand stage in front of a large marble building which appeared to head an enormous cemetery of sorts. Or this was what Cassius guessed it to be. Perhaps the marble building was a royal mausoleum.

Garnet, or whatever her name was, stood on the stage, as regal as the queen she now was. Military leaders stood upon the stage, as well as an array of other non-military personnel whose purpose Cassius could only guess. Maybe they were royalty, maybe clergy, maybe something else entirely.

Cassius went up and searched the stage. Maybe it was hidden there somewhere in order to coronate the new queen. He found nothing. Not gold, not silver, not even a stray jewel, anywhere on stage or any person thereon. The crown was completely gone.

Cassius stood there, frustrated but also a little bewildered. There was no way that anyone could have gotten here before him and stolen the crown. Considering how hard he was having to work to even get Titik to hire him for this, the Psiaco pirate wouldn't just turn around and offer the job to someone else. Would he? Pirate or not, that was traitorous even among thieves and outlaws.

The only other option, short of him just not looking in the right place, was that the Turitians had been warned and so hidden the crown. The only one who could have and would have warned them was Rifun.

Sometimes Cassius wished he had a little more love for mankind, a little more faith in his fellows. Sometimes he was glad he didn't.

Well then, the festivities were nice and all, but he wasn't here to pay respects. He was here to take them. Since his target was apparently missing, he had no reason to be here.

He opened a portal to the Wheel and stepped through, his distraction by circumstances leaving him unprepared for the feeling of running into a brick wall that was travel to the Wheel. He stumbled a bit in the portal room but caught himself before he went tumbling through another portal into an unknown world.

He made a few tours of the Wheel, looking for Titik or Pilory, to ask if they knew anything about this mystery. He could not find either of them, so he could not ask them anything. This was perhaps to be expected, but it did nothing for his disposition, and he angrily stomped around several Unengaged worlds before finally calming down enough to return to the ruins.

In an odd sort of way, navigating the dark tunnels around the ruins helped to calm his nerves some. Perhaps it was being able to vanish into the darkness, an ethereal sort of sensation, that there was more beyond what could be seen, and the shadows could take him there.

This was about as existential as he got before light penetrated the gloom and he was back in the open. The relative quiet of the ruins and darkness overhead from the fissure suggested that it was basically nighttime. Lanterns were lit throughout the city, casting an eerie orange glow over everything.

Cassius headed for the officers building which was also quiet. He headed straight for Rifun's chambers and let himself in, rather unceremoniously, the heavy stone door scraping noisily on the floor. Cassius silenced the noise using Sound, but the initial scuff was enough, for Rifun was awake and standing ready even before Cassius got through the door. Even when he recognized Cassius, he did not relax his posture.

"Something I can do for you?" he asked stiffly.

He slept only in a pair of boxers, and even in the dim light of a low fire, his burned, twisted flesh was not a pretty sight.

"You can stop meddling with my contracts," Cassius told him, moving toward him. "You can stop getting in my way."

Rifun had only to hold his hand out, and it was like the force of a battering ram struck Cassius square in the chest. He went stumbling back, the breath knocked out of him, until he finally fell on his seat. He Banded so he could recover quickly, but there was no secondary attack. He seriously considered going after Rifun anyway, but decided against it at the last moment.

"If you are referring to what happened at lunch, you may recall that I did not say two words to Titik, nor did I interfere in your 'contract' as you call it," Rifun said, cutting off Cassius and sitting on the end of the bed. "If you are referring to what happened afterwards, you may be relieved to know that even as I give you warnings and implore you to heed them, I am not so foolish as to think that I can restrain you. You will do as you will do. I simply try to curb your energy away from a straight line to destruction."

"Then you deny forewarning the Turitians about my contract?" Cassius challenged.

Rifun gave him a look. "What's the matter, Turitians don't wear crowns on their heads?" When Cassius advanced angrily, Rifun merely sighed and said, "I didn't forewarn them, no. But it doesn't take a college education to deduce that the only reason you are this angry is because you don't have Srori's crown."

Cassius frowned and folded his arms. "Srori has died, and I walked into the middle of his funeral procession. Outsiders aren't allowed, but that didn't stop me."

"No, I imagine it wouldn't."

"I searched the entire procession line and the stage where the new queen was going to be sworn in. No crown."

Rifun shrugged. "Well, I don't know what to tell you. Maybe try the palace next."

Cassius studied him intently. "And you're absolutely certain that you had nothing to do with it?"

"As sure as Srori is now dead." Rifun stood. "Now if you don't mind, I would like to get back to sleep."

Cassius grunted but left the room. What was he going to do, really? Fight, beat, and torture Rifun to make him talk? His body was testament to how well that would work. That was the problem with some people. It wasn't that they didn't know enough to be afraid, it was that they did know enough but they knew even more to push it aside and carry on anyway. Then the only option was death.

And, again, what was he going to do? If Rifun had or hadn't forewarned the Turitians, it didn't change the present problem. The crown, to Cassius' knowledge, was gone.

Well, whatever the reason for its disappearance, be it treachery or some cultural nuance he didn't know about, he wasn't going to return today. If the festivities went as long as the procession, it might be a few days before he could go back to look around.

Or maybe he should go now. Since everyone was at the party, that would mean less security and less hassle at the palace, right?

He stopped and mulled this over. He had been considering a short nap to get his head back on straight, but then again...

He did end up returning to Turit, and he did go to the palace that was less of a palace for a king or queen and more of a governmental building for assorted governing affairs. Whatever it was used for, it was basically empty save for a couple servants who were busy giving everything a thorough cleaning.

Cassius scoured every single room of the building, from the grandest foyer to the smallest broom closet. He searched under every rug, behind every curtain, tried to tap out secret compartments and hidden levers, used the Akari to uncover long-forgotten passageways. He found plenty of notable secrets of the old palace, but still no crown. He couldn't imagine that such a treasure would be truly so difficult to find. Generally hidden, heavily guarded, either of these made sense, but it was still something that the Turitians took pride in. They had to look up to this treasure and cultural identity, and if they did, then it had to be at least a little bit visible.

Or maybe it wasn't. Maybe there was no crown. Maybe it was lost, and that was why Titik wanted to find it. As much as the Book of Abilities was lost, so was Srori's crown. Titik wanted Cassius to find something impossible in order to motivate him to do the same.

Or maybe Cassius was just exhausted and needed to get some sleep. The palace was by no means small, and he was only one man. He'd Banded for a while, but as the search wore on, he'd decided that it was useless in an empty palace.

Then he figured that the funeral must have ended because people began returning. He'd Banded in order to prolong his search, but finally he could hold out no longer.

He returned to the ruins, again empty-handed, more grouchy than angry. The city was again alive with activity, which only made him more grumpy. When he reached the officers building and someone tried to get his attention, a single look was enough to excuse himself from whatever impending conversation was about to be had.

He headed for his chambers where he lay down to sleep. Still no crown. Not even a clue as to the whereabouts of the crown. He was running out of time. He didn't balk at a challenge, but he was more about force than finesse. He didn't have the patience that Rifun had. He needed to make friends with Titik in order to get the Book of Abilities. Get the Book of Abilities, take control of the Cult, get rid of the Borelians, scoop up the Time industry, and then...

And then what? This wasn't his plan, was it? What did he care for all of this? He thrived in this kind of chaos; why should he seek to bring order to it?

Well, he would figure that out later. And even so, he could always get the Book of Abilities, take control of the Cult, and then just get rid of the Borelians. He would make his own plans later. Right now he needed sleep.

He slept hard but did not recall whether he had any dreams. Sometimes that was for the best, he figured. As long as he woke up, he was good. If he woke up and wasn't in immediate danger, even better. If he woke up and had the time and ability to actually consider his next actions, and perhaps even plan a little ahead, well, he didn't want to curse his good luck by speaking it aloud.

He needed to find the crown, but how to go about it? He'd already searched the royals. He'd scoured the palace. Where could it be? Was he going to have to search all of Turit, including all of their ships, just to find it?

As he was meandering about his room, he happened to notice something on the floor near the door. The doors were too big to allow the slipping of paper underneath, so whoever had left it had been terribly quiet. Or else he'd been sleeping so hard that he hadn't noticed.

Whatever the case, he approached the paper and picked it up. He inwardly grimaced as he recognized Rifun's handwriting.

"By the way, the Turitians take the crowns of their kings and queens and 'coronate' their dead. Find Srori's tomb in the royal mausoleum; his crown will be on his statue."

The information was not so puzzling as Rifun's possible motives. Could this be a trap? After his whining about political fallout, was he actually willing to help? Had he decided that the Book of Abilities took precedence over minor feuds?

Trap or not, it was a lead, and Cassius hurried to investigate.

7 | Teny sy Asa

<h1>Words and Works</h1>

The Wheel of Time, 1964

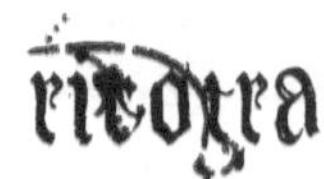

In an odd sort of way, Rifun actually liked Captain Titik. He was what the hippies on Earth might call a free spirit. He was bound by no man and no law but his own. True, he wasn't all that interested in peace as he raided and pillaged, but he seemed to genuinely enjoy himself and did not appear to regret his life choices.

Perhaps that was what made this whole debacle so puzzling, as it seemed to be a bit of a love triangle, or perhaps a square. Titik didn't like the Turitians—though whether this was truly personal, or more generalized as lawbreaker and law enforcement clashed, was up for debate—and likewise, the Turitians didn't like Titik. The Cult had an alliance with Turit, or at least the royal family Jalar. Titik wanted the crown of the now-former king of this royal family. Cassius, as part of the Cult, wanted to trade Titik for the Book of Abilities.

How was this all supposed to be balanced? If Titik were just stealing the crown, did the Cult have an obligation to warn the Turitians? Was the Cult expected to do police work for their allies? If Titik had asked for anything else for the Book of Abilities, would the Turitians have been offended? And considering that Titik was a rather famous defector, the Psiaco had to be on the lookout for him, right? Was there any way Rifun could appeal to them?

Politics could be confusing and even nauseating at times, Rifun thought as he returned to his chambers from the Wheel. He thought back to his time in the army. Working intelligence, he'd been privy to information that had occasionally gone from him straight to the general, or even from him straight to the Allied commanders, with very few or even no stops in between. It hadn't been his job to correct or interpret anything, simply record everything as-is and send it along. Let others make the decisions.

He greatly disagreed with some of those decisions, such as sending the British to invade Madagascar in order to keep it out of Japanese hands, but even so, his task had been very simple.

Now he was the one making the decisions. Right now, he had to decide whether to help an ally by forewarning them of treachery. If he did so, would that be considered betrayal to the Cult? True, Cassius was one of the leaders, but he was planning theft. Would it be seen as noble, that he would call out misconduct within his own ranks? Would it be seen as ignoble, that he would betray one of his own? If he did not warn the Turitians, would they blame him? Could he feign ignorance, given who the ultimate benefactor of this theft was, and who was tasked with carrying it out?

Or should he simply ignore the whole thing? This was, at its core, a feud between Turitian royalty and one Psiaco space pirate. There were plenty of small feuds among disagreeing species who were part of the Cult. While they were in the ruins, the only rule was put up or shut up. They were there to learn; take their disagreements elsewhere. The Turitians were Cult allies. Titik was not. Maybe if the Turitians wanted to get their crown back, they would have to learn the Akari in order to gain an edge over Titik.

But there was still that small problem of Cassius being the one to steal the crown. If he was smart, he might consider doing it anonymously, at least to keep the Cult's reputation in tact in the eyes of their allies. Let the crown magically show up in Titik's hands, let him and the Turitians fight it out.

But this was Cassius. As much as Cassius wasn't one for leadership and responsibility, he still liked the notoriety, being feared as an entity or untouchable god. He would want everyone to know that he had walked right into the Turitian palace and stolen the crown right from under their noses.

If they lost Turit as an ally, they were losing a vast area of influence to spread the Akari, as well as significant funding. The Wheel worked as well as any place to be able to increase their physical range of influence, but funds were a little harder to come by.

Another thought occurred to him then. What if they recruited Titik for funds?

He scoffed and shook his head. Ask a pirate to give away his treasure? Might as well ask a shark to give up its meal. But then, if Cassius could negotiate for the Book of Abilities and maybe entice Titik into at least considering the Akari, well...

Too many variables. Right now, he had to decide whether he was going to warn the Turitians.

Maybe it wasn't so much about whether he was going to warn the Turitians. Maybe it was him coming to a certain crossroads, where he could no longer feign ignorance to himself. He was going to have to make a choice and compromise his morals one way or another. Defend an ally, thereby betraying another leader and potentially giving up an opportunity to recover a priceless artifact, thereby betraying the Cult; or allow the other leader to hurt an ally, possibly lose that ally, taint the reputation of the Cult against future alliances, all for no guarantee that said artifact would be recovered.

But he'd been initially brought in to kill Cassius, and his intended actions were not so noble that they warranted such defense. Perhaps if there was a greater guarantee that Titik could produce the Book of Abilities, but he was either unable or unwilling. And as the Cult was already associated with at least one massacre and sabotage of the Wheel, their reputation was already unfriendly. Losing a stable, trusted ally was not a benefit, and there was again no guarantee on Titik's part to help them, even with the crown.

He had to warn the Turitians.

He returned to the Wheel briefly, just to see if Titik was still around, or perhaps his companion with the poor table manners. He found neither, and so continued on to Turit.

As he approached the governmental building, the whole city seemed all in a tizzy as people moved quickly from here to there, everyone appearing to be on the same urgent errand. When he reached the door, he was astonished to find himself barred from entry.

He made the appropriate turns and gestures. The last he knew, foreign guests were inferior only to the royal family and high military officers. Either he had committed an offense, or something else was going on.

"Why can I not enter?" he asked, trying to sound firm without being demanding.

"Our reluctant apologies, guest," one guard said sincerely, making more turns and gestures. "You have come at just an inopportune time. Beloved King Jalar de Srori has gone to walk with Ilir. Preparations for his second coronation must be made, and no visitors are permitted."

"Srori is dead?" Rifun echoed.

Why was he surprised? Srori had been terribly old and weak, wretchedly ill. He was king in title only, and Princess Aronet had assumed all such duties with all but the title.

An inopportune time indeed.

"My condolences to your people, but I must speak with...someone. Queen

Aronet perhaps."

"She is not queen yet, and your business will have to wait until after the ceremonies," the second guard told him.

"My business has to do with Srori. I must warn Aronet of a terrible plot that is to unfold during these ceremonies!"

That got the guards to pause and glance at each other at least.

"If the king has just died, how do you know that this plot is to unfold now?" the first guard asked.

Damn him and his logic.

"That business is for the new queen, or whomever I speak to."

The Turitian guards made certain gestures to each other, spoke only a few words, and then one of them disappeared into the building.

"The Commander General takes command between coronations. Lieutenant Lodit will inquire if she will receive you."

"Thank you," Rifun said, dipping his head graciously and making the equivalent Turitian gestures.

He stayed out of the way as best he could with all the people coming and going. Whatever preparations had to be made for the royal funeral, it promised to be a grand affair. And why not? From what Rifun could gather, just by his few interactions with the common Turitians, Srori had been a good king, one whose death may be mourned and not celebrated.

Would this pose any problems for Cassius and his attempts to steal Srori's crown? Would the crown be passed on to Aronet, or be buried with Srori? How big of a scene would Cassius cause to steal the crown? Would he do it discreetly? Could Rifun hope for that much? What if Cassius was already here? He knew how to take advantage of chaos. Even if there were many rules and traditions governing the burial of old kings and coronation of new ones, the whole affair still appeared very chaotic.

At long last, Lieutenant Lodit returned.

"Commander General Dira will receive you, but you only have ten minutes."

"It's all I need," Rifun said.

The Turitians were not cut out to be marathon runners, but that didn't mean they couldn't move fast when they wanted to. They moved swiftly to the third floor of the building where Commander General Dira was waiting. To Rifun's eyes, the room appeared quite large. For the Turitians, it may have been average to small.

"Rifun Ndolo," Dira acknowledged.

They exchanged greetings, the turns and gestures and formalities easily eating up two of the ten minutes.

"Lieutenant Lodit says that you know of a plot against us during the ceremonies," she went on finally. "How can this be? King Jalar de Srori walked on only a couple hours ago."

"Quite frankly, I was unaware of his passing, as was the perpetrator of this plot, but I've little doubt that the ceremonies will give him enough cover to pull off his heist. It may even entice him," Rifun said.

"And what is this plot?"

"Cassius is planning to steal Srori's crown."

"Cassius? Another leader of the Cult?"

"That is correct."

"Why would he do this?"

"He intends to trade it. The Cult is seeking a particular artifact, and the one who has this artifact—or claims to have it—is willing to part with it if he is given the crown."

Dira made several gestures. "I see." She paused. "Why are you going against one of your own?"

"This artifact seller only claims to have the item in question. He has given no proof of it. And I am not willing to risk tension between us for a hope and an unvetted promise."

"Hm..."

Alien body language was notoriously difficult to read, and this was only made more complicated by Turitian niceties.

"Who is this seller of artifacts?" she asked.

"An old friend of yours, I believe. One Captain Morain leRou Titik."

Turitians were humanoid, civilized, well-cultured, and well-mannered to a fault. That didn't mean that they, like humans, did not have a bestial side. As soon as Rifun said Titik's name, Dira dropped all pretense and spat a hiss, like a cat that's suddenly turned on its owner, lips drawing back to reveal rather sharp fangs. She growled for just a moment before apparently remembering her manners. She composed herself and took a breath.

"Are you certain of this?" she demanded.

"I was there for the negotiations myself," Rifun answered. He went on before she could speak. "I only knew that Cassius was seeking the artifact. I did not know from whom, or what price he was asking. I tried to dissuade Cassius, and when that failed, I came here."

A low rumble emanated from Dira's throat for just a moment. "He would like to get his hands on the crown." It was unclear whether Rifun was supposed to have heard the statement, so he kept silent. After a moment, she huffed a sigh and made more gestures. "Thank you for telling me this. I will arrange the necessary precautions."

He made a gesture of assent and relief.

"If I may ask," she said before he could leave, "what is this artifact? The Turitians control a rather large area of influence. If Titik is operating in these parts and with such dealers, we may have less...questionable methods of retrieving this artifact."

And the benefits of his decision began to make themselves known.

"It is a book. A journal. It details many secrets of the Akari, many of the more advanced abilities. It was written by Julianna's husband, Richard, the founder of the Cult."

"I see. A curious thing. I will be sure to tell our merchants to keep an eye out for it. The retrieval of this journal is the least we can do to keep Srori's crown safe."

"Happy to help."

Rifun figured it should have made him feel better and helped him to sleep when he returned to the ruins, but this was largely untrue. He lay awake for at least an hour, still wondering if he had done the right thing. But once again, he had been hired to kill Cassius.

He didn't realize he had fallen asleep until a loud, sudden noise jolted him awake, and he was jumping out of bed before his mind knew what he was doing.

It was Cassius, and he didn't look happy.

"Something I can do for you?" Rifun asked, both wary of the man's presence, and moderately annoyed at being woken up.

"You can stop meddling with my contracts," Cassius told him. "You can stop getting in my way."

Rifun barely heard the man, instead paying attention to his actions as he moved angrily toward him. Finally he invoked Force, an Energy ability that he was still uncoordinated in, and used it to push Cassius violently away from him. The killer stumbled back, used Time to right himself, but did not come in for a second aggression.

As expected, Cassius accused him of warning the Turitians. Rifun denied this, though he couldn't help but consider that the man wouldn't have been so angry if he'd managed to get the crown anyway. He might not have even suspected such treachery, but this anger could only mean that the plan had worked and the Turitians still possessed the crown.

This did not make the dark-skinned man any happier, however, even as he accused him again of warning the Turitians, to which Rifun again lied and denied it.

Cassius studied him intently. "And you're absolutely certain that you had nothing to do with it?"

"As sure as Srori is now dead." Rifun stood. "Now if you don't mind, I would like to get back to sleep."

There was a long moment of silence as they sized each other up, but Cassius was not known for his patience and he left the room.

Rifun waited a few more minutes, just in case the brute came back for a second round. Then he got back in bed, but found he could not sleep. He had no doubt that even if the king's death slowed Cassius down a step or two, he wouldn't be down for long. He would try again.

He lay there for a bit, maybe dozed off for an hour or so, then finally sat up and swung his legs over the side of the bed. Well, with dreams like his, who needed nightmares—and sleep—anyway? Might as well get something done. And he had an idea.

Years in the military and paramilitary had instilled a great sense of discipline within Rifun, complete with prioritization and a few annoying but unbreakable habits. Years in prison had instilled an equally great sense of both suspicion and exhaustion. Most often, he could overcome the latter with the former, but every so often the two bumped into each other, and he found himself sitting on the edge of his bed, knowing he needed to do something and having a plan formulating in his mind, and yet he lacked the motivation to get up and fulfill this plan.

This sensation lasted a good thirty seconds before discipline finally took over, and he started getting himself around, grabbing clothes and a comb.

As far as the rest of the ruins was concerned, it was the middle of the night. For the Turitians, however, it was still the late afternoon.

He should have guessed that death processions for a king would go longer than the average funeral service, and he was no stranger to lengthy funeral rites. But was there any way that he could speak to the Commander General? He was already barred from entry normally, and he figured that he was perhaps pushing his luck by coming back a second time.

Maybe he could wait a little while, just keep an eye on things until Cassius showed up.

The rites stretched on. Rifun watched from a distant rooftop as speech after speech after speech was made.

Finally, something started to happen. He could not make out the words, and his binoculars were only so powerful, but it seemed to be that Commander Dira produced the crown of Srori and, making more gestures that held little significance to Rifun, approached a statue of the deceased king which had clearly been carved in his younger years. With assistance and more words from almost-Queen Aronet, it appeared as though they coronated the statue. There was some big to-do, and then the statue was removed from the stage and taken inside the grand marble mausoleum.

Well now, that was something interesting to consider, and even before the plan had fully unfolded in his mind, Rifun was already opening a portal and retreating back to the ruins.

With the Turitians already being warned of Cassius' plans, they would certainly take extra precautions to keep Srori's crown safe. But if Rifun could bait him into trying again while the ceremonies were still going on, maybe the Turitians would be able to apprehend him.

Rifun headed to his chambers and grabbed some paper and utensils. It was a given that Cassius would try again, but maybe something could be done about it.

When he finished writing the note, he went to Cassius' chambers. Peeking inside, he found the man still asleep. Not wishing to disturb a sleeping giant, Rifun simply left the note on the floor and backed out, closing the door quietly.

"Ah, I didn't expect you to be awake."

His heart jumped, but he managed to calmly turn around to see Julianna approaching. She looked as prim and proper as ever, as though she'd just woken up and freshened herself for the day. Meanwhile, he felt as though he'd already been awake for a full day and then some. "Couldn't sleep. Figured I may as well be productive."

She nodded sympathetically. "The war or the torture?"

"Does it matter?"

"I suppose not."

They started walking through the building, moving and speaking leisurely, though Rifun erected a Sound barrier around them. He was as yet uncertain whether someone else could manipulate Sound in such a way so as to negate the barrier, but he decided not to dwell on it at the present moment.

"How goes the spiritual quest?" Julianna inquired pleasantly.

"I've been a bit distracted. I discovered the identity of Cassius' contact for the Book of Abilities."

"Oh? May I ask who it is?"

So Rifun relayed the events of the last day or so, with Captain Titik, the crown of Srori, the funeral procession, including his plan to snare Cassius.

"Do you really think it will work?" Julianna wondered.

"I don't know," Rifun admitted. "On the one hand, I had hoped that maybe Cassius would use a Disguise to pull off his heist, this way he could blame it on someone else—perhaps Titik himself—and so not jeopardize our alliance with the Turitians. On the other hand, with no guarantees that Titik even has the Book of Abilities or knowledge of its whereabouts, I decided to place the value of an established alliance over the value of uncertain information."

"Not an easy decision, certainly, but understandable." She nodded. "What do you expect will happen if Cassius does manage to pull off this heist and steal the crown of Srori?"

"The Turitians can't say they weren't warned. If they blame us, they expose their alliance with us and, tangentially, the Borelians. Not only that, but they only add credence to the idea that the Akari is vastly superior to mere Time and discredit themselves for not learning of it in order to counter it. I suppose they could sidestep the issue by declaring for the Akarin, but I doubt it. Easier for them to blame Titik, someone they are already pursuing and who hates them in return, and who will be the ultimate benefactor and possessor of the crown."

"Hm..." Julianna did not look convinced.

"I am not convinced that Titik has the Book of Abilities. I think Cassius was baiting us, to see what we would do if we thought he had an advantage."

"And so, in warning the Turitians and laying this trap, assuming it succeeds, then it may buy us time to follow his leads and see if they go anywhere," she finished.

"Precisely."

"And if this trap doesn't work?"

"Then, in the end, it is merely a feud between the Turitians and one Psiaco space pirate. If one wishes an advantage of the other, perhaps he should learn the Akari."

Julianna grinned. "Ah. A masterful plan indeed."

Rifun shook his head. "Hardly. It is what I have to work with. Once this saga plays out, then Cassius will return to sabotaging the Wheel and playing controlled opposition to the Borelians, and I..."

"You...what?"

"I shall continue on this spiritual quest of mine."

"Oh." She frowned but nodded. "I expect such a thing to be a personal endeavor, but do you mind if I ask about it?"

"As you yourself just pointed out. It is typically a personal endeavor."

"Does this have to do with your Book?"

"Among other things which I have recently experienced or discussed with others. But mortal commentary can only go so far into the realm of the immortal before both knowledge and wisdom become exhausted."

"This is true. I suppose I have no right to interfere in such matters."

"I will warn you, however, that I do not intend it to be an instance of meager bedtime prayers or morning meditation. I mean to lock myself away for an indefinite time to wholly pray and meditate."

Such a thing seemed to surprise her, and she was silent for a long moment. Then, "Well, I suppose we shall have to endure without you for a time."

"Cassius will be the agent of chaos, and chaos must reign for a time before the people are truly ready for peace. Even I tired of the insurgency after a time, when the noose tightened and the food ran low. I am certain the Cult will manage without me." He continued, "This is not to say that I shall ignore an attack or other great distress, but I am satisfied that we are in a good place, politically, for the time being."

"If you're sure," Julianna said hesitantly.

No, he wasn't sure, but it was, at its core, a leap of faith. Faith that the Author would handle things, and faith that she might see his willingness to not be consumed by the things of the world and instead seek a higher plane of existence. He was ready and willing. His mission was true, and he wanted his spirit to be pure. He wanted to touch the razana fully now, and not have to rely on Cassius and his personal demons to teach him. If there was anything that the Cult and the Akarin could agree on, it was that there was more than the Akari out there, and Rifun had a sneaking feeling that Cassius had found one of those other things, and it wasn't good. But if he could meditate and seek the Author, then maybe things could be put back to rights.

"As sure as I can be, which is a great deal better than not sure at all."

"And do you also have a plan for the Borelians?"

"Nothing new, as it relates to the Turitians. Perhaps the Author will show me something."

"I see."

Rifun dropped the Sound barrier and gave her a look. "Perhaps I'm out of touch with modern life, but I always thought women liked pious men? For some it means stability, for others in means power?"

"I thought I wasn't your type."

He felt his face flush with embarrassment. "Maybe not, but religion tends to be one of those topics that evokes emotions in even the most callous of people."

"Well, you're not wrong there. If it's my opinion that you are asking for...I think it's admirable that you are taking this seriously, that this is more than a mere job for you. But I worry over your intent to lock yourself away for several weeks or months or who knows how long."

"Why?"

"On the one hand, I wish to say that I find it extreme. Though certainly no more extreme than intentionally sabotaging the Wheel and all that."

"Are you afraid that I may see or learn something that would steer the Cult in a different direction than our current intent?"

She considered this for a moment, then nodded. "Yes, I suppose you could phrase it that way."

"But would you not want such correction from the Author, to be certain that we are in the right?"

"That may be so, but it is never fun to be told that you are in the wrong and must change, never mind trying to make the changes and explain this to the underlings."

He nodded. "I fully understand, believe me." He stepped in front of her and turned to face her. "But we need this. How shall it be if we grow too grand and successful, only to learn that it is all a lie? All backwards, and nothing as we have promised or preached?"

He could see that she was still uncertain, but finally she nodded. "You're right. If the reason the Cult broke away from the Akarin is that the Akarin no longer served the will of the Author, then we must make a point of seeking the will of the

Author and conforming to it."

"Precisely."

"Now then, how long do you expect to give for Cassius?"

"If he is successful, then he can sweat for a few minutes. If he is unsuccessful, I expect we shall know about it just as soon as he returns."

"What about Titik?"

"He'll give the crown to Titik, I'm sure, but he'll want to rub it in my face first."

"Well, I suppose that is to be expected."

"After he's done that, provided no catastrophes arise in the immediate wake of his scandal, then I will begin my quest."

Julianna said nothing, merely dipped her head and took her leave of him.

Bouncing from planet to planet, when those planets could have drastically different days and nights, could really mess with a person's Circadian rhythm, and Rifun was no exception. He'd also heard it said that the blind were especially susceptible. His blindsight may have kept him in check personally, but it did nothing for the varying planetary cycles. He'd been up since the wee hours of the Sadurnon morning, spent the better part of an afternoon to late evening on Turit, returned to Sadurnon where the ruins were in a lively midafternoon routine, and there was every chance he might have to return to Turit in the middle of the night. His body didn't know if it should feel normal, tired, or launch into sleep deprived delirium.

Instead he returned to his chambers where he spent a good hour or so preparing his shrine. He cleaned and straightened the colorful blanket that was spread out on the floor, spread a handwoven silk blanket over that, and laid many items upon it: two stones as a vatolahy, a lock of his hair in a straw hat, a wood carving, a bowl of rice, some smoked omby, a handful of ginger, a small cup of honey, some crushed up tree bark, and a dusting of dried leaves. He would add his Authored Book last, when he was ready to sit down and actually begin his quest.

When he left his room, he passed by Cassius' chambers. Curious, he Banded and opened the door. The room was empty; Cassius was gone, along with most of his tools of his trade. Was there any way to tell how long he'd been gone? Maybe, maybe not, but Rifun did not try to fool himself into thinking that such a theft was going to be a swift or easy heist. He would give it some time.

He debated going to bed. In the morning, he would find out whether Cassius had been successful and so weigh his options and duties before embarking on his quest. If Cassius were captured, well, he could sweat a little while. If not, then he would just have to assess any needed cleanup, maybe make nice with the Turitians, and then see if this adventure really did produce the Book of Abilities.

On the other hand, if Cassius did get the crown and escape, what if he did get the Book of Abilities without returning to rub in his victory? What happened then?

Quite frankly, nothing would change as far as Cassius was concerned. The Borelians, though, they could pose a problem if they read that book and learned from it. But, seeing how Cassius was hardly a friend or even willing ally of Isthim or the Borelians, that fear might be lessened for a time.

For a few moments, Rifun was unsure of his ability to step away from the Cult to pursue his meditation. Then he chastised himself for having such doubts. Were not all their actions at the whim and will of the Author? Did she not have control over all things? Did he somehow think that she would be a less effective ruler than him while he was away?

He was only staving off his meditation in order to tie up a few loose ends. That was it. If Cassius walked in the door right now, with or without the crown or the journal, as long as there was no fire, no war, no immediate danger, Rifun could retire to his chambers and stay there for a few weeks or months or however long this was going to take.

He didn't know who he was trying to convince, really, or what his panic was truly over. Maybe he ought to meditate a little now, just to calm his anxiety before it turned into something worse, something he couldn't control.

His disgust at the thought snapped him out of his anxious state well enough. He was a soldier, a survivor, a servant of the Author. He couldn't let his mind run away so. He had to remain alert and determined and in control of himself. It was perhaps the only way he was going to survive the coming revolution.

Determined not to start any new projects before his meditation, he deliberately ignored the political work left out on his table in his chambers. Indeed, he took care to do no more than organize it a bit and set it aside, revealing the stone beneath the pages. After that, he took a casual tour around the officers building, exchanging stiff pleasantries with the Borelians but otherwise avoiding them, before going out into the ruins.

The ruins were more of a city now, and a rather lively one at that. This was not a bad thing, though he wondered if it wouldn't be prudent to consider some sort of Disguise. Was that possible? To Disguise a city? It wasn't just about hiding the activity within, but masking the sound as well and making it uninteresting and even uninviting to curious cavers. But then, if they could Disguise a city, who was to say that they couldn't have other bases on other worlds? Expand recruiting as it were?

Well, that was a different trouble for a different day, and not something he could concern himself with in the here and now. His primary focus now was simply tying up loose ends between Cassius, the Turitians, and Titik. Nothing else mattered. The time for calming one's thoughts and anxieties began long before the actual meditation.

He returned to the officers building, wondering if he shouldn't go to Turit and see if anything was amiss. Maybe they really had captured Cassius and they were just waiting for him to come clean up the mess. Bail him out of jail as it were.

If that was the case, Rifun figured, returning to his chambers, then it could wait until morning. Maybe the spirits would show him something tonight.

He saw nothing, or nothing he wished to see, and woke up thinking only that he hoped the cleanup from this business of Srori's crown would be swift, because he greatly desired to pray and meditate for a while. At least for a few weeks.

When he asked around, no one had seen Cassius. When he checked the madman's chambers, they were exactly as they had been the day before. Could Rifun really hope that Cassius had been successfully apprehended? Maybe even executed?

Only one way to find out.

He got himself around and went to Turit. It appeared that the funeral procession had ended and life was back to normal. At the very least, he was able to enter the governmental building freely again and request an audience with Commander Dira. Due to the festivities of the previous day, however, her schedule was backed up and he could be waiting a while.

This was nothing that a little Time couldn't solve, Slow Banding his way through an extensive wait period. He was escorted to meet with Commander Dira soon enough. He would not consider himself to be an expert on alien body language, but if he had to guess, he might say that she looked rather smug and self-satisfied. Her turns and gestures reflected this.

"I take it the crown is safe?" Rifun wondered when formalities finally gave way to conversation.

"It is, thanks to your timely warning," Dira told him, still looking quite smug. "We replaced the real crown with a decoy. It is crafted similarly, but it is not Srori's crown."

"I will not ask for the details; I trust you to know how to take care of your own affairs. The question is, will Titik know the difference?"

She made a gesture. "Of course he will. He may be a pirate, but he is no fool. He was once considered one of the most promising students ever to attend Psia's Time Academy."

"What happened to him, do you know?"

Another gesture, one of indifference, similar to a shrug. "Greed. Lust. Short-sightedness. He chose the pleasures of the day over meaningful, long-term contributions to society."

"I know people like that. They deserve our pity."

"And justice, where need be." More smugness. "But if Cassius or Titik deserve anything now, it is only our laughter. Titik will not get what he wants and Cassius will be made the fool."

"I do not believe he will take kindly to such a thing."

"Nor do I, but perhaps he should then examine himself. Titik may be a pirate, but he is no fool. He knows his enemy. Cassius should perhaps educate himself in the same fashion."

Rifun laughed humorlessly. "Easier said than done, and you don't have to live with him." He sighed. "But all is well, then? Once Cassius finds out, he may return, looking for the real crown, just out of spite."

Dira made a gesture. "Do not worry yourself. Titik is not the only one who desires the crowns of our kings and queens."

"Maybe not, but you've never had to contend with the Akari."

"Are you certain? Please, leave our affairs to ourselves."

He made a gesture of submission. "Of course. I mean no offense."

A gesture of ease. "No, naturally not. But as I have said, all is well here. You need not concern yourself over trivial matters, and our alliance is in no jeopardy."

Rifun could only assent, and he did so gladly. This loose end tied up nicely. He made the appropriate turns, gestures, and farewells, and finally departed.

That couldn't have gone any better if he'd scripted it himself, except, perhaps for Cassius' apprehension or execution as royal Turitian guards defended their dead monarch with ruthless cunning and superiority. But, for what it was, it wasn't bad.

That also meant that Cassius had not returned to the ruins to parade his victory before the whole army, or at least before Rifun.

But then, why would he? Cassius was intent on taking the Book of Abilities for himself. If he'd taken the crown and then boasted of it to Rifun, then Rifun would invariably wish to go with him to meet Titik and make the exchange. By doing it this way, well, he was cutting out Rifun.

It was more annoying than anything, he thought. Potentially dangerous, if Titik really truly did possess the Book of Abilities. But then, if the crown that Cassius stole was not the crown Titik wanted, then by all accounts, the bargain was unfulfilled and the pirate would have no reason to turn over the Book of Abilities or its location. So things may not pan out as Cassius had hoped.

As much as he wanted to simply return to his chambers to begin his meditation, he did need to find out how far this went.

He returned to the officers building just to see if Cassius had returned while he'd been away. Such was not the case. The next step, then, would be the Wheel.

The good news was that the Wheel was still in tact when Rifun arrived. If Cassius had decided to destroy all of the balancers in a fit of rage over the crown, well, he hadn't done so. Yet. The movement of the crowds in the Wheel suggested heightened alert owing to recent events, but little more. If anything had happened, no one in the outer reaches of the Wheel was aware of it yet.

All but one marketplace—the one where the initial balancer incident had taken place—was back to normal operations, though crowds still seemed a bit thin, comparatively speaking. As for non-marketplaces, only the Archives remained closed. Rifun suspected that the Archives would remain closed for a while.

Before he turned away completely, however, movement caught his eye. He fully expected many secretaries to be moving about in the Archives, but he was not certain why the Borelians would take such an interest. Even as Grandfathers, their role had been fulfilled. They did not need to supervise the restoration of a library.

Curious, Rifun approached.

"Commander," he acknowledged, nodding once to Commander Misik. "Something going on here?"

"Restoration," Misik replied, his tone suggesting that he was lying, he knew he was lying, he knew Rifun knew he was lying, and he didn't care one bit. "The secretaries asked us to help move things and demonstrate the Akari to them."

"I see." Rifun gave Misik a look, and the commander responded in kind. "Carry on then."

He departed the Archives, leaving the conversation for another time. He couldn't get involved in something new. He couldn't. He was going to find Cassius, wrap up this thing with Titik, and start meditating.

He needed to meditate regardless, because he was starting to get frustrated about the whole thing.

He went to the Food Court, not intending to get food, but just to look around. The place was populated enough that he could generally hide within the ebb and flow of aliens, but it wasn't so crowded that he couldn't see three feet past the nearest hide. He followed the various currents as people moved through the Food Court, trying to pick out his party.

He did not see Cassius or Titik or any of Titik's crew, especially the one with the poor table manners. He got a table and waited a little bit longer. Wasn't as though anyone would miss him, given that time at home did not pass normally while one was in the Wheel. Still nothing happened.

Could Cassius have already come and spoken with Titik? Certainly, while Rifun had gone to Turit to speak with Commander Dira. But if the crown had been a fake, and Titik should have known, well, honestly, Rifun had expected a tiny bit more violence. Even if said violence had already ended, it didn't usually have such...minimal aftereffects. Take the balancers for example, or whatever Cassius had done. That was still being cleaned up.

On the other hand, Cassius getting violent over this would only showcase his ineptitude. He wouldn't want that.

Whatever had or hadn't happened, Rifun wasn't going to sit there forever. He stood, stretched, took one last look around the Food Court, then left. With any luck, if Cassius had somehow acquired the Book of Abilities, he wouldn't have completely abandoned the Cult. At the very least, he still had to return long enough to rub their faces in it. That would be the time to finally pull out all the stops and kill him.

As he was making his way through the Wheel to the portal room, something else caught his attention. It took a minute to push through the crowds to verify it, but it did seem to be Titik's crewman, the one with the poor table manners. He was unsure of the exact species, though it appeared birdlike. What he did know was that it had been with Titik, which meant the pirate was probably around here somewhere, and Cassius probably would be also.

He followed the crewman through the marketplace until the crowd broke enough that he could approach and get its attention.

"Oh, it's you," it said.

"I can be no one else," Rifun said. "And what about you?"

"What about me?"

"Well, pardon my manners, but I seem to have forgotten your name."

"Pilory. Lieutenant Pilory."

"You seem rather unsettled, Lieutenant Pilory. And since we seem to be on formal terms, you may address me as Adjudant-chef."

Her expression appeared annoyed, then relented.

"You are not Cassius. This much I can tell. And I thank the gods for it."

"You're hiding out from Titik," Rifun guessed. "I take it the exchange didn't go as planned?"

Pilory made a noise that was somewhere between a whistle, a twitter, a screech, and a laugh, and Rifun could only guess its social function. "Hardly. Cassius boasted of himself well enough, true. He even produced a verifiable Turitian crown."

"But it wasn't Srori's crown."

"No. How — ?" She cocked her head like a bird. "You warned the Turitians?"

"I saved our alliance is what I did," he informed her.

She studied him for a long moment. "You knew Titik didn't have the book that you're looking for."

"Not for certain. It was a calculated risk, which you have just confirmed paid off."

Pilory made a movement that appeared to mean affirmation.

"How did Titik take it?" Rifun asked.

"You've never seen an angry Psiaco I take it?"

"No, never."

"You don't want to. Psiaco like to portray themselves as greatly civilized, but they can be little better than the Urid when they get angry." She shifted her stance. "Although, he wasn't overly angry. He was impressed that Cassius managed to pull off the heist he did, but he was less than pleased that he didn't have the forethought to even research what he was going after."

Rifun nodded. "I see. What happened then?"

"Well, there was an argument and Titik removed himself."

"He doesn't fight much?"

"He's not a coward, if that's what you're implying." Pilory glared at him.

"Not at all," he assured her.

"People underestimate him, think he's dim and uncoordinated. Nothing could be further from the truth. He doesn't fight just to fight, although he has no qualms about complaining to any who will listen. He chooses his battles. He just didn't find Cassius a worthy opponent."

"And what of the Book of Abilities?"

Pilory made a motion like a shrug. "What of it? Titik never had it, to be honest. The crown of Srori was supposed to be payment for him to even passively search for it. Well, no payment, no service."

"What about the decoy crown?"

"Sitting in the treasure hold on the ship. It's still an authentic crown, worth at least a few umox."

So then, no Book of Abilities, no deal, no parting pleasantries, and not even a consolation prize. How had the Wheel escaped Cassius' wrath? What was he going to return to in the ruins?

"An unfortunate situation," Pilory went on, "but Titik isn't interested in long-term business or charity. Money is the only pleasure in the world." Even for an alien, he could detect a fair amount of sarcasm.

"So there's no chance of yet winning him to our cause?" Rifun inquired.

"He's pretty annoyed right now. I would wait a while before you spoke to him again about anything, even if he's back here on his pedestal lamenting the state of things. It may also be better if Cassius were not the next one to speak to him."

It was one of the better things to come from this conversation so far, but how would Cassius take it?

"I take it you've not seen Cassius since?" he asked.

"Titik removed himself, and so did I. You are correct, I am staying out of his way for the time being. No, I've not seen Cassius."

Rifun nodded. "All right. At any rate, safe travels."

"And you."

They separated on amiable terms to different places in the portal room.

Rifun returned quickly to the ruins but found nothing amiss at first glance. Nothing was burning down and he heard no sounds of distress. The officers building then.

As he made his way through the city, he spotted Cassius just walking up the steps to the officers building. He didn't look like he was on a rampage, so what...? Rifun wasn't sure if he should feel relieved or afraid for his life.

"So, where is it?" Rifun asked at Cassius' back once they were inside the officers building.

Cassius turned. "Where's what?"

"The Book of Abilities. Do you have it? Were you able to trade for it?"

"No." He shifted his stance. "Strange thing. The crown turned out to be a fake."

"A fake?"

"Oh, it was real enough Turitian craftsmanship, but it was not the crown of Srori."

"Are you sure you had the correct tomb?"

"Oh yes."

Rifun didn't like the man's demeanor. He was too calm after such a scathing insult. Still, he himself remained calm about it. "And Titik?"

"Took the crown eagerly enough, but never delivered."

"What are you going to do now then?"

"I haven't decided."

Rifun knew instantly that was a lie. Cassius knew exactly what he was going to do, and he wasn't going to tell Rifun.

"I see," Rifun said at last. "Well, when you do decide, don't tell me."

"Suddenly the political master of information doesn't want to know something?"

"I'm going to be gone for a while. Weeks, perhaps months."

"Going home for a vacation? More African countries to fail to liberate?"

Ouch. Rifun wouldn't deny it; he visibly flinched at that remark. Sure, Cassius failed to secure the Book of Abilities, but Rifun had failed to secure independence for his people.

"No. Consider it a religious pilgrimage."

Cassius stared at him as if searching for the punchline to a joke he didn't understand. Finally the dark-skinned man shook his head. "And it's going to take you weeks or months? Why do this now?"

"The Cult is in a stable position, both here and in our alliances. Isthim and Julianna have things managed here, and you have your mission to carry out in the Wheel. If I don't go now, I never will."

Again, Cassius could only stare at him. He probably had no concept of piety or the idea that any supernatural being could exercise power and control over him or his surroundings.

"If there is a major problem, I will return," Rifun sighed. "But this is something that must be done."

Cassius waved a hand dismissively. "Whatever. Your religion is your problem."

Rifun raised a brow. "At least I don't make you observe any fady in my presence."

"I don't know what that is, and quite frankly, I don't care. You pray to whatever god you think is going to help us. If he or she or they do help, then maybe I'll even thank them."

He turned and walked away, muttering something Rifun didn't care to consider.

Rifun sighed, rolled his eyes, but continued on, making for his chambers. Three steps into his walk, Julianna came alongside him.

"All is well with the Turitians, then?" she inquired.

"Yes. They were never worried," he assured her. "Titik is out of range for the time being. Cassius has plans he is not disclosing to me, but I suspect his mission will keep him occupied for a time."

"And no journal?"

"I'm afraid not."

While not surprising, he did not miss the look of dejection on her face either. "You're going to retreat into your meditation, then?"

"I am."

"I wish you well. Bring us some sort of insight, won't you?"

"I can only do as the Author wills, and I'll not fabricate anything."

"No, of course not."

They paused outside his chambers. He turned to her and lowered his voice. "Oh, and you may want to keep an eye on the Borelians."

"I already do," Julianna growled. "Shall I keep the other eye on them as well?"

"I don't know." He told her of the exchange in the Archives. "It could be nothing, but I suspect they could be up to something."

"In the Archives? What could they want there?"

"Information is a powerful thing. Now that the Archives have been shaken, it may be a chance for them to alter or remove some of that information with none being the wiser for it."

Julianna considered this, then nodded. "Fair enough. Anything else?"

"Try not to burn the place down."

He entered his chambers and closed the heavy stone door behind him. As if to make a point of it, he used Gravity to lift the heavy stone table and barricade the door further. He thought about, then moved all of the furniture except for the bed to reinforce the barricade.

He grabbed his Authored Book and went to his shrine. He closed his eyes, said a prayer, and laid the Book amid the other items. From there, he knelt, said another prayer, then shifted and bowed low.

The Caves of Meroian, 1964

Ọkọ̀kúmbọ̀

Cassius closed the door, then dumped out the contents of his bag, the false crown and handfuls of jewels scattering over his bed and rolling onto the floor.

It had gone like this:

Upon finding Rifun's note, Cassius had quickly grabbed his things and left the ruins, making for Turit. This was accomplished easily enough.

When he arrived on Turit, donning his Disguise so he could move about more or less freely, he discovered that while the funeral procession was still going on, it appeared to be wrapping up. To his eyes, it appeared as though the coronation of the new Queen Aronet was one of, if not the final item on the agenda.

It was a grand display, really. As one might expect from an incoming monarch, Aronet had been dressed in what probably passed as the nicest finery that could be owned and worn by any Turitian. In addition to very decorative bands, the streamers were so dazzling that Cassius might have mistaken it for a type of grass skirt made from tinsel. She also wore a shawl of some form, and other decorative clothing that he had never previously seen on any Turitian.

Watching from a distance, listening to conversation around him, he quickly learned that each crown was unique to the monarch, designed and crafted for them over many years as soon as they were selected as being in line for the throne, and even then, the crowns were not actually fashioned until that person was within three deaths of becoming king or queen.

So, theoretically, there could be several crowns hiding in the area worth stealing. What would happen if Cassius stole the crown belonging to the next person in line, then assassinated Queen Aronet? How would the next person be crowned?

It was a devious idea, but not one he was going to test this day. His concern now was with the crown of the previous king.

Really, all he had to do was wait for the ceremonies to end, and then he'd just walk into the mausoleum and take the crown. He could probably do that now. It might even make a bigger statement. But he was annoyed enough by this whole debacle that he either wanted this to go smoothly, which would require less security and such; or he was going to go on a full rampage and start killing indiscriminately.

In the present moment, he could still respect an alliance.

Actually crowning the new queen was a simple task that took only a minute or two. The speeches and other niceties that had to come afterwards took much longer, and nearly put Cassius to sleep. Even after the new queen was done speaking, others had to come up and speak, praising the new queen, as if they hadn't just given half-hour speeches only a few hours beforehand for the old king.

Sheesh, politics was exhausting. Cassius was reminded anew why he normally left this stuff to Rifun.

Or maybe it was that nice politics was boring. Polite politics was boring. Public politics was boring. All the stuff behind the scenes and in the gutters, well, that could be a bit more exciting. His deal with Titik, for example, he might classify as politics, just a different kind of politics. Just because one did not dine with kings did not mean he did not fight for his place in a subterranean pecking order.

All the same, this shit was boring as hell.

He waited around, listened, glanced at the mausoleum multiple times a minute, considered just going in and stealing the crown more than once, and waited some more. It was terribly dull, and every time he thought that things might just be wrapping up, someone else had to get up to speak. From the distance he was at, he couldn't make out what they were saying. He could use Sound to amplify it, he supposed, but he didn't care that much.

Eventually he grew tired of being patient. He wasn't going to go on a killing spree—the boredom of waiting had sapped his rage strength—but he was going to pass out if he had to endure this much longer. He couldn't even say that he'd been waiting that long, but boredom had a way of stretching out the moments.

So he picked his way back through the crowd, changing his Disguise several times so that he could not be reliably identified, not dropping the Disguise until he was well clear of the security line.

Once he was free to be himself once more, he Banded, bringing everything to a standstill. He was going to do what he should have done an hour ago.

He made his way back to the ceremonies and festivities, skirting the edge of the crowd and heading for the mausoleum. It was an enormous marble structure, almost as big as the palace, it seemed. With the stage set up before it and all the important people still giving speeches, the two regular door guards seemed almost laughable, and Cassius easily slipped by them. The enormous carved doors were remarkably light, and he had no trouble shutting them silently behind him.

Once inside the mausoleum, he discovered that it was not almost as big as the palace. It was bigger than the palace, by at least threefold, if not more. The structure aboveground was the palace, but a quick survey of the structure showed there to be seemingly endless catacombs and antechambers underground as well.

There had been some big ceremony to commit Srori's body to the mausoleum and whatever afterlife the Turitians believed in, but apparently the actual location of his body was not as easy as simply picking the next available stone bed. If he had to guess, Cassius would probably expect him to be buried in some family vault.

Question was, where was the family vault? The problem was that the Turitians, at least their royalty, didn't live in blood relative family units, but picked and chose their families. He didn't understand the criteria, but it could make things difficult for him.

On the other hand, he could just follow the apparent disturbances of the place. Muddy boots, for instance, that left a trail of dirt. A couple long hairs fallen from someone's head to the floor which was marble all over the aboveground structure and for at least two levels underground.

Once he hit the third sub-level, however, things got difficult. The marble walls vanished in favor of heavy stone. The floor turned to a slate-like rock, but clearly no one thought it important to sweep regularly, and it was well covered in dirt. He might have thought to simply follow footprints, except there were too many of them to say which ones were the most recent. Were there guards down here? Sure, he might expect a small contingent of soldiers to bring the dead king down here, but what reason would there be for them to travel down every corridor?

Well, he was in a Band anyway, so he could afford to look around a little. If every crown was unique to every monarch, well, there were plenty of monarchs down here. And who knew what other treasures they might be buried with? This could prove to be a profitable venture, whether he found the crown or not.

The marble mausoleum aboveground was about the size of the palace. A cursory inspection of the underground levels seemed to be about two or three times that size. Actually exploring them, well, after the first few miles of tunnels, switchbacks, dead-ends, vaults, atriums, and antechambers, Cassius was beginning to wonder if there might not be an entire underground city here.

He'd found plenty of tombs and bodies, that was for sure. He expected that Rifun might be able to exposit an entire history of the Turitians to make sense of it all, but the way Cassius saw it, there was a period of kings being buried with great wealth and treasure, just like the Egyptian pharaohs, then a period where they were buried with little more than tattered garments, and then a period that he couldn't even begin to describe or frame in any Terran context, and then a period of more modest burial treasures.

But one thing that remained constant through the centuries was that every monarch's tomb came complete with a stone statue of that monarch, and the statue was dressed in the likeness of the body and wore the monarch's crown. Well, he supposed that was the original intent. There were a couple of monarchs whose statues had been defaced in some way, suggesting they had not been well-loved, and any treasures missing.

Having opened up Srori's casket or sarcophagus, whatever one wanted to call it, Cassius knew the king hadn't been buried with much. His clothing had been regal with plenty of jewels, but there was little beyond what was on his body. He was also glad he did it, seeing how he couldn't read any of the writing. He wasn't even sure it was writing, as calligraphic as it was, swirling about in a dizzying array of patterns and pictures.

Didn't matter. He wasn't here for the culture; he wanted the crown. Cracking open the coffin had given him a good look at the dead king's clothes. Now he just needed to find the statue that matched.

Whatever wars and culture shifts had happened to the Turitians over the centuries, they still appeared to honor their traditions. Cassius didn't know the expected lifespan of Turitian royalty, but if it was at least as long as a human, then they had tombs dating back probably a thousand years. For as passive as Cassius was, even he couldn't help but be impressed. But only a little.

He smiled smugly to himself. Rifun would die to get into a place like this, he was sure. To study the history and everything else up close and personal. It would just wring him to think that an ingrate like Cassius traipsed about freely, observing but uncaring.

Well, such was the price of morality and its limitations. Why waste time waiting for permission? Hell, Cassius wasn't even going to ask for forgiveness.

But he really needed to find this damn crown. Band or not, he was bored and frustrated. He'd come across a few guards, but none of them had apparently been

Srori's pallbearers.

He continued down another level. And then another. Just how many levels did this mausoleum have? At this rate, he was going to hit groundwater. And still he kept going down and checking.

He must have missed something. Maybe he overlooked a chamber. Maybe he hadn't been paying attention. Maybe he'd somehow mistaken the king's clothing or his crown, or forgotten some distinguishing feature. There was no way that a recently dead king would be buried this far down. Unless he was somehow the secret twin brother of Turitian-Jesus—apparently his name was Ilir—with a ridiculously long lifespan, there was just no way.

More than a little annoyed, Cassius abandoned the idea of going even farther down and decided to retrace his steps instead. This time, he made a line in the dirt outside each tomb he inspected, and an X at the top of each stairway as he cleared the floors.

It also occurred to him, none too soon, that perhaps someone had deduced that he was here in a Band. Even if they didn't understand the Akari, they suspected that he was in a Band, and so they were constantly moving the king and his crown in order to frustrate Cassius' search. Even the very idea, never mind if it was true or not, was enough to infuriate him and make him speed up his search.

He reached the second sub-level, where dirt and slate finally gave way to fine marble once again. Depending on family lineage, however it worked here, he might believe that Srori could be this far down.

Seeing how the floor was solid again, he had no good way to mark the chambers as he inspected them, and he resorted to taking a streamer off of each statue and laying it on the ground outside.

Finally, returning to the first sub-level—and kicking himself for going on such a long, unnecessary search, although he did not discount the possibility of treachery— Cassius found Srori's antechamber. He remembered the cascade of bands and streamers well, and he'd committed the crown to memory. Well, basically.

He took the crown off the statue and placed it on his own head. Or, that was the intention. Turitian heads were a bit bigger than human heads, and the crown slid over his head to his shoulders with ease. Still looked good. It wasn't gold, but the metal was still polished and engraved with the same calligraphic lettering in a flowing, almost flowery pattern, interspersed with several fine jewels apparently to accent various features of the engraving.

Whatever the significance of the engraving, the writing, or the jewels, Cassius did not know. He briefly entertained the idea of asking Rifun to translate, or at least provide some context. At least then Cassius might present it to Titik with some smug knowledge of what he'd just stolen and from whom. But then, seeing how Titik was already an enemy of the Turitians and had requested the crown specifically, there was a chance that he already knew the history and significance.

Besides, Cassius didn't want to ask Rifun. This was his mission, and his alone. And he was going to finish it alone and fulfill the bargain on his own. He didn't need the other so-called leaders to hold his hand, or his chain as it felt some days. He was going to do this by himself and claim the prize for himself. Then see how the others felt about it, and about him.

His main objective complete, Cassius returned to a few of the more lavish burials and took a few small knick-knacks for himself. Just a few jewels and possibly a priceless artifact or two. Maybe he'd give them out as birthday gifts for the others. Ha!

As he finally hiked back up the stairs with the honest intent of leaving—still getting distracted here and there by the various tombs—he found himself wondering if Borelians observed such things. Birthday celebrations were very personal, individual affairs. This seemed antithetical to the Borelian collectivist mindset.

How would Isthim react, then, to such a gesture? Would it make her uncomfortable? Angry? Would it keep her separated from her brethren? Could there be some other repercussions for her? Could there be repercussions for him? Could he plead ignorance?

Well, he wasn't much of a gift giving person, so such a gesture would already be suspicious. He couldn't think of any way to make it convincing either.

Maybe an anonymous gift.

Maybe an anonymous gift to Rifun. Cassius had nothing to do with whatever book was left for him, but if that paranoid the man, what would continuing gifts do to him? Would he become even more paranoid? Would he think someone was after him? Would he figure it out? Would he think Cassius had left the book?

There were a number of ways he could milk this, and he smiled to himself as he emerged from the mausoleum into the still life of Turit. He took a few more things just because he could as he wandered through town before finally finding a quiet alley to release the Band.

In the many years that he'd used the Akari, he'd become quite proficient in its many uses, and he could Band with the best of them. That didn't mean they didn't still cause some problems, most notably headaches. Sometimes it didn't come about until after he released the Band.

It hit him with such force, he was momentarily stunned and stumbled a few steps, all the while looking around to make sure he hadn't actually been slugged in the head. After a few seconds, the worst of the pain cleared and he composed himself. He cast another long look around himself to make sure no one had seen him. It did not appear so.

Shaking his head and limbs, he decided to make a hasty exit.

With his headache now little more than a dull throb—or that was all he was going to admit to—he made several blind jumps before finally returning to the Wheel.

His intent was to send a message to Titik and let him know that his mission had been a success. This was unnecessary, for he found the Psiaco captain on his favorite soapbox in one of the marketplaces. His crowd was large, so Cassius could not get close, but he did spy Pilory a short distance away. Her expression was less than thrilled to see him, but she approached anyway.

"I know you're his lieutenant," Cassius said, "but are you also his babysitter?"

Pilory made an annoyed motion. "It feels like it sometimes. I'm in charge of the ship while he's gone, but once everything is taken care of, someone has to bring him back."

"What is he complaining about anyway? The Tacagans and the Gentleman Killers don't have as much of a hold as they used to. He can't be complaining about them."

"The Tacagans are only regrouping, as all politicians do. But the thugs, the Gentleman Killers, they never sleep. They just take independent contracts and keep the profits for themselves."

Cassius frowned. "To be expected, I suppose."

"Have you given up on the crown yet?"

"How could I, when it's safely in my possession as we speak?"

Pilory stared at him, antennae twitching as though they could sense lies. Even if they could, there were no lies here.

"You're serious," she stated.

"As dead as Srori himself," he told her. At her confused look, he clarified, "An

Earth expression. As serious as death."

She still seemed a bit confused, but finally said, "I will simply take your word for it, as it is not an important matter. But you do have it?"

"I intended to send a message to Titik to have him meet me here, but I see that is not necessary."

Pilory twittered a laugh. "Oh, it may still be necessary. It may be the only thing that gets him off his soapbox."

"Are things really that bad for space pirates?"

"It's not the pirating that's become difficult. It's the selling off of our goods. In the Time industry, if it's not the Hands or the Grandfathers, it's the Tacagans or Gentleman Killers. If it's not the Tacagans or Gentleman Killers, it's the Turitians. But it's the best profit margins for us."

"I didn't realize piracy was an expensive business."

"One of the most expensive, actually. And it's all in labor costs. Freedom is great and all, but when a man is hunted, he wants to indulge in each day because it could be his last. If he doesn't have the funds to indulge, he gets cranky."

Cassius nodded. "I know a thing or two about cranky men. Cranky women, too."

"Our raiding and black market dealing have set a high bar for the crew," Pilory went on. "The Tacagans changed all that."

"So what does Titik hope to accomplish? Most dealers I know don't want so much attention drawn to themselves or their prominent customers." Jora came to mind.

"Believe it or not, he's cataloging the crowd and scouting the marketplaces."

"Looking for the silent support."

"Exactly."

"I like it." Cassius shifted his stance. "Now, about the crown."

Pilory studied him for a moment, as if searching for the punchline to a joke. Finally, "I'll see if I can divert his attention. Meet in the Food Court, as before."

He dipped his head as graciously as he could manage and stepped away. He did not leave immediately, however, but turned to watch Pilory approach Titik. She waited a moment for a pause in his ranting before attempting to get his attention. This was not an easy feat as the Tibidi was quite a bit smaller than the large Psiaco pirate and had to keep an eye on four flamboyant arms.

Only when Pilory finally got Titik's attention did Cassius turn and leave the marketplace, heading for the Food Court. He passed several Gentleman Killers along the way, and not a few intentionally bumped into him, but none of them started anything. Maybe it had something to do with the lingering presence of the Borelians. They were not numerous, they were not obvious, but they were certainly a presence to be felt.

He had to get the Book of Abilities and take total command of the Cult. Fast. Then he would bring these slavers to their knees and...and...

Well, he really didn't have a plan beyond that. It would come to him eventually.

His face twitched involuntarily, though he pretended not to notice. No alien here would know it was out of the ordinary for a human.

He did not get any food at the Food Court, just picked a table and sat to wait patiently. He did a little people watching, and it wasn't long before Titik arrived, moving purposefully, Pilory hovering along behind him. The large alien plopped down across from Cassius with the same air of being a man in charge as he always had.

"My lieutenant tells me that you have a gift for me," he said casually, his four eyes sharp but mocking. Clearly he was expecting this to be a joke.

Cassius lifted his sack and laid it on the table. "Just a little something. It is our third date after all, or is it our fourth? I can't remember. Each time I go away I can't stop thinking about getting back to you."

Titik's expression turned to granite. "If this isn't what I hope it is, I'm going to kill you for such remarks."

But Cassius wasn't worried, and he kept his gaze locked onto Titik's — as best he could, seeing how he wasn't sure which eyes he was supposed to be looking at — as he opened the bag and brought out the crown.

Titik's eyes turned to the metal object inset with jewels. Confidently, Cassius slid it closer to him, then leaned back to watch the show.

At first, the pirate didn't move, but stayed very still and watched the crown, as though it might be a live animal about to attack. When he did move, it was slow and deliberate. He picked up the crown in one hand, then two, and brought it up to eye level. He then used his other two hands to carefully touch the crown and inspect it. He touched every contour, every edge, every face, every angle. He tapped the gems and turned it this way and that to examine them in the light.

Cassius had taken plenty of merchandise to Jora over the years, and he always appreciated the attention he got from the black market dealer. But watching Titik handle Srori's crown now was pure art, the way he inspected everything as though each piece by itself were pure gold, to say nothing of how priceless and awe-inspiring the piece as a whole must be.

He almost regretted giving it up, figured that maybe he should have at least taken a photo of himself wearing it, just so he could have proof that he had possessed and worn the crown of Srori at one time. Perhaps, if he established himself in Titik's good graces, then he could at least ask to wear the crown again, just long enough for that photo.

Finally, Titik set the crown on the table very carefully and regarded Cassius. They locked eyes for a long moment, Cassius casual, Titik tenacious.

"They said it couldn't be done," Cassius said after a long, admittedly uncomfortable, moment. He grinned.

"And they will still say that," Titik told him, his nerve unwavering.

Cassius blinked first, but he didn't move. "What do you mean?"

The pirate studied him, and Cassius found himself feeling more and more insecure about his position. Titik grabbed the crown with more carelessness than art and held it up. With all four hands in the air, he looked like a mythical monster come to life. "This is a fake, you fool!"

"Lies!" Cassius roared, standing suddenly. "I went to the mausoleum myself, I searched every damn level, every fucking tomb and corpse, and I took this crown from the statue of Srori himself!" He opened the bag and dumped out other things he'd stolen. "Tell me that all of these ancient relics are fake, too!"

Titik set the crown aside and went through the other goods, examining them carefully. Finally he leaned back in his seat, as casual as you please, and made his choffing sound that Cassius guessed was something akin to a laugh. So perhaps it had been a test, a way to see if he could handle being challenged, opposed, called a liar to his face.

Cassius sat down.

"The jewels are real enough," Titik stated. "The trinkets are indeed authentic. Even this crown is a real Turitian crown. But it is not the crown of Srori."

"How would you know? And why wouldn't it be? I took it from his tomb!"

"The Turitians are a patient people, but not a dumb people. And the royal family Jalar is perhaps the worst of all in their paranoia of such things, for they are seen by other royal families as 'young' at best and 'illegitimate' at worst. So they do what they can to ensure their cultural heritage is protected. It doesn't surprise that they should put a fake crown in Srori's tomb so soon after death, for just such an occasion."

"How do you know it isn't Srori's crown? Do you know what his crown is supposed to look like? Will you enlighten me?"

Titik made a motion that may have been interpreted as a shrug. "I know not what it looks like, but I know that each crown is a masterpiece. The craftsmen begin work just as soon as the next monarch is named at their age of nine, for it takes a great long time to make. Each jewel is cut and engraved in such a way that the main jewel has the name of the monarch and other jewels have the names of the predecessors, the family, even the successors if they are known in sufficient time. These jewels are fine, but the names do not match —"

"How do you know all this?"

"Because I take the time to study my enemies and learn from them. I, too, have been to the mausoleum. I am the reason they changed and strengthened their security measures."

Cassius didn't know what to do or say.

The Psiaco pirate stood and pushed the crown away like a moldy plate of food. "A daring endeavor nevertheless."

Cassius stumbled to his feet, tripping over the chair. "What about the Book of Abilities?"

"The trinket or heirloom you want me to find? Why should I do that? You have not delivered on your part of the bargain."

"But I proved my value."

"Your value, yes, which is why you get to keep your life despite your stupid comments earlier. And we may speak again in the future. But as I said, even I have been to the mausoleum. I have no need to seek out the Akari or this fabled religion of yours. It could not even tell you what my intellect and research told me."

He choffed a bit as he left. Pilory only gave him a sympathetic glance before following the pirate out of the Food Court.

Cassius just stood there, staring.

A fake? No! Impossible! There had to be a mistake! Or it was a trick. Titik didn't want to admit that someone was better than him, had done what he could not, so he was just saying it was a fake in order to avoid making good on his end of the bargain. That had to be it. There had to be some way that he could verify that this was Srori's crown.

But how to go about it? Titik was willing to admit that it was a Turitian crown, so whoever examined it would have to know more than that. They would have to know specifics. But who would have such intimate knowledge of modern Turitian crowns? And not only modern, but a crown from a literally just-deceased monarch?

He checked the Archives, but they were still closed. He probably could have forced his way in, but knew it would do no good if the information he needed was on a tablet that was still buried in any of the mountains stacked around the place.

He was just scouting out potential sources in the marketplaces when it occurred to him. Titik had said that the royal family Jalar was looked down upon by the other Turitian royal families, called either young or illegitimate. Maybe one of the more put off royal families could offer some insight.

It was certainly an interesting prospect. Now he just had to get an audience with a royal family.

Or maybe he should forget the whole thing, keep the crown for himself, and carry on with finding the Book of Abilities on his own. What did he care if Titik was on his side or not?

Because he needed more friends on his side, not politics to fuck around with and get taken over by Rifun. Bad enough Rifun almost took Titik from him, too.

So then, who to contact? Who held the biggest grudges against the royal family Jalar and would be perfectly fine with some alien asking to verify that he had stolen the correct crown?

Or maybe he should Disguise himself and act as an agent of one of these disgruntled competing families. How would that change things? Start a feud? A war? Wouldn't that be something? Let's see Rifun put things back together after that. Then he would have to choose between his pithy political alliances and the Book of Abilities. Put his faith where his mouth is for once.

But that still left him with the problem of finding the appropriate rival and deciding his approach. Hm...he might have to think about it a little first. He didn't need to lose Titik, the Turitians, and the Book of Abilities. Hey, he was capable of appreciating backup plans and maybe even making a few of his own. Occasionally.

"Cassius."

He turned to see Pilory approaching, hovering toward him until she got within a few paces where she landed and walked normally.

"What is it now?" Cassius asked. "Has Titik changed his mind?"

"Let me see the crown," she said.

"Why should I?"

"Because even if it's not Srori's, maybe I can tell you whose it is, or who made it. Might lead you to the real crown."

He shifted his stance. "Why would you do this?"

"Titik may not be overly interested in the Akari, but I am."

"Then why not join us? Forget Titik and —"

"That really wouldn't be proper. I happen to enjoy what I do. Is it not possible to learn and work at the same time?"

"Well...yes, you can do both."

"Then I will do both. Surely boasting of your alliances and armies means you must have some semblance of education going, even without the Book of Abilities. Teach me what you know, and I will try to sway the captain."

He searched her expression and body language — as if it meant anything to him — trying to decide whether there was something afoot, a trap being laid or some such thing. He could come up with nothing. Finally he nodded and slowly fished the crown from his bag and gave it to her.

Now knowing that it was real, Pilory did not have to do quite as thorough an inspection as Titik had done, although her handling of art and priceless artifacts was about as graceful and coordinated as her table manners. Even so, her keen, bird-like eyes seemed more well-suited to the task of deciphering whatever was engraved upon the crown's jewels.

"Rilor," she stated at last.

"What does that mean?" Cassius demanded. "I don't recall any Rilor being mentioned in the royal family."

"It's not the royal family, it's the craftsman. Gentleman Rilor."

"Do you know him? Or her?"

"Titik mentioned him once recently, just said that he was a master craftsman. Any craftsman tasked with making the royal crowns is sure to be paid well and perhaps even housed in or near the palace."

"Any craftsman tasked with making both the real crown and a convincing fake crown probably knows where the real one is hiding," Cassius finished.

"Exactly."

"It's worth a try." He nodded slowly, then paused. "If Rifun comes sniffing around, don't tell him any of this. Tell him the crown was a fake, we were all upset by it, the deal is off, whatever. Make him think it ended here. Tell him Titik took the crown anyway and stormed off."

Pilory made an affirmative gesture and began hovering, her wings creating a low, droning hum. "Will you teach me something, though, before you go? If you do find the crown, you can present that to him, and I can show him what I have learned. It will be far more convincing that way."

Cassius agreed, rather pleased with himself. A secret student. He liked this idea. Not someone sitting in Julianna's Sunday school class. Not someone under Isthim's merciless thumb. Not someone debating geopolitical philosophy with Rifun. A student of his own who wanted to learn things. Practical things.

Like many students who were already proficient in Time to some degree, he started her off with Bands, showing her the differences between Time and Akari Bands. Akari Bands were nearly invisible save for a tiny bit of visual distortion. They were also lighter and more flexible, able to be fine-tuned to a level far exceeding anything Time could do.

After sending her off with her newfound abilities, Cassius returned to the ruins. He ran into Rifun outside the officers building, but the wannabe African did not speak until they were both inside.

"So, where is it?"

Cassius turned and tried to assume a relaxed stance. "Where's what?"

"The Book of Abilities. Do you have it? Were you able to trade for it?"

"No." He shifted his stance. "Strange thing. The crown turned out to be a fake."

"A fake?"

"Oh, it was real enough Turitian craftsmanship, but it was not the crown of Srori."

"Are you sure you had the correct tomb?"

"Oh yes." Cassius tried to keep his voice level, but that seemed a little strange. Rifun would probably expect him to be raging mad, frothing at the mouth like a wild animal. Well, let him be nervous.

"And Titik?" Rifun asked.

"Took the crown eagerly enough, but never delivered."

"What are you going to do now then?"

"I haven't decided."

Rifun paused for a long moment. Did he know it was a lie? "I see. Well, when you do decide, don't tell me."

"Suddenly the political master of information doesn't want to know something?"

"I'm going to be gone for a while. Weeks, perhaps months."

"Going home for a vacation? More African countries to fail to liberate?"

He grinned as Rifun visibly flinched.

"No. Consider it a religious pilgrimage."

Cassius stared at him. A pilgrimage? Now? Where? For what? Sure they'd had a few setbacks—the crown being perhaps the most major one—but Rifun was already giving up and going to beg spiteful spirits for help? Finally he shook his head. "And it's going to take you weeks or months? Why do this now?"

"The Cult is in a stable position, both here and in our alliances. Isthim and Julianna have things managed here, and you have your mission to carry out in the Wheel. If I don't go now, I never will."

Again, Cassius could only stare at him. He'd known Rifun was soft in the head and generally weak-willed, but what was going on here? Did he have some terminal illness that somehow suddenly made him a philosopher?

"If there is a major problem, I will return," Rifun sighed. "But this is something that must be done."

Cassius waved a hand dismissively. "Whatever. Your religion is your problem."

Rifun raised a brow. "At least I don't make you observe any fady in my presence."

"I don't know what that is, and quite frankly, I don't care. You pray to whatever god you think is going to help us. If he or she or they do help, then maybe I'll even thank them."

He turned away as his face started throbbing.

"Dumb spirits," he grumbled.

Then he'd returned to his chambers and emptied his bag. Several handfuls of jewels and the fake crown tumbled out, scattering over the bed and rolling onto the floor. So close and yet so far, but at least he had a name. Rilor. Gentleman Rilor. Whether this was an honorable title because of his proximity to the royal family or some warning about the Gentleman Killers or simply a title lost in translation, he did not know.

Actually, Rifun's little pilgrimage might prove useful to Cassius. If Rifun was going to be gone on some quest, then Cassius wouldn't have to sneak around and work to keep information from him. He could do whatever he wanted on Turit and, short of starting any actual wars, Rifun wouldn't be looking over his shoulder and nagging him about political goings-on. If he was going to be gone weeks or even months, then as long as Cassius played his cards right and didn't get distracted by every minor thing, he might actually be able to retrieve the Book of Abilities with no one the wiser.

Yes, Rifun. You seek out your gods or your ancestors or whoever the fuck you pray to. Meanwhile, I'm going to get shit done.

He decided to wait until morning before considering his venture further. When he left his chambers, he found Rifun's door closed. Testing it gently, he found it locked and quite possibly barricaded. Good. Just to be sure, he went to Julianna's chambers.

She wasn't excited to see him, but she was tentatively cordial.

"Something I can help you with?" she asked. Probably she had been put in charge of Rifun's political affairs while he was away, but she was hardly a threat.

"Have you seen Rifun?" he demanded flatly.

"He's on a pilgrimage. Unless we're at war or the place is burning down, he doesn't want to be disturbed."

Exactly what he needed to hear.

He left without another word, meandering his way to the tunnels before opening his portals, traveling to Turit.

With the funeral and other festivities finished, Cassius was free to wander about the streets at his leisure. All evidence of the procession was gone, not a streamer or flower or candy wrapper or empty bottle to be found, and everyone went about his business as usual. If anyone knew who Cassius was or suspected what he'd done, or wanted to do, they gave no indication of it. And, Good Samaritans or not, Cassius suspected that even Turitian patience had limits and they would not hesitate to apprehend someone who had broken into the mausoleum to try and steal the crown of a recently-deceased monarch. They had a reputation to defend, after all, in the eyes of the other royal families.

He made his way toward the governmental building. He'd hoped that maybe there might be some sign pointing him to the local blacksmith or goldsmith or crownsmith or however Rilor styled himself. There were indeed plenty of signs, but the Turitian language made calligraphy look quite plain, and he couldn't make heads or tails of any of it.

Not wanting to waste time, he decided to just ask for directions instead, entering the governmental building and approaching the receptionist. He thought he got by on the turns well enough. He knew that all outsiders automatically qualified as superior, which was fine with him.

"Where can I find Gentleman Rilor?" he asked.

The receptionist gave him directions to what could have been classified as "the shed out back," as that was how it looked, compared to the splendor of the former palace.

Cassius pushed open the door, uncertain what he would find. He might have expected a small, hot room with a large oven, a fire roaring within and huge black bag of coal beside, an enormous steel anvil that weighed more than ten men, and an endless number of hammers, chisels, and assorted smithing tools. He would have even taken something like a jeweler's setup, with precious stones meticulously laid out, specific angles measured out with the utmost care, and an assortment of magnifying lenses that could show every detail and imperfection otherwise invisible to the naked eye.

What he got was something in between, not quite both, not quite either, and there was a third element that was entirely foreign to him. Not that he knew much about Turitian metalsmithing in the first place.

There was a large fire pit in the middle of the room, perhaps four or five feet high of brick. Cassius had to use Light and Thermodynamics to dim the blinding glow and see that it appeared to be several pits layered within and on top of each other. Hot coals bedded the bottom of the pit and there were several concentric rings, or perhaps cauldrons, of molten metal on top. A rack of tools stood off to one side beside the anvil that probably weighed more than ten men.

Along the wall near the entrance was a meticulously organized section of raw materials, from metal sheets to rods to raw ore, still with specks of dirt embedded. There was also a small collection of wood off to one side next to a polished wooden chest of innumerable tiny drawers, all with tiny locks. He guessed that was where the gems were stored. Saws and others large, crude implements were also laid out.

On another wall, to Cassius' left, were several mismatched tables. Beside one was a canister containing several large rolled up papers, probably schematics. Different projects, or pieces of projects, were laid out on the mismatched tables. Small hand tools were either laid out beside the pieces or put away in any of the small containers on the tables.

On the third wall, across from the entrance, was what Cassius immediately identified as the gem table, or tables as the case happened to be. He didn't know the names or specific functions of the various tools, but he knew that they were intended for cutting with deadly precision. And there were indeed several magnifying lens setups.

The fourth wall saw the finishing table, where pieces came together to form something amazing. There was nothing here at the moment.

There was also a door on the fourth wall, which Cassius guessed led directly to the governmental building.

The whole place was empty. Gentleman Rilor was nowhere to be seen.

Cassius knew a moment of frustration before deciding that this was the perfect opportunity to give the place a quick search. Maybe the good blacksmith had Srori's real crown handy, either disguising it as a work in progress, or perhaps polishing it up to make it look like new before it rotted for eternity in the mausoleum. He Banded.

He looked everywhere. Between and behind the raw materials, around the fire, under the tables, in drawers. He looked for secret panels, trap doors. He did indeed find one, a trap door in the floor, but the room below was empty. Cassius stood there for a moment in the darkness of the secret room, wondering if there might be more secret rooms or a secret tunnel leading into the palace or out of the city, but his searches came up cold.

Sighing, he climbed out of the secret room and gave a lazy look around. The only thing he hadn't really checked was the chest of drawers, but no crown was going to fit in there unless it got chopped up into little pieces.

Well, it was the only thing he had left.

It didn't take much to cause the locks to rust and disintegrate, and soon Cassius was wildly pulling out drawers. As expected, plenty of glittering gems, but no crown.

He would admit to taking a couple of the more exotic-looking gems.

He dropped the Band. Well, this had been a fantastic waste of time, even if only a few seconds had passed in actuality. He ran his tongue over his teeth. There had never been any guarantee that the smith would have it, or have knowledge of its whereabouts, but that didn't make him any less frustrated or annoyed.

As he was turning to leave, the door on the fourth wall, the one leading to the governmental building, jiggled and opened.

If it was Gentleman Rilor—and his magnifying headset suggested it was—there did not appear to be anything special about him. He was not paying attention as he entered the room, did not see Cassius, and did not hesitate to remove his belly band, this being akin to stripping naked, though Turitians did sport short hair. Rilor was clearly making himself comfortable in his own house.

Cassius decided to take the opportunity to don a Turitian Disguise.

The motion, a small human changing himself to look like a large Turitian, evidently registered in Rilor's peripheral vision. When he did look up, he spotted Cassius, and quickly replaced the band, making a number of turns and gestures of humiliation, submission, and forgiveness.

Cassius, in a flash of rage, used Force to throw the huge alien against the wall, and Gravity to pin him there.

"Gentleman Rilor, I presume," Cassius said.

The Turitian was stunned into silence for a long moment.

"Who are you?" Rilor asked once the shock wore off.

"My identity is not important," Cassius informed him sharply. He brought out the fake crown. "You made this, didn't you?"

"If that's what it says."

Using Matter, Cassius was able to restrict Rilor's windpipe to take in only the barest breaths. "I admit, I haven't dined with too many royal families, but I don't know too many of them who give their greatest projects to just any old craftsman."

Rilor squeaked in a breath. "Yes. I did it. I made it."

Cassius eased up just a little. "You were ordered to make a fake for Srori's tomb. In order to prevent devastating grave robbery so soon after the king's death. But the crown does not pass on to the next in line. Where is Srori's crown?"

"I don't know."

Still holding the smith against the wall with Gravity, Cassius went to the forge and studied it. Then he went to the box of crude tools near the raw materials and picked out a tool resembling a hatchet and a knife. He went to the forge and touched the blade of the tool to the molten metal, using a touch of his own Thermodynamics to ensure the blade heated up but did not melt itself. Then he went over to Rilor. If he touched the man directly with the needed force, his Disguise could be comprised. So he did it with the Akari, creating a secondary Gravity track to manipulate his arm and hand.

He cut off one of his fingers with the hot knife. Rilor shrieked, but with a Sound barrier, no one would hear.

"Torka bastard!" he gasped finally, his fur matted with sweat. "Have you no honor? No pride? Does your family even understand the meaning of such words?!"

Hm, so the Torka family seemed to be a very disgruntled rival of the Jalar family. He'd have to remember that.

"No," Cassius answered. "We don't." He made a show of studying the knife-hatchet, the blade still glowing. "I imagine any smith can have an accident. And I imagine that one lost finger is a small price to pay for your brilliance and position close to the Jalars, especially the new queen. But what about two fingers? Three? How about a hand?" He brought the glowing blade close to the flesh of Rilor's wrist.

"I don't know!" Rilor insisted, struggling to breathe amid his panic and the restriction Cassius still held on him. "I promise!"

"Crowns like this don't turn up overnight, which means you knew about the switch for a while, but the switch itself would have had to have been quick and quiet." Cassius backed up and looked around dramatically. "Is it here somewhere? Hidden in a drawer maybe?" He made a show of opening up several of the gem drawers. "In a table?" He opened up one of the drawers, then pretended to spot the trap door. "A secret room, perhaps?"

"It's not there," Rilor said.

Cassius turned around, facing him. "I'm not interested in where it is not. It is not in my hand. I want to know where it is."

"I don't know. I promise you. I was only commissioned to make a replacement."

Of course. Srori had been nearly ancient, and the crowns were begun when the next in line was named, as young as nine. Whoever had made the original crown was probably long dead.

That didn't mean Rilor was off the hook, and Cassius drew near once more.

"You made the replacement, yes, but you are the royal crown maker. If anything happens to a crown, you are responsible, are you not? Why wouldn't you be entrusted with it? You have to polish it up before burial at least, don't you?"

Even if that were untrue, Rilor couldn't admit to it. If the Torka family looked down on the Jalar family, then for the Jalar family to admit that they didn't care for the crowns of their monarchs would look terrible on them. Rilor's expression reflected this.

"But you're right," Cassius said suddenly, moving away again. He went to the forge, studied the fire, studied the hatchet-knife. "It wouldn't be kept here. Too easy to rob, given that you were gone and left this place unguarded for a long enough period that I could have taken it had it been here. But it's not."

He could feel Rilor try to relax.

Cassius turned around but did not leave his spot near the forge. "So then, who has it? The new queen? The commander general? Someone else?"

"Torka bastard," Rilor hissed, seeming to find some shred of courage within himself. "As your empire crumbles, you seek to steal power from others." He chuckled and made a few weak gestures. "But it's not working. And your family and your lands fade away as dust in a storm, as fake as that crown."

Even without knowing the details of this feud or other politics, Cassius found himself enraged by Rilor's words. Perhaps it was less about the words themselves and more about his defiance.

Snarling in rage, he took the hatchet-knife, dipped it in the forge afresh, then went and, without a second thought, severed Rilor's hand from his arm. This time, he didn't bother with a Sound barrier, and he let the man howl. He felt himself grow hard and he hoped it didn't diminish the Disguise.

He put the blade near the man's throat so that it singed the hairs.

"Guards are coming," Cassius hissed. "And if you want them to find a living smith, you're going to tell me what I need to know." He let that linger until he heard the heavy footsteps of the guards just outside the door. Then he Banded the two of them so that all was at a standstill.

"Where is the crown of Srori?"

9 | Mijanòna ary Mijoròa   Stop and Stand

The Caves of Meroian, 1964

Rifun lay on his bed and stared up at the ceiling.

He understood that spiritual quests took time and patience. He understood that it could be difficult to set aside the cares of the physical world and focus on the spiritual world.

He considered himself to be a very patient person. He'd done ten years in prison for no good reason after all, out of some misplaced sense of pride and nobility. And he had been willing to accept that it might take a few days to really set aside his physical worries. He wanted to know what was going on with Cassius and his side adventure with Srori's crown and Titik and the Book of Abilities, if that had truly ended. He wanted to know if Julianna was rising to the occasion in diplomacy or if she was being bullied, bets on the latter. He wanted to know if Isthim was remaining loyal to the Cult or her own people, and how she was doing in her position. But, once a few days passed and war did not spontaneously break out and the city didn't burn down, then maybe he would have an easier time letting go.

Those cares did fade away eventually. The outside world ceased to matter. All that mattered was what was inside his little room. And in his stomach. Which was nothing.

Rifun had fasted before, sometimes voluntarily, sometimes not. He knew what it felt like, and he'd thought he'd prepared for it. His activity level was down as low as he could make it without going comatose, he already had the slowed metabolism from his use of the Akari, and he'd mentally prepared to overcome the hunger pangs.

But it was now day six. His mind was not focused, for he still worried about outside goings-on. His stomach had quieted, but he knew that if he gave in even a little bit, it would start demanding food and become absolutely relentless. Even filling up on water was doing little for him in that regard.

It didn't help that his chambers happened to be on the outer part of the officers

154

building and had a small window that faced the ruins at large, thus bringing him a number of sounds and noise throughout the day. He'd tried a Sound barrier, but he couldn't hold it continuously, and the sudden noise when it failed was more of a distraction than allowing continuous noise, to say nothing of the headache and confusion afterwards.

He thought of his shrine, even looked at it. Everything was still in its place. It still looked very proper, exquisite even. It was a shrine's shrine. But he felt no peace for it. Of course, a shrine did not itself bring peace, only helped to foster the mentality. The problem, then, was on him.

But what could he do? He was not a stranger to fasting and meditation. Certainly he'd prayed to the ancestors many times as a child. True, his faith had severely wavered as he became an adult and the wars consumed his life, but he'd found purpose since finding the Akari and discovering the Author. The Book sitting there in the shrine was proof that someone out there at least acknowledged his existence, had written him into existence. So why was it so difficult to meditate and show a little gratitude for it? Why was it so hard to focus?

He stared at the ceiling. Almost every inch of the officers building, which used to be a temple for the ancient Elif, was covered in elaborate carvings depicting...well, something. Rifun had done some searching into the ancient peoples, but it was hardly his top priority. The one over his head appeared to be a great gathering of some form, and he figured he was fairly safe in his guess that the main figure in the middle was Difk, to whom this room had originally been dedicated.

He sat up.

Maybe that was the problem. Maybe it was because this room was a temple dedicated to false gods. Of course, now that he realized this, it all seemed very logical. The Akari allowed him to touch the razana, true, but the razana was the culmination of all life, the souls of the deceased and the power of the ancestor spirits. These gods had nothing to do with any of that.

He would have to return to Earth. He would return to Madagascar. Damn it all, but he would return to the family tombs and pray there. There he would be close to his ancestors. There he would touch the razana, meditate, pray, and there seek out the Author.

And perhaps that was part of his problem, too, he thought as he got out of bed. He didn't know what he wanted or expected out of this meditation and prayer. He had a hope— No, that wasn't it. Hope was an excellent thing to have when seeking out the spirits. What he'd had was a wish. A fancy. A fleeting conjuration of his mind, rather than a conviction of his soul. He would never presume to tell the spirits what to do or demand anything from them, but there was no reason for them to suffer a fool, so he could not approach them as a fool, uncertain, wishy-washy, not knowing who or what he was and so unable to become anything else.

He reached the grand barricade that he'd erected in front of his door and paused. He'd told them all that he would be gone for a while, holed up for his meditation. Why not just open a portal?

Well, for the same reason that everyone had to use the tunnels for portal travel, to make it more difficult to track down the Cult. If his portal were to be traced and re-opened, it could lead anyone straight to his chambers in the officers building in the heart of the Cult's operations. At the same time, humans didn't have that capability yet. Truthfully, few species did, and even the Grandfathers — well, before the Borelians — had been pretty lazy in its use.

He shook his head. No. He'd set the rules, and he would follow them. He had no reason not to in this instance. The reasoning was sound. He couldn't abandon all caution just because he'd come alive again.

Besides, he probably should tell at least Julianna. That way, if something did happen where he was needed, they weren't breaking down his door and all his furniture just to get to an empty room and then not know where he'd run off to.

He left the shrine as it was, but he returned the rest of the furniture to their proper locations. Then he opened the door.

A gust of cool, fresh air washed over him. True, his room had a window, but it was only very small, and covered with heavy curtains. He hadn't realized just how stale the air had become. What did that say about him, then? He hadn't bathed either. And now that he was up and around and moving and had a purpose, his stomach was starting to grumble a little. Now that he was thinking about it, his stomach started grumbling more.

Maybe he should just start over fresh. Get a bath, something to eat, refocus himself and his efforts.

As if on cue, Julianna strode around the corner. She stopped suddenly when she spotted him, then approached. Her expressions were always easy to read thanks to the scars outlining every movement of her face.

"The hermit emerges from his cave," she observed, trying to be polite and friendly while clearly upset over what he might expect to be his unwashed smell.

"Your spiritual quest was a success, then?"

"Ah, no," he admitted. "No success at all."

"Oh, I'm so sorry." She seemed genuinely distressed over it.

"I'm going home to Madagascar, to my family tombs," he told her. "Maybe I'll have better luck there."

Her expression turned puzzled, then neutral. "Of course. I suppose that makes sense."

He couldn't help but smirk. "Not to you. But it makes sense to me, and that is what I am going by."

She nodded uncertainly. "Do you still plan to be gone for weeks or months?"

"Yes."

"Well, do what you must, I suppose. But before you come back...at least take a bath."

"I intend to get both food and a bath before leaving. I will start fresh."

She said nothing to that, although her relief was obvious. She wished him well and moved off, returning to whatever errand she had been on before their encounter. Rifun, for his part, went about his own business. He figured to get a bath first before he ran into anyone else. Julianna was the most polite of the group. He had little doubt that Isthim or any of the Borelians would have much harsher words regarding his present hygienic state.

Once that was complete and he felt a little more human and a little less hermit, he also went about finding himself some food. Nothing too extreme, as he had gone without for six days, just enough to get some energy back in him and quiet his stomach.

He did not run into Cassius at all, which was both suspicious and fine with him. He passed by Isthim once in the officers building, but she said nothing more than a passing greeting and her expression was impossible to read. He also found this suspicious, but he forced himself not to dwell on it. He was still on his spiritual quest with the meditation and the praying, and he couldn't let his hard-fought battle for a clear mind be lost to a bunch of clutter that amounted only to suspicion and paranoia.

Of course, his mind wanted to take that thought and run with it to the horizon, but he clamped down on it and held only to his thoughts of getting home and going to the tombs.

The family tombs were not far from the old farm, and for all his intended dedication to only going to the tombs and continuing his quest, he couldn't help but at least walk by the place. Once upon a time, Nibe and Dabe had overseen a veritable mini-empire. They'd had vast herds of cattle, large tanimbary for rice, a few plots of vanilla, and before his death, Dabe had begun cultivating grapes for wine. The Andilan family was the ruling family of this area, at least as much as the French would allow.

Then the war broke out, and all the creative math that had helped them to dodge French taxes came back to bite them. The land had been confiscated by the French government and turned solely to rice and vanilla. Family and friends no longer worked the fields, but slaves bent their backs to the labor.

Rifun had hoped to inherit the land and reclaim his name and family, but the nationalists had failed in their Uprising, and he'd gone to prison.

These days, the old farm was still productive. It still produced rice and vanilla, although a small herd of cattle meandered their way here and there. He thought about inquiring as to who owned and managed the land, then decided against it. That was a quest for another day, one that could lead to more adventures. Maybe later, when he was not already occupied with other matters.

The tombs were not terribly far from the farm, only about a mile and a half. Time was, the tombs had been marvelously built and decorated, and famadihana celebrated appropriately every five years with lavish abandon. The war had seen much of that fall by the wayside. These days it appeared as though attempts had been made at cleaning things up and restoring them to their former glory.

He'd brought many things from his shrine, and he laid them out again, meticulously arranging them. When he was satisfied that all was in order, he bowed to pray as he had done so many times as a child. His head suddenly felt heavy, a fog of confusion settled over him, and for a moment, he was almost unsure where he was. He couldn't remember when he was, even, and he wondered, just for a moment, if perhaps he were a child again. Maybe even for the first time. Perhaps the spirits had given him a vision, a dream of the life he would lead if he pursued a path of vengeance against his stepfather, striking him and so being expelled from the community.

Then the feeling receded, and he couldn't help but feel a bit foolish. And sore, as his right shoulder reminded him that everything he had experienced had been very, very real. All the same, perhaps that feeling was a sign that he was doing the right thing, coming to the family tombs. He was a child again here, part of the family, welcomed into them.

This feeling of acceptance transferred to a welcome wave of relief, and he was finally able to relax and focus. Perhaps what also helped was that he was not here to really ask for or demand anything. He was not looking for explanations for wrongdoings or asking for divine intervention with a particular agenda. This time, he simply desired communication, and his intent was reverence and respect.

But there was a difference between praying in his room and coming here to the family tombs, emphasis being on the word family. He was not the only one who could visit, and certainly he was no longer a known family member.

After several hours of prayer, he could feel eyes on him. The good news was that it was terrible misfortune if he were to be disturbed, so unless he was desecrating the tombs, they would not advance on him, but it didn't make him any less uncomfortable. Likely they were circling, trying to determine his identity, or at least his clan. He had to be a mixed blood of some form; few tourists actually prayed at foreign tombs. But for him to bring gifts and set up as he did, he had to know something of the family, yet he was not recognized.

Now thoroughly distracted, Rifun sighed and sat up.

"Fantatro fa eo ianao," he said, not looking around. (I know you're there.)

He counted three sets of steps.

"Manao inona ianao?" one man asked. (What are you doing here?)

"Mivavakaho, manao ahoana ny endriny?" (Praying, what's it look like?)

All three were men, their features obviously Betsileo. One of them he thought bore a striking resemblance to a cousin he remembered from long ago. Perhaps a son or grandson, then. Damn, Rifun felt old, and yet he appeared of an age.

"Are these your ancestors?" the second man inquired testily.

"As a matter of fact they are," Rifun said, standing.

The three men glanced at one another, clearly unsure what to do or say. The first man spoke again. "Who are you? Whose relation?"

"Lalao Andilan."

Truthfully, he'd been hoping for something a little more dramatic than confused glances and a stare. It was the first man who said, "Lalao is our sister and cousin, and the elder Lalao Andilan died over forty years ago. She married a Tsimihety and lived in Mahitsy."

"But her firstborn son was not of this Tsimihety." Rifun almost added a few choice words about that particular Tsimihety, but decided to keep those thoughts to himself.

"Rivotra?" Now the third man spoke for the first time. "Rifun Ndolo, the Bastard of the VVS?" He took a step forward. "You are far too young to be him. His son, perhaps?"

Someone could have put a pickax in Rifun's head and he never would have known. He Banded instead, trying to figure out exactly what he was feeling. Perhaps the stark reality of his extended life, confronting the idea that he had lived so long — and would continue to live many more years — that he would have to start calling himself his own son in order to maintain access to the family tombs.

He simultaneously wanted to run away and fall down in prayer again. Instead, he took a breath and dropped the Band.

"Fanantenanirainy," Rifun lied. It seemed an appropriate name, one he would give to a son. If he had a son. Another feeling not readily identified passed through him, and then it was gone.

The men did not immediately embrace him, but he could see the hesitation at his presence melt away.

"We heard of your father," the first man said. "He did many noble things for the people, and it is shameful that he was not recognized for it."

"Thank you." Rifun cleared his throat. "I mean, he will be glad to hear it."

"He's still alive?" the second man wondered.

"He was only born in 1897. He's only..." How old was he? "Sixty-seven. Sixty-eight?" No, he couldn't pretend to be so old by any stretch of the imagination. But perhaps a Disguise...?

"Of course." The first man cleared his throat. "When you see him, you may tell him that he is welcome to return and pray at the tombs at any time."

Rifun dipped his head. "Thank you. I don't know that he will come. He is not well, and he has carried much hurt and shame with him to ever return."

"A tragedy," the second man said. "Perhaps some of the shame will be lifted by his return. But if he is not well, then he will know that all is well."

"Of course." Rifun shifted uneasily. "He has been distressed lately that he would not be buried in the family tomb."

"Nonsense," the third man proclaimed. "He is more than welcome. He is an Andilan."

"I will tell him. It will lighten his soul to hear it. And he would have to return then."

"And so it shall be," the first man said. "Until then. We apologize for interrupting your prayer."

"You were doing exactly as you should have been," Rifun assured him.

Nevertheless, the men made their own apologies to the spirits within and around the tomb before departing, leaving Rifun alone once more. He wondered whether he should have mentioned that he would be here for quite a while, then decided that they would figure it out eventually.

He returned to his previous position, bowed before the tombs, and found tears running down his cheeks. He breathed an enormous sigh of relief. He had been cleared. Vindicated. Accepted.

Did he dare reclaim his name?

No, not yet. Not when he'd just lied and said he was his own son, and that he was apparently still alive at nearly seventy years old. In order to avoid the confusion, he would have to wait a little while longer, until...until there was no one left to remember him. His cousin would be of an age as well—his true age, not his apparent age—and he would know well that something wasn't what it seemed.

All the same, he was finally recognized and accepted for his work, his role in defending the Malagasy in not one, not two, but three conflicts. Why shouldn't he announce himself and claim his name? He wouldn't be able to claim both his name and his achievements at the same time if he waited too much longer. At least if he Disguised himself as himself but older, then he could make things right before everyone he ever knew—more importantly, everyone who ever knew him—died.

That sounded like a good plan, but it would have to wait. For one, he'd just told his family that he was his own son and that he was living far away and didn't want to visit because he felt abandoned. He would have to wait a while, long enough for him as his own son to return home to tell him that all was well, then try to convince him to come back, and then wait for an undetermined length of time to either resolve or ignore his fabled health problems so he could return and perhaps die and be buried in the family tombs. But preferably without actually dying. And without himself as his son being there.

What the hell had he just gotten himself into?

He pondered this for a short time before remembering that he was supposed to be praying and meditating. He was here to seek the Author, touch the razana, perhaps even learn the secrets of the Akari that would allow him to be a Builder. He would worry about his personal problems later, assuming they even mattered anymore once his quest was complete.

And how would he know it was complete? There was a difference between three weeks and three months. Was he simply going to keep praying until the Author answered him? Was he arrogant for thinking he could force a spirit to do anything? Quite possibly. But where was the line between giving it his all and giving up, and being arrogant and not leaving until he got an answer?

He let out a breath and tried to focus. It wasn't about him. He was not the goal, he was the gateway. He was not here demanding some change to his tiny, physical, immaterial world. He was asking to just glimpse the eternal, the flow and power of the ancestors and spirits, the razana. He was coming to them, asking to know more about them, learn from them. He was here with an open mind and a desperate soul.

But are you prepared to consider that you might be wrong?

It was only a whisper of a thought, but it may as well have been a blow to the head. He did not move, but he felt terribly unprepared, and he could think of nothing else for a long time.

Was he prepared to consider that he might be wrong? Wrong about what? The Author? The Akari? The Cult? How could he be? He would not presume to understand the Author. That was why he was here. He wanted to know and understand. As for the Akari, if he were wrong, it would be obvious by now, wouldn't it? If it was supposed to be a living thing, then if he was misusing it, it would know and the Author would correct him. If it wasn't a living thing...

As for the Cult, he couldn't see how he was wrong there. He knew they had problems. He was working to solve those problems. And if getting rid of Cassius and the Borelians was wrong...to use a cliché, he didn't want to be right. Then he might have a problem with the Author and the Akari.

He considered this for a short time. What if he was wrong? What if the Author really was an advocate for chaos, destruction, and death? It might explain the decline of the Akarin as they embraced timid pacifism. It might explain the leadership of the Cult, himself included. As much as he was telling himself that he was working toward a peaceful resolution, he was no stranger to violence and killing. What if that was why he'd been chosen as a leader? What if that was what the Author expected of him?

He sighed and thought more on this. It didn't sound right. It didn't feel right. But that was why he was here. He wanted to learn what was right and true. No Julianna or Cassius. No Akarin. He wanted to go straight to the Author.

Are you prepared to consider that you might be wrong?

The question lurked in the recesses of his mind, but he was unsure how to approach it. What if he was wrong? What if he found the truth and didn't like it? Most people said that they would be able to handle it, and most people were wrong. Few could handle the truth if it meant straying too far from their comfortable feather bed of lies. He'd faced the ugly truth of war and torture and gotten out. What if facing the truth now meant going back to that?

Could he do it? Could he walk through the valley of the shadow of death? Again? If the Christians got anything right, it was that. And it seemed a very apt analogy to his predicament. Would he walk through the fire again in search of the truth on the other side? The thought was unnerving. He felt his skin grow warm, but he could not sweat well, and his anxiety increased. How much was the truth worth to him?

One of the goals of prayer, fasting, and meditation was also one of its pitfalls, and it was time. Time to consider such things on a deep, spiritual level. It was one thing which frightened those who understood into not meditating, and terrified those who did not understand and were unprepared for such things. Some people knew the price of meditation and were unwilling to pay it. Others did not know the price; they went into meditation expecting to find what they wanted to find: good vibes and positive energy.

Rifun knew enough that true meditation brought out the negative as much as the positive, sometimes even more, depending on what had to be brought to the surface. And it appeared that he had a lot to bring to the surface.

On the other hand, perhaps this was not a specific question, but a general one. Was he prepared to consider that he might be wrong? Could he take criticism? Could he take rebuke? Refute? Correction? Could he handle the idea that he was not omniscient and omnipotent? Perhaps that was the reasoning behind it. He was imperfect, and he knew it. Everyone knew that they were imperfect, but few were willing to admit it to such a degree that they would take correction from anyone else, much less the spirits. It was hard enough taking correction from one's family or friends, whom people could see, meet, and understand. It was harder to take correction from invisible spirits, especially one such as the Author. Even the Malagasy, who held the spirits and the ancestors in high regard, could have trouble taking correction from said spirits and ancestors.

It was one thing for a man to be corrected in minor issues concerning his personal business or relationships, but when considering the scale of the operation that he was a part of, he had to be able and willing to take correction. He had to learn to be flexible. He had to learn to work well with others.

If this were the only question he had, he might have been content to end his meditation at that point, or perhaps a little later after some appropriate prayers of thanks. But this was not the only question he had. Indeed, it wasn't even one that he had come bearing.

Nevertheless, it was promising, he thought, that he should begin to have such spiritual questions and deep considerations. It made him feel validated in his quest, hopeful that he would not be doomed to weeks or months of inexplicable and frustrating silence. He just couldn't allow his personal feelings to get in the way of whatever the spirits wanted to show him. He could be hopeful, but he still had to maintain a certain level of humility.

He remained where he was, considering that particular question a little while longer, but trying to allow himself to be open to other things as well.

At some point he fell asleep, and when he woke, he could feel someone nearby. He yawned once, then sat up, his back cramping in several odd locations. His neck was stiff and he got a good crack out of it when he turned to look around.

He spotted a young woman, appearing in her mid-twenties, standing about ten yards away, drawing nearer as he stretched. She was carrying a basket.

"I brought you some food," she said, getting within comfortable distance and kneeling, setting the basket in front of her and opening it. Inside was a bowl of rice, a few slices of bread, some jerky, and some fruit. "My brother said you were here praying."

"And fasting, too," Rifun informed her. "But I will not dishonor the family by refusing."

Dishonoring the family by refusing the offer of food would have brought such disgrace that observing a perfect fast would have meant nothing in the end.

Forcing his stiff joints to move, he sat and took up the food. "What's your name?"

"Lalao," she answered shyly. At his look—which he approximated as somewhere between stunned and suspicious—she went on, "My father would have been your father's cousin."

Rifun opened his mouth to say that his father was Tsimihety, but remembered himself at the last moment, simply replied, "I see," and took a bite of bread and rice.

"Your grandmother was a beloved part of the family. Your father was, too. Or he would have been."

"What happened to him? I've asked, but he's never said much."

Lalao frowned. "According to my father, your father, Rivotra, was treated very poorly by his father, or stepfather, I should say."

"Vala." The name was out before Rifun could call it back.

"Yes, that sounds familiar. Rivotra wanted so badly to prove himself that he joined the nationalists. Then he was arrested and sent to prison where he was beaten until he was eventually blinded. Vala hated him even more for it, so Rivotra fled to France for many years. Somehow he regained his sight. He returned home once, during the Uprising, to fight with the nationalists again, but..." She sighed. "He was arrested, along with other war prisoners, but eventually freed. No one knew what happened to him after that, but apparently he went to Europe."

Rifun nodded thoughtfully and swallowed his bite. "Sounds similar to what he told me. What little he's told me."

She shifted position. "My father said that the family should have done more to help your father."

"Like what?"

"I don't know. I never really asked him about it. Any time he talks about the Uprising and the family and everything else, he just says that things were complicated back then. Things were complicated, things were complicated. But I was just a little girl back then."

"Then you were one of the lucky ones," Rifun blurted, again speaking before thinking.

"Maybe, from some of the stories that I've heard about whole villages being slaughtered, families being put to the torch." Lalao shook her head and looked away.

"And our family arrested for tax evasion."

"That's right." She looked at him. "It's been a long road to recovery. My father talked about how your father's grandmother had a great empire with many cattle, productive tanimbary, and even grapes for wine. Then the French seized it all."

"Looks like we got it back, though." He bit into a piece of fruit.

"Well, it wasn't easy. I don't remember the details, but it was a hard fight to win."

"We won. That's all that matters."

She studied him for a long moment, her expression amused. He looked at her. "What?"

"You speak as though you already knew everything I was going to say, as though you have lived alongside us."

Rifun shook his head. "No. My father told me many stories." He added quickly, "Stories of the good times, the way things used to be, the way they were supposed to be."

Lalao laughed. "Is that so? Is that why you're here praying, and not at a European church?"

"My father holds no love for Christians."

"He must if he is living in Europe. Surely he must have married a Christian woman to have you."

Uh...shit.

"Not necessarily. Europe is full of irreligious people. My father says that the war did it to most of them."

"Well then, I pity them."

"You do?"

"Of course. Madagascar lived through its own war during the Uprising, and just as many people were killed, most of them not even soldiers on the front lines. Yet here we are, as faithful as ever to our ancestors and to God. They are all we have ever had, and they are all we have ever needed. But the Europeans idolize their great buildings and their many possessions, putting gods into these things that can be destroyed."

Rifun blinked. "You're saying we shouldn't take pride in the accomplishments of our ancestors, of our ancient kings and queens?"

"We may take pride in them, of course, but we should not make idols of them. Our souls are what matter, as we leave this world and take our place among the ancestors and the spirits."

"But the living are needed to tend to the dead. And what if the dead should be destroyed? What happened to the families whose tombs were desecrated by the French?"

Now Lalao looked uncertain. Then, "I don't know."

Rifun sighed. "I'm sorry. My father has strong feelings about such things, and I suppose I've picked up a few of those strong feelings."

She managed a small smile. "Well, those strong feelings are what drove your father to fight for his people." She nodded. "You should speak to him and get him to return, to make things right. If he wishes, I know he would be buried in the family tomb."

He nodded. "I'm sure he would like that."

She collected the empty dishes and set them back in the basket. "How long do you expect to be here?"

"Weeks," he answered, looking at the tomb. "Months."

"Surely you don't mean to stay out here the entire time?!"

"That was my original plan. I am attempting a spiritual quest through the ancestors. It helps when one prays at the place where the ancestors happen to be."

"As true as that may be, you can't simply lie here day and night with no food, no water, and simply passing out from exhaustion. The ancestors may hold the power of the spirits to help the family, but the ancestors have no reason to help someone who does not help his own family. And you are family."

Rifun was stunned by both her forcefulness and her logic, and he found that he had no rebuttal. Sensing this, Lalao got an unreadable but undeniably feminine look, and she stood, basket in hand. "Continue your prayers. I will speak to my father and others and see where we might set up a bed for you to sleep in, and what work we may find for you."

He watched her leave, unable to do much more than blink. The food had been a surprise, but this was an unexpected turn of events. Well, it couldn't be entirely unexpected, he supposed. After all, he was planning to be here for weeks or months. No one could be expected to just leave him be for those weeks or months, could they? But still, this was not part of his planned prayer, fasting, and meditation. It was one thing to share a lunch with a cousin just to keep him alive during this quest, but living and working with them?

Although she did have the right of it. Why should the ancestors grant him anything if he ignored the needs of his family? Everything he did was to be for the good of the family. Did that mean that his quest was in vain, seeing how he was lying about his identity and not intending to stick around to help his family more? What did the Author think of all of this? He glanced longingly at the tombs. Would he even be able to find out?

More uncertain than he wished to be, he stretched one last time and resumed his posture before the tombs. What did he pray for now? How did he pray? What did he ask for or hope to receive? Did the ancestors or the Author approve of what had just happened, what Lalao intended to happen? Could it be, perhaps, that the ancestors or the Author had sent her for such a purpose? Could they be testing him, testing his loyalties? Was he more dedicated to his religion and ignorant of his family, as he had seen in so many hypocritical ministers? Was it his job to prove that he would not be the same way?

The day grew hot as he considered this, and he was grateful for the intermittent shade from a few trees at various locations surrounding the tombs.

Lalao did not return that day, nor any other family members. Rifun again slept there at the tombs.

The next day was a bit cloudy, but he was thankful for it. He hated his light skin, how it burned and peeled so easily. This was not to say that his dark-skinned relatives did not have similar problems, but their skin did not turn bright red. Still, he remained where he was, continuing to pray.

It was after the heat of the day had passed and the light began to wane when Lalao and one of the three men from the other day—presumably her brother— returned to him. He moved slowly and stiffly, but sat up to face them.

"Our father consulted the shaman and the local pastor," Lalao said. "A place has been set aside for you. If you want it."

It was all Rifun could do not to jump up and run to the old farm. As it was, his stiff joints tempered his response as much as his force of will. After a moment of hesitation, he stood.

Helping and respecting the living was honoring the dead. That, and he really needed a bath. If he'd thought he'd looked and smelled bad after six days in the cool temple that was the officers building, that was nothing compared to only a few days here at the tombs, covered in sweat from the heat and the dirt kicked up by the wind. Who knew what he might look like in six days, or six weeks? That was a frightening thought.

Lalao and her brother, Tomas, talked the whole way back to the house.

"When the French seized the farm, they turned it into only rice and vanilla," Lalao told him. "Rice for their own soldiers and vanilla to export to pay the soldiers."

"Since we got it back, we've been able to reintroduce cattle to the land," Tomas continued. "And some of the old grapevines were not properly cleared away and they grew back, so they are being cultivated again."

"Who actually owns the land now?" Rifun asked.

"My father, Volana," Lalao answered. "He would be one of your father's cousins. He was initially imprisoned during the Uprising, but later sent to do labor in the fields. Afterwards, he returned to the farm and sued to win back the land."

"Quite frankly, he only won after we gained independence and could take our case to our own people in our own courts under our own law," Tomas said bitterly, then sighed. "But we shouldn't be ungrateful. We have the land back, and that's all that matters."

Rifun said nothing to that.

"And what of your father's family?" Lalao inquired. "Who is your mother? Do you have any siblings?"

Um...good question. "My mother is long dead. I have one sister. Her name is Julianna."

"Ah, an English name."

"Yes."

"When were you born?" Tomas asked quizzically. "Your father came to fight during the Uprising, but then he was imprisoned for many years. You are clearly too old to have been born afterwards."

Shit. And this is where my story falls apart. "My sister was born first. I was conceived before he left to come back here, and born while he was away. I did not know him for my childhood. Then my mother died, and we lived with her sister for a short while until he returned. And even our aunt said he was a different man. But he was able to raise us well."

"That's good," Lalao said warmly. "It sounds like he managed to be what his stepfather was not."

"Oh, he could be harsh at times, but he was good."

Actually, Rifun had no idea what kind of father he would be. The thought barely even registered as feasible at this point in time.

"And your sister, is she married?"

"She was, but her husband perished of illness before they had children." If a broken neck could be called illness.

"Is she as dedicated to the family?"

"She took after our mother and is quite English."

Tomas made a scoffing sort of sound but tried to cover it up with a cough. He asked quickly, "And you? Are you married?"

Rifun felt his face grow warm. "No."

"Why not? Do you have a girl in mind?"

"No, I've been busy with work."

Tomas waved a hand. "Bah! Such a European statement! Work. Always about work and materialism." He put a hand on Rifun's shoulder and it was all he could do not to hit it away or flinch away. "Family. Family is what is most important. Your time here will do you good, cousin."

They reached the farmhouse where an older man came out to meet them.

"Ah, so this is Fanantenanirainy," he said, grinning.

"Yes, sir," Rifun said meekly, suddenly unsure what to do or say.

"Ah, none of that 'sir' nonsense. Call me uncle or call me Volana, for that is my name." He put his hand on Rifun's other shoulder. Rifun's heart lurched into his throat. "Come inside. We'll get a bath for you and then sit down to eat."

There was obvious damage to the house, probably from years of neglect under French occupation, but there were also signs of repair. New bricks were set into walls, awaiting fresh red clay plaster. Old grass roofing was being slowly replaced by clay tiles. A foundation had been laid for a new room, truly a luxury on a house that was already of mansion status.

"The last time I—" He checked himself. "—heard my father talk about this place, he made it sound like it was in near ruins."

"Well, many things were destroyed during the war and the Uprising and the French occupation. This farm did take a beating. But we're coming back. We always do."

Rifun looked around as if seeing everything for the first time. Playing the role of Fanantenanirainy, he was. Certainly it had been many years since he had been near this place, and the last time he had been inside and dined here, he had been completely blind.

He didn't know what he had been expecting. Perhaps to see more things that reminded him of Nibe. But that was foolish, for she had been dead many years, and French occupiers would have destroyed anything left behind by the family.

"As loathe as I am to admit it, there were a few hidden blessings of the French taking over this place," Volana continued, moving off to another room. He pushed open the door. "The French enjoy their modern inventions and conveniences, so they installed indoor plumbing." He barked a laugh. "It's not quite as sophisticated as some of the systems in Tana or Fianar, but it works for us."

Before Rifun could take more than two steps toward the bathroom, Volana was taking him to another room.

"This is where the unmarried men sleep. We set up your mattress here. Take care to put the net over you."

"Right."

Volana took a step back and studied him. "Did you bring nothing with you? Did you really expect to spend weeks or months at the tombs with no clothes and no food?"

From a purely Earth-side point of view, it did sound extremely foolish. From a Time-side point of view, well, the food mattered less because of his slowed metabolism, but the clothes...well, yes, he supposed he had expected to simply spend day and night in prayer and meditation with few, if any, interruptions.

Volana waved a hand. "We'll get something for you."

"Misaotra," Rifun said, finding that he meant it more sincerely than he'd meant anything in his life. "Misaotra betsaka."

"You are most welcome. Tell me, why did you come? Coming to meet family is one thing, but to come to this place you've never seen, to the tombs of a family you have never met, to fast and meditate and pray...what drives you?"

"To be honest, I'm here on behalf of my father. And to find out where I come from, my place in the family."

"Ah." Volana nodded gravely. "Yes, feelings of frustration and abandonment are very powerful indeed, and it has unintended consequences on future generations. But it seems your father taught you well, if you know how to pray to the ancestors."

"How shall I do that, though, if I'm working here?"

The old man grinned. "Work here in the mornings, while it is still cool. We will show you everything you need to know. After lunch, go and pray to the ancestors. Then come and sleep with us here."

"I didn't realize that spiritual enlightenment could be scheduled in such a way."

Now Volana laughed heartily. "Ah, perhaps not as such. But the ancestors at the tombs are as much family as the family who work in the fields. Make time for both and you will be rewarded by both."

10 | Duro ati Wo   Wait and See

The Wheel of Time, 1964

kokumbo

The Food Court seemed to be the place to go when devising nefarious schemes. Hell, he himself had used it multiple times in recent weeks, and it seemed as though the Gentleman Killers used it as a popular hangout spot, too. It was as though the Food Court had been turned from a respectable restaurant into a rather shady establishment.

He looked around, surveyed the scene, studied who was meeting with whom, attempted to assess whether any of the meetings presently going on were likely to be an immediate threat to himself or his own contacts and clients.

At first he wasn't sure how things would change with Rifun going on his quest or whatever the fuck he was doing. Then he hated himself for allowing himself to be so bound and caught up in the man's comings and goings and actions or inaction. He was a leader, wasn't he? He was part of that council of four that ran the Cult. So why should he act subservient to any other member? He wasn't worried about Julianna, certainly. He wasn't worried about Isthim, at least, no more than any other Borelian. So why was he so concerned about Rifun?

The first day he may have slunk around like a cowed fool, but after a week of not having to worry about Rifun's concerns or negotiations or whatever else he had going on, Cassius was starting to feel more like himself again. Isthim trained the grunts so he didn't have to, and Julianna took care of the soft stuff. This left Cassius free to kill, maim, and destroy, just as they had agreed, with no one objecting who could do anything about it.

He took a drink. He didn't drink alcohol often; it dulled his senses, as it was supposed to do. But there were occasions when he might indulge a little. He was feeling good. He was feeling strong.

He was feeling free.

Well, maybe not entirely so. He was still part of the Cult and still beholden to the dark spirit.

He frowned and leaned back in his seat a bit. There was no pain from the bullet in his face, and every so often he wondered whether there wasn't some way to remove it without the dragon noticing. But how did he accomplish such a feat? How could one outwit the spirits? Maybe he ought to ask Rifun when he returned from his spiritual quest. Ha!

He took a drink.

Aside from the usual mischief he was expected to cause, he was also supposed to be the controlled opposition. Make it look like someone was striking back at them, perhaps with limited success, and see who could be drawn out of the shadows. Few men were bold enough to tackle evil by themselves, but if they saw someone else start the charge, they may follow. If Cassius could be the one to start that charge, lead some of the bolder followers into the light, he could turn around and scoop them up, destroy them, and discourage the weaker rebels from attempting anything themselves. And all the while, he would have nothing to fear from them, for he would be the one in control.

It was a nice fantasy, but much harder to put into practice. How much did they want to show off? How much did they want to expose? What happened if something went sideways and a secret got out? What if the Borelians attempted to thwart the plan and become a third party?

All things that would be dealt with as they came up. Cassius could not allow himself to be paralyzed by fear and indecision. He had to think on his feet and compensate on the fly. He would not let himself become as weak as Rifun.

He considered the situation with the crown of Srori. The smith, Rilor, had perished, refusing to give up the location of the real crown. Cassius had stayed just long enough to be spotted by the royal guards, exchange a few blows, some insults, and make a point of blaming the royal family Torka for the assassination before disappearing, first into the streets, and then into thin air as though he'd just ducked out through a portal.

If there had been any fallout against the Cult, Cassius had heard none of it. And considering Rilor had picked up on the rival family, rather than Cassius' plan, was it unreasonable to think that there might not have been other agents looking for Srori's crown?

On the one hand, he'd managed a relatively clean getaway.

On the other hand, he wasn't the only threat out there. The likes of Titik and Cassius were probably only ancillary concerns for the Jalar family compared to those like the Torka and other rival families.

He'd not yet met with Pilory for private instruction, and while he was not yet averse to the idea of having a secret student, he found himself wondering whether it was worthwhile to pursue the crown further. Did he really need or want Titik's help? What could the pirate do that he himself couldn't? What resources were somehow unique to the Psiaco pirate?

He shook his head and took another drink. He didn't need Titik. Although he might continue to pursue the crown. If he found it, he would make the pirate beg for it. Absolutely beg. And maybe Cassius wouldn't give it to him. He smiled at the thought. Pirate or not, Psiaco could be stuck up bastards with their advanced space technology and prestigious Time Academies. But like many races, they were conquerors and slavers, subjugating the Urid when they conquered their planet and made themselves kings. Like Isthim, Titik was an outcast, but no less a slaver deserving of death in the end.

See? He knew a few things, too. He knew how to do a little research and find other people's dirty laundry.

He finished off his drink, stood, and stretched. A few discreetly made note of his movements, though none rose to confront him. One also stood and exited the Food Court as nonchalantly as possible, never looking directly at him. Going about his own business? Or going to warn someone? Who could know? But it would make things exciting.

Cassius did not come to the Wheel merely to drink and watch people pass the day away in their own sinister dealings. He was here for several reasons, fulfilling several promises or contracts, none of them as pleasant as delivering newspapers to elderly patrons.

As he departed, he made eye contact with only one of those giving him sideways glances. The other party did not attack, did not move, and did not avert its gaze. Its intentions were impossible to determine beyond mere annoyance, hardly anything immediately hostile. So he was unlikely to get a knife in the back as he left the Food Court. Such a disappointment. And a pity. There was something to be said for being in the middle of the pack. There was always a challenge, whether above or from below.

He left the Food Court. It would be misleading to say that the Wheel was back to normal after the incident with the balancers, for it was not, although it appeared to be. People still went about on business, in the same way that poor souls and refugees still went to draw water from the well of a town decimated by aerial assault. Those people had nowhere else to go, and their only thought was satisfying basic needs and hoping to live another day.

Truly, Time was not a basic need. Billions of souls got along just fine without making trips to the Wheel, and Timekeepers were more than capable of dealing with Runners themselves; they just didn't like to get their hands dirty and preferred to turn them over to the Grandfathers for a more formal affair.

But there was another aspect of Time, and that was addiction. The lust for one more day of life. Just one more day. Just one more thing to accomplish, but only if one had the time, the days or weeks or months or years to devote. Just a little more time.

Even as he thought it, someone reached out to him, a panhandler begging for Time. Just a single Time Capsule. An hour. Just one Base Hour. Cassius ignored the beggar and continued on his way.

Those who populated the Wheel now were comprised more of the addicts than the common person. Business was still conducted normally, but there was very little difference between a rich alcoholic and a poor one, other than how much money one had to put toward their vice at any given moment.

In a way, it made this very easy. He got to cause chaos, and in doing so, he might kill not only a few Gentleman Killers who happened to be out and about, but a handful of worthless addicts as well. He should get an award for this, really, something to thank him for doing the universe a favor and cleaning up the most useless bottom feeders. He would even settle for a verbal thank you or a pat on the back for his service.

But such a thing would not come, he knew. He would just have to do this anonymously, with no thought to reward. How noble and humble of him. Rifun would be proud.

He wandered around the Wheel a bit. Not because he was lost, but because he was waiting for a cue. When rigging both position and controlled opposition, it helped to coordinate with those he would be "opposing," in this instance, the Borelians. More specifically, Isthim was leading this exercise, both because she knew how the Cult, how Cassius operated, and to prove herself to her fellows.

He wasn't sure how he felt about her getting back into her people's good graces, but now was not the time to dwell on it.

Finally he spotted her in one of the lower marketplaces. She must have been having the same thoughts he was. The place was well crowded with Time addicts.

Not all, certainly—there were a few honest patrons out and about, trying to keep things normal and sane—but enough that any deaths were well-deserved. And there was a good crop of Gentleman Killers to cut down as well; they were probably here to keep some order among the riffraff.

The first Gentleman Killer looked at him, then spotted Isthim and a few Borelians hanging around in different places. Before the man could say anything, Cassius tweaked the Gravity in the room.

It wasn't quite as dramatic as before, where he threw the entire Wheel in a blender and put it on high for thirty to forty-five seconds, but it was certainly jolting for anyone not expecting it to happen.

But Cassius and the Borelians were expecting it, and they had spent a good chunk of time working with Gravity so they might be able to offset the worst of the effects, if not negate them entirely.

It was rather satisfying to watch thousands of people go about their business one minute, only to suddenly scream in terror as their world was, quite literally, thrown upside down and to all sides of the three-dimensional planes. Meanwhile, Cassius and the Borelians used each other as gravitational anchor points to steady themselves in the center of the room as best they could and watch it all happen.

This was not to say that they were unaffected. As the room shook and tossed and turned, the Gravity going haywire and the balancers attempting to sort things back to rights, not a few people and objects were flung about. This was half the point of their stunt, after all. So while Isthim ducked as several large objects flew over her head, another Borelian failed to completely maneuver out of the way of a large booth and was knocked aside. This sent a reverberation through their anchoring system, and the Borelian tumbled away and broke free, now at the mercy of the quake.

Cassius was hit in the head by something small, but he refused to let go of his anchor. He'd experienced this sort of thing once before, and he had no desire to do it again. He was not only going to instigate this, but he was going to carry it and see it through to the end. He had to be ready to lead the retaliation, after all, and he couldn't do that if he was concussed.

Comparatively speaking, this tiny demonstration of power was but a child's block building tumbling to the floor, but for everyone caught in the middle, it may as well have been the grand demolition of an enormous skyscraper.

Only when the quake was nearly over, with the balancers finally settling things back as they should be, did Cassius and the others carefully dismantle their Gravity anchor system and allow themselves to touch the floor—or walls or ceiling—of the room. There was still a bit of shaking, and he briefly wondered what should happen if the balancers were unable to settle things. Then the aftershocks died down, and the room was still.

He went to his knees as if thrown off balance by a particularly violent tremor. He looked around. Chaos, debris, bodies, all of it very familiar. He strangled a groan as he hardened. He had done this. He had caused this chaos and destruction for his own ends, and now he would pretend to lead some kind of opposition against those he would pretend had done this, but whom he did not have to pretend to hate. It was almost too perfect. Too good to be true, and yet it was.

He slithered under a heap of debris, pushing aside a body and crawling over a mess of scattered Time Capsules.

He didn't know the name of the alien he Disguised himself as, only that it was bipedal and a little larger than the average human, with a face resembling an extremely wrinkly dog he'd once seen in a park somewhere. The skin was a dark green and a long, shaggy mane circled his head and swept down his back like a rug, covered badly by some loose clothing. He also had a tail that wasn't very long; it didn't even touch the ground.

What was important, though, was that he didn't look like himself, and he looked imposing, or he thought he did. He crawled out of the rubble, careful to Band and repair his Disguise as it frayed.

He stood and looked around, trying to act confused and a bit disoriented while surveying the scene, seeing who else was about. No use launching into a grand tirade and attempting to rally a fighting force if there was no one cognizant enough to fight beside him.

Some were already wandering about, a few clearly dazed, most fairly clear-headed given the circumstances. Many more were crawling out of the mess or helping others to do so.

Another aftershock caused the room to tremble, and not a few cries of shock and despair echoed through the air, but no more came of it. Things settled back to stillness, though there was a certain air of urgency to free those who remained trapped.

The portals, for the most part, appeared unaffected. A few had closed, but most remained open and undisturbed, if blocked by large piles of debris. There was some movement as rescuers from other areas of the Wheel forced their way through. These were mostly larger aliens who could clear a large area of debris with a single sweep of a large, meaty paw.

"Did you feel it?" someone demanded of one of these rescuers. "How bad is the damage elsewhere?"

"Minimal," the rescuer replied.

"How did this happen?" someone else wailed. "Is the Wheel falling into such disrepair? Are there no secretaries after the slaughters? Are they too afraid to work?"

"This must be the work of evildoers!" Cassius proclaimed, jumping into his role. In his alien body, he strode into a large clearing, trash and debris piled high around an area perhaps sixty feet across.

"But who?" a third person wondered. "The last time this happened, the whole Wheel was thrown into chaos."

"A warning, then," Cassius said. "The first time, a show of power that we mistook as 'disrepair.' Now they mean to grab our attention, let us know that they mean business!"

Every so often, Cassius wondered how idioms got translated across a universe of language and culture. Then he decided he didn't care as long as his message got across. A small crowd was gathering around him, and he was briefly reminded of Titik on his soapbox.

"Who is it, though?" the same person asked. "Surely they would be just as vulnerable as us during this time."

"Not if they had the power to negate it for themselves. The only way to do such a thing, to alter the Gravity, the Energy here, is by the Akari." Before anyone could protest, he pointed to the Borelians. He knew their attempts to sneak out were obvious and faked, but he hoped it was convincing for everyone else. "The Borelians are known allies of the Cult of the Akari! And they've not a scratch on their skins! They must have something to do with this!"

Cassius had hoped there might be a little more enthusiasm from the crowd to coax them to turn into a mob and then a riot. As it was, the Borelians by themselves commanded enough fear to make everyone but the most heartless bastards pause. That also seemed to include mobs.

Determined not to let this go to waste, he pushed through the crowd to confront the Borelians. Isthim took charge of the group and stopped to confront him. He wondered what would happen if he initiated the false fight and "accidentally" managed to kill one of them. Would it make a difference if Isthim were the one to die? By all rights, she was still an outcast, had been hunted by her own people. What would they do if he finished the job for them? What would happen if he killed Medik, her bitch of a cousin? Or Misik? It was what was expected, at least from Julianna and Rifun, but the first incident would be too obvious, wouldn't it? And this spontaneous riot would normally be too weak to pose a real threat. This was just to get them into the spotlight. The actual assassinations would come later.

"So what'll it be?" Cassius demanded. "Are you going to claim your prize? Make your demands? What is it you want?"

"Does our answer matter?" Isthim asked. "You've already made your decision."

Cassius chuckled. "Guess it doesn't matter. Only good Borelian's a dead Borelian anyway."

He didn't get quite the response he'd been hoping for. He'd envisioned a great mob enveloping the Borelians and eating them alive. As it was, he was the only one around to throw the first punch, with a few tentative thugs coming in a few seconds later.

Isthim and the others probably could have had them all subdued and executed in short order, but they let it play out a little, made it look like they were losing. This emboldened a few more from the crowd to try their hand at bruising Borelian flesh, but this was as far as it got. There was no riot, no army, and none of the Borelians got more than a minor scratch, and that from the debris still lying around.

Eventually, Cassius grew bored of the back and forth. He let himself be thrown to the ground where he slipped away amid another pile of debris. After a few seconds, he shed his Disguise and Banded to escape the room.

He dusted himself off and faced Julianna.

"All yours," he told her.

She nodded without saying a word to him, then motioned for her small army of humanitarians to flood into the wrecked room. He heard her gasp dramatically, then begin scolding everyone for the fighting. He could not make out her exact words, but he didn't need to. His work was done.

As promised, there was minimal damage outside the singular marketplace, a few things displaced but nothing destroyed. People whispered but there were no riots here.

It was a bit frustrating, honestly. Where was the passion, the drive, the fury that had so consumed the voters as the elections went sideways? It had been only a year—or maybe a little more—since that time. Had everyone forgotten? Did every species in the universe have such a short attention span and an even shorter memory? Had they somehow forgotten about the Tacagans and the Gentleman Killers? Would they even remember this incident in a week?

What was it going to take, exactly?

He returned to the ruins, uncertain what he expected to do. Isthim was probably off with her cohorts, scheming as Borelians do. Julianna was leading the charge in humanitarian efforts to both clean things up and make a good name for the Cult, craft some positive association. Rifun was gone, best forgotten.

His role in this event had been fulfilled, and yet he did not feel similarly. What did he do now? What was his part in the fallout? Did he want a part? Did he trust the others to handle things well? Not exactly. Did he want to go back and inject himself into the conversation? Hardly.

So he skulked around the officers building for a bit, mercifully empty of Borelians and pretty much anyone else. He ended up in the great hall where, at one time, thousands of primitive Elif had gathered to participate in some ritual to their ancient gods. Maybe it was a feast, perhaps a sacrifice, maybe both, or perhaps something never even conceived of by humans but of immense importance to the ancient Elif.

Now he stood alone amid great stone carvings and the fireplace large enough to build a small house. If the Elif had offered up sacrifices here, they must have been monstrous affairs. Had they offered up animals, or each other? What were the criteria?

"It's amazing the Elif have advanced as far as they have," a voice said behind him. He turned to see Isthim approaching. She stood beside him and studied the carvings over the hearth. "They valued their sacrifices so much they nearly drove themselves to extinction."

"So they did sacrifice each other."

"They sacrificed whatever they thought would please their gods."

Cassius frowned. "And what sacrifices are offered to Tujor, I wonder? Does the god of death value life?"

"The blood of our enemies," Isthim replied simply.

" 'Our' enemies? You've been accepted back, then."

"There is still some debate about that."

"How often does an exile earn back her commission?"

"How often does an exile escape the Hunters?"

Well, he couldn't argue that one. He shifted his stance and changed the subject. "So how was that for a first run at controlled opposition?"

"Sloppy," Isthim answered without missing a beat. "Obnoxious, rude, obvious, inorganic. The only good news is that most people, in the aftermath of such an event, are too stupid to think about this logically. Going forward, they will recall the gravitational event, the accusations which they will associate with the Borelians because of the visual aspect of it, the prolonged fight, and perhaps they will get a silly notion in their collective head that maybe we can be defeated."

"We root out the leaders of the organic movement, kill the resistance, move in and take over."

"Precisely."

"Speaking tactically, how long do you expect this to take?"

Isthim shrugged. "If the resistance organizes into a more central movement, it could be as little as a few months. If it becomes decentralized, we may be looking at years."

"If we're controlling the resistance, though—"

"Then it may remain centralized. If we lose control, if we push things too quickly, other leaders may slip away into the shadows. We have to draw them out, but it is not an instant thing. We must be patient hunters."

"We can't wait too long or else we'll fall asleep and give them a chance to overrun us. Has there been any reaction from the Tacagans or the Gentleman Killers?"

"I wouldn't know. We departed after Julianna calmed things down. I expect she will have more information in that regard."

Cassius rolled his eyes. "And a thousand words of fretting on either side of it if there is."

Isthim frowned. "If you had the words of the Author, why not write down the journals yourself and establish the Cult yourself? Why did you give the task to others?"

"Seems an odd question to ask, coming from a collectivist."

"Maybe so, but humans tend to value their individuality and their ability to outdo each other and do things by themselves."

"Well, even I may admit a weakness. I was never very good at writing and literature."

It was the truth, but not the real reason. If Isthim suspected anything of the sort, she did not say so aloud. Finally he gave her a look and said, "Delegation. I didn't expect things to go as horribly as they did."

The Borelian nodded but said nothing more on the matter.

They continued gazing at the carvings for a few minutes more. The main god was easy to pick out as he was the most prominent, but the rest of the scene was lost to time and history and someone who cared more than Cassius. It may have been a battle, or, seeing how the Elif apparently sacrificed each other, it may have been a festival of some sort with sacrifices as the main event. It was hard to tell.

"So what do you think of Rifun going off on his spiritual quest?" Cassius inquired casually, tired of staring at carvings yet not wanting to walk away first.

"If he is gone as long as Julianna says he expects to be gone, I should hope he finds something for his efforts, and for wasting our time."

"What do you mean wasting our time? He's helping the cause by getting out of the way."

"Yes, but he has left all of his responsibilities on us. How shall you or I attend to political affairs when we are busy trying to maneuver position and opposition? How shall Julianna attend to politics when she is so weak-willed, to say nothing of her role in humanitarian efforts after we have caused chaos?" Isthim snorted indignantly and shook her head. "No. Rifun has a role to play, and he is abandoning that role for this quest or pilgrimage of his. As I said, I hope he finds something for his efforts."

Cassius studied her for a long moment, but she kept her gaze deliberately on the carvings. Finally he said, "And...?"

She looked at him. "And what?"

"He's abandoning you for weeks to months, too."

Isthim's expression turned unreadable. "You bring this up again?"

He shrugged. "All I'm saying is that—"

"You are jealous and immature, and also uninformed. Borelian relations, especially with outsiders, hold no emotional connection or impact."

"That's what you say, but I think humans have rubbed off on you a little while you've lived among us."

She sighed and turned to face him. "What is it that you expect me to say? Do you expect me to pine after him? Weep at his absence? I will not because I have no such inclinations. Nor will I fall into your arms for comfort, for I hold no such emotions for you either. What you really want is to mate with me as he did just so you can say that you have, and because you expect to fare better than he did which would be another point of boast."

Cassius grinned. "You know me so well."

She made as if to leave. "Well, I am sorry to disappoint you, but such a thing is not happening today."

"But there is a chance in the future," he stated wolfishly.

She did not reply, just turned and left the building. Cassius stood there, dumbly grinning after her, for a long moment. She would be his someday, and it would be a willing partnership, not accidental as Rifun had done, but purposeful. It would both satisfy him and give him — and possibly her — a chance to snub his nose at the others, both in the Cult and the Borelians.

Until then, however, he just had to play his part. Cause trouble, then get upset about that trouble, cause more trouble, and let Julianna deal with the aftermath. Yes, he supposed that wasn't a bad arrangement. Probably he should have talked to Isthim about the next bit of trouble he would cause and coordinate their efforts, but he could do that another time. They couldn't do this back-to-back-to-back, after all. They had to allow a little bit of time for the denizens of the Wheel to process events and figure out their position on the matter, decide how to react.

It was several hours before Julianna returned, and another two before she was ready to hold a meeting. Not that Cassius especially enjoyed meetings, but this one might actually be pertinent to their operations. The three remaining Cult leaders as well as Commander Misik were in attendance.

"Seventeen people killed, dozens or hundreds more wounded to varying degrees," Julianna reported. "Plenty of damage and mayhem, but I know you all saw that. My people were able to fix most of it and get things almost back to normal."

"And what did you tell your people about what happened?" Misik inquired.

"I told them that it was the Akarin. The first incident with the balancers was the Tacagans as retaliation for the massacre. This, now, was the Akarin, trying to stay relevant even as we work to bring everything back into order under our rule. Our first step was compassionate efforts to restore the livelihood of the common folk, those who had no understanding of the nature of this three-way battle. Our next step is..." She made a gesture. "Well, I told them that our next step would be to better secure our hold so this does not happen again. So then." She looked around. "How do we better secure our hold?"

"How was the mob and failed attack by Cassius received in the aftermath?" Isthim asked.

"About as well as it was taken up initially. Some fear, skepticism, only a few bold actors."

"Nevertheless, an attack on our people cannot go unpunished," Misik said, looking at Isthim as if reminding her of some basic tenet of Borelian existence. "Regardless of the staged nature of this attack, the Council of Ancrath and the Great Admirals of the Fleet will expect a response."

"Against whom, exactly?" Julianna wondered.

"This attack was conducted in the Wheel of Time, presumably by Time Agents, or those of Engaged worlds. Or, as you have perpetuated, by the Akarin. And as we have recently overtaken the operations of the Grandfathers, it was affront on our position and title."

"Sounds like a good opportunity to capture a few early favorites for rebel leaders," Cassius commented.

"Too early for that," Isthim said. "You are the only possible candidate."

"Blaming the initial attack on the Akarin, we could bring in some of their leaders," Julianna suggested. "Actually drawing them into the fight might not be a bad idea."

"Agreed," Misik said. "If they believe their fight is with us or the Time industry, then that will leave the Cult free to deal with other matters."

Cassius did not miss the deliberate separation he gave the groups.

"And once we have the Akarin leaders held in the Judgment Wing, then what?" he asked casually.

"There were more than a few Gentleman Killers in that marketplace," Isthim stated. "Likely they will take offense at this attack, and they will be the most likely to organize into a resistance group first."

"It may also be that the Gentleman Killers will come after you," Julianna continued, "if they saw you involved, or even just as an excuse to come after you."

"I'll be happy to teach them another lesson in power and respect," Cassius said.

"Any ground they lose is ground we stand to gain." The proper Englishwoman shifted uncomfortably, suggesting she was about to compliment the man she hated most in the universe. "Considering how the Gentleman Killers were never well-liked in the first place, it may be that you could make a hero of yourself in this endeavor, if you play your cards right."

Now that was an interesting prospect. Considering the scars on her face, he could see how she might be annoyed by admitting such a thing.

"Has there been any word from Rifun?" Misik asked, sounding a bit annoyed.

"None, but we knew he would be gone," Julianna sighed. "He may play the politics well, but I don't know that he would care for this sort of thing. He acquires the pieces on the board, but he doesn't maneuver them. And I should hope that we are balanced enough that we do not rely overmuch on any one member of this council as it were."

"No, but if each man has a part to play, then the absence of that part ought to be noticed."

"Then you are free to go to him and lecture him on such things. But consider also that it is no one's job to babysit anyone else, and to lecture him on his part may be overstepping your own boundaries."

Two thoughts crossed Cassius' mind then. The first was that the look on Misik's face was immensely satisfying. The Borelians were not accustomed to being talked to in such a way. Slavers were never prepared for a slave to defy them, and even in an alliance, the Borelians still viewed the rest of them as slaves, or slave material.

The second thought was that Julianna certainly looked prim and proper — without question she had a record of poor decision-making — and yet, something about the way she was handling this conversation told Cassius that she was a quick study and rapidly learning the political ropes. Perhaps it was due in part to experience and in part to the removal of Rifun as her crutch, but the woman was learning. Cassius didn't do a lot of reading, but he'd lived through enough history to know that a learned woman could be the best leader anyone had ever seen, or else their worst nightmare.

The moment passed.

"It sounds as though we have our parts to play, then," Julianna stated finally.

"And what will your part be?" Misik asked quickly before they could adjourn.

She gave him the same look as before, that one of a slave defying her master. "My part is to ensure everything goes smoothly, to calm ruffled feathers and soothe fears, and to ensure that we come out looking like heroes that the people want, rather than the best alternative currently being offered, to be replaced as soon as another offer comes along."

Whether this answered satisfied Misik was impossible to tell, but he said nothing more about it.

"If there is nothing further, then we all have our tasks to arrange and delegate as necessary," Julianna said. "I call this meeting adjourned."

Misik and Isthim left quickly, perhaps to plot their fake revenge against the Wheel and the Time industry, or whatever remained of it. Considering there were no true Hands, the Tacagans were out of power, the Gentleman Killers scattered, and the Borelians themselves were the Grandfathers, just who were they planning to retaliate against? Well, it wasn't his problem.

He and Julianna lingered for a moment.

"We don't have to like each other to know that something is amiss with the Borelians," Julianna stated.

"There is always something amiss with the Borelians," Cassius said flatly. "It doesn't help that Isthim seems to have gotten back in their good graces, though it does clear up what the mystery could be."

"Oh? And what's that?"

"Slaving, what else? They're slavers. They're slavers, and slavers have power. What does anyone with power fear most? Losing that power. They have an opportunity to take more for themselves."

"They have had such opportunities in the past and never took them. What makes now so different?"

"I don't know, but just because it hasn't happened in the past doesn't mean it never will."

Julianna raised a brow. "You seem to be full of surprises and great leaps of introspection."

"Maybe Rifun's spirits are telling me something."

"Many people tell you many things; the more significant part of this is that you seem to be listening."

"I can learn a few things, too."

Before either of them could say more, he left the room. Maybe it was better to leave things a little ambiguous. Make her nervous, see what happened, what she did.

For his part, he was rather intrigued by the idea of making himself a hero, especially since someone else had brought up the possibility. All he had to do was play his cards right while murdering Gentleman Killers. That sounded doable, even for him. But what cards did he have, and how did he play them?

A thought occurred to him as he passed by one of the windows looking out into the ruined city. He noticed a group of Korin standing around, talking, and, if he had to hazard a guess, laughing. At least, that was what he guessed those sounds to be.

A group of Korin had joined the Cult, not as part of the political agreement between Rifun and the Korin leaders, but because they were Gentleman Killers, or they had been. He left the officers building and went to them.

"You there!" he called.

The group of Korin came to attention in a rather impressive manner. Unaccustomed to having such authority over someone in this way, Cassius momentarily faltered in his approach. He hoped they didn't notice.

"Who are you?" he asked, standing before them. There were four of them. Compared to other Korin he'd seen, he might have guessed that they were in their early to mid-twenties, comparing to human years.

"Surloff, sir," the first answered.

"Dubikoff," said the next.

"Barnoff," said the third.

"Kokriloff," said the last.

Cassius shifted his stance. "Am I to assume, then, that your snappy military responses mean that you are not the group formerly affiliated with the Gentleman Killers?"

The four Korin cast uncertain sideways glances at each other. Finally, one, Dubikoff, replied, "Regardless of our past affiliations, all Korin are taught respect."

"So was I, once. Yet here we are." Beat. "Exactly how close did you get with the other Gentleman Killers? How high were you on the food chain?"

More uncertain glances. It was Surloff who answered now.

"A lot of the others weren't too fond of us, often made fun of our sense and respect for balance in all things."

"Well, there don't tend to be too many other options other than alive or dead."

"They said that," Barnoff said, his tone tinged with acid. "And other things."

"All right, then. Would it make your sense of balance happy if you were to accompany me on a few missions against the Gentleman Killers? They didn't like me very much either, and they're not too happy with the Cult right now. If you were actually part of them, you may have useful information." He went on, "And if it does prove useful, and you help me in this, then I may be able to teach you a few more things about the Akari that Isthim can't."

Something he said must have struck that balance nerve because the four of them readily agreed. They then proceeded to inform him of the many ways they could benefit such missions, their talents and specialties. He noted that they boasted in such a way that they all balanced each other out. One was strong, but not fast. Another was fast, but not as smart with complex machines. A third had a way with machines, but was lacking in people skills. The fourth had tremendous skill with people, but lacked in strength. Perfectly in balance, as all things had to be in the Korin psyche.

"In two days, come meet with me, and we will go out on one of these missions I have told you about," Cassius told them. "We'll see what you're made of and how we can best utilize your respective talents." He added, "But tell no one of this just yet. Wait until afterwards."

The Korin made gestures of approval and departed, talking excitedly amongst themselves. He watched them walk down one of the streets and finally turn, vanishing from sight. Then he turned around and returned to the officers building.

Two days was more than enough time, he thought. He would have to pick a target, something relatively easy, just to test them out. If it worked out well, he would train them alongside Pilory. He would have his own secret school going, his own private army. How was that for taking responsibility, contributing to the cause, and making himself a hero?

Neither Julianna nor Isthim said anything about having witnessed him speaking to the Korin. In fact, he rarely saw them over the next couple of days as they were too engrossed in their own tasks. He mentioned only once to Julianna about even having a plan to move against one of the Gentleman Killers, and she did little more than acknowledge him. That was fine. He could operate on his own without someone holding his hand.

The morning of the second day, it occurred to him that he hadn't actually specified what he meant by "days," a problem that few ordinary people could appreciate. The days on Sadurnon were longer than Earth days, but that rarely mattered underground save for the brief hours that sunlight shone through the crevasse to the east, and even then, the Cult tended to run on Base Days. And how long were days on Irig? What if they didn't show up until later, or even another full day? What if they'd already come and found him gone?

What if they were only pretending to have left the Gentleman Killers, but were in fact double agents?

He dismissed that idea quickly. The Korin were not immune to deception, but it was harder to balance. Rifun had mentioned that once when speaking of his political dealings with them.

He decided to stay in his chambers and wait. It was around midday when the four Korin showed up at his door. Where before they had been dressed casually — or as casually as a humanoid rhino could manage — now they looked ready for battle. Well, why not? Irig was currently ruled by a war dynasty.

"I'm glad you are still intrigued by my offer," he said. He opened his door farther and stepped aside. "Please, come in."

11 | Fahanginana sy Faharetana

Fianarantsoa, 1964

Silence and Patience

R ifun woke and stared at the ceiling, or what he could see of it through the mosquito net. The sky was barely light enough to see by and already he could tell it was going to be dreadfully hot. His skin started itching at the thought of it, and he absently picked at a spot on his arm, trying to peel off the dead skin without agitating the painful burn that was made worse by the fact of his already melted flesh. He had tried several experiments with the Akari to stop his skin from burning, heal the burns more quickly, or even just make it less painful, but his greater priority always went to maintaining his Disguise. If he were to be his own son Fanantenanirainy, then there was no reason that he should have the burns and scars from his years of torture. He'd worn long sleeves and long pants on his arrival, but such was not appropriate for working the fields, and he'd had to come up with something quickly.

The Disguise was easy enough, really, for he was only using a simple trick of the eye in order to cover up his scars, and he could maintain it throughout the day providing he did not for some reason fall unconscious. Several times he thought about using Matter and making it permanent, but he couldn't bring himself to do it.

This was not to say that he did not seriously consider such a thing. Why shouldn't he reinvent himself in this way? Perhaps leave this place and return Disguised as an old man, put on some show about being accepted, maybe fake his death, then stay with the family as his fictional son, as Fan. He was welcome in the family, he could work and be productive, he could pray at the tombs, he could do everything he had ever envisioned. And this time, his country was free and independent, though for how much longer was unknown given the growing Communist movement.

In the early morning hours such as this, it was sorely tempting. It hurt to consider not doing it, in fact.

Perhaps that was what was meant by considering that he could be wrong. Maybe he'd been wrong to leave home. Maybe he would be wrong to return to the

Cult. Maybe he was wrong even thinking about leaving the Cult and doing these things that he wanted to do. The spirits had been silent beyond the simple, vague message of potentially being wrong.

He could hear the chickens outside. The rooster had been crowing for an hour, but now the hens were waking, most likely forcefully as a couple of the women went out to collect eggs. The milk cow lowed in greeting to the women, which was the alarm clock for the men.

The light grew brighter and the simple sounds of sleep gave way to the moans, groans, yawns, and stretches of wakefulness. Rifun found himself moaning, groaning, yawning, and stretching right along with them, with the only added step of donning his Disguise before pushing the net aside and standing, still stretching as he did so. Pleasantries were exchanged as everyone inquired after everyone's soundness of sleep as well as any dreams, especially spiritual ones.

From what Rifun could gather, most of the family had converted to Christianity, or else incorporated it in some way into the traditional beliefs. Few in the family held strictly to the old beliefs, and even they might be known to say a Hail Mary now and again. Only Rifun, as Fan, seemed to remain unilaterally faithful to the spirits and ancestors.

Rifun didn't bother to learn exact familial relations, but contented himself with knowing his elders, who were either aunts and uncles or grandparents, from his juniors, who were all cousins of some kind. Volana was his mother's nephew, Rifun's cousin. He had twin brothers, Mahafaly and Mahaleo, who also had some ownership of the farm, and a sister, Mirana, who lived close by and helped out often. From the four of them were twenty-six children, some who stayed to help on the farm, others who started their own farms, and a few who chose to move away.

Elisette was Volana's wife, and it was she who conducted the household chores, sending her daughters and nieces out to collect eggs, milk the cow, and gather whatever was needed to make breakfast. Like Volana, she had been arrested and imprisoned during the Uprising, but where her husband had been sent to work the fields, she had been made an indentured servant to a particular French commander and quickly became his household chef. Only a food taster had kept her from poisoning the man and his whole family, she'd said. She'd been a well-loved chef, but the commander had taken no chances.

And it had been his standing and authority that brought Elisette and Volana back together after the island finally gained independence. She had been working somewhere in the north country, and Volana had been sent from farm to farm to farm, neither one knowing the fate of the other for the entire Uprising, and for nearly a year afterwards. The French commander had somehow gotten word of the lawsuit records Volana had filed to win back the farm. Elisette promptly left his service and never looked back.

Now she and her daughters and nieces were busy preparing food for their own small army, Elisette directing them with the deft efficiency of someone who could direct anyone to any task whether they liked it or not. But the girls did not mind, and they talked and laughed among themselves as they worked.

For the part of the men, they stood upon the veranda overlooking the fields and discussed the work that had to be done that day. At this time of year, it was primarily maintenance. The ducks needed to be herded to the *tanimbary* while the cattle had to be driven to another field to graze. The grapes needed tending and the vanilla had to be weeded.

"Fan, why don't you help with the cattle?" Fanevy, one of many cousins, suggested. "You can help me bring up the rear and keep them moving."

Rifun agreed, for he had no reason to disagree, and he was grateful for a chance to be off of duck duty. He knew most of the chores, or he could guess well enough, but as his fictional son Fan, he had no knowledge of anything, so they gave him easy work, like herding the ducks or weeding the crops. On the occasion that they brought him in to work with the cattle, he had done well enough, and they told him this, but still he was mostly given chores fit for a child. The ducks didn't really need herding; looking at them in their pen, they knew well their job and where they had to go, and they wanted to go there. The *tanimbary* was full of snails and other insects to eat.

But before the family could do anything more than talk, they had to eat. It was custom, it was tradition, it was practically law. At least in was in Volana's household where Elisette ruled the kitchen.

Of course, with Elisette's cooking, no one was going to argue about eating a hearty meal before going out to work. As expected, Volana took the seat of honor in the northeast corner, his wife, brothers, and eldest children around him. From there, the generations fanned out, Rifun being given a spot in the northwest corner with Tomas and Lalao and others of similar age. Children sat in the southeast corner. Because of the large family, they had no need for servants or slaves, so the southwest corner remained unoccupied.

The Hands Pulling the Strings

For the first week or two, almost all conversation had been about Rifun, or rather, Fan. How was his father, what was he doing now, what was his disposition and feelings about the family? These questions, Rifun did not really have to lie, though he stretched the truth quite a bit on a few occasions. It was when they started asking about his fictional family that he sometimes had to Band to buy himself time to get his story straight. Who was his mother, his sister, his extended family? How was he raised? Did he have a good relationship with his father? Did he have an education, where did he work, did he have a wife and family of his own? What was life like in London? Had he ever been to France?

Naturally, telling them of his fictional life made them wish to learn more, and they most certainly insisted on bringing his father back to Madagascar in order to make amends before his death. And if he wished to be buried in the family tombs, then it would be done. Of course they wanted to meet his sister Julianna as well; she sounded simply lovely. He tried not to roll his eyes at that remark. The best he could do was inform them that she had little interest in her Malagasy heritage and instead had whole-heartedly embraced a proper English lifestyle.

No matter, said the Malagasy family. At the very least, she ought to meet the family, just to know that she had one. Then she could decide from there whether she truly wanted to ignore them.

Once the details of his life were exhausted, he spent another couple of weeks quizzing the lot of them on their lives. It wasn't difficult to portray ignorance of people, but he couldn't allow himself to know so much about certain events. Everything he knew about World War II and the Uprising and gaining independence had to come from "stories his father told." Because of his service and the things he experienced, he didn't say much.

So he had to listen to what others went through during that time. Most all of those who had been old enough had been imprisoned and punished in one way or another. Many of those who had been children had been sent by their families to the cities where the nationalists had their strongholds in an effort to keep them away from the burning and gunning happening in the rural villages. Rifun recalled how one of the buildings at the university where they'd holed up had been converted in something of a children's center to house all the orphaned or unaccompanied children. Those who hadn't even been born yet stayed silent and listened attentively.

"Did your father ever tell you about his time with the VVS in the twenties?"

Mahaleo asked.

Rifun shrugged. "Not really. He said that he'd been accused of being a traitor on both sides and sent to the chain gang with the rest of the nationalists."

"Well, that's true enough, I suppose. He was kind of a big deal, actually. Earned himself a name. He tell you what it was?"

"The Bastard of the VVS."

"That's right."

"He told me once that he couldn't decide if he loved or hated the name. One day it was a badge of honor, and the next day the only thing that saved his life was that none of the French believed that was who he was, and if they had believed him, they would have shot him outright rather than just imprison him."

Mahafely laughed. "True, true. Well, now that Madagascar is free, he may wear it with pride. Our grandmother, your great-grandmother, she told him once that he was not made different so that he could live like everyone else."

Rifun nodded, careful to keep his expression neutral. "He said that that was the only thing that kept him alive some days."

"Well, if you starve to death now, it's your own fault," Elisette interrupted loudly.

Food was spread out before them, and in no small portions. Rice was the main ingredient, as always, sitting in bowl large enough to bathe a small child. There were also several plates of eggs, half a dozen freshly chopped greens, a bowl of fruit, some crushed nuts, and a calf's worth of sausage. On top of all of this, there was even a fresh loaf of bread. Milk and fruit juice were passed out for beverages.

Plates were also set out at the ancestor shrine behind Volana, a tribute to the ancestors who sat among them as spirits. Specific dishes were prepared for specific ancestors, and as they were laid out, prayers of the living were murmured, most often asking for protection as they went about their work for the day. The food would remain there all day and taken away at night to be properly disposed of.

"Another day of blessed bounty," Volana said, kissing his wife as she walked by, still passing out dishes and drinks. Once everyone had everything they needed, she sat beside him and he continued. "Let us pray and thank God for this wonderful meal. And the hands that have brought it to us."

All heads save one dutifully bowed for the prayer. Rifun looked around, still mildly perplexed by the whole thing. A crucifix sat on the north wall not five feet from the shrine. Rifun could remember when the French Christians tried to destroy the shrines around Tana and Mahitsy and proclaimed damnation on those who went to the tombs to pray.

He'd been asked repeatedly why he was not a Christian, growing up under his European mother and aunt while his father was away. He'd used the excuse that he wanted to be like his father—minus his absence—and that meant observing all of the customs of his father's people. When his father returned from the war, he praised him and gave him further instruction in the old ways. He was not interested in learning the religion of those who had destroyed his country.

Some looked upon him with pity at such a remark, most of them mentioning they would pray for him. Others thought he was joking—though how they arrived at this conclusion was anyone's guess—and dismissed it as the fancies of youth. "Like father, like son," they said.

At the very least, no one could accuse him of being disrespectful. He was quiet and waited for the prayer to be over. Whenever someone sought to engage him on the subject, he remained calm throughout the discussion, though opinions were never swayed either way that he noticed. If nothing else, he thought they seemed a bit surprised that Europe was not as Christian as they had apparently been led to believe. He simply said that the wars did it. It was not a lie, he thought.

"Amen," Volana finished.

Heads lifted and the feeding frenzy began.

Fortune was not lost on Rifun as he partook in the feast. His family had fared exceptionally well in the aftermath of the war and the Uprising. The Betsileo were known not only for their kindness, but their intelligence and resilience, and the Malasay even more so. But there were plenty of families who were yet starving and begging for scraps. Whole villages had been destroyed, families ruined, and many came through the war with only their given names. Truthfully, he had been one of those people, freed from prison and having nothing more than the clothes on his back. His family had survived. Many had not.

This was not to say that the family was selfish, for they helped as many local families as they could, providing meat and eggs and fruit and even live animals to families in and around Fianarantsoa. But as they talked and laughed and ate, Rifun was very aware of how lucky they were, how their family had been blessed so mightily.

The country was independent, its people free. The family was back together and the farm was flourishing, almost as lively and productive as when he'd last seen

Nibe. He was comfortable with himself and accepted by the rest of the family.

What need did he have to remain with the Cult? He'd gone to them only in hopes of healing his scars, and he'd bounced back and forth between the Cult and the Akarin during a period of spiritual crisis, going with the Cult only out of some sense of justice and needing to kill Cassius. Now he'd gotten himself wrapped up in politics and negotiations and everything else. He didn't need that.

He'd come home to find spiritual meaning and enlightenment. Instead he'd found family and acceptance.

What if he was wrong? That was the question the spirits had posed to him when he'd first gone to the tombs. What if he'd been wrong about needing to understand the Akari, become a Builder, and go through all this nonsense with the Cult? What if he just needed to return home? He'd served his time, paid his dues, and now it was time to rest and enjoy the fruits of his labor with his family.

It was a grand sentiment, he thought, laughing at something that someone had said, and entirely within the realm of possibility. He glanced at Lalao who looked away, embarrassed. Strictly speaking, she was his first cousin once removed. Cousin marriages were rarer now than they had been, but not prohibited. And they were of an age. In his role as his own son, making them both great-grandchildren of Nibe, they were now second cousins, which would be acceptable.

Hum, perhaps it was only a fantasy, a desire to return to normal. He still went to the tombs to pray every day, and he still had to consider the effects Time and the Akari had on him. He had a lot of years left to live. As much as he liked Lalao, he liked his Akari abilities, too. Could he somehow introduce her to the Akari? Could he bring her into the light? Was it a good idea?

He took a drink of fruit juice and leaned back in his seat, listening to the hum of conversation around him. Interestingly, a Bible verse came to mind, though he could not recall its reference. What good does it do for a man to gain the world but forfeit his soul?

Was he willing to consider that he was wrong?

What if everything he needed was right here? What if his journey, his path walked along the edge of a knife, was at an end? It had to end at some point, why not now, why not here, with a loving family, prosperous farm, and a pretty girl? Maybe he should take his prayers in a new direction. After all, the Akarin mantra was "May the Author write you a happy ending." Maybe this was his happy ending.

Something about that didn't sit quite right, but it was a good thought to hang onto as breakfast came to a close and everyone began moving. All of the men, at least those thirteen and older, headed outside to the pasture.

Generally speaking, animals were not kept under strict lock and key like they were on European farms. Many times, fences were just a suggestion. In smaller villages, such fences did not even exist. Animals might be marked through scratching or brands to denote ownership, but otherwise cows and goats and sheep were free to roam where they wished.

For the Andilan farm, which was quite prosperous, fences had been erected more to keep the livestock out of certain places, like the *tanimbary* or the vineyards. When the French took over, they had more rigid fencing installed, sectioning off various swaths of land for rotational grazing. Volana had since adopted the practice and, finding it greatly beneficial to both land health and animal safety, now promoted it to other farmers, though with little success.

The zebu were loafing in a northeastern section of land. A couple of the younger boys ran ahead of the men, whooping and waving sticks to get their attention and get on their feet. As one large bull swung its huge head around, one of the boys, a fourteen year old named Faliarivo, went to his knees, leaning back and sliding under its horns, then popping right back up and running a short distance away.

"Hey, Faliarivo!" his father, Jaona, called. "You keep that up, you'll be married before you're twenty!"

The teenager laughed and continued rousing the cattle.

On Rifun's left side, Sambatra elbowed him in the ribs. "Your father told you about *savika*, right?"

"Yes. In great detail," Rifun replied, nodding. "Said that he was very good at it. Some girls even looked his way. But no family ever approved of him."

"Too bad," Jaona said, shaking his head. "Your father ever take any strikes?"

"Oh, of course. He showed me a scar on his back where he had taken a hit, said he was very lucky that it hadn't ruptured his kidney."

He remembered the incident, though it had all happened so fast he could not say he recalled many details.

"Where did he compete?" Sambatra asked. "I do not recall there being any *savika* tournaments outside of Betsileo land, especially so close to Tana."

"His mother brought him a couple times, when she wished to visit family and show him his heritage. But such trips were few and far between."

Indeed, he'd only ever competed three times, and none of them had been near Fianar, but in other villages. Of those three times, he'd only seen his mother's family twice, those who had decided to make the trip to watch him or compete themselves, and only once had he been able to have any kind of conversation with them. More often, he'd been trying to talk to girls. It was shortly after the third tournament that he'd gotten in an argument with his stepfather, struck him, and then left for Tana and the VVS.

"Maybe we should toss you in the ring, hm?" Volana suggested behind him.

"Dada, how would it be if we had to send a letter to Rivotra trying to explain why we sacrificed his son, who is inexperienced in such things, for *savika*?" Jaona scolded mildly.

"I'd be happy to try," Rifun jumped in before anyone could speak. "I'm sure he would approve of me at least trying."

The good news was, masquerading as his own son, if his skills proved to be a little rusty and subpar, no one could fault him for it. On the other hand, if he was still a decent contender, all the better for him.

Sadly, while one part of his mind said he was still fit for such activities, the more rational part of his mind told him not to push it. He was years, literally decades, out of practice and there was no telling if his blindsight could keep up, and he really didn't want to have to cheat with Time or the Akari.

"Well, for today, let's just get them moved," Jaona said.

It was not difficult, just time-consuming. The younger boys had gotten the cattle roused, but now they were beginning to wander to graze. Volana was too old to do any actual herding, but he could man the gates and the fences, closing off a few sections and opening others in order to herd the cows as gently as possible at first. Sometimes things went well, and other times they didn't.

Sambatra let out a shrill whistle followed by a great shout. He and a few others took the right flank while Jaona and three more skirted to the left. Fanevy made a motion to Rifun and they took the rear. They waved sticks and shouted, sometimes whistling, occasionally tapping a cow on the hind leg. Faliarivo and the other boys spread out with shiny objects in hand, waving them around to spook the cattle into moving.

The herd slowly figured themselves out, turning in one direction and going that way. The boys backed off. It was now on Rifun and Fanevy to keep them mobile, and on Sambatra and Jaona to keep them moving in the right direction.

Today proved to be one of the easier days. Except for one bull apparently being too close to another bull that didn't like him, followed by a small shoving match between the two, the herd moved from one paddock to another without incident, and no one was injured.

"Maybe next time we grab that spotted one and throw you in the ring with him, hm?" Volana said as he closed the gate, casting a knowing glance at Rifun. "What do you think about that?"

"Maybe I will," Rifun told him before anyone could object. "I can't let myself be outdone by fourteen year old boys." He looked at Faliarivo who grinned.

"Yes, you should practice," Jaona said. "Then you can bring your father back here to watch you compete."

"Perhaps."

The Betsileo prized family above all else, and his family seemed intent on doing everything they could to bring him, Rifun himself, back to Madagascar. With a Disguise in place to age himself, this could be done. But he couldn't be himself and his fictional son at the same time. He felt terribly disrespectful toward his family over the whole deal, but he couldn't think of a way to bring everything together.

Fence inspections had been done the day before, but they did it again anyway, just to be sure. Some of the younger men in the family liked to boast about how they had gotten the French to pay for many of the farm upgrades that they had been denied before independence. Such bragging did not go far beyond the fences as they returned to the house to consider some of the repairs that still had to be done because of French neglect, on top of finishing the new addition to the house.

It wasn't that the family didn't have money, but it was difficult to get supplies in good time. There were certain economic logistics that had to be fulfilled with national independence, all the little details that never mattered until suddenly they did.

They got done what they could, then headed inside for lunch. There was no want of food, and only the constant heavy labor, as well as the heat, kept Rifun from gaining a bunch of weight during his stay. Sometimes he wondered if he shouldn't be fasting, and his lack of observance of the ritual was the reason why the ancestors were not speaking to him.

He'd spoken to the family shaman a few times since his arrival. Seeing how many of the younger family were embracing Christianity, his role had been reduced to more of a ceremonial ritual, a decoration to be brought out at special events and holidays. But even he admitted that he now had a crucifix in his bag of charms and divination tools. He did not seem to embrace it fully, instead treating it as merely another service that he offered to the family.

As for his advice on why the ancestors were not speaking to him, the man had advised patience and commended him on his knowledge of the old ways. The way he said it, however, tipped off Rifun that the man was not entirely convinced of his role as Fanantenanirainy, son of Rivotra. If the shaman suspected who he really was, he did not say so out loud. Either he was trying to reconcile the age difference in his mind and did not wish to appear insane, or else he did not wish to disrespect someone who was clearly showing a little more power than him over aging and death.

The rest of the family made plans over lunch for afternoon chores, but Rifun did not join in, instead considering his time at the tombs. For the first time since his arrival, he found himself questioning his motives. What if he really was wrong? What if his focus should not be on how to master the Akari, become a Builder, and return to the Cult, but instead on how to best return to the family, become a part of family life again? He looked around at those gathered round the table, talking and laughing and carrying on.

There would always be someone in need of saving. Even he was not so naive as to think that all wars and conflicts would miraculously cease one day, or that his people would have smooth sailing and worry-free lives just because they were independent. No, now things got much harder. But he didn't need to be everybody's savior. What use was it to save the world and neglect his own home?

"You look deep in thought, Fan," Volana said. "Tell us, what is on your mind?"

Rifun blinked. Somehow, all eyes had turned on him. He awkwardly cleared his throat and answered, "Nothing. Just a sense that the spirits may speak to me today."

"Ah! Truly? Splendid! Always a good thing! And good for you, too, the way that you've been out there praying in sun and rain. Surely this has been a test of endurance, and you have endured."

"Yes, but now if they speak to me, I think I should be afraid and uncertain what to do," Rifun laughed.

Jaona grinned. "Yes, sometimes the biggest surprise of all is getting what we ask for."

"You will be fine," Volana told him. "It's a frightening thing, to be sure, since you did not grow up here. Yet your father seems to have taught you well enough that sometimes it almost feels like you did."

Rifun said nothing to that as his ears burned hot with embarrassment, and he hurriedly stuffed a bite of food in his mouth. The others got a good chuckle, then returned to their previous conversation. If only they knew. If only he felt that he could tell them. What would they do if he did confess to them that he was actually Rifun Ndolo? What would they say? What if they actually believed him?

Lunch ended. There was a short period for an afternoon nap, waiting out the heat of the day, and then they would reconvene for afternoon and evening work. For Rifun, he drank his fill of water, wished his family a pleasant afternoon, and left the house.

If there was any good news to be had, it was that there were a few trees around to provide relief from the worst of the heat, and Rifun made sure to take advantage of this, picking a spot where the sun would be hidden by one or more trees for most of the afternoon.

He laid out his stones and crystals and other divination charms. He laid out several offerings. He did not lay out his Book, in the event that someone walked by and happened to notice it. It was terribly bad luck—even curse worthy—to mess with an offering made at a tomb or shrine, but that didn't mean that they wouldn't go looking or ask questions later.

Once he got everything situated and arranged just so, he bowed to pray.

Some days, he had prayed earnestly with great oration and many words, pouring everything from his soul and mind as it came to him. He spoke of everything, or nearly so, being careful to disguise some of his words lest there be any eavesdroppers in the area to think him mad. He begged for guidance and answers, divine wisdom, visions, anything at all, just to let him know that they were paying him any mind.

Other days, he had bowed and lain there in absolute silence, hardly daring to breathe, focusing only on keeping his mind and soul open to the *razana* and the guidance and wisdom of the ancestors and spirits. Sometimes he invoked the Akari in this, hoping to make a connection, and other times he let it rest, content to let the spirits show him what they would.

So far the only thing he'd gotten had been the same question of whether he might be wrong. The spirits had never actually clarified what he might be wrong about, but after a few weeks, he thought he'd finally begun to understand. And if he was right, maybe the spirits would show him something more. There was no use teaching more advanced techniques to someone who couldn't grasp the basics, and what was basic to the spirits was woefully ascended compared to what most human minds were capable of and willing to perceive.

He felt good about approaching the spirits today. Perhaps it was a change of perspective or a change of heart that they had been waiting for, for his will to agree with theirs.

An hour passed.

And another.

He could not say that there was nothing different today compared to other days, for there was one distinct difference: the question of him being wrong seemed to have been removed from his mind. He could recall it, but it was like remembering a conversation versus presently engaging in one.

So if he was correct, and he had reached the conclusion the spirits had wanted him to reach, what was the next step? Why were they suddenly silent?

Or had he gotten it wrong? Had he turned away from the correct path rather than onto it? Seeing this, had the spirits given up? Why should he be so doubtful?

"So, are you ready to listen?"

Rifun's heart jumped, but he was slow to sit up. He hadn't heard anyone approach, but he knew the voice well. It belonged to Daniele Ivolo, the only human Dominion Timekeeper and the one who had trained him to be a Warden. He was sitting on a rock off to Rifun's left, between his position and the entrance to the tomb.

For a long minute, the two stared at each other. Ivolo remained kind, but Rifun was just confused. Finally he stood, went over to the former Roman soldier, and put a hand on his shoulder. Completely solid.

"Were you expecting an apparition?" Ivolo laughed as Rifun stepped back.

"You may have noticed that I've been praying," Rifun told him. "I don't know what to expect."

The man shrugged. "Well, that's fair enough, I suppose."

"Why are you here? How did you find me?"

Ivolo got off the rock. "Word gets around. I may not be Akarin, but I have friends who are. They mentioned that you were looking into Building. Given your association with the Cult, that could lead down a very dangerous path. I was concerned, thought I'd check on you. Took me a few days to track you down. Fan."

"I can't be myself, you know that."

"Oh, I'm not blaming you, not at all. I completely understand. It just made finding you a tiny bit more difficult. But then, the chickens come home to roost eventually, don't they?"

Rifun nodded. "And that's what I'm considering now."

"Oh?"

"I live with my family, Daniele. I'm a part of their lives. They're a part of mine. Lalao is of an age and unmarried. Or if not her, then others. I'm accepted. I've finally gotten what I've always wanted, and I don't want to pass it up."

Ivolo took a few steps back and leaned against the rock, folding his arms. "Well, this is a new take on things. Far cry from the man I remember training to become a Warden." He gestured to the offerings. "Can I assume, then, that all this is looking for approval from the spirits for such a decision?"

"They've challenged me for the last few weeks with a simple question. I believe I have answered it. I wish to know if I'm right."

The Roman nodded. "And what if you are?"

"Then I suppose I shall have to come up with a way to bring myself here as an old man, perhaps fake my death, and then I, as Fan, will stay here with my family."

"Sounds like a good plan. Does this mean that you would give up Time and the Akari?"

Rifun sighed. "I don't have an answer for that yet."

Ivolo stood up straight. "No, of course not. But I'm sure you will, in time. As long as the bridge is stable, it is not always required to see the other side."

"Quite the wise man yourself, hm? Two thousand years teach you that?"

He grinned. "No. Only three." He shifted his stance. "Speak humble words to one who is happy, that the roots of pride do not take hold. Speak true words to one who is curious, that they may see no error in you. Speak kind words to one who is sad, that they may see hope and shun despair. Speak bold words to one who is proud, that they may see a mirror and be confronted by their error. Speak no words to one who is angry, for one must smother a flame by depriving it of fuel." He shrugged. "Paraphrasing, of course."

Rifun nodded uncertainly. "Things have certainly changed around here. Mostly for the better."

"Yes, independence and freedom is a wonderful thing. Living with a loving family is unmatched."

"Do you have family? I don't recall that you did while we were training together."

"I didn't, but I do now. And, ah, let me say that sometimes being able to go dark is a blessing. Having two ex-wives is not something I would recommend. On the other hand, I love my three daughters." He appeared conflicted.

"Are any of them exposed to Time?" Rifun wondered.

"The oldest is only nine, so no."

"Are you going to expose them? Or at least tell them about it?"

"Honestly, I haven't decided. I'll cross that bridge when I come to it."

"But only if it's stable, right?"

Ivolo forced a laugh. "I suppose so. Certainly I cannot see the other side." He stretched a bit. "Well, I'm glad to see that you are doing well for yourself. Seems as though things are really improving for you. I wish you happy days and smooth sailing, and God bless your endeavors."

"May the Author write us all a happy ending," Rifun told him, reciting the mantra of the Akarin.

"Indeed."

Ivolo used a portal to depart the tombs, leaving Rifun alone once more.

Had that been his answer from the spirits? Had they brought his old mentor to him in order to communicate with him? After all, what were the odds that the same day he had his spiritual revelation, that Ivolo would show up and show all support for his decision?

Was that it, then? Did he just gather his things and go home?

Even if that were basically true, he ought to at least spend a little time thanking the ancestors for answering him, and in such a kind, straightforward way. He owed them that much. He was definitely going to be asking for more help to pull off his little switcheroo charade, killing himself but returning as his own son. Take nothing for granted, and always show appreciation.

He stayed at the tombs for another hour or so, thanking the spirits, but also delaying in case they had anything else to tell him, any more people to visit or any more questions to plant in his mind. The sun moved around and the shadows danced, and finally he sat up.

Carefully, he packed up his things, stood, stretched, winced at a pain in his shoulder, then departed.

Normally his prayers would see him at the tombs until nightfall. When he returned even before sunset, it caused quite the stir in the family.

"You were correct, then," Volana guessed. "The spirits spoke to you."

"Judging by the air in your steps, it seems to be good news," Sambatra observed.

"They did speak," Rifun told them. "I must return to London as soon as possible and fetch my father."

There was much ado about this, cheering and celebrating and whatnot, and Rifun was forced to wonder what the party would be like once he actually returned. The Malagasy, and especially the Betsileo, were not known for small parties.

But that was neither here nor there. Dinner was a grand affair that evening, every family member giving some message to Rifun for him to pass on to his father. He promised that he would, knowing that there was no way he was going to remember all the messages, or which message came from which person. Even so, he was right there receiving those messages, and they made him feel pretty special nonetheless.

"You should bring your sister, too," Elisette told him. "Even if she chose a more English lifestyle, she should at least meet the family. And we wish to meet her."

"I will do my best," Rifun promised.

It was all he could do. Truthfully, he wasn't even sure how he was going to break the news to Julianna. How did he tell her that he was leaving the Cult? If he kept her in the dark, then he would just return as himself and say that his daughter had adamantly refused and his son had had other obligations for the time being. Simple, easy to remember, and it cleared him from having to be both himself and his son at the same time. If he faked his death soon enough, he could still come back as his son.

He could work out the details later. He had a couple weeks to spare for his fake trip, the plane back home, convincing his father, packing, getting the necessary papers and whatnot, then flying back to Madagascar. He had time.

Famous last words, he was sure.

He helped with evening chores, then returned to the house to sit around outside and enjoy the coolness of the approaching night. Drinks were had and there was much lively conversation and merriment.

Yes. This must be it. He'd been wrong about the Cult, or at the very least, wrong to stay with them so long and assume a leadership position. That was not his destiny.

On the other hand, if that was not his destiny, then what was? What had been accomplished while he'd been away, really? Becoming a Warden Timekeeper? Good, but that benefited only him. Joining the Cult and assuming political leadership? While a difficult task that he had gracefully navigated, it was far from complete as the others began the next phase of their takeover of the Wheel. It might be that he had simply been tasked with getting them to that point—spirits knew that they'd been in shambles when he'd come along—but it felt...incomplete. After all, Julianna had brought him in with the intent of killing Cassius. He'd forced an alliance with Cassius in order to find the Book of Abilities. Neither of these things had been accomplished.

He took a drink and watched a couple of the teenage boys wrestle in the dirt. He remembered doing that with his brothers, always letting them win so they would have no excuse to hate him. Well, see how that worked out.

If he didn't return to the Cult, how likely were they to just let him walk away? He had no fear of Julianna. Cassius might be glad to be rid of him, but that didn't mean he might not return later to try and kill him, and possibly everyone in the house. Isthim probably wouldn't come after him; she held no lasting affections for him, and she would likely treat it just as a logistical issue. One soldier down, compensate in some other way. And they might see it as the removal of a barrier, since he was the political medium. It might make it easier for them to take over the Cult completely.

Hm...that didn't sound like a good thing. A Borelian was bad. A Time Agent Borelian was worse. An Akari-bearer Borelian? He was loathe to consider the ramifications.

But who was to say that it wouldn't have happened eventually?

Given the tumultuous start to the Cult and its notorious continuing instability, it probably never would have happened. Cassius running into Isthim was, for all intents and purposes, pure luck. The Akarin had been better run and the Borelians weren't exactly flocking to their doors.

Suddenly the idea of settling down with his family again felt a little less certain. Maybe he just had cold feet. Maybe it had to do with this whole bid to fake his death and live as his own son.

He thought about Nibe's words. Rivotra Andilan could stay on the farm, but he would never marry, never have children, and he would die at a young age. Did that still apply? Was there an expiration on that? Or was his life as Fan a way to sidestep it? Prophecies could be very confusing at times.

Well, as he'd figured before, he had a little time to think over the details. Maybe he would inform Julianna of his plans, see what she had to say about it. Might be that everything was running smoother without him there, and it was decided that it would be better for him to leave. That he could handle, he thought.

He took another drink, leaned back, and closed his eyes.

"Come now, Fan, you cannot be tired already," Jaona said, elbowing him. "You spent too many nights at the tombs for me to believe that, unless you slept there."

"No, I didn't," Rifun said, grinning.

"I think the drinks are taking a toll on him," Sambatra said on his other side. "I thought the British liked their pubs?"

"They do, but I don't normally partake." That, at least, was true.

"Well then, don't overdo it." Jaona took his glass. "You're already going to regret it come morning."

He knew. He didn't care.

It was well late in the night, or perhaps even early in the morning, when they finally remembered their need for sleep and decided to go inside. Rifun slipped under the mosquito net covering his mattress and stretched out as best he could. All around him were the sounds of boys and men settling in, all the bachelors of the family.

He thought about Lalao, in the women's room. Did she think about him the way he thought about her? He'd been too shy to broach the subject, while he'd still been praying and seeking answers. Now that he had a course of action, maybe he could bring it up. Once the death of Rivotra had been sufficiently mourned and he could return as Fan. It was still a bit strange, the thought of dating a girl with the same name as his mother, but he could get over that, he was sure.

He rolled over and settled in. With any luck, this whole endeavor would be wrapped up within a few months. And no one else in the family would have any idea what had transpired.

12 | Awọn Ọre ati Awọn Alabašepọ — Friends and Allies

The Caves of Meroian, 1964

kokumβo

The Gentleman Killers had been a force to be reckoned with when they'd had hierarchy and orders coming from the Tacagans. With the head of their operation effectively blown off, the underlings had scattered, only loosely regrouping into factions, much as things had been before the Tacagans took over after the rejected elections. This made them easy pickings for the decidedly less-gentlemanly killers whom they'd displaced.

The Korin mercenaries were surprisingly more ruthless than Cassius had expected them to be. He'd expected their innate sense of balance to be as much, if not more of a hindrance as a moral compass. This proved to be largely incorrect. Apparently there were loopholes in this balancing act that permitted them to act as mercenaries. In spite of this, or perhaps because of this, however, it made picking a target exceptionally difficult. Cassius had a list of names of lesser-ranked Gentleman Killers. He figured that it would be as simple as basic logistics of any assassination, but then that damn balancing had to come into play.

"Yu-bix killed thirty-five people after the elections," Kokriloff said. "We have twenty-eight between us. It will narrow the gap."

"But Rnluv Kril slaughtered what amounts to three baliks," Dubikoff argued. "If three of us go after him, the fourth can go after someone else."

Apparently balancing did not take outsiders into account, Cassius mused. But then, they had invoked one of those balancing loopholes to be able to include him in the plan, calling him the fulcrum of decision. A tiebreaker, in common vernacular.

Surloff shifted his stance. "We could also go after Murdi and Lordo, the twin assassins from Maronet. Certainly that would be a balanced affair."

Barnoff just nodded. "Agreed."

Cassius rubbed his face. "Why don't we plan to go after all of them? Three can go after Rnluv Kril while the fourth one and I go after Yubix. Once that's done, then we can go after the twin assassins."

The four Korin looked at each other, discussed this, and apparently determined that all the math and all the stars balanced out. Then there was a secondary discussion over who went with Cassius to kill Yu-bix. It was agreed that the honor belonged to Surloff. The reasoning for this was a rather drawn-out affair, one Cassius did not care to listen to. Actually, he was greatly annoyed by this whole debacle and figured that in the time it took the Korin to get ready, he probably could have killed all four Gentleman Killers plus a fifth as a bonus prize. But two things had never been clearer: first, the reason the Korin had been attracted to the more elegant breed of mercenary known as the Gentleman Killers; second, the reason they hadn't been highly regarded by them.

Then they were underway, and none too soon, for Cassius' patience had all but worn out. At least traveling with only one Korin meant he did not have to deal with group discussion for every minor decision. It was a wonder that each dynasty lasted only eighty-one years, or perhaps that was how long it took to balance things and pick the next ruling dynasty. And if odd numbers were unlucky, then why were nine and eighty-one sacred numbers? Bah, more cultural complexities he didn't care to learn.

Yu-bix Krelin was a Poyrai from Resil. Poyrai stood perhaps eight to ten feet tall and appeared insect-like in their otherwise humanoid physique, including a rather tough exoskeleton. All were brightly colored, either red, orange, or yellow, and some had wasp-like wings with full flight capabilities. In keeping with their insect qualities, Poyrai were also capable of lifting and carrying, with ease, up to fifty times their body weight. When the average male Poyrai weighed six hundred pounds, well, even a glancing blow might sting a little.

Another interesting tidbit about the Poyrai was that they had six distinct sexes. Yu-bix belonged to the one that had wings, was colored yellow, and preferred solitary living outside of mating season. This made it easier to track him down to an area of dense jungle vegetation and a rather large waterfall tumbling into a crystalline pool just ahead of frothing rapids.

"Tobar Poyrai prefer to live in the trees so they can attack prey from above and quickly fly off with it," Surloff said, walking behind Cassius as they pressed through dense vegetation.

"What's a tobar?" Cassius asked, irritably pushing aside a fern.

"The sexual distinction of Yu-bix Krelin. Few aliens have sexes outside of male and female—including your own—so the native words must be used."

"God, now you sound like Rifun."

"I did appropriate research."

"What does sexual distinction have to do with locating and killing someone? If they're destined to die, they're destined to die."

"It is simply something that came up in research."

Cassius scoffed, shook his head, and did not pursue the matter further. Dead was dead, and he was no archaeologist. Of course, what did he expect? Well-liked or not, Surloff had once been a Gentleman Killer, and such elegance and due diligence was expected of such people.

"Why do your people change your names with each dynasty?" he asked. "Doesn't it get confusing?"

"Not for us," Surloff replied expectedly. "Although it can be so for outsiders. And we understand. But it is a sign of respect and balance, harmony with the ruling dynasty."

"Why not just call yourself Irigian or something?"

He did not look back, but if noise was any indication, Surloff had stopped moving. "That would be terribly disrespectful to Irig, and disruptive to the balance of the cosmos. There must always be inside and outside. Above and below. Irig is outside and above. We must be inside and below."

Cassius paused and turned.

He did not get a chance to speak. Only the slightest gust of wind provided warning of the aerial attack, and only a heightened perception of Time and ability to Band saved Surloff from being a snack for a very large bipedal insect.

Without his prey, Yu-bix Krelin landed with a huge thud that shook the earth. Surloff slithered out of the way and went to stand beside Cassius who had drawn his knife.

"Well, well, well," Yu-bix said, straightening. "This is a surprise. I might have expected the little Korin to run away back to their own people and beg for forgiveness. That is a kind of balance, isn't it? Sin and forgiveness?"

Surloff snorted like a true rhino.

"No matter," the Poyrai went on. "I'll eat you all the same."

Cassius could see that he went for a Band and tried to fly at the same time. It was no difficult feat to rip apart Yu-bix's Band. Were he and Surloff average Timekeepers, this would have been potentially the extent of things. The Akari, however, allowed them to use Gravity to make it so Yu-bix was unable to fly.

The Poyrai, evidently unprepared for this sudden turn of events, paused for just a moment to panic. Cassius rushed forward, intending to stick it with his knife. Just before he got to Yu-bix, there was a Band, a great surge in gravitational strength, and a small earthquake that knocked him forward on his face a split-second before getting covered in sticky goo.

Cassius wasted no time, jumping up and looking for a fight. Instead, all he found was a squashed bug that had once been Yu-bix Krelin. Cassius whirled on Surloff who had not moved.

"I was ready to fight him!" he roared.

Surloff was unmoved. "The gravitational force that was simply keeping Yu-bix from flying would have been enough to kill you. Besides, our only goal was to ensure his death."

Cassius would not say that he did not Band so he could roar his frustration and possibly think about killing Surloff and blaming Yu-bix. He very nearly did it, too. He refrained only for the hope that he and the others might still be useful in the future. They still had to go after the twin assassins Murdi and Lordo after all.

Finally he dropped the Band and sighed. "Fine."

"Perhaps next time, we should discuss a plan of action beforehand," Surloff suggested.

His suggestion was probably genuine, but Cassius still hated him for it. He didn't research. He didn't plan. He figured out who his target was, where they were going to be, and then he went and killed them. No muss, no fuss, no balancing, no consulting stars, just death.

"Fine, whatever," Cassius repeated. "Yu-bix is dead and that's all that matters. We'll return to the ruins to wait for the others, and then, assuming no one is injured, we'll go after Murdi and Lordo."

For once, Surloff did not object or offer up any Korin insight, and the two of them returned to the ruins without incident. Barnoff, Dubikoff, and Kokriloff had not yet returned. Cassius took the opportunity to wash Yu-bix's entrails off him and inspect himself for any foreign germs or other microorganisms. Another benefit of the Akari, not having to worry about foreign diseases because he could isolate them within himself and eradicate them. Sure, such feats were feasible at the highest levels of Timekeeper and Harvester training, but the Akari made it so much easier.

Afterwards they headed to the officers building. It wasn't twenty minutes before the remaining three Korin mercenaries returned, looking no worse for wear.

"Success?" Cassius inquired politely.

"Most assuredly," Kokriloff reported. "All balanced well. Small injuries were sustained, but were then healed."

"Very good. And we're ready to go after Murdi and Lordo?"

"We should have a plan," Surloff and Dubikoff said simultaneously. The two looked at each other, made some gestures, and it was Dubikoff who continued speaking. "The twin assassins might have been the greatest of the Gentleman Killers except for their 'difficulty' in paying tithes to the Tacagans. Their lack of rank came not from lack of skill, but lack of dues."

Cassius frowned but nodded. "All right, then. What do you suggest?"

The twin assassins were Mishim from the planet Maronet, Quadrant Two, Parsec Eight, Sector Sixteen, System Forty-Three, Planet Ninety-Six. Maronet was occupied by the Lilir, although the two peoples had formed a sort of symbiotic relationship. Both peoples operated under mafia-style governments, and they had close dealings with the Gentleman Killers, so it was no wonder that Murdi and Lordo had fit right in, save for the unpaid taxes to the Tacagans.

As for Time, they were both Physician Harvesters. They couldn't kill at a touch as Cassius could when he'd been merely a Harvester, but they seemed to have perfected the art of face-transfer. It was a bleed-over ability, when the Akari had been diluted by the Time industry. Similar to Disguise, a skilled Harvester could take the DNA of a victim and, depending on his level of skill, either alter himself with it or even transfer it to someone else. All Harvesters eventually took on traits of the victims, although it was a slow process. Such intent was therefore reserved for either the highest levels of instruction or else the greatest stubbornness of a lesser student.

Just finding the twin assassins could prove a challenge, Cassius thought. The Akari had an ability called Test, which would reveal a temporary Disguise, but it was useless if the DNA had been permanently altered.

"Do we know if they have any current contracts?" he wondered aloud. "Maybe we can't pick them out in a crowd alone, but if we track them from a victim, we may have better luck."

"The last we knew of, Murdi and Lordo had retreated to Maronet to serve the Mishim solely, forsaking the Gentleman Killers," Dubikoff stated. "This could prove an advantage as our search area has shrunk, but Maronet is not the most hospitable to mercenary competition."

"Sounds like an excellent balancing of the scales, then," Cassius said snidely.

"Does anyone know where they live?"

No one did, though it was helpful to limit the possibilities to areas of Maronet solidly controlled by the Mishim. This was still a vast expanse of land, however, and Cassius allowed the Korin to go to the Archives in the Wheel to do their coveted research. After all, it was unbalanced to have experience only with no knowledge. If one gained knowledge, he could balance it out with experience, but not the other way around. Of course.

He told them to meet him at a certain place on Maronet, and they made their way to the tunnels to open their respective portals.

Maronet as a whole seemed to be a very bleak place, Cassius thought, or maybe it was just the particular city he'd chosen. It wasn't that they didn't have sunlight or brightly-colored vegetation, but the general atmosphere of the place was rather depressing. The social scene was not very social as everyone seemed to keep to pre-determined groups.

Of course, the Mishim ruled through the mafia. There were probably a dozen different factions or families vying for power here. He just had to find the one that hated the twin assassins enough to want them gone and not care who did the deed.

The Mishim were humanoid, but unlike some species that were perfectly comfortable running around with minimal clothing, or even no clothing at all, they spoke as much with their dress as any words. It was difficult to tell the average height and weight of the people, for it seemed as though this season's fashion revolved around how many layers one could possibly wear before being rendered nearly immobile. Cassius passed by several Mishim — their age and sex impossible to guess — who wore at least seven coats and a dozen hats all stacked on top of one another. Only through sheer exposure to them thanks to their work with the Gentleman Killers did he even know that their skin was almost like tree bark, and it was shed annually, like a snake.

He ducked into a business that looked a bit promising. He might have picked a tavern, if he were hunting someone on Earth, but given the latest fashion trends, he decided a coat store might be better. See, he could deduce things, too.

"Welcome," a man, presumably the store owner, or at least a common worker, greeted. He paused when he came around a rack of coats and saw Cassius. "Well now, we don't get too many visitors these days. A second layer of welcome to you."

"Thanks," Cassius said stiffly. "Unfortunately, I'm not here for a coat."

"I see. Well, you will notice that coats are all I have to sell." He gestured around generally, nodding to several browsing customers. "But perhaps I can give you directions to your destination?"

"Yes, perhaps you might. I'm looking for Murdi and Lordo."

Something about the man's posture and expression—hidden though it was amid several layers of scarves—told Cassius that this was not an ordinary coat store, and that the customers whom the man had nodded to had not been ordinary customers.

So it was that five bodies and one destroyed business later, Cassius was able to procure some information about the twin assassins' last known whereabouts and possible destination. He meandered out of the shop, leaving the owner tied to one of the racks, and ran into the Korin.

"I got information the hard way. You got it the polite way," Cassius said, pulling on a jacket that was much too big for him but he liked the looks of. "Let's see who was more productive."

His way turned out to be more productive, or so it seemed at the time. The Korin were able to find where the twin assassins had been born and their last official place of residence. Like the coat store, however, it was, at best, only a pretext meant to weed out amateur sleuths and give them a head start on escape if need be.

Cassius' information took them to a village about four hundred miles northeast of the city, where the layered fashion was not so insane. Here were the more common folk. It did not make them innocent of the mafia-style dealings that went on in Mishim government, but at least they were out of the lair of the beast.

If anyone knew who Cassius was, they didn't say anything. Nor did they raise an alarm to the sight of the four Korin mercenaries. But there was no disguising the looks; hatred and suspicion abounded. Of course there wouldn't be any outright violence. They were too polite and elegant for that. While the Mishim and Lilir might brag about rarely ever stepping foot on the battlefield, that didn't mean they didn't wage war. They just preferred to do it with politics and psychology.

Rifun would fit right in here, Cassius thought dryly.

It wasn't until they hit the proverbial town square that they started to get the feeling that something wasn't quite right, and it wasn't because they were walking down the wrong alley at the wrong time of day. Cassius paused, and the Korin did as well, noting how the townsfolk moved to surround them, though still at a relatively safe distance.

"Is this how you treat all your guests?" Cassius asked. "I can see why tourism is so bad."

"We knew the Tacagans would come," someone said.

The crowd parted and a Mishim approached wearing a fancy coat that Cassius could only guess was an official uniform of some kind. But if they ruled through the mafia, was an official policing force really necessary? They seemed to think so.

"I am no Tacagan," Cassius spat. "And my companions are certainly not Tacagans."

"No, but you are human, as the Tacagans are. And you are all known mercenaries."

"What of it?"

"The Mishim government has separated itself from the Tacagans and will conduct our own affairs. We will not be subject to Tacagan law and whim. But neither will we suffer the scum to degrade our good name, trying to take advantage of apparent chaos to attempt to better themselves and make decay live once more."

Only the sharp eye and sharper reflexes of one of the Korin saved them from being suddenly and swiftly assassinated, Banding the group so they could dodge a blow from behind.

The five of them took up a circle defense as two Mishim—all signs pointed to Murdi and Lordo—began circling them. Their fashion was out of sync with the rest of the people. They wore only a single layer of clothing, a simple shirt and pair of pants with a single long jacket over top, a single wide-brimmed hat (one twin having an enormous feather sticking out), and boots. But what Cassius was more interested in was the long, sharp metal they had in their hands, swords fashioned in the likeness of a katana, but with wickedly jagged edges designed for ripping flesh.

All of this appeared to be a distraction, however, as the twins began moving. Unlike Timekeepers who could use Bands to creatively make it appear as though they were everywhere and nowhere, the twins used portals to keep on the move and out of reach of anything Cassius and the Korin had to throw at them. One minute, Cassius was trying to use Gravity against one twin, and the next thing he knew, the twin was already across the square. Sometimes they opened tiny micro-portals, stabbing their swords through and catching one of them, slicing open an arm, a side. One of the Korin took a heavy blow to his horn which caused him to stumble off balance and crash into his fellow.

Just as Cassius was reaching for a Band to bring everything to a halt so he could kill the bastards with their own swords, the twins weaponized the portals. Rather than open a portal and step through, they took the portal itself and moved it. Five times in rapid succession, they flung a portal at the mercenaries, swallowing them up and sending them to all different places, all far away from Maronet.

Frustrated from the fight—or lack thereof—and disoriented from the rather unorthodox portal travel, Cassius found that the only thing he could do was sit down wherever it was that he'd landed.

He should have just done like Surloff had done with Yu-bix. Skip the formalities and the fight and just squash the bug.

But that was neither here nor there, and he got to his feet on unsteady legs. He could go back, he figured. Surprise them, Band, kill them, go home. Unfortunately, his strength and his interest had waned. He'd gotten in his fights for the day, killed plenty of scum to satisfy him. At the very least, he should find out where the Korin had ended up.

He returned to the ruins first, pleasantly surprised and not a little relieved that two of the four had apparently had the same idea. They waited for him outside the officers building, talking and looking both annoyed and worried.

"Well, you two made it," Cassius observed. "Where are the others?"

"We have not seen Barnoff or Kokriloff," Dubikoff stated. "But we are relieved to see that you are well."

"I'm alive." He huffed. "It hasn't been that long, and the unique portal travel was disorienting. Maybe they were more disoriented from it than we were. We'll give them a few more minutes."

"Murdi and Lordo were rather talented in their use of portals," Surloff mused. "I've not seen anything like that before."

"Indeed not," Dubikoff agreed. "Considering the nature of portals as the bridge between fixed points in..."

Cassius tuned them out as they delved into discussion and theories of portal travel. Maybe Barnoff and Kokriloff would return soon and spare him the lecture.

The missing Korin turned up about ten minutes later. They did look as though they hadn't fared as well as the rest of them when it came to the portals, but they were upright and talking, anyway.

"I'm just going to take a guess that you aren't enthusiastic about the prospect of returning to Maronet?" Cassius questioned.

"We should not return so soon," Surloff warned. "We should rest, regroup, take what we have learned and come up with a new plan."

"Some battles are won, and some are lost," Dubikoff agreed.

How the hell do your people wage war? Cassius wondered.

"We have succeeded in our earlier missions. We have learned much. We should do some practice of our own now, in the Akari," Kokriloff suggested.

It was the polite way of telling Cassius to make good on his end of the bargain and teach them something beyond what Isthim was teaching. It was the last thing he really felt like doing, and he would have to get a message to Pilory about it, too. He sighed but nodded. "Fine. Give me an hour to recuperate myself."

The Korin did not seem displeased by the idea, and Cassius retreated into the officers building, making for his chambers. Getting a message to Pilory was not difficult, but then he was left alone for a time. This may not have been a problem, except now he had to come up with some kind of lesson plan, like he was a teacher or something. Handing out candy and appetizers was one thing, something to string people along so he could either use them or else hand them off to Isthim. This time, he was the one they were actually coming to in order to learn something. And he'd promised them something spectacular, or at least outside of the common grunt work.

His grand idea of having secret students didn't sound so grand now, he thought, but it could still prove useful. Like Rifun, he just couldn't teach them everything. Give them something nice, as promised, but reserve the best for himself so he could kill them later if he had to.

He received Pilory's confirmation soon enough, but still had time left in his one hour.

He considered the incident on Maronet. His rage had been reduced to a frustrated simmer, tempered only by his own curiosity about the way the twins had used portals. He'd seen such skill only once before, a time he could not recall, but he had dismissed it as a fluke, an optical illusion, his brain trying to reconcile what it was seeing with what it wanted to see with what it thought it was seeing. This time, he'd been fully cognizant of his surroundings and the fight itself, and he knew what he'd seen.

Right there in the middle of his chambers, he opened a portal. To keep things safe, the destination was one of the tunnels outside the ruins, close enough to the cavern that there was still enough light to see what lay beyond.

Try as he might, he could not figure out how to move the portal. He may as well have tried to move any of the doorways in the officers building, and there he might have better luck. He could close the portal and reopen it well enough, but moving it seemed to be out of the question.

Perhaps he ought to go after the twin assassins by himself, capture them, and then force them to show him how such a thing was done.

No. He needed to learn it on his own. He couldn't stand the thought of mere Time Agents being able to do something he couldn't, not when he dictated the will of the Author and had the spirits themselves to train him. Clearly it was an advanced ability, but how did he go about mastering it? What were its secrets? Could it be something he had forgotten from the Book of Abilities? His interest in finding the journal suddenly jumped.

He did not get to debate this long before his hour apparently timed out and his entourage came looking for him. Damn their punctuality. It was better than keeping him waiting, he supposed.

"Where will we go to train?" Barnoff wondered.

"There's a spot outside the city that we can use for today," Cassius told him smoothly. Truthfully, he hadn't given it much thought. "We'll be out of the way of the rest of the recruits. I have one more to round up. I will meet you at the south gate."

The Korin agreed, and they parted ways.

Cassius met Pilory in the Wheel.

"Are you ready to learn something extraordinary?" he asked her.

"I am," she told him, her body language agreeing. "I hope to learn something to help myself, and if it's interesting enough, maybe I can convince Titik to give you another chance."

"Does he know you're here?"

"Everyone takes time to himself now and again. What someone does with his time doesn't matter, so long as it isn't theft or mutiny. Going after a little side treasure is more likely to get me in trouble if I don't share."

Cassius grinned. "I like how you think."

They returned to the ruins, Pilory initially skeptical of the dark portal and the tunnels. Cassius grabbed her hand to guide her through, but she was stiff as a board. Even when they emerged into the cavern and overlooked the ruins, she remained stiff, eyes darting about anxiously.

"The sun should be coming around soon," he told her, unsure if it was even true. "What's the matter? Don't like feeling trapped in a cage?"

"Tibidi don't do well underground," Pilory replied in a small voice. "The cavern is nice, but it's still...underground. That fissure is the only thing keeping me sane right now."

She followed him down the slope toward the city, hovering most of the way as if to reassure herself that she wasn't trapped.

"What's the difference between this place and Titik's ship? That's enclosed, and the only place to go is out into space."

"Yes, but there are many windows to see out into space, into the stars. Here, there's nothing. Only darkness. Only the cold cave walls."

This was probably the part in the conversation where Cassius ought to offer some encouragement, a feel-good sentiment, maybe a friendly reassurance. He wasn't good at those, and he found himself liking Pilory less and less. She no longer appeared to be the spunky go-getting space pirate with an attitude. Now she was just frightened prey in a trap.

He hoped she was a quick study and could show Titik something to bring him back around.

They met up with the Korin at the south gate. Cassius did not have a particular place picked out, but he knew of a large sandy area about a quarter mile or so around the lakeshore. Unless one wanted to fly or swim there, it could only be accessed from a narrow path and a short tunnel along the edge of the cavern. The clearing was about forty or fifty yards in diameter, the surrounding rock walls averaging sixteen feet tall when they weren't part of the cavern wall itself. With their proximity to the fissure, Cassius noted that Pilory seemed much more relaxed.

A thought crossed his mind. What if she got scared and took off through the fissure? Could Tibidi fly that high? If she somehow discerned the location of the ruins, would she tell, or could she keep a secret? Being a pirate and all, he imagined the latter. But just to be sure, should he induct her in as a full Cult member and give her all the rules?

Well, first he would assess her potential. It may be that she was an idiot and any further instruction would be wasted. He doubted this, as idiots didn't tend to last long as pirates, but he wanted to be sure.

As for the Korin, they looked ready and eager to learn, like four rhinos about to charge just for the fun of it. Good. He liked enthusiasm. He just hoped he wasn't digging himself a hole here, taking on students like this. He turned around, tried to judge whether they could be seen from the city. It didn't appear so, unless someone could see through solid rock, or if they happened to be flying above the city. Was there a way to Disguise a location? Could he somehow make it so that everything looked perfectly normal?

An investigation for another day, he decided. He didn't even know if or how this was going to work. He would worry about the more minor details later. He turned to face his class.

"If you're here today, it's because you want to learn something substantial," he began. "More than the baby steps Isthim is teaching." *And good riddance to her.* "If that's not why you're here, if you consider yourself to be an idiot and a fool, leave now."

No one moved.

Cassius nodded. "Good. All that said, things will be fast and hard. I expect you to learn swiftly. You can strengthen and refine in your own time, but here is where you will learn the basics. Understood?"

Variations of "yes, sir," were heard.

He had no clue what he was doing. He didn't even know what he was going to teach them. So he did what any good teacher in such a situation did. He made them demonstrate what they already knew. He first asked for the basics, and then he wanted them to perform what they perceived to be the most advanced or difficult trick they knew.

The Korin, having been exposed to and training in the Akari for a little while now, could work with Matter and Energy. One chose to demonstrate a Disguise in which he cycled through several Korin genetic traits in his DNA. Many jokes were made about how to make one's horn bigger. Another chose to demonstrate a Light ability he'd been working with on his own time with no formal instruction. The third showed off that he could take the water in the lake — or at least a small handful of it — and separate it into its base elements. The fourth took a rock and, sucking it dry of all its water, crumbled it to dust.

Pilory was not so talented, and she watched in awe of the Korin. When it came her turn to demonstrate her greatest ability, however, she was able to manage multiple micro-portals simultaneously with some skill, throwing rocks through them to simulate projectiles or other means.

"The best I've ever managed was eight," she said, "but my steady average is five."

"Comes in handy in space piracy, does it?" Cassius inquired, more curious than mocking.

"It can, yes. When your opponent expects grand opposition, sometimes the best way to get around it is with a small operation instead."

"Indeed."

He bade them return to their original positions. He knew what he wanted them to do.

"You've demonstrated a wide range of abilities and talents. And you've been brought here today because of your potential, because you want to learn more than whatever elementary teaching Isthim is giving the grunts. So today, we're going to Disguise the city."

The five students glanced at each other. It was Kokriloff who asked, "What do you mean?"

"I mean that the city itself is no longer in shambles. It is no longer a dead archaeological dig. But it should look that way to outsiders. We can't chance an exposure because someone got curious about what might be going on in otherwise empty caves."

"But Disguises are dependent on time, strength, and the abilities of the one who constructs it. And it's usually tied to DNA," Barnoff said. "How shall we Disguise rocks so that it lasts longer than a few hours?"

Cassius nodded. "It will take time to perfect a project of this scale. We're not going to finish today. But we will start it today. Consider this a class project for the year. Or the semester. Depends on how quickly you learn and apply."

The prospect seemed to intrigue them, and it relieved Cassius for it bought him time to figure out where he was going with this.

He hated to admit it, but Rifun had been right. He was unsatisfied with a realized action because he was too in love with the ideas in his head. Ideas could be manipulated and refined in a way that was uniquely impossible in the real world, regardless of any abilities they may possess. Everything in his head always went according to plan, and he could play God to an astronomical degree, giving himself a high like nothing else could.

Things were harder in the real world. There were too many variables to contend with, the most frustrating one being free will. There was also the aspect of time, having to wait for results. And actually having to work for those results. And the prospect, and sometimes reality, of failure. At least in his head, he could do anything, skip ahead in the timeline, go straight to the finish.

For example. He rather enjoyed the idea of having secret students and a secret army, and he could easily imagine taking ten thousand secretly-trained aliens to bear against, not only Rifun and Julianna, but also Isthim and the Borelians, and defeating and killing everyone. But in the present moment, in the real world, he had five people who were barely trained. Plus, if he put them to work Disguising the city, that wasn't keeping them very secret. Furthermore, what did he do afterwards? After he killed Rifun and Julianna and Isthim and the Borelians, what then? After the party, what happened next? It was like escaping to Africa. He'd done it. He'd delivered his people to their homeland. There was rejoicing and weeping...and then people just started leaving. Yes, they wanted to go home, but...would it have really been too much to ask for a little more worship?

"All right, stop here," he said.

He'd brought them to a rocky ledge overlooking the city. During the day, when the sun was over the fissure, it was easier to pick out the buildings and the wall and everything else. For the time being, the light was dim and fading fast. The only way to spot the buildings and such was by the lanterns and fires and any Light tricks going on. But, by all accounts, it was a living city.

"What would be your first step to Disguising the city?" he asked. "How would you make it so people would not give this a second look?"

"Too many lights," Dubikoff answered. "Light attracts the eye."

"All right, then. Let's turn off the lights. But only from our perspective, an outside perspective."

Cassius watched as the light bent, flickered, wavered, dimmed, scattered, but never truly went out. After a moment, it all came back.

"I'm sorry," Dubikoff puffed. "I've only just begun to consider Light and—"

"As I said before, this is going to be a difficult project and will not be completed today," Cassius said calmly. "But just consider that you are free to return to Isthim at any time if you want to give up."

That statement rattled the Korin a bit, and he tried several more times to turn off the lights. After the sixth attempt, Cassius grew bored and waved a hand. "Enough, enough. Besides the lights, what else would you do to turn someone's eye away?"

"The buildings," Surloff suggested.

"What about them?"

"They've been restored, or they're being restored. They should still appear as though they are in a ruined, broken down state."

"And how would you do this?"

The Korin shifted his stance. "I do not know. Rocks lack the DNA necessary for such manipulation."

"Ah, but DNA is only half the equation, else I should not be able to Disguise myself as a Qalik." Cassius did so briefly to make the point. "There is also the element of tricking the eye."

Surloff had far less success with his attempt at Disguising the city, and Cassius was truthfully, if silently, unsure how to help. Finally he told the Korin to cease his attempts. Perhaps they could all think on it a bit. Consider it homework.

"All right, what else can you think of?" he asked, looking at the three who had been standing there useless so far. "What else would cause someone to look away from this place, not pay attention?"

"Danger or bad energy vibrations," Pilory offered.

Cassius gave her a look.

"Do none of you feel the uk'cha?" she asked, looking around at them. "No?" Her wings fluttered, perhaps in embarrassment. "My antennae pick up on an incredible range of frequencies and vibrations. Some are measurable by common instruments found throughout the galaxies, across unrelated worlds and species. Others are measured only by very advanced races, and less advanced races believe them to be mythical or spiritual or something of that sort. The Tibidi call it the uk'cha."

Cassius could not discount the possibility that different species were able to perceive different things that humans could not based on their unique physiologies. But what she described was, as she herself put it, in the realm of the mythical or spiritual. On the other hand, given that he apparently served a spiritual dragon made of smoke and shadow, he couldn't say too much about mystical vibrations that could effect healing or frightening or anything else the hippies claimed they could do.

"So how does one manipulate this uk'cha?" he asked instead. "How do you cause a place to give off warning or danger vibrations, tell people to turn back by only a feeling or a gut instinct?"

"I have never done it," Pilory replied honestly. "I've never had to. I have heard that it can be done, but I would need some crystals and other materials. I would also have to research it more."

Sounded like an oxymoron to Cassius, but whatever. "Well, if you figure it out, let us know and you can try. If it is possible and we can ward people off with a feeling, then we may as well use every resource available to us."

If she was offended at his apparent dismissal of her uk'cha, she said nothing about it. Cassius looked at the remaining Korin. "And you two? What can you think of?"

"We would need to cut off the Sound as well," Barnoff said. "Noise coming from nowhere could be a deterrent, or it could be an invitation."

This was easily demonstrated. It was almost surreal, the way the distant hum of activity from the city was suddenly cut off. Cassius would not say that it was not disquieting, but he would never show his discomfort.

Then Sound returned, and all was back to normal. Pilory let out a breath and a couple of the Korin shuffled a step.

"How was that for your uk'cha?" Cassius inquired.

"It did change," Pilory said, fluffing her feathers, again perhaps for embarrassment. "Sound does indeed offer some comfort. But as one here stated, Sound coming from nowhere may present an element of fear. I imagine, then, that Sound and Light are linked to some degree in the uk'cha. As I said, I will have to learn more."

Cassius turned. "And you, Kokriloff? You've been silent so far. What can you come up with?"

"Smells," the Korin replied thoughtfully. "You can smell the people and the fires and everything else. This cave should smell empty, musty, and cold."

"And how would you erase the smells?"

"I don't know yet, but I feel like it may provide a framework for holding the Disguise in place."

"Smells?" Pilory wondered.

Kokriloff nodded but did not elaborate further.

"Does anyone else have anything to say?" Cassius asked, looking around. No one did. "All right, then."

He would have been more than happy to just leave it at that, tell everyone to scram, and walk away. But he supposed he should offer some encouragement or guidance. Assuming he wanted them to come back. Well, the Korin had their uses, and their business with the twin assassins remained unfinished. Pilory had slowly warmed up to the exercises, and she seemed to be awed enough and perhaps now dedicated enough to learn more to present to Titik to bring him back into the fold on finding the journal.

"You all did well today, for a first lesson," he said finally, feeling as though he were speaking a foreign tongue. "While this is a private class, I do not want you to simply box this up and stuff it away in the off hours. Think about it, practice it. I will gather you again when we will meet."

It was an awkward dismissal, but being different species had its advantages. The Korin departed, speaking eagerly amongst themselves. A few times, Cassius saw something about the view of the city change as they tried to Disguise it. At last the attempts stopped.

Pilory remained.

"Is there something you wanted?" Cassius asked.

"There is a lot to be learned here," she commented. "I am impressed."

"Glad I could accommodate your curiosity."

"I will be certain to practice and show Captain Titik what I have learned. And I will consult the crystals about the uk'cha."

"Yes, you do that."

She shifted her stance. "And I might even have a bit of information regarding the crown of Srori."

That gave him pause, and he raised a brow. "Oh? How is this?"

"A little gossip I picked up at a Hiktorian outpost."

"Hiktor? Sneaking around the Tacagans, are we?"

"Titik isn't as naive or aloof as some think he is. He's no fool, but sometimes it's more profitable to play the part."

Cassius nodded. "All right. So what about this information about the crown?"

"Rumor has it that the Turitians are planning a large space envoy to parade their new queen around to their neighbors and allies. It's a custom of theirs, when a new monarch comes to power. As part of this grand parade, which can last more than eighty days, the new monarch gives many gifts to these neighbors and allies to foster good will and keep the peace. Some of these gifts, especially for less advanced worlds, can be priceless artifacts."

"Rumor says that the crown of Srori will be one of those gifts?"

"Just a rumor."

With that, she turned and walked away, as at ease as he'd seen her since setting foot in the cavern.

Well now, that was a rumor that might be worth investigating, then. And if this was an eighty day parade that involved priceless artifacts, how would it be for him to show up to Titik bearing, not only the crown of Srori, but artifacts that the Psiaco pirate had only read about and drooled at through the proverbial glass window? He'd have the captain over a barrel with that one.

Again, an idea he could fall in love with, but how about its actual execution? Would he attempt to use a portal to sneak aboard their ship at various times and hope to find the crown? Did he want to take the time and effort to Disguise himself as part of the envoy? If he did that, he'd be gone for up to eighty days. Rifun was already basically AWOL. That would leave the Cult in the hands of Julianna and Isthim, and he didn't trust either of them not to muck things up while he was away.

Frustrated, he left the ledge where he'd trained his students and returned to the city. Was there any way to know for sure whether the crown would be one of the gifts given? Was there some sort of gift roster or ledger he could check, something that would detail which gifts went to which people? There might have been, except he couldn't read Turitian.

Maybe he should just keep an eye on it, see which planets they went to, and then follow up later. Surely the planets receiving these precious gifts wouldn't just stuff them in a back closet. No, they would put them on display in their own royal palaces or in a museum or in other places of prominence.

That sounded like a logical plan, he decided, and he wouldn't have to be gone for eighty days.

As he returned to the officers building, he happened to notice Julianna going about her business, and he changed course to intercept.

"What do you know about the Turitians? Specifically their royalty?" he asked.

She seemed unprepared for the question, and it was a moment before she answered, "Not much. Certainly not as much as Rifun. I know we're dealing with the royal family Jalar and that they just crowned a new queen. Otherwise, my experience with them is limited. Why do you ask?"

"Just some rumors I'd heard about the recent transition of power."

"Given that I've taken on most of Rifun's diplomatic responsibilities, should I be aware of these rumors?"

"I don't think that would be necessary."

"What you think is irrelevant. Tell me anyway and I'll decide."

He was rather taken aback by her tone, but he was also a tiny bit impressed by it, too. He replied, "I'd heard that the Turitians are having a space parade to show off their new queen to their neighbors and allies."

Julianna raised a brow. "Is that all? Doesn't seem like the kind of news you would be interested in. What are you really after?"

He ignored the question. "When is Rifun supposed to return? It's been over a month. Has anyone checked on him, made sure he's still alive?"

"Oh, he's alive. I've done a few cursory looks around his family's farm and tombs. He is very much alive."

"Is he praying or did he give us the slip?"

"He goes out to pray every afternoon. Where he's at in his spiritual quest, I don't know. I didn't want to bother him just yet."

Cassius grunted. "Fine. Not like we've needed him around here anyway."

He turned to leave, but he didn't get four steps before Julianna called after him. "What are you up to, Cassius? Where are you going?"

He paused and looked back at her. "You all wanted me to cause chaos, didn't you? Why are you complaining now that I am doing exactly that?"

Not waiting for a reply, he left and strode down the long stone corridor to his chambers. He needed to do a little investigating of his own, snoop around this Turitian royal envoy a bit, see if he couldn't pick apart these rumors. Who knew? Maybe an eighty-day vacation was exactly what he needed.

13 | Fahalalana sy Fahendrena   Knowledge and Wisdom

The Caves of Meroian, 1964

ritotra

Y ou want me to what?"

Rifun stood in Julianna's chambers. He'd returned to the ruins and spent another day or so in his own chambers, both praying and tidying as everything had been covered in a thick layer of dust. Back home, he'd told his family that he would do his best to convince his father to come visit, to make amends and such.

Now, about four days after emerging from his chambers, he'd finally approached Julianna with his idea.

"I want you to pretend to be my daughter."

She stared at him, as if searching for the punchline to a joke. He'd explained the situation, but she didn't seem to believe him. She took a breath.

"So, you went back to your family and your tombs, pretending to be your own son—understandable because of the age discrepancies—and now you're 'flying back to London' to convince yourself, your father, to return to the family to make amends. And you invented yourself a sister, and because of that, they want to meet her. And you told them that I'm your sister."

"Yes," Rifun said.

"You want me to escort you back to Madagascar as your daughter, meet your family, have you make amends or whatever it is that you're doing, and then we're going to 'fly back to London' again. What about your favorite son?"

"He was called to work, which is why you have to accompany me."

Julianna sighed and rubbed her eyes. "And this is just going to be for a few days, right? Maybe a week?" When he hesitated, her expression turned suspicious. "It is only a week, right? You had your spiritual epiphany, now you just have to wrap things up with your family?"

"I don't know," he admitted. "I don't know what's going to happen. However, seeing how I informed my relatives that you have done everything in your power to ignore this side of the family, it wouldn't be far-fetched for you to spend a few days there, come to greatly dislike it, and decide to leave early."

She sighed again and walked a short distance away. She folded her arms and turned to look at him. "It's a good thing you're a damn good politician, you know that? I hired you to kill Cassius, and you've done good work to stabilize the Cult in our political dealings. But I would be remiss if I didn't mention that I—and the others, Cassius, Isthim, and a few of the Borelians—have questioned your commitment in the past few weeks."

"And I would be lying if I didn't say that I have questioned it myself." He went on before she could speak. "But if nothing else, I have a chance to make amends with the family and win back my place in my family's tomb. I cannot expect you to understand the significance of such a thing, but I can ask you to respect it and help me achieve it."

A third sigh. Then, "Fine. Even for our lengthened years, we are still bound by time in some respects. I will accompany you back to your family farm in Madagascar, pretend to be your daughter for a few days or a week or however long I can stand it, and then we will return."

He did not miss her use of "we" when referring to the return trip, but he did not comment on it.

"Thank you," he told her sincerely.

"When do you expect to pull this off?" she asked.

"Give it a few more days. After all, I have to talk to myself to convince myself that it's safe for me to return after all these years. It may take a little persuasion on my part."

He left her chambers with a smirk.

When he got back to his room, he was surprised to find Isthim already there, waiting for him. This did not appear to be a social call, however, as she was dressed in full uniform, and not the old decorative one she'd kept with her for centuries in exile, either.

"Took you four days to welcome me home?" he asked.

"I had duties to attend to," she told him simply.

"Ah. And now you're here to lecture me on why I should have come back sooner, or perhaps not gone at all. Maybe you're going to mock my religious beliefs. Is that it?"

"Not yet. Actually, I require your assistance." She approached him.

"Really? How's that?"

She had him spent before his mind could fully comprehend that her skin had turned from pink to white, and the next thing he knew, she was helping his stumbling, drunken, endorphin-overloaded carcass to the bed where the most he could do was lie down and try to breathe.

"I missed you, too," he sighed. "At least you didn't try to kill me this time."

"It wasn't my pleasure I needed," Isthim told him. "It was yours."

He grinned and chuckled stupidly. "Cassius is still stalking you, is he? So you want to spite him before he leaves on his own little trip." He made a noise. "And here I thought you proclaimed yourself to be immune to such petty jealousy, fearless in the face of competing rivals."

He sucked in a breath as she touched him again, just one finger on his chest.

"Do I look fearful to you?" she asked soothingly.

The most he could do was a small shake of his head. When she got up from the bed, the best he could do was shift around a bit to watch her leave. He wanted to say something, but could find neither words nor breath.

He could only conclude that Isthim had somehow set the whole thing up because not thirty seconds after she'd left, Cassius entered. His expression spoke before his mouth.

"Isthim said you wanted to show me something," he stated. He noted Rifun's exhaustion. "Don't worry, don't get up. And you don't have to tell me either; I can guess."

And he left.

Rifun found himself wondering if Isthim wasn't trying to roundabout get him killed by making Cassius so upset that the only logical conclusion to this apparent one-sided jealousy was some kind of duel. Or maybe it was her way of trying to get him to kill Cassius before it got to that point. Julianna only hired him to do the job, but Isthim was forcing the issue. But who could know the minds of women, especially alien women?

At the very least, he thought, she wasn't asking for anything in return. If he wasn't trying to seduce or marry her, he figured he wasn't obligated to such things.

He found his mind going to Lalao. He wondered if she liked him as much as he liked her. Then he reminded himself that he would be returning Disguised as his elderly father, supposed to be married, at least widowed, and couldn't look at her like that. He would have to wait, play the part he'd written for himself, and return for her later. Maybe he could use his position as father, talk to Volana, and see about arranging a marriage. Wouldn't that be something?

But then, as himself, the only Disguise that he would need would be aging. He couldn't cover up his scars. But Fan had no scars, no burns from years of torture. Even a blind wife could tell the difference between smooth, youthful skin, and burned, twisted flesh.

On the other hand, he knew how to heal himself. He knew how to use Matter. He could do it. If he did win back his place in the tombs and arrange a marriage, thus securing his place in the family once more, maybe he really could live life as Fan. Fake the death of Rivotra, reappear as Fanantenanirainy, marry Lalao, and live well. Happily ever after, as the English liked to say.

Well, he would see how this meeting went between Rivotra and Volana first. None of it would matter if he were still denied access to the family, and especially the tombs. The family shaman still seemed to be suspicious of him, though his suspicions had not yet been articulated. Would the appearance of an aged Rivotra quell or exacerbate those suspicions? Only time would tell.

It was probably an hour before he got around and made himself presentable again, though presentable to whom...he did not know. He was only back for a short time, unsure if he was going to stay, so he did not wish to undertake any major projects, or any minor ones for that matter. Perhaps he ought to consider how he would start packing and moving his things if he did decide to stay with his family. What did he need? What did he want? What could or should he part with? He was not a hoarder or collector of things, but he had a reasonable number of items in his possession. Perhaps he should leave them to Isthim as a gift to end their relationship, whatever it was. Ha!

He rarely left the officers building over the next two days. He'd packed up many of his things, showing none of this to any of the other leaders, especially Julianna as he met her outside the city so they could leave.

"So the man we're going to meet—" she began.

"Volana."

"Volana. He is your mother's nephew?"

"Yes."

"So I am supposed to be of an age with his children, including this Lalao you like so much?" He felt his face turn red, and she continued, "You didn't have to say anything; I can tell. But wouldn't that make you cousins as well?"

"By technicality, first cousin once removed. A little fibbing and we're second cousins." He sighed. "It's strange to you, but it's not so strange to me."

Julianna made a noise. "Well, to be quite honest, it won't be difficult for me to play my role or show a bit of revulsion."

"It's not as if the English never had close family marriages."

She said nothing to that.

They entered the tunnels, and Rifun opened a portal back home. Even though he'd only been gone about a week, it felt like so much longer, and the homecoming felt so much warmer. He actually had something to come back to. Before, when he'd been released from prison, he'd walked among strangers in an alien land that had once been so familiar. Now, home had been returned to him. He took a breath, inhaling the beautiful smells of home and family. And they were about two miles out. How much greater would it be to see the farm once more?

"Good Lord, it's hot as blazes here," Julianna complained, interrupting the moment. She huffed an exasperated sigh and put a hand up to shield her eyes. With a Disguise covering her scars and making her younger, about thirty or so in appearance, she looked almost homely. "How do you stand it?"

They started walking.

"I always had a harder time because my lighter skin burned easier," Rifun said. "It's even harder now because my scarred skin doesn't sweat well and is even more sensitive to sunburns."

"And you want to live here?"

"It's home. Believe me, I was not so very impressed with London when I first lived there. Actually, I've never been impressed with London. But the weather was miserable."

Julianna barked a laugh. "Ha! Even Londoners will agree with you there."

"But it's home, is it not?"

She did not reply to this, but instead asked, "Does anyone in your family speak English?"

"Quite honestly, I don't know. I don't think so, not unless they were in the Army during the war, and even then it may have faded from disuse afterwards. But we already agreed that you shunned Malagasy—"

"And my French is passable at best," she finished. "Which is the truth." She smiled. "Honestly, after moving to the ruins and taking charge of things there with all of our...students, shall we say...it's a bit strange returning to Earth, to be among humans again. Strange, but entirely familiar. Like a homecoming of sorts, I suppose."

It was indeed, and it felt doubly so for Rifun. His Disguise was minimal, limited primarily to aging his facial features and graying his hair. His scarred flesh could be kept how it was, he had decided, and he could make his movements more pronounced, allowing the pain of past injuries to come to the forefront of his mind a little more. But, mentally, emotionally, spiritually, it was like removing a disguise. He could be himself again. He could talk about the VVS and the wars and going to Europe. He didn't have to hide behind, "Well my father told me..." It was, in a word, refreshing.

They were about a mile out when they were spotted, and by the time they reached the front door of the house, Volana was there to greet them.

"Rivotra! Tongasoa!" he said grandly, opening his arms wide. *"Havako, efa ela loatra!"* (Rivotra! Welcome! Cousin, it has been far too long!)

They embraced, and it briefly killed Rifun to have to force himself to make himself a little resigned about the whole thing. After all, he was just returning to Madagascar. The last time he'd seen it, he'd been tortured within an inch of his life and everything at home had been in shambles.

"Et tu dois être sa fille, Julianna," Volana continued, grinning. (And you must be his daughter, Julianna.)

"Oui, monsieur, je – " Julianna began, being cut off as he embraced her heartily, still quite strong for an old man. (Yes, sir, I—)

"Come in, come in." He hustled them into the house. "Where is Fan? Oh, he should have told us that you were coming so soon!"

"His long absence was not appreciated by his employer, so he had to stay behind this time," Rifun lied smoothly.

"Ah, I see. Come, come, don't be shy." Volana paused and huffed a sigh, looking twenty years younger. "It has been a long time, cousin. And you've not changed a bit. I don't know where to begin." He went on before Rifun could speak. "Your son told us that you are still very traditional. Maybe you would like to visit the tombs first?"

Rifun sighed and made a point of favoring an injury, as well as being leery of the outdoors. "Perhaps later when it has cooled off some. You ought to know as well as I do that age does no favors to a man's body."

Volana laughed. "No, it truly does not." He slapped him on the back and took a step back. "Well then, why don't I show you everything and introduce you to everyone in the family?"

If Julianna was acting uncertain and a little repulsed by the idea, she was certainly a world class actor. Rifun suspected that she was not acting. She was being polite, but this was a situation where she was both uncomfortable and desperate to leave. She would be gone before the week was out, he was sure. Which was fine. She wasn't needed for long, just long enough to sell his story.

Volana introduced Julianna to Elisette and some of the other women and left her in the house with them. Julianna Banded herself and Rifun briefly in order to voice her extreme displeasure, but he merely smirked, took down the Band, and left with Volana to go to the fields.

So it was that he was introduced to a family he'd been living with for the last month or so. Only the oldest generation remembered him in a physical sense, perhaps last seeing him when he'd visited Nibe. The next generation after that might have been aware of him from stories of the family. The generation after that, the one including Jaona's son Faliarivo, had maybe heard his name once or only just learned of his existence from the arrival of Fan.

With his return, family ties were reinforced and forged anew, though Rifun started to get the sense that he really might fare better with the younger generations as Fan.

As Rivotra, he had to talk about himself and his life, his experiences, and many of them were quite miserable. Everyone wanted to know what happened to him during and after the war and the Uprising. It wasn't something he wanted to talk about, and that he didn't have to lie about. He didn't want to show his scars or any of that. On top of that, he had to act his age, at least a little bit. He couldn't go running around with the young guns and jump in the *savika* ring. He had to sit back, occasionally flinch at an old wound, mind a few particular motions, and not look at the pretty young girls.

As Fan, he was free to act like a young man. He could run around with them, work hard, eat well, try his hand at *savika*, and try to catch Lalao's eye. He could talk about school and work and life in London, things which were both true and not painful to talk about. He didn't have to talk about war or torture or the terrible things he had seen. He could be the man he wanted to be.

It was a harder decision than some gave it credit for, he thought as they returned to the house. He'd gotten involved with the Cult because he wanted to heal his scars. He'd decided against it because he'd told himself that he wasn't ashamed of them, that they made him who he was.

What if he was wrong? And what if this was his chance to undo a number of bad decisions he'd made over the last fifteen to twenty years, or maybe longer? Maybe he'd done what he was supposed to do among stars and monsters, and somehow he'd taken it too far. Who could know in the grand scheme of things? Only the spirits and the ancestors had that much power.

And how would they feel about him faking his death? The Betsileo practiced *famadihana*. With all the death from the Uprising, it wouldn't be hard to find a body to use, to pass off as his own. But you couldn't fool the spirits like that.

This troubled him greatly as they entered the house, but Volana evidently took it as general discomfort over the whole current situation.

"Perhaps you are conflicted about their motives?" he guessed, then shook his head. "You are something of a legend in this family, Rivotra. After the Uprising, after we gained independence, no one knew where anyone was. No one knew who had died, who had survived, or, if they had survived, where they were. I will tell you the story of Elisette's return later, if she does not tell you herself. The last anyone knew of you, you had been imprisoned. And that was it. Most assumed you had died in there, and those who thought you might still be alive had no way of knowing where you might have gone. In the end, with all the uncertainty, we could only move on with what we had. We could not wait endlessly for something that might never happen. We had what we had, and we had to work with it.

"No one intentionally turned their back on you, Rivotra. No one knew what had become of you. And those of us who were there did everything we could to protect those who were not. Like you, we don't really talk about what happened, what we saw. And heard. And smelled. It's a new generation of people ignorant of those horrors. For better or worse, we don't know. Don't blame them if they seem naive and ignorant, because they are. If you must blame someone, blame us. Blame me."

Rifun shook his head. "There is no one to blame for the horror but the French. If there is anyone to blame here, it's me for abandoning the family."

Volana waved a hand. "Bah! Nonsense! I made my way here to find a farm in ruins, occupied by the French, and it was years of legal action before I got this back in our name. Otherwise we would be as poor and destitute as many of the families that we help. There is no way you could have known that we were going to restore our farm and our name to what it is today."

That much, at least, was true.

"It's all in the past, I suppose," Rifun said at last.

"Indeed it is!" Volana said, back in a cheerful mood, clapping his hands together. "What matters now is that you are home again, where you belong! I pray I can convince you to return here permanently, but regardless, we must have a feast to celebrate your return!"

Julianna, who was already having a difficult time of it in the kitchen or the garden with Elisette and the others, was less than thrilled at the idea and very nearly departed as soon as she heard the news.

"This coming from the humanitarian leader of the Cult?" Rifun asked her sarcastically in private conference.

"I'm happy to help those in need," she hissed through gritted teeth, "but I am no housewife or caterer for your welcome home party!"

"Come on, sweetie, can't you do something nice for your Papa? Can't you see how happy it would make me?"

Julianna Banded so she could slap him, and he Banded to avoid it, laughing hysterically while she just glared at him.

"God, I hate you sometimes. Was that the real point of this? To humiliate me?"

"Of course not," he told her sincerely. "I really do want to wrap up some family matters. This is all part of it." He sighed. "It's a people and a culture you don't know or understand, but you have to give it more than half a day." He smirked. "Maybe if you had listened to your Papa, you would not feel so out of place."

She took another swipe at him which he dodged easily.

He returned to Volana.

"Naturally it is too late to have the celebration today," his cousin said. "How long do you plan to stay?"

"More than a day, naturally," Rifun told him. "A week, a month, maybe more. I doubt Julianna will stay so long. I will be surprised if she lasts more than three days." He let out a breath. "She resents me for leaving, and we've not always seen eye to eye. I was surprised she agreed to come with me."

"Life's little miracles, no?"

"Speaking of miracles, seeing how the air has cooled off, I would like to visit the tombs before the sun goes down."

"Of course. Do you know the way?"

He did. Very well, in fact. But he could not admit to this. He feigned forgetfulness, and his cousin was more than happy to take him to the tombs.

"You have a place here, Rivotra," Volana told him. "If you wish it, you will be buried here, with your *nany*, and your *nenibe*, and your *dadabe*."

Rifun nodded slowly. "I wish only that it does not come so swiftly."

His cousin grinned. "Don't we all?" He put a hand up as if to touch his shoulder, then thought a moment, and lowered his hand. Rifun hoped his sigh of relief wasn't too obvious. "I will leave you to pray."

"Misaotra."

He waited a good five minutes after his cousin departed before setting out his offerings and bowing to pray. He felt honest again, if one wished to phrase it that way. He was coming before the ancestors as himself. Not that he hadn't been himself before, for his intent of spiritual guidance had never been insincere, but the living and the dead were all family, and it had felt terribly dishonest to lie to one part of the family and not the other. Something might be said for this charade of having Julianna for a daughter and Fan for a son, but...semantics. At least he himself, Rifun or Rivotra, was open and free before both sides.

And if he did decide to return, what did he do now about his name? His family all referred to him as Rivotra. Long ago, Nibe had said that Rivotra's place was on the farm while Rifun took to the stars. It seemed only logical that he should continue in this way and discard the name Rifun Ndolo. He would die as Rivotra Andilan and be resurrected as Fanantenanirainy Andilan. Rifun Ndolo would disappear into history, like a bad dream or unpleasant memory.

He paused and listened, looked around without moving his body. After batting it back and forth in his mind for a minute or two, he took a calculated risk and shed his Disguise. The only obvious change to the unlikely observer would be his hair, for his face was obscured by his posture and he had no other stark changes.

Doing this freed his soul as much as his body, and he prayed again, thanking the spirits and the ancestors for the opportunity to relive his life, but perhaps as it should have been, where he was accepted, appreciated, respected. His life under Vala's thumb had prepared him to face some harrowing challenges in life, but now it was time to settle down. Step off the battlefield and return home to peace time. He took an even breath and it let it out over a count of thirty.

His first inkling of being watched came only from gut intuition, the bestial sense that something wasn't quite right. He didn't move his body, but he did shift his mental focus from his prayers to his senses. Using Sound, he slowly stripped away the various environmental noises. The wind and rustling of leaves. The clacking of branches. The noise of humming, buzzing insects. The sound of feathers as birds took flight. He even stripped out the sound of his own breathing.

Someone or something was still breathing.

Madagascar did not have big cats like continental Africa, but that didn't mean there weren't predators. Attacks on humans were extremely rare, though, almost impossible on a healthy individual like himself.

The only thing that would stare at him for so long, then, other than an animal predator, was a human one.

Still using Sound, he was able to locate the source. To his left, about ten yards or so, where thick vegetation could easily obscure curious eyes.

About the only thing he couldn't do was identify his stalker, and he didn't want to attack someone who was merely curious but not hostile. Actually, he didn't feel like attacking someone, period. To do so at a tomb or a shrine of all places was to risk vengeance from the ancestors. Surely his stalker would understand this also.

Sighing, he sat up. If they'd been watching him this long, there was no reason to bother with his Disguise. He also released his use of Sound, the noise rushing at him like a wave.

"I know you are watching me," he said simply. "Show yourself before me and the ancestors."

For a long moment, there was no movement. Then, as if his stalker had debated whether to stay hidden and then decided against it, the bushes rustled.

It was Andrianary, the family shaman, who cautiously got to his feet. It was a surprise, and yet entirely expected. Who else should it be, after all?

"Why should a shaman have to sneak around the tombs?" Rifun asked, almost goaded.

"It is not the tombs I am wary of," the shaman said, straightening proudly, or as much as could be managed from a man who was pushing ninety. He took a step toward him. "You are not who you say you are."

"And who do I say I am?"

"I may answer, but the question is, do you know yourself? Rivotra Andilan? Rifun Ndolo? The Bastard of the VVS? Fanantenanirainy Andilan, perhaps?" He went on, "Please, do not deny it. It does not take a message from the ancestors to know that it is a lie. The woman isn't your daughter either, is she?"

Rifun took a breath and managed a level, "No."

The old man nodded once and approached slowly. "What are you? A ghost? A spirit?"

"Only a man who has touched the *razana* and paints with it."

"Impossible! Even I, who has served faithfully as a diviner and am nearly an ancestor myself, can only glimpse such greatness."

Somewhere in the back of his mind, Rifun worried that too great a shock to the old man could actually give him a heart attack and kill him. In the present moment, however, he was determined to prove the old man wrong, and the best way he could think to make such an impression, was to use a Disguise. He pushed all of his Malagasy genes to the forefront, darkening his skin and using a trick of the eye to darken his hair, so that he more resembled his mother.

With the shaman's mouth dragging on the ground, he then took a large stone near to his position, drained all of the water from it, and crumbled it to dust in his fist.

He released the Disguise, and his appearance gradually sorted itself out, but the old man remained rooted to his spot. For a moment, Rifun wondered whether he had actually killed him. Then Andrianary blinked, tried to move, stumbled, started falling as one might expect from an elder. Rather than jump to his aid, Rifun invoked Gravity and gently got the man upright again.

Regardless, the old man went to his knees, and then his seat, staring into nothing in Rifun's general direction. It was a long two minutes before he found his tongue.

"You...have been touched and gifted by Zanahy himself," he said hoarsely. He nodded slowly. "I understand now. The vision I saw...all those years ago when I divined your future."

"Stars and monsters," Rifun recited. "Kingship and treachery. A path walked along the edge of a knife." He nodded. "I know. I walked that path. I have completed that path, and I am coming home."

"No..." Andrianary whispered, shaking his head. "No, you're just getting started."

A certain sense of dread lodged itself in Rifun's gut. "What do you mean?"

"You are a man of two worlds. With the power to shape both. Stars and monsters. Kingship and treachery. These things are not by accident."

"I don't understand."

The shaman seemed just as perplexed, which was never a good sign. "These worlds...go far beyond what can be seen with the mortal eye. Two worlds. One divided. And you...a hand over all. Twisting the very fabric of space and time."

Rifun shifted position. "Why did you not tell Nibe more of this so she might have told me years ago? I might have made many different decisions."

"I know only what I know," Andrianary said. "And I know less than you. If I am correct, even you do not understand all that the spirits show you."

"Well, you would have the right of it. What is simple for the spirits is beyond the comprehension of the living."

"Except you are beginning to understand! The spirits have lengthened your years so you might learn and understand and be a powerful living force upon the mortal realm! But for what purpose, I do not know."

They sat in silence for a long moment.

"I thought I was done," Rifun sighed at last. "I thought I had fulfilled my calling and now had the opportunity to rest."

"You have too many years left in your great life," the shaman told him. "But I can tell you something."

"What's that?"

"As long as you think in such mortal terms, as long as you try to keep yourself anchored in the living realm rather than balanced between realms, you will never reach beyond the barrier of the spiritual. You have touched it, pulled on a fraction of the power that awaits, but for a pipe to bring forth water unto thirst, it must be balanced between the water and the drought and open to both." He continued before Rifun could protest. "You cannot abandon the spirits now, not when they have shown you so much. But that does not mean that you cannot have both for a time, a reward for faithfulness thus far."

"What do you mean? I can stay with the family?"

Andrianary nodded. "Yes. Stay with us. As yourself, as Rivotra. Come to the tombs, and I will help to channel the spirits, to make clear your confusions and answer your questions. You have great talent with the spirits, but stumble in your communication with the ancestors, whose guidance is crucial to your ascendance."

"I spoke with Nibe and my mother once, after they passed. It has been many years, though."

"When your faith was young, and your power growing, I imagine."

"Yes."

"I thought as much. You must return to such a time, when faith was young and malleable. I will help you in this."

"Can you teach me to be a Builder?"

The old man shook his head, but his countenance was light. "I do not believe I will do much teaching at all. I think the spirits and the ancestors will show you the most, more than any man has ever known. I think, in the end, you will be teaching me."

It was one of the greatest compliments one could receive from a shaman, and Rifun took it with pride.

"Though I am curious," the shaman went on. "I understand, perhaps, your need to lie about yourself. Few would believe you to be Rivotra Andilan and look so young. But why lie about Julianna?"

"I don't know," Rifun answered. "Maybe to make my story more tangible, believable, if I, whether as myself or my son, existed in more than a vacuum."

Andrianary nodded slowly. "Understandable, and yet..."

"What?"

"There is a ray of light and dark. No...it is as though a shadow touches something and casts light beyond it, how normally light casts a shadow."

"What does this have to do with Julianna?"

"This is unclear..."

"But does a shadow casting light indicate good or evil?"

The old man made a frustrated noise. "Things always appear backwards for you. Backwards, upside down, and mirrored. My sight in these matters is limited only by my understanding. I may impart a message, but it may be up to you to discern its meaning."

Rifun sighed. "I was afraid you might say something like that. But does this mean that I may reclaim my name?"

"Rivotra Andilan?" Rather than give him a definitive, joyful "yes," the old man made another noise. "As you live here, you may call yourself as such, for this is what your family will do. But Rifun Ndolo is the master of worlds."

"Do you know when I can be Rivotra Andilan again?"

"Only once the eyes of Rifun Ndolo have closed. And opened again."

"But my eyes are open. The spirits restored my sight."

"Not completely. But one day they will."

"And I shall see more into the spiritual realm?"

"Greatly so."

Rifun stood. "*Misaotra betsaka*. I came in search of answers and a way forward, and it has been revealed to me. How shall I repay you?"

"Teach me, and it will be all the reward I require."

Rifun helped the old man to his feet. Before they could leave, however,

Andrianary said, "It may be prudent, however, to speak not of this to your family."

"Of course."

"To that end, you may wish to repair your disguise."

Face burning red, Rifun did so, graying his hair, accentuating the lines of his face, and allowing some of his aches and pains to bleed through in his movements. Andrianary watched with awed silence. He raised a hand as if to touch his face, then lowered it again as Rifun retreated slightly.

"The Disguise can be broken," Rifun explained, "but the fear of touch is still mine."

"Of course," the shaman said quickly. "Of course, I apologize."

"It is not necessary to apologize to me. I am still learning these things myself."

"Maybe so, but one should show correct respect and deference to chosen ones of the spirits."

Rifun stepped in front of the shaman and faced him. He hesitated. "Andrianary, know that I mean no disrespect to you, the ancestors, the spirits, or anyone. But what would happen if I were to refuse to continue? Or perhaps if I am unable to advance myself, if I remain stubbornly anchored in the living realm?"

Andrianary blinked, as if unable to comprehend the question. If one was called by the spirits in this way, he could not, should not entertain such thoughts as refusal. Finally he found his tongue and answered, "Surely bad fortune would come upon the family. And as you have seen, the Andilan family has much to lose, as do other families if we are struck by such misfortune."

Rifun nodded. "Yes. I thought as much."

"Banish such thoughts from your mind, Rivotra," Andrianary warned. "Years ago you were given the rarest gift of all: a choice, a chance to choose your destiny. You have proven yourself trustworthy in that regard and now stand at the doorway to greater power than any living man has ever known. You must not squander it, but you also have to want it, more than anything."

"I do. I simply wish to be clear about it."

"Understandable." They began moving again. "But sometimes we must step out in faith when doubt clouds our vision, yes?"

Rifun thought back to Ivolo's words. "If the bridge is stable, it is not necessary to see the other side."

Andrianary pondered this a moment, then nodded. "Yes. An excellent analogy. Wise words. What happens, though, if the bridge is unstable?"

"Then I might recommend getting across as quickly as possible."

The old man barked a laugh. "Yes, that would be a prudent course of action, would it not?"

Rifun frowned. "What do you do if you find yourself on a bridge that you are not meant to cross, and the way back is blocked?"

"If going back is not an option, and staying in place is not an option, then your only course of action is forward. But here is something else to consider. What if you find someone else crossing the bridge going the opposite direction?" He added hastily, "Don't answer me now. Think on these things. As I said, by the end, you will be teaching me, I think. But I must still be the line of communication between you and the spirits."

"Of course. I mean no disrespect."

By the time they reached the farm, the sun had just disappeared below the tree line, and the shadows quickly gobbled up the land. Rifun found himself pondering the shaman's words, his vision. A shadow that cast a light. What did that mean? Who or what would be the source of the shadow? Who or what would be the medium, where darkness turned into light? He thought of a prism, splitting white light. Who or what would be the opposite, turning the rainbow back into white light?

Chores had been finished and dinner was just being laid out. Rifun and the shaman were given seats of honor, and Rifun had to remind himself that he couldn't just fall back into casual conversation. This was supposed to be his first family dinner in more than a decade; he couldn't know as much as he did about recent goings-on.

Not that he was able to get in much of a word edge-wise in any conversation. Everyone was more than happy to share stories of all kinds with him, and he learned a great deal more than he had just as Fan. His life demanded different tales as he understood different things.

Julianna was also given a seat of honor, though her look of stiff, just-masked terror and uncertainty was more genuine than her actual face; Rifun was still having to adjust himself to her smooth skin rather than her scars. If anyone else could see that she was not enjoying herself, no one said a word about it.

After dinner, Rifun spoke with Andrianary again just off the front step.

"When will you call again?" Rifun inquired.

"How long do you expect Julianna to stay?" the shaman wondered.

"Not long. It doesn't take a shaman to know she was uncomfortable."

"This is true. Send word to me when she leaves. It will be easier that way."

"How so?"

The old man shook his head. "Darkness clouds her, like a gathering storm in the distance. She has her own path to walk, but it would be best if she were not here to learn what the spirits have to teach you."

He spoke with dead seriousness, and Rifun could only agree. "Of course. I will send word. Shall we meet at the tombs again?"

"That would be a prudent thing to do. If one wishes to communicate with the spirits, one should go where they are."

They exchanged farewells, and Andrianary went on his way. Rifun watched him go, then moved through the house to the backyard where everyone had gathered for evening drinks and conversation. It was perhaps the only time Julianna looked even mildly at ease as Lalao and a couple other women of apparent age tried to engage her in simple French conversation. When she saw Rifun however, she made a motion to speak privately. They headed inside.

"The good news, in this case, no one speaks any English," she began flatly.

"What a concept, as no one here is English," Rifun said sarcastically.

Her temper flared. "I'm here because you asked for a favor. I'm not your wife, I'm not your cook, I'm not your babysitter. Now what is going on here, and when are we going home?"

Rifun sighed. "I am home, Julianna. You are free to leave at any time."

She blinked, her rage floundering. "You're actually leaving the Cult?"

"Not as such. The family shaman, Andrianary, he found me at the tombs. He knows who I am, what I'm doing. He is going to teach me how to Build."

Julianna blinked again. "Building? That's...are you sure?"

No. "As sure as I can be. This is what I came here for. For answers, for guidance, for understanding, and for learning. It has taken time, but such is the nature of the spirits as they assess those who ask for such power. I can't back out now."

She seemed conflicted, like she wanted to be mad at him but couldn't. She huffed a sigh. "Well, I suppose this is a good thing. Building is a great honor, an exclusive, high calling. I just thought..."

"What?"

"Nothing."

"You thought you would be the one to learn it."

"Something like that, yes. I mean, my husband did write the book on Akari abilities."

"He wrote it, but Cassius dictated it. I think he kept some things, the best things, for himself. This is a way around that, the Author giving me a way to learn those things. Not only will I be able to kill Cassius, but Building will allow us to make things how they are supposed to be." An image of the Core of the Wheel flashed through his mind. "We will be able to completely reform the Time industry. We can go against the Akarin, even."

She nodded slowly. "Yes, I suppose you're right. And perhaps there will be a way to retrieve the journal without needing to jump many years into the future."

"There is that as well."

"Very well. From my time in the Akarin, I know that Building is a very long, very involved, very patient study."

"Yes, but if we can avoid having to jump years into the future, we can afford to wait a little while here in this time. As long as you think you can keep things running smoothly in my absence."

"I've learned a lot in the last month."

"And how is Cassius faring? I know what I saw when I returned—not much— but what have you noticed?"

"He seems to have his own pet projects, but none of it appears to involve our overthrow, so I give him some leeway."

"Well, you know what they say about giving the devil an inch."

"We gave our army recruitment and training over to Isthim. I think the devil's taken more than an inch."

He couldn't disagree with that one. "Just know that I may be studying, but that doesn't mean I'm entirely indisposed."

"Duly noted. Actually, I think Cassius and Isthim will do well to balance each other out."

"Maybe. All the same, you can call on me if things take a turn for the worse."

She nodded and sighed. "I've got to be honest, Rifun. I don't like your family. Well, your family is fine, I suppose, but I don't like your culture."

"That's just because it's different and you're not used to it. I don't like your culture very much, but I lived in Europe for decades and survived. You have the option to leave at any time."

She gave him a couple more days just to be polite, but by the fourth morning, she was ready to either kill herself or Elisette and the other women. She removed herself as gracefully as she could, Rifun filling in the gaps of social niceties, and left just as soon as she could manage.

"At least she has met the family," Volana told him, evidently believing that Rifun was in some distress over her hasty departure. "She knows we are here and she may call on us if she ever has a need."

"Yes," Rifun said. "I suppose so."

"And what of you, cousin? What are your plans?"

"Julianna has made her decision. Fan, I know, wishes to return, though how feasible that is at this time, I don't know. I don't wish to be separated from them, but I do want to return here, to live and die here, to be buried in the tombs."

"Perhaps you should speak to Andrianary."

His indecision was obviously a front, but he played along with it anyway. He sent word to the shaman about Julianna's departure and they met at the tombs as agreed.

"Before anything," Rifun began, "I wish to know that this is the will of the spirits, that we will be communing with them, and that everything we discussed is what is meant to be. I do not like uncertainty, but I dislike chasing shadows more. I want to know that what I dedicate my time and my soul to is worth the effort."

"I suppose that depends on what you believe your end goal to be," the shaman told him. "The more you impose your will upon things, the less it will coincide with the will of the spirits, and uncertainty is always a certainty in such matters. Because men are fickle, the more he leans upon himself, the greater the uncertainty as his path becomes more unstable. It is never a mistake to follow the will of the spirits and heed their warnings and teachings, but you have to want it. In this, there will always be certainty. But there is one thing to consider in this."

"What's that?"

"Sometimes the most frightening thing of all is getting exactly what we ask for."

Rifun nodded. "You're not wrong there."

The old man managed a kind smile. "Perhaps you have been away from home for too long. Whether as yourself or your fabled son, I think your time home has done you good. Staying here will do you even more good."

"Maybe."

"Now then. Tell me truly, he who is both Rivotra Andilan and Rifun Ndolo. Do you want to pursue this path? Do you wish to continue to walk among stars and monsters, kingship and treachery? Do you wish to continue to walk along the edge of a knife?"

A choice. The ability to truly choose. To break out of the fixed destiny of men.

"I was not made different so I could live like everyone else," he recited sagely.

"Excellent," Andrianary said. "Let's begin."

฿okum฿o

If there had been any fallout from the murder of the royal crown maker, it didn't seem to affect the common laborer, and Cassius intentionally did not ask about it. If he started asking about them, someone might start asking about him. He didn't want to risk anything before he could secure the crown of Srori.

His initial mission had been to simply find some kind of roster or ledger detailing which gifts were going to which people when Queen Aronet made her debut on the galactic stage. He'd visited Turit several times, Banding for hours, almost whole days, so he could search the palace and government offices, the shipyards, the ships, anywhere that such a ledger might be hiding. He'd found plenty of important-looking papers, to be certain, but he still couldn't read their flowery writing. He could have been looking at exactly what he had been looking for, or just a list of regular maintenance duties. And the dragon spirit didn't seem to be able to be bothered to help him, give him any clue or guidance as to what to do or where to look.

He had returned to the ruins, annoyed, frustrated, wondering what he was going to do. That was when he learned that Rifun's spiritual quest had apparently panned out to the tune of going to be gone for months or years.

Cassius had asked Julianna directly if Rifun was actually going to come back, or if he was trying the polite letdown. Julianna had tried to insist that it was a temporary thing, that he was studying great things, but even he could see that she wasn't entirely certain.

He would also silently admit that he'd been rather upset with Rifun. What was he learning, exactly? Cassius had communed with the spirits. He had been the one to dictate what Richard had written in the journals. What more could there be, why was it going to take months or years to learn, and why hadn't he invited anyone else?

In the end, Cassius decided that Rifun had tried the polite letdown, for the sake of Julianna's tender heart. This did not bother Cassius any. Whether Rifun left the

Cult or did somehow return at some point in the future, he was out of the way for a good long time.

It probably meant that their deal was off, too, not that they'd been making much progress in that realm. Cassius seemed to have better leads there, and Titik was a pretty poor lead, he thought.

So it was that he found himself on Turit, Disguised as a Turitian in hopes of getting into the parade for Queen Aronet. Now that appropriate mourning had taken place following Srori's death and funeral, the new queen could be shown off to the rest of the universe.

He made himself out to be what amounted to a grunt, although the grunts for this kind of a job were greater than the grunts sweeping the streets. His job was simply ensuring that all treasures and gifts were undisturbed for the length of the trip and got to the appropriate recipients. If that didn't give him the greatest chance of finding the crown of Srori, assuming it was even on this trip, he didn't know what would.

He avoided others as much as possible, sticking to his duties like a loyal guard should. If he was going to be found out, it was because of his lack of social graces. Even as a human he failed in most social niceties. For a rigid society like the Turitians, with their almost endless permutations of possible gestures for a variety of situations, he was sure to mess up and, even if he wasn't outright discovered to be using a Disguise, at least get locked in jail for a while.

Maybe he could somehow turn this in his favor. If he intentionally went before the queen and intentionally doffed his Disguise, maybe he could turn this into a political affair. See what the Akari can do? What if I had been an assassin? What if I had intended to kill you? Or someone else important, like your general there? If you want to protect yourself from such things, maybe you ought to learn a bit about the Akari from us. And by us, I mean me.

There was actually a good length of time where he seriously considered such a move. It might even yank the political rug out from under Rifun—assuming he cared —and Julianna. On the other hand, did he really want to make allies out of the Turitians? The Good Samaritans of the universe? Sure they had vast influence and powerful markets, but they were so slow to do anything. Their patience was nauseating. Even Julianna had made mention of how exasperating it could be, and she was no portrait of initiative herself.

Still, there was something to be said for the aforementioned vast influence and powerful markets. They weren't quite as powerful in the Time industry as Cassius might hope; they afforded the Gentleman Killers a lot of leeway.

Maybe that was how he could spin this. Forget a personal alliance, maybe just a warning to get them to beef up security in the marketplaces in the Wheel and keep an eye on their outposts. Maybe it wasn't about turning them toward the Cult so much as away from the Akarin.

Regardless of whether he did or did not pursue this plan, he would have to wait until they were well underway before trying anything. It made a stronger point that way.

So he stayed where he was, overseeing the loading of the cargo, specifically the intended gifts. He had a ledger indicating the gifts, and he was supposed to check them off as they came aboard. He couldn't read a damn word, so he just checked off random lines. If they did an inspection later and someone else found something missing, well, obviously there was a thief aboard the ship. What else could it be? And, he figured, as long as the number of gifts matched up with the number of lines, he was at least in the ballpark of being correct.

Somehow, perhaps by provision of the Author alone, he made it through the loading process. He compared his ledger with that of his supervisor, confirmed that all gifts had been received, and was then given the task of securing everything, tying everything down so nothing was dislodged or broken during takeoff or landing.

Once that task was complete, he stood with the rest of the crew to welcome aboard the royal emissary. Knowing the appropriate gestures by heart was not necessary here, as he just copied what all the other grunts were doing. The queen paid them no mind except to briefly thank them and welcome them aboard. Cassius gave the appropriate response, again copying the others, and she moved on.

If he had hoped that it would be a load and go, he was sorely disappointed. It was probably another two to three hours before things were to the queen's liking and they could take off. Such minor details were not the concern of those in the cargo hold, though it was annoying.

In perhaps the wisest move of this mission yet, Cassius did not comment on it. If this was out of the ordinary, or if the other grunts were dismayed by the delays or disgruntled with the queen, they gave no indication of it. Maybe they loved their new queen, maybe this was something to be expected, or maybe they didn't care because they were paid by the hour. Whatever the case, for being a society that prized their precise social order and gestures, it could be difficult to get an emotional read on them.

Then, finally, the call came down for all hands to prepare for takeoff. Cassius had never been on an airplane before, but he'd heard that each flight was preceded by a short monologue welcoming passengers to the flight and giving instructions for how to behave on the plane and what to do in case of emergency. Apparently someone involved in the invention of planes had taken notes from the Turitians because whoever was on the PA gave about a twenty to thirty minute college-level lecture on the journey they were about to embark upon, followed by another ten minutes of what to do in case of emergency.

So about three hours after their scheduled departure time, the Turitian vessel, the RFJS Rusitan—apparently the name of the king who had been in power when the vessel was commissioned—launched from the Turitian home world, pushed through the relatively thin atmosphere of the slowly dying planet, and burst into space.

Cassius, who had been dutifully strapped into his launch seat, had thrown everything he had into Force, trying to minimize the shaking and rocking of the vessel. So while he did not get nauseous from the launch, he did exhaust himself. And this did not even begin to cover the potential nausea if he ever walked by a window and saw stars and the endless reaches of outer space. It was eleven days to their first destination. He took a breath and let it out slowly.

If there was any good news, it was that the royal party would probably never need to come to the cargo hold, nor would anyone else of importance. The most important person present was the supervisor, and he generally entrusted operations to the grunts so he could go play politics and make nice with upper management, or whatever it was he did.

That just left Cassius, whose Turitian name was Mardir, as well as two coworkers, Satchet, a female whose age might be guessed around thirty for a human, and Sroda, a young adolescent just maturing into adulthood. Satchet was considered superior to both Cassius and Sroda, but there were certain gestures that had to be observed for female superiors of her age. Similarly, there were certain gestures that had to be used for Sroda. He was just breaking into a new set of gestures himself now that he was considered an adult.

Cassius quickly decided that whoever the idiot was who had classified the gestures into merely "inferior" or "superior" was a moron who needed to be murdered slowly and painfully. A thousand ways to do this ran through his mind in about a minute.

The good news was that, at least on Sroda's part, everyone was pretty forgiving about getting it right and making the change from adolescent gestures to adult ones. The bad news was that Cassius wasn't well-versed in any of them, and he pretty much just copied whatever anyone else did. But on the bright side, if Rifun did ever come back, if Cassius survived this trip without being exposed, he would be a master of these infernal gestures, something he could lord over the smug bastard.

With the supervisor kissing ass in upper management, Satchet drew up the work schedule for the voyage. With security being their only job while in transit, one person could handle a shift just fine. When they were on a planet or meeting with important figures in space, there were other logistics to consider. Cassius just paid attention to the first leg of the journey for the time being.

When everything was worked out, Satchet began the first shift rotation, and Cassius and Sroda left the cargo hold.

"This is my first time leaving Turit," Sroda began conversationally, making a gesture that remarked ease and requested equality of conversation.

"Ever?" Cassius questioned, making an acceptance gesture.

"First time ever. I read a lot about space and the aliens we're in contact with—I've even seen a few when they come to the city to meet with the royals—but I've never gone anywhere."

"What about the Wheel of Time?"

Sroda made a noise that Cassius had learned was a Turitian laugh. "Me? A Time Agent? No, I don't think so."

"Why not? You don't seem like an idiot."

"No. Truthfully, I just missed out on the aptitude test. Just two more points and I would have had a chance."

Cassius elected not to say anything to that. He didn't know how these apparent tests worked, although, being an adult Turitian, it was reasonable to consider that he probably would have gone through the same aptitude test.

It was also apparent that only Time Agents could go to the Wheel.

"Have you ever been there?" Sroda wondered. "The Wheel of Time, I mean."

"Hm? Oh yes, I have. Many times."

"Even recently? I don't understand everything, but I've heard that there's a lot of chaos there right now. Tacagans and Gentleman Killers and the Cult of the Akari."

"Well, it's not pretty, say it that way," Cassius said diplomatically.

"Have you ever heard of the Akari? Well, being a Time Agent and all, I imagine you have."

"I have, yes."

"What is it?"

"It's an artifact of great power, giving the user the ability to manipulate not only Time, but Matter and Energy as well. The very fabric of the universe."

"Oh, wow!"

"Be careful, though," Cassius warned, almost grinning in spite of himself. "Such conversation is normally banned in the Wheel." He made a gesture he believed to be one of concern for his younger compatriot. "I wouldn't want you getting in trouble."

"No, of course not." Sroda made a gesture which Cassius did not know. "But I am curious. What kind of artifact is it?"

"A book. A journal of sorts. The Cult believes it contains holy text, the words of the original Akari-bearer, the words of the Author, and that it is essentially an instruction manual of how to obtain these forbidden abilities."

Sroda was utterly enthralled. "Amazing. Do you believe in such things?"

Cassius made an uncertain but dismissive gesture. "There is a lot going on in the Wheel right now. The Time industry is not what it once was. Something has to be responsible for it."

"If you met one of these Cult members who knew the secrets of the Akari, what would you do?"

"I'd want to sh—" Was shaking hands a thing? Were there any similar gestures? How would it be received? "I'd want to thank him."

"Why?"

"Just because something is settled doesn't mean it's stable. Or good. A building can be settled in the mud, but it will eventually sink. The Time industry was this way, a hovel town that fancied itself a royal city. These Akari-bearers, whoever they are, want to build something better. Imagine learning about all facets of Creation, Time, Matter, and Energy. The Hands of Time only had power over one, but it was their power, their rule. They don't want it yanked out from under them."

Sroda made a confused gesture. "Why not include Matter and Energy, then, and keep the Hands?"

"Well, quite frankly, most of them are dead now. But the Akari is about loyalty to oneself and one's people, righting past wrongs. The Hands demanded allegiance to them, to the industry."

"Oh."

Before the young lad could say more, Cassius said, "It's easier to explain and understand if you know the Time industry, understand how it works and what is expected of a Time Agent. If you don't understand these things, then I am wasting my breath."

"Oh," Sroda said, making an apologetic gesture. "That makes sense."

"Sometimes it's easier to not understand. Ignorance is bliss, as they say."

"Maybe."

"Focus on your mission here. If it's your first time leaving home, you don't want to mess it up by dreaming of other things."

"Of course!"

Sroda made some gestures and tripped over some departing phrases as he hurried off to do something or other. Cassius let him go, grateful to be rid of the pest.

He found his sleeping quarters easily enough. He hadn't quite figured out what he would have done if he'd had to bunk with someone. Like everything else about Time and the Akari, it couldn't be held while unconscious. About the only thing this didn't apply to was dream-walking. Disguises, however, would be lost, which meant Cassius would be sleeping as a human.

What if there were cameras? What if he did have to share? His sleeping quarters were small, even for a human, and no bigger than broom closet for a Turitian. Just enough room to lie down, sit on the edge of the bed, and turn around in order to adjust one's bands or perhaps don armor if needed.

Such arrangements didn't bother Cassius, for he always packed light whenever he traveled, but it left too much downtime. However, when he went to figure out lunch or dinner arrangements, he discovered that Time Agents did not eat with the rest of the crew. Because the Wheel of Time had the Food Court, and the Food Court was functioning again, all Time Agents were expected to eat there in order to conserve resources and minimize the needed supplies.

This also didn't bother Cassius because it would let him escape for a while if he needed to. But once again, it left a lot of downtime. Being a royal vessel, it did have amenities, but he couldn't exactly engage in contact sports while Disguised, and he didn't want to just sit around for the duration of the voyage, his time interspersed only occasionally by a duty shift or landing party.

This might be a short trip after all, he mused. He could take his duty shift and search for the crown of Srori. As soon as he found it, he could leave. He wasn't exactly missing out on anything. Wasn't as though he was going to get in trouble for it, since Mardir didn't exist, or not as Cassius was portraying him.

Some vacation. Oh well. He wasn't really into traveling or politics, and certainly not both at the same time. He'd find the crown, get in contact with Titik, get the journal, get rid of Julianna and Isthim, and be waiting and ready for Rifun to return so he could kill him, too. And if Rifun didn't return, well, it wasn't as though the man would be hard to find if he decided to kill him anyway.

Cassius checked his tiny room for cameras, and, upon his determination that he was not under constant surveillance, decided to lock the door and take a nap. If anyone needed him, they knew where to find him.

No one needed him, which was just as well because he slept like a rock, and he woke just in time to start his shift in the cargo hold. He relieved Sroda and watched the boy leave. He was way too eager, Cassius thought. Or maybe he himself was just too stubborn and cranky.

Whatever the case, he needed to start searching. There was a museum's worth of treasure in the hold right now. He'd better get started.

Nothing was supposed to be touched until it was needed to give away, and special locks on the crates could tattle on him. Not that he cared necessarily, seeing how he was only looking for one artifact and would leave as soon as he got it, never to be seen again as Mardir, but if this turned into a prolonged search, then he needed to be discreet.

For his first round of searching, he used a kind of vibration sonar he'd been working on. He didn't have the precision hearing or other extra senses of creatures that had inherent sonar capabilities, but he'd learned how to determine the general shape of an object in a box using Sound vibrations.

His tests thus far did not, however, include padding and packing material, and he was entirely unsuccessful in even guessing which crate could contain the crown, or anything remotely shaped like a crown.

If only he could read Turitian, at least enough to know the word "crown," how to spell "Srori," and the numeric system to identify the crate.

Biting his tongue and slowly sacrificing his pride, he returned to his normal post to consider his options.

Maybe he could use Light to manipulate X-rays. While that might technically work to search for the crown, he had not yet developed a way of actually seeing the X-rays, nor what they revealed.

Maybe he could use Electricity to mess with the locks. Unlock the crates, search through them, then just manipulate the locks so they didn't register the tampering and set off the alarm.

He went to one of the crates and studied the lock. He had no idea how it worked, and touching the Electricity in it yielded no simple answers. It was tied into a network with the other locks on the other crates and also into the ship's security systems. If he was going to tamper with the lock, he was going to have to manipulate a lot more than a single lock.

Maybe he should just go on a rampage, rip into everything, take what he needed and whatever caught his eye, and escape. Maybe he could somehow tie it back to his assassination of the crown maker and the Torka family. Ooh, wouldn't that be lovely? How would it be for a rival family to get this close to the new Jalar queen and make off with priceless treasure? How much chaos would ensue?

But he still needed that crown. And if he did cause that much chaos, without actually finding the crown, no doubt there would be repercussions that could make future missions that much more difficult.

He returned to his post.

His shift was otherwise uneventful, and he returned to his tiny quarters to weigh his options.

Going on a small rampage would be fun, but if the crown wasn't here, then it could cause problems in the future. He was already frustrated about this crown, and he wanted to end it here, in this mission, even if it meant jumping through a portal back to Turit to search for it there.

So then, he either needed to figure out how to bypass the security in the locks in order to do this stealthily, or he needed to learn Turitian so he knew which crate to break open first.

He thought back to Rifun and his ability to use Bands to separate a man's brain from his body, stop the signals from going back and forth, effectively paralyzing him. Could he do the same to a security lock? Would that register in the larger computer? That might be something he could look into, experiment on smaller gadgets.

Or he could wait, carry on with this eighty-day parade, and see which people got which gifts. Once he determined that, he could come back later and steal from someone with, hopefully, a little less sophisticated security in place.

Seeing how any option short of the blatant rampage involved a little bit of waiting, he decided to head to the Wheel to maybe possibly consider learning Turitian. At the very least, he wanted to know which way was up for their language. And the word "crown" wouldn't be bad to know either.

He gave up on that after about fifteen minutes. There was officially only one language in use on Turit, though there were eight recognized dialects, the one used by the people under Jalar rule being something of a bastard language between the "country" dialects and the "elite" dialects, which meant it had bits and pieces from all over the place. There were seventy-six letters, all with five different forms. Prose had eleven different stylistic forms ranging from "falling leaf" to "broad sun" to "spiral wind" and others. Poetry and songs had fifteen forms. The one Cassius believed to be the one used for official memos and documents such as he dealt with in the cargo hold was one of the simpler forms, called "dagger strike," though this was hardly a comfort.

The Turitian language was also built around adjectives, nouns being denoted by how one would describe a thing, verbs by how one might do a thing, which meant that a single word could be over a hundred characters long. When Cassius was finally able to find the word for "crown," he discovered that it roughly translated to "metal 'hard, metallic, possibly magnetic, earthen, stony, electric, shiny, malleable' with jewels 'clear, colored, stony, earthen, shiny, rock "earthen, hard," beautiful' sits 'stationary person "oneself" down' upon the head 'top "over, on," person "oneself", ' leader 'person "oneself," lead "motion others follow 'person "oneself" ' " ' "

And numbers? Not even an option. There were no special written numerals; everything was written out. Not only that, but there were five different ways to write out number-only sequences. At least three were in use in the cargo hold, depending on the medium and the author.

No wonder the Turitians were a patient people. It took at least half an hour just to say hello.

Well, skip that idea, then.

He returned to the ship. Learning the language was out. Way out. It was not something he would ever even consider, no matter how desperate he may be. He'll do the rampage and suffer the consequences first.

His next experiment, then, would be to see if he couldn't try to block the electricity in the locks, cut them off from the ship's security system long enough to peek in the crates. He would need to find other things to try out first, see if he couldn't adapt Rifun's little party trick.

In the meantime, he might just have to stick it out for a little bit, go with the flow, and, if necessary, watch and keep track of which people got which gifts.

It sounded almost like giving up. Giving up, going slow, plodding along with everyone else rather than doing it his way. Well, he could be open to new things every now and again. Rifun wasn't back at the ruins waiting for him and fretting about whatever trouble he was causing. He didn't have to worry about Julianna. And if Isthim tried anything, well, at least she didn't have the Book of Abilities. He'd find the crown, find the book, and carry on his merry way if he had to.

Besides, a vacation might do him some good. A change of pace, a new identity, a chance to do and be something other than who and what he was. It might be interesting, like the time he masqueraded as a white man to smuggle slaves along the Underground Railroad. That had been almost entirely stealth with very little violence, far cry from his instincts, but he had done it. He had done it for quite a while, months, even years. He could handle eighty days.

His next shift came around, and he was left there staring at crates full of priceless treasures and artifacts. It was like leaving an alcoholic in charge of a liquor store. He didn't need to destroy everything, just get a little peek here and there. Except he couldn't.

Day after day, he sat there. He was glad that his job didn't usually involve interacting with others, except the rare occasion when the supervisor came down from his own throne to make sure everything was in order, which it always was. Then he would vanish back to the clouds of royalty.

Cassius also did not typically socialize with others of the crew, although Sroda was usually happy to chitchat for a few minutes when they traded off their shifts.

Day after day after day.

Finally, on day eleven, right on schedule, they made their first stop. It was a planet called Kath, its residents called the Kolkath. They were cat-like creatures with fur that never stopped growing, so that the oldest Kolkath might have fur that dragged on the ground.

The Kolkath were just coming out of a great war. Apparently the war only ended because of the discovery of the Turitians. Life beyond their own planet ended things pretty quickly, or that was the story. The problem was that there were virtually no stable governments left. Majestic kingdoms had shattered into over five hundred territories, each with its own idea of rule. The Turitians had ended one war, yes, but perhaps started dozens of smaller skirmishes as various leaders had differing ideas on how to approach the larger universe.

The reason for the grand royal visit, then, was to assert Turitian authority and invite any and all interested factions into peace with them and each other. The Kolkath were no threat to the Turitians, true, but the Turitians weren't going to waste time trying to help those who didn't want to be helped.

Cassius was saved the inevitable embarrassment of selecting the wrong gifts by the fact that it was the supervisor's job to get them ready. Satchet was chosen to stay behind with the remaining gifts while Cassius and Sroda were chosen to accompany the supervisor and the rest of the royal emissary.

The delegation was meeting with some four hundred and ninety Kolkath, all of them leaders of their respective territories or similarly important figures. Every single person was getting a gift, and it wasn't entirely luck of the draw. Latecomers who didn't RSVP might have to suffer with a common door prize, but those whom the queen had been in contact with were getting some exceptionally exquisite gifts.

And if Cassius thought the turns and gestures and other social rituals were stringent among the Turitians, that was nothing compared to what they had to do when presenting the gifts. He and the others had rehearsed the gestures for days. It was an elaborate rhythm, almost like a dance that had to be performed while Queen Aronet gave her introductory speech, thanking all of the Kolkath leaders for coming, and presenting the gifts to them. It was an odd sort of workout, and Cassius knew that he would be feeling it in the morning.

He couldn't grip items too tightly while using his Disguise, so he was forced to use Gravity to move the gifts. He looked around at those gathered, wondering if anyone knew what he was doing, if anyone understood that the Akari was being used. Could they spot his Disguise? Did they understand how Test worked? No one raised any kind of alarm, but that didn't mean they didn't know.

It was a bit like Christmas, honestly, passing out presents. Even though Cassius only handled one in four of the artifacts, he made sure to keep an eye on the others to see if maybe...

And what do you know? There it was. Queen Aronet herself was just handing over the crown of Srori to one of the Kolkath delegates. Cassius Banded so he could commit the delegate's appearance to memory. Later he would head to the Wheel and see if the Archives had anything about who it was, where he or she was from, and where the crown was likely to be stored.

After the Turitians gave their gifts, the Kolkath presented the queen with gifts of their own. These, too, appeared to be of great historical and cultural value, things that had survived the war, anyway. Cassius didn't understand it, honestly. Why would you entrust your most valuable, utterly irreplaceable artifacts to other people, especially when those people were literally from another planet? What if something happened to those people—war, famine, natural disaster? If that happened, and only certain things could be saved, they're going to go for their own stuff, not something that came from a dusty old monastery on another world. Or maybe a thief decided to steal it. Then that priceless artifact would be lost.

Whatever the case, it wasn't his call. And he was going to be that thief that stole one of those priceless, irreplaceable artifacts because the new owners didn't have the security that the old ones did.

After the gift exchange was a grand parade in honor of the new queen's visit. Seeing how the Kolkath just got out of a massive world war, there wasn't much to crow about or put on display, but it was a spectacle nonetheless. Of course the queen got the best seat in the house, along with her entourage. Cassius, Sroda, and the other help were given second-best seats. But it could be worse. He could have been stuck in the cargo hold like Satchet and never known that the crown was dropped off here.

An enormous feast followed the parade, and here the royals parted ways from the help. Oh, Cassius and the others were permitted to eat their fill, but then they had to trade out with those left behind on the ship. Sroda was next on shift, so Cassius returned to his quarters where he could shed his Disguise and hop to the Wheel.

The Archives had been shaken only slightly in the last attack, nothing that meant they needed to close down for several weeks. Still, the secretaries were still busy putting things back in order. Or perhaps it was only busy work, trying to give their lives meaning with all the uncertainty of leadership these days.

He tracked down some information on Kath and the Kolkath inhabitants, hoping to find some mention of the current leaders. Unfortunately, the information he got came with the disclaimer than the tumult of war may make some information unreliable, and work is being done to keep records updated. Well, between war on Kath and unrest in the Wheel, such updates were less than lightning fast. He could not find anything, or more accurately, he didn't recognize any of the leaders that were pictured.

He returned to the ship, donned his Disguise, and activated the computer terminal in his quarters. He'd barely touched the thing seeing how he couldn't read the language and he didn't want to risk anyone overhearing something. He knew a few commands just from sheer exposure in the cargo bay, but most of it was lost on him.

After a good length of time just pressing buttons and seeing what it got him, he somehow stumbled onto what he believed to be the information he was looking for. It appeared to be a roster of all the delegates they were supposed to meet, with pictures. He managed to narrow it by species, but five hundred Kolkath was still a lot to go through.

He did not know male or female, but he was able to narrow it down first by fur color, silver and gray. He also knew from the length of the fur that the delegate was just hitting middle age, late thirties or early forties by human standards. This brought it down to twenty-three males and eleven females. Just going by what he committed to memory, he was able to eliminate seven more, but it was still too many.

The roster included all gifts intended to be bestowed to the delegates, but the damn language!

Well, he didn't come this far just to give up, and he reluctantly made another trip to the Wheel so he could again find the word for "crown" and attempt to copy it down. It was painstaking, both physically and mentally. When he again returned to the ship, he was ready to just go on the rampage. Crash the party, steal the gifts, and leave. Blame it on the Torka family if he had to.

His efforts proved fruitful, however, as he was able to match the word he had copied with one of the gifts.

"Computer, how do you pronounce the seventeenth candidate's name in the Kolkath language?" he asked innocently.

"Suri vur alAbanaki," came the computerized reply.

"And who is he?"

"Overseer of the Vault of Irdo."

"Vault, huh? Sounds like a high-security place. Sounds like a good place to hide priceless artifacts."

He got out of the computer and went about his duties, relieving Sroda at the proper time. Once the festivities dispersed and they were on their way, Cassius would wait a day, then slip out to steal the crown.

And why shouldn't the crown have gone to another planet to be placed in a well-guarded vault? Thieves hadn't even waited for the dead king's funeral before trying to steal it. It all seemed so obvious now, almost laughable. And here the thief stood, ready to pull off the heist right under their noses.

Or maybe he should wait until the crown was in the Vault. Sneak into the Vault and see what other treasures lay inside.

He decided against it only because he was feeling too impatient about his mission overall. After being humiliated by Titik and lurching about on this almost wild goose chase, he kind of just wanted it to be over. Maybe he would return later to raid the Vault. Then, at least, he wouldn't be potentially obligated to share his spoils. He wasn't part of the space pirate's crew; he could keep his treasure for himself.

The festivities went on for the rest of the day and most of the night. Cassius was almost relieved to be merely part of the help, that way he didn't have to entertain or be entertained by others. He could go about his day as normal. Leave all the politics and whatnot to the queen, or Rifun and Julianna as the case may be.

Even once the partying ended, it was another day before they were supposed to leave. This gave the royal entourage time to sleep off a hangover as well as meet privately with a select few diplomats.

Their next stop was thirteen days away, and the partying was rumored to be even grander for the simple fact that the Uuodi weren't just coming out of a war, and apparently they were just really good at parties and festivals.

As Cassius spent his time going through the itinerary for their trip, jumping back and forth to the Archives as needed in order to translate everything, he considered sticking around for the rest of the journey, if only to experience these great festivals and celebrations. And maybe he could nab other artifacts, too.

His impatience won out by the end of the day, and he was ready to jump the Vault keeper even before they departed. But he went through a similar song and dance as before, this time thanking the Kolkath for their hospitality, reaffirming peace, love, and rock and roll, and then enduring another harrowing launch. While he was sure that everything went smoothly, his stomach was not so convinced, and he decided that if he didn't have to endure any more space travel, then he wasn't going to try and fool himself. If he wanted to steal treasure, he would steal treasure. Fuck the pretext.

He slept off his discomfort, then pulled one last shift. It was his last chance to cause chaos, bust open the crates, take everything, and blame the Torka family.

Of all people to walk in on him busting the first lock, it was the supervisor.

"Mardir! What is the — ?!"

The Turitian language took so long to get through, was it any wonder that Cassius was able to kill the man before he got to the point of his sentence?

Between the breaking of the lock and the detection of weapon's fire within the ship, a security alert went up. It would take only a minute for the cargo hold to be swarming with guards.

He Banded so he could break open all the crates, but let it drop while he was collecting loot. He enjoyed the thrill of the chase, and there was no way he would be able to carry everything with him. He probably could have sent everything through portals, but he himself would need enough strength leftover to make an escape. He didn't know whether Turitians possessed the ability to track portals, but he didn't want to take any chances.

He raised his weapon as guards flowed into the hold. He had a decent stock of treasure, he decided.

"Lower your weapon!" one guard commanded.

Cassius didn't have enough experience with the Turitians to say how many times they would ask before they started shooting, but he wasn't worried. He did, however, lower his weapon. Instead of surrendering, however, he merely said, "The Torka family sends their regards."

With that, he opened a portal and jumped through, forcing it closed behind him. After a few jumps, he felt safe enough to return to his chambers in the officers building where he shed his Disguise and dumped his loot on his bed. He would sort it out later. He had a crown to steal, and if he was right, the Turitians were probably already on the phone with the Kolkath, warning them of the possible danger of a thief.

The problem was, the Kolkath would be told to expect a Turitian thief. For Cassius, though, it was much easier to build and hold a Kolkath Disguise.

By the time he returned to the place where all the delegations had met, Suri vur alAbanaki had already departed. With any luck, he hadn't heard about the crisis on the Turitian cruiser and wouldn't be expecting any foul play.

Irdo was as far west as west could get, but the biggest obstacle to get there was the Mighty Whiteclaw, a great river that was so wide it could not be crossed in a day, or so the old sayings went. New technology rendered that observation obsolete. Catching the Vault keeper on the crossing would have been like shooting fish in a barrel. As it was, the man blubbered and begged so pathetically, Cassius actually found himself inclined to spare him his life in exchange for the crown.

It seemed to put the man in some kind of moral or ethical dilemma, but killing one of his attendants made up his mind pretty quickly, and Cassius escaped with ease back to Sadurnon.

It was tempting to simply up and leave for the Wheel to meet with Titik, but he decided to hold off for about five minutes, just long enough to take a few of the treasures he'd stolen and distribute them among his friends. Friends being loosely applied, and referring only to Isthim, Julianna, and Rifun. The first two he left in their chambers. The last he left with Julianna with a note saying that it was intended for Rifun but Cassius wasn't going to go after him.

Maybe he could flush out whoever had left the gift for Rifun and discern their intentions.

He sent word to Titik through Pilory, and she responded quickly. An hour later, the three of them met on Titik's ship, right in the captain's quarters.

If the pirates were hurting because of events in the Wheel, Cassius was forced to wonder what their days of plenty looked like. The things he'd just stolen from the Turitians looked like pocket change compared to the loot in Titik's quarters. He was completely ignorant of any cultural significance of the more sculpted pieces, but just looking around, this was enough to buy a planet.

What, then, was the crown of Srori to Titik except a bragging right? All the same, Cassius turned over the piece.

Titik examined this second crown with the same precision and care as the first. Cassius wondered if his four eyes were the same as human eyes, or if he was capable of seeing beyond the human spectrum, and that was how he was able to examine the crown and declare it true or untrue.

After a minute or two, Cassius began to worry. What if this was another fake? Would the Turitians do that? Would they really send a fake crown as part of this diplomatic mission? Real enough, surely, to be valuable to the Kolkath and everyone else they were visiting, but still not the actual artifact? Would it be every gift, or just the one whose theft had already been attempted once? What would Titik do or say? The first time might be forgiven, but what about a second mistake? Cassius could almost say for sure that there would be no third attempt.

"Where did you get this?" Titik asked, still looking.

"I boarded the Turitian emissary taking the queen on a galactic parade. The crown was a gift to the Kolkath," he replied evenly.

"The Kolkath…" The Psiaco choffed as if laughing or thinking. "Ah, Turitians, the ibilik of the galaxy."

"You'll forgive me, the word doesn't translate."

"One who takes pity on a weak or helpless creature. It would be like a Psiaco caring for an Urid child." He set the crown on his desk. "You took it by force, then?"

"Of sorts. I traveled with them for two weeks, surveyed them, planned my move."

"A stowaway."

"A part of their crew." Cassius stood and backed up a couple steps. "The Akari can do many things, including…" He donned his Mardir Disguise. "Disguises."

Titik stood suddenly, a bestial sound like a snort coming from his nose as he tried to determine the threat level. Cassius released the Disguise and returned to his seat. "The further you get from your own species, the harder it is to pull off, but I managed to fool them for a while, long enough to figure out where the crown was and who it went to." He donned his Kolkath Disguise. "Then once the Turitians had gone, I returned to Kath and robbed the diplomat who had the crown."

Pilory said nothing, but her expression was quite eager as she looked back and forth between the two of them.

"So tell me," Cassius said, "was my effort worth it, or did I waste two weeks of my life?"

Titik said nothing for a long moment, just studied Cassius. Finally he pushed the crown to the side a bit, folding one set of arms across his chest and folding his other hands on the desk. "The crown is genuine. It is the true crown of Srori. But I am forced to wonder, with these abilities…if you can impersonate royalty, stop Time, and do all these wondrous things, why bother sneaking around? Why bother with plans or even weapons? Pilory tried to explain to me this concept of manipulating Gravity. So what is it that holds you back from achieving your ambitions? Why ask me for help with finding this trinket of yours?"

"It is only a manipulation of physics, not magic," Cassius told him. "The Akari can no sooner cause someone to fall madly in love with me than find lost car keys."

"The Borelians are known to manipulate people in such a way."

"Then people are no more than the sum of their parts, and the soul is useless."

"Some might say that you are quite a soulless character."

"They wouldn't be wrong. But we're getting off track. Will you help me or not?"

Titik leaned back, his alien expression difficult to read. Clearly he was accustomed to having things his own way all the time, and now he was teaming up with or working for someone else. He sighed. "What is it that you are looking for?"

"A journal. A leatherbound book about this big." Cassius vaguely made the dimensions with his hands. "It contains the original writings of Richard Brown, detailing the Akari and the Cult."

"Do you know anything about it, where it might be?"

"No, but I have reason to believe that it may be with a traitorous former member of the Cult, or it may have fallen into Akarin hands."

Titik grunted, evidently displeased. "Traitorous former members I can handle, but I don't like going near the Akarin."

"They have the same power we do, and they are our biggest obstacle to taking over the Time industry. We get that journal, that problem goes away. I am the most learned of the Cult, the most practiced, but we need that journal. I will take Pilory and train her, and she can train you if you wish. Once the journal is found, then it will be open to all."

The captain didn't look entirely convinced, but he couldn't deny what he'd just seen with his own four eyes. Finally, "You may train Pilory at your leisure, if she wishes, but she'll not abandon her duties here."

"Of course not, captain," Pilory promised.

"I will keep an eye out for this journal of yours. I'll let you know what I come up with. If I get the chance, I might even get it for you. Once it's in your hands, I expect payment for my part in this."

"Naturally, though isn't power enough of a motivator? Money is all well and good, but why live in fear of acquiring or spending it?"

Titik was about to say more when a communication came through, requesting the captain on the bridge.

"On my way," Titik said gruffly, standing. He looked at Cassius. "We will discuss my payment later, if this journal is indeed recovered."

Cassius nodded graciously. "Of course. I look forward to it."

Titik and Pilory departed, and Cassius returned to the ruins, feeling rather satisfied about the whole thing. He'd accomplished all of that by himself. No Rifun, no Julianna, and no Isthim. And he still had Pilory and the Korin as his secret students.

As he entered the city, he encountered Julianna apparently on her way out.

"Going somewhere?" he inquired.

"Meetings to attend," she replied, perhaps a little too quickly. "Rifun left so much for me to do."

"On that we can agree. Hardly a chance to get in a nap or pursue a hobby."

"Isn't that the truth? Was there something you needed?"

"I can't inquire after the well-being of my coworkers? We're all supposed to be working together, aren't we?"

Julianna gave him a look, then left without another word, Cassius watching after her. Only after he'd turned and continued on his way did he realize she hadn't said anything about the gifts he'd left.

15 | Fiofanana sy Fifehezana
Madagascar, 1965

Training and Discipline

Rifun sometimes wondered if the meditation wasn't just an excuse for Andrianary to take a nap. He wouldn't blame him, for the man was very old, but the snoring could be a bit of a distraction when he got really into it.

Still he dutifully went through his forms, the meditative Akari tai chi he'd developed. This was always preceded by prayers and offerings, thanking the ancestors for guiding him this far and asking for wisdom going forward.

He wouldn't say he didn't feel a little disappointment, that his journey wasn't over and he couldn't come home for real, but he would accept the wisdom of the spirits and carry on. And, looking back, he hadn't really accomplished much. His personal training had improved, and he had become quite adept at politics, but he hadn't done any of the things he'd promised others he would do, and it was a terrible thing to leave promises unfulfilled. And besides all of that, there was no way the Author would have shown him the Core of the Wheel just for him to walk away from it and retire to a cattle farm. He needed to do something about the Core, and to do that, he needed to become a Builder. He'd finally received his guidance, and now he had to really begin his training.

He slowly moved from one form to the next, keeping his breaths even, trying to ignore the sweat soaking his blindfold and the snores of the shaman. The day promised to be a hot one; the sun was barely up, he hadn't done any real work, and he was still feeling it. Simple existence was enough to make a man sick from the heat.

Finishing up his forms, he removed the blindfold and used it to wipe his face. As he tossed it aside, the shaman roused, yawned, stretched, and finally stood.

"Well, that was some excellent meditation, I think," he declared.

Rifun raised a brow but said nothing.

After another minute or two of the old man stretching, he again sat down in a heap, stating, "If we continue to do this, I should think that I will eventually reach a point where I will sit down and not get back up."

"I could try to help you with that," Rifun told him.

Andrianary waved a hand dismissively. "I'm too old for such things. I shall attain the knowledge and wisdom of the spirits the old-fashioned way. But you...I am more than happy to help you discover your way along this new path. For as long as I can."

"Of course. And I am grateful."

"I know you are. Now then, why don't you show me again how it is you make yourself older?"

For proclaiming himself too old to get mixed up in too much of this advanced sorcery, the old man was pretty obsessed with Rifun's Disguises, how he could change himself to merely appear older or younger, or even change himself entirely to what he might have looked like if only his Malagasy genes had overridden his French ones.

And he had shown the man how he Felt deep inside himself, delved all the way to his DNA to make these changes.

There was not a little irony in a witch doctor crying witchcraft.

Nevertheless, he went along with the old man's wishes, if only out of respect. Regardless of Rifun's Disguises and extended life, at this point, Andrianary was still older than him.

Personally, he thought he should be studying more in the realm of Energy. He utilized this somewhat through Thermodynamics, attempting to keep them both cool in the wretched heat, but there had to be more, some way to combine two or more Energies. Because of the volatile nature of most Energies, he was loathe to experiment haphazardly. But in order to do it at all, he needed to get away from Matter.

Matter was one of the first things a new Akari student learned, for the simple fact that it was easy to see the results and know that something was being accomplished, without risking upsetting natural physics, as could happen with Gravity, Sound, and other Energies. The problem came when the student stopped at Matter, enthralled with the spectacle and shunning greater power.

Andrianary was still enthralled with the spectacle, and there were times when he acted more like an eager spectator than a spiritual mentor. Still, Rifun indulged him, telling himself to be patient. He'd waited this long to get anything. There was every chance that there was some logic and purpose to this. Maybe he couldn't see it, and maybe the shaman couldn't either, but the spirits knew. The Author knew.

When he'd spoken of the Author to Andrianary, the old man had become thoughtful, if not a little perturbed. He likened it to the Christians and how they called their God "the Author and Perfecter of faith." Perhaps it was simply a translation error, seeing how he had first learned of this strange religion through an English speaker. Surely this manipulation of Creation and communing with the spirits came from Zanahy, the creator spirit. God would never allow men to have such power. After all, according to the Christians' own Bible, the last time they had tried something even remotely similar, He'd scrambled their languages.

It gave Rifun something to think about as he demonstrated one more Disguise before using Thermodynamics to cool them both off. The sun was well into the sky now.

"I'm impressed," Andrianary told him as they both sat down. "You've certainly come a long way since the last time you were here."

"Are we talking a couple months ago or a couple decades ago?" Rifun asked cheekily.

The old man gave him a look. "When you were here, yourself, not Fan." He shifted position. "When you were here last, speaking with Nibe, you hardly knew who you were. Of course, you are in a unique situation, a man of two names and two destinies. Such confusion! Even among the spirits and the ancestors there was great hubbub over you. But now here you are, a man who has found himself and knows himself so well he can change the very fabric of his being. The greatest of all control begins with control over oneself."

"I understand," Rifun said humbly.

"You must always know yourself, search yourself. Always have a plan. Be ready with your actions and reactions, whatever may come your way. Expect the unexpected and the outrageous. Even if victory seems certain, plan for defeat. Even if defeat seems certain, plan for victory."

"You've read Sun Tzu."

"Who's that?"

"A general and strategist from Ancient China. When you are strong, you must appear weak. When you are weak, you must appear strong."

"Sound advice, I think," Andrianary mused. "And applicable even outside of war. Applicable even within yourself. Always plan. Always know. Always plan for what you know and what you don't know." He shifted position again. "For example, what would you do if it were to start raining right now?"

"That's highly improbable, given the sun and sky the way it is."

"Improbable, not impossible. What would you do?"

"I might suggest we return to the farm early."

"For a mere sprinkle?"

"You didn't say how hard it was raining."

"No, but there are many possibilities, are there not?"

Rifun blinked. "For a light sprinkle, I would suggest we stay here and continue training, maybe wait until it passes, depending. Unless, of course, you wanted to leave—"

"What? You think I'm old or something?" Andrianary laughed. "Continue, please."

"If it turned into a heavy rain, I would suggest we return to the farm."

The old man was still grinning. "All for rain. A simple natural phenomenon, merely a fact of life."

"But there's a lot that goes into rain and storm systems," Rifun blurted.

Even as he said it, he knew where the old man was going with the lesson. He could see that Andrianary saw that he knew.

"Always be aware," the shaman said sagely. "I will say that it is impossible for a mere mortal to understand every single possibility and course of action, and many factors will lead to overlapping outcomes. But what is not impossible is for you to understand yourself and understand how you will act and react. Many spirits will tempt you, and many voices will whisper and shout at you. You must find the path of the future."

"But if the future is fixed—"

"The future is fixed for ordinary men of ordinary lives. Even many self-proclaimed extraordinary men are but ordinary. Why? Because they are just one man, one spirit, one life, one destiny. You are a man of two spirits, two lives, two destinies. You are an extraordinary person with the power to, not just follow the future, but to shape it."

Rifun went back on his elbows. "That's a lot of weight."

Andrianary nodded slowly. "It can feel like it, yes. But you already have a foot in the spirit realm and wield remarkable power and influence. The more you understand yourself, the more you will be able to influence and shape the world around you, and the more you will be able to bear." The old man's eyes were kind. "This is not a curse, Rivotra." Rifun looked up. "Your first step into this power was deflecting your stepfather's curse, turning it back on him, and embracing your dual nature."

"What is my next step, then?"

"We will return next week, as usual, and we will see about influencing the world around you."

Rifun stood and helped the shaman to his feet. Then he donned his Disguise—much to Andrianary's delight—and together they left the tombs.

Even though it was before noon, most of the people had already retreated inside their homes, having completed only the necessary chores. Rifun took Andrianary back to his humble residence, then headed back to his family's farm.

"Ah, welcome back, Rivotra," Volana greeted as he walked in the door. "Another successful journey to the tombs, then?"

"Of course," Rifun told him, gratefully accepting a glass of juice from Elisette who was busy preparing lunch.

"Like father, like son, I think, although Fan went out every day. Every afternoon, once the morning chores were done and he got something to eat, every day he went to pray."

"Yes, he told me. To my shame, I wasn't around when he was a child. He has a lot of catching up to do, and he frequently seeks the ancestors for guidance." Rifun sat in a heap in one of the chairs near Volana.

"Not a bad place to go, considering some of the social trends going on," Volana said.

"No, certainly not. I'm glad for his zeal. As for me—" He made a point of shifting position. "I don't know that my body would let me make so many trips."

His cousin nodded. "One of the pitfalls of getting older, that's for sure."

The nice thing about being himself and being able to act his age, Rifun could reminisce about his younger days and no one would think him strange or crazy for it. Granted, he didn't talk much about his time in prison, but he could talk to his cousin and the others about the war and the Uprising, get some different stories, some new perspectives. It was different talking to them as Rifun, when they could speak as equals about such things, versus talking to them as Fan who ought to have no first-hand knowledge of the atrocities that took place. It was refreshing.

"How is Faliarivo doing in his *savika* practice?" he asked, changing subjects.

"Ah, he is quite nimble, but he needs to work on the strength in his arms to be able to hang on," Volana answered, grinning.

"Fan told me that he wants to try it. I told him that he should watch a couple tournaments first, take notes. He's never seen one before, and I wouldn't want him to jump into one blindly."

"No, certainly not. But it's too bad he couldn't be here to see the one coming up in a few weeks."

"Does Faliarivo expect to compete?"

"Of course he does. He already has his father's blessing."

"Why am I not surprised?"

Lunch was called and all family members appeared out of the woodwork. Whether they had been talking, napping, or out doing whatever, a relatively empty house was suddenly full of people again.

Volana remained in his place of honor at the northeast corner, his wife beside him. Rifun was seated close to them, an honored elder. As per usual, Volana prayed, thanking God for food and family and asking a blessing on everyone who could be there and even those who couldn't.

"Amen," he finished.

Being an elder now, rather than a young whelp, Rifun was able to get to the food much sooner, just as soon as it got through Volana, Elisette, and a couple others. He didn't take much, true, but it was sort of a smug point of pride.

"Rivotra," Elisette began, "what is it you do every week with Andrianary? Were you very good friends before the war?"

"Not as such, I think," Rifun replied, "but he did have great faith in me, a particular vision of destiny he once had about me. He wants to teach me as much as he can about that vision before he joins the ancestors. If he teaches me well, then I may be able to speak to him even after that happens and learn even more."

"You see, Elisette?" Volana joked. "Destiny is not reserved for the young."

Elisette said nothing to that, though she was grinning hugely.

"Then may we all live to be as young as Rivotra," Sambatra laughed.

"Hear, hear," Jaona said, raising his glass halfway, as if unsure whether to make it a full toast. A few others met him.

Rifun Banded and cast a glance at Lalao. She hadn't toasted, but she was smiling nonetheless, and her sister beside her was in the middle of saying something. She was still beautiful and he was still greatly attracted to her, but he couldn't pursue her how he was, not unless he told her about the Akari and brought her into it.

Maybe next week he would ask Andrianary about Lalao's role in his future. Could he reveal these marvelous things to her? Should he? Absent his feelings being crushed, there was still the risk of absolutely ruining her life. Even he was not so blind as to think everyone was capable of, not just understanding, but simply accepting such power, such an expanded universe among the stars. What if he ruined her?

Well, that was neither here nor there at the moment, for he was still Rifun Ndolo. He would ask the shaman, either have the old man divine an answer or give him the guidance to divine the answer on his own. He could do nothing until then.

He looked away from Lalao and surveyed the rest of those gathered, everyone appearing to be in a fairly good mood. Having shaken off the worst of his uncertainty, Rifun dropped his Band and inserted himself back into the scene, purposely ignoring Lalao for a few seconds.

After lunch was the more normal time for a nap, and some took advantage of this. Rifun, as well as several others, who had done very little already because of the heat, elected to stay awake and play tabletop games, cards or dice.

It was this way for several days as the heat remained oppressively situated over the island. The first day or two, everyone was able to remain in fairly good spirits, whiling away the time and pursuing some hobbies. But as the heat lingered for three, four, into five days, when the warm air was so thick and compressed that it no longer really dissipated at night, spirits suffered.

Rifun was not immune to this, and even his talent with Thermodynamics was limited. There simply wasn't anywhere for the heat to go; he had nowhere to safely dispel it. It was easier at night—easier being a relative term—when he could force the heat simply up and out into the atmosphere, but the heavy stationary front remained.

A few times he tried to force it, but the weather was more complicated than simply hot or cold, rain or sunshine. What's more, it was all connected throughout the world, and anything he did at home could disrupt something over in India or China or anywhere. He didn't expect to cause any typhoons, tsunamis or earthquakes, necessarily, but he didn't want to cause bigger problems down the road. Some things were left to the control of the spirits for a reason. He was not that powerful yet, and he didn't need to push it before his time.

So he, like the rest of his people, suffered the heat.

When he went to Andrianary the next time for their weekly meeting, the old man humbly declined, saying that the heat had made him ill. His appearance and general disposition made this clear without the need for words. Rifun said he understood, did what he could to cool him down and take the edge off his discomfort, then went to the tombs by himself.

He spent the day praying, wondering if there were some way he could move the heat along, but if there were, the spirits did not see fit to impart such knowledge to him yet. In all honesty, that was fine with him, for the heat was making him a bit sick as well, and he did no more than pray. His physical movement was limited only to what was necessary. Perhaps it was his own misjudgment that said his Akari forms were not that necessary, or maybe the heat was getting to him.

Whatever the case, he returned home earlier than normal. No one commented on it. Indeed, very little was said as each person was wrapped up in his own ways of keeping cool. Elisette worked nonstop in the kitchen to ensure a constant supply of water and fruit juice, and Rifun grabbed one of these juices as he settled into a chair near an open door, silently begging for a breeze.

Twelve days into the suffocating heat wave, the front finally broke, and it was as though the heavens opened up and poured cool air upon the meager denizens inhabiting the planet, or at least the island. True, it was basically the same heat they normally had for the time of year, but the air temperature dropped a good five degrees and the humidity lifted, and it was like throwing off a heavy, unnecessary blanket.

There was much ado about the relief, including a great dinner party hosted by Volana and Elisette which spread from the house across the whole of the backyard and spilling into the first pasture which was, thankfully, empty of cattle.

The party might have ended around ten o'clock or so, except clouds rolled through the sky and a sprinkle graced the guests, causing even greater rejoicing, and things didn't wrap up until just before sunrise. Rifun was glad he didn't have any obligations outside the family — and even then he was not expected to do much since he was an elder — because some of the younger adults who worked did not look up to the task of going through another day after not having slept.

He spent the day basically lounging, on the one hand grateful for his Disguise, on the other hand frustrated by it. He liked being young and strong. He enjoyed his extended lifespan. He knew to respect his elders and defer to their wisdom, but what happened when the wisdom of age was combined with the strength of youth? So much could be accomplished! He had been chosen for this! So why did he feel so...lazy?

He brought up the question to Andrianary when they again met at the tombs. The old man looked better than he had, but he still seemed a bit fatigued.

"It is a war of nature, a war of will," the shaman told him. "Your common nature, your mortal nature, desires peace and ease of living, hence your elderly Rivotra Andilan Disguise and participation — or perhaps lack thereof — in chores and daily activities. Your spirit nature, your immortal nature, desires power and action, to rise higher than any man, even yourself, to break free of constriction."

"How do I fight it?" Rifun asked dumbly. "I want to be useful and powerful and help my family and my people. But I don't want to cut myself off from everything I fight for."

The old man nodded sympathetically. "Dual-spirited people are impossibly rare, and as such, it can be difficult to understand what is expected of you and how to balance it with your mortal nature. Oftentimes, a dual-spirited person will never meet another like him, to guide him."

"Why not write it down?"

As soon as the words were out of his mouth, Rifun knew what he had to do, although he didn't have to like it. Before he could dwell on it for too long, Andrianary spoke, laughing.

"Ah, cheeky child. If only it were that simple! But times change, and one knows not how the future may be influenced from one dual-spirited person to the next. Perhaps they exist only one at a time, isolated, in order to influence things only in their own time and no more. Not by the past, and not to the future." He went on before Rifun could speak. "And to that end, enough talk of possibilities and probabilities and what-ifs. Focus on the here and now and see what the spirits may reveal to you."

"Or reveal to you," Rifun said.

That was the day when he showed the old man Time. Once again, he wondered whether the shock of it might cause him to keel over. He demonstrated basic concepts like Fast and Slow Banding, Double Banding, and Pinpoint Banding. Some things, like an ability called Predict which allowed a Timekeeper to see and anticipate the path of a moving object, could not be shown. Other things, like his trick to paralyze Cassius and separate the time between signals sent from his brain and reaching his body, he would not show; at the very least, he couldn't demonstrate on the old man.

"Matter, Energy, and Time," the shaman mused as Rifun sat down to take a break. "The very nature of the universe. But only the physical one."

"All held together by one critical element," Rifun said. "Faith."

"The spirit. The *razana*." Andrianary nodded. "Exactly." He frowned. "So what is holding you back?"

"What do you mean?"

"You know a great many things. Even a fraction of this power would drive some men mad with lust for power and money and the pleasures of the world."

"I know a man like that, and he knows a great deal more than I do about this."

"What does he have that you don't?"

Rifun sighed. "Quite frankly I don't know. I know what I have that he doesn't. A moral compass, for starters."

"If Faith is what binds this all together, who or what does he place his Faith in?"

Rifun shifted position, thinking about the Book. "He claims to have spoken to a great spirit made of smoke and shadow, that it healed a mortal wound and so he pledged himself to its service, though rather grudgingly as he does not take kindly to serving others."

"Do you believe him to be a dual-spirit, such as yourself?"

"He is as flesh and blood as I am, and he has great power."

Andrianary grew serious. "But does he have two spirits?"

"I don't understand."

The old man made a motion as if trying to make sense of thoughts even he did not understand. "I want you to consider something, that maybe he is yet only single-spirited, and it may not be him."

"What do you mean?"

"Do you know whether he had Faith before his mortal wound?"

"Not to my knowledge."

"Then perhaps it is not that a man had two spirits that he must balance, but that an evil spirit was looking for a vessel. You say this man has no moral compass, and so his soul is void."

"Possession, then."

The shaman nodded gravely. "And if this is the case, and if he truly is more powerful than you, then simply killing the flesh will do nothing to stop this evil spirit."

Again, Rifun shifted position. "Are the ancestor spirits revealing this to you?"

The old man gave him a certain look. "No. They are revealing this to you. Through me. This is your destiny."

"To vanquish this evil spirit?"

"To root out the evil it has caused, vanquish it, send it back to Hell as it were."

"How should this be done? If killing the flesh is not enough, what must be done?"

"The answer to this is not straightforward, as you might imagine. It will take much prayer, much meditation, much discipline in seeking the spirits. You must train, use your abilities and discover new ones." He nodded. "It will help to ascertain the plans and intentions of this spirit; it may help guide your actions and reactions. Remember what we spoke of in regards to planning and being constantly aware."

"I remember," Rifun told him.

Andrianary stretched a leg. "Now that we have discerned your destiny, this true reason for your dual-spirited nature, I may be able to teach you a few things myself about driving out evil spirits. Understand, however, that anything I do, you must be able to give strength a hundredfold, if not more, for this is no ordinary spirit."

"I understand."

"Tell me, what is this man's name?"

"These days he goes by Cassius. He took the name..." Rifun paused. "He took the name after pledging himself to the spirit's service. It was the name of the man who mortally wounded him. He killed him."

The shaman nodded slowly. "And his name before?"

"He was a Yoruba man, his name Kokumbo. He said it means, 'this one shall not die.' "

"Mm. And indeed he hasn't."

Rifun frowned. "But could he really be possessed by this spirit? He was already quite evil by the time he made this pledge. He rather enjoyed killing."

"A fleshy husk devoid of soul and conscience makes an easy target for an evil spirit who intends an extended stay in our world."

He said nothing for a long minute. He could feel the old man's eyes boring into him, fiery youth hidden in a body too frail for its spirit. Finally, "What is the first step?"

Andrianary grinned. "You've already taken it. You stepped out in faith upon an unbelievable journey when no one, not even I, knew what to make of such an impossibility. Stars and monsters, kingship and treachery. A path walked upon the edge of a knife. When no one understood, you went anyway. That demonstrates amazing faith. Now you must pray and learn how to manifest this faith as power." He leaned back. "Return home for now. Pray each morning when you wake and each evening before you sleep. I think that by next week, you will have learned something."

Rifun did not argue with him, simply helped the old man to his feet and got him back home before heading to the farm.

His mind was spinning the same way it always did when trying to process such heady revelations. He hadn't understood it before, but it made a lot of sense. What if Cassius really was just a front for this evil spirit? For a man who had been obsessed with his birthright and his heritage to suddenly take a new name and identity without giving his old self a second thought, it only made sense if that man truly no longer existed, and such a spirit would have no need for the old life.

There were some details that didn't make sense and some questions that needed to be answered—such as why the evil spirit had wasted any time with Julianna—but if the answers were important, the ancestor spirits would reveal them in time. He'd just been delivered an earth-shattering revelation; he didn't know how much more he could handle at the moment.

With the heat finally broken, chores were being caught up at home, which meant no one was around when Rifun walked in the door, perhaps still appearing rather startled. Something about crossing the threshold into the house took the edge off his frazzled mind and anchored him back in the mortal world, and he was able to compose himself when the first person walked in the room.

It was Lalao.

"Oh, hello, Uncle Rivotra," she greeted. Technically they were cousins, but she called him uncle. "You're home early."

He Banded, if only to buy himself time to mentally transform into the uncle who was thirty-something years older than her, and not a cousin who was of an age and very, very attracted to her. Even when he released the Band, the best he could come up with was, "Well, there are still chores to be done and still some strength left in these limbs."

She grinned, grabbed a glass of water for herself and another for him, and sat down a moment at a small table near the door, wiping sweat from her brow. He joined her, again trying to be the uncle and not the cousin.

"I've been meaning to ask you something," she began.

"What's that?"

"Did Fan say anything about me to you?"

Rifun grinned. "Fan said a lot of things about a lot of people. What are you asking for specifically?"

"Did he...did he ever say he liked me? I mean, we spent a lot of time together and I usually caught him looking at me, at mealtime or from the yard. And not in a bad way. I mean, I kind of liked it. I was just wondering if he ever said anything."

"Well..." He shifted position and took a drink of water. "He may have mentioned something about it. And for as much as he takes after me, he is technically your cousin—you and I are technically cousins—and cousin marriage is frowned upon in London."

She shrugged. "We're second cousins. I mean, marriage between first cousins was common practice for...ages, even after the French came." She nodded. "But I understand what you mean." She took a drink. "Anyway, I was just curious."

Rifun chuckled. "I think you're a little more than just curious."

"Please don't tell him I said anything."

Too late for that. "Your secret's safe with me."

"*Misaotra*, Uncle Rivotra."

He let her go back outside first, then waited another minute or two before following.

Damn, he wanted her. He wanted to know her, he wanted to love her. If he wanted to be honest, the thought of marriage had crossed his mind a few times. But could he indulge? If he was going to go up against powerful evil spirits in possession of a soulless man, what right did he have to put Lalao in danger? Just because he didn't tell her, didn't mean that the spirits wouldn't know and seek to exploit their relationship. He was wary of his own personal defenses; if he had to protect both himself as well as her, and if he faltered for even a moment, the spirits could kill her.

He couldn't risk her life like that. If wouldn't be right. The way Andrianary made it sound, only a dual-spirited person could go up against this particular evil spirit. Even if he exposed her to Time and the Akari and got her into training, there was no way she would be strong enough to hold her own.

He should abandon the idea. It made logical sense on a number of levels. But he couldn't bring himself to summarily dismiss the possibility. There was no way he could just walk by her in the yard or see her at mealtime and not think about it. And if he did ever return as Fan, he couldn't suddenly be disinterested, cold and aloof. He couldn't shun her. He couldn't even make up a lie about having a girl back home, if only because he was playing both roles.

Why should he have these feelings now? After years of war and isolation and everything else taking up his time, why should they resurface now? It was terribly inconvenient to say the least. Here he was, being shown this great destiny, and love had to come strolling up the road. He couldn't fault love, for it was a noble thing, but for him? Here? Now?

He tried to go about his day as though nothing was wrong, and there were periods where he could push everything to the back of his mind. But as he lay down to sleep that night and thought about his prayers, doing everything as the shaman had instructed, he wondered. What was the pull of destiny, and what was a trick? Where did his true path lie, and what was a path to destruction? Where did he find greatness, and what was a distraction?

Again the question, what if he was wrong?

But the spirits would not lie, would they? Andrianary had been a reliable, trusted shaman for the family for many decades. He had discerned omens, divined futures, and left nothing to chance or uncertainty. He told the good news and the bad, gave good omens and warnings. He knew the power of the ancestors and the spirits, and if they had ever been upset with him, thought him deceitful, they would have done something about it years ago. Even if he had somehow tricked Rifun before with a false prophecy, surely the spirits would not allow him to do it again. All things had to be.

Rifun finished his prayers and lay there in the dark under his mosquito net, staring up at nothing for a long time.

When morning came, he did the same, saying his prayers and asking for guidance. Upon finishing, he rose with the rest of the family and went about his day. Lalao said no more about Fan, and Rifun made sure to stick to his own sex and age group when it came to chores or doing anything around the farm. He was her uncle, not her cousin. He was her elder, not her peer.

With the sweltering heat finally broken, things went back to normal. Chores got caught up, entertainment was had, and life was merry once more. Faliarivo trained desperately for the upcoming *savika* tournament, and many an evening were spent watching him in the makeshift pit, clinging to the hump of a large bull as it charged around the arena. He had the strength to hold on for the charge, but he lacked the dexterity needed to weather sudden jolts, jerks, and bucks. More than once he was thrown to the ground by a sudden stop, and his quick movements would startle the bull so that it ran over him in a panic before retreating.

Jaona helped his son out of the pit while Sambatra and a couple others opened the gate for the bull. Faliarivo was covered in dirt and bleeding from some minor wounds, but he was grinning ear to ear.

"You think a girl might notice me?" he asked, breathing heavily.

"I think they might," Jaona told him. "But you have to do more than one ride in one tournament."

"I know, but I have to start somewhere."

"As long as you don't start out in the hospital," Rifun told him. "Why don't you get yourself cleaned up? You'll be feeling it in the morning."

Faliarivo took off running back toward the house, just as energetic as when he'd first entered the pit. Jaona gave Rifun a look.

"What?" Rifun wondered.

"I get the feeling you don't approve of him competing in a couple weeks."

"Does it matter what I think? Your his father." Rifun went on before Jaona could speak. "Call it age, Jaona. All of my wounds are catching up to me. I feel them more now than I did when they happened. I feel everything as I see it, every fall and trample and gore. Cut an old man some slack."

Jaona did not seem entirely convinced, but it was an answer he could accept. Finally he nodded. "Well, you're not wrong there. Even I am starting to feel some new aches and old pains."

"It only gets better with each passing year."

Rifun clapped him on the shoulder and moved off.

Inside, Elisette was scolding Faliarivo for how filthy he'd gotten and a couple small wounds he'd sustained. The lad was still too excited to be much cowed, and he was still smiling even as Elisette finally sent him to wash himself.

"Oh, come now, Elisette," Volana said smoothly, "let the boy have some fun."

"I'm not denying him fun," she informed him. "I simply want him to get clean! Is that too much to ask?"

Rifun left the two of them to argue while he and others got ready for bed. Tonight he bowed to pray in front of the shrine. Why should he hide under his blankets as though ashamed of his ancestors? Did he not believe them capable of bestowing this promised power? Was it any more spectacular for him to pray versus using the Akari and molding the fabric of Creation?

No one said anything to him about it, and he headed to his bed soon enough.

The following morning was refreshingly cool, but he found himself holding a piece of paper in his hand. It hadn't been there last night. Curious, he opened it.

It was a note from Julianna, asking to meet him at the tombs at noon.

Well, clearly this wasn't a social call, a wayward daughter asking for forgiveness and a second chance to be with family. At the same time, it clearly wasn't an emergency of the highest order since this meeting came from a note slipped to him in the middle of the night.

But it wasn't like he had any major obligations for the day. He got breakfast, helped with morning chores, ate lunch, then made his way to the tombs.

Julianna sat on a rock looking rather annoyed.

"Took you long enough," she said sternly.

"If it were a true emergency, you wouldn't have been so kind about the message," he told her. "All it said was that you wanted to meet. What's this about?"

"Cassius is acting strange."

"And water is wet."

She shook her head. "No. He's secretive, elusive. This wouldn't bother me except Isthim has mentioned that a few of the grunts are disappearing regularly, and he always excuses them, bringing them back like lost hounds."

"Where are these missing grunts going?"

"They won't tell, and neither will Cassius." She shifted position. "Call me paranoid, but I think he's doing some training behind our backs."

"At face value, one might be able to come to that conclusion. But to what end? What would he need an army for that he couldn't do on his own?"

"That I haven't figured out. But there's more."

"Oh?" Rifun folded his arms.

She nodded. "He brought presents home the other day."

She tossed a sack to him which he caught effortlessly and opened. He may as well have unearthed King Tut's tomb and all the riches inside.

"Do we have a guess as to where they came from?"

"No, not exactly. He went missing for several weeks." Julianna huffed a sigh. "Interestingly and perhaps coincidentally enough, the Turitians had a bit of trouble on some grand royal parade for the new queen. Seems a rival family sent an undercover assassin or some such thing, and he got a hold of a number of priceless artifacts and trinkets, including the crown of Srori."

Rifun looked in the bag again. He was no expert on Turitian antiquities, but he wouldn't doubt that's what they were.

"Why, though?" he asked again. "Cassius doesn't need an army. He doesn't need money. He does things in order to show off, but to use a Disguise and go through some undercover operation... It has to serve some purpose. Which grunts are going missing? Are they regulars?"

"The Korin mercenaries were the first to go. A few others have since gone as well. Whatever he's doing, it seems to be a pretty exclusive club."

"And expensive." He tossed the bag back to her. "What do you want me to do about it?"

"At this point, nothing," she told him. "Quite frankly, there's nothing to do. I just wanted you to know so that if it turns into something, you're not playing catch-up."

"A point well-made, I thank you for it." He dipped his head. "Otherwise, how are things going between you and Isthim?"

"She's a bitch, but we've staked out our territories. She controls the army, and I control the Peace Corps. As long as we stay in our lanes..." She sighed and gave him a look. "If you want my opinion, I hope Cassius is raising this secret army or task force in order to get rid of the Borelians."

"It wouldn't be a bad idea," Rifun agreed.

"And what about you? How goes the quest to become a Builder?"

"Only just begun, although I believe I have cleared the first major hurdle."

"Do you mind if I ask what that is?"

He thought on Andrianary's words, about Julianna being a gathering storm, how it may be better if she didn't learn these skills. All the same, she had only asked a simple question, and he gave her a simple answer. "Purpose."

"Purpose?"

"What I am meant to do as a Builder."

Julianna nodded. The scars on her face made any expression mildly comical and moderately repulsive, but Rifun figured he knew her well enough to say she was both awed and dismayed. She admired that he was studying to be a Builder, but she had always expected that she would do the same. And here he was, a bastard from an inferior culture taking her prize. Actually, putting it in those terms made Rifun feel rather smugly satisfied about the whole thing.

"Well then," she said, standing and smoothing her dress, "I suppose I will leave you to your grand, metaphysical studies and return to the land of mere mortals."

"Timekeepers were gods and Harvesters witches to primitive peoples," Rifun said. "We both know how this works."

"Physically, yes. But there is still that element of Faith." She went on before he could say more. "Continue your studies. Depending on what Cassius has up his sleeve, we may need all the firepower we can muster."

He couldn't disagree with that. He wished her well and watched her leave, stepping through a portal and being swallowed into thin air.

The next day was his regular meeting with Andrianary, and he relayed events as best he could, fudging certain details to make it more plausible for the old man.

"So, this evil spirit possessing this soulless man has robbed royalty of their antiquities and is recruiting others to his side," the old man mused darkly. "But for what purpose?"

"Nothing good, I think," Rifun said.

"His strength grows while yours is only budding. As I am merely a guide and not a teacher, I am afraid that your progress may not only be slow, but terribly limited. We will require much prayer as well as fasting. This past week of prayer each morning and evening has brought this knowledge to you, but we must know more."

Rifun shifted uncomfortably. "What if I were to find another dual-spirited person? Someone who already has some of this knowledge, who could actually teach me?"

"Such people are exceedingly rare, as I have already told you, and may not even exist in each other's lifetimes. Where would you find such a man?"

"I might know of one."

How willing Andrew or Micaiah—assuming he was one—would be to help him, after everything that had happened, Rifun wasn't sure, but he couldn't not try. The Akarin weren't too fond of Cassius in the first place, so they might be willing to help depose a psychopathic tyrant. If they also took out Isthim, then maybe the Cult and the Akarin could come back together, or at least begin the peace process.

But first he had to find Andrew or Micaiah and convince them to help.

"If you do know of such a person, it would be wise to seek his counsel,"

Andrianary agreed. "And if there is such another person, and you two were to combine your strengths...Zanahy only knows the extent of this evil spirit that it takes two dual-spirited people to dispatch it."

Rifun elected not to inform the shaman that there were more Builders out there.

"Until then, we must proceed with your training with all speed."

"Have we intentionally been slow?" Rifun wondered.

"No," the shaman told him, "merely thorough, methodical. Just as you studied many classes and subjects in school in order to more greatly fulfill your education. But we appear to not have the time for such things, and must focus only on needs and essentials."

"Is there a way to entice the spirits to do this? Are they not the ones we are waiting on for instruction?"

No matter what the shaman answered, it would make him look bad, so he elected not to say anything at all. Instead he simply gestured for Rifun to begin his forms and prayers.

It did not seem to Rifun that anything changed that day. The spirits did not bombard him with divine messages, nor did they slap with him sudden insight and incredible power such that even the Akari paled in comparison. He did his forms and prayers, demonstrated what he knew, and did as Andrianary instructed, showing this or that ability.

The old man had a certain seriousness about him, but that was to be expected, Rifun supposed, with the news about Cassius. He hadn't even fallen asleep during forms. Rather, he seemed thoughtful, ponderous even. Like many elders, there was a youthful fire set deep in his wrinkles. In the case of Andrianary, perhaps it was not youthful fire, but spiritual fire, as if some curtain had been parted in his mind that he was finally beginning to understand and could help truly teach Rifun.

But to Rifun's eyes, very little progress was made, if any at all. He tried to take the old man's compliments at face value when things got wrapped up, but it was hard.

"A fine job," Andrianary told him, grinning as Rifun helped him to his feet. "I think we have both learned something remarkable today."

"The spirits showed you something?" Rifun wondered.

"Yes, but I must go home and dwell on it, seek the spirits of my own accord. When we meet again next week, I think I shall have much to teach you."

If Rifun was supposed to reciprocate this hope, then he was sorry to disappoint the old man. Nevertheless, he donned his Disguise and escorted the shaman back home. Neither said a word of what had transpired, simply wished each other good day and parted ways.

Rifun returned to the farmhouse where lunch was very nearly ready.

"Rivotra," Volana began lightly, "don't worry yourself about being buried in the family tombs. It will happen. But if you stay there so constantly, you shall see yourself to an early grave."

"Is that what you told Fan when he went to pray every day?" Rifun asked smartly.

Volana waved a hand. "Ah, I doubt he would have understood. You did well to teach him, Rivotra, but some things can only be truly learned when one grows up with it, and to a child's eyes, everything is true and absolute."

Rifun took his place at the table just as Elisette emerged from the kitchen with the first plates of food, Lalao close behind. He did not wish to ignore his cousin, but he couldn't just carry on as he was. And with the threat of Cassius and the evil spirit looming overhead, he knew that eventually, something was going to have to give.

16 | Tọjú ati Ki o Wá

En Route to Ikta, 1965

Hide and Seek

kokumbo

The Turitians had managed to make space travel bearable, making everything as comfortable and stable as if walking along the ground or in any common building. They would have had to, for the royal emissary had been expected to travel in the utmost style and convenience, with all the latest amenities. It was terribly bad for public relations if a member of the royal entourage stumbled off the spacecraft with violent space sickness.

Even Jora had a pretty smooth ride in his little one- or two-man craft, although it wasn't as though he didn't have the funds to ensure stability and comfort.

The Korin had yet to perfect this art, and Cassius spent a good deal of time lying in his bed and Slow Banding to try and pass the time.

He should have insisted on portal travel. But no. Had to do things logically, and God forbid things be off-balance for the damn Korin.

Their destination was Ikta, a planet not far from Sadurnon, speaking relatively. Unfortunately, the Iktarians were rather snooty about the use of Time and forbade all portal travel on the planet's surface. They were also sticklers about its use in their entire solar system. Ikta was the only inhabited planet in their system, and they decreed that all portals opened therein were to be investigated. All incoming travel had to be done the old-fashioned way, by spaceship. And just in case anyone thought to be clever and try to open a portal around their entire ship, the Iktarians would investigate that, too, if it happened within three systems of them, and any planets in these systems were either uninhabited or Unengaged. The only exception to this was for the handful of Time Agents on the Unengaged worlds who had to conduct their own business, but that did Cassius and the rest of them absolutely no good.

The Korin had taken them all aboard their own ship via portal, then used another portal on the ship to get as close to Ikta as possible. Now they just had to ride in like good little civilians.

It was probably why the twin assassins had chosen to hide on Ikta. A few favors, a few bribes, and they would know when anyone came looking for them. Which was why Cassius had suggested they use a portal anyway.

But no. It was unbalanced for the Korin. Cassius probably could have gone by himself anyway, but that would only put them more off-balance. Tip them too far and they were likely to fall over, leave and not return.

Some days he didn't care, and some days he did. He'd started out caring, at least enough to go along with the charade, but with each slosh of his brain as the ship rattled and jolted, he was caring less and less. Unfortunately, there was also less and less he could do about it.

As far as he was concerned, he only spent about nine hours onboard the hellish vessel before they reached the border of Iktarian space along an asteroid belt in the outer reaches of one of the three systems. Any space craft would have to slow down in order to navigate the belt, giving the Iktarians plenty of time to send smaller pods to intercept them.

"What is your destination?" one of these pod pilots demanded, his communication audio only.

"We're bound for Ikta," Cassius answered, grateful for the lack of visual; even someone who had never been exposed to humans would know that he did not look or feel well.

"What is your purpose to the mother planet?"

"Why else would a Korin of Irig vessel be here while under a war dynasty? We're here on a mission of bounty. The twin assassins, Murdi and Lordo, of Mishim, are hiding here, or so our source told us."

There was a silence that stretched so long, Cassius was forced to inquire whether they'd lost the transmission. Dubikoff, manning the communications systems, reported everything normal. Surloff and Barnoff, who did everything and anything having to do with engines and weapons, also reported nothing unusual from their vantage in the engine room. Kokriloff, the pilot and commander of this particular craft, had never had dealings with the Iktarians before and could offer no guesses. Pilory, acting as a kind of navigator as well as trainee, might have been able to help had the communication been visual, but her keen, bird-like eyes could not see through walls and bulkheads.

Probably the message was being relayed to specific people, those people paid off to warn the assassins from three solar systems away that someone had come hunting for them. All the more reason to have used a portal, Cassius mused.

Finally the pilot came back on the channel.

"You may proceed to Ikta, observing the following regulations."

If they had been able to get a move on from the moment they were given permission, they probably would have made it to Ikta in the time it took the pilot to recite all of the regulations and ordinances they were to follow, only to be told at the end that a written document would be transmitted to the vessel's computer so they could review it at their leisure and refer to it if anything came up.

Only Pilory seemed in any kind of good spirits when they at last cleared the asteroid belt and were able to speed up a little, hopefully reaching Ikta before the next century rolled around.

"They're already gone," Cassius grumbled as he stumbled back to his quarters, the ride only marginally smoother since travel through this system was limited to twenty-nine obors, whatever that converted to. He steadied himself in the doorway. "The rules and regulations were just to buy the assassins time to leave. And if we have to do this all over again on our way out..."

He collapsed into bed, frustrated. He closed his eyes and focused on Slow Banding, telling himself that Banding might be a little nauseating now, but it was nothing compared to hours on a clunking, unsteady ship. With that logic in mind, he was able to get a Band around himself.

It was Pilory who interrupted him. He thought it had been only about ten to fifteen minutes, but a good four hours had passed.

"We're at the border of the Iktar system," she told him. "The Iktarians want to talk to you."

"Kokriloff is the commander," Cassius growled, pulling himself out of bed yet again. He followed her out of his quarters, returning to the command cockpit. "What do they want? More rules and regulations to sign off on?"

"They want to verify all species aboard this vessel."

He sighed but said nothing more, instead choosing to be grateful that they were at least stopped. He scolded himself. Time was he could brave raging seas as easily as calm waters. What was it about space that made him so queasy? He'd tried more than once to Feel inside himself, pinpoint the part of his brain — or his stomach — that protested such a thing, but by the time it got to that point, he couldn't focus long enough to really figure out the problem.

They reached the command cockpit, the four of them making the small space noticeable.

This time they had visual communication, though the Ikta weren't much to behold, and all that was visible were their heads, their blue skin capturing anyone's attention. Their heads were incredibly narrow with a pronounced ridge running from chin up a near-vertical visage, arcing back only slightly. Holes on either side of this ridge at the top may have been breathing holes of some form, for they had no nose, only the ridge. With the angle of the face, the set of their enormous black eyes suggested they could see a great deal around them.

Perhaps the most peculiar thing, however, was the mouth. Or rather, mouths. Like the eyes, there was one on either side of the ridge, turned vertically, with no lips to speak of so that they might have been mistaken for much larger breathing holes. They also did not appear to have teeth as humans had teeth, but more like bristles, such as whales had.

Cassius noted how the Ikta appeared capable of holding two conversations at once, one on either side of them. It was rather dizzying to consider, and he found himself unsure just where to look or how to respond when they started talking to him, switching mouths at leisure.

"To whom and what am I addressing?" one of the Ikta began. There were five in the picture.

"Cassius Hand, human," Cassius replied, suddenly annoyed by the Ikta. "And you?"

"Biktora Revol, Iktarian. It has been made known that you seek the Mishim known as Murdi and Lordo."

"That's right," Cassius said, shifting his stance. "Do you happen to know where they're hiding? It will make our job easier and we'll be out of here just as fast as possible."

"When you arrive at Ikta, go to the Gelvor docking station. There you will receive further instructions."

The communication ended.

Cassius glanced at Kokriloff. "What the hell was that?"

"Permission, I believe."

"You're no help."

"They're transmitting coordinates to the Gelvor docking station," Dubikoff reported.

"Take us there," Kokriloff ordered.

"So what did they need me for?" Cassius grumbled, half to himself. Verify all the species, yeah, sure. Given their rules, regulations, and procedures, it was plausible, but still, he couldn't believe they were entirely innocent in all of this. Murdi and Lordo were long gone by now, he was certain.

It only took an hour to reach the docking station, or about five minutes via the Slow Band he finally managed. When they were at last secured and the engines powered down, Cassius had Pilory Fast Band him so he could recover at least some of his wits, though he told her it was to test her Akari Banding abilities, in the event they were needed while on Ikta.

Upon entering the station, they were given special gravity boots to help them stay on the ground, then escorted to a sort of processing center which put Cassius in mind of the Wheel, the secretaries at their dull jobs. The line moved swiftly at least, and Cassius stepped up to the counter to speak for the group.

"You arrived on the Korin of Irig vessel, correct?" the Ikta secretary confirmed.

"That's correct," Cassius said. "We're here looking for—"

His attention was taken by the Iktarian's hands. Four slender fingers, very much like a human's, but where there was normally a thumb, four more fingers extended out, like a second almost-hand. A strip of paper was printed out from a machine, ripped off, and handed to him, the secretary saying, "This is your destination, with coordinates. Move along."

Shouldn't they have to talk to someone? Get some kind of clearance? Was it really that easy to kill someone on Ikta? All you had to do was ask?

Apparently not, since the paper they were given was a map directing them to an office on the station. Cassius awkwardly knocked once and entered, the rest trailing behind.

"Ah, you must be the ones from the Korin of Irig vessel," the Iktarian greeted before they were even all in the room. "Here searching for Murdi and Lordo of Mishim."

"And who are you?" Cassius asked.

"Ruv Vilitar Gilin. Don't bother with introductions of yourselves, I already know. I was apprised of the situation when you entered our system."

"Do you know where Murdi and Lordo are?" Pilory inquired.

Ruv Gilin printed off a paper much as the secretary had. "Last we heard, they were in Irikor, or its outskirts anyway. Irikor is one of the oldest cities on Ikta, thousands of years old. And it shows. Ages and eons of overlapping architecture and technology, and a popular spot for tourists. Makes it easy to hide. A transport pod is already waiting for you in Bay 23."

He handed the paper to Cassius. It appeared to be a city map, but any and all writing was lost on him.

Cassius looked up. "How do we know this information is accurate? How do we know you haven't warned them ahead of time to get away and are sending us into a trap?"

"Ikta is only as good as its word, and we have had superb relations with the Hands of Time for centuries unbroken. Regardless of the state of the Wheel now, we must remain as loyal as possible to all Hands, past and present."

For half a second, Cassius couldn't figure out what that had to do with anything. Then he considered that he had once been a Hand. The Hand of the Hands, the Zero Hour. Finally he dipped his head. "Your loyalty and cooperation are noted and will be passed along."

"There is one rule which must be strictly observed, however."

Of course there was.

"And what is this rule?" Cassius asked, trying to suppress a sigh.

"There must be no killing on the planet's surface or on any Iktarian space station or ship."

Cassius blinked. "You do realize why we're here?"

"Yes, but that is our law. There must be no killing. You may take the twin assassins prisoner however you see fit, and you may dispatch them aboard your own vessel once you have left dock. But there will be no killing, or else you will face our judgment."

They were made to agree to the terms before being permitted to leave and continue their mission. The Korin went first, then Pilory, but Cassius stopped at the door and looked back. "Ruv Gilin, I must ask something."

"By all means."

"There are no Hands in power in the Wheel right now. Even the Tacagans and Gentleman Killers have been deposed for the time being. All that remains are the factions and a growing presence of the Cult of the Akari. Where do your loyalties really lie?"

Ruv Gilin chose his words carefully, but Cassius still wasn't sure how to look at him. "Our first loyalty is always to Ikta and our own people. After that, the Time industry has always been the most powerful force in the universe. With none claiming total control of the industry, we try to be hospitable to all."

"So you are saying that you were once loyal to the Tacagans and the Gentleman Killers, when they controlled the majority of the industry?"

"That may be an accurate assessment, although we do try to remain hospitable to all."

"And if the Cult of the Akari were to take over and control the industry?"

The Iktarian made a gesture Cassius did not understand. "It is not about loyalty to this group or that group, but loyalty to the industry that sustains us outside of Ikta. All that we have here—our space capabilities, our entire economy—is because of the wealth of the Time industry. Some call it blood money, others call it business."

"Like the Turitians, then."

"You could say that, although we are not so patient nor given to helping others."

Cassius frowned and nodded. "Fair enough. But I am forced to wonder, Murdi and Lordo are Gentleman Killers, or they were. And you just admitted to once supporting them. Would you so easily turn on us if the opportunity arose? If the winds of change shifted away from the Hands?" He put up a hand. "You don't have to answer."

He left the office, meeting up with the others in the common area.

"Something wrong?" Dubikoff inquired.

"Not yet," Cassius replied. "Kokriloff, how attached are you to your ship?"

"It needs many things, but it is reliable."

"That's not what I mean. If it were to be confiscated by the Iktarians, how devastated would you be?"

"It would be frustrating, but I hold no emotional bond with it." He seemed genuinely confused by the concept.

Cassius nodded. "Good."

"Has the ship been confiscated?" Pilory wondered.

"Not yet."

The station was divided into two major wings, one for space-faring vessels, and one for the transport pods that zipped back and forth between the planet and any of the space stations orbiting high above. As foretold, the pod in Bay 23 was expecting them, although it was a bit cramped with the four Korin, to say nothing of Cassius, Pilory, and the two Iktarian pilots.

Cassius' stomach did a flip, but entering the atmosphere proved to be little more than a bump in the road, and soon they were soaring high over the planet's surface.

Ikta was a very blue planet, as befitted its blue-skinned inhabitants, and if not for the shadows over the land, it might have been next to impossible to tell where land and water met.

"What can you tell us about Irikor?" Cassius inquired of their pilots.

"It's an ancient city," one answered, using its left mouth to speak to him while his right mouth seamlessly conversed with his copilot. "Thousands of years old. Some say it was the first Iktarian city ever built."

"What about these days?"

"A mismatched quilt of eons and dynasties, fortune and famine. Popular with tourists. The Great Spire has long been the symbol of hope and prosperity for our people."

The pilot went on to list several other points of interest, none of which concerned Cassius. He hoped the others didn't plan on doing any sightseeing while they were here. If they weren't allowed to kill Murdi and Lordo—and this point was up for debate, depending on how the confrontation went—then the longer they wandered around as stupid outsiders, the greater the chance the assassins would see them and flee, and Cassius and the others might never know it.

"Where are your shadier parts of town?" Cassius asked. "Where should tourists typically avoid?"

"The city is largely peaceful during the day, but the west side tends to get a bit rowdy after dark," the second pilot answered, speaking out of his right mouth while he conversed with his copilot with his left.

"How long until sundown?"

"Five Base Hours until sunset, but a majority of the city lights will remain active for another two hours."

Seven hours. The others were going to want to go sightseeing. Cassius just knew it. Fucking normal people.

They broke through the last layer of clouds and Irikor sprawled out before them. It didn't take a genius to figure out where the Great Spire was, for it reached a hundred feet above the tallest building with a giant shining thing on top. As sun dimmers went into effect on the pod's windshield, Cassius saw it appeared to be a great mirror array atop the spire. A huge wall surrounded the city, differences in craftsmanship testifying to all of the eons and battles it had witnessed. The city itself expanded far beyond the wall's confinement in, as the pilot had observed, a mismatched quilt of age and architecture.

"How many people live in Irikor?" Cassius asked.

"Eleven million Iktarians, another five million off-worlders."

Sixteen million people, plus who knew how many casual tourists, at least five million non-Iktarians, and they were looking for two Mishim. Needle, meet haystack.

Their landing was not as smooth as the Turitians' had been, but it was better than anything Kokriloff's ship had managed, and they departed no worse for wear. There was strict protocol to follow to usher people off the landing strip and away from the yard, but once beyond the gates, they were on their own.

From above, the city was huge and sprawling, and it didn't get any smaller seeing it from the ground.

"So where do we want to start?" Pilory wondered, looking around like a bright-eyed tourist.

"We should start with a base of operations," Cassius said. "It might take a little while to canvas the city; we should have a place to meet and compare notes, share information."

Normal people called this getting a hotel, and Pilory was happy to oblige. Despite the fact that their targets were probably hanging out in some seedy motel on the west side of town, Pilory insisted on finding something more on the high end, and she didn't even mind paying. The concierge thought it a bit strange that four Korin were checking in, but said nothing about it as they received their room keys.

Cassius hadn't been in such a nice hotel in a long time. Or rather, he assumed it was a nice place. The tables and chairs were hard to mistake for anything else, but these weren't regular rooms like one might find on Earth. Apparently the Ikta slept standing up in pod-like contraptions, and they expected everyone else to do the same.

Pilory, as his roommate, eagerly flitted from room to room.

"Shouldn't you be pirating with Titik?" he asked irritably.

"Ship's docked at Timtoy Station," she replied, unfazed. "I'm just taking shore leave."

"How long do you have?"

"Four Base Days."

He hoped it wouldn't take four days to find Murdi and Lordo. The only way to ensure that, then, would be to get started as soon as possible.

"All right, we should start with a general canvas of the city, try to get our bearings, establish some landmarks, and figure out the who's who of—" He paused. "Pilory!"

The Tibidi stopped and looked at him. "I'm listening, don't worry. Canvas the city, get our bearings, landmarks, and did you know there is an eating establishment on the ground floor of this place?"

Cassius blinked. "So what?"

"Come on. I know you're not going to let us go sightseeing, but we can at least enjoy one of the amenities I'm paying for." She emphasized the last bit.

"How about this? You and the Korin can go to dinner. I'm going to find a way to the Great Spire. Seems as good a place as any to start. Meet me there when you're done."

That seemed to brighten her mood and she went next door to get the Korin.

Sighing, Cassius left the hotel room. He shouldn't have brought them. Not only were they useless, but counterproductive. He was here to kill, not play games. When had he fallen from mercenary to babysitter? Oh, right, when he decided he wanted a secret army or something. Yeah, how was that working out?

Thankfully, the Iktarians seemed to be one of the few advanced civilizations that had invented elevators, making it much easier to get from the twenty-seventh floor to the ground, or vice versa as he considered the ride up.

He stepped off the elevator into the lobby area. Most of the walls were glass, letting in plenty of light, though most of it came from a mirror network set up around the city, the Great Spire being its main matrix or something. Pilory had made some comment about it to the concierge who was ready with the standard rundown of the network for the information and pleasure of all guests.

There were eight elevators in the lobby, ten concierge ports, a rather luxurious sitting area, and a hallway leading to any number of amenities, including Pilory's coveted restaurant.

But as Cassius did a quick glance around the room, he stopped dead in his tracks and stared. There. Just getting off one of the elevators. Could it honestly be? No. Yes. Not a chance. Could he really be so lucky?

"Hey! You!" he barked.

Naturally eighty percent of the room looked around, trying to figure out what the yelling was about. But it also attracted the attention of Murdi and Lordo, and as soon as eye contact was made, they bolted.

The twins made it to the doors first, barreling through and rudely pushing past several patrons. Cassius was close behind. Not being slowed by unsuspecting patrons, he raced through the opening they had made and managed to gain a few paces.

The Iktarians did not have cars as such, but they did utilize mass transit in the form of hoverpods, being very similar to the transport pods to the space stations, and they traveled along specific rail lines laid in the stony roads. If struck by one, it would certainly hurt, but it was also very possible to slide under them.

As the twins narrowly avoided a particular hoverpod, Cassius threw himself to the ground and rolled, popping up on the other side, losing whatever he had gained at the hotel, but little more. Whatever technology was used to make the hoverpods hover, it did not seem to have any adverse effects for the odd pedestrian.

The twins were Physician Harvesters, but they'd evidently learned a thing or two from the Timekeepers as they went into a Band. It was weak, hardly better than what a probationary could pull off, and Cassius easily pushed into its wake, effectively drafting behind them. Murdi and Lordo also only used regular, weak Time Bands, where Cassius used an Akari Band, and he quickly discovered a very unique and effective feature. Being in the Time Band wake, when he brought up his own Akari Band, the Akari Band began taking the energy out of the Time Band, fueling itself and diminishing the Time Band's power. Suddenly it was like running at the twins at a hundred miles an hour, how quickly he caught up, but he did not slow.

Instead, just a millisecond before he touched the twins, who either did not know or did not care about their Band being diminished, Cassius took the Band, inverted it, and popped it like a bubble. The Energy erupted, throwing the twins and a dozen passersby to the ground. Cassius merely slowed to a walk.

Murdi and Lordo were ready in the blink of an eye, suddenly on their feet and circling him, flesh-rending swords at the ready.

"Now, now," Cassius purred, "we all made an agreement not to kill on Iktarian soil."

"Then that was your own fault," Lordo spat.

Through some sixth sense, Cassius ducked and rolled just as a sword reached through a micro-portal into midair where his throat had been just a moment ago. He got up, jumping as another sword swiped at his feet. Did the Iktarian rule about no portal use extend to micro-portals as well?

Whatever the case, the twins apparently had no reservations about breaking the rules, which meant Cassius didn't either. Let the Iktarians gripe; he was no Hand or Zero Hour. He was the Cult of the Akari, and he would suffer no traitors. But first he had to survive this encounter.

He rolled on the ground, considering any number of tricks he could pull to neutralize the threat of steel. Then, the next time he saw a micro-portal open and a sword come through, he reached out for it. He Banded to buy himself time, flinching as the blade made the tiniest of incisions on his skin. He could see every edge along the deadly blade, and he found himself regretting his decision even as he followed through. He oxidized the metal, causing it to become brittle, rusting it in only a fraction of a second so that it crumbled around his hand, bits of rusted metal only giving him minor nicks.

It had been Murdi's sword, and the assassin stumbled, his weight and balance suddenly thrown off. He went down and Lordo tripped over him. They Banded so Cassius could not see them go to the ground, and when they were ready again, Murdi had his sword raised once more, now little more than a six-inch knife.

"Nice trick," Murdi said.

They struck again before Cassius could reply, and their fighting style did not seem terribly affected by a sudden lack of sword.

In his peripheral vision, Cassius deduced that some kind of law enforcement was arriving on scene. Well, they weren't going to interrupt his mission. He pulled the three of them into a Fast Band. At the first sign of disorientation from the twins, Cassius threw up a second Band around himself, grabbed Lordo's sword, and, using Thermodynamics, melted the blade into slag that dripped onto the swordsman's feet, eating through his shoes and feet like candy.

Lordo shrieked and went to the ground, wailing. Murdi seemed torn between advancing on Cassius again and tending to Lordo. He took one step toward Cassius, paused, looked at Lordo, looked at Cassius. His hand wavered ever so slightly. He looked at Lordo, looked at Cassius, looked at Lordo. Finally, he took a step toward Lordo, then, with incredible acrobatics, launched himself sideways in an impressive leap and twist, swinging ferociously at Cassius with his little knife and even cutting his arm when he put it up to protect himself.

Pain broke through the awed illusion, and Cassius grabbed Murdi's arm. He yanked the assassin out of the air, twisted Murdi's arm, feeling several bones break, and slammed him to the ground. Taking the knife from his limp hand, Cassius superheated the blade, then sliced off Murdi's hand, in much the same way he'd done to Rilor. While Murdi shrieked, Cassius forced the assassin to do an awkward roll over toward Lordo where he again inverted and popped the Band, effectively hitting them both with a hammer while they were down. They gasped for air, but made no further threatening movements.

He dropped the Band and the law enforcement squad arrived.

"What has happened here?!" one demanded.

"Talk to Ruv Gilin on Gelvor station. He'll have all the information," Cassius told them. "I'm just here to take out the trash, clean up a little pest problem as it were. You don't have to thank me."

"There is to be no killing on Ikta."

Cassius made a gesture. "Do they look dead to you?"

"We also detected portal activity in this area."

"Purely on them."

"We'll see what the cameras have to say about that."

Using a device reminisce of the Glass tablets in the Archives, the officers were able to bring up camera footage of the area, narrowing it down to three cameras that captured elements of the fight. With Murdi and Lordo still in pain on the ground, Cassius was cleared of any wrongdoing, as far as portal use went.

"We'll be taking them into custody," the officer said.

"But they're my prize," Cassius protested. "I didn't go through all the hassle to get here just to let them go."

"Our law has precedence here. We're taking them in." The lead officer made a motion to the others who were swift and efficient with their use of handcuffs.

Cassius was dumbfounded. "Do I get any compensation? Can I come back later to claim them once they've served their time in jail?"

"They're ours now."

"And how are you going to stop them from using portals, anyway, to escape?"

"Portal-inhibiting handcuffs," another officer answered. "Similar technology used in our keep."

"Then why don't you use that around your whole damn planet if you're such sticklers about it?" Cassius growled. "I want my prize. I'm not leaving empty-handed."

The lead officer gave him a look. "Then buy something from a souvenir stand."

Cassius was rather taken aback by the officer's words. He was ready to flout every rule right then, kill the officers, the assassins, and then escape via portal. With that beast straining against his will, he asked, "Can I at least come with you and ask them some questions of my own? I need information out of them, too."

It got him somewhere, at least, as the officer agreed and motioned for him to follow.

Pilory and the others could do their sightseeing around the Great Spire. Cassius was going to get something done.

He followed the officers to a specially-marked hoverpod and got in with them. A lesser officer had grabbed the swords, or what remained of them, and sat at the end opposite the prisoners. A third disappeared into a sectioned-off cockpit. There was the faintest whir of an engine, and then they were on their way.

"We will process them in our way," the lead officer told Cassius, his tone suggesting no room for discussion. "If they survive, then you may question them."

"Survive?" Cassius questioned, intrigued.

The police station was not just located in an eight-story building, it was the eight-story building. With the landscape the way it was, the entrance was on the third floor. The lobby or receiving room was hardly anything of note, and Cassius was made to wait there while the officers took Murdi and Lordo, almost passed out from the pain and damage to their hands or feet, back for processing.

Cassius recalled his time in Beaumaris Gaol. Things had been simpler back then. Commit a crime, especially a serious crime, and get treated like scum. It might have been easy to label Cassius a hypocrite for such things, but he never expected to be treated like a king. He'd been very pleased with his time on Rid in the prince's palace, but he never expected it to be the norm. He expected the lying, cheating, backstabbing, and everything that came with the criminal underworld. He expected it in jails and prisons also.

That was why people broke in jail. They told themselves that they were good, that they were better than this. They never thought they "deserved" it. They told themselves that things ought to be better, that they were being wronged. They never thought about making something out of it. Lemons and lemonade and all that.

He Slow Banded here and there, to pass the time, wondering just what Iktarian police processing looked like. Around the four-hour mark, Pilory and the Korin showed up.

"Took the long tour, did you?" Cassius asked before they spotted him.

"We went to the Great Spire," Surloff informed him, sounding annoyed. "You weren't there. We waited. We looked around. Finally we began a search. It was fate only that took us to the place where you apprehended Murdi and Lordo, a civilian giving us directions here."

"What are you doing here?" Pilory asked directly.

As Cassius opened his mouth, the door also opened, and the same lead officer as before stood there in the doorway.

"I'm asking them questions of my own," Cassius said. He looked at the officer.

"You may interrogate them at your leisure," the officer said.

Telling the rest of them to stay put, he followed the officer through the door, making sure to close the door loudly behind them.

While the outside looked crisp and clean, once behind the facade, the building had evidently been part of the oldest architecture of the city. It wasn't just floors that were different, but sections of floors, even individual rooms were different builds and styles, wood and stone and metal and things Cassius had no name for, all haphazardly thrown together and secured with bubble gum and tape. Rifun would have a field day with this place, Cassius thought.

They headed down to the first floor. Cassius was taken to a room with an airlock, where Murdi and Lordo were held behind some kind of energized bars.

"The outer door here will be locked, and I will be waiting on the other side," the officer said. "Should you wish it, the key to deactivate the field is right there." He indicated a fob hanging on the wall. "Knock on the door when you are ready."

And he left, locking the door behind him, leaving Cassius alone with the twin assassins. Lordo looked like he'd received only the barest of care for his wounds, and he was currently passed out on the bench. Murdi sat in a tiny space at the end of the bench, his arm and hand also hardly cared for beyond a makeshift splint and sling, his wrist stub cauterized grossly.

"What were you doing in that hotel?" Cassius blurted.

"What were you?" Murdi retorted. "You're scum. You don't fraternize with high rollers. You wouldn't expect us to, either. We figured you'd go slinking around the slums and gutters for a while. Assuming you ever thought to look out of your price range, we'd hear about it long before you got to us."

"I admit, I thought that was why you came to Ikta in the first place. Bribe a few officials in order to get news of anyone looking for you through the insufferable legal channels, anyone who opened an illegal portal, maybe bribe them some more so you could make a quick escape. Question is, why didn't you escape?"

"What does it matter to you?" Lordo grumbled, not as asleep as he looked. "What, you can't kill us outright so you're going to bore us to death?"

"Curious to know what my fellow mercenaries are up to these days since the breakup of the Gentleman Killers."

"Like you care," Murdi said, spitting at his feet. His off-colored phlegm sizzled against the energy field. "I read somewhere that that's a human insult."

"Your source wasn't wrong."

"But maybe we should be asking you a few questions instead. Like why you are coming after us, really. Who contracted you? We heard about Yu-bix and Rnluv."

Cassius grinned. "No one contracted me."

"Then what interest does the Cult of the Akari have in us? Surely you can understand the concept of going where the money is good. At the time, it was the Tacagans. Your own flesh and blood, if memory serves."

"They'd never admit to it," Cassius chuckled. "As for the Cult, I'm just cleaning up a few loose ends."

"Doing the dirty work the others don't want to do?" Lordo guessed.

"Something like that."

Murdi shifted position. "So what made you offer amnesty to the likes of the Korin, anyway?"

I'm asking myself that more and more. "They were already part of the Cult. Seems the regular Gentleman Killers thought they were too good for them. Why? Are you begging for mercy?"

"Who's begging? You should know the game by now. We're offering our services to the winner."

"What services? He can't walk and you can't fight."

"We haven't studied the Akari true, but if it can do half the things with half the prestige that you've demonstrated so far, Lordo's feet should be just fine, I think," Murdi said. "If you cared to help. As for my hand, you think we trained only one way?"

Cassius frowned and shifted his stance. "As I said. What services? And how do I know you won't go running to the Akarin next? Or back to the Tacagans? Or anyone else who may suddenly come into some power and fame?"

"There is some loyalty to be had for the one who bested us. And the one who heals us. And trains us. Everything we've done so far has been of our own accord and time. We've never done it any other way."

"And for the third and final time, I'll ask, what services?"

Murdi held him in a long stare, as if trying to feel out what kind of response was most likely to benefit him. Then, "Aside from fighting, we're very good at going places where others can't, getting information. We're not politicians, but we can go where they are, where they can go, and where they can't."

"Spies, then."

"Something like that, yes. We're skilled assassins, not bumbling mercenaries. Why do you think we were invited to be Gentleman Killers?"

Defiant to the last. Cassius found it rather amusing. He grabbed the fob from the wall and turned off the energized bars. Without a word, he stepped forward and touched both Murdi and Lordo. He Felt them. He Felt the damaged, tender flesh. He could sense every fiber as it knit itself back together however it could, every nerve that could relay only pain. He was not an expert on Mishim anatomy and physiology, but he thought he managed to do them some good, heal them up a bit, put things back to rights, perhaps prevent a little permanent damage.

With the twin assassins reeling from the experience, Cassius reinstated the energy field.

"A small show of good faith, in the event we decide to take you up on your offer." He shrugged as Murdi looked up at him, his expression twisted in rigid pain. "I can't just offer this kind of mercy without consulting the others. Quite frankly, the only reason I'm considering it at all is because it amuses me. Maybe the Iktarian no-kill rule has spared you and given you a second chance at life. Who can know?"

He turned, went through the airlock, then knocked on the door. A small slot in the door opened, the lead officer looking in. Then he opened the door and Cassius stepped out.

"That didn't take long," the officer observed mildly.

"How long will they be here?" Cassius inquired.

"The average time for this offense is seventy-two days."

"What are the rules for visiting?"

"Normally there are no visitors."

"What happens when they are released?"

"The door is opened and they are free to go."

Cassius nodded slowly. "Call me on day seventy. I may have something for them when they're ready to go."

The lead officer mentioned something about it being irregular, but did not make a fuss. He escorted Cassius back to the lobby where he picked up Pilory and the Korin and headed outside.

Once a fair distance from the police station, he stopped and turned.

"I brought you along so you could help me. I asked you to join me because I thought I might need your help, that your help might be unique, that your talents may be not only unique, but powerful, critical to this mission and others. I'm not here to be your tour guide or take you on exotic vacations. You can do that well enough on your own."

Pilory opened her mouth to speak but Cassius cut her off. "The details are not up for negotiation, nor do I enjoy playing give-and-take over such trivial matters. If you want to spend your money on nice things, by all means. But do it on your own time and don't try to buy favors with such small things. And know that today, we got lucky. Very, very lucky. I can't even describe how lucky we got except that it must have been the Author's will. But we can't rely on dumb luck. We have to be smart. And if I can't rely on the lot of you, then I must also be smart and get rid of that which is slowing me down. Is anything I'm saying unclear?"

No one said a word, and alien physiology meant Cassius couldn't tell whether they were sufficiently chastised.

"As I said, we got lucky. And as much as I enjoy gambling, I don't know how I feel about you five hanging around me while I do seeing how you were nowhere to be found until after the fight. So here's what we're going to do. We're going to return to Gelvor Station, we're going to get back on Kokriloff's ship, assuming it hasn't been confiscated for some reason, we're going to get the hell out of here, and we're going to return to the ruins where you will be put back with the regular grunts in the regular army where you belong until you decide that you want to be special again!"

Now they were looking a little more sullen.

Truth be told, Cassius was feeling rather relieved about the whole thing. It was an easy way to get rid of them without having to actually get rid of them. And if one or more of them did decide that they wanted to be special and learn what he had to teach, assuming he wanted to go back to teaching, then he would make them prove themselves in some way. Make them come to him. They blew it on their first chance, having him approach them, and they seemed to realize this. In the future, they would come to him, but they would have to really want it.

And speaking of training, where had Rifun gone off to? Julianna had said something about him starting more advanced studies, but advanced studies in what? Cattle ranching? If Murdi and Lordo did actually end up in his service, maybe he would send them to figure out what Rifun was up to.

The six of them returned to the shipyard where a transport pod took them to Gelvor Station. It was difficult to hang onto flaming anger when your stomach was upside down, and by the time Cassius pulled on the special station boots, his anger was at a low simmer, more of an agitated annoyance. Pilory and the Korin had not said a word the whole time, and they still did not as they found their way back to Ruv Gilin's office.

"Stay here," he commanded irritably. "And don't cause any trouble. Not that you could."

He knocked only once before entering the office. Ruv Gilin looked up from his desk. If Cassius had to pick an expression or emotion, it might be surprise.

"Back so soon?" the ruv inquired. "Did you forget something?"

"A minor hangup," Cassius told him, relaying the condensed version of events.

"Mm...so Murdi and Lordo are held by the police," Ruv Gilin mused. "An unfortunate turn of events."

"The officer said that it would be seventy-two days until their release. I'd like to be notified of it, with enough time to get here before they are loosed to their own whims."

"I make no guarantees, but I will attempt to arrange it."

"Good. I trust our ship is where we left it?"

"Of course."

The parking fees were obscene, even for the short time they'd been gone, but Cassius was more than happy to have Pilory pay the bill and show off all the money she commanded. He couldn't decide if her anger was directed at him or herself. If she was smart, she'd realize that she had only herself to blame.

Would this have any bearing on Titik's cooperation? Maybe, maybe not. He was the captain, not her, and he didn't seem one to suffer fools. If she admitted to what had happened, she would certainly look the fool.

Then they were boarding, surrendering their station boots to the Iktarian workers before sealing the airlock. Surloff and Barnoff went below to start up the engines while Cassius, Pilory, Dubikoff, and Kokriloff made for the command cockpit. The departure sequence was initiated, and in just a few minutes they were slowly maneuvering away from the docking port, the large hunk of space metal surprisingly nimble.

"Incoming communication from the station," Dubikoff reported. "Audio only."

"Let's hear it," Kokriloff said, still finessing his pilot controls.

"Korin of Irig vessel, Shon-dur zero-five-one-nine, you are clear of the docking port," a station official reported.

"Thank you, Gelvor Station. We'll be on our way."

"Be advised that there are forty-three other vessels currently docked at the station and thirteen more in transit in the immediate vicinity."

"Thank you for the information. Shon-dur zero-five-one-nine out."

Cassius hung around for a bit, trying to tell himself that he was needed and important in some way, trying to hang onto that last bit of power he had over them. But Kokriloff was the commander and pilot here, and he was the one who was going to transport them out of here so they could go home. In seventy-two days, was Cassius going to have to ask for his help again? Would he have to offer his teachings as payment?

No, of course not. He was one of the leaders of the Cult. He gave orders and others obeyed. He didn't beg and trade favors.

All the same, maybe he would make a point of not asking Kokriloff to transport him back.

Once they were well clear of the docking station, Cassius left the cockpit, trying to appear as though he had better things to do and he would leave everything to his underlings. Really he just wanted to reach his quarters before they started picking up speed so that he could Band in peace and get this nightmare over with.

He thought he managed the return trip well. Once again they were stopped at the border of the Iktar system, confirming that they were leaving and all was in order. They were also stopped at the asteroid belt, on the edge of Iktarian space. It was less of a "come again soon" and more of a "don't let the door hit you on the way out" kind of farewell. But they were not detained or questioned, and instead sent on their way.

Once they were a fair distance from the border, the six of them pooled their strength and managed to open a portal around the entire ship, taking them back to Irig. It was a terrible thing to do, and they spent an hour just getting their bearings before opening a smaller portal back to the tunnels which took them to the ruins.

"Report to Isthim," Cassius ordered before they could get far. "Make sure she knows what's happened and what I've said. Then you follow her orders. Understood?"

Any morale recovered during the flight home quickly dissolved, and the five underlings crept away to find Isthim.

Cassius, meanwhile, returned to the officers building, intending to sleep for a few days, at least. Instead, Julianna found him first.

"Ah, back so soon?" she asked. "I thought you expected to be gone for a week?"

"Luck was on our side," he replied.

"Excellent."

"If you have another name, it can wait a day."

At first she seemed puzzled. Finally she nodded once and said, "All right. I suppose it can. Let me know when you're ready to go."

Either she was too eager to give him a name of someone to kill, or he was grouchier than usual. Whatever the case, he needed to get some sleep.

Maybe he should have taken advantage of the ritzy hotel on Ikta.

17 | Lazao ary Mianara

Madagascar, 1965

Tell and Learn

With the threat of a powerful evil spirit and the might of the Akari now more tangible, Andrianary seemed to be far more interested in Rifun's meditations and trainings, and the old man no longer fell asleep while he was doing his forms. In fact, he asked about them, why he made certain motions, what they represented, why he did a sequence a particular way. He even made a few suggestions of his own, which he said would improve the flow and balance of the forms overall.

Andrianary did not know anything about how to use the Akari, but his connection to the spirits and his own willingness to serve, learn, and offer unique insight helped Rifun to focus his energies on where and how to train so he didn't waste his time going over things he already knew.

"And is all this helping you to find this other dual-spirited person?" the shaman inquired.

"I know where he may be, just not when," Rifun answered evasively.

Truthfully, he was a bit apprehensive about approaching Drew again, assuming he did nail down when he would be at the Akarin fortress. They hadn't parted on especially amicable terms the last time, and he wasn't exactly converting over to the Akarin. He was asking for help in destroying an evil force in the universe, true, but if Micaiah had been any indication, the Akarin could be a bit stiff-nosed about helping others deal with their problems.

"Perhaps you ought to go looking for him, then," Andrianary suggested, "and stop waiting for good fortune to fall into your lap."

Rifun took a piece of fruit and, combining a Gravity track with a Fast Band, tossed it a good ten feet away from his position and watched a decayed husk hit the ground and vanish into dust. He glanced at the shaman. "I have never expected good fortune to fall upon me in any manner, but if I rushed into things with mere hope, chances are good that I would be long dead." He tossed another piece of fruit.

"And yet sloth is often disguised as caution in the fearful."

Rifun turned to look at him. "What are you saying?"

"You are glad to have training; you are glad to have a teacher and support; you are glad to have a destiny. But you seem a bit fearful to pursue it. Why is that? I understand it may be intimidating to consider going up against such a powerful spirit, but your fearful human nature must not be allowed to overcome your more powerful spirit nature."

On the one hand, the old man had no understanding of the broader universe, the politics at play, the powers that existed. On the other hand, maybe he didn't need to.

"It was said once that a man's destiny is only as resolute as the actions he takes to get there," he said, quoting from one of the Authored Books.

"Wise words," Andrianary said, nodding. "And that is why you fear? Because the act will perhaps close a door that you can never return through?"

"Another man said that a bridge does not need to be seen in order to cross it; it only needs to be stable."

"Also wise. Fear of the unknown, then. Although you have faced this unknown before, when rendered blind and driven from your village. Perhaps, then, it is the fear of initiative and the desire of comfort."

Rifun didn't want to admit to it, though his silence betrayed him.

"Understandable, but foolish," the shaman told him. "And, quite frankly, selfish. You know all of this, Rivotra. We've been over this more than once, and it has gone from the reasonable musing of a conflicted man to the stubborn pride and selfishness of a fool. The idea that you would drag your feet so you can curl up in a soft bed at night while an evil spirit wreaks havoc upon the world! Honestly! And who is to say that this other dual-spirited person is not looking for help for his own problems, perhaps in a far more dire predicament than you, beset by his own great evil, waiting for someone to help him? And you would ignore him so you can look upon your cousin?"

There were times when Rifun hated his lighter skin, and his embarrassment was often the cause of it. "What do you mean?"

"I don't visit often, I know, but I remember you as Fan and how you pined after Lalao. I can't imagine you feel any different now; you just can't express it. It not only frustrates you, but it hinders your progress here!"

Rifun opened his mouth to speak, but the docile old man had come roaring to life.

"You are incredibly selfish to waste this gift! Your *nenibe* is ashamed of you!

You were not made different so you could plod along like the rest of us! You were given an exceptionally rare gift, the ability to choose! You were born of two worlds, made of two worlds, just not the worlds that everyone else sees. You were refined by fire through unspeakable trials and atrocities that would break other men, as a way of testing you, your resolve, your *fanahy*. What are you made of? Are you the broken warrior who is going to lay down his arms and retire into a life where he cannot rightfully pursue the girl he loves, cause his family outrageous grief by faking his death and resurrecting himself so that he can marry her, all to satisfy his own ends? Or are you a war hero who is made stronger by his victories so that he might help not only his own people, but now the people of the world? How should it be for this man to lay down his arms when it suits him, simply because he wants to, and not because he was ready to die for a cause he believed worthy? Do you no longer believe in death?"

"Of course I do," Rifun defended.

"Then why don't you act like it? Going against this evil spirit will certainly present the possibility of death, but ignoring the threat will assure it. Then where will you be?" He went on before Rifun could speak. "An embarrassment among the ancestors." He let that linger. "You have been redeemed among men. This is known. Your mortal life is complete. Now you must rise higher and let the spirits and ancestors speak your name long before you join them." He nodded, half to himself. "They will do that anyway. All that remains is for you to decide whether they will do this for good or for ill."

The old man stood with no help and turned to leave. "I think that's enough for today, at least for me."

"Do you want me to take you home?" Rifun offered helplessly.

Andrianary laughed and waved a hand. "I'll be fine. I haven't felt this good in years. You must be rubbing off on me, for which I am not complaining, no. Besides, you have some praying to do, I think, and maybe a trip to plan. You don't need my help for that."

And he left, the foliage closing behind him and obscuring him from view. Rifun still watched the spot for a minute, used Sound and Light and Thermodynamics to see if he might be hanging around still, to see if he might spy some powerful, magical thing. When he found nothing beyond some birds and lizards, he lay back on the rock he'd been sitting on and let out a breath.

That was not how he'd expected this to go, to put it mildly. But then, he could find nothing about it that was untrue in some way. Thousands of Malagasy had lived and died on the battlefield. Thousands had lived and died through prison. By that token, he was one of thousands. And he highly doubted that every one of them had been told that they walked a path of stars and monsters and been given universe-bending abilities. To cut himself off now really would be a selfish thing to do, especially given the revelation of the evil spirit within Cassius.

But where did he go from here? There was still much to learn from the spirits about the Akari, and Andrianary had proven an adept mentor. But if he was to act, if he wanted to put force behind his words and work, he couldn't just herd cattle and relax on the porch with Volana and the others and meet the shaman once a week like a Sunday school class. He would have to return to Sadurnon, return to the Cult, and start making things happen again. He would have to get involved.

It might have been an easy choice if he could just kill Cassius and call it a day. The spirits knew there were a number of times when he could have, perhaps should have. But this would have to be different if he wanted to kill the spirit and not just the body it inhabited.

He didn't have the answers, and the spirits weren't just going to, as Andrianary had so eloquently put it, just drop good fortune into his lap. He was going to have to take the initiative, prove that he was ready and capable of receiving the guidance that the spirits had to give. No use giving a map to a man who had no intention of taking the journey.

He returned home, each step feeling heavier than the last. He was finally home, and he was having to leave. Again. With any luck, it was only temporary. He did not expect that he could wrap things up in a few days, or even a few months, but he could do a year. He had some affairs to take care of in London, get his things in order so that he could return permanently, not just for a visit. It was an easy story, even a logical one. Maybe he could visit once or twice as Fan, just to check in.

But if he was away that long, whether as himself or his fictional son, what if Lalao got married? What if she got tired of waiting? What if she wanted to come visit him in London?

He shook his head. He couldn't be consumed with such selfish things. Even if he married her today, he would outlive her by a century. Even if she became an Akari-bearer today, she might not be ready in time to face this evil spirit, and he couldn't have his attention divided so. It would be better, therefore, for both of them, to not pursue this relationship. Rifun could not, obviously. Maybe Fan found another girl. Maybe Lalao found another boy. Whatever the case, it couldn't happen, for reasons as logical as they were logistical.

All the same, it killed him inside to admit it, and someone could have stabbed him in the heart and he wouldn't have known.

When he returned to the farm, everything was as he expected it to be. The last of the morning chores were being finished up, overseen by Volana. Elisette directed her kitchen crew with the ruthless efficiency of an army commander. Lunch would be served, and then they would retire to an afternoon nap before the evening chores.

He paused on the slope overlooking the land. The farm was stable and the family was strong. Things could handle his absence for a few years, maybe even a few decades, though he did not anticipate being gone quite that long.

He descended the slope and entered the house. Elisette was just heading out to ring the bell, and Volana walked in the back door a moment later.

"Well, there he is! Right on time!" He put an arm around Rifun's shoulders. "You know, when the boys see you coming back down the road from your time with the shaman, they know it's almost lunch time, and they start packing up—whether the chores are done or not! Oh, we scold them and tell them to finish the chores, but we appreciate the notice, too."

They sat at the table as more people came filtering in from the fields, washing hands and chatting amiably. Everyone sat in his place, a prayer was said, and food made its way around.

"You seem troubled, Rivotra," Sambatra observed. "A bad omen from the spirits today?"

Rifun shook his head. "No. A bit of a chastisement from Andrianary. My fault, really. But I do have to return to London as well."

"Whatever for?" Elisette asked.

"My dear, he's stayed with us for quite a while, but he has a life back in London," Volana said. He looked at Rifun. "A home, surely, at least?"

"An apartment, anyway, not much of a home. I do intend to return, but I have to get some affairs in order so that I can make a more permanent residence here. And I have to explain things to my kids. Fan will surely understand. It's Julianna I'm worried about."

Elisette waved a hand. "Oh, of course. Please, take all the time you need, and leave nothing on bad terms if you can help it."

"I never intend it."

He hated lying to his family, and he didn't like how easy it had become. Would it really be so difficult to have Andrianary explain things to them, about the Akari, being dual-spirited, and this grand quest he had to embark upon? If the old man understood, surely they would as well. Maybe they weren't as in tune with the spirits as the two of them, but they could absolutely respect that the spirits and ancestors held greater power than anyone truly understood.

Maybe it was because he didn't want to alienate himself. He'd always been treated poorly because of who he was, thought less of. While he did not want that at all, neither did he want to be put on a great pedestal, out of reach of the common man, or common family member. He didn't want to be thought of as so great that he had nothing in common with his own family.

Easier to have them believe that he was returning to London to take care of affairs. If things went well, he could vanquish this evil spirit and return with no one truly the wiser, save those involved and Andrianary.

He spent the afternoon packing, not that he had much. He'd brought little and acquired even less since his stay. He was frequently interrupted by family members who wished to speak with him, asking this or that about life in London, how long did he expect to be gone, could he perhaps procure a certain item for them as a souvenir, could he take this or that message to Fan or Julianna. He went along with as much as he could, the guilt piling up as much as the lies.

He prayed fervently that this wouldn't take too long, that he could wrap this up in a matter of weeks or months. Good fortune may not fall from the sky, but did it really have to hide in the deepest, darkest holes guarded by the biggest, meanest beasts imaginable?

By evening, he was back on the porch with Volana.

"You really think it will be a year before you return?" his cousin wondered. "I thought everything in Europe was about speed. Fast, fast, fast, quick, quick, quick, now, now, now. Everything must be done—" He slapped his knee. "—right now!"

"In the social and business scene, yes," Rifun told him. "In the courts, however, things move very slowly. Painfully slow, actually. And they don't like it when people leave."

Volana grumbled a rare anger. "Yes, the great empires of the world are loathe to lose anything they call their own, be it land, sea, sky, or person."

"Or space."

His cousin, who had raised his glass to drink, laugh-choked, and brought the glass down. "Exactly! Exactly true!" He coughed and shook his head. "Good God, the nerve of some people. To claim...space. The stars themselves. Shall it be a crime, then, to look upon this constellation or that one?" He pointed in turn. "I never thought I'd see the day."

Rifun grinned. "There were plenty of days I never thought I'd see." He raised his glass. "Most of them ordinary." He took a drink.

Volana nodded. "Well, however long it takes, a month or a year or a decade, know that you are always welcome home." He punched Rifun in the arm. "And don't be afraid to call or write a letter. We're not as savage as the Europeans seem to think we are. We know how to use a telephone and how to write, although I believe writing a letter may be the cheaper option."

Rifun laughed. "I'll see what I can do. And maybe Fan will come back for a visit, too."

"I think Lalao would like that very much. She fancies your boy, you know."

"She may have mentioned something of the sort in a...roundabout way."

"Ah, don't let her looks fool you, or how she goes about her day with Elisette and the others. She's a shy girl when it comes to admitting that she likes a boy. Always has been that way."

Rifun raised a brow. "Do you think it would work?"

"I don't see why not. They're second cousins, and even that is permitted in London."

"What if he doesn't come? Does she expect to wait for him forever?"

Volana waved a hand. "Oh, who is to know? They were acquainted for a month. She may wait a while, or she may not. There's the next *savika* tournament to consider, too, and I'm sorry you're going to miss it."

Oh, that was happening, wasn't it? Maybe he could put off— No. He had to stop being selfish. Get this taken care of, then he would have whole lifetimes to watch the *savika* tournaments.

"There will be more in the future, I'm sure," Rifun told him. "But I can't have this hanging over my head."

"I understand." He raised his glass. "Cheers, cousin."

Rifun raised his glass, clinked it to Volana's, and drank.

The following morning he said goodbye to everyone after breakfast, then headed out on the road. He stopped once at Andrianary's house to quietly confirm that they would continue their weekly meetings. When the shaman asked how this would be, Rifun simply told him not to worry and left it at that.

So it was that he'd woken up under a mosquito net that morning, and by noon he was back staring at stone carvings in an ancient temple on a world galaxies away.

He unpacked his things and went to work tidying up his chambers, the mindless chore helping to reset his focus. He was no longer on Earth. At the moment, he was back on Sadurnon. He was among aliens and Time and the Akari again. He was among those who understood the broader universe. He didn't have to pretend anymore, at least about that. He could be open and honest about everything except the thing that lurked under Cassius' skin. That he was still having trouble understanding himself, never mind having to explain it to anyone else.

He did not tell anyone he was back just yet. First he wanted to get to the Akarin fortress and find Drew, figure out where he stood on things and make a plan from there. Given how Julianna and Isthim felt about Cassius in the first place, he figured it safe to assume they wouldn't have too many objections.

Once things were back how he liked them, including his shrine, he opened a portal to the fortress. Even though he hadn't opened too many portals in the last few months, his practice in other Energy abilities seemed to have strengthened his resolve against their normal ill effects.

While he'd been effectively barred from coming to the fortress for recreational purposes, he couldn't imagine that diplomatic dealings were off-limits. If his suspicions were right, all he would have to do to get someone's attention would be to stand there in the first atrium off the portal room at the base of the primary staircase.

There were four staircases, really, the fortress being set up as a square, each corner being a large atrium with an enormous open staircase in the center. The portal room happened to lead to the southwest staircase, so that was the most used.

He heard the man long before he saw him, and when Rifun saw that it was a human, he concluded that this was Doug Templeton, one of the council members.

"Ah, yes, I see him now! Thank you very much!" the man was saying, speaking to someone in the corridor a good fifty yards away.

He wasn't especially tall, though he had the appearance and disposition of being able to sell water to a shark after beating it in single combat underwater while bleeding.

"You must be Rifun!" he said, still about ten yards away, already holding out a hand. "I've heard a lot about you!"

"Forgive me, but I don't shake hands," Rifun informed him politely.

"No?" It slowed the man down about a fraction of a second until he finally stopped, uncomfortably close if Rifun wanted to admit it, and he took half a step back. "Bow, then?" The short man executed a flawless Japanese bow.

"Flattered, but no," Rifun said. "A simple hello will do. You must be Doug—"

"Doug Templeton! That's me! Commander of the Akarin, part of the council, and incredibly handsome, at your service, sir. As I've said, I've heard a lot about you, and the last I heard, you were asked to leave by one of our more senior members. What brings you back this way?"

"A bit of a problem. I was actually hoping to speak to this member. Drew was his name, I believe. Or I have also had dealings with Micaiah."

Doug nodded emphatically. "Yup, I know them both. Quite well, actually." He appeared thoughtful for a moment, as if considering whether he shouldn't ask Rifun to leave anyway. Finally he said, "Come on then! Follow me! I might have an idea of where they're hiding."

The stairs never got any easier, and using Gravity could be hazardous if tracks got crossed. They got off on the third floor and began the hunt amid a fantastical maze of rooms. If Rifun remembered right, this was the floor for meeting rooms, nonessential paperwork, and other inconsequential business items.

"So, Rifun, did I hear you're from Madagascar?!" Doug asked loudly, because quiet, or even normal, was apparently not his default setting.

"That's right," Rifun replied, already exhausted by the short man and immensely grateful that Micaiah had found him first when he'd made his first visit.

"Very nice, very nice. See my story is a bit of an interesting one. My ma was British, my da American. Ma went to South Africa as a little girl with her family, basically born and raised there except she wasn't actually born there. Da was a soldier who happened to get sent to the area. Next thing you know, they fall in love, they're married, they travel a bit while he's in the Army, have both my sisters while on the road. Then Da gets out of the Army and they decide to go back to South Africa. And that's where I was born and raised."

"My father was a rapist who I never met, my stepfather hated me and threw me out of the village, and my mother died in childbirth and I was never told."

The man never faltered, and the biggest indication he gave that he even understood the implications of Rifun's words was little more than a scuffed half-step as he carried on, ten feet tall and king of the world.

"Beautiful place, South Africa," he went on, as if he hadn't heard. "Ever been there?"

Rifun stifled a sigh. "No."

"Too bad. Of course, I don't know that I'd go there now with things the way they are. But once things settle down, I'm sure it will be very pleasant to visit. Now then, I haven't been to Madagascar, but I have been to — ah, here they are!"

Like Rifun, Drew and Micaiah had likely heard Doug coming long before they saw him, so they were not caught off-guard by his appearance. They were, however, visibly uncomfortable when they saw Rifun.

"Let's take this discussion to a meeting room, shall we?!" Doug suggested, herding them into a side room that could have housed an entire congress.

Once in the meeting room, a Sound barrier was erected and the more naive aspect of Doug's personality melted away, although this did not diminish his normal volume in any way. Rifun was forced to wonder if the man didn't have some kind of hearing impairment.

"Now then, why don't we just lay it all out on the table!"

"The last time you were here, I warned you of what would happen if the Cult continued its antics," Drew began, taking a few steps away from Doug and trying not to grimace.

"In my defense, I haven't been around for the last...I can't even count the months now," Rifun said calmly.

"You've left the Cult, then?" Micaiah questioned, looking both skeptical and suddenly thrown off-balance mentally.

"Did a bit of soul-searching, you might say. A spirit quest, to use modern vernacular. And I find myself with a bit of a problem."

"What's that?"

He spent the better part of an hour explaining his journey, starting with the Core of the Wheel and ending with his dressing down by Andrianary, making sure to emphasize the part about Cassius and the Shadows.

When he was finished, the three Akarin glanced at each other and gave him many hard stares, as if looking for the punchline to some joke, or the reveal to a great mystery. Personally, Rifun thought he'd just revealed a mystery. What was left to uncover? Well, when it came to the world of the spirits, maybe it was better not to ask that question.

It was Drew who spoke first.

"We read your Book," he started slowly. "I think I speak for everyone when I say that it was a shock to see you featured in a Book. Not only you, but Cassius—or Kokumbo—as well. So we are aware of this deal with the devil. Combined with what we know of these Shadows and Whites, as told in *The Lone Wolf,* it makes a certain amount of sense."

"Then you will help?" Rifun asked. "You don't sound too eager to be rid of a menace you have been decrying for months or years."

"To give credit to your shaman, killing a body does nothing to harm a demon. If it were as simple as cutting his throat in the middle of the night, I doubt you would be here asking for our help."

"That much, at least, is true. But once again, you don't sound too eager to go against him. Whatever Cassius has been up to in the last few months or a year, he obviously isn't slowing down. The longer we delay, the more powerful he gets."

Still the Akarin hesitated, Doug both mercifully and worryingly silent.

"Our hesitation is not him, or not entirely," Micaiah said. "We'll be making plans for him, don't worry about that. Our hesitation is you."

"Me?" Rifun wondered. "Because I still believe in the journals?"

"If Cassius were possessed by a spirit at the time of the journals, and if he dictated the journals, why would the journals be true? Why would you want to follow them?"

"Richard was attempting to understand the spirits. The spirits speak a language we cannot comprehend. Cassius merely bridged that gap."

"Once again, why would you want to follow a book written by an evil spirit?"

"What makes my Bands evil and yours not?" Rifun challenged. "Why should my Disguises be evil and yours not? We're not calling for ritualistic blood sacrifice, simply a clearer understanding."

"So clear that only those possessed by evil spirits and those who are naturally dual-spirited can hope to understand it?" Drew threw in.

"And your Builders are any different?"

"Builders are chosen by the Author, but they are not required to be anything special."

Rifun sighed. "We're arguing semantics at this point. Are you going to help me or not?"

"While it would prove to be an advantage in the short-term," Doug began thoughtfully, "we must consider the power vacuum he would leave behind. Good or evil, he is a very large, very powerful force in the universe right now. What would take his place?"

Again all three Akarin looked at Rifun.

"And this begs the next question," Doug continued, "even before all of this...spiritual revelation, you knew he was a menace. As your Book reveals, you have had many opportunities to kill him. Why haven't you? The only logical explanation, once again revealed in the Book, suggests that you are using him as a buffer against the Borelians and others who would come after the Cult. Maybe even the Akarin as well. And why not? He's a large, loud, boisterous target. His sudden demise would surely be projected loud enough for you to escape."

"And if you hate the Cult so much, what do you care if that dam breaks?" Rifun asked.

"Because we are not unaffected," Drew told him, giving him a look. "The Tacagans and the Gentleman Killers are well diminished in their power because of Cassius, but that's not to say they couldn't make a comeback if he were removed. Barring that, it could be the Borelians, I don't know which is worse."

Rifun shifted his stance and folded his arms. "What, pray tell, do you expect to happen? Politics and war have been the norm the universe over. What makes this special? What would make you happy? Why don't you take advantage of the chaos and try to impose your own order? Things seem to be going well for you."

"Absolute power corrupts absolutely. We have our own troubles. More power would only amplify them." Drew shifted his stance to match Rifun's. "As to your question, we're working out a way to put Hands back into power again, get things back to roughly the way they were."

"Because that was anyone's idea of a well-oiled machine."

"Would you rather have squabbling factions?" Micaiah asked. "We may be well here. The Cult may be well to walk around where you are. But the average Time Agent? Terrified to go to the Wheel. Who knows when or where a fight may break out? Or maybe someone will sabotage another gravitational balancer. Or maybe someone new will come to power and make things worse. The imagination is the worst of all tyrants."

"So you're going to not impose your will by imposing your will about what you think others want or need?" Rifun said, raising a brow.

"Are you not suggesting the same?"

"Maybe, but at least I'm not hiding behind a righteous facade and pretending humility."

"Pride goeth before destruction."

Rifun glared at all three of them. "Doesn't it, though?" He straightened. "I can see I'm wasting my time here, dealing with humble cowards. But at least it has been confirmed that the Akarin value safety over the truth." He continued before any of them could protest. "You would rather deal with a comfortable lie ruling the majority because it is no threat to you."

"The journals are also a lie, and the Cult is a threat," Micaiah butted in. "And we will be fighting against you in this, if you pursue it."

"Once again, standing there, rattling your sabers and shouting vicious words, but taking no action. You prepare for the lion but are terribly susceptible to the snake."

The tension was broken awkwardly as Doug chuckled. It wasn't a nervous sound, either, but he appeared to be genuinely amused, and it caught the rest of them rather off-guard.

"What's so funny?" Micaiah asked.

Doug stopped laughing, but he was still grinning as he looked at Rifun. "And if the Cult were as powerful as you say, beyond Cassius—if you were actually a threat, why have you not made your move, taken over the Time industry fully? Granted, Cassius has been cleaning house rather effectively, but what's stopping you from taking over completely?" He grew serious once more. "I think it's because he is the only one who is as powerful as you claim. He is the only one who has any real advanced abilities that are a threat to anything and anyone. It's another reason you haven't killed him, because he is the only truly fearsome weapon in your arsenal, the only one who can put teeth to the Cult's claims. Considering that two of your sacred journals are currently lost—the location of which one is known—I'm guessing that—"

Rifun cut his merriment short, using Force to throw everyone to the ground.

The thing about Time or the Akari was that they seemed to still be bound by the laws of physics. Like Matter, Energy could not be created or destroyed. Using Force, therefore, required a significant amount of Energy, which most often came from the user. But the element of surprise was enough for Rifun to be able to Band and recover enough that he would be able to walk straight.

From there he created a Gravity track. This would have normally been nothing for Drew or Micaiah to break, if they had any experience with Gravity, but he tweaked it a little, weaving the track between them, whom he held down under heavy gravity, and Doug, whom he lifted. He modified it so that the energies were dependent, with a tiny focal point in the middle. If Drew or Micaiah attempted to lift the Gravity, it would put pressure on Doug, and it would kill him before they broke free. The same went in the opposite direction, if Doug tried to break free.

Just for good measure, he also increased the humidity around Drew and Micaiah, making it even harder for them to breathe as they lay on the ground, gasping as though pinned under many tons of rock despite there being nothing there. For Doug, he removed some of the oxygen, not enough that he would be completely lethargic, but he would feel it.

Rifun let them try to break the Gravity, both sides quickly discovering the nature of the track and how it held them in bondage to each other. Probably they were already considering ways to get around this little trick, so he would have to make this quick.

"I'm in no mood to play games," Rifun said, looking up at Doug who hovered probably two feet off the ground. "And I don't like to be mocked. I have tried to reach out, to be reasonable, to have a discussion. You all seem to be under the impression that simply reading your Books and listening to a few pithy encouragements ought to be enough to win over everyone, and that pacifism is the answer to any conflict. It may serve the weak-willed just fine, but then there are the rest of us. We are not interested in building sandcastles, we wish to be master masons. We wish—I wish to know, to understand. And when I reach out, I am given nothing but discouragement, derogatory remarks, and an invitation to join.

"And when push comes to shove, you declare yourselves neutral even as you work to reestablish the very institution that got us into this mess in the first place. What, then, is your purpose? What is your use in this universe? You have the power to reshape the universe and yet you sit on the sidelines selling concessions and profiting off chaos, sweeping up the weak-willed and terrified, giving lost sheep a flock to join without ever addressing the wolves and instead making yourself a bigger target. You claim to be ashamed of and opposed to the practices of the Time industry, yet you profit from it, and those drippings are a little too juicy to pass up because if you didn't have a master feeding you then you would have to feed yourselves, or, spirits forbid, put your money where your mouth is and actually rely on the Author.

"I think there is more here than meets the eye, but I can't say what that is just yet. Regardless, I'm done with it. Things will not go back to the way they were. I'll leave it up to you to decide how you want to respond, but know that the clock is ticking, and you won't have forever to think about it."

Between the use of Force, the Gravity track, and all the other minor party tricks he was holding, Rifun was growing considerably weaker with each breath. He never let it show, or he tried not to, and he held it all the way to the door, not releasing his hostages until it was already swinging shut behind him.

There were no shouts behind him. No security was called. No one stopped him in the halls or on the stairs, though most seemed to sense his bad mood and got out of his way. By the time he reached the main floor, he actually felt strong enough to open a decent portal, though he would have done so anyway. You couldn't just walk away from a situation like that, then ask for a ten minute break while you called a taxi. He took the jump just as soon as he could, making multiple jumps before finally landing in the tunnels.

The darkness was a welcome thing, and Rifun sat against the cool stone wall for a minute just trying to collect his head. His injury throbbed and his eyes ached. He may have fallen asleep briefly, he wasn't sure, but his sickness cleared up enough that he could stand and be on his way.

He was done with the olive branches and the peace talks. He was tired of listening to the Akarin whine and hum and haw and all the while degrade those they perceived as beneath them, sitting on their white horses. He was tired of being seen as "less than" because of things either outside his control, or because no one saw fit to educate him properly. How could he learn if all the teachers thought him too dumb to understand, all the while telling him to "just read the Books" and he'd get it.

Sometimes the most frightening thing in the world was getting what you asked for. Well, he decided, he was going to give people what they asked for.

He broke into the cavern where the city lay in ruins. This might not have been so startling, given that they were indeed ruins, except they had made much progress in the last couple years to bring it back to life. Had something happened? Had they been discovered? Could his meeting with Doug and the others have been a distraction? If so, the Akarin were not only going to get what they asked for, but also what they deserved.

He ran down to the ruins. When he reached the gate and went through, however, it was like breaking through a waterfall and the city came to life around him.

A Disguise? Around a city? It was brilliant and needed and also very, very difficult to do. Personally, Rifun had thought it impossible. Well, he would be able to ask about it soon enough, he figured.

He found Isthim easily enough, training a group of grunts. They appeared relieved when she dismissed them early and headed to the officers building at his request.

Julianna took a little searching, but he found her outside the city near the lake where something of a refugee camp had been set up. Many were Time Agents who had become displaced and out of sorts with all the chaos in the Wheel, whether caused by Cassius, the Tacagans, or the Gentleman Killers. They promised that once their wounds were treated, they would head home, wherever home happened to be. A few were interested in learning more about the Cult and the Akari. Still some were Akarin, or former Akarin, who, like Rifun, thought the Akarin were too pacifist, too cowardly, too passive about the whole thing, and wanted to take more direct action.

He directed Julianna to the officers building for a meeting, then went looking for Cassius.

That was a little tougher, and only the sudden dispersal of the Disguise over the city gave Rifun any hint that Cassius was still in the cavern somewhere. After some fruitless searching, he turned to Light and Thermodynamics, looking for any body heat in the cavern outside the ruins, using Light as a screen to visualize heat signatures. He found numerous small flying animals, like bats, on the ceiling and in various crevices. Finally he spotted a mass of heat big enough to be human on a ledge overlooking the city. Not wanting to waste time, he used Gravity to get himself up there where he did indeed find Cassius.

"Impressive work," Rifun complimented.

"I know how to do it," Cassius said, sounding both tired and frustrated, "but I don't know how to hold it, detach it from myself and make it permanent."

"Well, think about it over a break. Meeting in the officers building. Now."

He did not wait for assent or argument, just saw himself back to the ground and all the way to the officers building without looking back.

Isthim and Julianna were like a couple of wet cats just waiting for an excuse to claw each other, and Rifun's appearance seemed to smooth at least a few ruffled feathers. Cassius joined them a moment later.

"You said this was urgent," Isthim began, looking at Rifun. "Has something happened?"

"Did your spiritual journey to become a Builder reveal something?" Julianna asked.

"Yes and yes, though the personal matters of my spiritual journey will not be revealed, thank you," Rifun told them. He relayed the events from his meeting with the Akarin, including his scathing indictment of them.

"This is my third, if not fourth, attempt at peaceful resolution," he said. "I have no more patience and am too exhausted to pretend otherwise. Here is the situation: because of the Book, they know two of our journals are missing. They know where we are hiding. I can only conclude that either they are too weak themselves to expose us, or they think we are too weak to fight against such leverage."

"We don't have the army to storm such a stronghold," Isthim informed him.

"Maybe not now, but one day. But I'm not proposing storming their castle. They want the Time industry back to the way it was, we're going to remind them what that means. Cassius, I want you to arrange a kidnapping. Bring me Micaiah Durvin."

"Why him?" Julianna inquired. "Why not Doug or Drew or anyone else on the council?"

"Because Micaiah has Authored Books. I want him to show me what that means, where his Faith truly lies." Rifun looked at Isthim. "With the Borelians in charge of the Grandfathers, I trust they'll be able to arrange a suitable Time Trial."

Isthim, her eyes glittering with excitement, simply dipped her head once.

"We're going to make a point about this," he went on. "Julianna, you know the Akarin fortress well enough. Use a Disguise if you wish, but I want you to go in there and take the Book about us. *The Hands of Time, Book One, In the Hands of the Enemy.* The copyright isn't for another sixty years, so I think we'll be set for a while. While you're at it, just do a quick search and see if maybe they don't happen to have some other property that belongs to us."

"And what about our location?" Julianna wondered. "We may stop new readers from knowing where we are, but if we start moving like this, it'll be an act of war, and guaranteed they will expose us and the Elif."

"To whom, exactly?" Cassius asked. "We are the Grandfathers. The Time industry will do nothing. If they want to do something about it, they'll have to do it themselves. They've already proven to be too cowardly to try it."

"It's still a loose end we can't afford," Rifun agreed. He looked at Isthim. "How many ith-colored Borelians can you round up?"

She looked thoughtful. "It depends on how precise you want them to be."

"What's ith?" Julianna asked.

"In the unskilled, it merely clouds the memory and erases the feeling of danger," Isthim informed her. "Skilled wielders may erase precise memories." She looked at Rifun. "But the physical encoding of memories in the brain is far more complex than it seems. We may call up a memory of any time at any point, but the physiology of it, the wielder would have to know at what point the person acquired the knowledge of our location."

"I received the Book about a year or so ago," Rifun said. "Does that help?"

The Borelian frowned. "It's something to work with at least. At the same time, clouding the memories of the Akarin for the last year or so, it would make them less of a danger to us."

"Exactly."

"I'll see who I can find."

"And once this is all accomplished?" Julianna asked. "Then what?"

"Then we need to go after the journals," Rifun said. "Clouding the memories of the Akarin should buy us some time, assuming they are not in possession of them. Cassius, what happened to your lead?"

"Still working on it," was all the man said.

"All right, fine. We'll focus on the Time Trial first."

"I might know a few grunts who want to prove themselves."

"Be careful," Rifun warned severely. "Micaiah Durvin has an identical twin who isn't an Akari-bearer. We don't need to punish the wrong man. Is that understood?"

"They'll understand it perfectly."

"Good. Does anyone not understand what's going on?"

"Do we think the Bat and the Day will cooperate with the Time Trial?" Julianna wondered. "They've been incredibly loyal to the Hands, and they're immune to Time. They may pose a threat if they decide to oppose us."

"This is a Time industry proceeding," Isthim said. "The Grandfathers are making the official arrest and rendering the official verdict and sentencing. They won't be able to refuse. In the absence of the Hands, we will also preside over the questioning."

With no other objections, Isthim and Cassius were the first to leave, looking excited to finally have something to do that might make some progress. Rifun and Julianna remained.

"What does it mean when you have both Books and journals and you're breaking into Building?" Rifun asked.

"It means that you've ascended beyond what Richard or I ever thought possible, what the Akarin believe to be possible," Julianna told him. "The Author had many stories of her Beloved characters, all of whom had great power and were unique in their own right."

"You think I may be one of them?"

"Who am I to say? But I think you will take us further than we've ever been."

"Considering we've never been anywhere, anyone could accomplish this."

She cleared her throat. "Well, I've been playing the humanitarian well enough, I think—"

He grinned. "And yet you still won't cook dinner for me."

She gave him a look. "I've been playing the humanitarian well enough, but I think I will be glad to have a bit of revenge on the Akarin."

"We all have our petty indulgences."

"When do you suppose you will tell Cassius about the Book of Abilities? Or do you think you will kill him first?"

"I haven't decided, but I have a certain stirring that it will be soon, and things will unfold as they are meant to be."

Julianna nodded, grinning. "They always do." She turned to leave, but looked back when she got to the door. "Thank you, Rifun. I knew I could trust you."

He wanted to believe her. Truly he did. But he was not in the business of trust. Right now, he was in the business of getting things done.

18 | Kolu ati Padasehin

Vancouver, 1965

Attack and Retreat

W ith their sentence served on Ikta, the twin assassins were more than happy to
pledge themselves to Cassius. They did not say what jail on Ikta was like,
but their demeanor said it was not a tale they wished to share.

Once they were rescued from Ikta and settled in their new accommodations in
the ruins, Cassius approached them with their first task, the one to prove their
loyalty. The idea of not only going against the Akarin, but kidnapping one of their
leaders, proved to be both terrifying and thrilling.

Being in jail for a total of seventy-nine Iktarian days helped to speed along the
process of learning to fight with new handicaps. Murdi was well adept with a knife
in his off-hand, and Lordo had learned new stances to accommodate his terrible
limp. Going against the Akarin would show whether they had learned enough. If so,
Cassius completed the mission and the twin assassins redeemed themselves. If not,
well, he got rid of his rivals anyway.

Nevertheless, he accompanied them on the initial reconnaissance mission. It
wasn't too difficult to Disguise a Mishim as a human. Differences in physique could
be hidden with proper clothing, and skin was merely a trick of the eye.

Micaiah Durvin lived with his girlfriend and twin brother in Vancouver, British
Columbia. To be more precise, he lived with his girlfriend, and his twin brother
lived in the apartment across the hall. It was easy to tell the twins apart: Micaiah
was obviously into working out and strength training while his twin, Micah, was
obviously not. Micah was not fat, but he was small and skinny compared to his
bodybuilder brother.

Cassius and the twin assassins had Disguised themselves simply as average
humans, loitering around the twins' apartments just long enough to tell who was
who and where they lived. Then they regrouped outside.

"The woman is called Aklaq White Bear," Murdi said. "She is also Akarin, and
not to be trifled with."

"Is that so?" Cassius said. "Well then, maybe we'll make this a two-for-one deal."

They stuck around a while longer, but the twin brothers did nothing of note that they could readily observe. As the clock ticked eight, Cassius and the twin assassins returned to the ruins.

"How perfect that twin assassins should go against twin warriors," Lordo was commenting as they walked through the city.

"Please tell me things don't have to be balanced with you like they do the Korin," Cassius said irritably, on the verge of begging.

"No, of course not," Murdi assured him. "But you have to appreciate the irony and the...poetic justice."

"You know them, then?"

"They're upstanding Time Agents in their own right."

"So the brother is aware of things."

"Oh, yes, just not the Akarin."

Cassius paused and looked at them. "Why would Micaiah not tell his own twin brother about the Akarin, of which he seems to be a rather prominent member?"

The twin assassins shrugged.

"None of our business," Murdi said. "And he may be dead soon anyway."

Cassius grinned. "That's the spirit."

He dismissed them and headed to the officers building. As much as he disliked Rifun and thought his whole spiritual quest thing a little annoying and a lot hokey, he was glad that the man had come back swinging, assuming he'd had to return at all. At least now they seemed to have a plan of action.

He found the light-skinned man about a block from the building, heading the same direction. Cassius fell in beside him.

"You don't have the giddiness I would expect from a successful kidnapping," Rifun said. "What is it?"

"Seems as though Micaiah Durvin's girlfriend is Aklaq White Bear," Cassius told him, noting how Rifun's expression turned thoughtful. "She is Akarin as well. Prominent, apparently, in some circles." He paused. "Did you know this?"

"I'd heard the name. I didn't know the relation, however. It is a bit of interesting news, though."

"Should we make it a two-for-one? If we can't get his twin brother, at least his beloved."

Rifun grinned. "No. That makes things too easy. We force them together, it strengthens their resolve and leaves no room for panic. We take him, first he has to decide whether he wants her there for her strength and abilities or not in order to save her life. He leaves her, it weakens her, divides his attention as he is faced with the possibility he may never see her again. He takes her, she has to either watch as he fights for his life and cannot help, or he has to watch as she is potentially punished for his iniquities." He gave Cassius a look. "Basic psychology."

Something only normal people could understand, apparently.

"In layman's terms," he continued, "no. No two-for-one deal. Leave her out of it. Let them decide."

Cassius grunted but agreed.

"Otherwise, it sounds like you're making progress. Keep it up."

He moved on with whatever his work was while Cassius stopped and finally moved off elsewhere.

So, no girlfriend. It made things a little easier, then, only having to kidnap one Akarin instead of two. That was fine with Cassius, although he wondered how well he could pad his reputation with two Akarin in his clutches. But whatever, there was a plan at least. He could go along with a plan. Running out here and there chasing down Gentleman Killers and the odd side contract was getting boring anyway.

He started off again, making for the officers building at a snail's pace.

He spent a little time considering his team. Murdi and Lordo were in it to redeem themselves in some fashion, ingratiate themselves and find a place in the Cult. Maybe there was planned betrayal in there somewhere, maybe not. The Korin hadn't approached him directly, but it was hardly a coincidence that almost every time he turned around while walking through the city, he saw one or more of them, always trying to act casual and definitely not get his attention. Such cowardly tactics hardly seemed befitting of a monstrous race, but who was he to judge? Pilory hadn't contacted him and was absent more often than not from training. Her excuses varied, but Isthim suspected great shame and humiliation to be a driving factor and actually requested she be thrown out. Cassius refused.

Was there anyone else he could ask? Recruiting was up and morale seemed to be high. So far the followers had been divided into senior and junior classes, with various ranks therein, if only to make it seem like there was somewhere to go in their training. They needed the Book of Abilities. Their only saving grace that made it so they didn't look like complete asses was that former Akarin typically knew more advanced techniques that were in turn passed on to others. And what about Rifun? Had he learned anything while away?

Cassius abandoned his path to the officers building, instead turning and making his way back around to the training grounds. In old times, the ancient Elif may have used the open courtyards as simple recreational areas, festival arenas, or fights to the death and blood sacrifice to the gods for all he knew. These days it was filled with various grunts all learning and practicing elements of the Akari, but in a militaristic fashion.

He observed their movements. Everything was done on ten-day cycles, and physical and Akari training was only done a few days in this time period. In these times, Isthim had once reported that a unit was done on Time, another on Matter, and another on Energy.

If he didn't know that two journals were missing and they were running a bare bones operation in the logistics and ideological departments, he never would have guessed that most of it was a front, busywork to make others believe they were far more powerful than they were.

He watched as two aliens, terribly mismatched in size, sparred against one another. He could not name the species readily, but he was impressed. The larger alien did not waste his time and energy with wild movements, instead calculating his moves, trying to time them with the smaller alien who did well to exploit his own size as well as his opponent's. The first round was straight physical fighting, but the second round introduced basic Time Bands into the mix. This was more difficult to watch as a spectator, but he did so anyway.

The third round introduced Matter, strictly non-lethal at this stage. The favorite party trick appeared to involve messing with an opponent's clothing, if he wore any, so that he became tangled and tripped up by them. This was easy for the smaller alien to accomplish as he caused the fabric in some of the larger alien's clothing to wear out and tear open, creating a trip hazard. When the larger alien went down, the smaller alien then grabbed unaffected pieces of fabric and stretched them farther than they normally could, wrapping up his opponent and effectively mummifying him.

The fourth round introduced Energy, and Thermodynamics seemed to be the element of choice, causing minor burns to irritate or distract an opponent. The smaller alien also seemed to be rather adept at Sound, masking his normal movements while projecting decoys here and there to confuse the larger alien. The larger alien, meanwhile, fumbled with some kind of Light ability, apparently attempting to blind the smaller alien but having limited success.

"Critiquing?"

Cassius turned as Isthim walked up beside him.

"Observing," he replied. "Want to make sure there's a reason we're doing this."

"Having doubts?"

"About the journals and the Cult? No. About them?" He grunted. "I guess I was expecting more."

"Given that the objective is to not appear as a sole military force, they cannot be treated as such."

He shifted his stance. "How does it work on your world? How did the Borelians become a military superpower if you never fought amongst yourselves before going into space? That's where a warrior learns and is refined is on the battlefield."

"Brelix is not a hospitable world, nor are the creatures that live there alongside us," Isthim informed him. "Battle is not merely against one's own kind, but against other creatures seeking to kill you. Mental fortitude is tested not only in battle, but in fear and anger and starvation and desperation. A child learns early on that life is a battle, that he must fight and win or be destroyed."

"Yet you're too lazy to grow your own food and need slaves to do it for you so you're free to conquer other peoples."

"I would not expect you to understand the needs and politics of Brelix. And if all you're going to do is complain, then my time will be better spent elsewhere."

He waved a hand and she departed. He wondered how it would be, if he subdued her. If he forced her. Would it change anything about her attitude?

In the end, he stayed where he was, watching the grunts until they lined up for finishing forms and finally dismissed. None of them had particularly stood out to him as someone he wanted to train specially. Well, not everyone could be special. He would keep looking, assuming he wanted to.

He returned to the officers building and made for his chambers. It might be a good idea to get in a nap before going on this daring escapade. He had little doubt that kidnapping an Akarin member would be a little more challenging that your average mercenary, and Murdi and Lordo had been no picnic. Yu-bix hadn't been much fun, either, but that was more because the fight had been over too soon. There was a delicate balance with these things.

He was woken up by a pounding at his door; the muffled voice might have been Julianna. Grouchily, he got out of bed and yanked the door open, using Gravity to assist with such a feat, and the scarred woman very nearly fell forward into him.

"You're quite the sleeper," she said, standing and self-consciously smoothing her dress and hair.

"What do you want?" Cassius demanded.

"Some information that may be pertinent to your mission."

"What is it?"

"There's some movement within the Akarin. I went there in Disguise to look for the Book and the journals—"

"Did you get them?" Cassius interrupted.

She nodded. "I got the Book, yes, it's safely stored. I have reason to believe, however, that they may possess at least one of the journals."

"Do you know which one?"

"I don't."

"What makes you so sure of this?"

She took a calming breath. "Andrew O'Dell is a Builder. A damn good one, too. He was one of the ones Rifun was talking to the other day. No doubt the Akarin took that little disagreement as something akin to a threat because the Akarin have mobilized."

"They're going to attack?" Cassius demanded.

"No, not yet. Right now, they're only assessing the situation and moving assets. All the important stuff is stored in the upper levels, and they have safeguards to seal off the levels of the fortress if they ever came under siege. They also brought out the Trackers, the Akarin hounds of war. I wouldn't expect you to understand what all of this entails, but I noticed Andrew moving against the crowd, talking to Micaiah as well as Nathan Wilde, another Builder. Micaiah left them to help with the fortifications, but Andrew and Nathan kept going, and I lost them on the second floor; my guess is they were heading to the portal room.

"Before you ask, I already told Isthim about this. She's got some of her people going after them, and she's rounding up more of the ith-colored Borelians in hopes of getting to their memories, clouding them, erasing them, whatever, in hopes of deescalating the activity."

"And I should grab my people and go after Micaiah," Cassius concluded.

"Exactly," Julianna said. "I don't know where he's gone, but I imagine he has to go home at some point."

He agreed and she departed.

Well then, seemed as though things were moving a little faster than anticipated. That was all right, though, as long as they were smart about it. With any luck, Isthim would be able to head off the Builders and get the journal back, assuming that was what was going on. With even greater luck, it would indeed be a journal. With phenomenal luck, it would be the Book of Abilities. How quaint that the Akarin should have what they so sought after.

But that was neither here nor there. Cassius had to step up his mission, and he had to do it now.

He stormed out of the officers building, sweeping through the streets until he came upon the house shared by Murdi and Lordo. It had only the crudest of wooden doors and simple cloth curtains over the window beside it. He banged on the door and ripped the curtains aside, poking his head through the window to look around.

There was movement in the house and a moment later the twin assassins were standing at attention, or as "at attention" as they could manage, being rather unaccustomed to taking military-style orders.

"We're moving," Cassius told them. "Now."

He turned and stalked off without another word and without even looking to see how well they were following. A minute later the assassins caught up to him, Lordo limping horridly.

"What's going on?" Murdi asked.

Cassius relayed the events of the last ten minutes to them, ending with, "We need to find and capture Micaiah Durvin now."

"Where is our starting point going to be? Surely you're not thinking about going to the Akarin fortress?"

"Of course not. Even if we did use Disguises to follow him, he would have every advantage and many friends to call on. No, we're going to check out his Earth-side haunts. He won't risk exposing the public of an Unengaged world."

He could sense the hesitation in the twin assassins, but it was Lordo who gave it voice. "So we're out jumping and running about on a terribly urgent mission—which I agree is of great importance—just so we can do everything we just did yesterday?"

Cassius stopped, whirled around, and gave a fierce kick to Lordo's foot. The twin assassin barked in pain and quickly snapped his mouth shut, making an ungodly noise in his throat.

"Any more questions?" Cassius hissed. He gave each one a long, hard stare. "No? I didn't think so. This is the plan. This is what we're doing. If you don't want to participate, then I'll just drop you off somewhere and you can make your own way."

Neither Mishim said a word, instead obediently falling in behind him. He did not slow his pace, but they did, as Lordo limped along like an injured dog. Why did he always have to get stuck with the rejects? Just once Cassius wanted to go on a mission with someone of his own caliber, his own mindset. No balancing, no tourism, no handicaps, no fretting, no monologues, no analyses, no moral compass, no nothing. Go, do, kill. Just once.

But he had what he had. He slowed his pace only once he got deep into the tunnels and total blackness enveloped them. Once he ensured that they all three were present, he opened a portal. They jumped through three or four before finally landing on Earth.

Once again, they were in Vancouver, in an alley where they could don Disguises without issue. Cassius appeared to be any average white male on the street. Murdi was Disguised as some wounded war veteran, maybe Cassius' fake brother. Lordo, with his limp, was an older man, maybe their fake father. They made quite the trio walking down the street, but to anyone who didn't know, well, they didn't need to know.

"We need to make this quick and quiet," Cassius said, using Sound so that the conversation stayed among the three of them. "If the Akarin are mobilizing in any fashion, they'll be on high alert, and they might suspect that someone will try something. We can't let him send for help or get a warning to anyone else."

"Are we just going after him, or Aklaq White Bear as well?" Murdi asked.

"Just him. Part of him not calling for help or getting out a warning means we may have to wait for him to be alone, when she isn't around to back him up. That's not a major point, but if we can do it, we should."

The Mishim agreed and they continued down the street, dropping the Sound bubble as if nothing were amiss. Just an old man and his two grown sons out for a pleasant stroll. Of course, Cassius had no idea what an old man and his two grown sons would talk about while on a pleasant stroll, so their silence may have been a bit off to any observers. He just had to hope that Micaiah wasn't one of those observers and hit them with Test, exposing their Disguises while they wouldn't even know.

They walked by the apartment building where Micaiah lived. Cassius didn't know what he drove, so the best they could do was go inside and look, letting themselves in and casually heading upstairs. Just some new tenants, nothing suspicious here.

Stopping in front of the appropriate apartment, Cassius used Sound to listen inside the apartment. Words, shuffling of things, even a squeaky floor would be amplified. There was nothing. They waited a whole minute. Still nothing. Unless both he and his girlfriend worked the night shift and slept during the day — in which case there should still be sounds from rolling over in bed or snoring — they clearly weren't home.

"We'll wait outside," Cassius decided.

There was a little ice cream parlor about half a block from the apartment building. The three of them all got an item and went to sit on a bench within view of the building's main entrance.

"This is the lactation of your species?" Murdi questioned, studying his dish of chocolate ice cream topped with sprinkles.

"No, it comes from cows, a big, dumb, grass-eating animal," Cassius said, licking off his cone. "It's mixed with sugar and cocoa and a few other things, and it's eaten."

"Is it not possible to make ice cream from the lactation of humans?" Lordo wondered. "Do humans lactate?"

"Of course we do. Women, females do. It's how babies are fed."

"Why not make ice cream from your own lactation, then?"

Cassius blinked. Then, "I don't know. Humans can't produce milk on the scale required for — you know what? I'm not having this conversation."

"Where does one find a cow?" Murdi went on. "How is someone expected to take milk from a wild animal?"

"They're not wild. They're domesticated, kept on farms, specifically so they can be milked. You're telling me the Mishim don't have farms or any domestic animals?"

"Of course we do. Animals are kept for meat and serve a variety of functions in society. But never has it been considered to use the milk of an animal in such a way. Mostly because a creature's lactation is specific to its species and toxic to others."

"So much for adoption," Cassius murmured, taking a bite of his cone.

"But it is enjoyable," Murdi added, as if he thought he'd offended Cassius. "You say this is a popular dessert?"

"It is. Always a treat for a hot summer day."

Actually it was overcast, promising later rain.

"And what is this 'cone' made of?" Lordo asked, studying the papery cake-like edible.

Cassius sighed and rubbed his eyes. Why did he always get stuck with the idiots? Curiosity would kill the cat and leave their target alive. "I don't know. It's not something I ever cared to know." He stuffed the last of his own cone in his mouth to intentionally stop himself from speaking.

"On Maronet, there is a fruit called a tobrikor," Murdi said. "It is purple on the outside and may be pink or blue on the inside. It is either cooked and mashed, or chopped fresh, and mixed with the sap of a lubiv tree. Then it is shaped into balls to be eaten, or it can be baked more, wrapped in the lubiv tree's leaves. It is also a delicious dessert."

"Next time I visit, I'll be sure to try it," Cassius said absently.

"Target from the west," Lordo stated casually, if suddenly.

His posture never broke from where he still enjoyed his ice cream cone. Murdi also remained fixated on his dish. Nevertheless, Cassius saw how they positioned themselves so as to watch down the road where Micaiah and Aklaq walked toward the apartment building. If the couple ever suspected they were being watched, they gave no indication of it.

"Finish your ice cream," Cassius told the twins as they began to rise. "Give them ten seconds to think they're home safe."

Lordo had his cone finished in two bites while Murdi's ice cream had basically melted to the point where he was forced to drink it. With that sixty second head start, Cassius figured that Micaiah and Aklaq were probably well in their apartment by now. Talking, laughing, chatting about wherever they had been and whatever they had done. All accounts indicated that they'd probably been in the Akarin fortress, but they had to keep up appearances for the neighbors.

The trio crossed the street and again let themselves in the building. This time, other than managing their Disguises, they made no pretense about being a kindly old man and his sons. This time, they were on a mission.

They saw no one in the halls and stopped only briefly outside the apartment, again using Sound to listen and verify. And if they were discussing happenings in the Akarin fortress, Cassius bet that they would talk more about it now in the privacy of their own home versus being under the gun. See? Cassius knew psychology things, too.

"I don't know," Micaiah was saying, voice thick with an Irish accent. "And it's better that way."

"And what if something happens to Andrew or Nathan?" a female, Aklaq, asked. "How will anyone know where to go or where to look or what to do?"

"Then it's better that way, too. Maybe the journal will get lost to history." Pause. "You can give me the look all you want, it won't change anything. I don't know where they're taking it. They said something about meeting up with a third party, and that's all."

"What did they want to talk to you for, then?"

"Because I've had more interactions with Rifun, and I was there when he threatened us. They just wanted to know if I remembered anything Andrew didn't, or if I knew anything else."

"I wish I had been there. I would have given him something to make him think twice about this obscene...whatever it is he's on. Quest, crusade, I don't know. I would have done something."

"Do you think I didn't try?" Pause. "No, no, tell me. You think I didn't try to save myself, Andrew, or Doug? I had no idea what was going to happen. For all I knew, he was going to kill us. You think I wouldn't want to stop that?"

"I didn't say that."

"Seems like you meant something like it."

"I didn't say that."

Cassius grinned. Ah, the best time to conquer, when your targets had already divided themselves. He glanced at Murdi and Lordo, and the three of them shed their Disguises half a second before Cassius kicked in the door.

Micaiah was a Timekeeper in addition to being Akarin, and the first thing Cassius knew he would reach for was a Band so he could slow things down and figure out what was going on. Cassius felt the Band as merely a pinprick for a tiny fraction of a second, but he latched onto it, expanding the Band and bringing himself and the twin assassins inside.

The Band negated, the trio of attackers did not stop to introduce themselves or gloat, but moved seamlessly into the attack. Murdi immediately engaged Aklaq, distracting her while Cassius and Lordo went for Micaiah.

With Lordo's limp, a smart opponent would consider him the weaker of the pair and work on dispatching him quickly in order to focus on Cassius who was arguably the greater threat. Micaiah followed this line of reasoning to a T, turning and, attempting to use his skills as a prize fighter, going after Lordo, looking for his weakness, be it hip, knee, ankle, or foot.

Cassius seized on this opportunity, going around to the side and reaching for him, hoping to get in a good grasp and maybe use that nervous system trick that Rifun had tried to pull on him.

Micaiah pulled a clever trick, then. With one hand on Lordo, he siphoned the assassin's Energy and then drove his elbow back into Cassius' ribs, using the extra kinetic energy to throw Cassius off without actually expending any of his own energy. Cassius went back into the sofa and Lordo stumbled back to the door, dropping to the ground, suddenly exhausted despite the fight just beginning.

Micaiah turned as if to help his girlfriend who was still fighting Murdi in close quarters in the hall, fists and a small knife making dents and slashes in the wall. Cassius used a trick of Gravity, latching onto Micaiah and then using himself as a greater gravitational force, pulling the large Irishman back. He let go of the Gravity track before Micaiah could slam into him, but the Akarin was no fool. Once he realized what was happening, he went with the force instead of fighting it. When the pull released, he again tried to use the momentum to land another crushing blow, but Cassius managed to Band and slip out of the way.

His Band wasn't perfect, though, and Micaiah seized on it, stopping Cassius from getting all the way clear. Shoulder met hip, and Micaiah also used Gravity to his advantage, trying to force his weight into Cassius, maybe to pin him, maybe to shatter his pelvis. His intentions were neither clear nor relevant as he was suddenly rolled off, Lordo taking his knife and driving it into the man's bicep.

Micaiah lost all concentration in the flow of battle, and the best he could do was scramble away to the other side of the small living room. Cassius let him go as he himself stood and got together with Lordo. The problem was, now Micaiah had a weapon, as he pulled the knife from its place in his bicep, using Matter and Time to knit the wounded flesh back together so that it was like it never even happened.

"I'm just going to take a guess and say you're Cassius," the Irishman said, breathing heavily.

"Being right doesn't get you anything," Cassius told him, immediately launching into another attack.

His first trick was to reach for Thermodynamics and melt the blade as Micaiah swung it at him, catching the blade in his left hand, Time slowing it down, Matter keeping him safe. Micaiah was not fooled, however, and managed to turn the attack back on him. As the blade heated up, just before it reached the point where blade integrity degraded, Micaiah both distracted Cassius with a wild, obvious, projected attack from his other fist, and inverted the Thermodynamic bubble, causing it to burst. The blade remained hot, and with the distraction, he was able to force the blade forward, straight through the hole in Cassius' fist, so that the blade slid between arm and chest, slicing open skin but puncturing nothing.

While it was a point for Micaiah, it also put him in a very bad position. Cassius locked up Micaiah's shoulder and upper arm while Lordo took the blade, stuck it in the man's forearm and twisted, mangling flesh and bone.

Micaiah cried out in pain, but even that was a distraction as he slipped his left leg between Cassius' legs, hooked his left foot around Cassius' right ankle, then used his knee to collapse Cassius' stance, forcing them both to the ground again. Again he tried to use Gravity to force the situation, but Cassius grabbed onto the track and, as Micaiah had inverted his Thermodynamics, Cassius inverted his Gravity.

Micaiah hit the ceiling, and none too gracefully. Cassius removed the track entirely, and it was all the Irishman could do to control his fall. He hit the ground and rolled. As he did, Cassius gave him a good old-fashioned kick to the head. Micaiah grunted and kept rolling, managing to get back up and face them. Gritting his teeth, he again pulled out the knife, but there wasn't time for him to set a broken arm. His back was to the door, Cassius and Lordo were in the living room, and Murdi was just emerging from the hallway.

"Where's Kayla?" Micaiah demanded.

"She's sleeping," Murdi answered.

All things considered, the assassin's answer may have actually been truthful. Micaiah did not see it this way, however, and instead chose the route of irrational vengeance, using Gravity to launch himself clear of the kitchen island and plow into the mercenary.

Murdi let this happen, folding around Micaiah like a blanket. Lordo went to assist his brother, and together they effectively smothered Micaiah between them. Cassius watched, fascinated, startling as the Mishim threw themselves apart, screeching in pain. Micaiah, sweaty, exhausted, and still with a broken arm, stood.

"Two down, one to go," he breathed.

"And here we tried to do things the nice way," Cassius sighed.

With only a flick of his wrist for dramatic effect, Cassius hit Micaiah with a terrible show of Force, blasting the Irishman all the way down the hall and through a door. It cost him most of his strength, but that would be recovered soon enough. He Banded and went down the hall where Micaiah was just landing on the floor amid a field of debris. With the kinetic energy of the fall suspended around him, he was able to touch it and recover some of that energy for himself. When he released the Band, the man and the debris simply dropped to the ground, affected by no more force than simple Gravity.

Cassius touched Micaiah again, using Matter to Feel him, all the way to his muscles, nerves, and the individual cells. Even with such great abilities, he still didn't fully understand how the body made and used energy. He might be able to recite the process, but there was still a tiny bit that was sheer magic. Faith, if you will.

He sapped Micaiah of all strength and ability to fight back. When Cassius was done, Micaiah could barely lift his head, and if he opened his mouth to speak, all that came out was a yawn. He lazily lifted a hand, reaching for Cassius as if to try and do the same in reverse, but Cassius easily slipped out of reach and sat down.

"As much as my reputation precedes me, believe me when I say we're not here to kill you. If we had been, you would have been dead by now," Cassius told him.

"A warning, then," Micaiah breathed, breaking into another yawn which he seemed very displeased with.

"Mm...yes and no. Maybe. I don't know. I just do as I'm told."

"By an evil spirit."

Cassius grinned. "That's up for debate."

He stood. Micaiah tried to push himself up, get into any position except vulnerable on the floor. A simple bit of Gravity held him down, and a little Thermodynamics to warm him up kept him comfortable and compliant. It didn't take five minutes for him to fall asleep. Or unconscious, anyway.

Cassius went out to the living room where the Mishim twins were still curled up feebly, nursing whatever wounds had been inflicted on them.

"What did he do to you?" Cassius asked, rolling Lordo onto his back with a foot. The assassin was trembling.

"I...I...I..d-don't know," the assassin whimpered.

He touched Lordo and Felt him. He didn't understand Mishim physiology, so unless he was bleeding internally, he wouldn't know if anything was really wrong or if Micaiah had simply used an overwhelming pain sensation. He didn't find anything obvious. He went to Murdi.

"Do you know what he did?"

Murdi looked almost asleep, but just before Cassius repeated the question, answered, "I think it was just simply pain. Taking the nerves of our new wounds and sending fresh pain through them."

"You mean you didn't use Time to heal them through?"

"The Iktarians have Time-suppressant technology. After so many days, when the worst of the pain was gone and we had begun new training, the thought simply passed us by."

Cassius grabbed Murdi's less-than-dexterous stump. The assassin made guttural noises of agony, but did little more than writhe in slow motion. After a moment, Cassius used Matter to knit together any damaged flesh, and Time to finish off the healing process. Then he went back to Lordo and did the same thing to his feet.

Why did he always get stuck with the idiots?

Another minute went by and the twin assassins got themselves together.

"Are you ready?" Cassius asked irritably.

They agreed, and the three of them returned to the bedroom.

Aklaq, or Kayla as Micaiah had called her, was, true to Murdi's word, sleeping soundly in the bed. Micaiah was still passed out at the end of the bed.

"Did you put her in bed, or was that pure coincidence?" Cassius asked, looking at Aklaq and then at Murdi.

Murdi shrugged. "She was not our target. It was only polite."

Cassius sighed. "Gentleman Killers to the last."

It was Murdi who hefted Micaiah over his shoulder, and Cassius and Lordo who opened the portal to the Wheel and forced it closed once they were through.

For as much as Rifun wanted to keep things as quiet as possible, the Akarin had forced their hand just a little, and Cassius hoped that parading Micaiah's unconscious carcass through the Wheel would get back to them. Of course, it wasn't as if they wouldn't find out about it, once Aklaq woke up and went to report the attack. Maybe they should have taken her, too, whatever Rifun said.

Oh well, they were here now. They took Micaiah to the Judgment Wing where Misik himself was waiting.

"Impressive," he commented, though his true level of intrigue seemed to be far beneath the standing of the word. "Take him back."

The trio of attackers was given a two-way stamp while Micaiah was given a one-way stamp. From the main lobby, they headed through an enormous doorway which resembled a bank vault door and down a great corridor which led to another bank vault door. The room on the other side of this door had three smaller doors. The one on the right led to private rooms. The one in the middle led to the actual prison. The one on the left, which they chose, led to what amounted to holding cells as well as the minor courts.

Of course, Time Trials were no small affairs. If not for this being such a planned operation, Micaiah might have been waiting here a while.

They dropped him off to the waiting Borelians, then left without another word. Misik gave them hardly more than a nod as they left the Judgment Wing entirely.

"Now what?" Murdi inquired.

"You return to the ruins and wait," Cassius answered. "Your part is done for now. Stick to your training schedule, like normal. I will be working with the other leaders to move this all forward."

They returned to Sadurnon where the twin assassins went their own way and Cassius made for the officers building. Turning the corner down the back corridor, he almost ran into Rifun.

"Ah, just the man I was looking for."

"Oh?" Cassius raised a brow.

"We're having a meeting. Just need you to join us."

Cassius sighed inwardly as he followed Rifun. Another meeting. Were they even allowed to take a shit without having a meeting first? He had to admit, it had actually been pretty nice with Rifun gone, not having to listen to politics or go to meetings or anything of the sort. Everyone had a job. They knew what it was. They got it done. Why did they need all these meetings suddenly?

Well, it was kind of a high priority mission and everything. Kidnapping an Akarin, erasing memories, staging a Time Trial, none of these were little events.

All the same. So many meetings.

Julianna and Isthim were already in the room, and no time was wasted when the men joined them.

"So Micaiah is captured?" Julianna asked of Cassius.

"He is," Cassius told her. "Currently sitting in a cell under the watchful eye of Misik and his grunts." He gave a pointed look at Isthim.

Julianna shifted her stance. "How do we know he can't escape? The Judgment Wing may have Time-inhibitors, but the Akari is not bound by such rules."

"Then I guess we get to find out whose Akari is the real one, or whom the Author favors," Rifun stated. "Is that not how the Akarin conduct their proceedings? Give the accused a chance to escape, and if he does, the Author clearly favors him enough to warrant his evasion of justice?" He gave her a look. "If he is still there in the morning, I intend to speak with him." He looked at Isthim. "And your people?"

"The team that went after Andrew and Nathan has not yet reported back, but it is not a worrisome thing at this time. As for the ith team, they are still conducting operations in the Akarin fortress."

"How is this done exactly?" Julianna wondered. "The Borelians and the Akarin have been at odds for as long as I can remember."

"We never knew where their fortress was, before the Akari. Similarly, we never had the use of Disguises. Factoring in many elements of this particular mission, it may be a day or two before it may be considered complete."

"That won't work," Cassius said. "It needs to get done faster. Micaiah's girlfriend was there for the fight. If she goes back to the fortress and tells them of the attack, the panic could expose your people. Or if Andrew and Nathan get a message back. Which, in eavesdropping on a bit of conversation, they were supposed to meet a third party to deliver the journal."

"I will pass the information along, but we cannot move faster than we are. Once this meeting is done, I will again join them, but it cannot be rushed."

"If the concern is simply the girl waking up and going back to tell them—which I don't know why it makes that big of a difference anyway seeing how they are already preparing for siege," Julianna said, "then why not continue to babysit her and make sure she doesn't wake up so soon? Or better yet, why not use ith on her to cloud her memories of the attack, make her forget, make her not question why her boyfriend is gone?"

Thankfully, Isthim agreed to the memory alteration before Cassius agreed to the babysitting, though he knew he was going to have to point her in the direction of the apartment.

"And what about you?" Julianna continued, looking at Rifun. "What are you doing in all of this?"

"Brushing up on the Laws of Time," Rifun answered. "Talking to the Bat and the Day."

"Will they help us?"

"They're onboard. Actually, they seem quite enthusiastic about it."

"Really? They're actually capable of real emotion?"

"It seems they are. In the morning, I will go and speak with Micaiah, and then we'll proceed with the trial."

"And what are you trying to get out of him?"

"I don't know yet, but our conversations have always been interesting. I don't see why this one should be any less. Regardless, he is going through the Time Trial."

"Considering the possibility that he read our Book," Isthim said slowly, "should we cloud his memory as well?"

"Why waste the effort? He won't survive the Time Trial anyway," Cassius scoffed. "The success rate for humans is somewhere around one or two percent."

"But not zero," Rifun told him. "We can't take the chance that he does survive. And I highly doubt we're going to be friends if he does come out the other side. He'll tell everyone where we are. Akarin, Tacagan, Gentleman Killer, he'll bring Hell to bear against us. Yes, we should cloud his memory."

"But we want him to know that he is on trial and why he's there," Julianna quipped.

"He is on trial because we put him there. He defied the Grandfathers, defied Time, defied us. Now he gets a chance to put his money where his mouth is and prove his awesome power." Rifun gave Cassius a sideways glance. "And if he couldn't defeat a psychopath and two cripples, I don't see what chance he has against the Bat or the Day."

If it was meant to be a compliment, Cassius was having a hard time accepting it as such.

"And even if he does miraculously survive," Rifun went on, "then he will have made his point, we will have made our point, and the Akarin will be crippled themselves because of their sudden, inexplicable memory loss."

"We're not going to kill him anyway?" Isthim questioned.

"To what end? We still don't have the journals. There is a bit of politics at play here."

"And when will these petty politics end?" Cassius whined.

Rifun turned to fully face him. "When we have crushed the Time industry. It's down for the count, ripe for the picking. We just have to take it. We take over the Time industry, take over the many hordes of Time Agents, teach them the journals and our Akari, then move against the Akarin and finally swat that fly."

"First we need the journals," Julianna said, giving Rifun a pointed look.

"I have a pretty good guess that once Isthim's teams catch up with Andrew and Nathan, and their mysterious third party, we'll know where they are. If they don't have them, they know who does."

It all sounded so simple. But sounding simple and being simple were often two different things.

"Any questions?" Rifun wondered.

No one said anything, and they were dismissed.

Cassius returned to his chambers, actually quite pleased with himself for the day's events, even if they hadn't gone quite as planned. Sure, they got Micaiah in the end, but why did he always get stuck with the idiots? What fool didn't heal himself just as soon as he could? Rifun may have had some noble lie he told himself, but his wounds were skin-deep. What excuse did Murdi and Lordo have?

Well, it didn't matter anymore. Their mission was complete, and Micaiah was going to a Time Trial, one of the most brutal and unfair events to take place in the Time industry. And Cassius was going to be present to watch it all.

Maybe he could talk to Rifun and convince him to let him get in another swing or two. Maybe he could deal the killing blow.

There was no good way to know the exact time Rifun went to see Micaiah in the Judgment Wing, but since it was the first thing he did after a good night's rest, he elected to say it was "early the next morning."

The Judgment Wing was in no manner of disarray, so if anything had happened in the night, not only had it already been cleaned up, but he hadn't been told about it. When he got back to the holding cells, he found Micaiah sitting against the wall, eyes closed.

"Still here?" Rifun questioned.

Micaiah opened his eyes and gave him a cat's regard. "I figured that if Cassius and the other two went to such lengths to do this, I could at least humor you by staying put and listening to your ultimatum."

"Ultimatum? What makes you think I have one of those? Or any left to give, I should say?"

"Because if you wanted me dead, you would have done it already."

Rifun grinned and shook his head. "No. I have no ultimatum for you."

Now Micaiah stood and approached the bars, though he remained just out of arm's reach. "Pretty good leap, isn't it? To go from wondering about the meaning of it all, one's future, to suddenly attacking and imprisoning rivals?"

"You say this as though it happened in some sort of vacuum, that it was unprovoked." Rifun shifted his stance. "I came to you many times, looking for answers, for support. I asked for help. And you wouldn't do it. Wouldn't budge an inch. You sit on your horse while the rest of us labor away under the hot sun."

"You are not a victim here," Micaiah interrupted. "You made your choices. Our stronghold remains a stronghold because we remain firm in our beliefs and our stances. You leave one cupboard open and the rats get in. And rats multiply quickly, and soon, no more food."

"You consider me vermin, then."

Micaiah sighed. "Not you. Only this ridiculous ideology, taking bits and pieces from here and there and wherever you can find to tell you that you are something special."

"And having Authored Books never stroked your ego." Rifun raised a brow. "Does your brother know about them?"

"No."

"Really? So it only applies to Akari-bearers, then?"

"I don't know why I got one and Micah didn't. I'd rather leave him out of this."

"Why? Are the politics of the Akarin really so horrible? What will he think when —"

"He isn't an Akari-bearer. He wasn't chosen, I was."

"Then by that token, seeing how I received a Book and Cassius did not, seeing how I am becoming a Builder and he is not, I am also an Akari-bearer, chosen by the Author. And yet you would deny me help and strike down my offer of peace and reconciliation between our groups."

Micaiah took an even breath, but his expression was anything but kind. "As long as you follow those damned journals, we have nothing in common."

Rifun nodded slowly. "Good. I'm actually glad you feel that way. Makes this next bit a little easier."

"You're going to kill me?"

"No. At least, not so directly, and you do have a chance to survive. When I leave here, you will be formally charged with aiding and abetting an enemy of the Laws of Time, the Akarin. You know, since you flout most of their other rules and most Akarin are listed as Runners, which means aiding and abetting a fugitive as well. And your chosen punishment will be a Time Trial."

Micaiah went pale.

"You do remember that little clause, don't you?" Rifun needled. "It's right in the Laws of Time. I can show it to you if you want. I remember you said you wanted to reinstall the Hands, reestablish the Time industry. I'm just reminding you of what that means."

"But—"

"Do you think they're going to thank you, even if you did pull it off? Do you think the Hands would somehow forge an alliance with the Akarin, or just let you keep your cozy little fortress on the edge of the universe? Maybe for a short time, as things get sorted out. But one day, one or more Hands is going to grow suspicious of you, and they're going to think either two things: First, Akari-bearers are powerful enough to take out and install into power whomever they please, so they must be dealt with. Second, Akari-bearers are too pacifist to fight back, which makes them excellent targets to flex Time industry muscles and instill a little fear into the common folk. And then what?

"We are at a crossroads. Akari-bearers have a chance to make things right, just as they were before the First Rebuild. We've always had the upper hand, now we have a chance to use it."

"A broken upper hand," Micaiah stated. "And you're insane."

"Those who speak beyond the mortal world are often called as such, so I will take it as a compliment."

"It wasn't."

"As much as they don't want to admit it, the Time industry needs Akari-bearers. But we don't need the Time industry. Get rid of it. Get rid of the corruption, the lies."

"And everything in the Cult is roses and sunshine?" Micaiah wondered. "I doubt it. None of you four leaders trust each other, and having more power won't change that." He sighed. "I don't fully understand what's going on here, or what's going on there. I don't know why the Author wrote a Book about you or where it's heading. But I do know that what is happening here is far cry from normal and cannot be accepted as such."

"Then why write it? Why write a book about your enemies?"

"Why study history except to learn from it? I don't presume to know her intentions."

"Then don't. This is what is happening. You will go on trial. If you die, justice is served and a point has been made. If you survive, take it back to the Akarin as a warning. If you remember to."

"What's that supposed to mean?"

Rifun did not answer. He turned and left him there and made his way out of the holding cells, back to the booking area. Three Borelians were busy with office work. One was yellow, one green, and one of a color that could not be perceived by humans. He motioned for the latter two.

"How skilled are you in your toxins?" he asked.

"I have been trained extensively," the green one said.

The other one did not look so confident and admitted, "I am not so skilled."

He looked at the first. "When the Time Trial is over and they have lost, I want you to break their clocks. And you are permitted to fuck with them as much as you wish in Time before killing them."

They agreed eagerly, even the younger one. Rifun regarded her. "What toxin are you?"

"Ith, but I am more skilled in my second toxin, urlo," she replied.

"Sidakvar batil," Rifun stated.

"That's right."

"Carry on, and see about honing your skills in ith as well. We may need them more in the future."

He did not stay to hear her reply, simply left the Judgment Wing and made for the Seat of the Hands. With no Hands to preside over Wheel functions and most of the smaller factions choosing to base their operations in the various Auctionhouses, the Seat was actually fairly empty, with exception of a few secretaries and a couple loiterers making shady deals.

He found Isthim inside, her voice echoing in the presently empty arena as she directed her cohorts here and there, preparing for the trial. The Bat and the Day were also present. While their expressions remained as impassive as ever, they moved with an energy that one might describe as being enthusiastic. Of course, they'd been out of work for two years; why shouldn't they be happy to be useful again?

"Everything in the fortress is wrapped up?" he asked Isthim.

"It is, and neatly so," she confirmed. "Micaiah Durvin?"

"Detained rather snugly in the Judgment Wing, claims to still be here only out of curiosity. We'll see how long that lasts once the trial is underway. Considering the stakes and how he will simply be trying to stay alive, I can't imagine that he and the others will wish to stick around for long. No doubt they will try to make plans for victory or escape, even revenge. But even if he were to return to the fortress, their disarray will keep all of them too busy to notice us."

"I was thinking something similar."

Rifun looked around. "It appears that things are just about ready here."

"They are. All that needs to be done, then, is for him to call his Stake and his witnesses."

"Let me know when everything is ready to proceed. I'm going to take a walk around the Wheel, see if I can't bring in a few spectators to witness our great takeover of the Wheel."

Isthim got a look, then, as she pushed her white toxin and lightly touched him. Rifun made a strangled sort of sound but did not fight it.

"Even you have to know it's embarrassing to walk around like this now," he told her as she lifted her finger and reverted back to her favorite pink toxin.

"Wear it with pride that a Borelian gave it to you willingly," she countered.

And he did, although it wasn't as though ninety-nine percent of the aliens in the Wheel would understand. Some had zero qualms about such things in public.

He managed to gather a sizable crowd, though their reasons and expectations could only be guessed at. Maybe some thought it was a feud between rival factions that was finally going to be settled. Maybe some thought it was getting back to some semblance of normal, when the Hands ruled. Maybe some thought that the person who had caused this whole mess was finally being put on trial. Maybe some were just interested in a bloodbath. Who could know?

Whatever the case, it wouldn't be an empty courtroom. Rifun took a seat beside Isthim who sat amid fifty-one Grandfathers, stand-ins for the fifty-one Hands who normally presided. Farther down, closer to the arena itself, was Cassius. Maybe they should thrown him into the arena as a third Juror, along with the Bat and the Day. Rifun did not see Julianna, but that was no surprise; she wasn't given to blood sport.

In the arena, a portion had been sectioned off, maybe ten by twenty yards. This was where the Accused would stand to answer questions. Anything he answered, one of his witnesses, called Testimonies, would have to corroborate. If the answer was satisfactory, the trial moved on to the next question. If it was unsatisfactory, the Accused would be forced to fight either the Bat or the Day in alternating order. At any time, he could call his Stake to stand in for him, to fight for him for one round as a double-or-nothing gamble; if the Stake won, everyone went free instantly. If not, everyone was put to death immediately. If he chose not to do this and still survived all fifty-one questions, the Accused and his entourage could go free. If he didn't survive, his Stake and Testimonies were also put to death.

No one could say anymore where the Time Trial had originated, or why it was rigged to be so unfair, more spectacle than true justice. Whatever the cause, it clearly wasn't going to die if anyone had their way and took full control of the Time industry.

The general din of the crowd suddenly got louder as the Stake and Witnesses were led into the arena, behind the sectioned off area. Rifun studied them. It wasn't a stretch of the imagination to think his Stake was his twin brother Micah, though he was decidedly less buff. As for his Testimonies, Rifun guessed that the woman was Aklaq White Bear.

Hm. *Chasing the White Bear.* Another of the Authored Books. There was a connection there, Rifun was certain.

The second Testimony was Doug Templeton, and the third was Andrew.

Say one thing for Micaiah, he was either an idiot, or a professional high-stakes gambler, risking his twin brother, his girlfriend, an Akarin council member, and a Builder. Too bad it had to come to this.

Then the Accused himself was brought in. He didn't look as though he'd been beaten, but his movements were a little dazed. Maybe he'd bene roughed up a bit by the green and ith Borelians, just enough to disorient him a bit, make him more compliant. When he turned to face Rifun, however, his gaze was clear. He might not have all the details or the whys, but he knew what was happening and who brought him here.

Rifun let the crowd have their time to mock and jeer at Micaiah and his entourage, a good two or three minutes before finally putting his hands up and calling for quiet.

"Miach Meagher," he began, using Micaiah's true birth name, "you stand here, Accused, charged with aiding and abetting an enemy of the Time industry. The Akarin are known heretics, and their members often classified as Runners, whom you routinely assist in flouting the Laws of Time which you yourself have claimed to uphold, being a Master Timekeeper yourself. How do you plead?"

"Not guilty," Micaiah answered, still glaring at him.

"You have as your Stake, Aklaq White Bear, is that correct?"

"That's right."

"And your Testimonies are your twin brother MacEoghan Meagher, Doug Templeton, and Andrew O'Dell. Also correct?"

"Yes."

Rifun shifted his stance and addressed the crowd. "In the absence of the Hands of Time, the Grandfathers will preside over these proceedings. Fifty-one Grandfathers will each ask one question. After each question, the Accused must answer or forfeit the question. For each answer, one of the Testimonies must corroborate, or he will forfeit the question. If the answer and the corroboration are satisfactory to the Grandfather who asked the question, the trial will proceed and the next Grandfather will ask his or her question. If a question is forfeited, or if an answer and corroboration is unsatisfactory to the Grandfather, the Accused must prove his worth, by the oath of the stars—" A fancy way of saying by divine intervention, let the gods show who was worthy. "—in single combat against the Jurors, either the Bat or the Day. He need not kill them, merely best them in the round. Then the questioning will continue.

"At any time, the Accused may call his Stake to fight for him in single combat. If the Stake wins, the Accused and the rest of the party will go free. If the Stake loses, all will be put to death.

"If the Accused survives all fifty-one questions and any and all combat with the Jurors, then he and his entourage are declared innocent and are free to go."

He looked around at those gathered, from the spectators, to the Grandfathers, to the Accused and his entourage. Time Trials were rare things because they took up so much damn time, and they were notoriously unfair, truly a last-ditch effort for someone looking to escape a death sentence, or even clock-breaking.

The spectators seemed eager enough, he thought. For once, this was an organized blood sport, and they were not a potential target. This time, they got to witness someone else's demise. And, again, this was something, while barbaric, almost normal. Sure, the presence of the Borelians as the Grandfathers, sitting in place of absent Hands, was perhaps a bit disquieting, but it was normal. Like children who played stickball in the middle of a battlefield where grass hadn't covered up the bomb craters yet, and indeed more could fall at any time.

As for the Borelians themselves, they reveled in their role with nearly rambunctious enthusiasm. On the one hand, it was a break from the mundane office work that normally occupied their time as Grandfathers. On the other hand, it was very much like their own court system, or so Rifun understood. The way Isthim told it, the Borelians had a very large part in the early years of the Wheel, when the Time industry was still being sorted out, and they helped shape the justice system. While Rifun had no reason to disbelieve her, he was fairly certain that the story was greatly embellished. The Borelians were not known for their modesty, after all, and it would be insulting to insinuate that it had been the other way around, that they had modeled their justice system after the Time industry.

Looking down into the arena, the Bat and the Day had resumed their impassive expressions, although their dispositions suggested that they were ready for this to begin, and they were just waiting for one of the Grandfathers to declare something unsatisfactory.

Micaiah was still glaring at Rifun, though his posture was not so rigid as the Jurors' off to either side of him. Behind him, just outside the designated area, his twin brother also looked rather displeased by the whole thing, but also afraid, and his lack of bodybuilding made him look small compared to Micaiah and absolutely puny compared to the Bat or the Day.

Aklaq White Bear was the epitome of a woman scorned, and it was tough to say just whom she was angrier with. Oh, he could imagine that she was mad at him, Rifun, and the Cult and everyone else involved in this show. But it looked as though there was also quite a reservoir of anger against Micaiah. And why not? She probably had hopes and dreams and plans for her life, and here she was facing life and death because her boyfriend couldn't even fend off a couple of assassins.

Doug Templeton was mixed. His posture spoke of his arrogance and boisterous personality, but the set of his jaw and the wrinkling of his brow suggested that he was thinking hard. Was he plotting escape? Looking for some kind of loophole in the rules? Rifun had only interacted with him the one time, but he seemed to have a solid mind in that skull of his. Was his obnoxious personality naturally occurring, then, or simply a front so people didn't suspect his brilliance?

Only Andrew O'Dell held the posture of a man who was thinking beyond the present moment, beyond what was around him. He was seeing the big picture, the whole forest. He gazed at Rifun, and when their eyes met, they both understood what was happening. Something beyond the mere physical was unfolding. Something absolute was taking place. There were no mortal words to describe it, and for a long moment, the two dual-spirited men met each other beyond the physical world.

The moment passed, and the world around them became more real. The sights, sounds, smells, all of it bringing Rifun back to the mortal world and the present moment, where a man, his brother, and his three friends were on trial for their lives.

"Are there any questions before we begin?" he inquired. "Any involved may speak."

"How do we know you'll keep your word," Doug asked, "and let us go free if we pass this ridiculous test of yours?"

Rifun raised a brow. "I am a man of my word, I assure you. If I say that you shall go free, then you shall go free."

"How do we know that you will not simply recapture us?" Aklaq demanded icily.

"To what end? Clearly you would have proven yourselves innocent and certainly worthy opponents."

"So what do we get if we win?" Micaiah wondered.

"Quite frankly, you get your lives. And a valuable lesson, I think."

"What lesson is that?"

Rifun sighed and shifted position. "Are we going to begin, or shall we debate philosophy all day?"

"Your show," Micaiah said. "Your call."

Rifun sat up. "And so it is." He glanced at Isthim. "I think we're ready to begin, don't you?"

She dipped her head once and stood. She started into a short speech, some recitation of how the questioning was to proceed, but Rifun was more intrigued by those in the arena. In particular, he wondered about Micah. Why had Micaiah never spoken of the Akari to his own twin brother? The reasons might be personal, true, but to never mention it once, and then to suddenly call on him for a Time Trial? The logic behind it might have been understandable, that one brother sticks up for the other, but Micah was so far outgunned, he may as well have brought a knife to a bomb fight.

Just for kicks and giggles, Rifun decided to use Test, a little thing that could penetrate a Disguise. It would reveal, to him only, the person beneath the facade, if there was indeed a facade.

And there it was. Micah Durvin was not Micah Durvin. This was a man of similar apparent age as the rest of them, not a bodybuilder like Micaiah but still a threat to a petty thief. Black hair, brown eyes, nothing exceptionally special about him. But who was he?

Isthim sat down from her speech, and the questioning began. Rifun leaned over to her.

"One of these things is not like the other," he murmured. "Micah Durvin is not who he appears to be. My guess is it's another Akarin."

Isthim made as if to stand, but Rifun put a hand on her arm. "No, don't. I want to see how this plays out. He's only a Testimony, so it's not as though he'll be in combat."

"It's still a trick," Isthim growled.

"What is life without a little spontaneity? If it becomes a problem, we'll deal with it. Until then, enjoy the show."

She still seemed annoyed, but did not say anything more about it. Likely she also Tested so-called "Micah," but she said nothing about this either. Rifun simply leaned back and watched. *Who are you, not-Micah?*

His attention was taken by a sudden uptick in volume from the spectators. One of the Grandfathers had apparently deemed an answer unsatisfactory, thus pitting Micaiah against a Juror, the Bat up first.

The Bat was frightening just by its mere presence, and even Rifun would admit to being a bit intimidated by it. Having to fight it as part of the Apprentice Timekeeper review was petrifying, more so when one considered just how much it was holding back so it didn't clobber someone into dust, little more than a smear on the floor. Rifun imagined that the Bat was relieved to be able to let loose every so often and go full strength, but to see it go after Micaiah with such determination put the absolute fear of God in Rifun.

He glanced down at Cassius. The man was a psychopath with an unhealthy lust for death, but he was manageable. Rifun hadn't quite worked out where the man ended and the spirit began, if indeed there remained a distinction, but there was still a part of him that was human, subject to the same flaws and psychology as any ordinary human being. Even if he were little more than a shell for an evil spirit to occupy, with no trace of the human Kokumbo left in him, he still acted like a human, somewhat.

The Bat and the Day were not so comforting. If there was a Hell, the Bat was probably its gatekeeper, or perhaps a sentry, looking upon the affairs of men and mortals across the universe and reporting back to the Devil whenever he went off shift. The Day could easily fill a warden's role, if Hell had prisons. Rifun couldn't pinpoint any one thing that made him feel this way about them. Other aliens were large, others were ugly, others were strong, others were fast, others were intimidating, others were all of these things wrapped up and tied with a bow. Rather it seemed to be more of a gut instinct, something that his spiritual self sensed, a higher awareness that the Bat and the Day were not natural.

Micaiah didn't stand much of a chance against either of them, and after four rounds, he seemed to develop a bit of a strategy from it. Rather than fight for all he was worth, thereby tiring himself quickly and just making everything hurt that much more, he seemed to be trying to lose quickly. Surrender and hope to fight another day.

After question ten, Isthim leaned over to Rifun.

"So, is this it?" she asked. "Are we officially asserting ourselves as masters of the Time industry?"

"Mm, if that's what the people think, then I won't be scrambling to crush such rumors," he replied.

"What more do we need? We hold the cards of justice and punishment. We have allies who have taken over the markets. Our enemies are a non-issue, and the Akarin have been rendered useless. What more do we need to accomplish before we finally declare victory?"

Rifun sighed, thought a moment, then motioned for her to follow him. They left the Inner Sanctum, but remained in the vicinity of the Seat.

"I suppose I could have used a Sound Barrier in there, but I didn't want to risk one of the Akarin down there thwarting it," he said, now erecting a Sound Barrier.

"Fair enough," Isthim acknowledged. "But again. What more needs to be done?"

"We need to find the missing journals. Did your teams recover anything?"

She huffed. "They have yet to report back to me about it."

"Considering that Andrew O'Dell is right inside that arena, either he palmed it or passed it off, which means your teams are either still looking or are too ashamed to admit failure."

"Holding out will garner a worse punishment than admission," Isthim said testily.

"And here we are with no journals and no reports," Rifun told her. "Fine. We declare victory today. We have the fear to maintain it for a while, but we don't have the numbers or the strength to hold it. Even the Tacagans could topple us, if they got clever enough. The Akarin are in disarray now, but it won't stay that way for long, I think, and they still have the greater numbers and the greater power. The converts who teach what they know help, but it's not enough. We take over the Time industry, even if the Akarin don't remember Sadurnon, it won't matter because we'll be here like sitting ducks with a huge target on our back."

"The teams—"

"Will only find one journal if they're lucky!"

Isthim's expression turned puzzled for a moment. Then came the realization. "You know where one of them is."

"Yes," he sighed. "I do. The Book of Abilities."

Her hand shot out and got a lot closer to his throat than he was really comfortable with. He could almost imagine her hissing like a cat. "How long have you known?"

"Over a year." He went on before she could speak. "You think I haven't wanted to go get it? You think I haven't considered a hundred different ways to try and make it discreet? Because I have. I've thought about it a lot."

She studied him intently, and finally lowered her hand. "Thinking on it for a year...it's not an easy place to get to, is it?" She paused. "Where is the Book of Abilities?"

"Hidden in the Time Trap where Cassius chased Julianna over a century ago. She hid it there in the cave, in a pile of bones so it can't be easily found."

A moment of silence stretched out between them. Isthim took a step back and Rifun found he could breathe normally again. Alliance or not, mated or not, it was unnerving to be so close to a Borelian. She nodded slowly.

"Whoever goes and gets it is going to be gone a long time. Months, even years."

"Yes," he stated. "It's not something that can be done haphazardly or thoughtlessly. The Cult should be stable enough to go a length of time without one or more of its leaders, but—"

"—the key to stabilizing and strengthening the Cult lies in that very cave," Isthim finished. "This is why you departed for a year, to see if we were ready for such a thing."

He made a sound. "Ah, no, not really, but I'll take the compliment."

"All the same, preparations should be made to retrieve it."

"I'm not disagreeing, but I would like to hear the report from your teams first. And I have some loose ends of my own to wrap up."

Isthim frowned. "Why do you maintain such ties to your Earth-side life?"

"I'm fixing some things that went wrong, most of them being not my fault. I want to do it while there are still people alive who remember me as the man I am, or was."

She did not say anything to that, just made an indifferent grunting sound. "Well, once the teams have returned and your other 'loose ends' have been dealt with, then we shall see about this oh-so-important journal, hm? Or perhaps I shall go after it myself."

"Or perhaps Julianna should do it since she's the one who hid it and might have a better idea of where it is, minimizing the time lost." He continued, "We'll sort it out once this is taken care of. We're kind of in the middle of a trial."

She couldn't argue that one, and they returned to their seats.

It was impossible to say which question they were on. Down below, Micaiah wasn't looking so hot. He looked like he'd gone at least a few rounds with both the Bat and the Day, and it was difficult to say just how effective his lose quickly scheme was working. Might be that it was the only reason he was still standing upright, or it might be what got him killed in the end. There was only one good way to find out.

"The answer is satisfactory," the current presiding Grandfather declared.

Micaiah and his entourage breathed a collective sigh of relief.

The next Grandfather stood.

"Where is the Akarin stronghold located?"

Micaiah sighed and rubbed his face. He did it again. Finally he said, "I don't know."

The Grandfather looked at the Testimonies. It was Doug who spoke, and he had no trouble making himself heard. "Few know where the fortress is truly located. It is not public information."

To no one's surprise, this answer was considered unsatisfactory, and the Day stepped out of the shadows.

Despite looking very different—the Bat appearing as a huge, humanoid bat; the Day looking like a giraffe and a peacock had a love affair, then got tangled in some jungle vines—the two of them had very similar fighting styles. The Bat used its wings and the Day used its peacock-like feathers as a means of distraction, dazzling and confusing an opponent long enough to strike. The Bat relied on sharp claws and brute strength, and the Day, while it had arms to use and they did have some strength, preferred to strike with its long neck and head that was about as friendly as a ten ton boulder.

Micaiah went down hard, coughing and gasping for air. The Bat and the Day both began shrieking the most ungodly noises known in the universe, causing an uproar even among the spectators. Rifun put up a Sound Barrier around himself and Isthim, not letting it down until the posture of the Jurors changed and they seemed to be speaking. They talked over each other in absurd, almost demonic, voices, complaining that Micaiah was using the Akari to heal himself and should be disqualified and executed immediately.

Rifun did not tolerate this for long, standing and, using Sound, shouted, "Silence!"

The spectators grumbled, the Bat hissed, the Day made some unintelligible noise, but everyone quieted.

"There are no rules in a Time Trial concerning use of the Akari," Rifun began slowly. "Time Trials were designed for the Time industry which has dismissed its use, even its very existence." He put his hands out just a bit. "The rules and proceedings of a Time Trial cannot be officially altered except by a vote from the ruling body. Normally this would be our beloved Hands. You will all note that we are short a few Hands in order to make that vote.

"So then, who is the ruling body? Is there a ruling body at all? I can say anything I want, but what authority have I? What authority has anyone here? The only recognized body here who could make such decisions is the Grandfathers, who also happen to be presiding over this trial. Therefore, we will conduct our affairs in an orderly manner and take it to the ruling body." He folded his hands and looked over the fifty-one Grandfathers. "Ruling Grandfathers, what say you? Shall Miach Meagher be permitted to use the Akari, and to what extent?"

By this time, Micaiah had finished doing whatever it was he had done to heal himself, and was standing again. He still looked like he'd gone a few more rounds than he wanted and was not excited by the knowledge that he would no doubt have to go a few more before it was all over, but at least he was upright and breathing.

The Grandfathers conversed among themselves for a moment, perhaps more than a few moments as Rifun noticed the use of a Band. When they were done, Isthim, being the head of this particular operation, spoke for the group.

"Miach Meagher is permitted to use the Akari in whatever way he sees fit within the scope of this trial. If he believes in the Author, then let us see whether the Author also believes in him."

This did not please the Jurors any, but the Akarin entourage seemed almost perplexed by it. Clearly they'd been expecting a terrible shutdown and an even worse fight going forward. Instead, they'd been given every tool they might need in order to survive this ordeal. They were suspicious. Rifun didn't blame them. He'd be suspicious, too, if their places were reversed.

The questioning continued, and the answers were almost always unsatisfactory. Rifun wondered what Micaiah was thinking. If he answered truthfully to many of the questions, he was betraying the Akarin, or at least giving away a lot of information. If he lied, well, he was lying, basically having to denounce the Akarin in front of everyone. Was he running on fear, or was this part of the plan?

How strong is your faith, Miach Meagher? Which is more noble, the lie that possibly lets you live and fight another day, or the truth that betrays your friends but frees your soul? If you love your life, you will lose it. But if you lose your life for the sake of the Author... Rifun smirked.

Another unsatisfactory answer, and the Bat came out to play. Now knowing that Micaiah was free to use the Akari, it held nothing back, and Rifun was forced to wonder just how much more power it had to give. It seemed to have no end to this reservoir, just an endless tide of strength and speed, a great wind that never let up but only got more powerful.

Suddenly Micaiah's strategy to intentionally lose was no longer an option, for the Bat seemed intent on going for the kill, but somehow always pulling up just short of that final blow. It was not illegal for the Juror to kill the Accused, for that was why the success rate was so low overall, and for humans, it was hardly worth mentioning. Perhaps the Bat, and the Day, derived some sick pleasure from tormenting Micaiah, daring him to use the Akari, punishing him for doing so, punishing him more for not doing so. They were like cats playing with their prey, getting all the joy they could before having to make the decision to end its life.

Rifun glanced down at Cassius, sitting on the edge of his seat and nearly falling into the arena. How badly he must want to be down there, doing the same. Was there some law that there could only be two Jurors? What were the requirements? If it was bloodlust only, Cassius was surely the top contender. If there were other conditions, well, Rifun wouldn't put it past him to try to meet them.

Isthim stood, now her turn to ask a question. Was she the final questioner? This trial seemed to be over awfully quick, or else Rifun had been too distracted to pay that close attention.

"Is it true that not all of your Testimonies here today are who they claim to be?" she inquired.

Rifun smirked as he looked down at the Accused and his entourage. Micaiah was no longer standing, but rather sitting on the ground with his knees drawn up, looking ready to fall asleep. He might have been bleeding or bruised, except he'd healed any injuries as he'd taken them. Tears in his clothing were the only indication he'd suffered any fleshly damage. That and a couple broken fingers which he'd been nursing, trying to slowly heal them during the times of questioning without permanently disfiguring himself and losing precious dexterity.

"How do you expect me to answer that?" the Irishman asked.

Isthim grinned. "Let me rephrase. Are all of your Testimonies here today honest about their identities?"

"We already established who they are, yes."

"Your wordplay will not save you. The Testimony posing as your twin brother MacEoghan Meagher is not actually MacEoghan Meagher, is it?"

There was some murmuring in the crowd.

"In fact," Isthim went on, "it is in fact another one of the Akarin using an ability called Disguise." She paused to let the murmuring get louder. "And if not for our ability called Test, which penetrates this Disguise, no one ever would have known."

The thing about it, though, Test could penetrate a Disguise and alert the user of the target's treachery, but it couldn't actually do anything about it. Disguise was an internal ability, unlike something like a Band which was external. To force a Disguise to fall, the target had to be touched, forcefully, or even knocked out.

The so-called Micah was gracious, however, and dropped the Disguise of his own free will, ignoring the uproar from the crowd and glaring at Isthim, then at Rifun.

"Identify yourself," Isthim commanded.

"My name is Nathan Wilde," the man announced.

Another Builder, Rifun mused. Intriguing. Two Builders, a council member, a former council member, and a notorious Akarin member, all in the same place, all on death row if things went poorly. Were they really so arrogant, or was it the only thing keeping Micaiah alive right now?

Rifun put up a Band around himself and Isthim. Not looking at her, he asked, "What question are we on, dear?"

"This is the final one."

"Mm...this is too easy."

"You think we should have forbade use of the Akari?"

"No. Actually, I think your reasoning was quite delightful. Your exposing of Mr. Wilde here was also quite exceptional, certainly a good dose of poison in the Akarin's public relations well. But this is boring. The stakes don't seem to be high enough."

"Their lives?"

He frowned. "It's lacking something. We should give the spectators a show after all, and every good show has a grand finale. As it is, all they're going to do is stand there helplessly, as they have been doing, while Micaiah again bests the Day."

"What do you suggest?"

Rifun looked around, his gaze settling on Cassius. He grinned. "Send Cassius in there as a Juror. The three Jurors against the five Akarin. Let's see what happens."

He dropped the Band, shifting position and reorienting himself to the scene around him which roared back to life.

"This is a violation of the rules!" Isthim declared, turning her attention back to the matter at hand and looking directly at Nathan. "As such, the answer is unsatisfactory and punishment will be met with justice! Both Jurors will face off against the Accused and his entire consort, the punishment being execution." She looked down at Cassius. "You may join them if you wish."

She didn't even finish the statement before he was hopping into the arena, landing just behind the Day who was advancing on the Akarin. Micaiah scrambled over the barrier between him and his entourage, their side of the arena much larger than his.

At this motion, the Bat spread its massive wings, a good twenty feet across, and launched into the air, clearing the barrier with ease and leading the charge. Cassius simply used Gravity to throw himself over the barrier, landing with the softness of a cat and leading the ground charge. The Day might have had trouble with the climb because of its awkward body shape, but it somehow used the vines tangled around its body as viable appendages, hoisting itself over the obstacle.

As soon as the Day hit the ground on the other side, the vines shot out like wild tentacles, grabbing Andrew, Doug, and Nathan and swinging them high in the air like ragdolls. The Bat dove like a hawk, barreling into Aklaq like a battering ram and sweeping her off the ground. Meanwhile, Cassius engaged Micaiah on the ground, apparently thrilled to have a second go at the Irishman.

It all happened too fast for Rifun to keep track of everything at once. He saw Andrew whip out a knife and stab at the vine holding him, but either the vine had no pain senses or else the Day just didn't care. Doug was trying to fight it using Gravity and other assorted Akari abilities. Nathan got the upper hand on his vine, using Time to age it until it withered and crumbled, sending him a good twenty feet to the ground, a death sentence if not for Gravity. Once on the ground, he ran toward the Day.

Elsewhere, Aklaq was using every trick she had to keep the Bat from ripping her throat out with its teeth, all while still soaring around the arena at incredible speeds. She managed to get a good kick into its belly, buying her enough time and space to use some manner of Force. It ripped them wildly apart, sending them both tumbling toward the ground. The Bat regained its composure in midair and again went after Aklaq. It reached for her, to snatch her out of midair before she hit the ground, but then she reached for Gravity. She made two tracks, one to slow her descent, and another that, when the Bat struck it, sent it skyward with a screech of surprise.

From there she went to help Andrew who was fighting the Day. He'd gotten free and Doug had gone to help Micaiah, but Nathan was again captured, being crushed in the Day's vines. Like a hydra, any time a vine was cut off or withered and died, two more grew in its place. Of course there had to be a limit to how many the Day could grow and handle, but regeneration was a terrible ability to fight against.

She distracted the Day long enough for Andrew to stab it in the back as best he could. More vines shot toward him in some sort of self-defense, and it was unclear just whether he'd hit anything vital. With the Day now taken with its more immediate self-defense, Aklaq was able to free Nathan who dropped, unconscious, to the ground like a sack of potatoes.

The Bat made its reentry then, diving toward Aklaq and Nathan like a meteor. At that moment, in one fluid motion, Aklaq looked over and shouted to Andrew who tossed her his knife which she put up at just the right time to spear the Bat right between the ribs where a human's heart would be, though on the opposite side.

It still crashed into her, and they went rolling on the ground. Aklaq broke first, but the Bat and its massive size just kept going, the enormous beast making burbled shrieks of pain.

The Day became distracted by this, making it too easy for Andrew, who had produced another knife, to stick it in its enormous throat.

Suddenly realizing that the odds had shifted, Cassius paused and looked around. He glanced at Micaiah, dodged a blow, and pranced back a good ten paces.

The Akarin regrouped, all of them exhausted and sweaty.

Cassius, meanwhile, went to the Day, blood burbling from its massive throat. He knelt beside it and pulled the knife from its throat. Rifun was too far away to hear if he said anything. Probably gloating. Then he stood, went to the Bat, and did the same, pulling the knife from its chest and gloating. Finally he stood and went to stand a good twenty paces from the Akarin, as if ready to face them in final combat. All things considered, it actually felt like a pretty even fight.

The Akarin, however, looked a little perplexed, and even annoyed. Couldn't

Cassius see what had just happened? Didn't he realize the fight was over? Was he really going to risk his own death over this? Could they do this some other time?

Then something happened, and Rifun wasn't sure whether to call it miraculous or demonic. The Day and the Bat both stood up. Completely healed and renewed. The Bat took in a deep breath and let out a high-pitched shriek that echoed around the arena long after he ceased vocalizing. The Day extended its vines menacingly.

The Inner Sanctum went dead quiet. What had just happened? Had Cassius simply healed the Jurors, or had he actually resurrected them? It had to be healing, right? The Akari was powerful, but surely not so powerful as to bring forth resurrection?

The Akari, maybe, but what about the evil spirit that lurked within Cassius? If it had resurrected him from certain death, why couldn't it do the same to the Bat and the Day? What, then, did that say about their natures? Rifun swallowed nervously and shifted position, trying to play it off.

The Akarin decided it best to take no more chances, and they made a hasty exit, defying the Time inhibitors and using the Akari to open a portal to somewhere safe.

All that came after was a blur. Isthim declared the Accused and his entourage guilty but suspended, and messily dismissed the crowd that was already close to rioting if for no other reason than sheer fear, everyone trying to make sense of what happened. From there, she and Rifun made their own hasty exit, returning to the officers building just as soon as possible.

"He had to have healed them," Isthim was saying, following Rifun to the meeting room. "From our vantage, we could not adequately ascertain their life status. That's all."

"It's more than that," Rifun insisted. "The Bat and the Day are not natural. Everyone knows this. Why should they be so belligerent about the Akari and be healed from it?"

"Don't look a gift horse in the mouth?"

He shook his head. "No. I don't think so."

"Why?"

"Call it intuition. Spiritual intuition. Evil can no more be helped by good than good can be helped by evil. They couldn't accept help from the Akari if they wanted to."

She folded her arms. "More of this evil spirit you say resides within Cassius?"

"If the Bat and the Day are cut from the same cloth, and if the spirit really did resurrect or possess Cassius, why shouldn't it have such power over others of its kind?"

"Then what does that say about the Akari we teach, since it's based on Cassius' words?"

"Cassius words, but Richard's hand, and Richard and Julianna were Akarin. It's not about the words, but how they're used. 'Damn' has many different uses based on the intent of the user. The word itself is not evil." He paused and sighed. "Cassius made a choice in regards to the spirit. Maybe the Bat and the Day made the same choice in their own way a long time ago. I don't know. But it's just an alteration, a twisting of things. Cassius, or the spirit, has twisted the Akari to his own ends."

"And what do you plan to do about it? You've had plenty of opportunities to kill him."

Rifun shook his head. "Just killing the body isn't enough. The spirit will move on to someone else." He could tell Isthim was becoming less and less impressed. He sighed. "Leave the killing to me, please."

Isthim gave him a look. "You think maybe you're taking this a little too far?"

"You think maybe you're not looking far enough?" he countered. "Look beyond the physical. There is something more here."

Her expression did not waver. "I still think you're overreacting to events." She let her arms drop to her sides. "I will continue on as we have planned and wait for word from my teams. Given that Andrew was indeed at the trial, he had to have handed off the journal to someone else. They'll figure out who it was."

This brought Rifun's mind back to the present and he nodded. "Yes. Of course. Thank you."

He left the meeting room, mind still spinning. He went to his chambers, closed the door, and bowed to pray at his shrine. He wasn't seeking guidance so much as simply an anchor to calm his soul. Maybe he was overreacting a little. Something deep down said he wasn't.

Once his heart rate had returned to normal and he could breathe again, Rifun stood and went to his bed to sit and think. Next step, wait for word from Isthim's teams on the location of the journal, or at least its whereabouts. Once that was done and the journal was safely in their possession, then they would have to make a plan on how to retrieve the Book of Abilities from the Time Trap. That would determine their next move as it pertained to the Time industry.

With this little stunt today, and especially Cassius' healing or resurrection of the Bat and the Day, the Cult was pretty well cemented in as the major power in town. With any luck, it bought them enough time to go after the Book of Abilities.

Before he knew it, he was asleep.

It was one of those rare, awkward times when he knew he was asleep and yet dreamed nothing. And in that sleepy, almost mystical part of the psyche, he found himself making some connection between the sleeping mind, the neuroelectrical field the Hands used to project images into the Seat for the testing of Apprentices, and the visions he'd had that had apparently been true visions defying that field.

Suddenly he found himself in another person's dreams. How he knew this, he could not say for sure except through simple dream logic.

He was standing in some room. An apartment. Simple enough. Homey enough. Someone was washing dishes at the sink. Judging by shape, it was Micaiah.

"It's nice, isn't it?" Rifun said.

Micaiah whirled around, dropping the dish, a plate, and it shattered on the floor.

"What? How?" The large Irishman blinked and shook his head as if coming awake, as disoriented as Rifun had first been. "Is...where...you...? Are you...dream-walking to me?"

"What does it look like?"

Micaiah let out a breath. "Fuck. Been a long time since anyone's done that and..."

"I'm not the first one you wanted to see?"

"No." He paused. "But what did you mean, about it being nice?"

"Something normal, after a very abnormal day. A nice sleep, a good dream, dreaming of something normal."

"What did Cassius do?"

"Quite honestly, I don't know. And what does it matter to you? You're not going to take any action against him. You're not big into gambling, you can't predict the repercussions, so you're going to sit on your hands and wait for someone else to do something, then complain when they do it."

Micaiah hesitated.

"And if you want my opinion, I don't care what you do. You can sit it out, you can fight, you can bicker, you can whine. We're moving in for the kill, and we're going to take control of the Time industry."

"We can't let you do that."

Rifun shook his head and grinned. "I don't think you understand the situation. Red lines are nothing. Words are nothing. Society is merely an agreed-upon fiction unless there is action to back up your words. You rattle your sabers, but I don't think there is any blade attached to the hilt. So by all means, whine, complain, give us warnings and red lines and tsk your fingers to the bone. But we are moving forward. We put teeth to our threats, as today has proven."

Micaiah shifted his stance. "So we've gone from searching for answers, to attempts and peace and reconciliation, to ultimatums."

"And what have you done this whole time, I wonder?"

"I really don't think you understand what's happening, what you're doing."

"At least I am doing." Rifun continued before Micaiah could speak. "Admirable work in the trial today. Let's see if you can keep it up."

He wasn't sure just how he removed himself from Micaiah's dream, but he did, and he found himself blinking awake and staring at the ceiling in his chambers. Had that happened? Well, Micaiah seemed to know what was happening, so it must be something the Akari could do.

He didn't know how long he'd slept, but he found Isthim still awake in her chambers, everything neat and orderly as one would expect from a soldier.

"When it's convenient for you or one of your people, I want you to cloud Micaiah's memories. Actually all five of them, if they weren't already," Rifun stated.

"Do you want them to forget the Time Trial?" Isthim inquired.

"Oh no. No, I want them to remember that. Every detail, if it's possible. But cloud the rest, like the others."

"Consider it done."

He dipped his head and departed. He didn't know where he was going or what he intended to do, but his spirit was still disturbed and he craved peace. And as much as he wanted to have never witnessed it, he also never wanted to forget the image of Cassius resurrecting the Bat and the Day.

20 | Okunkun ati Ojiji   Darkness and Shadows

The Wheel of Time, 1965

kokumbo

No one ever asked Cassius exactly what he'd done to the Bat and the Day, and if they had, he wouldn't have known what to answer. Had he simply healed their fatal wounds, or had he actually resurrected them in some fashion? If it had been the former, then it would have been a bit more plausible. If the latter, well, he certainly wouldn't have been able to do that on his own; it would have had to have been the spirit of smoke and shadow.

Of course, after that little stunt, the Akarin had fled like cowards. The crowd had erupted into chaos, Isthim tried to bring back some semblance of order, at least enough to declare the proceedings terminated, and then it was anyone's game.

Cassius had stuck with the Bat and the Day initially, just to ride out the tide of fear. They stood in a small alcove in the arena, watching it unfold from relative safety. He breathed it in deep, savored it, enjoyed himself, then figured he should probably return to the ruins eventually. Before he left, the Bat put an enormous clawed hand on his shoulder.

"Whenever you are ready to take control, we are with you," it said in a voice that rumbled like thunder. "We know others who would follow as well."

Cassius glanced at him and then at the Day a step behind and to the right. He nodded once. "I'll make a note of it. Does this agreement have an expiration date?"

"Time is irrelevant," the Bat rumbled on. "So long as the goal remains the same."

"I'll be sure to pass it along."

The Bat lifted his hand and made a gesture that Cassius had never seen before but knew instinctively that it was a sign of, not just deference, but reverence. He simultaneously felt confusion and immense pride, a sense of receiving something that need not be earned but was inherently deserved. Was the Bat aware of the dark spirit? Were they connected somehow?

Cassius left the arena and made his way back to the ruins. Actually he'd fully expected a meeting of some sort, but found nothing. Julianna was tending her duties in the refugee camp that had sprung up outside the ruins, and Isthim was yelling at some grunts about their poor performance. He didn't even see Rifun. And no one chastised him about missing a meeting, either. Quite frankly, it threw him off just a little. Why wouldn't they want a meeting? Wouldn't they want to discuss the trial, how it went, how the Akarin escaped, how the Bat and the Day had been rescued from death? Wouldn't they want to figure out what to do next?

He returned to his chambers but found nothing amiss. No gifts, no letters, no angry mob. It was exactly as if the last twenty-four hours had never happened. The Wheel was in chaos. Why was it nothing but a Sunday afternoon here? Shouldn't they be doing something?

Well, the others may have been content to slide back into mundane boredom, but his blood was hot and he was still too excited from the trial to let that much energy go to waste. They were known in the Wheel now. And if they wanted to hold onto the power they just wrested and remain the ones in control, they had to keep going. They had to continue to clean house. There were still a few Hand candidates from the elections who needed mopping up, to say nothing of the Gentleman Killers still holding onto tiny empires, or the Tacagans lurking in the shadows. Plus there might be a few dissenters who had opposed the Time Trial.

He went out into the ruins, among the grunts and the soldiers and everyone in between. His first stop was Murdi and Lordo's house. He banged on the door and was rewarded with a timely answer from Lordo.

"Feel up to a bit of house cleaning?" he asked.

The Mishim blinked. "I feel like this is a euphemism, and you are not literally asking us to clean a house."

"You want to kill something? It won't be as difficult as Micaiah, I promise."

Lordo glanced inside at Murdi, then back at Cassius. "We're in. When?"

"Just as soon as I round up a few more hands. We're not losing this momentum, and it has to be utterly explosive. It'll require more than just me. Meet me at the entrance to the tunnel in one hour if you're interested."

They promised him they would, and he moved on.

It wasn't difficult to track down the four Korin, though they were in the middle of drills. He watched them for a good ten minutes. Had they improved any? Had their attitude changed any? It was difficult to say, for they were expected to be serious when in drills. Out in the field, they tended to get lax.

For as much as Cassius had promised himself that he was going to make them come begging to him to be reinstated as something special, if he wanted big and explosive, something to span more than just one room in the Wheel, he was going to need help.

Finally he pulled the Korin out of drills and off to the side.

"You look good down there," he said, hoping it sounded like a genuine compliment and not just words he hoped would start things off right. "Have you thought about our last encounter?"

Their guilty looks said it as much as their words.

"Good. If you're ready, I have another job for you. There will be others, and it will be a large, coordinated effort. If you're interested, be at the entrance to the tunnels in half an hour."

The Korin went from guilty to enthusiastic in a matter of a moment, though they were quick to contain it and try to accept his offer in a more professional manner. It seemed to be an improvement anyway, or an attempt at one. Cassius moved on.

Pilory was nowhere to be found in the ruins, and it sounded as though she'd basically given up or deserted. The good news was that even if she'd sneaked away from the Cult, she was too in love with her day job to be anywhere else.

He didn't stow away on Titik's ship, or set foot on it at all. All he really did was write a note, open a micro-portal, hope he got the right room, and drop it through. Like the others, if she was interested, she would be at the correct place at the correct time. He wasn't going to wait around and hope she showed up. He would plan based on what he had, not what he needed.

Then he set about packing up a few things. And a few things was all he had. It had been a while since he'd been to see Jora, at least since Juris. He should go back and see if the arms dealer had gotten anything interesting in stock. That would really spice things up. Hm, maybe another time, if the momentum started to wane too soon.

Once he was as packed and ready as he would ever be, he left his chambers, swept out of the officers building, and made for the tunnels outside the city. Murdi and Lordo were there, as were the Korin, and they all appeared to be getting along. He did not see Pilory. Well, perhaps that was to be expected.

"I trust you all heard about the Time Trial earlier today?" Cassius began, approaching the group.

Murdi and Lordo evidently hadn't, and the Korin filled them in. Cassius could only conclude that storytelling was reserved for the peace dynasties, for the alien rhinos made it sound like a rather dull, inconsequential affair, rather than the grand spectacle of blood and dark miracles and chaos that it had turned out to be.

"What are we doing, then?" Murdi inquired.

"We're going to do a little more mop up. Thanks to Isthim, the Akarin are in disarray. I think the Gentleman Killers have been pretty well subdued, but we should make sure of that. The Tacagans have been unusually quiet lately; I want to know what they're up to and make sure they got the memo that we're in charge now. And there are a few Hand candidates still running around that need to be taken care of."

"Do we have a list of targets?" Lordo wondered.

Cassius handed the twins a short list and to the Korin he gave another list. "If you complete it, let me know. I'm sure we'll have made more enemies by that time."

"What about you?" Surloff asked.

"I will be investigating the Tacagans, assessing whether they are a threat to us and figuring out what they're up to."

"Do you expect to be there long?" Murdi asked. "The Tacagans are sticklers about who comes and goes from their planet, and outsiders are not well-regarded. Nor could we ask after you, I assume, because they will not be aware of your presence."

"You are very perceptive," Cassius told him. "No, I don't plan on being there long, just long enough. Either they're not a threat, and I can move on to those who are, or they are a threat, and I intend to neutralize it."

Even he knew it would not be so simple or easy, but he wasn't interested in playing twenty questions.

The problem then became that none of the mercenaries could read English, so he had to read the lists to them and they rewrote the lists of names in their own languages. What was it about written language that the Akari couldn't seem to manage? How did all the species of the Akarin read the Authored Books?

Well, it wasn't something he was going to worry about today. He had a snooty society of genetically modified assholes to infiltrate.

Tacaga was larger than Earth with a population of 21 billion, all of them concentrated in one of nineteen cities across six continents. The capital city of Lip boasted four billion people in an area about the size of Texas. No one was permitted outside the cities for any reason. Every single thing they could possibly need, from clothing to building materials to food itself, was either artificially manufactured, gotten from the Wheel, or traded with another alien species in a neighboring star system. Absolutely no contact was had with the world outside the cities and the enclosed super trains that connected them. If the people desired nature, carefully cultivated parks provided this leisurely recreation.

Even the people were artificially manufactured, or partially so. Genetic modification had been all but perfected, and the Tacagans were born pre-programmed with not only their looks, but their entire life planned out based on political, economic, and social forecasts. If there was a projected need for construction workers in twenty years, then more embryos would be pre-programmed to have the traits desirable for construction work. Or office work. Or scientific research. Or whatever the need was projected to be. Compared to the average Earthling, Tacagans were remarkably strong and fit, every muscle and organ operating at peak human efficiency. Skin tone was the defining distinction between cities, as cities closer to the poles required citizens to be able to absorb more sunlight, while those from cities closer to the equator needed protection from it. Cassius had little doubt that something was being engineered either for the cities' domes or the atmosphere itself which would negate the need for varying skins and make the genetic modification that much smoother and more streamlined.

Until then, he figured that his strong physique would not be out of the ordinary, and his dark skin would identify him as being from a more equatorial city. He did not believe that he couldn't be identified as an outsider to some degree—perhaps the Tacagans all had the same nose because it optimized oxygen intake—but from a distance he wouldn't be as readily discerned as the Mishim or the Korin—definitely the Korin—would have been.

With no one permitted outside the domes and train tunnels, it stood to reason that there be no doors into or out of Lip. Cassius stood on a rise about five hundred yards away, peeking around a tree with binoculars. It wasn't that he expected a great army to come after him, but he didn't feel like finding out the hard way what kind of defenses the city had. The Akari could do many things, but it couldn't protect him from his own stupidity. A measure of caution was warranted.

Despite humanity as a whole being Unengaged, the Tacagans were very much Engaged. Portals would be nothing new for them. They couldn't be spooked by alien encounters, not when they traded with aliens in their own territory.

Cassius spotted a bit of greenery, enough to make him believe that it was a park. That would be his best bet to get inside.

He opened a portal to that spot and stepped through. It was indeed a park. Well, it was an oasis of greenery, anyway. In order to keep things efficient, the whole city was level, made up of boxes, squares, patterns, and precise angles. The park was similarly done. The ground was as flat as flat could get, without even an artificially-built hill to break up the horizontal monotony. Trees and bushes were planted at precise intervals in specific patterns, everything cut and trimmed just so. Cassius had to touch a tree just to reassure himself that it was real. He wasn't a nature loving hippie, but even he was disappointed to find that it wasn't even a real tree. Artificially manufactured, just like everything else. Even the grass was fake.

More annoyed than he thought he should be, Cassius left the park, wholly uncertain just where he was going. His best bet would be some sort of governmental center, but he didn't expect the Tacagans to build anything terribly special to house their government. It, too, would be bland, rigid, precise, and efficient.

Lip was closer to the equator, so many of its residents had darker skin, though not so black as his. It did not seem to be out of the ordinary, then, for him to ask for directions from a random store owner.

"The nearest internal train station is twelve blocks north from here," the man told him. "You can find a bike shop about one block from here. When you get to the train station, follow the blue line."

Cassius left the store and headed north. He Banded and looked around. There were no cars or similar motor vehicle transportation within the city. Short trips were made via bicycle, and crossing the city was done via a network of internal sky trains that moved overhead at breakneck speeds but entirely silent. The intercity trains were four times the size, but equally as silent. There may have been special portal stations for people to use, but Cassius did not see anything in the immediate vicinity, and he didn't want to ask and potentially brand himself an outsider.

Furthermore, he was uncertain of the law enforcement situation on Tacaga. He saw no uniformed policemen or military anywhere, walking or on bicycle. Absolutely none. Seeing how the Tacagans were far from perfect people, he could only conclude that any and all law enforcement was secret, plainclothes. Anyone could be a cop, so behavior was incentivized through fear.

He might have come to like this place except for how damn rigid and precise it was. Few people enjoyed the same level of chaos that he did, but most would be nauseated by the precision and the chaos vacuum of this place. Just one imperfection, one flaw. A cobblestone out of place, a person with a scar. He would take anything, but found nothing. Nothing but rigid perfection.

He dropped the Band and continued on, hurrying, breathing uneasy, nearly panicking from the perfection. He didn't like this place. He didn't like how it made him feel. He needed to carry out his mission as fast as possible. If he knew where the governmental building was, maybe he could just jump through a portal, kill who he needed to kill, and get out.

The train station was an enormous hub of activity, and the sheer volume of it was almost like chaos, and it helped to calm some of his nerves. To his outsider eyes, it was a mess. For the Tacagans, it was probably the most efficient method to move a lot of people a lot of places quickly. He would take what he could get.

There were no maps that he saw, but there were plenty of small tables littered about the room—less littered and more precise intervals, actually. Cassius might have mistaken them as bland, efficient seating, but he saw several people go up to them and touch them. When they did this, interactive maps came to life and transport lines could be discerned.

Cassius walked up to one of these tables as if he knew what he was doing, touching the panel so that it lit up. A map came up, complete with a whole host of labels as well as a menu.

The Tacagans were descendants of the Ancient Greeks and, later, the Romans. Their language reflected this as it was combined Greek and Latin letters and almost readable.

Cassius' only saving grace was that he had studied both Latin and Greek, long ago when he was still a slave owned by a Christian minister—and even a bit from the master he'd killed, who had also been well-versed in classical languages. True, after a hundred years or so, he'd forgotten almost all of it from a conversational standpoint, but with his knowledge of English and how it liked to borrow and steal a lot of foreign words, he was able to puzzle out most of the program.

He figured out where the blue line was, when it ran, how to get to it, everything he needed to know including a bit that said the train docked inside the actual governmental building so that workers didn't have to navigate any more city traffic.

Well that made things almost too easy, he thought, closing out the program. He looked around for the appropriate signs and followed them to the train he needed. No one checked tickets, no one asked him to verify his identity or give a valid reason for going to the governmental building. If there was any security to be found, it was either inside the building itself, something to screen the workers, or else it was the worst security he had ever seen from such an advanced society. Given how careful the Tacagans had been about the auctions and their relationship with the Gentleman Killers, he doubted they were so naive. But then, who would be able to touch them in their own home?

Whatever the case, he got on the train with the rest of the blue line riders, choosing a seat close to the door as it shut. Among the other passengers, no small talk was heard.

Then the doors opened again and people started moving. He stood. Had they gone anywhere? He hadn't felt anything, not a jump or jolt, and he hadn't heard any roar or hum of an engine. There was no way...

And yet there was. When he looked out the doors, they had indeed gone somewhere. He didn't know where they were, but if the blue line traveled right into the governmental building, then this was not his stop. He sat back down. Well, now that he knew that he wouldn't know when they were moving, he would have to pay attention to the doors. Maybe that was why there was no small talk.

People filtered off and on again. The doors closed, and a few seconds later, they opened, revealing a whole new part of the city, as if by magic. Cassius tried not to react to it. Whatever city he was supposed to be from likely had the exact same thing. This shouldn't be anything new to him. Given how bland the city itself was, it wasn't as though there was even any scenery to enjoy to justify any amazement.

The fourth stop proved to be the governmental building, the train pulling into a rather dark station. Only one set of doors opened to a small platform which led immediately to a set of double doors. On the other side of these doors was the security checkpoint Cassius had been waiting for.

Did he want to Band and slip right through? Did he want to pretend to be some emissary, impersonate Rifun as much as anyone else? Did he just want to kill everyone and announce his presence with the spilling of blood? So many possibilities. He got off the train with about a dozen other people and made sure to be the last one in line.

The basic procedure appeared to be handing over an identification card of some form, followed by a blood sample, similar to how one gave a sample in order to access the translator dispenser in the Wheel. So regardless of any smooth talking, Cassius was going to be found out. His options were narrowing considerably and would be based on simply how the security guards reacted.

Cassius stepped up to the desk. He did not hand over a card, but simply stuck his finger in the little machine, feeling the needle stab his flesh and take a blood sample. The guard, alerted immediately to some mischief from his lack of card and other social graces he supposed were expected, simply stared at his computer screen as it told him, in no uncertain terms, that this person was not Tacagan. He pressed a button and the screen went blank. Then he looked at Cassius.

"How did you get here?"

"By train, how else?" Cassius replied, grinning. "I got in the city via portal, the same way I got on your planet."

Before he could say more, two dozen armed guards rushed into the room. Ah, the good old silent alarm. Whether it had been set off because of the DNA discrepancies or if the guard had done it in some sneaky way did not matter. Cassius simply shifted his stance and looked around at them.

"So, the Tacagans are not completely helpless," he chuckled. "We were beginning to worry."

"Identify yourself," one guard ordered.

Still grinning, he answered, "My name is Kokumbo. This one shall not die." He gave them all a regard. "But I cannot say the same for you."

The Tacagan guards were smart, give them that. They knew enough to Band before firing, trying to negate his reflexes and subvert his expectations. Even Cassius would silently admit that he had been unprepared for that little trick. So small and yet so essential. A lesser Timekeeper might have been taken by surprise and so turned into Swiss cheese.

But Cassius was not a lesser Timekeeper. He was able to get up a Band that allowed him to see the movement of the projectiles, all fired within three feet of his body. They were not lead balls or bullets, nor were they pure energy. Rather, it seemed to be some combination of the two, a five-claw-shaped, solid, spinning projectile containing a type of energy that Cassius could not readily identify, but he was willing to bet that it would hurt regardless.

He had no desire to test out the effectiveness of these things on his own body, and he was willing to bet that the skin-tight armor the guards wore would shield against them. Instead, he decided to make things interesting. He opened up microportals around himself, in the paths of the vicious projectiles, leading to the busy streets outside.

As soon as the guards realized what was happening, they scrambled to force the portals closed or else redirect them, but they were either too slow and clumsy, or they didn't realize that there was a difference between Time portals and Akari portals. Did they even realize he was using the Akari? Poor, stupid fools.

"State your business," the same guard said, his orders holding far less weight than they had only a moment ago.

"Oh, now you want to know why I'm here? Only after a dozen civilians have died unnecessarily." Cassius gave him a look. "I'm here to make sure you Tacagans aren't going to interfere in any more of my business. But I think this little welcome party has proven otherwise."

He located the source of the energy in their firearms. He couldn't identify it specifically, nor give the chemistry or physics behind it, but he knew that, like all energy mediums, it had to be kept in balance. Throwing it off balance was as simple as Thermodynamics. He took the heat from the guards themselves and funneled it into the energy concentrater, the thing that would ignite each round as it was fired. The guards chilled quickly and began shaking, losing fine motor control and most control over their bodies. A few collapsed, still shaking.

Then they hit the final part of hypothermia, the paradoxical sweating, the last burst of thermodynamic energy the body used to try and save itself. Cassius stole that energy, too, and pushed it into the firearms.

The explosions that the overloaded concentraters caused was quite a spectacular sight, with blue flame, electricity, plasma, and sparks flying everywhere. It blew holes through the guards and melted what was left, Cassius stepping away a good ten paces so he wasn't caught in the line of fire.

The surrounding floor and walls were not unaffected by the display, and a fire suppression system kicked on. It was not so much about overhead sprinklers as it was some sort of liquid leaking out of a strip along the top of the walls, coating everything in a slimy film. The air chilled significantly just from the release of this liquid, and individual spouts in the ceiling doused specific fires not reached by the wall and floor slime.

This would not go unnoticed, Cassius knew, and the Tacagans probably had cameras everywhere, just more discreetly than their Terran cousins. Someone, or a lot of someones, would be coming. He grinned as he made his way across the slick floor, sliding, trying not to fall, carefully stepping over the charred remains of the guards, feeling relieved when he hit solid ground again.

He did not know his way around this building. He did not know if the entire building was dedicated to government function, or just select floors. He did not know where the governing body met, if they were even here, or who they were or what they looked like.

That was all right, he figured. It had been a while since he'd had a good bloodbath. All the planning and sneaking around and picking off targets one by one was nice, and sometimes it got him a little extra cash, but there was just no good substitute for carnage every once in a while. He felt himself grow hard, but told himself to wait until afterwards.

He didn't know the function of his next victim. He just rounded a corner and happened to see the young man walking against him in the hall. Dead. A Band of Time that aged him two hundred years in only a second.

Another man in the next hall. Dead, Gravity throwing him from wall to wall and ceiling to floor until he was unrecognizable.

He might have passed by his third victim, except her shirt was brightly colored and he saw it in his peripheral vision as he passed by a certain room. She appeared to be trying to hurry up and finish whatever she was working on, perhaps given evacuation orders because there was a madman on the loose in the building.

He used Sound to muffle her scream, and Force to knock her away from the desk and any alarms she might try to trigger. She hit the wall and tried to scramble away, but Cassius was on her in a second. He put his hand over her mouth with such force he might have broken teeth. With the Sound barrier still up, her weeping was silent as he forced himself on her, cutting her throat half a moment before he released.

When he stood, he could hear heavy footsteps running down the hall. So, the cavalry had arrived. Thinking fast, he stuffed the girl's body under the desk, then used Disguise to take her appearance. He ran out of the room, trying to figure out how to run like someone who was a foot shorter, a hundred and fifty pounds lighter, and with a more curvy body than he was accustomed to. Impersonating Julianna on stage was one thing, but trying to pass off as a damsel in distress was not his forte. Maybe he should ask Rifun for acting lessons. Ha!

He skidded to a stop when he finally found the armed guards running down the hall. Initially they raised their weapons, then lowered them when they saw it was only a helpless woman.

"Clear the area!" one guard said irritably.

"I know, I'm sorry!" Cassius-as-the-woman said, hoping he could manage a few tears. "I just had something I needed —"

"Keep moving!" another guard snapped. "Go to the vault!"

He nodded vigorously and slipped through the line of guards, doing everything he could to keep his Disguise in tact. He wanted to ask where the vault was, except it was probably part of the employee handbook that everyone already knew. In case of emergency, go to the vault. He ran off down the hall and turned the corner, mercifully the only corner available to him. Once there, he Banded and peeked back around. The guards were moving off.

Cassius shed his Disguise and kept moving. The vault. The vault, the vault, the vault. Where would the vault be? Logic might dictate that it would be underground, except people seemed to forget that there was no air underground in the event of building collapse. Granted, falling any number of stories was no guarantee of safety, but Cassius figured he would rather take his chances. He still remembered being in the cellar of the master's house and being smoked out. Underground, there was nowhere to go.

With everyone evacuated to this vault, the building was rather empty. This made it easier for him to get to a desk and hope that there was some building plan evacuation route stored somewhere in the computer system. His bumbling of Latin and Greek only served to get him lost this time, and he found no such plans.

"Who are you?"

Cassius' head snapped up at a voice, and he saw a man standing on the other side of the room.

"You're not Priscilla," the man stated.

"Am I not?" Cassius asked.

He donned the same female Disguise he'd worn to get through the guards. The man went pale and took off running. Cassius gave chase.

In a way, Tacagans were almost worthy opponents, just for the fact that they actually had the physique and the training to make things a challenge. Any common office worker on Earth would be lazy, slow, probably overweight, and easily overtaken. This Tacagan, however, was a track star.

The only reason Cassius did not Band and kill him immediately, was because he was also willing to bet that the man was still heading for the vault. When overcome by fear, single-mindedness took over. The vault was safety; therefore, head for the vault. Didn't matter that the threat was literally following you and you were leading him straight to your safe place, if you could reach that fabled finish line, you would be safe. Some kind of magic would keep danger out and you in.

See? Cassius knew a few things about psychology, too.

They went up four flights of stairs, Cassius causing the man to panic even more when he decided to use a Gravity track to bypass the steps completely. Now fear had turned to desperation. The man burst through the door and ran straight into a wall, tripping over a table and going to the floor. Cassius pounced like a wild cat, pinning the man with Gravity as much as his weight, and elected to simply starve the man of oxygen. His face turned red, then purple, then black.

Cassius got off the man and looked around. This was a little more promising, he thought. Where the rest of the building had looked like standard offices, this was a bit more...regal. More like what he would expect from the ruling body of an entire planet. Floors polished to a mirror shine, ornate rugs, paintings of famous figures adorning the walls, and other indulgences of the rich and famous. No doubt the receiving or deliberation chambers were close by, but where was the vault?

It was easier to find than he thought it should have been, and that only because there would be no other reason to post guards on some random, insignificant doorway. These guards, all five of them, were clearly the last line of defense, and no doubt specially engineered for their sole purpose in life. The average Tacagan was fit; these guys were absolute bodybuilders.

They did not see him at first, and Cassius Banded so he could sneak back a few steps and don his damsel in distress Disguise. He would be happy to challenge the guards, but only after he completed his goal. He wouldn't put it past the Tacagans to have yet another secret exit or other method of escape, even if it was just straight portal use.

He ran out of his hiding spot.

"Let me in!" he cried. "Please, I know I'm late, let me in!"

Four of the guards fanned out to ensure no one else was coming, or that the madman wasn't nearby. The fifth guard, once given the all clear, turned and fumbled with a special lock. Then the door was open and Cassius was herded inside.

First there was a set of stairs that took him down a floor, then some twisting corridors, and then another set of stairs going down another floor. Then there was another door with another beefy guard. The guard opened the door without a word and slammed it shut behind Cassius.

The vault was not as spacious and luxurious as one might have expected, but Cassius was willing to bet that the vault was hidden in the middle of the building for a reason. No one would suspect it. All the corridors, all the rooms and offices, the royal floor with all the posh indulgence, it was all a distraction.

Very clever, Cassius thought.

The room was maybe fifty by fifty, as industrial as one might expect, with a single, continuous bench running along each wall as the only apparent comfort. In one corner, a group of people had clustered together. Judging by their attire, how much nicer it seemed compared to everyone else, Cassius guessed this was the governing body.

There was something else about the vault, and it took him a second to figure out what it was. There was a Suppression field in place, hindering all Time abilities. Probably this was to keep any madmen from pulling a clever trick, but did they not realize it also made themselves defenseless against those with even greater power? Well, such was the fate of any who dismissed what they did not want to believe. It would just make his job easier.

"Lucienne!" someone exclaimed.

Cassius guessed this was the name of the woman he'd killed, and he could only guess at the significance of the man who pushed through the throng of people to get to her.

At the last possible moment, Cassius dropped his Disguise. The man stopped dead in his tracks, and suddenly there was a ten foot radius around Cassius, a luxury in the small room. The governing body eventually caught on to something amiss, for their murmuring died down, and they all turned to look.

"And who are you?" one of them demanded.

Cassius donned his Julianna Disguise. "I think you know who I am." He dropped it again. "At the very least, you must have heard of me."

"The Auctionhouse massacre," a woman sneered. "Yes, we heard. Some of us are the replacements for the people you killed that day. Are you here to kill more of us?"

"That's one thought I had, yes. I just want to make sure you understand who holds the power, and make sure you don't interfere in our affairs."

"Religious zealots," someone spat.

"You deny what you see with your own eyes," Cassius sighed. "Sad."

"We'll figure out your secrets one day. There is always a trick to it."

"I'm glad you are so confident in your beliefs, because today is the day you get to test them."

For all he knew, the stone that the vault was made from was a hundred thousand times stronger than anything used on Earth. For all he knew, the metal that the building overall was made from could cut diamonds like a warm knife through butter. For all he knew, he was going to kill himself before he even scratched one of the people in here.

But that didn't mean he wasn't going to try. Heat, to draw the water out of the stone and the metal. As the air became thick and muggy, he forced it into their lungs. People began coughing, choking. Cassius knelt on the ground and Felt the stone, felt its composition. It was impressive, but not entirely indestructible. While the Tacagans around him struggled, he began picking apart the stone, degrading the composition. Then he reached farther, into the metal of the building. It, too, was stronger than anything currently known on Earth, but not impervious to a little alchemal manipulation. Through all of this, he continued his use of Thermodynamics, drying out the stone and the metal, then forcing the water into the Tacagans' lungs using both Matter and Energy.

The building gave a loud groan, and the stone vault cracked. A few people choked a scream but quickly swallowed more water. Still playing with the metal and dabbling in true alchemy, moving the protons, neutrons, and electrons of the metal, Cassius had just enough sense to Band a split second before the explosion. Of course, Bands were notoriously finicky about containing Energy, and it was all he could do to redirect the energy into a portal behind him.

He lost his hold on all of his work, and suddenly he found himself flung backwards through the portal which snapped shut just as soon as his last toe cleared the threshold.

He did not get to see the building collapse, or hear the crunch of bones as the vault caved in around the Tacagan leaders. The best he could do, once he was a bit more recovered from the ordeal, was don a quick Disguise and return to Lip to witness the aftermath. The entire building had collapsed, and the unexplained explosion had also taken down three more buildings and damaged half a dozen more.

Cassius did not stick around long. Even if some of the leaders had survived, which he doubted, they would be in no shape to retaliate any time soon. He returned to the ruins and collapsed into bed for a nap.

When he woke some hours later, he learned that none of his team had returned yet. That was fine with him. But when he left his chambers, he ran into Rifun who, in spite of whatever errand he was on, turned and fell into step with him.

"We heard some interesting news from Tacaga," he stated. "You wouldn't happen to know anything about it, would you?"

"I may know some rumors," Cassius replied. "What are the updates?"

"Thirty-four Governors dead, the rest in critical condition. Four hundred or so workers and civilians confirmed dead, and hundreds more as yet unaccounted for. Six buildings destroyed, another four damaged beyond repair, and another six damaged extensively."

"Sounds like they're going to be busy for quite a while, all of their attention is going to be turned inward."

"So it would seem."

Cassius stopped and faced Rifun. "Why do I feel like I'm going to be blamed for this? And I don't mean because I'm the one who did it." He continued before Rifun could speak. "May I remind you that you are the one who instigated a Time Trial?"

"I'm not denying it," Rifun said, "nor am I blaming you for anything. You may have just bought us a significant amount of time. But how is your little special forces team doing?"

"Have you heard something?"

"No, nothing of importance."

"Then don't interfere with them. It's me and my team that's buying us time and eliminating our enemies."

"And you're doing a fine job. How much longer do you expect you'll need?"

Cassius studied Rifun. Normally people who embarked on spiritual quests, especially extended ones, returned with a heightened sense of morality. Rifun seemed to have done the opposite, discarded his morals and gone ahead with a Time Trial and now praising the work of Cassius and his team of mercenaries. Was this reverse psychology?

"I don't know," he answered finally. "We're narrowing down the list, and a lot of people know they're on it. They'll be harder to catch."

"Keep me apprised of your status," Rifun said, moving to leave. "I may need your help with something."

Now he was asking for help? From him? Watching him walk away, Cassius hit him with Test, just to make sure it wasn't Julianna or Isthim or anyone else in Disguise. The Test came back negative; that was Rifun. Just what had he learned on his spiritual quest? How did Cassius get in on that?

By the end of the day, no one on his team had returned. He found himself wondering at what point he should be worried. His task had been fairly easy, all things considered. It was easy to blow up a building because buildings didn't move. People could be harder to pin down. After all, look at how long it had taken him to catch up to and subdue the twin assassins. And that was with him in the lead. Leaving his team to their own devices, it might be a little while before they came back.

On the other hand, maybe he would receive a gift one day and it would be the heads of his team members. That was also a viable option.

He headed out to find Isthim and watch as she drilled the grunts. He did not spot the Korin among them. Once the groups were divided into smaller teams, she joined him at the perimeter.

"I heard about Tacaga," she said.

"Many people have," Cassius replied.

"The Akarin are disabled, the Tacagans impaired, the Gentleman Killers dwindled to almost nothing."

"I expect we'll be taking over the Time industry soon, then."

"One would hope."

Cassius glanced at her. "I'll bite. What do you mean?"

"What if we weren't going to take over?" Isthim postulated.

"Do you know something I don't?"

"We still don't have the Book of Abilities."

"Who needs that when we have me? We take over the Time industry, then worry about that."

"What if we couldn't?"

Now Cassius turned to face her. "I don't appreciate playing twenty questions. What are you trying to say?" He put up a Sound barrier to prove his point.

"I know where the Book of Abilities is."

"Where? And how did you find out?"

"Rifun told me. At the trial. He's known for over a year. Julianna has never not known."

Fury erupted in Cassius and he made several angry paces. After a minute or two, he calmed down and asked, "Where is it?"

"It is still in the cave where you chased her. She hid it in the darkness, in some bones."

He made several more angry passes. Then, "Why...? No, I know why. The perfect paradox. Anyone who takes the time to go get it is losing time. Years, maybe decades. But why not tell me?"

"They didn't know what you would do, and they didn't want to risk losing you."

He mulled over the likelihood of that explanation. Without him, they would be nothing, still squabbling in turf disputes with the Tacagans and Gentleman Killers. Rifun and Julianna wouldn't want to get their hands dirty like that, and they wouldn't want to give any more power to Isthim and the Borelians than necessary. So they did need him. But then why wouldn't one of them go and get it? Hell, Rifun had already been gone for a year and the Cult had survived. Julianna was hardly needed at all except as the wife of the founder.

"Then why are you telling me?" he asked at last. "Wouldn't this be considered lovers' confidentiality? Pillow talk?"

He quickly found himself on the ground, the life being choked out of him, and Isthim hadn't laid a finger on him. She kept him this way for a good sixty seconds, enough for him to cease the worst of his flailing and gasping.

"I am telling you because I have decided it important for you to know," she said as he stood. "And because I do not intend to waste this opportunity as so many other opportunities have been wasted." She hissed the word. "They expect that if you find out, that you will be angry enough to go after it yourself."

"And that's what you want me to do?" he coughed, standing shakily.

"No. That would be foolish and stupid. But it would provide you with the leverage to control a meeting and the path forward, if you called the others together and brought it up right away."

Cassius thought about this.

"Furthermore," Isthim went on, "my teams have also returned, and they have news of the third journal. I've not told the others yet."

"This sounds promising."

"I will discuss it at the meeting, but I want you to call it."

After a moment of batting it back and forth, he finally nodded. "Fine. We'll see how this goes."

He dropped the Sound barrier half a second before Isthim enveloped them in a Band. Before he could say anything, she'd turned white and was touching him. It was only the lightest touch, but it brought him to his knees. Then she was pink again.

"Consider it a gift in good faith," she said.

Then she dissolved the Band and walked away, heading for the officers building.

Cassius remained on his knees, head spinning, wondering just how it was that no-contact sex could feel that good. Raping that woman earlier had been immature, teenage, virgin sex in comparison.

After a few moments, he got to his feet. As he also made for the officers building, he found himself thinking that it was too bad Rifun hadn't been around to conveniently witness it. Maybe next time.

He found Julianna in the refugee camp where she'd become something of a Mother Theresa. He simply informed her of the meeting and departed, not waiting for questions.

He again ran into Rifun in the officers building, this time in his chambers.

"I'm calling a meeting," Cassius announced.

Rifun looked up from his work and glanced at Cassius, saying nothing. His expression said that he was unprepared both for the meeting and the one who was calling it. What was going on? All the same, he nodded and mentioned he'd be there in just a minute.

He told Isthim about the meeting just for show, so it wasn't too obvious that they had discussed this very thing not fifteen minutes before. She simply said she would be there.

Ten minutes later, three of them were assembled in the meeting room, the great stone table keeping them a respectable distance from each other. Julianna was the last to arrive, saying something about being in the middle of some humanitarian project and whatnot.

"All right," Rifun began, "I suppose we—"

"I hear that you three know where the Book of Abilities is," Cassius interrupted icily. "I hear you've known for a while." He glanced at each of them. "Why didn't anyone see fit to tell me?"

21 | Miomana ary Reseo Lahatra

Prepare and Persuade

The Caves of Meroian, 1965

For a long moment, no one said a word. Rifun knew immediately that Isthim had been the one to tell Cassius, but what he could not figure out was why.

Julianna tried to pull him into a Band, but Cassius ripped it out of her control and shredded it like a mad dog, shouting, "No! No private conferences! No secret meetings! What else are you keeping from me?! Why let me continue in this charade?!"

Again there was a moment of silence. It was Julianna who spoke.

"Quite frankly, Cassius, we didn't trust you. We didn't know what you would do. We fully expected that you would run off to the cave, go searching for the journal, and end up stuck there for years or decades or even another century. You were the only one who had read it in its entirety and understood most, if not all, of its teachings, so we needed you for that."

"And also to carry out the heavy lifting," Rifun continued. "The assassinations, the massacres, and so on."

"Because you were too cowardly."

"Every army has its mad dog," Isthim quipped.

"Is that all I am to you?" Cassius snarled. "A mad dog that you can call for on a whim and put down when he's no longer needed? If anything ever happened to me, then it would signal to you to protect your own asses and get the hell out of dodge, isn't that right? I'm your fucking canary, aren't I? The Borelians, the Gentleman Killers..." He shook his head.

"But look at what you've accomplished," Rifun said, now finally meeting him. "We've taken the Time industry. All that remains is a little more house cleaning and system-wide implementation."

"Implementation of what? So far, all I've seen is a lot of talk, a lot of planning, a little bit of action, but almost no follow-through. Passing up chance after chance, wasting opportunities right and left! We're powerful, yes, but we're a powerful joke!"

"The Book of Philosophy gives the why," Julianna said evenly. "The Book of Commands gives the structure. Once we find that, we'll have the means of altering the Laws of Time, rewriting them completely instead of simply changing words here and there and bandaging a broken system."

"And the Book of Commands was found," Isthim cut in. All eyes turned on her. "I received a report from my people that the third party was apprehended and the journal seized."

Julianna put her hands together and grinned. "Lovely!"

"Who was it, just for curiosity's sake?" Rifun asked.

"An Ururian named Abbal Duma T'Akhar Mureel Sibon," Isthim answered.

Julianna made a face. "I remember him. I don't know if he was ever truly Akarin, or just playing as one. He was a thief and a trickster besides."

"Indeed. He managed to get away, but the journal was recovered."

"Where is it?" Cassius growled.

"In safekeeping in one of the temples in Ancrath, until we decide what we're doing about the Book of Abilities."

"We all want it," Rifun stated. "We can't all go get it."

"I want to get it," Cassius said. "I'm tired of being betrayed and shoved aside."

"We need you to continue your cleanup. You already know what's in the journal. You possess the greatest abilities to keep our adversaries in line if and when they do pop up again. Julianna is the one who hid it; she knows where it is, so she'll cause the least disruption in time. Meanwhile, the rest of us can manage things on the home front, securing the Time industry, implementing the Book of Commands, and everything else."

"But—"

"He's right," Isthim said sternly. "Your absence would be noted."

Cassius gave her a look. "If we're taking over the Time industry, then shouldn't we have a bunch of new recruits to train up and protect us?"

"Without the Book of Abilities?"

"It's a paradox," Julianna sighed. "And I admit it. This is not how things were supposed to go. But I do know where I hid the journal. Rifun has the right of it, that I will be the fastest in and out, minimizing the time needed to rule strictly through fear." She gave a genuine, if grudging look at Isthim. "And the people aren't so helpless. Even those with the barest understanding of Matter and Energy have an edge over those bound only to Time." She looked at Cassius. "But you are the most powerful one here, and you would be able to keep our enemies at bay until I get back."

"And I can smooth things over politically when we start doling out spoils to our various allies," Rifun said. "That will shore up more tangible asset protection."

Cassius still looked greatly displeased by the whole thing. Rifun didn't blame him, but he got the distinct feeling that retaliation was not out of the question.

"Your mercenaries may continue to do their work," Julianna was saying. "You may continue to do your work, ensuring that any who stood against us pay the price for their rebellion. All others are welcome to join."

"And when you return?"

"Then we shall implement more new rules and more curriculum. It shouldn't be long. A few years, if that. Even the strongest of soldiers here have much to learn yet, and those who are former Akarin are able to add in what they know."

"And you are certain of this?" Isthim asked. "You know where the journal is, and you know how to get to it swiftly and easily?"

"I do. I will make preparations for this expedition immediately."

"What kind of preparations?" Cassius wondered. "What more do you need than a flashlight?"

"A torch will only let me see," Julianna informed him. "But I want to study the Time Trap itself, see if I can't make sense of it and perhaps figure out a way to lessen its effects."

"Do you want help with that?" Rifun inquired.

She nodded. "A second set of eyes and a more talented will wouldn't hurt, thank you."

"I will return to Brelix and retrieve the Book of Commands," Isthim said. "When you enter the Trap, we will begin the conversion of the Laws of Time into the Commands of the Akari."

"I'll make sure everyone else stays out of our way," Cassius grumbled, leaving the meeting without so much as an official adjournment.

Rifun and the two women watched him go, but no one made a move to stop him. If anything, it was a relief to have him gone. Even after their little deception, everyone had come out alive. Rifun turned to them.

"Who told him and why?" he demanded.

"I did," Isthim said, meeting him head-on. "We needed the push. Right now is the prime moment to pluck this fruit. I couldn't just sit around and wait for you to deliberate and debate and overcome your moral and ethical dilemmas. We had to take the opportunity, and we had to do it now. And you will notice that we have a real plan that will see us to the finish, and we are all, as you say, on the same page. No doubt, in his anger, Cassius will go on a killing spree, speeding up this cleanup that must still be done. Julianna is going to retrieve the journal, which will in turn help me. And you are no longer on the hook for any moral hangups you may still have."

Rifun let out a breath and looked away. "And what if he does decide to go get it himself? He isn't much for sharing."

"From his point of view, neither are we."

"You're siding with him now?"

"Are you jealous?"

He blinked.

"We have one journal," Isthim began evenly. "Another is in safekeeping. We know the location of the third. What is stopping us, honestly? Our excuses are running out, which means it is either some kind of moral restraint or simple apathy."

"She is right," Julianna said. "We've fallen in love with our ideas and would rather live with a safe fantasy rather than push for a reality that has the potential to be disappointing or amazing beyond our wildest dreams. But it's the uncertainty that stalls."

"Exactly. I simply provided the push. You get to decide how you're going to land."

With that, Isthim also departed, leaving Rifun and Julianna to stare at each other across the great stone table.

"I had hoped," she said after a moment of silence, "that this matter might have remained confidential until your own plans were fulfilled."

"Plans changed," he replied weakly. "Besides, it doesn't mean that those plans can't still be fulfilled."

"I expect that I will hear more about this when you come to help me survey the cave?"

"When did you want to leave to do this?"

"No time like the present. Meet me at the entrance to the tunnels in ten minutes."

Rifun agreed and left the meeting room, heading for his chambers. He wasn't sure for what, although he bowed at his shrine to offer up a quick prayer for guidance.

Not much later, he was hiking the trail up to the cave, pushing aside branches for Julianna who was hardly dressed for any sort of outdoorsmanship.

"Well, not much has changed," she huffed when they finally stood in front of the thing.

It was a simple hole in the side of the mountain, a boulder rolled almost all the way across the entrance, trees felled in front of the rest, though so rotted that it didn't seem to matter. A child or a thin person would have little or no trouble slipping inside. Someone of Cassius' bulk would have quite the squeeze.

"I know how the Trap was formed," Rifun said, "but who blocked off the entrance?"

"No one knows for sure," Julianna answered, "and I've never gone looking for the answer."

He went to the entrance and peered over the rotted trees which reached about to his navel. "Whoever it was didn't do the best job. Close, but just not good enough."

The Bands inside the cave were near-blinding due to their strength, to say nothing of how they twisted, moved, and writhed, like a tangle of snakes.

"Maybe, but it's served us well enough," Julianna said behind him. "Or it will."

She didn't see the look he had, and he worked to make sure it had gone neutral by the time he turned around. "Where do you want to start, then?"

"Well, I happen to know that the Trap doesn't actually begin until near darkness, so we can at least step inside and get a better look rather than trying to peer through a hole in the fence as it were."

He agreed and helped her over the fallen logs. She had almost no trouble getting through the opening and quickly signaled for him to join her. He had a little more difficulty sliding through. He was never in danger of becoming stuck, but it was a tad uncomfortable. Then he was through. He went to stand beside Julianna who had a hand up to shield her eyes from the dazzling display of color.

"Here I thought I was going to need a torch," she commented. "I think I shall instead need sunglasses."

"Did it look different when you came in here a hundred years ago?" Rifun wondered.

"I was running for my life at that time, thank you. As for your question, no, it didn't." She huffed a sigh. "I was sort of hoping it might. At least then it would give me something. Something other than how it doesn't change. But once you get through the mess of Bands there, it does taper off into total cave darkness after a bit. If you start here and follow the wall to the...right." She paused and thought a moment. "Yes. To the right. If you follow the wall to the right, it will eventually lead to an opening which takes you to another tunnel. The bones are in an alcove there, and you can just barely make them out. The opening is at the very edge of the light, and the alcove is almost completely shrouded. You would have to have superior eyesight to truly make it out."

"If not for the Time Trap we're staring at, I might consider that a challenge."

They stood there staring at it for a long moment, before turning away, blinking and trying to clear spots. After a second, still staring at the boulder, Julianna said, "All right, Rifun Ndolo, I know you didn't come with me just because you're a gentleman to help me in and out of this cave." She looked at him. "Why did you tell Isthim the whereabouts of the journal?"

"Equal parts playing the rumor mill and testing loyalty," Rifun answered. "I wanted to know how she and Cassius were getting along. Had our canary begun to make friends with our enemies?"

"And testing loyalty?"

"There is no reason her teams should have taken that long to hunt down the journal."

"You think they had it a lot sooner?"

He nodded. "I do. By giving up the Book of Abilities, she would have to admit to having the Book of Commands."

"She couldn't admit her teams were incompetent, but she couldn't rightly get the Book of Abilities without possessing the Book of Commands," Julianna finished. "Very clever. A gamble, but a clever one. The problem now is that we have three parties all vying for the Book of Abilities, and everyone knows where it is."

"Which is why I suggested we send the smallest of us through the minefield."

Her expression turned stunned. "I beg your pardon?"

"Cassius is threatened by Isthim. Isthim is threatened by Cassius. I'm threatened by both, and they're both threatened by me. We're constantly standing in a triangle, a gun in each hand, each one pointed at the other two. We're gridlocked. No one expects you to take the journal and run. Cassius would hunt you. Isthim would hunt you —"

"Would you hunt me?" she interrupted. "Would you chase me across ocean and galaxy to get the Book of Abilities?"

"Not with ill intent toward you," he told her smoothly. "And anyway, I think I'm learning just as much if not more from my own training."

He put his hands on the rock faces and hoisted himself onto the logs, squeezing through the opening before turning and offering a hand to Julianna.

"Still on your quest to become a Builder?" she asked, slipping easily through the hole and carefully getting down to the ground.

"Just because I am not living with my family at this time does not mean I am not training," Rifun answered, dropping beside her. "In fact, being back has allowed me to concentrate my efforts."

"I see. Making progress, I trust?"

"I'd like to believe so, or else I would have thought harder about telling Isthim about the Book of Abilities."

"Well, I will choose to view that as a good thing."

He looked out over the valley, the view just starting to become obscured by trees. "Just think. By the time you get back, we'll have secured our hold on the Time industry, and, with any luck, I will be a Builder. And you'll have the Book of Abilities to share with the grunts and fully validate our claims."

She gave him a look. "As much as I would like to share your optimism, I've learned to be cautious about such things, especially when this infernal Time Trap is involved."

He nodded. "Not a bad thing, to be cautious."

"And what about you? Are you just being cautious when it comes to actually eliminating Cassius? And what about Isthim and the Borelians?"

"The Borelians, yes, for it would be prudent to keep them friendly until we have the Book of Commands."

"And Cassius?"

Rifun hesitated. "I do not expect you to understand, but there is a darkness within him."

Julianna folded her arms. "Most people believe in evil to some degree, I think."

"Yes, but this type of evil..." He paused. "Simply killing the body isn't enough. The evil within him would only move on to someone else, and I don't fancy chasing it around or suddenly finding myself resolutely against it in battle if it landed in, say, one of the Gentleman Killers or one of the Tacagans or even a Borelian. It must be dealt with carefully, which is another thing I am exploring in my Building studies."

The concept of angels and demons was not foreign to most people. Most cultures had some iteration of good and bad spirits. But most people were also much happier when those concepts remained just that, concepts, and didn't actually intrude upon daily life. Or, even better, when good and evil could be confined to the mortal realm, assigned to mortal beings that could be defeated by mortal means and required no extra care or faith when it came to dealing with them. Rifun had no such luxury, but he could see Julianna was moderately skeptical. In a way, this offended him, given that she'd likely been raised Christian and she'd helped to found a group based around something and someone commonly dismissed by the larger universe as a false religion.

"Whatever you intend to do," she said at last, "don't wait long to do it. As the Cult grows, and as we solidify our holdings, it's only feeding Cassius. It's grown beyond himself; he has a team now. Evil begets evil."

"I'm not unaware of this, believe me. I expect it won't be long before I am his next target, whether for keeping information from him or some other offense."

"And regardless of any Akari abilities, he is still a very powerful Harvester who can kill at a touch."

"I've not forgotten this either. Trust me, I am very aware of the many ways that someone can kill me, especially Cassius."

Julianna nodded. "Of course. I'm not your mother, I shouldn't be harping on you like this."

Rifun shrugged as he put one foot on a rock and leaned forward, looking over the cliff. "At least one person in the Cult can pretend to like and care for me."

"You think I'm pretending? What about that olive branch of trust, which you betrayed?"

"I made a calculated move. As for the olive branch of trust, I am extending it back to you by sending you to get the Book of Abilities. Who knows? You might run off with it in the end."

"So much for sending the weakest through the minefield."

He put up a finger. "I said the smallest, not the weakest. Sometimes the smallest are the most devious and cunning."

She nodded once. "If that's a compliment, then thank you. If it's not, lie to me."

He grinned and straightened. "I'll never tell."

"No, of course not."

He got off the rock and started back toward the trail. "At any rate, we did the survey. You are free to continue looking around, but I have other work to do, preparations to make while you're gone."

"Things will change drastically while I'm gone, will they?"

He looked back. She hadn't moved. "No more than they did while I was gone."

She did not say anything to that, nor did she follow him, and a moment later, he was well out of range.

There really wasn't much of a trail here, actually. As far as he knew, this was all private property, though abandoned. He still went for a short hike, passing by an old, dilapidated cabin and barn that looked ready to blow over in the next windstorm. He intended to pass it by, but he found himself investigating it instead.

He found himself wondering if there were any people buried nearby. Certainly there were no cemeteries out this far, or there wouldn't have been a hundred or two hundred years ago. What spirits haunted this place? His hand hovered inches from the wooden wall of the cabin as he considered this. He hadn't brought any offerings, and he didn't need to disturb any more evil spirits or vengeful ancestors against him. He wasn't sure how these spirits, from a world and people so far removed from his own, would react to his presence, but he didn't need to push his luck.

He backed up and away from the area, bowing once and asking forgiveness of any spirits he had disturbed. Then he turned and quickly departed, walking only a short distance into the trees before opening a portal and stepping through, eventually making his way back to the tunnels and the ruins.

His first stop was his chambers where he laid an offering at his shrine, again asking forgiveness for potentially disturbing a sacred area and reaffirming his belief in and loyalty to his home spirits and ancestors.

Once he was satisfied that appropriate reparations had been made, he left the officers building and walked among the ruins, the city come back to life. He found Isthim drilling grunts, and he stopped to watch.

It was impressive, really, to see how she combined the Akari in with military tactics and combat training. Another part of him wondered if things weren't a little imbalanced. The Akari was a way of life, something to take with you in all aspects of your day, not merely in combat. Julianna had been supervising studies in the Book of Philosophy, which included learning English. If she left, would that fall by the wayside? He hadn't thought to ask if she'd found a replacement. He hoped she would be considerate enough to announce when she was leaving. On the other hand, if she was really that worried about Cassius and Isthim, she might not. Not like a two-day head start would matter in the Time Trap, but it was the psychology of it, he figured.

He watched until drills were over. Isthim approached him.

"Inspecting the troops?" she inquired, her tone impossible to determine.

"I don't know how I feel about calling them 'troops' necessarily, and with Julianna leaving, it seems I will not only be dealing with politics, but humanitarian efforts as well."

"Good to know you've taken those efforts upon yourself. I was wondering about that myself."

Rifun raised a brow. "Oh really?"

"No."

Now he frowned and nodded. "Humor. Glad to see you're still working on that aspect of your personality."

She gave him a look.

"I'm telling you, it's your best feature," he continued.

She sighed. "Is there something you want, or are you going to waste both our time with meaningless flattery?"

"Did your teams happen to report on anything else, during or after their pursuit of the journal?" Rifun asked.

"No. Should they have?"

"I just want to be sure we didn't miss anyone in their little scheme."

"The Ururian did escape, but the journal was the prize."

"Even so, I'm sure Cassius would like to make a point to all involved parties about, well, being involved."

Now she looked thoughtful. After a moment, she said, "No. To my knowledge, everything went exactly as it was described. If there were other handlers between Andrew and the Ururian, that knowledge is lost."

"Too bad."

He was turning to leave when Isthim spoke again.

"Do you intend to move against the Akarin? Once we have fully taken over the Time industry?"

He paused, hesitated. Then, "I don't know. I expect it may come to that."

"You don't want to."

Now he turned back. "Quite honestly, I don't know what I want. Any hopes I had of reunification perished when they refused to assist me or us against a very credible, very dangerous threat. Their pacifism is nauseating and now I understand well how their decay led to the creation of the Cult in the first place. On the other hand, I have seen first-hand what it looks like when one group strives to dominate or destroy another."

"I have led many campaigns to this effect," Isthim cut in, her tone bragging.

"Yes, I'm sure you have. Thing is, I've been on the receiving end of those campaigns." He paused. "I suppose, if I could wish for anything, it would be that we could simply stay out of each other's way. They have a great distaste for the Time industry, even if they won't admit to it, and their hesitation means they are not easily or quickly moved to action. They'll wring their hands to the bone and still not come to a decision." He went on before she could speak. "And yet, I get the feeling that you and your people won't be satisfied with such a thing."

"*Dijik* must be destroyed, and we finally have the tools to do so."

"Why destroy? At the very least, why not enslave?"

"The Ul Ik Zol—"

"—have proclaimed it so," he finished. He sighed. "All right."

She gave him a look. "Why do you scoff when I repeat a decree of the Ul Ik Zol, yet you spent a year fervently seeking your spirits?"

"Because I was looking for the spirits themselves, not a middle man. Middle men always have an agenda."

"Does that not make us middle men to those beneath us?" She gestured toward the area where the grunts had been training only a few minutes prior. "Do they not have faith that we teach them correctly from the journals? Do you not have faith that Richard and Julianna recorded appropriately what Cassius dictated? Do you not have faith that Cassius dictated correctly?"

Rifun huffed a breath. "All right, your point is made. I still prefer speaking to the spirits directly, though."

"And the dead, for which you have also criticized me."

"Speaking to the dead is not the same as worshiping death itself."

"Isn't it? If your ancestors are more powerful than you, wouldn't asking for their assistance and seeking their wisdom be the longing for death that you might have the same power? In your quest to become a Builder in this way, are you not seeking the power of the dead?"

"The *razana* is the power of life, the tide of life and reality itself," Rifun cut in. "Not death. And anyway, how do I always get sucked into philosophical discussions with you?"

"Because you are constantly trying to justify yourself that you are not like me, like us. You want to make yourself out to be superior, so that when the time comes and you attempt to get rid of us, you feel vindicated." Her expression was one of smug satisfaction. "We are not blind."

It was almost a veiled threat, and Rifun chose to leave it before it turned into a real threat, or a real action. He left her and meandered through the city, unsure of his destination. It wasn't unreasonable to believe that Isthim and the Borelians had deduced that the Cult wanted to be rid of them. Was this simply standard practice among all their business deals, knowing the other party probably wasn't a very willing participant? Or was it more serious and her words were actually a subtle warning that they were going to make the first move?

Just one more thing to consider with the politics he was once again in charge of. As much as he might have enjoyed telling Cassius that he had full permission and blessing to kill every last one of the Borelians currently among them—still no more than the original team picked out by Misik and the Ul Ik Zol—he had little doubt that the Great Admirals on Brelix would not take too kindly to that. Was there a way to make it look like an accident?

Although, speaking of politics, he probably should make the rounds, go back to all their allies and make sure they were still, well, allied with them. The Korin, the Turitians, and he should probably make nice with their Elif landlords, too. Assuming Julianna hadn't left yet, or even if she had, he would have to get the rundown on the refugee camp that had been growing for a while now. He wasn't opposed to helping the downtrodden, but he would prefer it if the downtrodden stayed on their own planets to get help or contributed to the Cult a little more. He didn't want to have to approach the Turitians to ask for money for leeches. Sure, supplies could be salvaged for free thanks to the Akari, but they couldn't let the camp spiral out of control and attract attention to these supposed "ruins."

He wondered if Cassius had made any progress on his Disguise for the city. That way, at least if anyone did come snooping down here, be they curious folk who thought something fishy was going on here, or common cavers, they wouldn't actually see anything until they were right on the city. And if someone decided to be an ambitious archaeologist, well, they would deal with that once they got there.

He went outside the city walls, took a cursory glance through the camp, and departed as fast as possible before he got caught up in something. He needed to make a plan and get things under control, put people to work.

But first, he had to play politics in order to ensure the rest of them could keep working. He'd pay a visit to the Elif first, then the Turitians, and on down the line until his schedule was once again filled with meetings and notes to remember which promises he'd made and to whom.

He knew a moment of despair, and he longed to return to the farm. Move the cows, repair the fence, build the house, enjoy Elisette's marvelous food, listen to the stories and tell a few of his own.

But the evil spirit would not go away because he backed down from the fight. He had to jump back into the water and take care of it before he settled down. How selfish would he have to be to abandon his duty? Maybe once Julianna had returned with the Book of Abilities, then he would return.

Until then, he had meetings to schedule.

His meeting with the Elif was put off for several weeks. Apparently they had some big to-do that they were managing and couldn't be bothered by something that, by all accounts, wasn't bothering them. Rifun chose to take that as a compliment and moved on.

The Turitians were more than happy to receive him, and Queen Aronet and Commander Dira were able to coordinate an impromptu meeting with him within an hour of his arrival. He made the appropriate turns and gestures, and made sure to congratulate Aronet on her ascent into the crown.

"If I may observe," the queen began as they finally sat down, "Julianna is not one who negotiates well. Were I a more devious leader from a more dishonest family, much would have been stripped from you by now."

Rifun faltered only slightly, replying, "You are not the only one to observe such flaws in her, but she has a good heart."

"This is not in doubt, but I do not envy you having to follow up with your other allies."

This was not how he wanted to start off his getting back into politics tour.

"Did she offend you in some way?" he inquired. "Has she offered your spoils to other allies?"

"She offered the training of your people to Commander Dira, just as soon as the Borelians had been...released, I think is the term she used." Even for a Turitian queen, Rifun could see Aronet was unimpressed. "We are not fools. The Borelians are not so easily disposed of."

"It was a poorly done deal before my time, and getting out of it has been a rather intricate dance."

"All the same, if another family were to learn of her words and her offer, it could mean disaster for us. And you."

Rifun glanced back and forth between the two women, and it hit him that they were the only three at the table. Where were the princes and princesses and dukes and duchesses? They seemed to sense the recognition on his face. It was Dira who spoke.

"During our queen's announcement procession, it was made known that the royal family Torka had infiltrated our very own royal cruiser. The impostor stole several artifacts that were to be gifts to diplomats and allies. Before that, an assassin killed our royal crown maker. That is an insult you cannot hope to understand."

"All the same, I'm sorry to hear about it," Rifun offered.

"It is our understanding that the Akari has an ability which allows one to see through an impostor's disguise," Aronet went on. "Is this true?"

"It is." Just for his own sanity, he Tested both Turitians at the table, as well as the four guards in the room. They were all clean.

"I want Commander Dira to be trained in this ability. And others, as time permits. Our family is under attack. So far, we've managed to keep the news to a minimum and downplay the damage, but we cannot allow others to think they can do the same. The Torka family is crumbling, and this may be an attempt to salvage their honor. Other families are not so frail."

Rifun nodded. "I understand."

"Do this, and we will see to it that the Cult of the Akari has everything it needs to usurp the Hands of Time and reform the Time industry."

" 'Usurp' ? Forgive me for saying, but that's a rather divisive word from a patient people."

"A *hitipfoalikortigaintisordinaevidorpfaefelivunatoir* is slow to rouse, slow to move, but when it does, it is nearly unstoppable and capable of some of the most violent acts known among beasts."

And to think some people had a hard time wrapping their mouths around some French sounds. Rifun found himself briefly wondering at the lag time of translation. With how long Turitian words could get, what was the exact wait time between a word spoken and a word understood?

"We'll be happy to teach you," he assured them.

"Not 'we,' " Aronet told him. "This training is to be kept confidential. While I am certain that your council is competent and confident in your goals, we cannot risk our security in this way. If, for instance, Julianna were to say something and the wrong person overheard, well, the universe is not so big as people would like to believe."

"If it's any comfort, Julianna is taking a vacation for a while, but I understand your point."

"We want you and you only to train Commander Dira. You will meet every nine Base Days, rescheduling as her time demands."

He leaned back in his seat. "Who am I to refuse an order from a queen?"

"Good. You will begin in exactly three days."

"Understood. If I may ask, though, if things are as...unstable as you make it sound, why not get a hold of me sooner? I was not entirely unreachable. I myself was studying even greater things about the Akari."

"Building, yes. Julianna informed us of this. But as you said, we are a patient people. And if this power you were studying is as grand as she makes it out to be, then there ought to be no trouble calling upon you if things do become dire."

And there's the catch, Rifun thought. But being assured of all necessary resources was nothing to sneeze at. Besides, there were worse monarchs in the universe than Queen Aronet, and Commander Dira would no doubt be an intelligent, reasonable, competent pupil.

"Of course," he agreed. "I would be happy to assist."

"Then we have an understanding."

"Was there anything else you wished to discuss?"

"As a matter of fact, there is." Both the queen and the commander made gestures that Rifun believed indicated some form of annoyance and distrust. "Understanding that there are many rumors running about in the chaos that is the Wheel of Time, I am offering no conclusions or condemnation." Conversations that started out this way rarely ended well. "But there is one particular rumor going around that one of your people, Cassius, is in business with Captain Morain leRou Titik."

"The space pirate?"

"And a notorious pest for our merchants."

Rifun hesitated and chose his words carefully. "It doesn't surprise that Cassius would be seen in the company of such a character, but what does it have to do with you, if I may be so bold?"

"Is Titik part of the Cult?"

"To my knowledge, no."

"Good. And until Commander Dira becomes proficient in these Akari teachings that would allow us to defend against him, should he ever come to learn, it will stay that way."

"Of course. And I will investigate the matter fully."

"See that you do, but again, it could be just one of the many unsubstantiated rumors of the Wheel."

"For our sake, let's hope so."

Their expressions were impossible to determine, but they made gestures of muted acceptance.

"Was there anything else that you wanted to bring to my attention?" Rifun asked, not sure that he wanted to know the answer.

"Not at this time. We are grateful for your return."

"As am I. Now as to the nature of my visit, I simply wished to ensure that our negotiations remained reliable. We are assuming control of the Wheel and should have it secured within a couple of years, if that."

"Why so long?" Commander Dira wondered. "I am certain that if I become proficient in the Akari, or passable even, then I may bring other trusted soldiers to —"

"It's nothing like that. Believe me when I say that we are whole-heartedly grateful for your gift of resources, but the thing we seek is not something you can provide. Consider it a matter of faith or religion. This is what Julianna is going to find. Think of it as a rallying point for the Cult."

"Do we have the honor of knowing what this artifact is?"

"A journal, one written by Richard himself, detailing everything about the Akari and its uses."

"Sounds fascinating."

"Let us return to the negotiations," Aronet suggested.

"Apologies. Were there other terms you wanted to discuss?" Rifun asked.

"We want control of the Scouts. Scouts will allow us to expand our markets more extensively than simple market control will."

"I see."

"We would also like certain...immunities in the markets."

"Immunities?"

"Perhaps I should phrase it another way. We would like to conduct business how we see fit without having to bow to the Merchants and the Hands."

Rifun nodded. "Ah. Yes, that is understandable. You can be assured that when we take over, it will no longer be about loyalty to a business. You are not employees of the Time industry, you are your own business, your own market, free to conduct your affairs how you will."

"That is all we ask for. Is it not a simple request?"

"The small man asks to govern his own affairs. The big man hears his control being taken away."

"And so it is," the queen acknowledged. "I am glad we could come to an understanding. We await your signal to fully take over the Scouts."

"Understand that it may not be Scouting as it has been in the past."

The queen made a noise that Rifun assumed was a laugh, for it was accompanied by a gesture of amusement. "The Scouts have always conducted their own affairs in their own ways with little regard for the Laws or the Hands of Time."

"Then what makes you think you can control them?"

"Maybe 'control' is too strong of a word," Dira replied. "We just want to be the first to review their information on new worlds and discoveries."

The royal family Jalar may have been threatened by physical attacks, but it was clear that this young line didn't claw its way out of commonhood by being foolish.

"I cannot presume to speak for the Scouts, for they are an entity all their own. If they choose to work with you in such a way, then I will not stop them," Rifun said at last.

"Perhaps that is all we can ask, then," Aronet said graciously.

There were more pleasantries and minor details, but otherwise, the most serious part of the negotiations were quickly over with, and Rifun left feeling good about the Cult's alliance with the Turitians, or at least the royal family Jalar.

No other dignitaries and leaders were so enthralled by his arrival that they upended their schedules just to meet with him, and soon his schedule was dotted with dates and times and places and people. With everything planned out and demanding his attention, Rifun was free to return to the ruins. He made his way to the officers building where he did not see Cassius, though he did find Julianna in her chambers.

"I was wondering if perhaps you wanted to get a head start on things," he said, announcing his presence and standing in the doorway.

"No, not yet," she said, glancing at him briefly. "I wanted to get everything cleaned up and locked down before I go. Make sure there's no food left that could mold or precious heirlooms that could go to rot."

"I'm sure I could find a new grunt out there who could work off some punishment by coming in and playing maid for a day. Barring that, I could look in every so often."

She grinned and shook her head. "I'm sure you could, but I want to minimize the trauma."

He entered the room and shut the door. "I had a meeting with the Turitians earlier."

"Oh? How did that go?"

"Well, for one, they would like to meet with me and only me going forward."

Julianna's face turned bright red. "Yes, I admit, I'm not the best negotiator in the universe."

"They also told me about a rumor they'd heard about Cassius getting into business with a space pirate named Titik. Do you know anything about it?"

She straightened and turned toward him. "I knew that someone from his crew was interested in the Akari and was coming to train. Isthim said she dropped out, though. Said she might have done all right except she and Cassius had some kind of argument, or that's what she thought."

"This crewman was one of Cassius' groupies, then?"

"Yes. What does this have to do with the Turitians?"

"Titik is a bit of a thorn in their side, and they don't want him to have the Akari."

"They're welcome to learn and train."

"They're dealing with their own internal problems right now." He added quickly, "They're still our allies, and they'll keep up any resources we need. They just can't do much more than that. Also, they want oversight of the Scouts."

Julianna grinned, scoffed, and looked away. "Ah, that will be the day, that anyone tells the Scouts what to do."

"I told them that if the Scouts choose to follow them, I wasn't going to stop it."

"That's the only way it's going to work."

Rifun nodded and let the silence stretch out for a minute or two, looking casually around the room. Then, "When do you expect to leave?"

"Soon," she answered. "In the next day or two. Why? Are you planning a surprise going away party?"

"Hardly. I just want to make sure you make it into the cave."

"Ah, I see." Her expression was doubtful. She turned her attention back to her work. "So, what will you do once I'm gone?"

"My meeting schedule is fairly full for the next few weeks," he answered. "The Elif, the Korin, the Turitians want to meet again, more properly this time. And I suppose I'll be keeping an eye on Cassius and Isthim, making sure they don't cause too much trouble."

"That much is true. Isthim, I fear, will enjoy leadership a little too much once our hold in the Wheel is secure. Cassius...I don't know. For as brutal as he is, he's never struck me as the...administrative type. The field of battle, perhaps, but not so much the nuance of daily life as a leader."

"You'll notice that he isn't the one scheduling meetings and doing paperwork here."

"Yes, but right now, he's still useful. He still has a purpose. What will he do once our goal has been met and we no longer have to destroy everything that moves?"

Rifun grinned and shook his head. "I don't think you understand how history works. I don't know of any power that has come into being and never been challenged."

"Yes, but once the conquest is over, then what?"

"I don't know, but I do know that we will not go unchallenged. Someone will mobilize against us. Cassius may end up being our top general."

Julianna gave him a look. "Cassius is not a leader of armies. Isthim would more likely be the general. She's training the grunts, she has the mind and, dare I say it, the talent for it. Cassius is a mercenary. He works alone, or, at best, with a small group. He does what Isthim and an army can't do."

Rifun huffed a sigh. "I don't know. I don't know what his place will be. We may just have to wait and see how he reacts to it."

"He was the Zero Hour once. He was once the ultimate governing authority of the universe. He could have done literally anything, and very few could have stopped him. What did he do? He would have rathered been either in a grimy old gaol torturing prisoners, or out killing others just for fun. Because being the Zero Hour and having that authority bored him."

"I'm not saying you're wrong. But back then, he was doing it alone, and he was still playing by Time industry rules. This time, I can handle the mundane, Isthim can handle the formal military, you, once you return, can handle the humanitarian efforts, and he...I don't know. Maybe he can be in charge of the Judgment Wing. Let him be the head guard, that way he can torture all the prisoners he wants; we can't say we won't have any."

She seemed uncertain, but all she could do was assent. "Well, like you said, we'll just have to wait and see. Counting chickens and all that."

"Agreed. With any luck, he won't be a problem."

He gave her a look which she understood, nodding wordlessly. "Yes. Well, I still have a few last-minute items to take care of before I'm gone for a few years. I have to say goodbye to some of the children in the camp."

He opened the door and stepped aside. "Of course. I don't mean to hold you up."

She exited the room and he followed, closing the door behind him, and they parted ways. While Julianna went off to say goodbye to her adopted children, Rifun headed back out to talk to Isthim. He wasn't overly concerned with whom Cassius spent his time with, within reason, but he was interested in this little club he was forming.

As Queen Aronet had said, it was only a rumor, and things may not have been as bad as they first appeared to the Turitians who were dealing with other problems. Besides, there could be another, more interesting angle to this, depending on what Cassius said. If Rifun managed to track down this crewman of Titik's who had been a groupie of Cassius', there could be something in the works. He didn't know what, but if there was a way to direct Cassius and keep him occupied during or after the takeover, then he was much less of a risk to them and their operation.

After searching throughout the ruins — twice — with no luck, Rifun returned to the officers building and found Isthim in her chambers, a rare moment of solitude for her. She looked up from whatever she was doing.

"What?" she asked.

"I have a few questions about one of your grunts. Specifically one who's been hanging around with Cassius."

The Caves of Meroian, 1965

After Rifun and Julianna left the cave, Cassius went there to survey it for himself. Why shouldn't he just go get the Book of Abilities? If Julianna was going to be the one coming in after him, well, it wasn't as though she was much of a threat. Maybe he would follow her in, have her lead him right to the journal, kill her, get out, and leave her there for all eternity. Wasn't as though anyone was really going to find her. Or miss her, for that matter.

And if anyone put up a fuss over it, well, who cared, really? He could take the journal for himself. He could take full control of the Cult. Get rid of Rifun and his moral dilemmas. Maybe he would even keep Isthim and the Borelians. Or maybe he wouldn't. Maybe he would forsake the Cult entirely, take over the Time industry himself, and recreate it in his own image. He would keep the journal secret and use it as a kind of magic to threaten the people with.

The shadow spirit was not happy with his erratic decision-making. If not for the bullet in his face that still threatened his very existence, Cassius wouldn't care about that either. It was one of the reasons he didn't act on every impulse, and probably the only reason he decided against following Julianna into the cave, killing her, and taking the journal.

But what was he supposed to do with himself? A quick jaunt into the cave for her was months or years out here. Rifun was taking care of the politics, and good riddance to him. Isthim had the army and her people to ensure a more or less peaceful transition and security of power. What was he supposed to do, crowd control? Being a mercenary was great and all, but he enjoyed working for himself, working for chaos. He led riots and opposition for their own sake, just to cause some havoc that the Cult had to quell. He wasn't some lap dog to be summoned when someone stepped out of line.

It was like the Gentleman Killers and the Tacagans all over again. He didn't conform to their ideals, so he ended up an outcast. But he couldn't very well destroy the Cult. He could, but the dark spirit wouldn't allow it.

What, then, was his purpose?

He'd had crises like this before. They usually didn't last too long because something interesting would happen and his services would be needed.

Maybe he could take up a second persona, whether through Disguise or Harvesting, and sell his services to those who would challenge the Cult. Maybe he would carry out the contract, maybe he would give the Cult some kind of forewarning. Play both sides, that way he always won. He rather enjoyed this idea. Seeing how his face wasn't throbbing with the reminder that his life was in someone else's hands, the dark spirit evidently approved of this as well.

As he said before. These kinds of crises never lasted long. Sometimes they produced his greatest ideas.

His next decision, then, would be whether to tell the others, and when. If he told them now, there was every chance they would disapprove and tell him not to do it. On the other hand, seeing how he'd basically been doing that already with the controlled opposition, the likelihood of their disapproval was minimal. Actually, they might even praise it. Then they wouldn't have to wonder where their next threat was coming from.

Did he want to tell them now, then, or get in a few of these back and forth contracts first? It wasn't as though he had to prove that he could kill; this was more than abundantly clear. The test would be of his loyalty. He could play as many sides as he wanted, but would he remain loyal to the Cult, or the highest bidder? Would he really tell the others of a plot to kill them, or otherwise undermine their efforts? Or would he ensure that those efforts succeeded and that Rifun and Isthim "accidentally" perished? That would be the real test.

Maybe he would get in a few contracts first. That way, when the others raised those objections, he could let them know of the times he'd already been hired to cause destruction for them and didn't. Wouldn't that throw them off?

It sounded like a good plan. The hard part was putting it into practice. So many little details. Did he uses Disguises, or did he want to go back to Harvesting? If he used a Disguise to sell an image, then he could use Harvesting as his method of operation to sell the persona and, in changing his appearance through the Harvesting, reduce his need for the Disguise.

He returned to his chambers in the officers building and stood in front of a mirror, trying out different Disguises. Maneuvering between Disguises and Harvesting meant that he would have to remain human. But he couldn't very well be mistaken for himself. Most aliens couldn't distinguish well between humans, and one of his most defining features was his skin.

He hated giving up his dark skin, but he had to sell the image. Maybe this was a bad idea. He would assimilate characteristics of his victims through Harvesting if those characteristics were compatible with his DNA. Even years ago when he'd been killing only humans, it had taken a lot of killing and a lot of effort to change his skin back and forth like that. If he spent even half the time doing any killing—and it was more likely to be about a fifth of that—it was going to take a long time to change. Throw in the contracts that would go against aliens, such as Isthim, and others whose DNA was wholly incompatible, and he wasn't going to change hardly at all.

He dropped his current iteration and studied his reflection. Maybe it was his own ego, but he was quite a handsome man. Dark-skinned, strong, confident. Why should he be anything else except that he needed to sell an image that just wasn't him? No one would believe that Calis Cutthroat would betray the Cult a second time. The first time, maybe. Fool me twice, shame on me.

But then, he only needed to help get the Cult into power and root out the less obvious threats. The Tacagans and Gentleman Killers had played their hands early, but they weren't the only ones with cards. Some were just more patient. Expose them, and he wouldn't have to pretend to betray the Cult because there would be no one to betray them to.

Still a touch uneasy, he donned another Disguise. South American, he figured, with caramel skin, black hair, and a thick mustache. Migrant worker, not especially bulky, but strong nonetheless, and with endurance that allowed him to work for sixteen or more hours a day. Yes, this would work out just fine.

Now then, what to do about his little task force? They'd been happy enough to be utilized again, brought back into his good graces, and they had done everything he'd asked, with no expensive hotels or other sightseeing. He couldn't just leave them hanging. Maybe they would be his innocent friends in the Cult who he talked to every once in a while. Then he could get information in and out without making it obvious that he was funneling information to Rifun or Isthim or anyone important.

Yes, this all seemed to be coming together nicely. He nodded to himself, still wearing his Disguise, rather impressed with his mustache and his plan. Now he just needed to find his people.

The Korin were gone, but Murdi and Lordo were practicing their Akari maneuvers in the secluded alcove by the lake where Cassius had taken the Korin.

They paused in their maneuvers when they saw him approach, still in Disguise.

"Hello," Murdi began, half-friendly, half-challenging. "Can we do something for you?"

"Yes, you can," Cassius answered, his voice accented. "You can learn this face. You can learn this voice. Because you will be taking information to and from me for the foreseeable future."

He dropped his Disguise. Murdi blinked, and Lordo stumbled, though whether it had been from his injured feet was difficult to guess. Cassius went on, "I'm going to be doing some work which will require me to be Disguised. If I have to meet anyone, it can't be Rifun or Isthim. You have a history with the Gentleman Killers, which makes you an excellent gateway in and out for information."

"What kind of information?" Murdi asked.

"All kinds. I'll tell you what I know and who to pass it along to, and then I'll tell you what I need to get back. Think you can handle that?"

The twins glanced at each other.

"Is this off the record?" Lordo wondered.

"For the time being. Depends on the information and how things go."

The twins glanced at each other again. It was Murdi who answered, "Sounds good to us. Is there anyone else who needs to know about this?"

"If there is, I'll make sure they know. But I don't anticipate so."

He again confirmed their support, then left the sandy alcove. Perhaps it was a good thing he'd found Murdi and Lordo and not the Korin. At least the twin assassins wouldn't be so bound up over balancing everything out. On the other hand, the give and take of information might provide the perfect fulcrum of balance for the Korin and make them more reliable for it. Time would tell, but for now, they were out.

He did not tell any of the others that he was heading out. He didn't want to have to tell them why, and he certainly didn't know how long he would be gone. They might worry, they might fret, but if he got in a couple good contracts and foiled plots, then when he did finally reveal his antics, they might be a little more trusting, too.

He waited until he was in the tunnels before donning his Disguise. If anyone saw him coming or going from his portals, they would never be able to identify him, or so he hoped. So it was that it wasn't Cassius who ended up in the wheel, but Alvaro Alvarez.

It wasn't the most creative name ever, but he liked the way it sounded, how it repeated and made the name seem more important. It wasn't enough to say it only once, no, you had to say it again for good measure.

So he made his way to the marketplaces. The lower marketplaces were in remarkably good order, all things considering. It wasn't quite as pristine as a luxury hotel, but it was a respectable street market. The common man didn't have to worry about being jumped, beaten, robbed, and murdered in broad daylight. The dead of night was a different story, but it was good otherwise.

The middle marketplaces were about the same, really, despite their better wares. Whoever was controlling the lower and intermediate marketplaces was evidently trying to make the buying and selling process identical between the two. Of course, basic commerce such as buying and selling was not a difficult concept, but, like competing stores selling the same wares, it was all about the details. Now that new management had come in to consolidate the chains, everything was expected to be the same no matter the store.

The auctions were open for business, but the atmosphere here was different. When he tried to enter one, he was denied.

"Are you an invited guest to this auction?" the door guard inquired.

"Since when do the auctions require invitations?" Cassius-as-Alvaro asked. "The Tacagans are out of power."

"That may be but new power always fills the void. Do you have an invitation?"

"Yeah? And who's the power in this auction?"

"I'm afraid if you don't have an invitation, I can't give that information away."

Smart man. Smart power. Cassius-as-Alvaro shifted his stance. "So how does one obtain one of these sacred invitations?"

"You must be invited." Even for an alien, the guard looked very smug about it.

"Yes, that's what an invitation is. How do I get an invitation?"

"You must be invited."

"There must be some sort of miscommunication here, because you're repeating yourself, and you're saying the same words. How do I get an invitation? An invitation means I've already been invited."

"Yes. You must be invited to be invited."

"Is it the same for all auctions?"

"It is."

So it was a two-step process, a sort of verification. Whoever was running the auctions now was being extremely cautious about it. It was a good thing to do, a smart thing, after what happened to the Tacagans and the Gentleman Killers, but it was also very frustrating for those who sought to try something like that again.

He could have killed the guard and busted in anyway, he figured, but he decided against it. Maybe he should make sure that it wasn't Rifun who installed this two-step verification as a means of protecting them, the Cult.

He backed down. He didn't think the guard could look any more smug, but apparently he could as his eyes laughed at him all the way out of the Auctionhouse Hub.

Cassius tried to go back to the other marketplaces and ascertain the state of things there, but either there was nothing out of the ordinary, or else the auctions really bothered him that much. He was on his way to the portal room so he could make his way back to the ruins and ask Rifun about any political dealings, when he made a detour to the wares marketplace instead.

It hadn't changed much, at least from the customer point of view, but if there were any major rule changes, the best people to ask would be the ones avoiding them as much as possible.

Jora's legal business hadn't changed any. He was still a carpet and rug dealer, of some form, anyway. The Ferulian's unusually small eyes got huge when he saw Cassius shed his Alvaro Disguise, and the two of them retreated to a more private area to talk. Portable portals were still illegal, but who was going to know, really? And it could have been that the new power in town was not above bribery.

Once out of the plush comfort of the rug palace, Jora's illegal smuggling business appeared to be either suffering or booming. Suffering, because he didn't have much stock. Booming, because it was in apparent high demand.

"It's been far too long, my friend," Jora said. "I thought perhaps something had happened to you on Juris, perhaps you had angered them somehow. Maybe you were injured or killed or some other fate. And then I heard about the Time Trial."

"A few have tried," Cassius told him casually, scanning the sparse wares laid out on the table. "But I've been busy with other endeavors. The contracts that I have taken haven't required such...bold, brutal obviousness."

"Well, a few more are going to try again soon, I think."

"Oh? What do you know?"

Jora made an expression that Cassius thought was supposed to be a smile. "Only because you're still my best, most reliable supplier and customer." He went around the table. "For the most part, I think it's just talk. Time Trials are intimidating. Lots of people don't like to be intimidated or bullied. Few have the *abuji* to carry out their threats."

"I'm interested in the ones that do," Cassius said. "What are the Tacagans and the Gentleman Killers up to?"

Jora waved a hand. "The Gentleman Killers don't matter much anymore. They've scattered and hold no loyalty beyond their current contract. Standard business."

"And the Tacagans?"

"Well, they had a bit of an incident on their world. Seems as though their entire planetary leadership was taken out in one blow. You wouldn't know anything about that, would you?"

"I might."

"That's what I thought. Anyway, seems they're under new management now."

"That didn't take long."

"Why should it? As paranoid as those bastards are, I'm surprised you got the jump on them the first time, never mind a second time."

"Fool me twice, shame on me," Cassius said, grinning.

"Whatever the case, they have their leadership back again, and they're out for blood."

"So they are the ones back in charge of the auctions."

Jora made a gesture. "They could be. It wouldn't surprise me."

Cassius raised a brow. "You don't know?"

"No one knows. The process for getting an invitation is damn difficult. None of my little spies have been successful."

"Then maybe there are spies stalking your spies."

"With everything going on? Wouldn't surprise me. I tell them to be careful, but it is physically impossible to plan for every possible contingency. Of course you know that means that whatever you've got going on with your skin and hair, you can't do that again because now they know that trick."

Damn. "Of course. That doesn't mean I don't have more Disguises."

Jora sighed. "I'm afraid I don't have much to give you. You and your Cult may take the lower and intermediate marketplaces. You may even have the wares marketplace. But whatever is going on in those auctions, I can't imagine it's going to stay contained forever."

"No, it won't." Cassius frowned. "Even if your spies can't get in, what do they say about who goes to these auctions? Who gets invited? What sort of person?"

"The same kinds of people who normally frequent the auctions. Rich, snobbish, entitled to the universe and everything in it, think it revolves around them. If there is anything of note, it's that the only security they have appears to be external, or else the guards are camping inside. Whoever it is, they're not employing Gentleman Killers or your run-of-the-mill mercenary."

"Is there another kind?"

"I don't know. If I could get in, I would tell you. But as a friendly word of warning, don't let that pot simmer too long."

"You think the Borelian Grandfathers couldn't handle things if they got a little messy?"

"I'm saying that the more this fighting goes on, the fewer people and the fewer markets there will be to control. You may end up the king of an empty castle."

Cassius shook his head. "No. Greed brings them back. It always does."

"True as that may be..." Jora sighed again. "Finally taking control of the majority of the Wheel is a good start. But whatever lies behind those auction doors isn't going to stay there forever. Just a friendly word of warning."

Cassius nodded. "Thanks." He turned to leave. "If you ever do hear what's going on in there..."

"You'll be the first to know. After me."

"I would expect nothing less."

He donned his Alvaro Disguise and departed as though nothing had ever happened. Even if there were spies around, cataloging who he was and who he pretended to be, he might as well be consistent. And being anonymous had its advantages, too.

He really didn't want to go back to the ruins and crawl before Rifun to ask for information. He didn't want to have to explain why he needed this information. There was every chance that he should have already known this information but didn't because he'd missing a meeting or stormed out of one before it was finished or in some other way made himself scarce when such information was being imparted to the others. He didn't like having to be a team player, but having a team had its advantages.

After a short time simply wandering through the various marketplaces—passing not a few times through the Auctionhouse Hub just to see if there might be any kind of non-violent opening to exploit—Cassius finally made up his mind to return to the ruins. He didn't know what excuse he would use, but he needed that information before going in there and killing everything in sight again.

In spite of his bad mood, Cassius made sure to avoid Murdi and Lordo. He didn't need them asking questions about why he was apparently disregarding everything he'd said to them just a few hours ago. Not that he had any obligation to answer them or explain how or why plans may have changed, but he didn't want to lose that avenue.

He found Rifun in his chambers, sitting at a table, looking over some paperwork. A dozen different ways to kill him flashed through Cassius' mind, but he forced himself to politely knock on the door.

"Yes?" Rifun wondered, not looking up.

"I have a question," Cassius said loudly, perhaps trying to spook the man a little.

If he was surprised that it was Cassius being polite and knocking, rather than Julianna, he gave no indication of it, instead saying, "I may have an answer."

Cassius huffed a sigh. "Who did you give the Auctions to?"

Now Rifun looked up, but not at Cassius. He paused only briefly before answering, "Why do you ask?"

"Because I just had a very interesting encounter there, trying to get in, and I want to know who to report to management."

Rifun barked a laugh. "Ha! How interestingly phrased."

"Well?" Cassius pressed, stepping into the room.

Now the man looked at him. "I don't know. It doesn't matter who I promised it to, because every single one of them has backed out. Sudden disinterest, internal affairs taking precedence, other matters undisclosed. I couldn't give away the Auctions if I tried. And I am trying." He leaned back in his seat and folded his arms. "What have you found out?"

"You have to be invited just to get an invitation, and I was denied both as myself and in a Disguise—" Not true, but he didn't need to know that. "—and none of my sources have been able to get inside, or get a mole of their own inside."

Rifun's expression turned both serious and impressed. "I'm impressed by their security. I'm guessing no one quite knows how to get an invitation either, right?"

"That's right. The only common theme of those who have been observed around the Auctions is that they're rich, snobbish, self-entitled assholes."

"That doesn't narrow it down much, unfortunately, as there are plenty of common folk who act the same way."

Couldn't deny that one. "Who do you think it is, then? There can't be nothing going on in the Auctions."

Rifun sat up. "Oh, I agree. The question is, who? On the one hand, the Tacagans have the power, the pull, and the technology to ensure exclusivity. But they shouldn't be able to penetrate a Disguise. On the other hand, the Akarin can penetrate a Disguise, but Isthim and the others scrambled their memories, so they shouldn't have been able to mobilize like this, or they shouldn't have been able to keep hold of it if they held it beforehand. Given that this occurred after the Time Trial, I would say that the Akarin are an unlikely culprit."

"The sudden disinterest may come from those offended by the use of a Time Trial," Julianna said suddenly.

Both men turned to see her standing in the doorway.

"A few, maybe," Rifun said, "but all of them? Even those who had no qualms about it?"

She frowned but said nothing.

"So," Cassius continued, looking again at Rifun, "if I go in there and kill everything in sight, I won't be disrupting any of your plans or alliances?" He said the words with some distaste.

"No," Rifun answered, his tone hardly reassuring. "But I would not recommend going in there and killing everything in sight."

"Why not?"

"Because we're going to do it as a unified force. An army, not a ballistic mercenary." He met Cassius' gaze. "We move on the rest of the Wheel we've already claimed as our own. The marketplaces, the Judgment Wing...with the Borelians as the Grandfathers, that alone should deter most threats, even without the Akari. Once we've secured our own territory, then we take the rest of the field."

"That shouldn't take long," Julianna commented.

" 'Should' is a wonderful word," Rifun sighed. "It holds so much potential."

"Why should it take long?" Cassius asked. "We already hold it. It's ours. We post some Borelian guards, let the Turitians or whoever operate the marketplaces...what's the hangup?"

"I didn't say there was a hangup. I am simply trying to avoid becoming overly optimistic."

Julianna sighed. "Rifun, you could win a race, be handed a medal and a trophy, and you still wouldn't be optimistic about your chances. For once, I agree with Cassius. We've got two-thirds of the Wheel, if not more. The Auctions shouldn't pose much of a threat, regardless of who it is holed up behind those doors."

For once, the man looked surprised. Actually, Cassius was pretty surprised, too, that Julianna would agree with him. He tried to play it off as some kind of planned collaboration, or at the very least, not surprised.

"One step at a time," Rifun said evasively. "We take what we have first."

"Agreed," Julianna said delightfully, grinning grotesquely. "I expect I will enter the cave first thing in the morning. I'll try to make it quick, but no matter what, I'll be gone for a bit. While I'm going after our prize, you will be securing the Wheel."

"We'll take our two-thirds, secure it with the Borelians. Once everything is instituted as planned, Isthim will lead the charge against the Auctions and whoever is hiding in there, assuming they haven't come out on their own, as I suspect they might."

"Do I get a part in this plan?" Cassius asked.

"You can lead with Isthim. I'm sure she'll be happy to let you run free through the battlefield."

His tone and intentions were impossible to determine, but Cassius wasn't going to ask for clarification. Sometimes ambiguity worked out much better.

"And what about the rest?" Julianna wondered. "Will we move our operations to the Wheel, or shall we stay here in these infernal, dank caves?"

"I rather enjoy the Caves of Meroian," Rifun told her. "And until we hold the whole Wheel, I've no intentions of giving up this base, nor disclosing its location. If something were to go wrong, we'll need a place to retreat. Even if we did take the Wheel in its entirety, I still wouldn't want to give this up for similar reasons."

She huffed and folded her arms. "I can't deny your logic—"

"When you return from the Time Trap, there will be a place prepared for you that is delightful and lovely and not in a cave."

This appeared to satisfy her, for she did not say more about it.

Now Rifun turned to Cassius. "If you're looking for something to do, get with Isthim and see what she has for prepared forces. Tell her what's going on with the Auctions, and come up with a plan for how to deal with it. I will be focusing on the logistics side of things and ensuring everyone is happy and gets what they want from this."

"I don't envy you," Julianna quipped.

Cassius said nothing to that, and he left the room, if only because he had everything he needed. He had confirmation that Rifun had no hand in what was going on in the Auctionhouse. He had permission to kill everything inside the Auctionhouse. And he had just enough ambiguity to do it however he wanted.

He still sought out Isthim and brought her up to speed on things. Her emotional reaction was difficult to judge, but there was a certain element of relief, that something was actually happening. Cassius could relate.

"Securing the Wheel will be a non-issue," she declared. "It's practically done anyway except for a tangible presence. Do we have any information on who may be holed up inside the Auctions? Even a guess?"

"The Tacagans have the influence and the technology. The Akarin can penetrate a Disguise," Cassius answered.

"They identified you, then."

"Well, no."

"Did you ever consider Disguising yourself as someone who can get into the Auctions?"

Cassius felt the blood rush to his face, and he hated it. "Well, no."

"No, of course not," Isthim sighed. "What does an elephant know of stealth?"

"I'll go try it," he growled.

Isthim may have said something to his back, but he deliberately ignored her. Of course that would have been a smart thing to do. It may have even saved him the trouble of having to crawl back to Rifun to ask if he knew anything. He could have gotten the information, killed everyone inside, and then they could have taken the entire Wheel in one fell swoop.

Well, they could still probably do that, if it was easy enough for him to kill everyone. Maybe he would do that without permission. Just present the opposition's head on a platter to the others, watch them turn pale, take some stuttering gratitude, and watch them take the Wheel.

Or maybe not. Yes, he could kill everyone and get the thrill, but why should he do all the dirty work? Why not force them to get their hands dirty a little? Force the grunts to fight and use their abilities. Force Rifun to give the order to attack.

Maybe he would let them live. At least for now.

So it was that an hour later, he was back in the Wheel, attempting to discreetly observe the comings and goings from the Auctions, waiting for any compatible species that he could use as a Disguise. The first problem was that there wasn't a steady flow of traffic. It was all or nothing, presumably as auctions started and ended. The second problem was that there was a limited number of species who were compatible with humans, enough to pull off a Disguise for a decent length of time, anyway. He could do just about anything for a few seconds, but to walk around and interact would require crafting DNA and Matter at a more sophisticated level.

Finally he found one. It was a Qalik, humanoid, with mottled greenish skin, large eyes, and hair that was more like vines. It wasn't the best species for human compatibility, but it would work for a few hours.

He trailed the Qalik through the Wheel. The Qalik headed for the portal room, returned its translator, then started down one of the rows of portals, heading for home. Once a safe distance from the front of the room, Cassius jumped him, Banding and beating him up before he knew what was happening. Cassius stripped him of his clothes and all belongings before pushing him through a random portal and forcing it closed.

From there, Cassius retreated to Jora's tent, then slipped through his illegal portable portal into his black market room in order to craft the Disguise. The Ferulian watched, greatly impressed, but refused when Cassius offered to teach him Disguise and more through the Akari.

"I have a perfectly happy life how I am," Jora told him. "It's bad enough dealing with Time politics. Now you want me to add more? Please."

Once the skin had been perfected, Cassius put on the clothes and examined the belongings. Most held no significance to him, but he did manage to find what he believed to be an ID of some form. He couldn't read it, but it might help in some way, even if it was only valid at the local fitness center.

Then it was back to the Auctions. He didn't have to wait long before another group of invited guests started into the hub. He joined the group and noticed something a bit peculiar. Being out of practice with simple Time abilities, it took him a second to identify what it was. There was a Suppression field around the group. Time abilities were utterly useless. More than that, it was an extremely sophisticated Suppression field that blocked those on the outside from using abilities against them, which meant a Timekeeper couldn't stand across the room and use his abilities inside the group, perhaps to steal an invitation.

Few species in the universe had technology this sophisticated. The fact that the technology was in use was notable in itself.

He was not barred from entry into the hub, but as they approached the door to the particular auction they were invited to, the group slowed and began to reassemble itself, slowly forming a line. Looking ahead, Cassius saw that a secretary was taking DNA samples while a second secretary was verifying invitations.

His first thought was to kill everything and force his way in.

His second thought was to just leave and come at it from a different angle later.

His third thought was to see what the local gossip was first.

"I don't see why we have to keep doing this," he whined, trying to sound as snobbish as possible. "Don't they have eyes? Can't they see who we are?"

One person grumbled something of an agreement, while another replied, "You know as well as we do that trust is an earned commodity."

"I am no one's slave for meager wages. Isn't money enough?"

"Not yet," someone else said.

The line moved ever closer to the checkpoint. Cassius pressed harder. "When will it be enough? When will we be able to stop sneaking around like paranoid fools?"

"With luck, soon."

"Well, I heard a rumor that the Cult of the Akari is supposed to take over two-thirds of the Wheel. What then? They'll undoubtedly come after us."

"The Tacagans can handle them. We've a stronghold here to do our business for the time being."

"How can they 'handle them' better now compared to the first time, when they were slaughtered in an auction? Or the second time, when they were butchered in their own government building?"

"Well, they—"

"Next!" A voice barked.

Before anyone could say more, it was his turn to be verified. He had no invitation to give, and his DNA was mismatched. Before the secretary could sound an alarm, Cassius had drawn a knife and cut its throat, then shed his Disguise.

Instant pandemonium erupted within the group, but Cassius ignored it—painfully—and walked away, frustrated. He was frustrated that he hadn't gotten more information, but he was also frustrated that all the effort he'd put into getting to Tacaga and murdering their leadership seemed to have gone to waste. What was the point of massacring hundreds of people if they could be replaced in less than twenty-four hours? Hadn't his skill and stealth bought them any advantage? Did everything really have to be about stealth politics?

Briefly he considered cornering the person he'd been speaking to, interrogating them and demanding more information. But when he looked around, that person had vanished. He or she probably hadn't gone far, but with the mood he was in, he'd probably kill them before getting any good intelligence.

He did not return to Jora's tent, nor did he head for the ruins. Instead, he made for Earth. It had been some time since he'd visited his home planet, and it was still chaotic enough in the middle of the 1960's that it afforded him a few excuses to kill and relieve some stress. True, he might not affect the outcome of any war here, but it helped to calm him down some, enough to make his way back to the ruins without killing anyone there.

Even then, his first stop was not the actual ruins, but the ledge that overlooked them, where he'd asked his team to attempt to Disguise the city so that it looked like the dusty ruins it used to be.

He managed to do it, Disguise the city. It even held for a few minutes. He just couldn't figure out how to hand it off or stabilize it so it could stand on its own without needing him holding it in place every hour of every day. Well, maybe he could figure it out later.

He found Rifun and Isthim in the middle of a discussion in the street near the officers building.

"It's the Tacagans," Cassius said, butting in.

Rifun and Isthim looked at him.

"The Auctions?" Cassius reminded them. "Something we just discussed an hour or so ago?"

"It's been nine hours," Rifun stated. "Judging by your bloody attire, things didn't go well and you killed everything inside."

Cassius glanced at his clothes. Then, "No. You would have been proud of my restraint. I waited until I was back on Earth before killing things. Do you want my report or not?"

They motioned for him to continue, and he did so, explaining what he'd done and what he'd found.

"Well, that puts my mind at ease," Rifun said when he was finished. "Means the Akarin are well out of the way for the time being, and I don't expect the Tacagans to give us much trouble. You can't fight what you deny exists."

"We can proceed as planned," Isthim agreed. She gave Cassius a hard regard. "Good work."

It sounded halting, scripted, and forced, but it almost resembled a compliment, and that was big coming from her.

"Excellent," Rifun continued. "Then in the morning, after Julianna leaves, I will go ahead to our allies and inform them of the situation. First come, first serve on the spoils. Isthim, you will prepare your people for the more immediate security needs. As for the general foot soldiers, I don't expect they will have to fight, but just their presence will make a point. Once we have things secured, then we can bring out the Book of Commands and start making changes."

"And if we do meet resistance?" Isthim inquired.

He raised a brow. "Are we going to turn around and go home just because they ask us to? Ignore them once; I imagine there will be some frustration, and grumbling is normal. Dogs can bark all day, but they make no difference until they actually bite. If anyone gives you trouble after that, assert power as the Grandfathers, take them to the Judgment Wing, and we'll sort them out later. Once we get the Book of Commands, we'll see what it has to say regarding laws and punishment." He looked at Cassius. "If you want, we'll even let you dole it out."

Cassius shifted his stance. "You're allowing this?"

"If punishment be fair and just for laws broken, then who am I to stand in the way?" Rifun indicated his scarred arms. "I was punished for simply existing. Existence has no law. We have laws."

Once more, ambiguity worked in Cassius' favor, and he didn't question it.

With everyone having an assignment, they were able to walk away confidently. Finally, there seemed to be a plan and a realistic method of execution. No more wishing and hoping and mildly dreaming about how they wanted things to be. Things were actually happening.

And at the end of the day, it was Cassius and Isthim who made them happen. Because they got things done. They were able and willing to do the things that others didn't want to do, whether it was killing the opposition or sharing pertinent information such as the location of the Book of Abilities. That right there could have spared them a year or more of tedious tail-chasing.

Cassius turned around and went after Isthim, catching up to her in the officers building.

"We made this happen you know," he began. "Me and you. Once information was shared freely."

"Yes, that does tend to help things," Isthim agreed flatly.

"Trust is key to any operation that wants to run smoothly."

"And suddenly you're preaching trust?" She stopped and looked at him. "I've no time or patience for games. What do you want?"

"Why don't we take this back to how it started? Me and you. We know the location of the Book of Abilities. Once the Wheel is secure, your people will have control of security. You can go in after Julianna, get rid of her, take the journal. I'll dispatch Rifun and his tedious politics. Who cares about the Turitians or the Korin or whoever else? Me and you, as it should have been."

Her expression was severe, if cold. "Your offer would be intriguing, if you had any semblance of stability or sanity. But you remain loud, unpredictable, disloyal, and untrustworthy. You do well as the bloody soldier we need to oversee the prison and the asylum of the Judgment Wing, but I would not leave so much power to you."

She turned as if to walk away, but Cassius went on, "So you would rather go along with Julianna and her humanitarian efforts? Or Rifun and whatever the hell he's thinking? We're doers, you and I."

"You are a doer. Rifun is a thinker. I am the balance between you. It is how things got done. Not merely by action, but by strategy. This is the plan we have, and this is the plan we will execute."

And she walked away.

Cassius stared after her, but his thoughts were interrupted as he suddenly hit the floor, all strength and control draining from his body. Then it returned, but only as a searing tidal wave of agony. He opened his mouth, but only a pathetic, strangled sort of sound could be heard. Then the pain receded, but he still had no control over his body.

He heard footsteps, and someone knelt beside him.

"It's an awkward thing." It was Rifun. "To stumble upon a conversation that seems to be an attempt at plotting my demise. Of course, logic would dictate that I dispose of you here and now. Rid myself of the threat, and the Cult of your stupidity and bloodlust. And I could do it, just as I could have done it years ago when I first pulled this trick on you."

Cassius contorted involuntarily as another wave of agony ripped through him.

"But I have need of you still. At least for a little while. For one, I want to know why you're still hanging around a certain Psiaco space pirate and his crew. Two, I'm a little curious what your special team is up to lately. And three, your excursion into the Auctions earlier has inspired me with a new idea."

Without losing his grip on whatever paralysis he had on Cassius, Rifun also managed to use Gravity to move paralyzed Cassius to his chambers and close the door so they wouldn't be disturbed. There he erected a Sound barrier. Once Cassius was safely arranged on his bed, Rifun continued.

"Let's talk about that first order of business then, about you and Captain Titik. Granted, it started out as only a rumor, seeing how you supposedly went your separate ways after the debacle with the crown of Srori, but then Isthim gave me some very interesting information about one of his crew being part of your secret little team."

He moved the paralysis, keeping Cassius down but allowing him to breathe and speak fully. Without this deprivation causing him to panic, Cassius was able to trace the paralysis. Before he could break it, Rifun put a finger on his cheek, right over the bullet.

"Think carefully about what you're about to do."

Cassius huffed. Then, "If you don't know, Titik is more than an opportunistic pirate. He's a treasure hunter. I went to him to see if he could find the Book of Abilities. As payment, he wanted the crown of Srori."

"This I know; I was there. But I was told that it was a fake and you departed from him. Have you been working for the family Torka?"

Cassius chuckled. "Hardly. They assigned that blame all on their own. I just went with it. Figured that if they turned their sights inward, it wouldn't affect your diplomacy."

"Thanks for the consideration." His tone was sarcastic. "You got the crown, then."

"That's right, and I turned it over to Titik."

"Have you informed him lately that his searching will be in vain?"

"No. Pilory and I had a bit of a disagreement. I've not seen her, nor sent any messages to her or through her, nor have I spoken to Titik. He said he would keep an eye out for it, but he's wary of the Akarin."

Rifun frowned. "What does Titik know of the Akari? What is his level of interest?"

"Minimal, or else I expect he'd be here, or Pilory at least, to learn and teach the others. His only interest is money, treasure, the pleasures of the world. I don't think he would be actively looking for the journal, but if he happened across it, he might remember to tell us."

"I see. Now what about this team of yours? What are they up to lately?"

"Nothing. The Korin annoyed me with their incessant talk of balancing. Murdi and Lordo were useful for getting to the Gentleman Killers, up until there were no more Gentleman Killers. Pilory was my door to Titik, but I don't know where that stands now."

"Maybe we'll have to knock on the door and see who answers," Rifun suggested. "Get in touch with him, see if he'll meet with us."

"Wouldn't that affect your diplomatic relations with the Turitians?"

"Eggs and baskets, Cassius, you know how that goes." He shifted position. "Speaking of which. Now let's talk about this brilliant idea I had regarding your proficiency with Disguises."

23 | Ataovy sy Takatrao

West Virginia, 1965

Do and Understand

Living in dark caves could cause someone to appreciate the little things in life, Rifun thought, like a beautiful sunrise. Not just a bit of light coming in through a crevasse in the ceiling, but a true sunrise, the glowing orange ball rising over the tops of trees and mountains. He leaned forward on one knee, his foot propped up on a boulder.

He'd gone to the cave early by himself for just such an occasion. It wasn't home, but he was grateful for an Earth sunrise all the same. Funny how one's perspective could change. But then, given what he'd been through, was he really all that surprised?

"Do you see the sunrise as we do?"

He turned to see Julianna approaching. She stood beside him as the sun lifted itself over the tops of the trees.

"The color becomes more gray toward the horizon," he admitted, "and the sky is rather muted. But it is no less beautiful simply because I have to use my imagination."

"The undiscovered poet." She grinned.

"I doubt that. I write plays, not prose or poetry."

"Too bad." She folded her arms. "Strange to consider that I shall miss dozens or even hundreds of these, yet I will perceive it only as a few minutes at most."

Rifun straightened from his position. "I know more than a few people who would wish for such an opportunity, to skip parts of their lives. Jump ahead a day, a month, a year. Always the next thing. That will make it better. If only we could skip to the weekend. Or get through the holidays. Or some other event. Then everything will be all right. But then they're only faced with new troubles of a new day."

Julianna raised a brow. "Are you sure you're not a poet in secret?"

"I think the word you're looking for is philosopher. Time makes philosophers of all of us in the end, I think."

"Contemplating death already?"

"Contemplating life."

"Reincarnation, then? I didn't think that was part of your beliefs."

"Lost souls may become a moth or a butterfly, but the rest join the ancestor spirits and eventually melt into the great power of creation known as the razana."

"I see. And what does this have to do with being a philosopher?"

"As a person ages, his connection to the spirits grows. It is why elders are so wise and able to see and do things that ordinary men cannot. I have aged as any man does, yet retain the energy of youth to harness the razana, not merely report it."

"And your spirits teach you the secrets of Building."

"The Author uses them to teach me these things, yes."

He couldn't tell how sincere her interest was, but she was polite at least. "I see. Then I expect great things from you when I return."

"I can only try," he told her.

They went to the mouth of the cave, where all the splendor of the sunrise could not well penetrate the boulder and logs blocking most of the entrance. The only light came from the twisting tangle of Bands that comprised the Time Trap and Julianna's small flashlight. Looking at her, Rifun thought she seemed a bit uncertain.

"You expect Cassius to come after you," he stated.

"The thought had crossed my mind," she admitted. "I'm having flashbacks of the last time I was in this cave."

"A few days ago?" He meant it as a joke, but her expression said she was not amused. "You won't be gone that long. In and out. A few minutes for you, a few months for the rest of us, maybe a year. In that time, we'll be so busy with running the Wheel—including Cassius—that he won't have time to give you a second thought."

She sighed. "I know you mean well, but you'll forgive me for not being the most heartened at your words."

"Our day is pretty full today, and then I have him on some other business for a while," Rifun went on. "If you want, since Isthim is going to be taking care of the force aspect of things, I'll stay here for a day or two."

Julianna waved a hand. "Oh... Please, Rifun, I'm not a child hiding from monsters under my bed."

"You're right. You're hiding from a very real threat."

Another wave. "Pah! Enough of this. I will be doing this myself, thank you." She gave him a look. "But I thank you for the concern and the thought." She looked at the cave and squared her shoulders. "Well then. No time like the present to get started, and I do not want to waste time seeing how it will suddenly become a very precious commodity."

"Be swift," Rifun said, helping her over the logs. "Be safe. More time will be wasted in foolish haste that results in injury or death than simple caution."

She made a noise as she hit the ground on the other side. "I'm telling you, Rifun, I think there's a bit of a poet in you."

"Maybe I'll practice and write something for you while you're gone."

"I would like that." She let out another breath. "Very well. Wish me luck. Or sense. Whichever I need more of."

Both, Rifun thought, but he did not say this out loud. He watched her walk toward the Time Trap and the twisting Bands, curious whether he would actually see her when the leviathan got a hold of her and took her into a new time differential. He did not see this moment, for the brightly-colored Bands swallowed her before he could see it, and there was nothing but cave darkness after that.

He watched a few minutes more before turning away. That was it. Her mission was underway. He looked around the clearing. Cassius did not jump out of the bushes and nothing appeared out of the ordinary. If anyone was going to try anything, they would probably wait a few weeks, once the idea of her mission was well on the back burner and forgotten. He couldn't wait around that long, so he would just have to trust that things went as planned.

He made his way through the trees and down the hillside, emerging back in the clearing where the old farmstead still stood, abandoned long ago. Having learned his lesson the last time, he did not approach and disturb the lingering spirits. He paid them greeting, then opened a series of portals to return to the ruins.

The ruins were all up in a frenzy of activity as Isthim, Misik, and several well-trained students worked to round everyone up and get them ready for the formal invasion of the Wheel. Compared to the maneuvers he'd had to perform while in the army, it was a little awkward, but maybe that was because these grunts were all different species compared to uniform human soldiers. Given that their commanders were Borelian officers, even an Admiral, it was almost impressive to watch. Once again, these were many species having to work together rather than something homogeneous, but Isthim made it work. Her specialty was combat, but she appeared to have trained them to walk in parades, too, which was essentially what they would be doing.

He finally caught up to Isthim in the street, heading for a repaired stairwell leading to the top of the wall, as if going to survey her charges from above.

"Julianna is out," he reported. "Waiting on your orders."

She did not say anything as they jogged up the steps and started walking along the wall, the parapets in various stages of repair. Finally they reached a spot that allowed them to look out over the courtyard where the grunts had assembled.

When in the streets going about everyday life, it was easy to think that they were little better than small boys playing with toy guns and wooden swords. Some days, that was how Rifun felt about it as they fumbled with half-learned abilities and patchwork commands and philosophies. But when viewed from above, all of Isthim's hard work to bring them together as something of a functioning army appeared to have paid off.

"They're not ready," she said in a low voice, looking over them. "When push comes to shove, a man falls back on his reflexes and what he knows well. Too few know the Akari well. If things turn ugly, they will default to their Time training, assuming they have any. And a well-trained Time Agent will overpower a poorly-trained Akari-bearer."

"Between your people and Cassius, I don't think things will get too ugly."

"It takes only a moment of stupid courage to spark true resistance. If one falls, others will get the idea to attack."

"Then punishment ought to be swift and severe. Pink Borelians can be used to flank the army as it moves, making people compliant. Ith can make them feel good, lose their sense of danger. Nit can make them too tired to fight well."

Isthim gave him a look and dipped her head once. "We think much alike. Many of these measures are already in place. But nothing is foolproof."

"That's where faith comes in, I suppose. If the Author doesn't like what we're doing, she is well within her power to stop us, don't you think?"

She nodded once. "So it is."

"When the time comes, I'll be right behind you."

He turned and walked back along the wall. Behind him, Isthim started in on some speech or another. It didn't sound so much like an inspiring rally to war as more of a giving of instructions now that she had them all assembled and was at a better vantage to address them.

He returned to his chambers and picked up his schedule of meetings. He was supposed to have met with a dozen different species over the next few weeks to discuss this and that. Well, meetings could be dull and unproductive. Now was the time to challenge them, to force them to make good on their word to support the Cult.

Actually, he thought he was being pretty generous, not calling them out until they were doing their victory parade through the Wheel. But then, if they didn't show their support during the parade, when would they? Such wishy-washy allies would have to be dealt with.

It was also a good time to watch these parading allies and try to discern who was most likely to commit treachery. Who was proud to be an ally, and who was simply in it for the benefits? Who would drop out, run away, sell them out when the going got tough or a counteroffer became more profitable?

Rifun frowned. They were promising the ability to be loyal to one's people, rather than a business. Was punishing the opposition going against that principle? He thought about it a moment and decided it wasn't. Being loyal to one's people meant leaving a common business alone. A florist had no say or stake in a war. A restauranteur cared not whom he served. So it was that the Cult and the Akari would work for anyone. It was the product, not the power, just as Time should have been the product, not the power. Let the people use it how they would according to their own laws, just another tool in the toolbox or weapon in the arsenal.

This would undoubtedly cause problems on some Unengaged worlds, he thought as he left the officers building once more. But ignorance was a disease far more tragic. Rip off the blindfold and let everyone see. Let them see that they were not alone in the universe. Let them see that great wonders existed, both naturally and technologically. Let them see that magic was real, and it was called the Akari. Let them see that there was a Creator out there, and it was the Author.

He returned to the wall as Isthim was wrapping up her speech, effectively giving the order to move out. He stopped her briefly.

"You lead the charge," he told her. "I'll follow up with the politicians."

"Between the two," she said, "I like my job better." She paused and gave him a look. "I'll see you later when this is all over. Come visit me."

He raised a brow. "Now we're getting into invitations? What happened to not having an emotional attachment to your partners?"

"Maybe you are rubbing off on me."

"Personally, I'd rather be rubbing on you."

"Later."

And she moved past him.

While Rifun's first and foremost thought was pretty well spoken for, his second thought was to look around for Cassius. He didn't see him, but that didn't mean much, considering the crowd. If Cassius had seen their little exchange, and Rifun's reaction to it, there was no telling what he would do. The best Rifun might hope for was a little resistance that required violence that somehow got Cassius killed.

But if it were that easy, he wouldn't have been needed, nor would he have to learn Building just to try and eek out an advantage over the dark spirit.

He watched the army move out and found his thoughts flooded with memories of Madagascar. All the formations and drills they'd done in the army. Their sad retreat from Antsrinana Bay. The British taking over operations. The French reclaiming land lost to the rebels. All of it done by blood and celebrated in formation, at least to start.

He closed his eyes and leaned against the parapet, pinching the bridge of his nose, as if it might help. They would go in, conquer, hope it would be peaceful. Any who resisted would be thrown in prison to be dealt with later.

Weeks in prison.

Convicted according to the laws of the enemy.

Ten years of torture.

This wasn't like that, he told himself, straightening, grimacing against both real and phantom pains in his body. The Malagasy had been perfectly capable of self rule. They'd done it for centuries before the Europeans came. The Time industry was chaos and factions and petty crime lords. The Tacagans were self-righteous imperialists who sought to lord themselves over the perceived lesser species of the universe.

This wasn't like that. They were just trying to smooth things out. One product, one rule. No more Hands, fallible politicians swayed by this or that. Only the Author. No more Time to be bought and sold, craved and addicted and greedy. Only the Akari. Open and available to all.

This wasn't like that.

Suddenly self-conscious, Rifun went back to his chambers to change into a long-sleeve shirt. It didn't take any time out of his day, really, since the army was still in the process of leaving. How Isthim had planned on moving an entire army from the city to the Wheel while still maintaining the secrecy of the caves and the anonymity of the Elif, he did not know, but few details escaped her notice.

It was still another fifteen minutes before he left, walking through the city which had become ruins again, dark and devoid of most life, save for the camp outside the walls and a small contingency force to protect them, in the event that things turned catastrophic.

He made it to the tunnels unmolested, and from there began his journey to each of their allies. The Turitians needed only a quick memo, and Commander Dira was more than happy to jump on the opportunity to parade their alliance and assert Turitian — more specifically, royal family Jalar — control. Whatever was going on between the Jalar and Torka families — exacerbated in no small way thanks to Cassius — this show of force was just what they were looking for.

The Korin were also fairly easy to motivate. If they had no current enemies, they could only spend their war dynasty years sharpening their horns on each other. Apparently, this alliance and takeover was little more than alleviating boredom and maybe a few extra benefits.

The Elif maintained a polite distance, if only to avoid giving away their close quarters arrangements.

The Grunjor were perhaps the most difficult to rouse. It was a wonder Rifun had secured them at all, assuming "secure" was the right word to use. They were a race of sentient rock beings, literally built from a special kind of rock on their world. At some point in the process, known only to them, the rocks became a sentient being, at which point it was given a name and an assignment. They were generally slow to move and even slower to act. Being rock, they were damn near indestructible. They were also incredibly single-minded, having few thoughts outside of their life's assignment, ninety-nine percent of which involved straight physical labor. They barely understood even the concept of war, didn't understand why the little, soft, fleshy beings fought over this and that. Even their entry into Time was unprecedented, seeing how the Grunjor, being rock, could live for thousands of years. Their motivations for doing anything, and especially anything outside their own world, their own norm, were entirely a mystery.

Somehow, Rifun was able to get two Grunjor to join the rest of the Cult allies in the Wheel. Having them would also be a minor show of force, and they could act as shields, he supposed.

There were some allies who vehemently protested being forced into the spotlight, especially on such short notice. Some claimed that they had to clear it with other leaders or supervisors. Others said something about other political ties and tensions and whatnot. The excuses were seemingly endless. A few chastised him for making such a bold move without getting their permission, which was quite laughable.

In the end, he managed to gather representatives from a dozen different worlds who were willing to be seen with the Cult in public on short notice. He made mental notes of where the rest of their so-called allies fell, silently determining whether the excuses given were understandable or cowardly.

Rifun and these allied leaders entered the portal room of the Wheel only moments after the last of the army left the portal room for one of the lower marketplaces. It seemed to be a logical enough progression, and the allied group followed. He didn't know the exact parade route Isthim had planned, but he held his head up high and pretended like he did. Pretended like this was all part of the plan that all the leaders knew about. He and the allies caught up to the army, keeping a good ten paces between them.

By this time, most of the resistance, if there had been any, had already been dealt with and quelled. Perhaps it had been by force, or perhaps Isthim had sent some of her skilled people along to drug the crowd into quiet compliance. Whatever the case, walking through the lower marketplaces truly was like walking along a parade route. People stood behind or beside the booths, watching the people pass by. A few seemed annoyed, a few seemed hopeful, but judging by the passive acceptance of the majority of the population, Rifun guessed that the Borelians had indeed drugged them. He could only hope that they had merely quieted their sense of danger, resistance, and aggression, and hadn't made it so they wouldn't even remember what was happening. This was a grand event, a change in leadership and a turning point for the Wheel of Time. What use was that if everyone forgot about it?

The parade snaked its way through the lower marketplaces, then wound its way into the intermediate marketplaces. It even wove into and out of the Auctionhouse hub.

Here the crowd was a little more on edge, and a line of Grandfathers stood between the Auctionhouse guards and the Cult parade. How effective the standoff was, or the methods for keeping it nonviolent, were unknown, and Rifun did not ask as he passed by. He could tell the other allied leaders were a little uneasy, passing by the Borelians, but then they were out of the Auctions and everything went back to normal.

Truthfully, Rifun was a bit disoriented about the parade. Before, he'd either been convict or soldier. He'd been part of the spectacle, making a show of force or being an example to others who might try what he had. Simply being the leader, he didn't know what to do. There was no formation to keep, nor did he bow to the will of others. And he was certainly no pageant queen to smile and wave to adoring fans. This time, he was the leader. Problem was, as a soldier, he'd never been close enough to the leaders to see what they had done during parades. Probably a greater show of force. But what did politicians do?

Smile and wave. He sighed inwardly. He didn't want to smile and wave. He was here to observe, take notes, not get killed, and figure out what to do next.

Fine, great, they had the Wheel. Now what?

Well, next they took the Book of Commands and started rewriting the Laws of Time.

Because that was going to be simple.

The meandering parade finally made its way into the Seat of the Hands. The Cult soldiers amassed in the open arena while Isthim, Cassius, Misik, and a few others looked down upon them from the place where the Hands normally dictated their will. As the last of the parade ended, the soldiers packing in ever tighter, Rifun and the allied diplomats joined the other leaders. Once this was done, the common population of the Wheel was permitted in around the fringes of the open space and spilling outside the Seat proper. The Grandfathers got in defensive positions, but Rifun found this was probably unnecessary.

"Do you still think my decisions to be mistakes?" Isthim questioned lightly as Rifun took his place beside her and looked out over the crowd. Cassius stood on her other side.

"That remains to be seen in the long-term," Rifun answered. He looked at her. "But in the short-term, it appears as though my indecision was the greater error."

"That's an odd way of apologizing to and thanking me."

"We're in the middle of consequences right now. Judgment of them will have to be made after the fact."

"You just can't give it up, can you? Can't admit that my plan was better."

He grinned and looked out at the crowd again. "What can I say? In the world I come from, men and women are different entities."

"Sometimes seeing things differently is how things get done."

"Seeing things differently is how people get shot. Or exiled."

"Yet here we are."

Indeed, Rifun thought.

It was Isthim who led the charge, using Gravity to step up and address those gathered. She praised the soldiers, the Grandfathers, Rifun and Cassius and Julianna, the Akari, the Author, everyone just short of the Academy. All the same, it wasn't the best speech Rifun had ever heard. She was good at the pep talks, and had there been an actual battle, it might have been the most magnificent speech in the history of the universe. But this wasn't a pep talk, nor was it a speech at the conclusion of a war or battle. This was more of a recitation of events, how the Cult of the Akari had grown from a few people in a living room to the most powerful, unstoppable force in the universe, conquering the immovable object that was the Time industry.

Perhaps another reason for Rifun's lack of enthusiasm came from having to listen to the speech through the digital voice assist which made her sound like she spoke through fan blades. It didn't quite capture the power or nuance necessary for a truly rousing speech. This wasn't to say that the actual composition was bad or that she didn't elicit cheers when appropriate. Maybe Rifun was applying too much theater logic. There was an art to the performance and getting the audience to respond as desired. He wasn't really responding.

Once Isthim was done with her speech, Rifun took her place to address those gathered. She was the emotional and psychological speaker. His speech was a little more practical, detailing some of the logistical changes.

The minute details were unimportant for the common man to know, but it was important to know who was going to be running the show. The Turitians had a fairly singular claim to the Scouts, and a majority of the control over exports and outposts. Rarely were Time Capsules permitted to be bought and sold outside of the Wheel, but there were a few exceptions, and the Turitians now oversaw those exceptions.

As for the marketplaces, well, those were a little harder to divide up because too many species wanted too much power over too little pie. Some species had been utterly irate at the thought of sharing and so backed out. A few even turned on the Cult. Rifun made a note of who those were. Others wanted other perks and benefits in exchange for having to share.

Too few of them understood what Rifun and the others were trying to do. The Time industry was not going to be this monolithic power structure at the center of the universe anymore. The people were going to be the power. They were going to power the industry. They were going to come to the Wheel to learn the journals, study the Akari, understand the nature of the universe, manipulate it down to the last atom. They would build civilizations from their very will. Time would become absolutely irrelevant. Rifun expected that in just a few decades, there wouldn't even be marketplaces anymore. There would be study halls and training facilities.

For those who thought that too many species would use the power for ill, he had one simple rebuttal: if war could be boiled down to finite resources, what happened when those resources were no longer finite? What if a man really could turn sand into water in the desert? What if he could turn stones into loaves of bread? When the hungry could be fed, not by conquering and stealing, not by gross negligence, but by simply creating food, how many problems would that solve? When entire worlds could be terraformed, shaped into whatever people needed, what greatness could be achieved?

When everyone had the power of Creation, what could be achieved?

There would be a learning process and many growing pains, yes. He was not so terribly naive as to think that years or generations of paranoia or selfishness could be undone at the snap of a finger, but a caterpillar could not become a butterfly without sacrificing its former self.

But as he'd told Isthim, they were in the middle of one set of consequences at the moment. Every decision they made from here on would carry its own consequences, big and small. They had to think, plan, prepare, and execute. What if there was no resistance? What if there was heavy resistance? What if the Akarin crumbled? What if they somehow overcame the effects of Isthim's ith teams? What if something completely wild and unpredictable happened?

The Cult crowd was remarkably attentive. And why shouldn't they be? They were learning astounding things, things they'd long believed mythical, from the Hands, or unattainable, by the Akarin. And now they were standing on the rubble of an industry everyone in the entire universe agreed was corrupt. They should feel proud of themselves, Rifun thought. They were the victors of history.

As for the rest of the crowd, be they common Time Agent, some spy for the Tacagans or the Akarin, their demeanor ranged from little better than a standing vegetable, to somewhat annoyed, like watching someone take the last parking spot that you were definitely going for. Rifun wasn't sure of the specifics, but he expected some of the more vegetative crowd to rouse a bit, as there were far too few Grandfathers to be able to control a crowd this size, and such specific portions, too.

And who knew? Maybe there would be some converts from this little display. The greatest enemy existed only in the mind, where the imagination could conjure up vast horrors that superseded anything physically possible. Once an enemy was revealed, sometimes it turned out that he wasn't the enemy after all.

Maybe some people had expected to be rounded up, imprisoned, tortured, and executed just for the crime of existing. Now that they were here, not imprisoned, fully in tact, and alive, maybe some of those phantasmal demons had dissipated. Maybe they would see what was really going on here. Maybe they would understand and accept that this was what needed to happen. Not another election bandaid, but a brand new system rooted in a stable ideology that existed outside of mortal man's control.

Whatever the case, whether or not they accepted the Cult or the Akari or the Author, at least there was no rioting or violence. There wasn't even a heckler in the crowd that Rifun could see or hear.

He wrapped up his speech and backed down. There was a good deal of cheering, some excited chatter, but no one called for his blood or his head on a platter. He didn't realize just how anxious he was about it until it was over and he could breathe again.

It was Queen Jalar de Aronet who took the stage now. Rifun could see that she was incredibly nervous about stepping out in faith upon the Gravity track, but her movements remained confidently graceful. She introduced herself, made her appropriate turns and gestures with all the beauty of a ballet dancer, and announced the reception that would be taking place in the Food Court just as soon as she was done speaking. Given that her only task had been to announce the reception, that time was considerably short, and it seemed to be something that everyone could get excited about.

The Seat of the Hands cleared out faster than Rifun thought possible. He noted how Cassius went forward and pressed himself into the crowd. Of course the parade would have heightened security, but what about the after party? Rifun was happy to leave general security to the Borelians, and the quiet removal of instigators to Cassius.

"So, this was your official announcement of our alliance," Rifun observed as Aronet came up beside him.

"Asserting ourselves as the ruler of the Scouts and the masters of the outposts," the Turitian queen said. "And a warning to the other royal families."

"Do you expect trouble because of this?"

"Undoubtedly. But we are prepared. You remember our agreement?"

"Of course."

"We will expect you to honor it. Until then."

She made some more turns and gestures, then departed, all without having looked at him even once. On his other side, Rifun thought Isthim seemed a bit displeased with the exchange.

"The Turitians ask for much," she observed mildly.

"No more or less than any other species," Rifun told her. "And Aronet is the queen. She is accustomed to issuing decrees and having her orders followed."

"Do we follow her orders?"

"I have found nothing she has said to be unreasonable. And I expect that, in due time, alliances will no longer matter."

"In due time, perhaps. But in the present, they are still essential."

"In the present," Rifun sighed, "we have a party to attend."

He offered her his arm. She gave him a look and ignored it, instead turning and leaving the Seat. He sighed again and caught up to her.

"You couldn't give me that honor, could you?"

"I am not your subservient," she said.

"No, but you are my partner."

"Is that gesture not one of submission?"

"It means that the two people are a pair, an item, a single article."

"Then why not offer your arm to Cassius?"

"For one, he's not here. And for two, it's only done between a man and a woman. Or it was, last I checked."

"Then you see me as your mate."

Rifun felt his face turn bright red, and he hated it. He Banded to buy himself time to calm down and come up with an answer, but the best he could do was, "It was a gesture of kindness. And don't pretend you didn't know that. You lived on Earth long enough to pick up on plenty of social customs."

"Many of them foolish, even idiotic."

"Yet here we are."

They entered the Food Court together, but Isthim was not on his arm, nor was she by his side for very long before she got distracted by something and made an excuse to leave.

This was not to say that Rifun was just left alone and ignored like the sad bachelor in the corner, no. He was quite the celebrity, in fact, to the point where it became impossible for him to get any food. The common grunts and soldiers wanted to thank him for a variety of things, some of which he had nothing to do with. The allied leaders all wanted to have meetings with him, all of them suddenly of the utmost importance. A few others who were not allies wanted to know what exactly was going on, how to become allied, or at least how to not be a target.

It was simple, he told them. Don't get in the way. Their loyalty ought to be to their own people, their own way of life. The Time industry, or this new industry, the Akari industry, was not the end-all of the universe. It was going to be the business it was originally meant to be, service to the people, not to itself. It would not be an entity unto itself. Its product would be knowledge, and it would be up to the people to decide how to use it.

This seemed to be a rather grand idea, and many more wished to know more about the Akari and the Cult. A few questioned him about the difference between the Cult and the Akarin and what happened to that little spat. Rifun simply observed that the Cult was here and the Akarin was not. Therefore, the Author's favor was clear. If they wanted to know more, they would be happy to teach them.

The whole party felt as though it lasted for days, but maybe that was because Rifun wasn't accustomed to being so important at this type of function. While the foot soldiers were getting drunk and having a grand old time, he was having mini-meetings with the political powers of the universe. How perspective changed!

Only fatigue told Rifun otherwise, although the party didn't appear to show any signs of dying down or letting up any time soon. It truly might carry on for days. But that was for the footmen. Let them party, let them celebrate. Let the Grandfathers haul their stupid, drunk asses to jail for the night. He was going to get some sleep, and then he had meetings to attend, and other things.

He hadn't seen Cassius at all since the Seat, and Rifun concluded that he'd probably gone to the Judgment Wing to start his new job as head guard. The man wasn't much of a wine and cheese person. And Isthim he hadn't seen for a couple hours. Well, it wasn't as though he needed their permission to come or go. Anyone who'd wanted to speak to him had basically done so already, and he managed to snag a few hors d'ouvres before heading out.

The party had spilled out of the Food Court into the surrounding area, but the rest of the Wheel was hauntingly quiet. It wasn't deserted, as some Merchants still had their stands and wares, and a few people wandered from place to place, but it was practically a ghost town compared to normal. Only the wares marketplace seemed to have any semblance of life.

He went to the portal room, briefly debating whether the series of elusive jumps and portals into the dark tunnels was really necessary anymore to return to the ruins. He decided it was, for the time being, at least until they'd rooted out the last of their credible threats, including the Tacagans hiding in the Auctionhouse.

The ruins were not as empty as when he'd left; a respectable number of grunts had returned, either because they were drunk or they were trying to avoid becoming that drunk. Being this far from the party, Rifun barked orders at the bumbling idiots to get back to their beds and keep their antics out of the streets. Anyone passed out drunk on the ground received a rude awakening and similar orders.

By the time he reached the officers building, he was the one with a headache. He crawled into bed, tried to get comfortable, but found little reprieve. The caves were already dim and his fire was low, but he used Light anyway to take it down to total darkness, yet his mind was still active, trying to process the events of the day.

They'd done it. They'd conquered the Time industry and pushed the Akarin out the door. Once the festivities died down — or, indeed, even before — then they would rework the industry so it was no longer its own entity. It was not the destination, but a stop on the journey.

This romantic notion helped him get to sleep, but perhaps it was a little too romantic, for the next thing he knew, his body was responding in an unexpected way. Unsure if he was dreaming or lingering in the fog between consciousness and unconsciousness, he sighed, rolled onto his back, moved his hand down, and opened his eyes.

He startled at a dark figure hovering over him, and immediately went into defense mode, using Imprint to distract his foe with several phantom strikes while he Banded to put distance between himself and it, who he fully expected to be Cassius.

But the figure did not attack, and when his eyes finally adjusted to the light from his dying fire in the great stone hearth, he saw it was only Isthim. He relaxed, but only a little.

"Just a test, right?" he guessed, finding the air to breathe again. "Keeping me on my toes?"

"Something like that," she said.

"What are you doing here? Haven't you heard of knocking?"

"I did knock. You didn't answer. First I had to make sure no one had gotten to you at the reception."

He paused, then shrugged and nodded. "All right, fair enough, I suppose. Everything is well, then, I take it?"

"The reception has devolved into raucous debauchery, but there's no war, if that's what you're asking."

"That's what counts, I suppose, though we might have to have a chat with the grunts and lay down a few ground rules for conduct."

"Of course." She nodded once, her expression saying that some of these rules may have already been implemented and enforced just in the last few hours. Rifun decided to leave that to her. She was the one training the army, not him.

"And was there something else you needed?" he wondered.

"Something I wanted."

As she walked toward him, he noted that she was wearing far less than she had been at the reception. She no longer wore her uniform or any kind of battle gear, though it was a terrible overstatement to call what she wore merely "casual." Her skin was its natural pink, though why she chose this method of seduction over her white toxin was anyone's guess.

"You're in heat again?" Rifun asked, his voice breaking.

"No," she answered simply, her sincerity and truthfulness difficult to judge. "But I want you to do something."

"And what's that?"

"I want you to do as you did in the Arena that one day, where you touched me skin-to-skin and didn't die." She gave him a look that was impossible to interpret. "Skin-to-skin contact is uncommon even among Borelians, and utterly unheard of among slave species. I want to do it again."

"And you want me to do this all over your body while distracted by other things?"

She got close to him. His stomach tightened and he felt sweat snake down the back of his neck.

"Yes," she whispered. "I want you to show me your finesse, your control. Your dominance."

She had to have been lying about being in heat, Rifun thought, but he couldn't just say no to her, could he?

Well, maybe she'd been telling the truth. He wouldn't say it wasn't good; all the universe would know him for a liar. It was very good. It just wasn't a bestial, ultra-sexual, near-death experience that left him catatonic for days followed by a months-long recovery. Part of this, he figured, was a certain fear of death that overpowered even her hypersexual influence over him, as he tried to keep skin-to-skin contact absolutely harmless. He did manage it, though, first using a Time barrier to separate the oil transfer, and then using Matter to temporarily shut down the oil glands in her body.

When deprived of the toxic oils, the Borelian second skin was nearly transparent, if papery, giving Isthim a rather elderly look that also helped to kill off enough desire to keep Rifun lucid. The first skin beneath, very much like human skin, was a sort of sickly gray, or it could have also been one of the colors humans could not perceive. Combined, Isthim looked a bit like a corpse, perhaps a mummy. This, too, killed off some desire. Actually, it killed off a great portion of his desire, leaving him only slightly more aroused than he might be with a high-end escort.

Nevertheless, he got the job done, and he wasn't kissing death, which was a good thing seeing how Julianna wasn't around to save him if something had gone wrong.

Even so, he held Isthim in her defenseless state for a minute longer while she lay beside him. Her horns proved a barrier to cuddling, but Rifun wasn't exactly opposed to a little space between them.

"I've never done this before," she said.

"What? This? We did it a couple years ago. You almost killed me," he reminded her.

"I've never experienced pleasure before."

"What do you mean?"

"A Borelian is immune to her own toxins, and usually those of her parents. I am immune to everything. It is part of what makes a *vodrak* so feared. But those with sexual abilities experience no pleasure for themselves, and males are often sterile."

"I guess I never thought of it that way."

"But something about what you did, stopping the oils, it opened up that experience for me."

"Glad I could oblige."

She sat up and regarded him, his hand still around her wrist, keeping the toxins at bay. "I will remember this, as I wish to experience it again."

Rifun raised a brow. "Are you asking for a second date? Is this proper among your people? Am I not just a slave species?"

"As you may have noticed, I tend to do things as I see fit."

"Hm, maybe humans are rubbing off on you."

"Maybe they are."

She stood now, taking her wrist from his grasp. It was a good three minutes before her second skin had filled out again and she was bright pink once more. But even after she left, he couldn't shake the image of the gray, papery mummy.

Eventually, he got back to sleep, and this time it was a full, deep sleep. He did not remember any dreams, and when he woke, he actually felt quite rested.

When he left the officers building, everything was slowly coming back to life. The morning after was kicking in as those who partied a little too hard were now paying for it. Rifun was sure he would find Isthim barking orders and running drills, if only to punish those who had engaged in such buffoonery.

Actually, he found several drills going on, but they were led by the appointed unit and group leaders, and Isthim was nowhere to be found. Nor was Cassius. Well, Cassius was probably still enjoying his new status as head guard of the prison. But what about Isthim?

The next logical place to check was the Wheel.

Activity was slow but normal in the marketplaces, which was a good sign that people hadn't been completely run off, nor were they in instant, open rebellion. The area around the Food Court looked like a frat house the morning after, but at least it wasn't a battlefield in the evening.

The Seat of the Hands was sparsely populated, the Grandfathers doing a good job of keeping unwanted entities out. They confirmed that Isthim had come by that morning, but could not direct him to her exact location within the Seat. This might have been a problem if there were more people out and about, but for the moment, it was merely a minor inconvenience.

It was actually the Bat who pointed him in the right direction, having spoken to Isthim only moments before Rifun's arrival. He caught up to her as she was on some urgent mission, her expression saying that someone was in for some severe punishment when she got a hold of them, a sharp contrast to her presence in his chambers earlier.

"We have a problem," she said lowly, not breaking stride or looking at him.

"What problem?" he wondered. "Rebellion?"

She thrust something toward him. He fumbled the object, missed a step, and only just kept himself in stride with her. It was a journal. It looked very much like the Book of Philosophy. When he opened it, he recognized Richard's handwriting.

"Is this the Book of Commands?" he asked, feeling a bit foolish.

"What do you notice about it?" Isthim demanded sharply.

They left the Seat proper and crossed the outer courtyard, heading for the exit portal. She stopped and he followed suit, facing her while still looking at the journal. She put up a Sound barrier.

"When you open up the Book of Philosophy, what's the first thing you have to do?" she asked.

"You have to unlock it," Rifun said, his brain putting things together even as he spoke the words.

He stared at her, and she nodded.

"It's a fake. Quite frankly, it's not even a very good one."

"But your teams—"

"Retrieved a journal of such a size and shape and texture and approximate contents. But they were not Akari-bearers. They did not understand Imprint."

Rifun let out a breath. "Can we still use it?"

She raised a brow and made a gesture toward the book. Rifun opened up to a page and read silently, " 'To deal with traitors, shuffle the deck of cards twice, add three—' " He sighed. "All right, fine. What about the one who had it? It was an Ururian, wasn't it? Abbal Duma something? Your team has to have a record of it. Or Andrew. He was the Akarin who presumably gave it to him."

"I've informed Misik of the situation. He said he would handle things with the Ururian. But we have to keep this as quiet as possible."

Rifun dipped his head. "Agreed. We didn't just conquer the Time industry only to be thwarted by a fake copy. What about Andrew?"

"Disappeared, and with the Akarin still in a collective memory fog, they're all pretty useless, too."

"Damn."

"Do we have any other avenues to explore?"

Rifun huffed a sigh and thought a moment. Finally he nodded. "Yes. Yes, we do. In fact, Cassius and I are going to meet with him in the next day or two. We'll hear what he has to say, see if we can't persuade him to help us. Then I think we need to convene an emergency meeting and figure out what to do about this missing journal."

Isthim made a sound. "Cassius was more than eager to memorize the Book of Abilities. His inability to lead or take orders suggests he didn't give the same thought to the Book of Commands."

"Maybe so, and we may have to make some stuff up for a while. Call it a long transition, whatever we have to do. At least until Julianna returns. I get the feeling that she may be our best resource there."

"Indeed."

Rifun nodded. "Let me know if your teams turn up the Ururian."

He left the Seat of the Hands and returned to the Judgment Wing. As expected, he found Cassius in the asylum, the deepest, darkest part of the prison.

"Here to make sure I'm treating them humanely?" the dark-skinned man asked snidely.

"We have a problem. And you're going to help fix it."

The Wheel of Time, 1965

kokumßo

Y ou're shitting me," Cassius said incredulously, grinning for no good reason and kind of wanting to stab something at that moment.

"I am not," Rifun sighed. "Believe me, I wish I were."

"You're fucking telling me that the journal the Borelians retrieved...was a fake."

"That's exactly what I'm telling you."

Cassius shook his head, still grinning. "Well, some hunters they are."

"They're hunters of prey, of people. Not trinkets and treasure," Rifun said. "And they're currently going after the Ururian who gave them the fake."

"Assuming they find him."

"Yes. But you know someone who is a hunter of trinkets and treasure."

"Titik."

"That's right."

"I haven't had much time to contact Pilory, and I haven't seen her. I don't know that she's much into parades and festivities; petty pickpocketing seems beneath Titik and his crew."

"Be polite first, and knock on the door. If no one answers, we're going in by force."

Cassius raised a brow. "Why? Titik isn't the only space pirate or treasure hunter out there."

"No, but you don't choose to associate with just any lowlife who happens across your path," Rifun said. "There's a reason you chose him, and I think it's because he's the best in the business who isn't also a threat to us. We'll start with him."

Cassius sighed. "Fine. Give me a day or two. Surely there are other logistical or diplomatic matters you have to attend to?"

Rifun assented without a fight, but his demeanor said that this wasn't an issue he was going to walk away from quickly or just put on a back burner to forget about.

It was several prisoners later before Cassius actually got around to considering the situation. The Book of Commands was a fake. Not only that, but it was a bad fake, full of sarcasm, witticisms, and blatant disrespect. Hardly something they could use to rewrite the Laws of Time. They would, of course, or they would say they were. They would just do it more slowly, Rifun said, coming up with the new rules as a process and not a complete replacement. Make it a slower transition, easier for the average Time Agent to absorb, digest, and adapt to. Or that would be the excuse.

In the meantime, they either had to find the Ururian who duped them, or the journal itself. The Borelians were going after the Ururian, and apparently they were hunting with a real vengeance this time. And somehow, Rifun expected either Cassius, Titik, or both, to be able to produce the journal itself.

Cassius sent a message to Pilory, using a microportal to drop her a letter directly, but he really wasn't holding out much hope. Space pirates were notoriously adverse to organized military campaigns, which was exactly what the Cult had pulled off just the day before with the parade and the takeover of the Wheel. Space pirates also tended to live for the moment. Carpe diem and all that, seeing how any day truly could be their last.

So he spent the day in the Judgment Wing. The Borelians had done a decent job of keeping dissent to a minimum, whether through straight fear or the toxins they produced. Those who were of a strong enough will to power through the side effects had been rounded up and brought to the Judgment Wing. Being that they were able to offset the side effects of the Borelian toxins, they were automatically considered a danger and a threat, which meant Cassius was free to beat them as much as he thought necessary to reinforce the point that there was someone new in charge.

Some broke easily, and occasionally Cassius showed mercy. There were enough Tacagan loyalists to capture his attention and challenge his strength that he figured he could afford a little mercy. Maybe it would confuse the opposition, too, if there were tales of woe and conflicting tales of mercy. The difference between Isthim and Julianna. Confuse the people, make the Cult more sympathetic, divide and conquer.

He left the Judgment Wing that day more because he was tired rather than boredom or running out of prisoners. He could get used to this job, he thought, as long as the others didn't try to micromanage him. He expected Isthim would be his biggest defender—and perhaps there was some irony in that—and Julianna his biggest critic, though she was hardly a threat. Rifun might object, but only if he knew what was going on. The man seemed busy enough that as long as it wasn't a public problem, he could live with it, or at least ignore it for a while. Out of sight and out of mind and all that.

The Wheel hadn't burned down during or after the parade or festivities, and the Auctions were silent for the time being. Cassius paused and studied the guards, made eye contact with a few of them. What were they thinking? Did they know who they worked for? What were the Tacagans thinking? Had they planned for this sudden maneuver? How would they respond? What was their real motivation for wanting the Wheel for themselves in the first place? Opportunity in the wake of destruction was one thing, but this was a coordinated effort against a ruling power.

He thought back to his time as the Zero Hour. The corruption was hardly a secret, even among the commoners. Being in the middle of it, it was obvious enough that it was like a wife meeting all of her husband's secret mistresses, and all of them celebrating every holiday, birthday, and anniversary together. Keep it together for the sake of the kids, but there was plenty of malice behind the scenes.

The Tacagans had indeed been one of the players in this corruption, though a much smaller one. They tended to control the less important Hands—Hand of Winking, Hand of Parental Governance, Hand of New Blood, Hand of Portal Maintenance—those that many did not view as significant and simply a filler in order to make up the required fifty-one Hands. If the Tacagans had the ability to run everything, why had they waited until now to make a move?

Well, that was beyond his scope of interest. People told him who to kill, and he did it. He was put in charge of the prison, and he was enjoying every minute of it so far. He had to clean up a mess that the others had made, and he would do his best— for a price, of course. He didn't know what he would demand in return, if he did get his hands on the Book of Commands before they did, but he would want something.

He moved on from the Auctions and headed for the portal room. Secrecy was still warranted for travel to and from the city, if only because of the lingering threat from the Tacagans. It was frustrating for anyone who was tired and just wanted to get to bed, but he grudgingly observed the need for secrecy, jumping through several portals before finally landing in the darkness of the tunnels and making his way toward the light and the cavern where the city lay.

Most of the army had returned, and it seemed as though most of them were hungover, however that looked for a particular species. Some appeared to have been punished for it, put through drills in spite of or because of their hungover state, and others were smart enough to not let themselves be found right away. If anyone had not gotten drunk or hungover, or engaged in other stupid or embarrassing antics, Cassius figured it was safe to bet that they got the day off from drills and chores.

He let everyone be, and he made his way to the officers building. He did not see the Korin, nor Murdi and Lordo, and that was fine with him. He might see to them later once this fiasco with the Book of Commands was taken care of.

No one approached him; indeed, the officers building seemed quite empty. That was fine, too. Meant he might actually get a halfway peaceful nap, barring whatever was going on outside.

He might have expected that after their takeover and his promotion as head guard that the spirit might visit him and offer him some congratulations. Or, since the spirit didn't seem big on gratitude, at least a little guidance. What did they do now? What did they do about the journal? Which of the other leaders should he assassinate first, and when? But he saw nothing, dreamed nothing. The spirit did not visit. He didn't even get so much as a twitch in his face where the bullet still rested to let him know whether the spirit was pleased with him. All was quiet, and Cassius found himself a bit uneasy about it.

Of course, he wasn't going to admit this out loud. He simply freshened himself up a bit after his nap, then left his chambers to carry on about his day.

He had just exited the officers building when he spotted Pilory at the bottom of the steps, and they met halfway.

"Your message said it was important," she began.

"Where have you been?" Cassius demanded.

She met his gaze. "I decided that the Akari just wasn't for me."

"You seemed eager enough before."

"I'm not a soldier, Cassius. I'm not someone you can just order around simply because you say so. I'm a pirate. Respect is earned." Her wings fluttered and she hovered over the ground. "And if you called me here just to give me a lecture on—"

"We need your help."

She made a gesture. "Oh, now you need my help?"

"Actually, we need your captain's help."

"Of course. More treasure hunting?"

"That will be discussed with your captain. And if he needs an incentive, you can let him know that there's money involved."

Pilory didn't look overly impressed, but sighed and assented. "Fine. Only because you found the crown of Srori." She turned as if to leave, then looked back. "But know that he isn't too happy about the deal you made the Turitians."

"Something we'll discuss, I'm sure."

She gave him a look. "I'll let him know you want to talk. If he agrees, I'll let you know the time and place."

"Tell him it will be both me and Rifun."

She agreed and departed, looking none too pleased.

Cassius returned to the Wheel and spent another day with the prisoners. Some were leftover from before the takeover, and Cassius derived much pleasure from forcing them to make the case for why they should be pardoned now that there was a new regime in power. Most simply said that they could be of great help, but few specified how. A few at least attempted a creative answer, and Cassius did allow them to go free, saying that if they were brought back to the prison for any reason, there would be hell to pay. One prisoner who particularly annoyed Cassius was set free with this warning, but Cassius only waited about thirty seconds before sending a Grandfather after him, saying to just make something up if he had to. That prisoner was brought back, speedily tried and convicted, and Cassius finished out his day with a grand round of beatings and torture.

He might have expected it to be a day or so before Pilory got back to him, and another day before Titik would agree to meet. In reality, it was four days before Pilory left him a note, and another two days before the actual meeting.

By this time, the worst of the panic over the missing Book of Commands had ebbed, though Isthim's hunters had had no luck in locating the Ururian.

As for Rifun, arguably the worst kneejerk offender, he was busying himself with making sure their allies all played nice with each other in the Wheel, occasionally eeking out a new command in order to smooth some ruffled feathers. Even just thinking about it, Cassius was glad he was no longer the Zero Hour. He was happy to stay in the prison. At least there, the lines were more clearly defined: guard, guarded, torturer, tortured.

Actually, Rifun seemed grateful for the opportunity to get away from the Wheel, even if it was only for a short time.

"What makes this different from any of your meetings with the allies on their own worlds?" Cassius wondered. They were in his chambers, and Cassius had just shared the time and date of the meeting with Titik.

"Because there are no diplomatic pretenses here," Rifun answered. "Titik may be the king of his own castle, but he's still a wanted criminal, and he knows it. He may be a lord of the underworld, but when it comes to a fight, he's all he's got."

"So we're going to intimidate him?"

"Only a little. Do you have a problem with that?"

"Not in the least."

"That's what I thought."

Two days later, the two men met up with Pilory outside the ruins. They followed her into the tunnels where, courteous enough to still honor their secrecy, she opened several portals before finally setting foot on Titik's ship.

"You must be a skilled Time Agent to be able to hop through portals on and off a moving ship," Rifun observed mildly. "Even if you're going by feel rather than coordinates, it's no small feat."

"No different than jumping from planet to planet, hurtling through space around their respective suns," Pilory said, her tone a bit boastful. "Actually, it may be a bit easier since the ship isn't usually moving as fast as a planet."

"True, but planets have a predictable orbit. Ships don't."

"Fair enough. So I'd say it's a draw."

Always diplomatic, always charming, Cassius thought grudgingly. It had its uses in politics, but did he really have to use it on Cassius' contacts? This was the pit of lowlifes, the scum of the universe. Why should they respond to such high society frivolity as if it meant something to them? Was it just to make them feel better about themselves?

"You know, many Time Agent skills, from all disciplines, have their origins and explanations in the Akari," Rifun went on. "Portals are not merely a magical effort of will, but a manipulation of Energy. Being able to open a blind portal based on feel alone is theorized by some to have its origins in Gravity, the forces of the universe working uniquely on a celestial body to cause it to move as it does."

"Is that so?" Pilory sounded genuinely intrigued, much to Cassius' chagrin. "And what of Disguises? DNA can only go so far, especially between species, but the only thing I've heard concerning the rest is merely 'trick of the eye.' Sounds quite a bit like magic to me."

Rifun shrugged casually. "Maybe it is. It's been said that magic is merely science we haven't discovered yet. On the other hand, if everything could be quantified, what use would there be for God?"

"You come from a monotheistic people, then?"

"Me personally? Not as such. No, the ancestors and the spirits have great power, and Zanahy is the creator spirit."

Pilory made a sweeping gesture. "I come from a particular tribe that observes a vast pantheon of sky gods and many earth spirits."

"And how does Time and the Akari appear to them, or by them?"

"Magic. The sky gods blame the earth spirits, and the earth spirits blame the sky gods. When my people were introduced to Time over a century ago, there were many wars. Factions loyal to the sky gods, factions loyal to the earth spirits, factions proclaiming peace, factions proclaiming atheism. Other tribes with other gods and spirits also armed themselves with weapons and philosophy."

"Have these wars resolved?"

"An armistice was called about fifty years ago. There are still skirmishes here and there, and there are divisions and countries now where there did not used to be divisions and countries. And yet..." She tilted her head like a bird, looking thoughtful. "While there is great animosity between the factions, the people within the factions seem...happier."

"They're free to self-govern without having to accommodate the demands of a minority," Rifun commented.

"I suppose you could say it that way. They have their own identity, something that binds them together. A rallying point, as it were."

"Well, take it from me that it's not an end point. It's a balance. My people were conquered once. Under French rule, we were all Malagasy. That was our identity. That was our rallying point. But once we were free, or close to it, that comradery fell away. It was no longer just Malagasy, but I am Betsileo, you are Merina, he is Sakalava. The divisions began again, and we were overrun by our enemies. It took many years before we were freed."

"Are you still Malagasy? Or are you Betsileo?"

Rifun blinked. "Both."

"But if the Betsileo and the Merina and the Sakalava do not get along, why force the issue? Why not allow the people to go their separate ways?"

"To what end? Shall we divide over every petty disagreement? If the Betsileo seceded, shall we then divide by region? By village? My mother was a Betsileo woman who married a Tsimihety man. Should my brothers and sisters be forced to choose a loyalty?"

"And what of you? Are you not Tsimihety also?"

Rifun's face turned bright red. "No. No, my father was one of the French conquerors. I never knew him."

"Then you have chosen. Others will as well."

"You can't ask people to choose like that." He went on before Pilory could speak. "The Akarin have divided over every petty disagreement. There are a dozen factions, maybe more."

"Is the Cult not one of those factions?"

"An offshoot, maybe, now guided by the journals, not the Authored Books. And we seek to end the need to choose loyalty to the Time industry, or any industry, or loyalty to one's people."

"Then what happens when someone challenges you for power, and people choose it? What happens when people choose not to learn the Akari? What if they choose not to learn it from you? If you are a product, then you have no need for forceful power except that you wish to remove the ability to choose. If you are a religion, then you need a following, and few religions stay quiet for long, especially in the face of heresy, which you have declared the Akarin to be." She stopped in front of a door and looked at them. "I'm not saying we won't help you, if captain agrees to it. I'm only asking that you examine your motives."

"This coming from a pirate?" Cassius wondered.

Pilory gave him a look. "No matter who is in power, most people consider stealing and plundering a crime, and so we live outside their laws. Sometimes it gives us a unique perspective."

She knocked on the door and a gruff voice bid them enter. Rifun and Cassius entered, but Pilory remained outside, saying, "I'll leave it to you three to discuss and decide what you need to do."

Then she was gone.

Titik's quarters hadn't changed much, not that Cassius expected them to. They were still nicer than his own chambers in the officers building, possibly even nicer than the chambers he'd had when working for the Burid prince.

"Cassius," Titik acknowledged, standing behind his desk. He looked at Rifun. "Rifun."

"Captain Titik," Rifun greeted.

The Psiaco appeared to be in a rather grumpy mood, Cassius thought. Good. Let him. See how Rifun responded to that. See if diplomacy worked in the presence of those who were not so kind and cordial, who would kill you themselves rather than hire someone else later.

"Pilory said you had some matters you wished to discuss with me," he went on, cutting right to the chase. "If I heard right, you just gave control of the Scouts and outposts to the Turitians." At least two of his eyes trained on Cassius as he said it. "So tell me why you suddenly need my help."

"Because the Turitians are nice and patient," Rifun began, his tone switching so fast it gave Cassius pause. "We don't have time for nice and patient. And if I'm right, what we're looking for won't turn up in nice and patient channels."

Now Titik looked at Cassius fully. "Are you still looking for that little book of yours?"

"We are," Cassius said. "This time we even have a lead."

"Oh, now that is a helpful bit of information." The captain's tone was dripping sarcasm. "Do tell."

"We thought we had it," Rifun explained. "Borelian hunters had tracked down an Ururian and seized a journal which, by the description we gave, was a match. When opened, however, it proved to be a fake, and the Ururian got away."

Both Cassius and Rifun startled as Titik burst into a laugh so mighty it might have shaken the ship. It was a fuller, richer laugh than one might have expected from the grizzled old Psiaco pirate, and he wiped a tear from his eye. He paused, took a breath, then burst into laughter again. Somehow, Cassius could imagine a group of crewmen outside, ears pressed against the door, wondering what was so funny.

"Are you quite done?" Rifun wondered as Titik quieted again.

The captain replied with another, smaller, shorter, quieter round of laughter. By now he had all four hands out to steady him on his desk, and three eyes had tears leaking from them. He panted like a dog for a moment, his body occasionally shaking with a residual giggle, then finally looked at them. Cassius thought he was going to laugh again, but then he spoke.

"By the gods, that's the funniest thing I think I've heard in ten years. Not only did the Borelian hunters get bested, but it was an Ururian who did it." He laughed again. "Gods...if it wasn't so absurd, I might not believe you."

"We're happy to brighten your day," Rifun said, his tone tough to judge. "Can we get back to business?"

Titik plopped down in his chair and motioned for them to do the same, saying, "I admit, I was in a rather foul mood, but you have made me see the sun again." He let out a breath. "Now then, do you know for certain that this Ururian has the real journal you seek?"

"No," Rifun admitted grudgingly.

"Well then, we have a problem, don't we?"

"The last person we knew who had it was a human named Andrew O'Dell. Unfortunately, he's gone missing, too."

"Well, this is a problem, too, isn't it?" Titik shifted position. "Cassius pulled off the impossible, and he brought me the crown of Srori. You have made me laugh as I have not done in a year." He made a gesture. "I am inclined to listen to any offer you may have to make it worth my while to search for this little book of yours."

"Did Pilory show you nothing of the Akari?" Cassius wondered.

Titik waved a hand. "I have little interest in your magic or your religion. Money is the only pleasure in the world." He continued before either could protest. "Psia has some of the most prestigious Time Academies in the quadrant. I was top of my class. But what good does more Time do if all those years are empty? What good does it do me to have a thousand years left in my lifetime if I am to be killed in battle next month?" He shook his head. "No. Money. Money is the only pleasure in the world."

"Then how shall we negotiate?" Rifun asked. "How is it that we can offer you something you have no trouble in procuring on your own? Even Cassius risking his life and our diplomacy with the Turitians for your stupid crown meant nothing to you. So either you're just another cheap, second-rate coward, or you're a cheap, second-rate, lying coward."

There was a flash of a Band, and suddenly Titik was twisted in all kinds of knots over his desk, Rifun leaning on him, helped by Gravity, with a knife to Titik's throat. If Cassius was right, it was Titik's own knife. The captain gasped for breath as he was tangled up, his neck bent back so that it was difficult to breathe, and his eyes were wide with an animalistic panic. Rifun looked like he'd hardly broken a sweat.

"Do you want money or do you want treasure?" Cassius asked, leaning forward to look Titik in the eye. "You know what I want? I want payment for that crown I got you."

"Or we can open up a portal right here, right now, and bring the Turitians right alongside your ship," Rifun went on. "From what Cassius tells me, your ship would fit well in one of their cargo holds."

Titik made a sound that was somewhere between a hiss and a snarl. After a moment of consideration, Rifun removed the knife and let Titik get back to rights. Four arms and two legs untwisted themselves, and Titik slunk back into his chair. Rifun set the knife on the desk, but no one moved to take it.

"We're not asking for a share of your plunder," Cassius said. "We're not saying that you have to stop your pirating operations or commit to a life of charity."

"All we want is one little journal," Rifun said. "There are search parties out for the human Andrew. The Borelians are going after the Ururian, but there's no reason he wouldn't have offloaded the real journal just as soon as he could, assuming he had it."

Titik's jovial mood was now fully gone, and he seemed to be in an even worse mood than when they'd walked in. He studied them, his anger surprisingly muted.

"Where did the hunters catch the Ururian?" he asked after a long moment of consideration.

Rifun gave him the approximate location.

"Do they know the style of ship he was piloting?"

"Small craft, two or three crew maximum."

Titik thought about this for a moment. "Ururians have no home world. They were conquered and enslaved thousands of years ago. Some exist in cohabited colonies on various worlds that will take them, but there is no centralized planet they call their own."

"Why not?" Rifun inquired.

The pirate made a gesture that Cassius interpreted as a shrug. "Who knows? Quite frankly, I don't care. Ururians are good for labor, good for entertainment, anything that doesn't require a solid civilization to achieve. They're much like the Urid, except the Ururians are a bit more evolved in my opinion. Maybe they're related. Who knows? Many end up as slaves or servants, depending on their home colony and their neighbors. If there is anything that they rally behind, it's the names of their fathers. They have exceptionally long names, if only because they insist on being called by their name, their father's name, his father's name, as far back as seven generations. Maybe more, depending on the person. Failure to do so is considered extremely rude, sacrilege at worst."

"If he was in a small pod, he couldn't have gone very far," Cassius said.

"No, indeed not," Titik agreed. "If he was running around Quadrant One, there are any number of places he could have gone. Does anyone happen to know his skill in Time?"

"Rumors say he was one of the Akarin," Rifun told him. "How true that is or how proficient, we don't know."

"Enough to elude the hunters," Titik chuckled. He grew serious again. "If he is somewhat proficient, he may be able to open a portal around a small craft such as he was piloting."

"But if not, then he may still be in Quadrant One," Cassius finished. "With the coordinates, could you tell us where he may have gone?"

Titik's computer mapped out the rough area where the Ururian had been captured.

"The closest inhabited world is this one, Mobid, but they're fairly hostile to outsiders. Unless it was an emergency landing, even an Ururian knows to stay away from there. But the next closest is a world in the same solar system. Dimic, it's called."

"I don't know anything about Dimic," Rifun said.

"Friendly people, but it's a water world. Only about five percent of the planet's surface is dry. The people themselves have unusually watery skin."

"Not impossible then. How are they on space travel?"

"The Dimica themselves are not especially advanced, but the Mobidians have outposts there for trade and travel."

"So it's possible he could have picked up something there. Is there anywhere else he might have gone?"

Titik grunted. "For a small craft such as his, he might have made it to the next system, depending on its capabilities, but his better bet would have been to go to Dimic and get passage on a Mobidian freighter or some other ship."

Rifun nodded. "Looks like you have your work cut out for you."

The captain looked ready to protest, but Cassius spoke first. "Why do you think you're going to weasel your way out of this?" He stood. "I went to great lengths to find the crown of Srori, yet you treat it like nothing. Just another trophy, and one you didn't even have to win." He put his hands on Titik's desk and leaned in close. "Do you treat all prospective sources this way?"

"Money is the only pleasure in the world," Titik growled. "And I could die any day."

"Anyone can die for a cause," Rifun told him sagely. "It's much harder to live with the failure."

"And I have to say, I'm surprised that you don't want a piece of this pie," Cassius went on. "Time may be inconsequential to you, but what about Matter? Energy? Why wouldn't you want to learn these same abilities that the Turitians are? Because once they do, your little party tricks from the Academy won't save you." When Titik hesitated — just for a split-second, but he did — Cassius pressed harder. "What do you really want? Yes, money is the only pleasure in the world, but what would really make you happy? You know what I think? I think you want to be able to take this little rust bucket of a ship and go against one of those Turitian cruisers. And win. I think that's what you really want."

Titik's glare was enough of an answer.

"You're not going to get it by sitting where you are. Because even as you have abandoned Time, time has abandoned you. You might have a few extra years of strength and youth from your days at the Academy, but let's face it, you are getting old. You won't be able to keep this up forever. One day, you won't be able to command, won't be able to lead. Your crew is going to dump you like the rotten potatoes you are and sail off into the stars on another adventure, leaving you behind. Maybe you'll have money, but then one day it'll run out. Then what? You'll just be someone who used to be fearsome. Who used to have a name.

"Or maybe you'll have a run-in with the Turitians. And they'll be able to split the universe like the gods themselves, and nothing you do can stop it. You might have been able to save yourself and your crew, had you learned the same secrets, but then, I guess we'll never know. And then you'll be gone. Just someone who used to be fearsome. Who used to have a name."

Cassius would not say that he was a great orator, and he certainly did not possess the suave charisma of Rifun when it came to diplomacy, but he couldn't deny that his words had an effect on the Psiaco captain.

The three men stared at each other for a long moment across Titik's desk. Finally the captain reached forward and pressed a button on his computer.

"Silva!"

"Captain," came the acknowledgment.

"Set a new course. Four-one-six, nine-seven, three-four-four. Twelve dolja."

"Aye, sir."

He released the button and leaned back in his seat, glowering at Rifun and Cassius who relaxed their postures. Cassius sat down.

"I hate you," Titik said. "And for that, I respect you as well." He huffed a sigh.

"We will set course for Dimic and see what we can find."

"Thank you," Rifun said graciously.

"The Turitians are also in Quadrant One, however. Their presence is well-known. I expect that with this new power you gave them—" He said this rather distastefully. "—their presence will be even more known. If they are learning this Akari of yours, I'm not inclined to get in any skirmishes with them. We'll investigate Dimic and the Mobidian outposts, but if the Turitians come around, I'm not eager to risk my life for this book of yours."

"Of course." Rifun stood and Cassius followed. "We have a few meetings of our own to tend to in the next day or so. After that, we will let you decide how you wish to proceed in learning the Akari. We are not exclusive, and I'm sure you do not wish to be outgunned by the Turitians all the time."

"Get off my ship," Titik spat.

Rifun gave him a dramatic bow, and he and Cassius left the captain's quarters.

Pilory was waiting for them outside, leaning against the bulkhead beside the door.

"How much of that did you hear?" Cassius asked.

"Dimic, huh?" she replied. "You know, it'd be a shame if a rumor got out that the mighty and fearsome Borelians got blindsided by an Ururian."

"It would be a shame," Rifun agreed. "A real embarrassment for them."

She gave him a look. "You sound like you want such a rumor to get out."

He grinned. "At least wait until after you've been to Dimic and investigated the outposts. Who knows? If the Ururian is hiding there, how much more embarrassing would it be that you captured him and not them?"

Her expression turned a bit smug, Cassius thought, but she agreed to wait until after the outpost. She took the lead and started off through the ship, the men in tow.

"You really know how to play a good game," she told them. "Not too many people can intimidate the captain like that. And no one gives him orders."

"We're not ordering anything," Rifun said. "We're just trying to make a simple, polite request."

"Well, he's a hunter of treasure, not trinkets."

"You can't tell me there's no treasure to be found in Quadrant One."

"No, but there's no Turitians in Quadrant Three," Pilory replied. "At least, not yet." Her tone was accusing.

"We'll see what happens."

She didn't seem pleased with the answer, but she did not say anything more about it. Instead, when they reached the cargo hold, she simply said, "I will let you know when we reach Dimic, and I'll let you know what we find. It really shouldn't be more than a few days. Depending on what we do or don't find, captain will expect a speedy response. He doesn't like lingering in Turitian space."

"We'll keep it in mind," Rifun promised.

"See that you do."

With that, they departed, eventually landing back in the tunnels and making their way to the dim light of the cavern.

"I think that went well," Rifun commented. "And you were even the one who convinced Titik to help us."

"You're welcome," Cassius said, only half-sarcastic. "So what do we do now? What meetings do you have to attend?"

"We are going to have a meeting. Us three leaders. We know what Titik is doing. I want to get an update from Isthim on her teams. Then we have to decide how we're going to proceed. We promised to rewrite the Laws of Time, replace them with what was in the Book of Commands. Without the Book of Commands, however, we have to come up with another strategy, unless you happened to have memorized that one, too?"

Cassius grunted but shook his head.

"That's what I thought. We need to come up with something in the meantime."

"And when is this meeting taking place?"

"Tomorrow morning. I'll find Isthim, and then I suggest we come up with some reasonable rewrites for the Laws of Time. Anything you do remember would be helpful."

"I'll think about it. I might remember a few things."

He wandered off before Rifun could say more, all the while thinking that maybe they should have waited on sending Julianna into the cave until she confirmed that the Book of Commands had been authentic. Oh well, just another blunder in their rise to power. Cassius sighed. There was no way they should have been able to accomplish all that they had except for some sort of divine intervention, whether it was the Author or the dark spirit. But then, why couldn't this intervention have blessed them with better planning and fewer blunders? There were setbacks, and then there were these unforgivable mistakes, some of which he himself had made.

Whatever the case, this was what they were dealing with now. All their plans to replace the Laws of Time with the Book of Commands were now shelved in favor of just making up something that sounded good and logical, at least until the Book of Commands was found, or Julianna returned, and pray she remember what was in it.

Well, the meeting wasn't happening now, and he really wasn't feeling like sitting down and just thinking about things. He might have more luck remembering if he was out doing something. And by that, well, he could put in a few hours at the prison. There had to be someone there worth torturing. Maybe he would remember all the commands that said he couldn't do this or couldn't do that. Not that he would voice those commands; he would just say he forgot those ones. And if the Book of Commands did turn up and someone pointed that out, well, down in the asylum, no one could hear you scream. Even if they could, no one would dare attempt a rescue.

So Cassius returned to the Wheel. In a week since the takeover, things were still a little slow in the markets, but most of the allies had figured out their place in the various marketplaces. So far, everything was still Time-based. Rifun gave the diplomatic reason as being that the people just needed something familiar for a short time. They needed to see that the Cult of the Akari was not a hostile takeover force out to enslave everyone. People could still go to the markets and carry out their day-to-day activities.

Once the Laws of Time started to get rewritten and new commands issued, that would change. Depending on the status of the Book of Commands, that change could come either fast or slow. Isthim was currently weeding out her instructor students, intending to have at least three ready to go, ready to take over the Arena and start teaching the Akari, slowly phasing out simple Time. Eventually, Time Capsules would no longer be needed, and the Time industry would slowly turn into more of an Akari Academy.

As for Cassius, well, there would always be troublemakers and rebellion, and he would be happily waiting in the prison, ready to deal with those who stepped out of line. That was his duty, his niche, his part of the leadership. Actually, he rather enjoyed the idea. Maybe things were finally starting to come together. Maybe he had found his place in the universe. It had only taken a couple centuries, but maybe he had finally accomplished that goal he'd never really realized he'd had.

It put him in a good mood, actually, and he tortured his prisoners that day with a special kind of sadistic glee.

It was easy for him to lose track of time while in the prison, Normally it wouldn't matter, seeing how the Wheel remained in its state of relative temporal fixation. He didn't know if that was a thing, but it sounded good to him. No matter how much time one spent in the Wheel, as long as his original portal remained open, no time would pass at home. He didn't understand how it worked. Rifun had tried to explain it once with his theories on Time and Gravity and this and that, but Cassius had no patience for it. With the secrecy they proclaimed they needed for the ruins and everything, and the many jumps they made to ensure they couldn't be tracked, most of them ended up closing their portals just out of habit. For him, well, it helped to pass the time between dull meetings. Sometimes it was helpful, being able to actually pass the time rather than spend hours or days in a place, only to return to the exact same point in time from the place you left.

If he had any complaints, it was that he was running out of prisoners. No, he didn't kill all of them, but with all the uncertainty in the Wheel with the change of power and whatnot, people were going to great lengths to be good and not find out what kind of court system the Cult intended to implement. In a way that was a good thing, Cassius figured, because that meant the common man didn't yet realize that the Cult didn't know what kind of court system it intended to implement either.

And it all came back to that stupid book. Why did it always come back to a book? Why were people so affected by little scribbles on paper? What power did books have over people that these little ink blots on a flammable surface could cause so much misery and suffering? What power did a book have to reward someone for reading it, or punish them for not? If any god out there cared enough about people to want to communicate, why wait hundreds or thousands of years to communicate? And if any god didn't care, well, why bother to communicate at all?

Cassius hated it when things turned philosophical, but there really were some things that he just didn't understand. Even he, who communed with the dark spirit and spoke the words of Richard's journals, found it all very confusing. Why him? Why now? What purpose was being served that couldn't have been done five hundred years sooner, or three hundred years later? And the Akarin and their Authored Books. Their earliest scripts were set only in the eighteenth century. Did the Author not care about humanity until then? What changed? How were there other Books listed that didn't exist yet? What happened to all the people who had died in the centuries beforehand? Hell, what happened to them now?

He tortured a few more prisoners just to vent some of his frustration, but the questions remained, and he found himself wondering what the point was of looking for the Book of Commands. Who cared, really? He had spoken the words, but those words hadn't existed until he spoke them. What about everything before that? What about everything now, when the book was missing and so may as well have not existed? The only thing that was continuous in life was death. People marched toward death every day. Why shouldn't they write their own rules and fight for every scrap of Time they could get?

His face throbbed a bit, but he paid it little mind. He wasn't going to try to undermine the Cult or the others' efforts to retrieve the Book of Commands and so impose their will on the universe. He was no humanitarian. And, really, this existential crisis, like all the rest of them, would eventually subside.

Briefly he found himself considering the Grunjor. Sentient rock beings who, upon receiving their spark or breath of life, however it was done, needed only a name and a task, and they were content. Or they seemed to be content. Most people assumed they were content. The Grunjor didn't really give any indication one way or the other. But if they were content, Cassius wondered if it wouldn't be better to be a Grunjor.

After a while, he left the prison. He again meandered past the Auctions. Very little activity had been seen around them since the parade, and it appeared that anyone who was staunchly against the Cult had taken shelter there. It wasn't unreasonable to think that it had been turned from a house of business into a place of war, but nothing seemed to be happening that warranted Cassius' attention, and he passed them by, making sure to make eye contact with all of the guards, as he always did.

With nothing else to distract him, he returned to the ruins.

It did not appear that he'd missed the meeting, but if something had come up, or if he had been late, it wasn't as though they didn't know where to find him.

He didn't see Rifun, and Isthim was busy with the grunts. Cassius greatly suspected that the two were regular lovers now, though how he could prove this, he was not sure, and how this was accomplished, he did not know. On the one hand, one small mistake and Rifun could be dead instantly. On the other hand, what ever happened to Isthim being attracted to his strength and power and callous disregard for pain and life itself? Had she gone soft? Had he? Had it simply been a ploy, a way to get into a group that would have excluded her and her people otherwise? Had her time among humans changed her?

He didn't like it. If he wanted to be honest, yes, he was jealous. But the more he thought about it, the less he wanted Isthim. She betrayed her people, then went back to them. She almost killed Rifun, and now they were probably sleeping together. She was a whore. Not that Cassius cared about her morals or lack thereof, but he wasn't going to share a woman with Rifun. A thousand other men, fine, but not him.

Maybe he should look at Isthim's cousin, the orange one. Those women hated each other. What better way to get under Isthim's skin than by sleeping with her cousin? And if she was irritable about it, who knew how Rifun would react?

Now he just had to figure out how to pull off the sex without dying in the process. He couldn't very well ask Rifun how he did it. Maybe if he took the bold approach and went after Isthim's cousin with the same brash fearlessness that got her interested, her cousin would show him a few tricks. After all, if there was any "safe" color for humans, it was orange. The side effects varied and were typically mild compared to the rest of the toxins.

It also just so happened that Medik's room was next to Isthim's, just to spite Isthim and try to goad her into a fight for the most petty offenses. When Cassius knocked and looked inside, however, he did not see Medik anywhere. He rarely visited any of the Borelians in their chambers, but he knew enough that they were sparse decorators, and it was difficult to say whether Medik had been around lately or perhaps moved out, either to the Wheel or back home to Brelix.

Mildly annoyed, he shut the door and walked away. It wasn't as if he couldn't try again later, but he didn't like putting off plans. He wanted to have sex with a Borelian, and he wanted to do it now. But one was busy, the other was gone, and the rest were male. Hey, Cassius may have been a soulless son of a bitch with no moral compass, but even he had standards.

He stopped in front of Julianna's door, her chambers locked up tight. He could go after her. Cut her up a little more, take his pleasure, take the journal for himself, maybe kill her this time. Then he could say that he had the longest-running bout of sex of any human in history. Rifun had a few days with Isthim, well, he'd take a few months or even a few years with Julianna. Ha!

The thought did hold a certain appeal, but then, that would be months or years that the prison would run without him. Without him and with Isthim. Rifun and Isthim, running things together and with no opposition. There was no way he could allow that to happen.

He'd try Medik again later. In the meantime, they had to figure out how to retrieve the Book of Commands — before Julianna got back and saw the mess they'd made.

25 | Mifanakalo Hevitra sy Manapa-Kevitra   Discuss and Decide

The Caves of Meroian, 1965

N o one was happy, but there was no one to blame but themselves.

If you want something done right, you have to do it yourself, Rifun thought, looking at the others around the table. Isthim made no effort to conceal her displeasure, and Cassius looked particularly annoyed.

They were the only ones gathered, for they were the only ones who knew. They hadn't told anyone else about their blunders. It would look terribly weak and foolish to the Borelians, and they couldn't risk the Tacagans trying something if they thought they had an opening. They had to keep this as quiet as possible.

"I have taken command of the teams myself," Isthim said. "I have taken care of the necessary paperwork with the Great Admirals, and they are mine to command for the foreseeable future. They are sworn to secrecy, and even they do not know the end goal. All they know is that they are to hunt down the Ururian Abbal Duma T'Akhar Mureel Sibon and bring him to us. He is to be alive, but in what condition...I let them have discretion."

Rifun saw Cassius' expression turn smug.

"Do they have any leads?" Rifun asked.

"They are currently scouting in the area where they originally caught him. The only worlds he could have made it to in his craft, barring use of portals, is either Mobid or Dimic."

"The Mobidians don't like outsiders." Rifun shifted his stance. "Unless his ship was damaged in some way? Did the teams attack him the first time?"

Isthim gave him a certain haughty, self-righteous look. "Spare parts are always needed. There is rarely a need to damage a ship to disable it. We have other means of detaining people."

"So unless he deliberately went to Mobid, maybe hoping to hide and hoping that pursuers wouldn't want to deal with the Mobidians' bad attitude toward outsiders, his best option, barring portals, would be Dimic."

"As I said, my teams are investigating."

Cassius shifted position. "Do we even know that he has the journal? Julianna said that Abbal Duma whatever his name is, he's a thief and a trickster besides. May not have even been a real Akarin."

"It's all we have to go on at the moment," Rifun told him. "Personally, I'd like to find Andrew O'Dell. Maybe they tried to pull a fast one on us."

"I can go back to Micaiah's apartment," Cassius offered. "Maybe he was in on it."

Rifun nodded. "That's not a bad idea. And why not check on the others who were at the Time Trial? I get the feeling that they might have all been in on this." He looked at Isthim. "Did your ith teams get to them?"

She dipped her head. "Yes, as ordered."

"Damn." Rifun frowned. "We may have shot ourselves in the foot with that one. They may have conspired, and then we may have erased their memories about the conspiracy. Even if we do find them, they may genuinely know nothing about it." He sighed. "I'm guessing that it can't be reversed."

"Unlike other toxins and functions that can be restored based on the body's DNA recreating normal function, memories, once the chemical encoding is lost, cannot be recreated."

"Damn."

"It may not be as bad as you think," Cassius said.

Rifun looked at him. "How so?"

"If one of them, say Micaiah, has the journal in his bedroom, he may not remember its significance. He may not remember how he got it, why it's there, or why he should protect it. So if I happen to find it and take it, he will probably put up less of a fight."

Rifun nodded. "I like how you think. Given the dynamics of those who were at the Time Trial, my money is either on Andrew or Doug."

"Why them?" Isthim wondered.

He looked at her. "Andrew is a Builder, so he has the greatest power to defend it, or try to destroy it. Also, he's the one who's disappeared. But Doug is Akarin Council; they may have wanted to get a look at it." He glanced back at Cassius. "Check all of them, just to be sure, but my money's on one of those two."

Cassius raised a brow. "How discreet do you want me to be?"

"If they have no memory of the journals, or if it's simply unimportant to them, then let's keep it that way. We don't want to get them riled up and coming after us after all the trouble we just went through to get them out of our hair." He paused. "Now, if they do remember everything and come after you with a holy vengeance, then by all means."

The dark-skinned man grinned and nodded once.

"In the meantime," Rifun went on, "we need to come up with something to rewrite the Laws of Time. We've put it off saying that people needed time to adjust, and I know that a few new rules have been put in place, but those have mostly been in response to some transition incidents between allies, rather than true commands and rewrites. Cassius, do you remember anything?"

"Nothing that would make sense without more baseline rules," he answered.

"What about you, Isthim? You must have at least glanced through the Book of Commands once."

"A century ago," she replied. "Contrary to popular belief, Borelians do not have infallible memories."

Rifun sighed and rolled his eyes. "Just perfect. All right, fine. Has anyone come up with anything to, as they say, fake it until we make it? What about the Book of Philosophy? Where's that?"

It was kept safe and sound in Julianna's chambers. Only because Rifun had helped to set up the barriers in her chambers did he know how to disable them and get in. The room wasn't booby-trapped necessarily, but it would be obvious that someone had haphazardly attempted to break in. Unless, of course, he knew how to undo everything.

With no one else part of the meeting, the three leaders elected to simply continue their discussion in the empty chambers.

"Even if it's just philosophy and sagely wisdom, we should be able to glean a few commands from them," Rifun reasoned. "Sun Tzu did not write the rules of war, but his observations certainly paved the way for them."

"Perhaps," Isthim suggested as he flipped through the pages, "the most radical thing we can do at the moment, and to buy us some more time, is not to attempt to implement new rules or overwrite the existing rules, but to simply erase some of them. Cut the ropes, unlock the chains—"

"Bold words from a slaver," Cassius threw in casually.

She gave him a look. "Cause chaos. Make people afraid of the chaos. Then when we do start to implement new rules, they will more readily receive them. Otherwise, we run the risk of rebellion at worst, and simple confusion at best."

"Same idea that got people to embrace the Gentleman Killers," Cassius said, shrugging. "People crave safety because their lavish, carefree lifestyle depends on it. Turn a loyal, domestic animal loose and it will seek out a new master rather than look after itself."

"Given enough time, all animals will turn feral," Rifun pointed out, "but you're not wrong. And there are plenty of masters out there waiting to scoop up lost animals. My concern is the Tacagans. People went to the Gentleman Killers because there was no one else. This time, the Tacagans are waiting, and they're making no secret of it. We're not anarchists; we've just temporarily lost our rulebook. But we can't let others know that. Furthermore, our allies running the marketplaces and so on are still operating under the old rules. If we yank the rug out from under them, they have no way to operate and no reason to remain allied with us." He continued before Isthim could protest. "This doesn't meant that the Laws of Time couldn't use a bit of pruning."

He sighed and again flipped lazily through the Book of Philosophy, hoping for something that might catch his attention and inspire even just one new command to implement. Something. Anything.

When did a character-building setback turn into a sign that this wasn't what they were supposed to be doing? He remembered something from long ago, a teacher at his school or maybe a pastor, that when God really wanted you to do or not do something, He asked nicely only once. Did the Author operate on the same principle? But then, why bring them this far only to get hung up on such a comparatively minor detail?

Or could this be a test of some kind? What happened when they didn't have the journals? Were they able to function without man's written word? Could they get by without Cassius, without Julianna? Maybe they had become too dependent on each other, and not dependent enough on the Author. They were looking too inwardly, too materialistically, when they should be looking outward.

Maybe if they stopped panicking and started working with what they had, the Author would give them what they needed. Seemed logical enough. It also seemed to be the only clear course of action.

"I'll sift through the Laws of Time and see what can be removed without incident," Isthim stated, as if reading his thoughts. "That alone may win us converts."

"Agreed," Rifun said. "We tell people that we've come to unshackle them from loyalty to a business, well, let's start by removing some of the unnecessary rules and obligations. I'll do a bit of searching myself in the Book of Philosophy, see if I can't come up with a little something. It may not be in the Book of Commands, but as long as it's plausible and doesn't conflict with anything else, we can get away with it."

"I'll go after the people from the Time Trial," Cassius confirmed. "See what they're up to and go searching through their homes."

Rifun pointed at him. "Don't engage unless they come after you. If they don't remember us, we don't need to give them a reason to going forward."

"I'll be careful."

Rifun had his doubts, but said nothing more about it.

"The Grandfathers will also go after the Ururian," Isthim said, "but for other reasons."

"Like what?"

"I'm sure I can find something in the Laws of Time as I'm going through them. As long as the reasons don't coincide, and as long as it's uninvolved Grandfathers who go after him, the chances of anyone discovering our blunder are low. It will put pressure on him from two sides."

"Julianna said he was a thief and a trickster," Cassius said. "He's bound to have broken some rules."

"If that's so, and considering his apparent reputation as such," Rifun continued, "then he already knows how to play the game and elude the authorities. He's demonstrated that for us beautifully."

"Maybe so, but it will still put pressure on him and limit his options," Isthim repeated. "If Cassius continues his travels through the dark side of the Time industry and all its underbelly inhabitants, he may come upon him by chance anyway."

"I look forward to meeting him," Cassius chuckled.

"No matter what, we need to keep this as discreet as possible," Rifun said severely. "If word gets out, and if it becomes a big enough issue, and if people ask why we're gunning for him so badly—especially if we're using only a minor offense as an excuse—I don't see any reason why he wouldn't suddenly make public what happened, that he managed to pull a fast one on us. If people—if the Tacagans— find out that we're missing the Book of Commands, or some similar thing, they could try to exploit it. I doubt very much that our entire army would turn on us, seeing how we've been operating very well for some time now, but it is still a weakness, a gap in our armor as it were."

"I don't know Ururians well," Isthim began, her tone a bit stiff, "but from what I do know about them in general as well as the reports from his first apprehension, it suggests that if he feels backed into a corner, he will create a spectacle in order to distract the hunter and try to get away. If he feels cornered between us and the Grandfathers, he would likely attempt such a maneuver, make our weakness public in order to distract our attention while he flees yet again."

"Well then we can't let ourselves get distracted, can we?" Rifun looked at Cassius. "If he does try such a thing, how do you feel about keeping an eye on him in spite of whatever fireworks he sets off?"

"Gladly," Cassius promised.

Isthim shifted her stance. "As the saying goes, playing the devil's advocate, what if we catch him and he doesn't have the Book of Commands? And the Akarin don't either, or not that they can easily remember or we can easily find?"

Rifun gave her a look. "Well then we're going to have a problem, aren't we?"

"We should plan as if that is a possibility. Otherwise, we're going to end up right back here."

He nodded. "This much is true. Similarly, the Akarin may indeed remember the journal and, if they have it, may already be squirreling it away in some other hole."

"Or they've destroyed it."

"Well you're in a good mood today. Can we get something constructive done, please?"

Now she gave him a look, but said nothing more.

"Regardless of whether or not they've destroyed it, or even who has it, if we can't wrap this up quickly, then we should turn our focus on those who are the greatest threat to us and who could exploit it. Namely, before we announce to the universe that we have, once again, blundered our way into the spotlight and are missing key elements of our whole doctrine, we should get rid of the Tacagans who are, at the moment, the greatest rallying point for opposition. We do that, then we can always blame them for the theft of the Book of Commands. It will make it easier to muster the troops to finish them off, if they have that extra little push."

"Why not say that now?" Cassius wondered.

Rifun raised a brow. "And admit that we may have partied too hard after the parade and festivities and left our gates so wide open and undefended that some Tacagan just waltzed in and nabbed it? Considering that we're not even camped in the Wheel, it seems a bit suspect, don't you think?"

"Then they didn't waltz in and nab it. Why not play the Judas card?"

There was a long silence. Finally Rifun asked, "What do you mean?"

"Judas Iscariot? Betrayed—"

"I know the reference, thank you. What do you propose for us, though?"

"Wildly crying traitor produces paranoia," Isthim said slowly. "While necessary when there is indeed a traitor among us, who can be defined, identified, and rooted out, if it turns into a witch hunt, it only serves to weaken us. The Tacagans will no doubt seek to exploit that."

"Similarly, our victory, the festivities, and the influx of interested recruits would more likely be the time that we are taking in traitors, spies, and double agents. I would expect information leaks to begin within a few weeks, some minor, distracting usurpation or assassination attempts in a few months, and a true attempted overthrow in about a year or so." He went on before Cassius could speak. "That's not to say that we won't ever need to play the Judas card, but that day is not today."

Cassius grunted.

"I know you were hoping for someone special to torture," Rifun sighed. "Just be patient. When the small spies and impostors start making themselves known, I will send them directly to you."

"But this doesn't resolve the issue of what we're going to do if this endeavor with the Book of Commands becomes more drawn-out than we are very comfortable with," Isthim said, bringing them back on track.

"We turn our attention to the Tacagans, assuming they haven't already come out of their hiding spot in the Auctions. I'm certain that in your training of the new recruits, you'll be able to spot some budding traitors. You can coordinate with Cassius as to who they are and how much of a threat they pose. Keep an eye on them unless you believe them to be an extreme risk. Otherwise, when we attack the Tacagans, or when they attack us, we'll have a few options as to who to blame when the Book of Commands turns up missing."

"And if we do end up with an extreme threat?"

Rifun made a gesture. "As you said, crying traitor is necessary when we have one to produce. And it may send a message to the less threatening ones." He paused. "Of course, we can hope that there are no such spies and traitors among us, but I think that, given the number of times Andrew O'Dell alone has managed to fool the Cult, it is folly to think such a thing. We can only hope that the four of us, even Julianna in her absence, remain loyal."

No one said anything to that.

"Now then, we all have our assignments," he said, straightening. "Let's hope for the best and prepare for the worst. And above all, discretion. When we are weak, we must appear strong. Remain strong before our adversaries and infallible to our troops and those under our protection."

"And indomitable to those who have already attacked and failed," Cassius added.

Rifun dipped his head once. "Any questions?"

Isthim looked like she had a few things to say, but she did not voice them aloud.

"All right, then. We'll see what happens. Either we find the journal or we don't; either we attack the Tacagans or they attack us. In the meantime, we have our duties. Adjourned."

They left the meeting room. Cassius stalked off to either return to the Wheel to torture someone or else go rifling through the homes of those who had been at the Time Trial. With any luck, they remembered just enough about the journal to know where it was, or where it could be, but not enough to want to defend it or start another major conflict. Rifun could have kicked himself. They'd gotten too cocky and ended up shooting themselves in the foot. How did the Author suffer such fools? Was there a purpose to this, or was this simply some sort of comic relief, or maybe a teaching moment?

Isthim, however, followed him to his chambers and softly closed the door behind her. Rifun went to his small bookshelf, but she stayed near the door.

"Sorry to say, but I'm not much in the mood right now," he told her, picking up the Book of Philosophy. "Naturally, you could change that mood arbitrarily, but I think you enjoy the chase."

"Why are humans such contradictions?" she asked.

He laughed, closed the book, and turned to face her. "If you ever figure it out, let me know. As a human myself, even I can't figure it out some days." He reopened the book and started flipping through pages. "But something tells me that you had a specific instance on your mind that you want to discuss."

He could feel her stare.

"You were a traitor once," she stated.

Now he slammed the book shut and looked up, but not at her.

She continued, "You attempted to infiltrate a group you disliked. You were caught. You were punished."

He turned a stiff neck and fixed her in a hard stare. "That's called being a spy. I was not a traitor. I did not betray my people. Ever. Not the first time, not the second, and certainly not the third."

"It causes you severe mental anguish still," Isthim observed. "Sometimes it becomes physical. You proclaim the nobility of your own deeds, yet seek to punish others for the same."

"And you think we should allow spies and traitors into our midst?"

She frowned and made a sort of shrugging gesture, made difficult by her horns. "Of course not. I am simply confused by this contradictory hypocrisy."

"And Borelians are perfect and noble?" Rifun asked, feeling the anger burn beneath his scars. "You were the one who was actually labeled a traitor by your own people. You were the one who sought to learn *dijik* arts."

"Yet my motivations and actions were in line with my people's needs and values. The Borelians are one, a single, unified entity."

Rifun took an even breath and approached her. "You don't understand because you've not been defeated. You've never been subjugated. You've never been enslaved. Once you've been there, you'll do anything to avoid going back. Sometimes that produces contradictions."

"And as you are the one who was defeated, subjugated, and enslaved, and who hates the ones who did it to him, what gives you the authority to impose such a thing on others?"

"What authority do you have to enslave others?"

"The command of Tujor and the Council of Ancrath and the Great Admirals of the Fleet and the Ul Ik Zol. We are Borelians, set apart from the rest of the universe."

Rifun shook his head. "Yet you don't conquer. The power to enslave the universe, whether by vessel or portal, and you don't do it. Why?" He studied her. "Are you backing out on us? Are you...afraid? Are you afraid of power?"

"We do not expand our power beyond our ability to control," Isthim informed him. She gave him a look. "I want to ensure that we are not doing the same here. Nor do I want you to falter in a moment of weakness."

He Banded and looked at her. She was pink, and he was aware of her toxins, so he was not affected by the side effects. There was certainly no passive compliance in him at the moment. After a moment, he let out a breath and released the Band.

"You're questioning me intentionally," he stated.

She nodded once. "Yes. I want you to know where you stand, what you believe, where your loyalties lie, and what your priorities are. Such things are easier to contemplate here and now, especially as you read the Book of Philosophy, rather than in the heat of the moment."

He huffed a sigh and gave her a look. "I don't know whether to kiss you or slap you."

"You can thank me by making a decision. We are at a critical point of growth, and we must have everyone on board for this to work."

"I know. Now if you'll excuse me, I have some reading to do."

She regarded him a moment longer before turning and letting herself out, the door closing with remarkable silence save for the single click of it shutting.

He stood there a good five minutes, just breathing and trying to sort things out in his mind. The whole exchange seemed to be a contradiction. He knew why she'd done it. He couldn't say that he blamed her, or even that he wasn't grateful; it was almost endearing, for a Borelian.

When it came right down to it, he supposed that he really just hated that it needed to be brought up and discussed at all. He took a calming breath and closed his eyes.

Immediately he was assaulted with memories of the Uprising. The pain, the screams, the death, the torture. He was able to keep it under control in that he did not smell the burn and the rot, nor did it dance before his eyes when he opened them again, but there were days when his control lapsed, even just for a moment, and tore his mind apart.

He looked at the Book of Philosophy in his hands, glanced at the window behind him where he knew the army lived and trained.

This isn't like that, he told himself. *We're liberating people from slavery. We're saving them from the folly of addiction and loyalty to corrupt bureaucrats. But you can't just let spies and traitors run free, or they'll turn everything back on itself and the corruption will not only become worse, but harder to fight the next time.*

He went to the window and pushed aside the curtain. Everything appeared normal. Isthim had the view of the training grounds, as one might expect, but for him, he had a view of the street and several houses that had weathered the ages better than some, needing little repair. A few people meandered about, talking and appearing well at ease.

This isn't like that, he told himself, turning away and letting the curtain drop. *We're not prioritizing one people over another. We're not putting ourselves over everything. We want people to be equal, to be free, to make their own choices. We only want to guide them, to help them along the way. We want to make them see.*

He couldn't let Isthim turn the army into a machine of conquest. He couldn't let Cassius become the secret police, murdering in the dark, especially when he would do it just because he got bored.

And yet, at this time, the army was necessary. Cassius was necessary. Weren't they? Of course they were. The army had been necessary to throw off the French, and it would have been—well, maybe not dissolved, but scaled down, once the people were free. Similarly, once the Wheel was under their full control and they no longer had to worry about major threats like the Tacagans, then they could dismiss part of their army. They were studying peaceful things. Akari things. Things of the Author. Once everyone was on the same page, force was no longer necessary.

They just had to get people to accept the Akari. It was a bitter pill, perhaps, but necessary. Those who did would come to understand. Those who didn't would be powerless to stop them anyway.

And the Akarin? Once they saw how well things were going, they wouldn't dare to disrupt it.

This isn't like that, he told himself. *It's far better.* He would lead his people to their salvation this time. He would lead the Cult.

He prayed at his shrine for a few minutes, then took the Book of Philosophy to his bed to read for a bit.

Comparing the beliefs he'd grown up with to the philosophy Richard had written of in his journal made Rifun feel a bit more at ease about the situation, and he figured that he could glean a few rules and commands from what he was reading to apply to the Laws of Time. Or rewrite them, he supposed. Time was no longer king here; it was now the Akari. The Hands of Time were no longer the end-all authority in the universe, but the Author. It would take time to make the necessary adjustments, but they would be better off for it in the long run.

Still, he was hopeful that Isthim would be able to strip away some of the more useless Laws of Time, if for no other reason than to win over some of the more pliable minds. The new rules would then guide them and rein in the more rigid minds.

He was also hopeful that the Book of Commands would be returned swiftly and in good order. Few could outrun a Borelian hunter for that long; the only reason Isthim had been successful was because she'd had intimate knowledge of their tactics; the Ururian had no such luxury. Even if he was trying to be crafty with portal usage, the hunters would be upon him soon enough.

They just had to weather a little uncertainty, keep an eye on the Tacagans, and all would be well in the end. They would have this wrapped up by the end of the year.

He set the book aside, stood, stretched, walked around, and went to the window again. As before, everything was normal, but he was far less apprehensive.

After considering his options for a few minutes, he turned and left his chambers. He did not seek out Isthim or Cassius, nor did he run into them on his way out of the officers building. Around him, city life seemed to be dwindling into the later hours, when some might decide to retire while others were just waking. The overt excitement of the parade and the festivities seemed to have mostly burned off, but there remained a spring in the step and a pride about the eye.

He nodded to himself. They should feel proud, he thought. They'd done it. They'd won. The greatest pride seemed to come from those who had been former Akarin. Years of fractured leadership and rigid pacifism, and for what? What had it ever accomplished? But this, now, this was something they could point to and say they had helped. They'd done this. They'd overthrown a corrupt regime and brought peace. Yes, they should feel proud.

Not a few of the grunts came to attention—with varying degrees of precision— as he walked by, though plenty more just stared at him, wide-eyed, as if they couldn't believe that he was a real person. He acknowledged them all in turn without breaking stride and left the city feeling as though everything had been accomplished and there was nothing left to do.

This was a lie, of course, as there was plenty yet to do. The Book of Commands had to be found, the Tacagans dealt with, but he actually felt as though it could be done. It was not just another chore list of things that had to get done, it was a list of tasks to accomplish, goals to achieve, and he had the means and the power to do it all.

The darkness of the tunnels swallowed him, and the twitch of apprehension he felt at it was enough to draw him back to reality, like a fish on a line. There was work to be done.

He did not return to the family farm, but took himself straight to the tombs.

There he prayed and made offerings, thanking the ancestors and the spirits for their guidance, asking for their help, just enough to complete his task.

"You've nearly succeeded, then?"

Reflexive Banding bought Rifun time to at least manage his Disguise as well as calm himself somewhat and look around to see who had spoken. When he saw it was only the shaman, he relaxed, released his Band, and shed his Disguise.

"My apologies," Andrianary said humbly, putting his hands up a bit as he approached, looking a bit unsteady. "I did not mean to startle you. Normally you are very perceptive; I thought you had already sensed me."

Rifun took an even breath. "I have a lot on my mind, a lot to do."

"Things have changed since we last met?" The old man sat down hard on a rock.

"How did you know I was here?" Rifun wondered.

Andrianary chuckled. "I didn't, not really. But I figured that if the spirits led me to be at this place at this time, there were few reasons for it. You were one of those reasons."

Couldn't argue that one.

"So then," he went on. "Things have changed?"

Rifun hesitated, then said, "The Book of Commands is missing."

"This is one of the three books written by the spirits, yes?"

Rifun had not disclosed everything to the shaman. He did not try to explain the Time industry or alien worlds or any of that, and he made only the vaguest of references to the Cult of the Akari and their operations. The Akari he understood well, and he understood Cassius and the shadow spirit. All the old man knew about the journals was that they were supposedly books written by the spirits. Cassius and the dark spirit wanted them, but so did Rifun and the other dual-spirited people, the good ones who touched the *razana*.

"That's right," he replied. "Not the most important one, but any of them impart great knowledge."

"Understandable. What do you mean it's gone missing?"

"We thought we had it, but it was a fake, planted to throw us off."

Andrianary frowned and nodded slowly. "I see. Do you believe Cassius may have a lead on it and is trying to distract you?"

"It's not out of the realm of possibility. We have a good idea where it is, so it's just a matter of getting there first."

"Hm." The shaman continued to nod. "I have this small inkling that this place is shrouded in darkness."

"You think he already has it?" Rifun asked.

The old man shook his head. "No. Not as such. It is the same, but different." He sighed and his expression appeared in some disquiet. "These things, I have no words for them, no good way to describe them."

Rifun knelt before him. "May I look in your mind and see what you see?"

Andrianary hesitated for only a moment before agreeing.

It was similar to Feel, but where Feel used Matter, the ability that Rifun called See used Energy. It was a kind of waking dream-walk, he supposed, manipulating the electricity and energy of the brain, connecting their minds so that Rifun could see and feel what the shaman saw and felt. Like his blindsight, it was not true sight or touch, but more of an impression in real time.

He touched the shaman's knee and, as gently as he could manage, Felt him. He started out this way, noting that the old man was weaker than before, with the beginning of sickness spreading throughout his body. It was when he touched the spinal cord that he switched to Energy and went to the brain to See.

It was as though someone wrapped a heavy blanket around him, covered him, smothered him. He felt the darkness as much as he saw it, and no light could penetrate if it tried. When he opened his mouth—unsure if he was doing so in the waking world or if he'd slipped into some sort of vision—his sinuses and lungs were accosted by acid, like swallowing thorns. He closed his mouth, but the damage was done. When he moved, tried to reach out, there was a flash of light...

...and he was falling backwards, hitting the ground in an ungraceful heap. He was coughing uncontrollably, trying to rid his body of acid and thorns that no longer stung, thus confusing his senses even more, and he was completely blind for a good two minutes. As he finally relaxed and listened, he noted that Andrianary was having some difficulty breathing.

Rifun fought his way to a sitting position and put his hand on the old man's knee once more.

"Elder, I felt the sickness in you," he said. "Will you let me help?"

Andrianary waved a hand. "I am an old man, Rivotra. I am grateful for each day, and I am ready to join the ancestors." He put his hand on Rifun's head. "Fear not, for even in death, I will still help you."

Rifun sat back on the ground, more intentionally this time. "That light. What was it?"

The shaman barked a laugh. "You went through all that effort so you could explain it to me, remember? I don't understand these things, Rivotra. This is beyond me, beyond the living except for those like you. You must be the teacher now. Tell me, what was the darkness?"

Rifun opened his mouth, and he could have sworn he tasted just a tinge of acid, or perhaps just vinegar, still on his lips. He swallowed nervously, opened his mouth again, but it was a long moment before he found any words.

"Death," he said finally. "And the acid was the rot that eats away at the flesh of humanity while living. Living death."

"Mm," Andrianary mused. He frowned. "These are such simple words you use. But the feel of it...!" He made a double fist for all he was worth, which wasn't much for a man so ancient. "There was...there was power and-and-and force and...anger, even. Yes, there was anger. An uncontrollable rage such that the stars tremble and fear to shine! And suffocating smoke and shadow like a smothering blanket." He made a sound of frustration. "These words...far too simple for this evil darkness!"

Rifun nodded slowly. "Agreed."

The old man gave him a look. "Does this mean that the dark spirit already has this book you seek?"

"I don't think so." Rifun shifted position. "And actually, I think I have an idea of what I should do."

"Truly?"

He nodded. "I do." He stood. "It won't be easy, but if I'm right, it's time for me to truly break into Building."

Andrianary beamed. "Oh, so lovely! Ah, I never thought I would see such splendor in my lifetime."

"Perhaps that is why the spirits have granted you such a long life," Rifun told him cheekily.

"Ah, watch yourself, Rivotra." The shaman's tone was still light-hearted. "Remember that I shall still join the ancestors before you. I may be befuddled for the moment, but soon enough, I will know more than you could understand this side of the grave, even being dual-spirited."

"Is that a challenge? Because you know I enjoy learning, and I'm a quick study."

"Don't become arrogant." Now his tone was a little cooler. "There is far more power to be had, but it comes from both good and bad spirits, as this man Cassius has demonstrated. Do not kill his body only to take on this dark spirit yourself."

"Of course not," Rifun replied humbly. "I meant no offense."

The shaman nodded, a small smile on his lips. "Of course not. Just remember who and what you are. The power you wield is not for the foolish or faint-hearted, and arrogance is a vice of lesser men. Be confident in what you do know, and do it well, but there will always be more to learn."

Rifun assented.

"Now then," Andrianary huffed, sounding more upbeat, "what do you suppose you will need for this Building of yours? How shall you prepare?"

Actually, Rifun had no real idea what he needed or how to prepare. Usually, in the stories, that part was glossed over, and that was assuming they even remotely resembled what he was going to be trying to do. But, when all else failed, ask the spirits for help. If they were the ones showing him how to tap into and work this power, they ought to have some idea how it was to be done.

"I will need an offering," he said finally. "More than simply going before one ancestor or asking for a specific favor, I will require a full offering with blessings." He nodded once. "This must be done before anything else can take place."

Andrianary groaned as he got to his feet, waving off Rifun when he tried to help. "I'll see what I can do. Must it be done immediately, or can you come back tomorrow?"

"As soon as possible."

The old man looked a bit distressed by this, but the shaman knew better than to argue. He took a breath, nodded, and promised to be back before sunset.

Rifun elected to Slow Band the time, but the shaman returned much sooner than he had really expected. He led a cow pulling a small cart. On the small cart was a goat and a crate of three chickens, as well as an assortment of ritualistic accessories: beads, shells, bones, rocks, gems, knives, and so on. There was also a small jar of rice, a small jar of honey, and a few fruits and vegetables.

"I wasn't sure what the spirits would want," the shaman said, "so I grabbed everything."

It was then that Rifun considered that he probably should have spent his time asking the spirits what kind of offering or sacrifice they expected, rather than impatiently Banding.

"The cow will witness," he stated, the words erupting from his mouth before he fully understood them, as though someone spoke for him. "The goat will be sacrificed with the chickens."

He then directed Andrianary on how things were to be set up, the arrangement of the beads and gems, the bones and rocks, and which knives to use and for what purpose.

It was a strange sensation, giving orders to a shaman like that. No one told a shaman or a diviner what to do. And yet it felt right. He had the power and authority to do these things. Andrianary knew it, and he was bowing to it. This pleased Rifun in a way he could not describe, as though this feeling, this rightness, were on the same level as the darkness and light from the earlier vision. This was from the spirits, and that transcended anything the old man could have said to him.

The goat was led forward so that it stood before the entrance to the tomb where it was tied off to a small tree. One chicken was tied by its leg to one side of the goat's neck, and a second chicken on its other side. The third chicken was tied between the goat's horns. All three were squawking and difficult to manage, but once they realized they weren't getting away, they simply went limp.

Rifun himself picked up the blooding knife. There was nothing particularly special about it except for the purple paint on its wooden grip. He walked up behind the goat, facing the tombs.

"Ancestors," he began, "you've not brought me this far to give up now. But in order to continue, I know that I must let go of the weight of this world and this life."

He grabbed the chicken on the goat's right. It flapped its wings a few times and clucked which made the others get antsy which made the goat snort and stomp a hoof, but Rifun paid it no mind.

"For the VVS," he stated.

He cut off the chicken's head. The sudden wild death movements from the headless carcass spooked the goat, but it could go nowhere.

As if in a dream, he simply moved around to the goat's other side and grabbed the chicken on its left.

"For the Army," he said.

He beheaded the second chicken. Again the wild movements scared the goat which screamed and pulled against its ties, to no avail.

Now Rifun put the goat between his legs and took hold of the third chicken, far less twitchy since it was tied to both horns.

"For the Uprising."

The third head fell on the goat's nose. The goat threw its head back and might have caught Rifun, except, even in his trance-like state, he was able to move patiently out of the way. Then he grabbed the goat's horns and pulled the head back.

"I go forward into lands unknown to this world, unknown to all the living," he went on. "I enter into darkness to defeat the living shadows that lay beyond the reach of mortal men. And I slay them."

He cut the goat's throat in a single, swift slice. Blood drenched the tree where it had been tied and splattered on the surrounding rocks. It touched the beads and the rocks and the gems and the shells and especially the bones. The goat's front legs buckled and it collapsed from beneath Rifun. Still its neck pulsed blood, staining his shoes and the hem of his pants, but it mattered not; his clothes were already speckled red from the violent thrashing of the chicken carcasses, still tied to the dead goat.

Only when the blood had stopped completely did Rifun move forward. Beyond the beads and shells and other accessories, the rice, fruits, and vegetables were laid out, untouched by the blood. Rifun got down on his knees before the food and picked up the bowl of food.

"And now," he finished, "I take what is mine."

He tipped up the bowl and ate. Behind him, he knew Andrianary made some sort of sound of protest but quickly strangled it within himself. It was unconscionable to eat of food intended for the ancestors. To do so was to risk the wrath of the ancestors and all the spirits, cursing oneself and even one's family.

But Rifun was beyond that. This was him taking his place as a dual-spirited, living soul, taking his place as a Builder, challenging any vengeful spirits and eager to take them on. This was inviting the dark spirit that was within Cassius to come and face him. This was his ascent into the spirit realm without ever leaving the realm of men.

When he finished the food, he sat there with his eyes closed, simply savoring the moment. No spirits came to challenge him, but neither did he have any visions as he might have hoped. He would not say he was not disappointed, for he might have hoped to speak to his mother or Nibe, to know that he was doing the right thing. But then, the spirits had guided him this far. Why wouldn't this be the right thing? Such precision in one's sacrifice and offering was not made without guidance from the spirits after all.

Finally he opened his eyes. The dishes lay empty before him, and the tomb was as silent as ever.

Slowly, he got to his feet. As he did, he turned his face in the direction of the sun...and passed out.

Pain registered before anything else when he finally came to, and he quickly had it localized to his old head injury. As he sat up, he put a hand to the back of his head and found the bare spot. Touching it, he found the folded skin and misshapen bone. If he put a little pressure on it, he found pain. Looking around, he still saw the impressions of his blindsight, not true vision. He also felt an aching in his shoulder and collarbone from his old bullet wound. Looking at himself, he still bore the scars of torture.

He tried not to feel disappointment, tried to dismiss it as reflexive and even childish. He was still a mortal man, of course he would feel pain. But he had made the sacrifices, shed those parts of his life, stepped out of the mortal world and into the spirit world. Should he not have something to truly show for it?

He took an even breath. That was what the Akari was for. He was fully able to heal himself, always had been. But perhaps that was all a foolish fantasy, a connection to his past lives. Mere men bore scars. The spirits had no scars.

But that did not mean they could not feel pain or be killed. He was on a quest to do just that. And why shouldn't he show off his might? Why shouldn't he show the world, the universe, that he could not be brought down so easily? He had eaten the food of offering, challenged the spirits. Why should he hide from that? Why should he face the spirits but cower from men?

Finally he got to his feet and looked around. Flies had gathered in huge swarms to crawl over the chickens and the goat and the great quantities of blood spilled from them. The cow still stood in its yoke on the cart, pointed tongue licking its nose, large eyes watching him with only passing interest.

Then he saw the shaman.

Without thinking, Rifun clumsily leapt from his spot, landed in sticky half-congealed blood and a swarm of flies, slipped, put a hand perfectly in another mess of blood and flies, skidded forward, finally righted himself and reached the old man.

Andrianary was dead.

He lay on his back beside the cart, eyes blankly staring off at something in the trees, mouth hung slack so that flies buzzed in and out. He was cold, rigid, and pale.

Rifun stood suddenly and whirled around to face the tombs, unsure exactly what he was intending to do. Was this punishment from the spirits for eating the food? Had his challenge been answered? Had Andrianary paid the price for his arrogance? Or was this simply a willing sacrifice? Had Andrianary known this would happen? Had Rifun gained something from his death? If Rifun was a living soul, intent on Building and weaving with the *razana*, a power only beholden to the spirits, had a human life been necessary for him to procure that power?

He didn't know what to do. He knew Andrianary's family tombs were some distance away, and the old man had earned every right afforded to him for a funeral. Did he don his elderly Disguise, go to town, find someone, tell them what happened? Did he use his youthful Disguise, claim himself as Fan, and try to explain? It was not necessary for people to know or understand what had taken place here, although such heady animistic displays were rarer than they used to be. But still. What did he do or say?

In the end, he donned his elderly Disguise, went to town, and fetched Andrianary's wife and children. The shaman's demise overshadowed the sudden appearance of Rivotra Andilan.

The old man's body was taken away, and another, younger, shaman was called in to properly dispose of the remains of the ceremony. Any remaining spectators were shooed from the area so it could be cleansed, and Rifun returned to the town with everyone else.

Andrianary's death was already popular gossip by the time they got back, but it wasn't long before someone called him out.

"Rivotra!"

He turned to see Sambatra approaching, expression both confused and ecstatic. The younger man pulled him into a grand embrace.

"Why didn't you tell us you were returning?"

"I wanted to surprise you," Rifun offered lamely.

"Well, you've certainly done that. Did you hear about Andrianary? He just died this morning."

"I know. I've paid my respects for the time being. At least until the funeral."

Sambatra nodded somberly. "Good. I know you were close with him in the end."

"His presence will be missed, but his power remains," Rifun said with certainty. "And he had great spiritual power."

"Yes, he did." Sambatra nodded again, then clapped Rifun on the shoulder. "But now, we have other matters to attend to, like your sudden return. Things are taken care of in London, then?"

He should have masqueraded as his son. "I believe so. I may have to go back once or twice more to settle things. And to see Fan and Julianna."

"Of course, of course. No rush. We're always happy to have you; you know that." Sambatra looked around, expression puzzled. "Do you have luggage or bags of some sort?"

He definitely should have masqueraded as his son. Rifun cleared his throat. "I seem to have misplaced them in all the excitement around Andrianary."

Sambatra grinned. "Let's look around a bit. I'm sure they haven't run off."

Rifun managed to ditch his cousin long enough to open a swift series of portals back to the tunnels where he Banded to get back to the city and his chambers where he hastily packed a couple of bags, wrote an even quicker note saying that he would be gone for a few days, then ran back out of the city, into the tunnels, dropped the Band, and opened another series of portals back to town.

"Found them," he said, emerging from a narrow passage between two houses and praying no one had seen him and that he did not appear to be winded for what was, to others, a very short search. "As I said, only misplaced."

"Wonderful," Sambatra said, grinning. "Here, let me take them for you."

"You can take one," Rifun told him. "I can't let myself get so old so fast."

His cousin laughed heartily. "Ah, Rivotra. You have had far too much European influence, I think. Come. Let us get you back where you belong, among family."

Offense and Defense

kokumbo

Cassius started with Micaiah's apartment, if only because he already knew where it was and how to get in. It was as simple as using Magnetism to manipulate the keyhole and unlock the door when Micaiah and his girlfriend weren't home.

As expected, the place had been cleaned up since the previous attack and bore the marks of regular housecleaning. Although, as Cassius snooped in every cabinet and cupboard, looked in every cookie jar and tested every laminated floorboard and tile for trapdoors, he noted that something about it seemed off, but he couldn't say just what.

It wasn't until he got to the bedroom that he figured it out. All of her clothes were gone. Clothes, jewelry, knickknacks, decor, everything about the apartment that was feminine had been removed. Had they split up after the Time Trial because he'd named her as the Stake? Had they simply woken up the morning after the ith Borelians got to them and each one had no idea who the other was?

Whatever the case, she was gone and the journal was nowhere to be found.

He checked the twin brother's apartment, too, just in case Micaiah had thought to get creative. No luck there either.

Next he went to Doug's house and was momentarily overwhelmed by the sheer vanity of the man. Cassius could remember a time when rich, esteemed men had portraits of themselves hung over the mantel. Doug seemed to think that he needed to see himself on every wall, not just over the mantel. The man was literally everywhere, with almost no common decor or even blank wall space. Some were actual photos, others were paintings, and some were prints such as one might see in a newspaper or at a movie theater. The content of these self-aggrandizing illustrations ranged from simple, semi-humble photos, to imagining himself as the great heroes and leaders of history, to making himself out to be a romantic hero of fiction, to more pornographic visuals tucked away in the bedroom he evidently called his own.

Cassius wouldn't say he didn't have an ego, and he'd accused Rifun of having a big ego on more than one occasion. Rifun was practically a priest taking a vow of modesty, poverty, and silence compared to this.

It was also very, very unnerving to have so many eyes of Doug watching him as he rifled through cupboards, dressers, and boxes, and checked for false floors and walls to no avail. He was actually relieved when he finished his search, although disappointed that the journal wasn't here, either. Cassius was surprised, actually, and wondered, if Doug did get his hands on it, whether he wouldn't go through and replace Richard or the Author herself with his own likeness. If not for the sheer fact that the Books had appeared before Doug's existence, Cassius might have expected Doug to be the Author, masquerading as a deity and building an entire religion around himself, but not saying so in some false show of piety.

Nathan Wilde was the next home he visited, though it took small effort to find. His was a refreshing reset compared to the ego that was Doug's house. Nathan appeared to be very modest, needing little more than two bedrooms, a bathroom, a kitchen, and a small living room. He had no pictures of himself save for those in which he posed with others. Given that almost all of those other people were children who ranged in age from five to fifteen, give or take, with hundreds of photos and almost no duplicate children, Cassius might have guessed that he did some kind of social work.

So he'd gone from overwhelming ego to nauseating philanthropy. Lovely. And somehow he and Doug had been able to work together to fend off the Bat, the Day, and him, Cassius, at the Time Trial? Seemed unlikely except that Cassius had been there and witnessed it.

Everywhere he looked, there were more pictures and other feel-good mementos, frames with awards for being a decent human being, boxes and chests full of heartfelt letters of joy and happiness and love for all the good work he did and what a good influence he was. Briefly, Cassius wondered how the man would react if he got home that night to find that his house had burned down, and with it, all the pictures and awards and letters.

But for all that, there was still no journal. Well, there were plenty of journals as the man appeared to have developed a habit of writing about his day in painstakingly specific detail. Cassius looked through these journals, hoping for some painstaking specific details on the whereabouts of the Book of Commands, but he wrote down nothing as it related to Time or the Akari. All the books, all the albums, all the paper and letters, all the books in his bookcase, and still there was nothing to go on.

His search for hidden doors in walls and floor yielded only an access panel that took him into a crawlspace beneath the house. Everything appeared standard, if a bit moldy, and still there was no evidence of the journal.

As for Andrew O'Dell, Cassius couldn't even figure out what planet he was living on, much less a specific street address. The man had ghosted off of Earth some hundred years ago and left no trace of his existence. Because he was fully Akarin with no ties to the Time industry for yet another hundred years or so, Archive records were even more useless.

He set that aside in favor of trying to track down Aklaq White Bear, hoping that her more recent departure from Micaiah's apartment would yield more current and more fruitful results.

This was not the case. Perhaps it was too soon after her departure, that she hadn't established herself elsewhere; there was no paper trail to follow because there was no destination to seek.

Frustrated, Cassius returned to the ruins. He approached Rifun's chambers, knocked, got no answer. When he tried the door, it was locked. This proved no challenge for him, but he found the room empty anyway. He was just about to leave when something caught his eye. It was a note left on his table, remarkably clean considering his normal state of mind.

"Returning to Earth for a short time. Will be back as soon as possible. Not tied up, so you can fetch me if needed. -Rifun"

Cassius rolled his eyes. Rifun couldn't rightly be called a traitor, but that didn't mean he wasn't useless sometimes.

But the nice thing about being human was that he didn't have to figure out a Disguise or brush up on etiquette when making social calls to Earth. It wasn't hard to find the Andilan farm, though he did have to do a double-take when he saw Rifun, sitting on the back porch with others he assumed were family members.

For one, he was remarkably white compared to the others. When Cassius had seen him in London, he was a bit darker compared to other Londoners, and to Julianna. Now he stuck out like, well, like a white man among Africans. And he was old. Cassius knew it was a Disguise—or he hoped it was—but it was a stunning change, to see him aged from a young and ambitious twenty-something to a frail and withered sixty- or seventy-something, however old he was supposed to be. His hair was gray, face lined with wrinkles, large scars twisted grotesquely by wrinkles and small scars almost nonexistent because of them. And he appeared happy. Genuinely happy. He said something, someone replied, he laughed, a pretty young woman stepped out of the house with a tray of drinks, and he accepted one with a smile.

This was where the man wanted to be, Cassius realized. This was the life he never had, the one he'd always wanted.

Rage and intense jealousy greater than anything Cassius had ever known flared through him. His heart and lungs contorted so that he could not breathe and yet felt the need to scream obscenities and blasphemy to the sky and every god that inhabited it.

He tempered this murderous rage only with the thought that maybe he should leave Rifun alone. Maybe if the man stayed away for another year, he wouldn't come back the next time. Maybe he would get overly sentimental and stay for a good ten years or so, to finish out his "natural" lifespan. Barring that, maybe he would be trampled by a cow or killed in some other normal way. Disease also did wonders, though the Akari typically rendered such a thing moot.

Cassius turned and started walking away, got ten steps into it when he stopped, turned back around, and made his way toward the farm. After a good fifteen steps, he stopped again. What did he need Rifun for anyway? What could Rifun do that he or Isthim couldn't?

He watched Rifun a bit longer before finally turning and actually walking away. He wouldn't disturb the man, would hope that he stayed away for good this time, and he wouldn't tell Isthim about this new development. They could do things just fine on their own.

As always, she was overseeing something to do with the army. He waited until she was done speaking with Misik and two of her other comrades before approaching.

"Have you found the journal?" she asked.

He grunted and shook his head. "No. All of the Earth homes are empty. I can't even find Andrew O'Dell. I need to go to the Akarin fortress. Finding coordinates are impossible, but your teams have been there."

Isthim raised a brow. "It would be unwise to send more Borelians to that place; it may disrupt the way the ith left it."

"Won't that fade anyway?"

"Yes, but why rush?" She went on before he could protest. "Why not ask Rifun? He's been there more than my people have; he will have an easier time getting you there."

"He's busy," Cassius offered lamely. He sighed. "I don't need anyone to go with me. I just need to get in, see if Andrew or any of the others have any lockers or safes or other secret hideaways that they might have used there to hide the journal."

"All the better reason to ask Rifun who has been there multiple times."

"I don't want to ask Rifun!" Cassius snapped.

Isthim blinked. Then, "Fine. I will open a portal there for you. Like any natural place, the portal will not stay open. You will have to get back on your own."

"That's fine, just get me there!"

She agreed, and they made for the tunnels to begin the series of jumps. Why was she so insistent that he ask Rifun for help? Why couldn't she do it? He wasn't asking for her to go on a raid with him; he just needed transportation. Like going anywhere by feel rather than coordinates, it was just easier to be shown by someone who had already been there rather than try to make the jump blind.

A series of jumps, and then he was in the Akarin fortress. Or he hoped he was. Any portal was taxing, blind portals even more so, but there was something about going to the Akarin fortress that sapped the life out of him. Was this how they remained unconquered, that they drained the energy of everyone coming in so that they could not fight?

Well, at the very least, he was not assaulted. When he finally picked himself up off the floor, he found that he was in a room covered in metal plates with large tubes running along the walls, as if protecting wires for electricity, or perhaps running water.

He stumbled his way toward the only opening he saw, a large doorway opening up into an amazing atrium big enough to fit the officers building and then some. In the center, an enormous stone staircase spiraled its way upwards, and two large, long corridors branched off from two walls. There also seemed to be some kind of smaller opening off to his right, but it appeared gated. There were no guards, but Cassius didn't want to press his luck.

The Borelian teams had swept through the fortress like a storm, or so they boasted. Because of the nature of their toxins, they had only to worry about ranged threats, those outside their sphere of influence, but it had been only a minor concern. The ith Borelians had done their best to erase almost all memory of the Cult of the

Akari and anything they'd heard concerning them beyond a subconscious thought that they were no danger and to ignore them. They'd also muddled the memories surrounding the function of the Akarin at large, confusing people as to who was in power, why, how they functioned and operated. Simple logic dictated that there would be extensive infighting, thus keeping the Akarin busy even without smoothing over and erasing any fears they may have had about the Cult.

Cassius had suggested erasing everything about the Akarin, who they were, what they believed, what they learned, and get them out of the way completely. Bring them over to the Cult and teach them there, tell them that the Cult was how things had always been. Seemed simple enough to him, and even Isthim and Misik agreed.

Rifun and Julianna did not. Julianna's fear was that they would come across the Books and realize what had happened, or at least question it. That would only fracture them back into the Cult and the Akarin, and all progress would be lost. Even if they destroyed the current Books, who was to say that more would not appear? Obviously it seemed as though they would, given that there were more listed in the front of the Books. Rifun agreed with her, saying that if they could bring everything to a smoother, more peaceful resolution now, with the Books and memories mostly in tact, the reformation, alliance, subjugation, however it formed, would be stronger for longer.

They could have wiped out their single greatest credible enemy in one shot, but, somehow, doing it the hard way was morally superior, spiritually righteous. Chivalrous, even. Cassius briefly wondered about the feasibility of asking for forgiveness over permission. Asking permission seemed to be going nowhere, least of all forward. But he was still a Harvester; he could still kill at a touch.

Because of the nature of the Borelian attack, they had been warned that there could be lingering side effects. Touching something second-hand from a Borelian was the same as being exposed to their offgas, and they had touched a lot of stuff in their raids. So Cassius did his best not to touch anything, though he also wondered how long the secondhand touch was effective, and how many people had to touch the toxin secondhand before there was nothing left. If enough people touched the same doorknob, it couldn't be as effective at the last person as it had been for the first.

With the population somewhat depleted, and no one who was present apparently knowing who he was, he was free to move about the fortress relatively unharmed. Not a few people stopped and stared at him, even alien countenances conveying an expression of desperate familiarity, knowing that they knew him but unable to say how. A few bristled at him, some latent instinct reminding them that he was dangerous, but he discovered that if he also pretended to be ignorant of everyone else, stuck in the same memory fog as them, then he was more likely to be left alone.

Not that this was terribly difficult, given that he didn't know the layout of the fortress, and he spent a great deal of time being lost. Of course, this afforded him an excellent opportunity to check every nook and cranny, except he couldn't be sure that he didn't forget any, or that he didn't check some two or three or more times.

He went floor by floor. Recreation, barracks, meeting rooms, more barracks.

He blanched when he got to the fifth floor and found the Archives. It wouldn't be as bad as having to search through the Wheel Archives, but that didn't mean he was excited for it.

He found plenty of leatherbound books, plenty of journals, plenty of leatherbound journals. None of them were the Book of Commands. The time it took to search the Archives alone put him in a monstrous mood, plus the time on the other floors, and he still had two more to go.

Cassius got distracted on the sixth floor, but it did help his mood. It was always a good day to find a weapons cache. Some things he could identify, some things he couldn't. He promised to return and help himself to a few things, maybe take them to Jora and see what he could get, or what he could use them for.

The seventh floor was food stores. He wasn't in much of a mood to search through every single container, but wouldn't it be perfect to hide the journal in a crate of oranges? Who was going to randomly pop open a crate of oranges? And if it got taken down to the cafeteria, well, the cooks might know what to do with it. Maybe.

It sounded absurd, but Cassius wasn't going to be outdone. The last thing he needed was to ignore this place, ignore the crate of oranges, and then have it turn up later in the crate of oranges. Rifun would never let him live it down.

But there was no journal, just a lot of food that was probably going to spoil now that he'd broken open the containers.

Standing there on the southeast staircase, he ran over in his mind everything he'd done. Had he truly searched everywhere? After a full day of searching, it was hard to say. There were a lot of stones for one man to overturn, and he'd used every trick he knew: Gravity, Magnetism, Light, Sound, Force, Thermodynamics, Electricity, even some he had no good name for except that he could do it. He'd scoured the Archives, but maybe he'd missed something? He couldn't believe that the trail ended here.

Displeased with his results but not wanting to go back and search through everything yet again today, he headed down the stairs. Once at the bottom, he made his way through the south corridor to the southwest staircase, where the portal room lay like an unwanted mole off to the side.

He elected to go to the Wheel for a bit, sit, think, eat, maybe see if the Wheel Archives had anything at all on the Akarin fortress. Surely a place that big had some secret rooms to dig through. He hadn't even found evidence of Andrew O'Dell, not that he knew what to look for. He headed to the Food Court to grab a bite to eat. It wasn't so much that he was hungry, as he just wanted to taste something.

Just as he was going to step up to the counter to order his meal, there was a tremor beneath his feet, like the outer ring of an earthquake many miles away. Then there was a sound like a distant explosion and the whole room was thrown sideways. As Cassius reached for Gravity, the room gave another huge lurch. The forces changed again and he lost the track.

He tumbled through the air only briefly before striking something. He coughed once before something else hit him. He could hardly say which way was up except that the Food Court had normal directions, and up was not where up was supposed to be.

Whatever had happened, though, its effects appeared to have run their course. Cassius slammed hard into something which he discovered was an alien with rather tough skin. It made a sound that he discerned was both displeasure as well as pain. Cassius slid off the thing, fought for balance amid a sudden dune of debris, and looked around.

"Down" appeared to be centrally located around one corner of what used to be a wall and ceiling vertex, but other than that, the room as a whole was in tact. Looking "up" at the new ceiling, Cassius spotted the exit portal. It wasn't even where it was supposed to be, and it didn't look especially stable.

Not wanting to get trapped in the Food Court, he immediately invoked Gravity, thinking only afterwards that it really could have made things much worse, depending on what had happened. But, he reasoned with himself, as he soared upward to the portal, it hadn't made things worse, and he was well on his way to being free.

He threw himself through the portal, heedless of any danger on the other side. Where there should have been floor, he was met with open air once more, and normal gravity took over. This time, he was able to save himself, erecting a Gravity track and slowing himself before he slammed into another pile of debris.

At the very least, he'd landed in the right room; the portal hadn't been redirected in some manner.

Looking around, this room wasn't much better. Normally it, too, had standard directions as it led to several different wings, but now everything was off-kilter. Actually, the Food Court was off-kilter. This room had been shaken by a giant.

Amid the destruction and debris, a variety of aliens picking themselves up and digging for those trapped in the carnage, Cassius' attention turned toward the Auctions. The portal appeared to still be in tact. Carefully rearranging his Gravity track, he floated his way there.

There was no way the Tacagans had learned the Akari; that would mean submitting to the idea of a deity-like figure. Given that he'd just been to the Akarin fortress and wasted a day or more of his life there, it couldn't be them. Or rather, it wouldn't be their army necessarily. That meant they were dealing with a traitor, or else something physical. Maybe this time it really was the Tacagans going after the gravitational balancers.

The thought actually gave him pause, if only because it made the Tacagans appear as a worthy enemy. They did not cower behind morals or some notion of higher ground other than their own inherent superiority. If there was an advantage to be had, they would take it. If they could undermine or attempt to match their opponent's obviously superior abilities, they would do so. Winning was the only objective. Kill as many enemies as possible, save as many of your own as possible, and any bystanders who got in the way, well, they shouldn't have.

For a moment, it was almost tempting.to offer his services, but he refrained. Even if they did accept his offer, it would only be to use him as a tool. A lackey. A slave. Useful only to betray his own people and deliver to the Tacagans a victory, but nothing more.

Even as he thought it, there was activity from the portal leading to the Auctionhouse hub. It was nearly impossible to say how many Tacagans swarmed out, owing largely to their near-uniformity of appearance. There were male and female Tacagans, light-skinned and dark-skinned Tacagans, a few in between, but there was virtually no individuality beyond this. They were all of a height and weight, within two inches and ten pounds. They all had the same forehead, nose, chin, eyes, hair. It was almost like an army of clones. Within fifty years, they just might be, he thought. It was enough to confuse him, and before he knew it, the whole room was full of Tacagans.

One of them stepped up and seemed to take charge. How they knew who was who and who was in charge was beyond Cassius.

"What has happened here?!" the Tacagan demanded.

"I might ask the same of you," Cassius retorted, the words spilling out of his mouth before his mind knew what he was saying. He gestured around at the carnage in the room. "Nice trick. How'd you do it? Playing with the gravitational balancers again?"

The Tacagan gave him a hard regard. "This coming from the one who has seen fit to massacre innocents and upend the Time industry twice in one century, all in the name of some deity?"

"In the name of destroying a deity."

He could see his answer both puzzled and amused the Tacagan. "Which deity is that, then?"

"Greed. And the Hands of Time were its priests."

The Tacagan frowned. "Well, true as that may be, one god is the same as any other. Yours is no more real or powerful than theirs."

In a flash, Cassius had enveloped the Tacagan in a special kind of Double Band. The man would only perceive a few seconds going by, and yet his body aged until he was gray, then white, then dead, then decayed, and finally nothing but dust, disappearing into the wreckage in the room even before Cassius had fully released the Band.

He saw some of the other Tacagans go wide-eyed and pale. A few swallowed nervously. A few started backing away slowly. So, they hadn't edited out the fear instinct yet. Good. That would make what came next much easier. Maybe it would send a message to any watching at home. Maybe it would send a message to their leaders.

The only drawback to that powerful of a Double Band, was that if he moderated the power, he could only use it on half a dozen more victims before the army swarmed him. On the other hand, if he threw everything he had into the Bands, he could pick off the attackers at hardly a blink, aging them and turning them to dust, but it cost him a great deal of strength so that he had little left in reserve when the rest reached him.

The nice thing, though, was that this wasn't an entire army. He elected to throw everything he had into the Double Bands. It was not necessary to use hand gestures as though he were some kind of street magician, but it certainly added a nice effect when he met an attacker's gaze and pointed at them. He enjoyed watching them go pale, maybe skid to a stop or try to evade, as if Time or the Akari were simple projectiles to be dodged.

They didn't scream as they died and turned to dust. The most they got was a gasp or a puff of air. One, two, four at a time, Cassius took them down, draining his energy like pouring water. He didn't have an actual body count to say how many he killed in this way, and still some had decided to flee and fight another day, but his odds were looking better all the time as the Tacagans rushed him.

All of this took place in about the space of two or three seconds. Then, as the Tacagans reached for their Time abilities, most of them Timekeepers, he had to divert his attention from creating his own Double Bands and focus on ripping apart his enemies' Bands before they could get close enough to cut his throat.

At the first touch of an enemy upon his skin, he reached for his old Harvesting abilities, taking them at a touch and absorbing their years into himself. But while it saved him from that particular person, it cost him time and energy as his body tried to absorb the years and the energies that went with it, readjusting his bodily processes to compensate.

In that time, only reflexive Banding saved him from a similar fate, and he was reduced to slithering away from outstretched hands that wished him great bodily harm, and other, less pleasant, fates.

Once he was more than four inches from any enemy, Cassius was able to intentionally wrap himself in a Fast Band and breathe. The Tacagans would never be able to break into his Akari Band, so he could relax a moment, gather his strength.

After a minute or two, he was able to sit up and look around. The number of Tacagans had dwindled from several hundred to perhaps seventy-five. How many he'd killed and how many had fled was impossible to say. All the same, one against seventy-five was not what one might call fair. The only reason he was surviving right now was because of the Akari.

He stood. He could go around to each of them, touch them, Harvest them instantly. There were also a few less dramatic things he could do that wouldn't expend too much energy. Or he could simply reach for Gravity and crush them all instantly. That would solve things very quickly and require very little effort on his part.

Weighing his options, he decided that he was just tired and cranky enough to do it. He'd been cheated out of his lunch, after all. Considering how little Time Agents or Akari-bearers ate, such an act became a much more heinous crime than normal.

With a bit of smug spite, Cassius released his Band, waited two seconds for everyone to slow down, stop, look around, and figure out where he was. Once all their attention was on him once more, he reached for Gravity, and simply crushed them. Bones crunched, bodies burst into pieces of flesh covered in blood. Everything beneath them collapsed as well, compacting down into a thin layer of unidentifiable debris.

His tremendous manipulation of Gravity, however, in an already unstable environment, cost him. The room shook again, flipping and spinning around faster than any object of its size had a right to. Caught off-guard, Cassius was thrown into the air, blinded by the splintered, ashy, bloody debris floating around like dust on the wind. He smacked something hard, rolled, fell, was thrown in the air again, landed hard, and did not move.

The room trembled a bit more like the aftershocks of an earthquake, but once he was satisfied that he was not going to be launched lengthwise across a football field, Cassius dared to move, getting to his knees and then his feet.

Every surface of the room appeared coated with the blood of the Tacagans, and the glittery, ashy, fleshy debris floated around like a snowglobe. He could not instantly spot any portals, nor could he speak to orientation or destination, so the instant he found a viable exit, he started walking toward it.

He found himself in the Auctionhouse hub. Now that he was out of the other room, he was suddenly very aware of the blood and debris that coated him, as though he'd been tarred and feathered with the flesh of a thousand other people. In a way, he supposed he was.

But now that he was clear and could see, he found this room to be filled with Tacagans as well. They stared at him. He stared at them. Aliens or the same species. Depending on who you asked.

"So," he huffed, trying to appear mildly winded, when in reality, he could have slept right there on the floor. He met the gazes of half a dozen Tacagans. "Who's next?"

Apparently the Tacagans were not in a generous, volunteering mood that day. A few fled quickly back into the Auctions, but most gave him hostile glares as they slunk back into their little stronghold.

This had been a test, Cassius mused, watching them leave. They wanted to know how the Cult would react to an attack. What were their strengths, their weaknesses? What was their response time, and who were their heavy hitters? Given that Cassius had managed to take on a few hundred by himself—and he hoped he'd appeared strong and ready for more—what did that say about the rest of them? With any luck, the Tacagans would believe that the grunts were just as strong, or near enough. And with the Borelians as allies, that was a whole new wild card to consider.

Cassius did not stick around to help with any kind of cleanup or restoration. He wasn't Julianna. He just stopped the mess from getting worse. Isthim or Rifun or someone else would oversee it. But in order for that to happen, they needed to know what had just transpired.

God help him, he was going to have to call a meeting.

He put this off as long as possible, first telling himself he needed a bath to rid himself of the blood and ash. If he took long enough, maybe someone else would get around to telling the others and they would call him to a meeting instead. Unfortunately, this did not happen. He bathed as long as he could stand, until the water and air could not be distinguished by temperature, and still no one came to fetch him.

Grudgingly, he made himself presentable and went out to find Isthim. She was not difficult to locate, and he figured that in the time it took him to drag Rifun back to the ruins, she would be ready also.

He again found himself watching Rifun from afar. It was now late in the evening. Dinner appeared to have come and gone, and now everyone had settled in for conversation and various card games. Sighing, Cassius went around and walked up to the front door and knocked.

He did not recognize the man who answered, but logic dictated that this was the head of the household as he appeared to be the oldest one in the vicinity.

"Puis-je vous aider?" the man inquired. (Can I help you?)

Cassius did not speak French, but he could guess the meaning. "I'm looking for Rifun."

As soon as he began speaking, there was some commotion inside the house. By the time Cassius said his name, Rifun appeared. Cassius was still stunned by his older appearance, and he had to remind himself it was only a Disguise.

"*Fantatrao izy?*" the older man asked. (You know him?)

"*Eny,*" Rifun said, nodding emphatically. He put a hand on the man's shoulder. "*Ao tsara, Volana.*" (It's all right, Volana.)

The man turned and opened his mouth as if to yell something into the house, but Rifun cut him off. "*Tsy, Volana, mba miangavy re.* I'm sure he just wants to have a quick word." (No, Volana, please.)

Before the man could protest, Rifun had edged his way past him and shut the front door. As a show for the prying eyes at the windows, Rifun put an arm around Cassius' shoulders and made a show of amiable conversation, at least until they were out of sight and earshot. Then they ducked off the road, into a cluster of trees, and Rifun shed his Disguise.

"What's wrong?" he demanded. "Has the Book of Commands been retrieved?"

"Not yet, but the Tacagans made a move today," Cassius reported. "We're having a meeting."

Rifun sighed and glanced back toward the road. He frowned, looked uncertain, then nodded. "All right. Give me a few minutes and I'll be there."

And he vanished back into the undergrowth, heading for home. Cassius stared after him. Was it really a good idea to bring him into this? Why not just let him be and hope that he didn't come back? Wasn't as though he contributed much anyway. Cassius and Isthim were the ones doing all the heavy lifting; Rifun just played politics and made nice, the photogenic face on the billboard, and he wasn't even that photogenic.

An hour later, the three of them were assembled in the officers building. Joining them were Misik, Medik, and a couple other Borelians whose names Cassius couldn't recall at the moment as he reported the day's events in excruciating detail.

"A test," Isthim stated when he had finished. "They want to see how we'll react."

"Fortunate that Cassius was present, then," Rifun said. "He may have bought us some time."

"The Tacagans don't seem all that interested in gore and torture," Cassius mentioned casually.

"War is a fine thing for those who have never witnessed it," Rifun mused. "Like many conquerors, they believe themselves too..." His expression contorted as he searched for the right word. "Too noble for such barbarism. They prefer sheer intimidation, bullying with words, leaving the physicality to an army who, having the same lifestyle, is too ill-prepared to face the stark reality juxtaposed against the romantic notions implanted in their brains by their white-gloved overlords."

All the Borelians raised a brow.

"What the fuck was that?" Cassius asked bluntly.

"Simply an observation made at the level of higher education. But in a nutshell, no, the Tacagans do not enjoy gore and torture. They leave that to their secret police who ensure that all average citizens stay in line with the whims of the governing body. But the secret police do not an army make, and even their common soldiers are comparatively soft."

"Maybe so, but they seem to have perfected the art of working smarter, not harder," Isthim said.

"Indeed they have," Rifun agreed. "Where are we on our search?"

"Still searching, but I have removed several hundred unnecessary Laws of Time from the rosters."

"Excellent. I have a few of my own to add, I think. And I imagine some of our allies may have a few words for me, some of them perhaps unsavory."

"So we're just going to ignore the Tacagans?" Cassius wondered.

"Of course not." Rifun looked at him. "As I said, it was fortunate that you were present for this attack, that you could stave off their assault and give them a few severe blows to remember us by. It may buy us time, but we cannot be idle, nor ignorant. And we shouldn't pass up the opportunity to make ourselves look like the better option, win hearts and minds of common people."

"Julianna left several people in charge of the refugee camp and the humanitarian teams," Isthim offered awkwardly.

Rifun shook his head. "No. Not good enough. Being targeted makes them martyrs and vilifies the Tacagans, but we need to do better. We need to make sure the Wheel itself is safe and that there are those ready to respond to any attack." He looked at Misik. "Your people do well as Grandfathers, but too few are trained in the Akari." At Isthim. "I want you to assemble security teams. Akari-bearers only. I want at least one very well-trained person to lead the group, three or four under him. I want them to assure the average people that their business is safe. In the event that it isn't safe, they'll be right there to defend the people. If they happen to have some downtime, or if they just want to win some PR points, have them do fun demonstrations; show the people that the Akari isn't scary."

Isthim noticeably blanched at the thought of the "fun demonstrations" but did not argue. Cassius also noticed how while Isthim was grimacing, Medik was smirking at her cousin.

"Cassius."

Cassius looked up as Rifun said his name. "Yes?"

"I'm sure you're doing very well as head prison guard, and I'm sure you wouldn't want to do any other job in the world, but if you find the time, maybe make a couple of runs at the Tacagans in the Auctions. They tested us; it's only fair that we should return the favor. I'll leave it up to you how you want to accomplish this."

He didn't have to be told twice.

The meeting ended shortly thereafter, the Borelians filing out of the room first and going their separate ways. Cassius caught up to Medik in the corridor.

"I saw you smirking at your cousin," he commented.

"Fun was never Isthim's strong suit," Medik replied, smirking even as she said it. "I don't know that she has a strong suit, actually."

"Evading your hunters, maybe?"

"Ha! Is it a talent or a curse to be a traitor?"

"Then why are you here if not to help?"

She gave him a look. "I am here to ensure that she remains loyal to Brelix and her people." Her expression twisted. "I'm the one who cut her vocal chords, you know."

"I didn't know," Cassius said, and it was true. They reached the door to her chambers. She went in confidently, but he stayed only a step inside the room. "Sounds like you enjoy gore and torture. Even a little?"

"Your description of how you dealt with the Tacagans was most intriguing."

"I seem to have that effect on your people."

"What effect?"

"Bringing out your curiosity, but being too fearsome to approach."

Medik laughed. "Ha! Fearsome? What have I to fear of you?"

"That I could kill you and I don't even have to touch you," he said simply, closing the door behind him and approaching. "Unlike you who is limited to physical touch and whatever your paltry Time abilities let you do."

She reached for a Band, but it was a simple Time Band, and it was nothing for him to rip it away from her. They did this several times before Cassius erected the Band. If she tried anything to penetrate it, it wasn't strong enough to even register on his senses, and he got directly in front of her before releasing the Band.

"You're an orange *tevak*," he stated. "Means it's your only color. And from everything I've read —"

"I'm surprised you know how to read," she spat.

"I'm full of surprises." He grabbed her arms. "Orange doesn't affect humans. Whatever it is that your toxin is supposed to do, humans just don't have the organ or sensory or whatever it is that you're supposed to be able to manipulate. That makes you utterly harmless."

She lurched her head forward, massive ram horns colliding with his jaw and shoulders. He fell back on his seat, quickly using Time and Matter to heal himself, flipping over just in time to throw up a Sound barrier so she couldn't call for help. A simple inversion of Gravity near the door made it so she bounced back, unable to reach the handle.

Cassius stood and went to her. He grabbed her and wrestled her away from the door. She was strong, he would give her that. If not for a few tricks up his sleeve, she probably could have beaten him in straight physical combat.

He didn't need to tie Medik to her bed. Physical restraints were unnecessary when Gravity itself could be invoked as a restraint. Or Magnetism, too, given how much metal she was wearing, adorning herself as if to show off to Isthim.

As he studied her, he put a hand on one horn and Felt her. He was not as precise as Rifun, able to play people like a puppet, but he could guess well enough, he supposed.

"Now then, let's see how you enjoy being manipulated," he hissed.

As he forced himself on her, he used Feel and Energy to manipulate different parts of her brain. He didn't know exactly what he was doing or her experiences, but the more she shrieked, the more he enjoyed himself. He Banded himself several times just so he could keep going. Only when she quieted did he stop.

He did not do anything more after that, just adjusted himself, dropped all the Bands, the Sound barrier, and whatever else he'd been holding, turned and left. No one said anything. No one confronted him. As he left the officers building, no one came running up from behind to accuse him, and he went on his merry way, disappearing into the tunnels and going to the Wheel.

In the few hours since the attack, some minimal repair work had been started.

Feeling pretty good about himself, Cassius decided to show off some more, using Gravity to move the heavy objects, Magnetism to place them precisely, and Time to get it done in only a few minutes. The balancers were still being repaired, and the Gravity made things a bit shaky and uncertain, but things got done with only minor injuries.

If Rifun was looking for PR, well, Cassius won them some PR. The evil Tacagans had again attempted to sabotage the Wheel, and again the Cult was there to save the day. What was that definition of insanity again? Or was it controlled opposition? He didn't know. He didn't care. Point was, unless the Tacagans had some trump card that could somehow overpower the need for help from the average citizen, the need for greater training both physically and mentally for their soldiers, and the need to learn the Akari and all its universe-bending power, they weren't going to win in the long run. They weren't even winning in the short run.

He considered doing as Rifun had suggested and testing the Tacagan army, then decided against it. They would be weary both physically and mentally, true, but he'd had a full day. He needed to give himself a break every once in a while. So instead, he returned to the prison and assumed his position as head guard.

He'd go after the Tacagans in a day or two. They could take a day to try and figure out what had happened, what they'd seen, try to reconcile their memories with their accepted worldview. It would keep them up at night, Cassius was sure, at least a few of them. Once they'd turned everything over in their minds, filed everything away in nice, tight, neat, organized boxes, then Cassius would come through and kick those boxes all over the floor again, scattering the contents.

It was a fun thought to have, and he savored it even as he punished his prisoners. It was also kind of fun to be in charge of a prison where the inmates could be any one of so many different species in the universe. Each one had strengths and weaknesses, different pain tolerances. It was like a game to try and figure it all out.

Hell, he'd had so much fun today, it was like something out of a dream. If he could build his perfect day, short of having lost his lunch thanks to the Tacagans, well, this probably would have been it. Somebody pinch him, because he really couldn't take much more of this fun. He was going to be the ninety year old man who had a heart attack because he'd convinced himself that he could do it just one more time in his life.

Even that thought made him smile, and he found himself wondering if maybe orange Borelians didn't have some kind of effect on humans; it was just more subtle than any of the others. Well, if that was the case, he could at least die happy.

But he didn't drop dead. Not there in the prison, not anywhere on his way out of the Wheel. He didn't lose a portal and perish in the unknown dimension between dimensions, assuming such a place existed. He returned to the ruins as he always did.

He did not see Isthim with the army. Actually, Misik appeared to be the one in charge at the moment. Cassius avoided him and headed for the officers building.

Rifun's chamber door was closed, and Cassius wondered if he was out doing his politics and such, or if he'd returned home for a good night's sleep with his family. Cassius frowned. Rifun was going to have to choose one day. He was sure of it. He hoped the man chose to stay away. Stay away, stay home, stop getting involved, and just die. No more politics and playing nice. If the man couldn't handle a little skirmish and a little blood, then he ought to stay out of the way.

Medik's door was still closed, as was Isthim's next door. Cassius made for his chambers, shutting the door and doing huge stretches and yawns on his way to his bed. Yes, today had been a good day. He was satisfied with it, in more than one respect. He got under the blanket and relaxed, stretching again.

Just as he closed his eyes, he heard a voice.

"I hope it was worth it."

Cassius flew out of bed, throwing up a Band and grabbing Light, illuminating the entire room like the middle of the day on the savanna. There, in the corner near his bed, unflinching, was Isthim. She leaned against the wall, arms crossed, looking as displeased as he'd ever seen her.

"What?" was all his mind could find to say, letting the Band slip away.

Gradually he let the Light fade into something more tolerable.

She straightened, let her arms drop, and approached.

"Medik is dead," Isthim stated bluntly. "It doesn't take an ith to know that you killed her."

"What does ith have to do with it?"

"I searched her last memories. You raped her. More than that, you fucked up her brain so much she had an aneurysm and died."

Cassius frowned but nodded. "Knowing that, I would absolutely say it was worth it. And what do you care? You hated her."

"There are many names I could call her, many things I could say. But above all, she was a Borelian. And you, a slave species, have violated and killed her."

"I am no one's slave."

"You will be if the others find out."

Cassius raised a brow. "You haven't told them?"

Isthim stopped about three feet from him and huffed a sigh. "No. If I were to tell them, this alliance would be instantly dissolved, and everyone here would be taken into slavery. Entire species would be at risk."

"Surprised you care."

"I don't. But this is the only chance I have to bring the Akari to my people. It is the first time that my people are learning something considered *dijik*. I don't expect you to understand how monumental this is, and I'm not going to lose it."

Cassius folded his arms. "Sounds like quite a conundrum, then. For you, I mean."

She glowered at him. "If we are to repair this mess—"

"We?"

"You caused the problem. You're going to help. She will have to die a hero's death."

He raised a brow. "Sorry to say, but she's already dead."

"Then we'll have to arrange the fight quickly. I hope you haven't attacked the Tacagans just yet."

"As a matter of fact, I haven't."

She sighed again, glowered at him a bit longer, then motioned for him to follow. They went to Medik's room where the deceased lay in a more respectful pose than what Cassius had left her. Isthim quietly closed the door behind them.

"I will grab some experienced fighters from the ranks. You will lead an attack on the Tacagans. At the right time, I will leave her body where it can be found. A bit of ith can fudge the details of how she got there."

"And what will you say?" Cassius asked.

"She wanted to lead an attack. I denied her. She went anyway just to spite me."

"Would that be an acceptable explanation for Misik and the others?"

"Is that your problem?"

"It is if my only other option is slavery."

Isthim gave him a look. "They will believe it."

It seemed he had no choice but to trust her. Reluctantly, he agreed. It wasn't that he didn't want to attack the Tacagans; he just mistrusted her intentions.

"Go now," she instructed him. "The others will be waiting for you in the Wheel."

"You preplanned this, then?" Cassius wondered.

"To an extent. You said it yourself, your only other option is slavery. I know you don't particularly enjoy that thought, so I decided to get everything in place in advance. Once things are well underway, I will bring her body and arrange it so."

Now he gave her a look, then stormed out of Medik's chambers.

He just had to tell himself that he was going to attack the Tacagans. On top of that, he was going to have a small army behind him this time. This wasn't just a little skirmish, this would be a full battle. It would be like the night he revolted against the slave master. Hunting in the darkness, two opponents feeling each other out, striking when they believed they had the advantage, and finally cornering their prey.

He actually didn't remember much of anything about the revolt anymore. He knew he'd hated one of the other slaves, but he couldn't say why, or even what his name had been. All that remained was the feeling. The thrill, the rush, the art of the chase and the kill.

On his way out, he grabbed Murdi and Lordo, as well as the Korin. In the event Isthim had something planned to stage his death in this little exercise, he wanted to have someone watching his back, maybe give him a shot at thwarting the clandestine assassination attempt.

"And when we're done," he concluded as he and his small task force entered the tunnels, "I want you to hunt down anyone who tries to flee. Kill them and kill anyone in the place where they try to run and hide. If they try to give you names of allies or higher commanders, take the names, then kill all of them."

As promised, there was a group waiting for him outside the Auctionhouse hub, in a room that looked a little less damaged. Through the portal, Cassius could see the Tacagans had also amassed a small force, evidently watching and waiting to see what they would do. He could also see that they still appeared tired from earlier, and far less cocky. They eyed him in particular with a measurable degree of caution.

"You know the plan?" Cassius asked, hoping he sounded like a commander who had known about this attack well in advance and had it all planned out. He really preferred the unplanned attacks, but even he knew the value of garnering some respect.

"We know," one leader said. He was an Obezod, big, bulky, and nothing that anyone would want to mess around with in a dark alley.

Cassius glanced at the twin assassins as well as the Korin. "Are you ready?"

They gave him an affirmative, and he was mercifully spared from having to listen to some lecture on balance from the Korin as he turned and led the charge through the portal.

They didn't stop just in the Auctionhouse hub. Like the point of a needle, Cassius threaded his way through the mass of Tacagans in the hub, making a path for the Obezod to act as a spearhead. Following him, the force that Isthim had assembled — perhaps five hundred strong — flooded into the hub.

They overwhelmed the Tacagans who beat a hasty retreat through the multiple Auction portals.

Isthim had probably designed a brilliant strategy, dividing various groups according to their strengths, weaknesses, training, and so on. Each one of those groups was probably assigned to specific Auction target with a specific plan or goal, whether they were to actually retrieve something or just cause havoc. Each of the leaders probably knew and understood this plan, and they expected the other leaders to know it as well. Maybe they understood the greater workings or only their own role, Cassius did not know.

But for his part, Cassius only desired chaos and death. He chose one of the Auctions and bulled his way in, Murdi, Lordo, and the Korin following him like a loyal pack of hounds — or rhinos, as the case may be.

Cassius did far less Banding this time around, instead opting for more hand-to-hand combat, feeling flesh and blood tear in close proximity. And yet, in the midst of the chaos that he himself helped to create, he noted that there was a sort of pattern to the movements of the Tacagans as their stronghold was breached. Of course, in the midst of the chaos that he himself helped to create, he was not prepared to process these patterns, nor ascribe to them any significance and react to them.

The force of five hundred was a battering tidal wave in the Auctionhouse hub. But as the groups were forced to split up into the different Auctions — of which there were actually dozens in number — their effectiveness swiftly diminished. There wasn't just a skeleton force guarding the Auctions, nor were the rooms populated with frightened women and children. There was indeed a standing army hidden in the Auctions, and a dozen Cult members with only basic skills were not much of a match. Cassius might have been able to take on a hundred or so for a while, but no one else present even approached his level of skill.

The other groups were probably being massacred.

As the walls started to close in, Cassius finally ordered the retreat. He did not want to, though he was fully aware that it had been part of the plan.

He did not stop to see where the twin assassins or the Korin were. He did not stop until he was clear of the hub, and even then he did not pause long, just kept going to the portal room. Later he would learn that Barnoff had been killed, his body borne back by his fellows even amid a hail of Time and physical attacks.

But in the moment, his only care was getting to Isthim to ensure the plan had been a success. He didn't fancy going up against the Tacagans a third time that day because someone made a stupid mistake.

He did not find her immediately, but by the time he got himself cleaned up, she had returned to the ruins and appeared to be relaxing in her chambers.

"And?" he demanded.

"The plan worked," she reported. He half-expected her to swirl a glass of wine. "My cousin is no more, a fool, but a brave fool. She will be honored appropriately."

"The rest of us are safe then?"

"For the time being, assuming you don't do anything else so foolish."

Cassius folded his arms and shifted his stance. "Do you know the numbers?"

"I don't know how many Tacagans were killed; they aren't keen on releasing such statistics. As for us, we lost only a dozen."

"That's good, right?"

She grinned. "We lost a dozen loyalists. We also eliminated a couple hundred traitors. Yes, that is very good."

27 | Manasitrana sy Mandrovitra

Mend and Tear

The Wheel of Time, 1966

Say one thing for Isthim, she knew how to knock out two or more birds with one stone. Taking care of Medik as well as a good crop of traitors and spies, that was no small feat.

Retrieving the Book of Commands, however, was proving far more elusive. Keeping the war with the Tacagans going, therefore, was their only viable distraction from this otherwise glaring error.

It was a terrible thing to consider, Rifun thought, but they had no other good options. What made it worse was that they probably could have subdued the Tacagans in only a few good raids, at least enough to kick them out of the Auctionhouse.

On the one hand, defeating them quickly meant not having the excuse of "war time" rules, which could be amended as necessary, and so needing the "everyday rules" which the Book of Commands, which they did not have, would provide. The absence of the journal would be discovered. This would embolden other enemies, and it would drastically cut morale among their own.

On the other hand, as they ruled the Wheel, cut out some Laws of Time and changed others, the Tacagans routinely berated them, demanding to know on what authority they claimed the Time industry, demanding to see their rulebook, which they did not have.

But at least with the insults and the demands, it could go both ways. The Tacagans had no more real authority than anyone else, except whatever superiority they concocted in their collective heads. They were a bit like the Borelians in the size of their ego, just without the toxic skin.

If there was any drawback to prolonging the conflict, it was that it called into question the superiority of the Akari. When it was no longer about Time, but Matter and Energy, why were they having difficulties at all?

"A human Timekeeper may advance from probationary to Master in a matter of a few years," Rifun said, addressing a meeting of their allies in the old Seat of the

Hands. "A Harvester may advance even faster. These are simple, basic things to learn as far as Time is concerned. For humans, it feeds the desire for fast progress, easy gratification. I myself learned how to Band in only a day.

"The Akari is not so simple, nor should it be carelessly toyed with. Yes, our people have been training longer, but there is so much more to learn, and it must be done at a controlled pace. Time is a trivial matter when compared to touching the energy of a star or the molecular structure of another living thing."

The only one who wasn't really arguing with him was Queen Aronet, but Rifun figured that she had the greatest understanding of how things worked. He had little doubt that Commander Dira was reporting everything she learned to her queen.

As for the rest of them, few leaders had actually been interested in learning the Akari for themselves, content to let bright-eyed underlings pursue some mystical dream of controlling the universe while they played politics to advance themselves.

"So was it for caution or ignorance that Barnoff is dead?" the Korin leader, Kerloff, asked pointedly.

"I do not know the exact abilities of each person, but even I know that the Akari cannot bring back the dead. I'm sorry. As to the manner of his death, without having been there, I cannot presume to say what went wrong, nor what could have been done to prevent it. Sometimes, that's just what war is."

"Including sacrificing hundreds of your own?" the Shatai leader, Milfor, wondered. "That is not the most promising start to a war."

"That operation was strictly comprised of spies and traitors under the command of loyal leaders," Rifun informed her. "Isthim was very diligent in her rooting out of the disloyal, and she figured out a way to both deal with them and test the Tacagans." He added quickly, "Cassius' role in that operation was strictly superficial."

Everyone liked to focus on the losses and not the victories.

"As far as the learning and acquisition of knowledge goes," he went on, "the Shatai may be our greatest asset. The knowledge and memories of your entire species are passed down from one generation to the next, cutting out a lot of basic learning time in subsequent generations."

"A misunderstanding of the process," Milfor said, "but true in principle. Am I correct to assume that he who learns the most the fastest will be more quickly put into power?"

"Depends on how you define power," Rifun replied. "If you mean military ranking, then yes, the more talented will rise faster. If you are speaking of political negotiations, well, we're all friends here." He gave her a look.

He didn't mind having the Shatai for an ally, and they were handy in their own way in a fight. But there was something unnerving about the thought of having a bunch of them in positions of military power. Maybe it was their appearance. They were flying creatures, yet they defied all laws of flight and aviation. To any casual observer, they appeared as little more than skeletons covered in thin, gray or black skin, formed in the shape of either a bat, manta ray, or deformed dragon, depending on who you asked. Actually, there was no way they should have been able to exist at all, never mind fly, at least that Rifun could see.

From what he understood, the Shatai hatched from eggs, and the saliva from the adults not only fueled their growth, but imparted all the memories and knowledge of all previous generations. Of course the natural lifespan of a Shatai was only about four to ten years, but with hundreds or thousands of years of collective memories and knowledge, what was a decade? Given their use of Time and, now, the Akari, was death even a concept for them still?

"War may be good for a time," Kerloff said, "but it is imprudent and unwise for it to last forever."

"It won't last forever," Rifun told him. "I wouldn't even really call it a war. Minor skirmishes, petty disagreements, a show of force as it were. Hardly a war."

Considering the Korin were ruled by war dynasties for eighty-one years, he didn't have a lot of room to talk, Rifun thought. What, then, did he consider a long or short war?

"You intend to end these 'skirmishes' rather soon, then?" Aronet inquired politely. "War itself may be an industry, but it strangles all other markets."

That got murmurs and gestures of agreement from everyone else in the room.

"Every intention," Rifun told her, unsure just how truthful he was being. "However, it should be noted, for those who don't know, that Tacaga has a very large standing army. If they truly wanted to, they could overrun us as we stand. I do not know their reasons for not doing so."

"All the more reason to end this war quickly," Kerloff stated. "If they grow bored, and they have the means to wipe you out, they will, and they will come after us as your allies."

"I don't doubt that."

"Could there be nothing gained from an alliance with them instead?" Aronet questioned.

Rifun grinned and shook his head. "No. As much as the Tacagans proclaim it a lie, they are still human. But they consider themselves to be superior to average 'Neanderthal' humans such as myself. As long as three of the four leaders of the Cult are inferior human beings — or even just one of the four leaders — they will not ally themselves with us. They will not take orders from me or anyone else who takes order from me or the others. Furthermore, they consider the Akari a religion, and they have vowed to eradicate all religion if possible."

"They should be destroyed as quickly as possible, then," Milfor said decisively. "I will send one thousand more Shatai to train. It may take years to become fully trained, but everything they learn will be passed down quickly, decreasing the time needed to train future generations. Even if something were to happen now, there will be a fully-trained army ready for them in only a few years' time."

The others also promised to send more to train, though whether this was from some sudden sense of loyalty and justice, or because they, too, felt uneasy about the Shatai was anybody's guess. Still, Rifun wasn't going to turn it down. He would have to tell Isthim and Misik to be prepared for a sudden influx of students. Wouldn't that make them happy?

They took a break from the meeting. While most lingered in various places around the Seat, Rifun elected to leave the area entirely, for some different scenery as well as to inspect any damage in the Wheel.

The Tacagans' favorite trick seemed to be sabotaging the gravitational balancers, as if they hadn't well-observed the Cult using Gravity to either avoid, offset, or negate this tactic. When it worked well, it did a lot of damage and minimized the response time of the Cult, yet it wasn't a big killer; there were rarely more than a few casualties from that trick alone. Was it just to bait them into a fight?

And when the Cult did respond, the Tacagans almost always retreated to the Auctions. This tactic was not a foolish one, for it divided the Cult's forces and drew them straight into enemy territory. But overall, the playbook was getting very, very predictable. Surely the Tacagans had engineered more military strategies into their superior brains than that.

If they were testing the Cult, the first few skirmishes should have given them sufficient data to change their tactics appropriately. If they were waiting to call in the rest of their huge standing army, well, what were they waiting for? If it was simply to act as a distraction, what were they trying to distract them from?

The Tacagans wouldn't be going after the journals, would they? They might, if only to burn or otherwise destroy them. Demoralize the Cult, make it easier to win the war and ensure that the chance of a resurgence was low.

Could that be the reason that the Tacagans were demanding to see the Book of Commands? Because they knew the Cult didn't have it? But how would they know?

Unless they themselves had the Book of Commands. Maybe that was why Isthim's hunters hadn't found the Ururian. He'd delivered the Book of Commands to the Tacagans and was under their protection.

Maybe that was why the Tacagans kept luring the Cult into the Auctions. It wasn't just about strategy, but maybe they were seeing if they would actually go far enough to find the Ururian and see the Book of Commands in their possession.

The last part seemed a bit far-fetched, but the rest had a thread of logic to it.

He returned to the Seat where the others had basically meandered their way back to the room to continue the meeting.

"Apologies for being a bit late, but there's been a change of plans," he said, sweeping into the room like a monsoon. "If you would be so kind, I would politely request that you remove yourselves from the Wheel entirely."

"Has something happened?" Aronet wondered.

"Not yet, but it's about to. Now then, we can stand here discussing it, in which case I cannot guarantee your safety, or you can leave and we will continue this meeting another time."

For as much as Rifun hated war, soldiers were at least a little more snappy when it came to such suggestions and the thought of impending doom. Politicians were just so darn slow, as if the world or the universe waited on their every word and no bad thing could happen until they were safely out of the way.

Strictly speaking, in this case, it could, because it was fully dependent on Rifun. But they didn't need to know that. And, really, the Tacagans could still attack at any time. Having so many allied leaders in the same place was a dangerous gamble any day of the week.

Eventually they got themselves to move. Rifun waited only long enough to see them out of the Seat before making for the Arena where Isthim and Misik had moved a large portion of their training operations. He pulled Isthim aside into one of the rooms.

"We need an attack force ready to go," he told her. "Somewhere between one and ten thousand, I think."

"We don't have that many ready to go," she informed him. "And even if we did, that's a large variance. What's going on?"

He explained his theory of the Tacagans having the Book of Commands. "So far, it's always been them attacking us, them baiting us. They control the maneuvers. If we attack them, we might be able to rattle them a little and get a better look inside the Auctions."

"True as that may be, how will it be different from any other skirmish? They may be caught by surprise, but they are by no means defenseless."

"No, but I'm going to give us a little advantage. We'll need to evacuate everyone who isn't attacking."

"That will leave us entirely exposed; the Tacagans could overrun us!"

"And not doing so could get everyone killed!" Rifun snapped. He let out a breath. "I'm going to touch the Core of the Wheel."

"What?" Isthim hissed.

He nodded. "I'm going to Build."

"You've never done that before. You could get everyone killed!"

"Which is why we need to evacuate everyone except the attack force. Worst case scenario, yes, everyone dies."

"Worst case scenario, the Wheel itself is obliterated and the entire universe collapses! So if by 'everyone' you mean literally everyone everywhere in the entire universe, then, yes, that is the worst case scenario. Everyone dies."

"I'm sure you won't feel a thing."

She gave him a look. "And this is the best plan you could come up with? For a theory you don't even know is correct?"

"If the Tacagans have the Book of Commands, then I'm going to give us every advantage to get it back," Rifun said. "If they don't have it, then touching the Core of the Wheel and manipulating things at a level beyond what their technology can replicate, that will send a message in its own right."

She still had the look on her face. Finally, "Fine. I'll tell Misik and we'll begin the evacuation. We'll get your fighting force ready. Just understand that the window between evacuation and attack can't be too big."

"Why not?" Rifun wondered, walking away. "Maybe we can bait them into our territory for once."

If she said anything to his back, he didn't hear it, and it wasn't until he was out of the Arena entirely that he realized what he'd just proposed.

The Core of the Wheel was, in reality, very poorly named. It wasn't just the center of the Wheel that powered all its operations, it was, in essence, the center of the universe. It was why the Wheel was so fucked up and terrible to behold. All the dimensions and black holes and energies of the universe all converged on this one spot, twisted and formed into something habitable, yet held together by only a single pin. It was why portals were so taxing and so dangerous, why time did not matter, why gravity could be manipulated so easily as to make everything a viable surface.

Now Rifun was going to have to hold all of that together on his own while trying to move the pin to a new spot. From what he understood, any casual observer would be driven to death upon seeing the Core of the Wheel. Only those chosen by the Author could look upon it and live, and only a Builder had any hope of successful manipulation.

The Author had shown him the Core of the Wheel, and Andrianary and the spirits had shown him Building when the Akarin would not. This was only a minor test, to find the Book of Commands and be rid of the Tacagans. If this proved successful, and assuming he didn't end up a vegetable, once he got a better feel for how things worked, then he would come back later and do some real Building, make the Wheel as it had been at the start of things. Maybe he could kick the Tacagans out of the Wheel from the inside.

For the moment, he helped with evacuation, ensuring everyone got the message and got out. Once the majority of people were clear and Isthim began assembling the attacking force, Rifun announced that he was going below. Isthim gave him a look, looked like she wanted to say something, refrained, and returned to her work.

The Wheel was eerily empty. They'd even sent the secretaries home, those who would go, anyway. The Bat and the Day remained at their posts in the Seat, refusing to leave. A few others proclaimed no homes to return to. But whatever the exception, the general rule was that everyone was gone save for those Isthim was assigning to attack.

He hadn't needed to tell her the cue to look for. If he was going to touch the Core of the Wheel, the consequences would be enough to give them an idea. Depending on the scale of those consequences, they would either launch their attack, or everyone everywhere in the universe would be dead or dying.

On the other hand, he thought as he entered the Archives, maybe nothing would happen. Maybe he wasn't yet skilled enough to be a Builder. Maybe the Author would deny him for impure motives. What kind of an ass would he look like then?

He shook his head. No. He was ready. He was right. He'd had the visions, made the sacrifices. Andrianary had given up his life so that he could cross this threshold. If this minor test proved unfruitful, then there was no point in pursuing things further, Book of Commands or no, Book of Abilities or no.

Fewer people made navigating the Archives faster, but hardly easier. The Archive attendants had been some of the most stubborn secretaries to get moving. The librarians had their order, and with each skirmish and damage to the gravitational balancers somewhere in the Wheel, they were working overtime to keep everything organized. Now he was going to touch the Core of the Wheel? Everything could be destroyed! Or worse, misplaced!

For as tragic as it sounded, he still got them to evacuate, promising to help them himself if even a single tablet was out of place when they returned.

Looking around at the dizzying tessellation of libraries within libraries as far as the eye could see and to the best ability of the human brain to comprehend, Rifun wondered if that had been a wise offer to make.

Somewhere in the back corners of the Archives, he finally found the employees only staircase, twisting down into another dimension of the Wheel, the room with many corridors, including one that was nearly invisible except for those aware of its existence.

It was this corridor that Rifun chose, pushing past whatever magic or technology forbade any ordinary person from walking into the darkness. Maybe it was technology similar to the neuroelectrical field in the Seat, the one which generated the hallucinations drawn from the brains of Time Agents hoping to advance in their fields. Maybe it was something deeper, connected to the Akari in ways now long lost.

Breaching the barrier was not enough. That was only the door, and what lay beyond was the real test. It was not a maze or some physical challenge or even a succession of ever more creative booby traps. Such things were easy, and some could be negated by a particular alien's size or other physical characteristics.

Fear on the other hand was inherent in all living things. It was purely primal, embedded deep within the body, within the very soul. Fear would be tapped into, seized, manipulated. Whatever it was that governed this corridor and its barrier, it was a powerful force to be reckoned with.

Briefly, in a moment of clarity, Rifun reached for the Akari. Perhaps if he could locate some bit of technology, he might disable it, at least long enough for this expedition. Or, if it was some Time or Akari force, he could negate it for a while.

He wasn't sure what he touched, but he instantly knew it was a bad idea. He lost his hold on the Akari, his whole body seizing up in stark naked fear until he was utterly paralyzed. He couldn't explain it exactly, but he almost had the feeling of something going through him, not like an electric current, but something living. It snaked through him, slithered just under his skin and through his face, and only once it had gone was he able to breathe again, his chest expanding like a drowning man gasping for air but finding precious little.

He waited there for a long moment. He knew he had to keep moving, but that knowledge, and the motivation behind it, felt as far away as the exit, and he longed to run.

He didn't know how much time had passed, didn't know whether it really mattered. Gradually, as the paralysis left his limbs and he began walking again, the unadulterated terror gave way to waves of despair and self-doubt. He'd taken too long. The window had been left open. The Tacagans would be attacking. He was too late. Even if he did make it to the Core, there would be nothing left to save. Even if he tried, he was only going to collapse the Core and the Wheel and the entire universe, leaving everything and everyone everywhere dead or dying.

He'd never done this before. What made him think he could do this? What made him think he was ready? What if the Author rejected his attempts? What if this was her way of trying to get him to turn back before he destroyed the universe? Would she intervene before it got to that point?

Of course. She had to. There were more Books to be had, and their copyrights were well into the 2000's.

This moment of clarity helped to clear away the worst of the doubt and lingering fear. He took a breath and kept moving, focusing on that small bit of knowledge.

But then, would that not make the Books true? The doubt came roaring back for a second round.

The Books and the journals don't have to be mutually exclusive, he told himself. *It was one of those Books that led me here, because I understood it. I tried to heal the rift, but the Akarin wouldn't listen. I can't judge the authenticity of a work against the insincerity of its followers.*

And what if you are wrong? What if this is the Author trying to get you to turn back?

I'm only trying to help my people. That can't be wrong. I've already determined that I won't destroy the universe.

Yes, but there's more than just the universe that you're messing with.

If she wanted to stop me, she could have done it before I got this far, before I got this powerful. She could have shown me a vision at the tombs, told me to stop or given me other guidance. She can stop Cassius at any time with the stroke of a pen or stroke of a key. The fact that she hasn't means that this is what I am meant to do.

His train of thought was cut short as his foot met open air. His breath caught for a moment, and then relaxed when his foot found a step. Stairs. Right.

Clearing his throat, he began his descent.

He startled when something touched the bottom of his foot. The tar. Right. He knew he'd forgotten, yet he felt foolish for it. He should have remembered. He should have remembered all of this, but he didn't, and it came back now only as a half-remembered dream.

The fear began creeping up on him once more as he went deeper, the tar climbing over his feet to his ankles, his knees, touching the tips of his fingers so that he instinctively raised his arms. Not that it did much good since he knew that he would have to be submerged, and for a short while, too, if he remembered correctly.

The tar rose to his chest so that he could not breathe. His heart raced and his skin crawled. He could hold his arms up no more, and he let them drop.

There was nothing actually, physically there. He felt nothing, no tar upon his fingers or his clothes or anywhere on his body. But the resistance, the murk, the pull, everything but the texture.

Fear, the only thing inherent in every living thing in the universe. Whoever had constructed this part of the Wheel originally had known a thing or two about psychology.

The tar reached his chin. Rifun stopped for only a moment before allowing himself to be submerged. He fully expected to inhale a mouth full of sticky tar as he opened his mouth to breathe, but he took in only air.

Still he descended the steps, wondering how much time had passed. What was going on above? Would he truly be too late to help? Would his efforts come in the nick of time to save his army? Would it provide some kind of emphasis to his victorious army that the Cult was not an enemy to take lightly?

He still couldn't breathe. He began to feel dizzy. He stopped and forced himself to take several deep breaths, his lungs expanding to find sweet, merciful air, yet it felt like a terribly strenuous workout.

Once the worst of the dizziness subsided, he refocused his efforts on moving more quickly. He'd taken too much time already, indulged far too long in fear and self-doubt. He had to help his people.

This was easier said than done, and his stubborn resolve lasted only until the heaviness of the tar suddenly burst and he found himself falling. Briefly he recalled that this was to be expected; it had happened before. He also needed to think fast because the ground was coming up quick.

He managed to keep his head from smacking hard against the floor this time, but it didn't make the rest of his body feel much better. Still, he was able to breathe again, and his next few movements were uncoordinated caricatures as he tried to breathe, stand, and assess himself for injuries all at the same time.

Once he got himself coordinated, he straightened and turned to face the Core of the Wheel. Lesser men probably went mad just at the sight of it. How else should an ordinary mortal react to the nexus of Creation? But his unique vision had allowed him to look upon it and, rather than be driven mad, be inspired.

This did not mean he was not still in awe of it as he approached the edge of the platform and leaned against the railing. Curious, he looked down. There was no end in sight, just light as far as he could see. This was the same as he looked up, and then left and right. Simply nothing but the eternity of time and the universe.

The Core itself was, perhaps fittingly, shaped like a ball, or maybe more like a wrapped candy as energy flowed into and out of it, twisting tightly at both points. Where this energy came from or where it went was anyone's guess, but Rifun figured that these were the pins binding all the dimensions and threading together all the points of the far side of every black hole, leading all to this point.

Access to the Core of the Wheel and the entirety of the universe, and he wanted to play a few party tricks on some mean kids upstairs. It sounded terribly petty, almost rude, not to the mean children, but to the Core. Asking the strongest man in the world to open a door, or the fastest man to run across the room, an insult to the talents they possessed.

But Rifun retained enough of his mind to know that he did not know the power of the Core, and if he got too cocky, he really could kill himself and everyone and everything everywhere in the universe. He did need to exercise some measure of caution, let this be a test run, and he could figure it out from there what he needed or wanted to do.

He studied the Core, looked up and down the platform, didn't see anything that might indicate just how one actually initiated manipulation of the Core. That was done from here, right? Was there a door or some other room that he'd missed? Was a sacrifice truly warranted, that he had to throw himself off the platform into the Core itself? He couldn't very well reach it from here, or it didn't appear he could.

Cautiously, he reached out, looking at the Core as if it could read his intentions.

And something reached back. Before he had time to process it, it was as though he'd been pulled straight off the platform, clean out of his shoes, and sucked into the Core itself.

He had no body, only consciousness, and his mind exploded with a cacophony of images he could not begin to comprehend. Stars and planets and galaxies and clusters of galaxies and nebulae and space formations he had no name for, nor could he begin to describe. As soon as the image was there, it was gone, with a million more he knew he'd missed, all of it flowing together in the brilliant dalliance that was Creation, such a vast and unknowable thing to mortals, merely the backyard of even greater beings. Zanahy, the Author, someone else, whoever or whatever was out there Rifun could not even begin to describe. To say that he glimpsed only the tip of the iceberg was to give himself too much credit, for this was but one tiny snowflake upon an entire galaxy wrapped in ice.

Across the universe, stars and planets moved in terrible harmony, like leaves upon endless rivers, the current flowing in the ebb and rise of time and gravity and forces yet undiscovered by humanity. These rivers diverted here and there, some moving quickly, others barely budging, flowing toward any number of black holes, where all things were swallowed into nothing, twisted, reformed, and spit back out again, pure and unblemished, to continue the cycle.

And here the energies were focused, a special place carved out, like an air pocket in an underwater network, where time did not matter, where gravity could be molded at will.

And this Core, this mighty thing which could drive anyone utterly mad, was but a small stream flowing through. The power and energy that surrounded this place, that surrounded the Wheel, was unbelievably more intense. The Core was but a pleasant brook compared to a massive typhoon.

Suddenly it made sense why portal travel was so difficult, and why it had taken so long to perfect—and even then, it was far from perfect. The torrent of energy that someone had to bypass to shrink the distance from one place to another was stunning. It was amazing it was even possible.

This thought helped to bring Rifun's focus back to the present moment. Whenever that was. He was almost certain that a great amount of time had passed in only the few seconds he had perceived. If that was the case, did he even have a mission anymore?

At some point, he realized he had a body again. How much time had that realization cost him?

Well, better late than never, he decided.

Was there something he had to do, then, to begin the process? Where did he even start? Was it a matter of will? Was the Core somehow sentient? Did it know his thoughts? Was that how it knew to take him in? Was the Core itself responsible for the tar that engulfed the stairs, the fear that draped itself over the corridor, the creature that snaked its way through him when he tried to fight back, the sixth sense that kept this place invisible to those unworthy?

As Rifun moved his hands, feeling very much like a child still in the womb, he began to feel things. He did not see the Wheel, but he began to notice patterns within the energy, like strings on an instrument. If he plucked a string a certain way, he could do certain things.

Learning everything there was to learn about how it worked would take a lifetime and a half.

He felt very much like a child beating on piano keys to the chagrin of all within earshot, knowing that what he intended to produce was a master symphony to a standing ovation.

His shame and humiliating lack of knowledge put an end to whatever he'd been doing. His only comfort was that he did not appear to have destroyed the universe and everything in it. Sighing, he moved, found the rest of the his body, right where it was supposed to be, and pushed out of his place within the Core of the Wheel, emerging from the womb of Creation.

The next thing he knew, he was back on the platform. He did not feel tired or energetic. He did not feel hopeful or humiliated. For a long ten seconds, he simply existed. Just another thing in the universe.

Finally he stood, turned, looked at the Core. It looked the same as it did before, but did he expect anything else?

Without a word and hardly a thought in his head, he returned to the place he'd landed after falling off the stairs. Looking up, he could see just the bottom two steps. He created a Gravity track, got himself back on the staircase, and headed up.

Leaving the Core and returning to the Wheel proper, there was no tar, no resistance, no fear whatsoever. He was just walking up the stairs and then walking down any ordinary corridor. But if he stopped and turned to look back, the fear would start to creep back in, little by little. But when he turned and continued walking away, it melted away.

He didn't know what he expected to find when he got back to the Wheel. He wasn't even sure how much time had passed. For his part, he might have guessed half an hour at the most, but that was assuming that time worked the same when he was in the Core. Standing on the platform, probably. Actually touching the Core of Creation? There was no way he'd only been gone half an hour. He might expect a few months at the most. Once he'd gotten his head back together, he did what he'd gone to do and got out.

His first bit of relief came when he ascended into the Archives and discovered that things appeared to be in order. Cases were not knocked over, tablets remained firmly on their shelves. At least he wouldn't be spending the next two years helping to replace all of them.

One indication he got that he may have been gone a little longer than intended was that there were patrons in the library again. Even if he'd been gone a full day, there was no way that people would have come back so soon. Well, a few might have, but not this many. This was beyond post-takeover levels; this was almost normal.

He left the Archives and stopped to look around a bit. Some time had definitely passed. He might have expected the normal run of Cult members intermixed with the more daring Time Agents intent on going about their business as usual. This, however, was quite busy, and he could not readily identify any Cult members.

Now he began to know a bit of fear. Had the Tacagans overrun them? Were they in charge now? Could a different group be in charge? What happened to the Cult? Where were Cassius and Isthim?

Of course! The Judgment Wing!

With trepidation dogging his heels, he made his way to the Judgment Wing. If he found any comfort, if it could be called that, it was that the Borelians appeared to still run things here. If anyone were to overrun the Cult, there was no way they'd leave the Borelians in charge here, right? Some gave him startled looks, but most wore the usual expression of disdain. He tried to appear friendly and non-threatening as he made his way back to the processing room.

"I'm looking for Isthim, have you seen her?" he inquired politely.

"Not recently," the desk clerk answered blandly.

Good. Then she was still alive, and she was still overseeing things here.

Maybe the Cult had been victorious and, with no wars to frighten people away, things got better, hence all the people. Maybe there was some kind of celebration to bring them back. Maybe the Book of Commands had been found, new rules had been implemented, and everyone was happy again. Not everything had to be doom and gloom.

To that end, he skipped going to the prison to look for Cassius. There would be nothing but doom and gloom coming from him, and Rifun wasn't fond of the idea of finding him in a good mood. If they had been victorious over the Tacagans, Cassius was going to have a lot of prisoners to torture. No, he would skip the prison.

He went instead to the portal room. Being uncertain of current safety protocols, he decided to go with what he knew, opening a series of portals until he landed in the tunnels that took him to the cavern housing the Ruins of Meroian.

The ruins lay in their normal spot, but they appeared dead, empty. Had the Cult been moved somewhere else?

He ducked as a shadow swept over him. Looking up, he saw it was several Shatai, the eerie, black skeletons gliding through the air like shadows. So Milfor had made good on her promise to send more. But seeing how Rifun doubted the Shatai would want to conquer the Elif—although their caves may have held some appeal to the bat-like creatures—then the Cult should still be nearby, right?

He elected to try the city. Maybe someone had left a note for him, explaining what had happened.

Or what if they'd given him up for dead? Maybe they thought he'd perished in the Core. Well, word would get back to Isthim eventually that he was looking for her, so that would be a surprise.

He went to the main gate and entered the city.

Like walking through a beaded curtain, the Disguise around the city trembled only for a moment, and he walked into a city that was even more lively and bustling than when he'd left. He had to stop to take it all in. He turned around to study the Disguise. Invisible from the outside, appearing as only a hazy, yellow, fogged dome barely visible on the inside.

Walking through the city, it still had some of the stiffness of a military encampment, but there was also an air of excitement, the hustle and bustle of a city, a real city. It was a bit like the Wheel, really, except there were no overcrowded marketplaces or greedy vendors or anything of the sort. There was comradery, friendship, two concepts Rifun was surprised the Borelians knew anything about at all, never mind how to inspire them in others.

Trying not to gawk like a new recruit, he headed purposefully for the officers building. It did not appear to have changed. Once out of the city streets, the lights dimmed, the sounds became muffled, and the air was stale and business-like.

He did not meet anyone in the halls—a relief, to be honest—and he found his chambers locked up and secured well. He carefully undid the barriers and opened the door.

Judging by the amount of dust, he'd been gone for probably those few months he'd figured. Some things had been tidied or put away, but otherwise, it was as he'd left it.

"You're back."

He turned at Isthim's voice. She did not appear to have changed a bit, although the surprise in her voice and on her face was entirely genuine. If she'd had something in hand, she might have dropped it.

"I have deduced from various clues that I have been gone a lot longer than I have perceived," he started. "First off, just tell me, how long have I been gone?"

For a long moment, she didn't answer, apparently still stunned by his appearance. Had he really been given up for dead? Was this his resurrection?

Finally she blinked and shook her head, a statue coming to life. "No one knew what to expect, but when nothing happened, Cassius led the charge anyway. I don't blame him."

"Did we win?"

"Depends on how you define win. We didn't wipe out the Tacagan army. We barely made a dent. They didn't have the Book of Commands, nor did we find the Ururian."

He shook his head, trying to bring everything together, still feeling very disoriented. "But the Wheel. Everything looks...happy."

Isthim took a breath and collected herself. "Rifun, you've been gone for more than two years."

He blinked. Waited for some kind of punchline. Felt foolish for expecting such a thing from a Borelian. "What?"

"On Earth, the year would be 1969 I believe. I don't know the month."

Rifun shook his head. "No. I only perceived half an hour, maybe an hour if I want to be really generous. I thought that time may have stretched a little at certain points, but..." He ran a hand through his hair. "A few weeks I would believe. A few months, maybe, just looking around the Wheel. But you're telling me that it's been over two years?"

"Almost three, but yes."

"Now, is that three Earth years or three Base years?"

"Does it matter?"

He let out a breath. "I guess not. It's still a lot longer than I expected. A lot longer than I had really hoped." He frowned. "I didn't mean to be gone so long. I told Volana that...and Lalao..." He shook his head. "They're going to think something's happened to me."

"Something has happened to you," Isthim stated. "I think we'd all like to hear about it."

After a long minute, he nodded. "You want to hear about my experience, and I need to get caught up on the last couple years."

"I'll call a meeting."

She turned, but he called after her. "Wait." She stopped and looked at him. "Not yet. I'm too tired. Just the shock of everything has kept me going, but I do need sleep after what I just did."

Isthim simply dipped her head and closed the door behind her.

It was a lie, really. Rifun wasn't tired; he was barely fatigued. But he needed time to process everything and think about what he was going to do next. Back home, after going out with Cassius, Rifun had lied to his family and said that the two of them were going to Tana to do some touring, some visiting and whatnot. They'd be gone a few days, maybe a week. It had been an excuse for him to get back and deal with whatever Tacagan shenanigans had been going on. He'd bought himself a week or so. He might be able to fudge a few weeks. A few months would be hard, but doable.

Two years? He couldn't even begin to conceive of a lie that big. What was his excuse going to be? Illness? Well, why hadn't he written? Spontaneous world traveling? Well, why hadn't he written or sent postcards? Gone home for family issues with his kids? Well, why hadn't he written?

And Lalao. No word from Fan in almost three years. She must hate him. What excuse did he have? For not visiting, he probably had plenty of excuses. For not writing? None at all.

What was he going to do? What was he going to tell them? How could he even face them now?

He ended up lumbering his way to his bed and sitting down. A man could be the savior of the universe, but if he had no family, he had less than a beggar. He'd returned home, fiddled with his Disguises and his excuses, integrated himself back into the family looking for redemption, and he'd managed to squander it in less than an hour. Or two years as the case may be. He didn't know anymore. He didn't know what to think.

Suddenly he found that he was indeed very tired. More than that, he was exhausted and not a little confused. Maybe he just needed a good night's sleep, something to calm his nerves and help his mind figure things out. Maybe he would have a vision, some guidance as to what he should do. Maybe the spirits would show him the things that had happened since he'd been away. Maybe they would show him how to make things right.

Yawning, Rifun used the Akari to collect the dust in his room, send it into the hearth that hadn't seen a fire in over two years, and set it ablaze. The sudden flash of an inferno lasted only a moment, but there was some exceptionally dry wood nearby which he used to feed it. The chill quickly diminished, but he had to go out several times to fetch more wood. Once the room was good and warm, he returned to his bed, stripped down to his underclothes, crawled under the blanket, and fell asleep.

28 | Idorikodo ati Daduro

Hang and Suspend

The Wheel of Time, 1969

kokumbo

Cassius was in the asylum when he received word that Rifun was alive and back on Sadurnon.

He didn't exactly go rushing out to meet him and throw a welcome home party, say it that way.

Really, he would have preferred it if Rifun had perished in the Core. The mission was accomplished, Rifun felt fulfilled or something, and there was no political fallout to be had. Sometimes an accident truly was just an accident. They would move on.

They had all waited, for a time, Isthim longer than Cassius. He made one trip to Madagascar just to sneak around and see if he'd slipped away in the aftermath, but even the family seemed rather distraught over his disappearance. After that, Cassius had simply given up and gone back to work.

There were a lot fewer meetings, say it that way.

Over the following months, various allies sent their condolences in whatever fashion their culture demanded. For some, it was a simple note. For others, it was everything short of a grand funeral. The point remained that Rifun was gone, and they moved on.

Now the son of a bitch was back. Wonderful. No doubt there would be a meeting about it. As long as it stayed a meeting and they didn't expect to have a party, too. Although the Borelians weren't big on parties, at least with other species, especially with other species as the center figure.

Still, Cassius did not leave his asylum until Isthim herself came and got him.

"I assume by now you've heard," she stated.

"Our glorious master of meetings, dazzler of diplomats, and powerhouse of politics has returned from the ether to grace us with his eternal wisdom?" Cassius guessed.

"One might think you enjoyed having him gone."

"It did make things simpler."

"Regardless, he needs to be brought back up to speed on things."

"You mean the Core of the Wheel didn't impart the wisdom and knowledge of all time and all things?" He noted her expression. "Fine, fine, I'm coming."

Grudgingly, he followed her out of the asylum, out of the Wheel, back to the ruins.

"How much has he been told?" Cassius wondered as they traversed the streets.

"Only that he's been gone for almost three years. I was prepared to brief him, but he proclaimed fatigue and wished to have a meeting later on so that he could be informed by everyone at the same time of what he's missed."

It made sense. At the same time, it could also make for a long meeting. Well, if this was just to catch Rifun up, maybe Cassius would volunteer to go first so that he could leave once he was done. He didn't need to be reminded of the last three years; he'd lived it.

Rifun and Misik were the only ones in the room when Isthim and Cassius entered. Other than a general air of disorientation, Rifun did not appear any worse for wear after whatever he'd been through.

What was the Core of the Wheel like? What did it look like? What did it feel like? How did someone manipulate it? Maybe Rifun could share his experiences first so that Cassius could learn, and then he himself would give his accounts of the last three years, and then he could leave to pursue his own agenda.

"Minor things I have learned," Rifun began, without so much as a "long time, no see" or other greetings. "But I need to know more. What has happened in the last few years?" He looked at Isthim. "What happened after I left for the Core?"

Well, so much for Cassius being able to speak first.

"The attack force waited for some sort of signal from you. We didn't know how it would come, but given the nature of the Core, we did not believe that we would miss it," Isthim told him. "But the Tacagans did take notice of the evacuation, and they took notice of our force. They attacked us. But the differences between that fight and previous fights gave us the advantage, and small task forces were able to go in and more thoroughly search for either the Ururian or the Book of Commands."

"Which you've already informed me was unsuccessful," Rifun said.

"Yes. However, on conclusion of the fighting, there were great tremors throughout the Wheel, very much like the disruption of the gravitational balancers, but not so catastrophically destructive."

"For a while there was peace," Misik jumped in. "Or rather, there was little or no fighting, though the Tacagans continued to hold the Auctions. They even allowed one to open up so that the markets could resume. The lower markets are good, but the Auctions are where the money really moves."

Rifun nodded. "It certainly looks like things are bustling again."

"Oh, they are," Misik agreed. "The markets are doing very, very well."

Rifun raised a brow. "I sense a bit of sarcasm in your voice."

"They are doing well," Isthim echoed, "but it's causing problems for us."

"How so?"

"We still don't have the Book of Commands. We have rescinded some rules, made others, but we have nothing to point to as our authority. With the Tacagans apparently backing down, we can no longer use the excuse of war or wartime rules."

Rifun looked around. "And Julianna isn't back with the Book of Abilities either, is she?"

"No. The Shatai are useful in building a trained army quickly—they were the ones who perfected the Dome of Disguise over the city—but we're running out of things to show them, and we have no cause to use it if we did. The Tacagans took that away from us, and we're in no shape to forcibly go after them. You have said it yourself that the Tacagans could overwhelm us by sheer numbers and a bit of ingenuity."

"So they're killing us with kindness. Backing out of the war so that our own flaws are exposed. With no Book of Abilities, we can't train an army. With no Book of Commands, we have no authority. Power has always rested with money in the Time industry, so that's where everyone is defaulting. Open up a few Auctions, get the money flowing, the average civilian settles down, gets comfortable, no longer cares about politics and war."

"Exactly. And some of our allies, the less devoted ones, are also enjoying this newfound power, seeing how you gave them great control over certain markets. Some have gotten a little too comfortable, I think. They're not in open rebellion, for there is little to rebel against, but they offer great resistance whenever the rules change in favor of the Cult or the Akari over the markets."

Rifun frowned. "I can't be entirely sure, but I'm getting a whiff of mole. Observation and deduction may tell the Tacagans that we're not as airtight as we proclaim to be, but these are very targeted maneuvers."

"Agreed," Misik said. "And there is more cause to believe that this is a coordinated effort. Someone, or multiple someones, have begun hunting down the old Hand candidates, those who somehow survived the first few bloody waves in the aftermath of the elections."

"Your old mentor Daniele Ivolo included," Isthim threw in.

Cassius saw Rifun blink, but he did not do more than that. Instead, he said, "Daniele was a Dominion Timekeeper, claimed to witness the resurrection of Jesus Himself. It would be next to impossible for anyone to get the jump on him." He let out a breath. "What are the Akarin up to? After three years, they must have some semblance of order back in their lives."

"They've been remarkably quiet, but it wouldn't surprise if they had some hand in this."

"Can't take us out themselves, so they back the Tacagans instead. Enemy of my enemy. These little maneuvers mean as little bloodshed as possible, and we collapse under our own house of cards." He swore and shook his head. "We should have waited. Should have waited until we actually had everything in hand."

No one said anything to that.

Finally Rifun said, "If we have anything to look forward to, it's that Julianna really should be returning soon. She said a few months, I would expect a year. Three years...any day now, she's going to appear. She has to."

"And then what?" Misik wondered. "We are already more powerful than most every army in the universe save for our limited numbers. We need nothing save for the structure to uphold our authority."

"And your teams have found nothing?" Rifun challenged in a rare flash of anger. "I understand how Isthim may have given you the slip, but anyone else? A day, a week, a month if they're exceptional. But a year and a half, two years? Longer? Who is this Ururian that he seems to have vanished from existence and made fools of the most feared people in the universe? Twice!"

Misik straightened suddenly, his expression indignant, but he couldn't deny it. Cassius couldn't stop himself from a small smile and even a low chuckle.

Misik caught it, and he turned his gaze on Cassius. Then back to Rifun. Then Cassius. Then to Isthim.

"We will not stand for this. This entire endeavor — alliance is too kind of a word — has been nothing but blunder after blunder, embarrassing mistake after embarrassing mistake. I'll not waste my time on this any longer."

He swept around the table with grand flourish, pausing at the door just long enough to add, "If you do manage to do anything right in the near future, maybe we'll take notice. Until then, I suggest you not cross paths with the Grandfathers of the Time industry."

Then he was gone.

Isthim frowned and looked at Rifun. "He's been threatening this for over six months. But promises can only go so far, and I suppose his limit has been reached."

"At least he didn't throw us into slavery."

"Yet." Isthim made a gesture. "Consider it a good and rare thing that he considers this alliance—and if he did not consider it as such, we would not be standing here—a worthwhile pursuit still, that he will return to the table once we have demonstrated that we can make good on our greater goals. He likes the training, but the politics and planning leave much to be desired."

"And how will the others react?"

"I'm still here. Anyone who wishes to stay and train will be permitted to do so, I imagine. It's just a matter of political logistics. We'll get no support from Ancrath."

"Not that we were getting much from them before. And he still seems pleased with arrangements as the Grandfathers."

"Ancrath likes it. That's all that matters."

"There are benefits to being in charge of the justice system."

"The problem is that it's morphing back into the Laws of Time. We need the Book of Commands. We need the Book of Abilities."

"And if I could conjure them out of thin air, do you think I wouldn't have done so by now?"

Isthim gave him a look that said she had her doubts.

"Does this mean I'm out of a job?" Cassius threw in, leaning lazily on the table. "Is Misik going to kick me out of the asylum or lock me up with the rest of them?"

"I don't know," Isthim sighed, "you'll have to ask him or go find out for yourself."

It was a dismissal, one Cassius was too happy to take. Given that he hadn't actually contributed to the conversation, he wondered why he'd been summoned at all. Yes, the war was over, or at least suspended for the time being, but was there no value in knowing how certain things were accomplished? Did no one care about the "minor skirmishes" as Misik had so eloquently put it? Was there nothing to be learned from them, or was Cassius simply an expendable grunt?

Maybe Rifun would ask him about the details later, once he wasn't distracted by his girlfriend. Isthim hadn't exactly roamed the halls weeping when Rifun was declared missing, presumed dead, nor did she fling herself on him for comfort, but she had seemed rather distracted and disoriented for a little while afterwards.

Cassius returned to the Wheel and made for the Judgment Wing. Misik had wasted no time as there appeared to be a rather large meeting going on right there in the lobby for all to witness.

He never actually said that the Borelians were breaking from their alliance with the Cult, but even Cassius could tell that his language certainly skirted that line. The commander stood with his back to Cassius, the Borelians gathered on the other side of the room.

"Are there any questions?" the commander asked finally. "Is anyone confused?"

Cassius raised his hand but didn't wait to be called on. "Does that mean I'm out of a job?"

Misik turned, his posture and expression suggesting he hadn't expected anyone to be behind him, nor for that person to be Cassius of all people. He regained his composure quickly and answered, "You are free to act as you see fit, as befits your position."

It wasn't much of an answer, but Cassius chose to interpret it as being able to keep his job and continue to torture prisoners. He just wasn't sure how he felt about the sudden less-than-chummy relationship they now faced.

He decided to hold off, at least for the rest of the day, possibly the next couple of days depending on how things panned out. Maybe Misik would miss having the Cult around and want to come back. Maybe the Council of Ancrath or the Admirals would force him. Or maybe he would enjoy being free of the restraints of an alliance and do something terrible. Whatever the case, Cassius didn't want to get caught unawares in the middle of a sudden battlefield. He would jump into the fray, but he didn't want to be surprised from behind.

So he returned to the ruins, avoiding the officers building just so he could avoid Rifun. Damn it, he was already feeling the bastard's return. He was back to avoiding, slinking around, just waiting to be called in for some meeting or other fretting. Why couldn't he ever walk freely with that man around?

Worse, what was he supposed to do with his time now? He couldn't just walk around freely, and he couldn't hide in the asylum. He hadn't completely given up on the idea of a small, private task force of his own making and training, but his interest in it came and went. Berkloff had been sent as a replacement for Barnoff, and that particular Korin was proving to be especially ruthless, which Cassius liked, and he enjoyed training him. But, like all Korin, he had a tragic compulsivity toward balance.

As for the other three, they seemed to regard Berkloff as a higher rank—the reason for this, Cassius did not know, since he thought Berkloff younger and more inexperienced—and did not integrate him as an equal among themselves. All odd numbers were unlucky for the Korin, and having only three of them really miffed their sense of balance, and Cassius may as well have been trying to train brand new greenhorns, no pun intended.

All this to say that the Korin were no longer terribly reliable when it came to a privately-trained and maintained force.

Murdi and Lordo, while they appreciated the training of the Cult, helped in small operations, and were glad to keep their location a secret, wandered off to do their own thing more often than not. They were not Gentleman Killers—those had been effectively phased out—but they held no real loyalties to anyone or anything, except, perhaps, each other. Cassius suspected they were the ones who had killed Ivolo.

Pilory had returned a time or two. She informed on any progress or potential leads as to the Book of Commands, maybe learned a thing or two, and then departed without much ceremony.

Others had come and gone as well, as he discovered exceptional talent among the grunts or when he found he needed a particular skill set. But his little task force was hardly what one might call functional.

So, really, he was left completely alone in a large crowd. This might not bother him so much, except he now had to contend with Rifun's return and all the political hell it would bring, and had already brought, if the Borelians were any indication.

Why couldn't the man have died? It had made everything so much easier. Without Julianna worrying like a woman and Rifun fretting over morality and spirituality and whatever he had going on at home, things had run smoothly. So smoothly, in fact, it was like the last two years had just glided by.

Cassius soon found himself in the secret cove where he'd been training his private force. Maybe he should start fresh, find aliens and people as ruthless as he was, but without the restraints of morality. The Shatai would be perfect, except they learned almost too fast. When new generations contained all the knowledge and memories of their ancestors, there were new Shatai recruits who already knew more than some of the instructors. And that knowledge was spreading even faster among the Shatai. There were supposedly some internal politics between them and a neighboring species, the Iuri, but as far as Cassius was concerned, that was all ancient blood feuds and things he didn't care about.

Of course, there were plenty of species now represented among the Cult. But so many of them—all of them, in fact—had some sort of moral or religious system that hindered them. They, the Cult, were supposed to be freeing people from such things, to let them live how they wanted. They were literally giving away, for free, the power to manipulate Creation. And still they wanted to play morals?

Cassius skipped a rock, watching it sail almost into the darkness before sinking. It wasn't water in the lake; it was denser than that, and not advised to ingest, though short swims were permissible for some species, humans included, provided one got a thorough bath in actual water afterwards. Cassius didn't swim, wasn't overly fond of large bodies of water in the first place.

"Almost three years and you have nothing to say to me."

Cassius turned at the sound of Rifun's voice.

"Were you expecting a welcome home party?" Cassius skipped another rock.

"No." Rifun walked up and stood beside him, looking over the lake. "But I imagine that my sudden resurrection may have thrown the proverbial wrench into any plans you may have had. I might have expected your private army to grow in the last two years, yet here you are, skipping rocks alone by the lake. The being alone does not surprise, but I never imagined you to be a rock skipper."

"The denser liquid helps," Cassius informed him snidely.

"I imagine it does. And your task force?"

"Annoying. Unnecessary. Disbanded."

Rifun did not appear satisfied with the answer, but he nodded anyway. "I see." He shifted his stance. "Isthim says the Akarin have been quiet. It is not unreasonable to think they have a hand in attempting to shift the Wheel back toward the power of the Time industry."

"By backing the sworn enemies of all religion in the universe and the assassinations of any and all former Hands and Hand candidates?" Cassius grinned. "I knew the ith Borelians caused them some confusion; I didn't know they had completely erased their identity."

"Having the Cult in power means the Akarin must take a stand and actually put some weight behind their words, power to their truth. They must actually act and do everything they say they must do. Why? Because we are a single, unified force. Reinstalling the Time industry means they can be fat, lazy, passive pacifists again. They can go back to griping and complaining, rattling their sabers and threatening this and that—assuming they ever get that far—but playing politics just like the rest of them. And the Hands are too divided in their competing interests to care. But as long as everyone is playing petty politics, it is just children in the sandbox. At the end of the day, everyone goes home and gets tucked in by Mommy and Daddy, their respective ideologies calmly assuring them that they are the ones in the right and everyone else is the bully."

"Damn, I missed your poetry." Another rock skipped across the lake.

"I sense some sarcasm in your voice."

"Only some? I must be out of practice since you've been gone." He went on before Rifun could speak. "Are the Borelians back, then? Have you gone to woo Misik with your charming words and debonair demeanor?"

"I'm surprised you were aware of the existence of that word, but no. I will let Misik be the king of his own castle for a little while, let Borelian politics play out a little. What I really want right now is to get some insight into the Akarin and the Tacagans, find out how much they're working together, if at all, and just generally see what they're doing."

"You're a Builder, aren't you? You can use a Disguise, same as I can."

"Yes, but you look bored. Did Misik relieve you of your guard duties?"

"No, but I decided it might be better to avoid the place for a day or two." Cassius turned to face him. "Why are you asking me? Really?"

"You remember that idea we talked about, a short time before I left? Just before we went to see Captain Titik?"

"You talked about it. I wasn't listening much."

"Yes, this I can tell. I—"

"You said something about infiltrating the Akarin." Cassius folded his arms. "It may surprise you to learn that I'm not much of a virtuous soul. I wasn't exactly fighting Julianna to be captain of the humanitarian team."

"No, but you do have something else in great abundance," Rifun said. "Ego."

"Hm...I'm not sure if I should be offended."

"Everything that I've seen—and I have no reason to believe it's changed—suggests that Doug may be a leader for his organizational and tactical skills, but he's not well-liked on a personal level."

"We don't even know if that's true anymore."

"Which is why it should be investigated."

Cassius blinked and shook his head. "Wait, you want me to impersonate Doug?"

"You have the strength, you have the ego, you have the skill with the Akari, and you're not overly concerned with people's opinions of you. Yes, I may be able to do a physical Disguise, but you know me—" Rifun shrugged. "—I'm too much of a people person."

"You want me to impersonate a man who masturbates to pornographic images of himself?"

"You're a necrophiliac, what do you care?"

"You say that like I don't have standards."

"Death is a pretty low standard, don't you think? At least Doug thinks highly of himself." Rifun went on before Cassius could protest. "I'm not asking you to throw parties. Just get in and look around a bit. See what they're up to, if they really are backing the Tacagans."

"Wouldn't it be better to infiltrate the Tacagans?"

"Given the number of times you've assassinated their entire governing body, I don't think that would be a good idea. They might get suspicious. I think I would be the better candidate in that case."

"And who will you be impersonating?"

Rifun seemed caught off-guard by the question, but he answered, "I don't know yet. I'll have to do a bit of research, see what my options are."

"What options?" Cassius wondered. "They're all genetically-engineered assholes who live in big cities and think the universe revolves around them. They disdain religion while making themselves gods, and they don't enjoy being told what to do even as they seek to control others. What more do you need to know?"

"Who will I be impersonating? Who do they represent? Who do they answer to? What is their daily life like? What is their political stance? Not to say that you shouldn't do a bit of research as well. At least stalk Doug a little."

Cassius blanched. "Why are we doing this? Honestly, why? Is there some plan behind it, or is it to satisfy your curiosity?"

Rifun gave him a look as though he'd just sprouted a third arm. "Do you realize how close we were? Do you understand what we almost had?"

Cassius shook his head. "That's not the point. The question is, do you understand what we have? Now, here. We have the power to shape the universe. You touched the Core of the Wheel; you did what the Akarin said couldn't be done without them. You are a Builder. You have power. I have power. We have power. We have an army. That is what we have. But we don't use it!"

"We need the Book—"

"We need nothing!" Cassius said loudly, erecting a Sound barrier so it didn't carry across the lake. "We don't need any of that. The Tacagans fancy themselves gods; we are gods. We decide the rules. We decide the punishments. We decide the morals. We dictate our own stories! And here you are, worrying over rules and spirits and morals. What can anyone do to us? Really? What prison can hold us? What blade can cut us? What toxin can hurt us?"

"You may disdain morals, but they are—"

"They are what we make them! Morals and rules and right and wrong are what we say they are! What are you afraid of? What do you have to fear? No slaver will ever be master over me again. No torturer will ever take fire or blade to you again."

Rifun gave him a look. "I fear the one thing we cannot dictate: eternity."

Cassius grinned, shook his head, shifted his stance, and sighed. "Is that it? Your immortal soul?"

"I may be a Builder, but I am not the Creator."

"Why not? Are you afraid to try? Are you afraid to take that step?"

"And what has been stopping you from pursuing this goal, hm? We are yet mortal men bound to the Author. We can do nothing she does not permit."

"And why should such a great master give away all her secrets? Why would Isthim train a soldier in how to defeat her? Except that would make for a better soldier, for if anyone were to defeat Isthim, then a defending soldier must also be able to beat that opponent as well. But if he remains behind that last wall of training, then he is doomed."

"You would dictate morality to God?"

Cassius shrugged. "I would. And I would dictate to all—"

"Then why are we here?" Rifun interrupted.

"Excuse me?"

"You were once the Zero Hour, and you had the power of the Akari then. Why didn't you dictate then? Why didn't you keep everything to yourself, forget Richard and Julianna, and rule unilaterally? Why not, hm? Was it not exciting enough? Did you get bored? Was being the almighty ruler of the universe not everything you thought it would be? More power won't make it less boring."

Cassius gave him a look. "You're rather argumentative since you got back. First Misik, and now me. Did you scare off Isthim, too?"

"Maybe the Core of the Wheel showed me a few things."

"Oh, so now you're a wise man, too. A prophet."

"All the progress we achieved up to the point of my leaving has been steadily slipping away. I'm trying to fix that. To do that, we need to know the positions of our enemies, see if they are collaborating, how, and what their end goal is. If the Tacagans and the Akarin are somehow in league together, well, it won't take much to poison that well, I think. But we have to act quickly." He sighed. "And I have to think of something to patch things up with my family."

"Now you want to leave," Cassius said flatly.

"I want to make things right, and I want to be buried in the family tombs. I just need to come up with something for where I've been for the last two years and why. It shouldn't take long, and I don't even have anything to tell them yet."

"Well, at least let us know before you leave next time. Don't need you wandering off a cliff."

He himself wasn't sure how much of a threat he intended, but Rifun appeared to take it as such and filed it away appropriately. Instead of replying to it, he changed the subject. "So, will you go and impersonate Doug?"

Cassius sighed and gave him a hard regard. "I will go and investigate his life a little, and I'll go snooping around the Akarin fortress a little—as someone entirely unimportant first—and then I'll make my decision on how far I want to take it."

Rifun nodded. "Well, it's a start. I'll go to the Wheel Archives and see what I can find for current events on or concerning Tacaga."

Cassius sighed again. "Why bother? Why go through these charades, these shows? Tacaga has a population of twenty billion—"

"Twenty-one," Rifun corrected.

"They have a lot of people, and a massive standing army. But they live in domed cities. It wouldn't be hard to turn those glass domes into runaway greenhouses, or even giant magnifying glasses. Burn them like ants. Solve our problems, and the problems of probably a few other peoples, if not the whole of the Time industry."

Now Rifun gave him a look. "And why didn't you do that when you went to assassinate their Governors? Why did you bother with the charades and the shows? If you berate me for morality, what is stopping you? Except, maybe, that you have no power that the Author does not give you. And if she doesn't want you committing genocide against twenty-one billion humans, then she's not going to let that happen."

Without another word, he turned and walked away, leaving Cassius standing there at the edge of the lake.

Cassius didn't know what to think. He went to assassinate the Governors because he'd wanted to. It had been necessary at the time. He supposed he could have done everything he'd just said, but he didn't...why?

He skipped a stone but turned and walked away before he could see how far it got. He dropped the Sound barrier but played with Light a little to guide him back toward the city.

Why didn't he just go and kill all the Tacagans? It would certainly save everyone a lot of trouble. It might even save lives in the future, then he would be a hero. Ha!

So what was holding him back? Morals? Hardly. Twenty-one billion would be an impressive record. He could do it on the planet, go city by city, or maybe he could commandeer a space craft, change the physics of their system, and completely destroy the planet. Tacaga was in Quadrant Five, one of the least-populated quadrants, so by the time any effects would be noticed by anyone else, it would be years. Generations. Probably.

Maybe it was boredom. Twenty-one billion would be an impressive record, but...then what? The only thing he would be able to do after that was...he wasn't sure what. There were probably other worlds out there with explosive populations he could destroy.

But then what?

A stray thought crossed his mind. He'd read Rifun's Book while he'd been away, found it at his little shrine. He'd learned a lot about the man, his inner thoughts and schemes. Rifun had had plenty of chances to kill him, as he'd been hired to do, including just now at the lake. What was holding him back? It wasn't as though he hadn't killed men before; his time as a revolutionary had proven that. Even for all his morals, he seemed to understand the concept of analyzing risks and benefits: the risk of keeping Cassius alive, the benefits of killing him.

Was it the Author's will, then, that he, Cassius, should live? Given the number of times Cassius had let Rifun walk away, including just now at the lake, did she also intend for him to live? Were they actually supposed to work together somehow? For what purpose? And where did Isthim and Julianna fit in all of this?

Damn it, he hated it when things got philosophical. The only way he could get away from that dull line of thought was to do something. Well, he couldn't go back to the asylum yet, so his only option presently was to do what he'd said he'd do and do a little sneaking around the Akarin fortress.

He went with a simple human Disguise, easy to manage, less likely to be given away by incidental mishaps.

He hadn't set foot in the fortress since before Rifun left. He hadn't wanted to, and it had never been deemed necessary, at least as far as he was concerned.

Back then, in the aftermath of the ith Borelians clouding everyone's memories, things had seemed empty, a bit dreamy, even. People were not hostile, but they were very uncomfortable with the gaps in their memories.

In almost three years since then, things looked rather robust. People moved about with purpose and confidence, not the confused, glassy stare of someone who knew they should probably remember you but didn't know whether they should remember you as friendly or unfriendly. Latent logic suggested friendly, but there was no way to know for sure.

All of that seemed to have cleared up. Even if the people didn't have those memories, they were making new memories, and things were settling down. Cassius suddenly found his curiosity severely piqued, and he wondered what had changed.

Even with a chunk of memories missing, a man's personality didn't change. In fact, it was when he had no memories to rely on and inform him what to do, what is acceptable or not, that his true personality was revealed. So if Doug's self-obsession had been merely a front—for whatever reason it was beneficial for everyone to believe you were that obsessed with yourself—then maybe the memory loss had jarred that facade just a little. Even if it hadn't been a front, penetrating one's psyche like the Borelians had, robbing a man of his memories, could shake a man, too, make him question things and cause him to change.

None of this appeared to be the case with Doug Templeton. Or maybe his facade really was just that perfect that no one cared. He was loud, he was boisterous, he was more than full of himself, and people were just too happy to have him gone...until they needed him.

Maybe he could impersonate Doug, assuming his position in the Akarin was still important. He wasn't going to pretend to be a self-satisfying Narcissist for nothing, and Doug's home art collection left much to be desired.

So Cassius casually kept an eye on Doug as he made his way around the fortress. It wasn't difficult to know where he was, or where he was going, or who he was talking to, or what he was talking about, or any of his intentions. His end of any conversation could be clearly heard thirty yards away. If he had suffered at all because of the ith Borelians, he wasn't showing it in the least.

He was either fearless, stupid, or things really were just that calm again as he strode up to a Kiboz.

"Ah, Marlek!" he boomed, his voice echoing down the stairwell. "Good to know my message reached you!"

"How could it not?" the Kiboz, Marlek, asked. Even for its alien physiology, Cassius thought it seemed a bit stressed at being found by Doug.

"Indeed! So listen, how about we follow up on that in the next day or two, hm? I know you've got some festival coming up and if I had realized it before I sent the message, I would have held off. I mean no offense, really, but at least this way you know about it and no one is getting blindsided, am I right? I'll get with you later about it. You go enjoy your festival!"

And he just kept right on moving. Cassius wasn't even sure he'd really stopped, but the Kiboz looked relieved to have him gone.

Cassius followed Doug around the fortress for some time. On the one hand, he could safely guess that the man still held some position of authority. On the other hand, he wasn't exactly rushing off to secret meetings or other official goings-on. He really seemed to be just socializing. For a moment, Cassius was surprised the man knew how to socialize with other people and didn't instead spend his time talking to himself in the mirror. Or maybe he did and this was him going out among the peasants as it were.

How did this guy get to be the leader of a group that was supposed to be about humility and helping people? Were people willfully blind, or did he possess some great skill that literally could not be found anywhere else in the universe?

There was no way the Tacagans were negotiating with a guy like this. It was impossible. If the sanity of any normal creature was challenged just by his socializing, Tacagan egos wouldn't allow him to do much more than walk in the room, never mind sit down at a table and talk politics. Just watching him was exhausting. Cassius dreaded the thought of impersonating him.

On the other hand, having that boisterous of a personality, that hated of a reputation, and that ability to wrestle in a captive audience, that could provide some form of entertainment. Of course, Cassius would want some kind of goal or end date, some way he could definitively shed his Disguise, or else someone was going to get hurt, probably a lot of someones.

There were no meetings to be had, not even an on-the-spot, glad-I-ran-into-you kind of thing. No messages were passed on, no hidden passages unlocked. The man didn't even return a library book.

But then, just as Cassius was ready to give up and go home, Doug did do something that made his time worthwhile.

The last time Cassius was in the fortress, he'd assumed there were only seven aboveground floors (if they could be called aboveground). Doug showed him that there were, in fact, eight.

It was only accessible from the northeast staircase, and it was narrower than the rest. Not by a lot, but noticeably so. Judging by the lack of traffic, this was intended only for the council, or those of sufficient importance, anyway. Finally, he was getting what he came for. Now then, how to get it without this ending in a massacre, and also massacring his chances of future information?

He'd learned a few valuable lessons about Light over the years. It was both particle and wave, which was why it was notoriously difficult to manipulate. But, if you were able to master it, and if you did it right, you could render yourself nearly invisible while standing. It was next to impossible to hold while moving because of all the shifting shadows, but standing he could pull off, especially with the shadows from the ceiling to hide any imperfections in his Light bending.

He Banded to get as close to Doug as possible, then implemented his Light cloak. Once he had it adjusted as best he could get it, he released the Band.

Doug did not bother to knock on the double doors when he approached, nor did Cassius hear anyone rebuke him for it. Once Doug was out of sight, Cassius followed him in. His Light cloak shimmered and faded, but he let it go, Banding to get in the room and look around.

The room itself was pretty sparse, little furniture beyond a table and a few chairs. It didn't even look like a proper meeting room. Another door stood off to one side, but, upon inspection, led to little more than a broom closet.

But it was the apparatus in the back of the room that got his attention. There stood on the floor a control panel of some form, and from the ceiling and through the floor, bearing the resemblance of an hourglass in style, was like an enclosure of pure Energy whose properties and purpose Cassius could only begin to guess at. It was the only light source in the room at present, and it glowed such a white-blue that it could probably blind someone.

Was this the core of the Akarin fortress? Was this how they maintained their atmosphere? Was it connected to the Akari in any way?

On the control panel, he noticed, was only a single button. Appropriately, it was red. It was covered in a box protected by another box that appeared to be locked and sealed. Whatever the button did, it wasn't something that was to be pushed carelessly.

Doug did nothing special in the room. Did a little sweeping, a little dusting, an inspection of the control panel and the energy contained in the hourglass, apparently found nothing of interest, and moved on.

But all Cassius could think was, The man does his own housekeeping? Around here, he might have expected grunts. At home, Cassius might have been expecting scantily-clad French nurses. And there was no way that Doug came all the way here to sweep and wouldn't do it at home. Would he? Why was Cassius even worried about this?

Other than discovering this almost-secret level and room and contraption, nothing of interest happened. It appeared to be little more than a day of socializing and light housekeeping.

Cassius followed Doug back down the stairs, all the way back to the portal room. Doug left first, and then Cassius, each man to his destination.

Without the asylum, Cassius again returned to the ruins. He did not find Rifun right away, figured he was still in the Wheel Archives doing his research and catching up on the last three years.

Cassius spent the time wondering whether he shouldn't keep this little tidbit of knowledge to himself. The machine may not have done anything special today, but if it had to be hidden on an almost-secret floor of the fortress, hidden behind closed doors and seemingly understood to be off-limits to everyone except a select few, then it had to be somewhat important, right?

But how would squirreling away such knowledge actually help him? What leverage did it pose against Rifun? Basically none. If he did tell, Rifun, though, the man might be able to do the dirty work and research what that machine was and figure out how to use it against the Akarin. If it was linked to atmospheric constants in the fortress, well, a man was suddenly very willing to negotiate when you were all that stood between him and sucking all the oxygen out of the room.

It was a good two days before Cassius actually saw Rifun in the officers building again, and another two before they could meet.

"Settling things with your family?" Cassius guessed, closing the door to his chambers behind him.

"Um...actually I haven't been to see them yet," Rifun admitted. "I've been working on other things."

"Impersonating Tacagans?"

"I've narrowed down my options to a few likely candidates. Unless you discovered something that will save all of us a lot of time and resources?"

Cassius told the story of his trailing Doug, noting that life for the Akarin appeared to have gone back to mostly normal.

"Did they appear to be mobilizing in any way?" Rifun asked.

"If they were, then Doug has no part in it. There were no meetings, no deals, no secrets, nothing but socializing and..."

Rifun raised a brow. "And...?"

"I followed him to a room. I figured there were seven floors in the fortress, plus the sub-levels. As it turns out, there are eight."

Cassius could not begin to describe the satisfaction at seeing he had Rifun's full attention. For once, he seemed to know something this political man of higher learning did not as he said, "Go on."

"There's another level, accessible only from the northeast staircase. This level has only one room. There's some kind of contraption in this room that's conducting a lot of energy through it, and it has a control panel with only one button. That button is locked down and barricaded so it can't be accidentally pressed." He described it in detail as best he could.

Rifun's expression twisted into deep thoughtfulness. "Interesting..."

"I thought so, too."

"And what was Doug doing in this room with this contraption?"

"Housecleaning, of all things. Sweeping, dusting, average light housework, which I thought was odd for him."

"Maybe, maybe not. And maybe..." His thoughtfulness turned into a smirk. "We may have found our Judas."

"You think Doug will betray the Akarin willingly?" Cassius wondered.

"If he believed he was doing the right thing, maybe. But I have a theory that needs to be investigated first."

"What theory is that, pray tell? I may make another trip to the fortress."

"Do you know the origin story of the Akarin and the Wheel? Whether true or not, I don't quite know, but have you heard it?"

"No," Cassius said flatly.

"The Wheel itself is the fulcrum of all the black holes in the universe, twisted together into something relatively stable. The Akarin believe that the Wheel was created for them by the Author. It was their safe haven where they could live in peace yet reach all corners of the universe. This place was initially accessible only by the Akarin."

"Let me guess. Some people got greedy and arrogant, started attacking others and asserting dominance. Author gets mad, kicks them out of their Garden of Eden, dilutes the Akari down into what we know as Timekeeping and Harvesting and all that, and the Wheel is turned into the hub of the Time industry."

Rifun nodded. "Exactly. A perfect fall from grace story. I don't know how true it is, but what is true is that no one—not even the Akarin themselves—know where their present-day fortress is truly located. The coordinates are rumored to be lost. The fortress is entirely underground, no passage to the surface."

"So that contraption is what's keeping them alive," Cassius said. "Atmosphere and whatnot, like I thought."

"Maybe, but I think it's more," Rifun murmured. "Thinking of some of the things I saw in the Core—and I remember less than a sliver compared to a tree—and some things I've heard around the city, it may be far more than mere atmosphere."

Cassius grinned. "If that's the case, then we've got them by the balls. They'll do anything we tell them."

"Well, before we do anything too extreme, such as pressing buttons that are heavily fortified against accidental touches, I want to know what's going to happen when we do decide to press it." He turned and made as if to leave.

"Do I still have to impersonate Doug?" Cassius wondered.

Rifun paused and looked back at him. "For the time being, no. Having this little ace in the hole may save you. At the same time, depending on what that contraption does, I'm a little suspicious about why and how you were able to access it so easily, Akari or no Akari."

Cassius shrugged. "People leave dangerous weapons lying around all the time. They just expect that other people have the morals to not pick it up and use it."

Rifun said nothing to that and departed.

Actually, Cassius felt pretty good about himself. Not only had he found an apparent Achilles' heel for the Akarin, but he'd also discovered something that Rifun didn't already know. He made the discovery. Him. Not only that, but because of that, he might not have to impersonate a man who got aroused by his own reflection. Everyone was winning today. Well, not everyone. He seemed to be the only one who was winning right now, but that was all that mattered, right?

Feeling in a pretty good mood, Cassius went to the Wheel and strode down to the Judgment Wing and the asylum. No one stopped him. No one questioned him. No one objected when he started picking out his favorite tools of the trade and ordering that prisoners be brought to him.

29 | Mandinika sy Mitatitra

Observe and Report

The Caves of Meroian, 1969

W hat exactly are you saying, Milfor?" Rifun asked.

The Shatai leader fluttered her wings, though it was more like rattling bones together. "I'm saying that whoever presses that button can destroy the entire Akarin."

Rifun blinked and shook his head. "Why would they leave it so exposed, though?"

"Who says they did? What are the odds that the leader of the Akarin would show the leader of the Cult directly to this grand weapon of mass destruction? I am not Akarin and never will be, but even I know Doug Templeton's reputation. Do you think he does his own housekeeping?"

"He knew Cassius was following him. It was bait."

" 'Come and get it,' he says. 'Here it is, now come and take it.' " Milfor shifted. "Guarantee that if Cassius had gotten close and actually threatened to push it, Doug would have stopped him, or tried to."

Rifun frowned. "They're trying to tempt us out into the open. They know we're losing ground in the Wheel. The Tacagans don't stand much of a chance except on an economic and technological level, which the Wheel provides, but the Akarin may be a match for us in the field. They just want to bring us to their home field." He let out a breath. "So they are working together."

"They may not be formal allies, but they appear to have a common interest," Milfor agreed.

"But if what you're saying is true, why haven't your people attacked the Akarin?"

"They're stronger than they look. And that fortress, while built by and for the Shatai — no matter what the Iuri claim — is full of traps and snares, to say nothing of anything they've invented since they kicked us out. Don't think that we haven't tried in the past. The beauty and curse of generational memory is never forgetting a grudge."

Rifun thanked her and she went on her way, not bothering to use the door but sweeping out through the window in his chambers. He took an even breath, stared at the floor for a moment, then glanced at Isthim.

"So, the Akarin have dirty secrets after all," he mused.

"Destroying an entire planet, driving the Kitir to near-extinction, now holding it all together at the edge of a black hole, just one button push away from falling into oblivion," Isthim said.

"One hell of an Achilles heel."

"Agreed, and surely they are not unaware of this."

"Means they're cocky," Rifun stated, standing. "Means they expect an easy fight, an easy victory. Expose your greatest weakness because you think your enemy is not able to exploit it."

"You intend to attack them, then?" Her expression was surprised.

"Oh, I'm not going to go running into their little trap they've set. I'll let them sweat a little first. We should make our own plans, don't you think? After all, the Akarin are only one front. They may have the power, but the Tacagans still have the numbers."

"So where are you going?"

"To do some thinking and planning."

This was what he told her. He even told it to himself, as if he might believe it.

What he actually did was return to Madagascar. He had a plan to see what the family thought of his disappearance, if it was even worth trying to return as himself or his fictional son.

So as far as Volana was concerned, a complete stranger knocked on his door that afternoon.

"I'm looking for Rifun Ndolo," he said, trying to appear optimistic. "I'm an old friend of his, and I'd heard he'd made his way back here finally."

Volana's expression fell as soon as he heard Rifun's name, and he chuckled sadly. "I'm afraid you are about three years too late, my friend."

"He's dead? I'm sorry, I didn't hear about it. Of course, that doesn't surprise me. That I didn't hear about it, I mean. Quite frankly, I didn't think anything could take him down, but time makes mockery of our youth, doesn't it?"

"Yes, it does. No, he's not dead, or not that anyone has been able to prove. He's missing. After three years, at his age, well, it wouldn't surprise me if he were dead."

"Holding out hope, then." Rifun nodded slowly.

"The shaman says he is still alive. His soul still walks among the living. It is the only reason we have not had a memorial for him, but I cannot think of why he wouldn't come back."

"Where did he go?"

"North, on a sort of vacation, with another old friend of his. Does the name Kokumbo mean anything to you?"

Rifun shook his head. "I'm afraid it doesn't. What could have happened to him? Is anyone doing anything?"

"There were searches at first, yes. But the police and the government don't have the resources it used to, and few at the higher levels want to go looking for an old half-blood, ex-revolutionary, possible-traitor." He spat to show his opinion of the titles.

There was something the old man wanted to say, but straight-up fear was holding him back. Later research would reveal that Madagascar had gone full Communist. Prosperity plummeted, paranoia abounded, and fear was thicker than the humidity in the air.

"I see. Well, I'm sorry to hear he's missing. If I happen to run into him, I'll point him this way," Rifun promised.

Volana thanked him and watched him leave. No mention was made of his fictional son Fan, and Rifun figured that if his fictional son had heard of the real persecution of mixed-bloods, he would stay as far away as possible so he didn't end up missing like his father.

So even if he could go back, he still probably couldn't. If the government found him, he could be dragged away for real. He had no desire to see the inside of yet another shithole prison, and he didn't want to alienate his family by breaking his Disguise and revealing his Akari prowess. He wanted to keep this part of his life normal. And yet, did he really want to go out with such a whimper, that he simply "went missing," was never found, never buried?

In an odd turn of events, it bought him a little time to think on it some more; he didn't need to go rushing home as he'd feared.

At least according to his Disguise, however, he was able to pass as a full-blood Malagasy. He had no identification whatsoever, but he wasn't worried. There was nothing tying him to his family, so they were not in danger.

He decided to head into the city, into Fianarantsoa, just to see how things had changed. Madagascar had known periods of grand wealth and prosperity, and periods of destitution. But always, whether free or subjugated, at peace or at war, the Malagasy had their pride and identity.

City life was recognizable, although it more resembled the early periods of the Uprising, when power was uncertain, changes swift, and there was no time to argue or try to keep up. A woman hurried her children across the street, frantic despite minimal traffic and older offspring who knew how to accomplish this simple task. A couple of men did their best to appear cheerful in conversation and yet deliberately avoided eye contact with a couple of policemen on the corner.

Rifun, safely on the sidewalk, startled as a car blared its horn when it was driving past him. As he continued to walk, another car, this one parked, also honked its horn. The owner of the car, not three steps away, also jumped, hurrying to dig out keys. He waved a pardoning hand which Rifun returned.

A few clouds rolled over the sun, enough to provide some tangible relief from the heat, though Rifun ducked into a business anyway.

It turned out to be a small cafe, well and busy and almost normal. He found a seat in a back corner. His army training reminded him that this was a tactically advantageous position as it gave him a good view of all patrons and all exits. Strategically, however, it was bad practice to be backed into a corner.

The sconce on the wall beside his table got brighter. Then it got even brighter. Just as he averted his gaze, it fizzled and went out completely.

A waitress walked over at that moment, though whether she'd been drawn to his appearance or the light was uncertain.

"I thank you for the consideration of brightening the lights over here when someone is seated, but I think it may have been a bit much," he told her, trying to come across as light-hearted and joking.

"That wasn't me," the waitress said. "Or anyone that I know of." She sighed. "I suppose it's just..."

"Just...?" Rifun prodded.

"Nothing," she said quickly. "Things are great. We'll just have to see about getting that light fixed, won't we?" Her effort was genuine, even if her smile was not. "Now then, what can I get for you?"

"I haven't seen a menu yet."

"Oh, sorry, sorry."

She shook her head, hastily retrieved a menu, and left him to browse.

He really wasn't hungry, so he just got something light. Not that he could have gotten something terribly filling; the menu itself was rather limited. But he didn't complain. It was home, and it was comfort food.

He paid for his meal by Banding and pilfering a bit of cash from another patron who looked like he could afford to give alms now and again. Then Rifun thanked his waitress and headed back onto the street.

The sun was going down and, in the nicer part of town, the street lights were flickering to life. He took a moment to breathe in the smell of home before deciding that an evening stroll might help to clear his head and help him think.

He turned north, toward the university, but instead of clearing his head, the walk began to muddle it. He would look to one side or the other, fully expecting to see chaos and garbage, the side effects of war and siege. He expected to find carnage, walking wounded, walking dead. He expected to see the uniforms of the French, the tatters of the Malagasy. Supplies running low, food nearly gone, morale nonexistent.

The closer he got to the university, the more his mind played tricks on him. There was what he remembered and what he now saw. But because his vision was taken as mere impression, his mind's eye could not distinguish between the two. Only factual knowledge told him that the university was not a bullet-riddled battlefield, but it did little to convince his soul.

He paused outside the campus, staring at the splendor of architecture, fortitude, and Malagasy pride. He remembered studying here. He remembered holing up here. He remembered almost dying here.

The street lamps on either side of him brightened, then dimmed. Then he saw the lights down the walk of the campus did the same in succession, as if showing him the way in. It was perhaps the only thing that brought him back to the present moment. He glanced at the lights on the street, then at the ones lining the walk into campus. First the lights brightened in succession. Then they started to go out and come back on in succession.

He looked around at any other lights on the street or on campus that he could see. None of them were acting strangely. And how was it that he should also have issues with the light in the cafe?

Briefly he examined himself, to make sure he wasn't doing anything to manipulate the lights. He didn't find anything, from Light to Electricity to basic Energy that he might have been tapping into. Whatever was going on was either coincidence, some fancy programming that he happened to stumble across, or there was someone else nearby doing this with the Akari.

Rifun hesitated. Cassius had been led right to the Akarin Achilles heel as a challenge, a taunt. Could this be something similar? Was someone trying to lead him somewhere, get him alone? But if that were the case, why here? Wouldn't it be better to get him alone in the wilderness? The middle of a city was hardly a spot for subtlety.

Unless it was a challenge to him. Divide his attention between defending himself and keeping it out of public eye. That would be a decent idea for a smart assailant.

Well, he was a Builder now. As Cassius had postulated, what did he have to fear? He had seen through time and space, glimpsed marvels that wouldn't be known to humanity for centuries and touched the Core of the Wheel, the Core of Creation. What was he worried about a petty thug?

So then, time to see where the lights took him. Who was waiting for him at the end of the road?

Whoever it was, upon seeing that he was following the lead, or the bait, started to make the clues and cues a little less obvious. Not a few people had stopped and stared at the long line of street lamps brightening or darkening in succession like a cinema marquee. But once that line of lights ran out, coming to a five-way intersection, Rifun had to start searching for his next clue, which he took to be a particular lamp that brightened whenever he looked in that direction.

At some point, when he passed through a dark spot on the road, he altered his Disguise to be younger so he could blend in with others on campus. There was no real reason an elderly man should be wandering around a college campus at night.

The paths twisted and turned, and soon he found himself standing in front of the library. It seemed a likely spot for an ambush, he supposed, especially if his opponent was trying to distract him with keeping things quiet.

All right, then, he decided, *let's see what we've got here.*

It was late, less than an hour before the library closed, but there were still pockets of students here and there doing some last-minute studying. A few more were huddled around a brand new computer, green characters glowing on a black screen. The librarian gave them a disapproving look but said nothing. Instead she turned her gaze to Rifun.

"Help you find something?" she asked.

"Architecture," he answered automatically, momentarily feeling like a student again and wondering when his next exam was. As this sensation swept through him, he also realized he knew where his books would be located. He'd only checked them out dozens of times while in class.

Even so, the librarian gave him directions and sent him on his way. He found himself grateful that she hadn't asked for any kind of ID, but something told him that if he'd made it this far, then he was probably already cleared to be here and go about his business. At least, that was his hope. Wouldn't matter anyway if a fight broke out.

He navigated his way through the stacks of books. As he came to a back wall and turned right, there was another new computer to his left, tucked into an alcove. As he walked past, the screen turned on and things began happening.

Looking around to ensure no one was nearby, Rifun paused and went to the computer. The brightness of the screen and the contrast of the colors confused his vision, but he was able to see that a square appeared on the screen. It was white, and black squiggles that turned out to be letters began appearing.

These computers were nowhere near as sophisticated or easy to use as the Glass tablets in the Wheel Archives. Those he could navigate like a map and read like a book. This screen and the tower and the board of letters and the round thing on a cord that evidently made it so you could move the thing on the screen...it was way too much. There was too much coordination required for this supposedly simple machine, and it overwhelmed his brain, trying to process the glowing input.

But it was the words that got his attention. After several incoherent lines, intelligence emerged.

Rifun. Rifun. Rifun, it's me.

"Who's me?" he asked aloud.

Rifun, it's Julianna.

"What?"

It's Julianna. Julianna Brown. Richard's wife.

He blinked and shook his head. "I don't understand." He looked around. "Where are you?"

More text appeared on the screen.

I'm right here.

"You're inside the computer?" He inspected the screen and the tower, but unless she'd magically shrunk, there was no way she was going to fit except in pieces.

No, the text read. I'm...it's difficult to explain, but I think... I think I'm stuck in another dimension.

Rifun Banded. "What do you mean you're stuck in another dimension?"

Nothing happened. No text appeared, nor did anything else. He waited a few minutes, just in case, but when nothing more happened, he dropped the Band. When he did that, more text appeared.

I don't have access to Time. Anything you do, like Banding, I can't be part of. I also can't use Time, not as the Time industry does. But I can use the Akari.

He put up a Sound barrier, if only so he could speak without anyone thinking he was nuts.

"How do I know it's you and not some prank? What happened to your mission?"

I went into the cave as planned. I moved as fast as I could, but when I got to the miner's bones, there was no journal.

"What do you mean, there was no journal?"

It wasn't there, and the bones had been scattered.

"So someone else got to it first."

I thought, somehow, maybe, that either you or Cassius or Isthim had gotten it, or, Author forbid, one of the Akarin had figured it out and gone after it.

"We don't have it," Rifun admitted sorely.

Whatever the case, it wasn't there. I didn't want to waste time going back out, so I thought that maybe I could just open a portal and get out, whether back to the outside or back to the ruins. But it backfired.

"The portal closed on you and you vanished."

Yes. Apparently, there is a very real, very livable dimension here. I can see and hear everything that's going on, just as if I'm there, but I can't interact. I'm basically a ghost.

"Are you all right?"

I'm fine. Really. But I can't open portals and go places. As I said, Time doesn't work, but the Akari does. But, with lack of portals, and because Earth isn't Engaged, the population of this dimension is almost nil.

"Not too many people to talk to, huh?"

Almost none, in fact. I've been wandering around, waiting for you to show up. I discovered that I can manipulate the Energy in these computers, the electrical signals.

"So you toyed with the Electricity in the street lights, too."

Exactly. I was so happy you showed up. Cassius and Isthim haven't returned to Earth at all that I've seen. Where have you been for three years? I'm guessing you already know your family is worried sick.

"And I'm guessing that you know the explanation they're living with for the moment."

The Communists, yes. Where have you been, though?

"It's kind of a long story, but to summarize, I became a Builder and touched the Core of the Wheel."

Oh, marvelous! Simply fantastic! Then the Cult is in full control of the Time industry? Has it been abolished yet? We really should change the name. "Cult" has such insidious implications.

Rifun sighed. "No. The Cult doesn't have control. Actually, we've lost quite a bit of control since I touched the Core."

Whatever are you talking about?

He gave her the rundown as he understood it. They confounded the Akarin and beat back the Tacagans, but then their enemies changed tactics and were working more subtly.

What about the Book of Commands? Why didn't you take command with that?

"Because we don't have it. The one Isthim's teams found was a fake, a mockery is what I should say, and the trickster has vanished. We did what we could. We trimmed down the Laws of Time, implemented our own rules, our own order, but the Tacagans have since subverted this. We could only promise our allies power; the Tacagans can offer them money, and the Akarin can offer them normalcy."

The text on the screen did not allow for appropriate approximation of reactions, though Rifun could hazard a guess at what Julianna was doing or saying at that moment. But all that came across was, Educating the masses means little if the leaders do not follow. We need to win them back.

"We need the Book of Commands and the Book of Abilities, or else we'll just ride this carousel around again and again, each time losing respect and credibility until we are nothing more than a revolving side show. We must maintain our integrity and our dignity and stop rushing into things."

For a long moment, there was no new text on the screen. Rifun looked away and rubbed his eyes, trying to make the glowing squiggles stop squirming.

You have a point, Julianna typed at last. But how do you suggest going about it? If Isthim's teams are already on the hunt for the Book of Commands — as well

AS THIS CAPTAIN TITIK, UNSAVORY CHARACTER THOUGH HE MAY BE — THEN WHAT MORE CAN BE DONE THERE?

"That may just be a waiting game. And I'm willing to wait—we may have to wait, as we must also search for the Book of Abilities." He took an even breath. "Do we know for a fact that the Akarin have the journal?"

NO. AND, WHILE I CANNOT EXPLAIN IT, THERE IS A UNIQUE ASPECT TO THIS DIMENSION THAT ALLOWS FOR CERTAIN ELEMENTS OF TRAVELING IN TIME.

"What do you mean? Can you go back and—?"

NO. I CANNOT ACTUALLY TRAVEL PER SE, BUT I CAN OBSERVE THINGS THAT HAVE HAPPENED IN THE PAST.

"Do you know who took the journal?" Rifun asked pointedly.

NO. THERE HAVE BEEN MANY PEOPLE WHO HAVE GONE TO THE CAVE OVER THE YEARS, BUT NONE OF THEM APPEAR TO HAVE FOUND THE JOURNAL.

"Then the logical place to begin would be at the source, the last-known location."

I'M NOT GOING BACK INTO THAT CAVE. I DON'T EVEN KNOW IF THE BANDS WOULD AFFECT ME, BUT I'M NOT KEEN ON FINDING OUT. IF YOU GO IN THERE, THEN THAT'S ANOTHER SPAN OF TIME WHERE OUR ENEMIES MAY SEIZE CONTROL OF THE WHEEL!

"They can have it. At least for the time being. Integrity and dignity, Julianna. We can't let our image degrade by folly. But if we allow ourselves a retreat as a strategy, let the Tacagans and the Akarin get comfortable again, then we can regroup, rethink, and attack again when we actually have full force, full power, and the words of the Author behind us."

Again there was a long stretch of silence.

Then, YOU ARE A BETTER TACTICIAN THAN I, AND I SEE THE WISDOM BEHIND YOUR SUGGESTION. I CAN'T OPEN A PORTAL TO SADURNON AND JOIN YOU IN THE MEETING THAT I EXPECT YOU'LL WANT TO HAVE OVER THIS.

"We'll need a better meeting spot than this, though," Rifun pointed out. "Typing and speaking in English is good because few here know the language, but it's still too public. And..." He hesitated. "I don't know or understand what's going on with the politics of my country right now, but I don't feel that it is the safest place."

I'M SORRY TO HEAR THAT. HONESTLY, I ONLY CHOSE THIS PLACE BECAUSE IT WAS PUBLIC AND HAD COMPUTERS (TO MY SURPRISE). I WAS TRYING ANYTHING AND EVERYTHING TO GET YOUR ATTENTION, BUT IF IT'S TOO SUBTLE, THEN IT'S JUST LIFE. IF IT'S TOO OBVIOUS, IT ATTRACTS MORE ATTENTION THAN I WANT.

"And the cinema marquee?"

More enticing than car horns and a single light in a cafe.

"You have a point. But computers are so new and not very widespread. It's not like I can just walk into any house or business and find one. And if I can't Band, then we'll have to meet someplace we won't be disturbed for a while."

You've been to the cave, right? You know where it is.

"Yes, it's in the United States."

Specifically, it's just outside the city of Charleston in the state of West Virginia. Charleston has a public library with a couple computers. If you're intent on going into that infernal cave, then it may be prudent to converse a little closer to that locale.

"I'll agree to that."

When shall we meet?

"I think a week should do. We'll get everyone rounded up and have a meeting to discuss this little revelation I've just had, that one of our leaders is trapped in the Land In-Between and the Book of Abilities is missing, too. I'm sure it will all go over just fine."

Oh, absolutely.

Text did not allow for proper sarcastic intonation, but Rifun imagined it was there.

"At the very least, we know what happened to you. The others were getting worried."

I'm sure they were worried. About the Book of Abilities.

"They were worried, that's all that matters. Now we just have to come up with a rescue plan."

You mean you do intend to rescue me? I wouldn't put it past the others to simply go after the Book of Abilities and leave me here.

"Someone has to deal with the humanitarian work."

Oh, very funny.

"Cassius lacks a certain empathy, and Isthim's bedside manner is terrible."

She doesn't stick around for pillow talk?

"That's low, even for you."

Ha ha.

"I'll see you in Charleston in a week."

All right. I'll see you then. Thank you, Rifun.

"For what?"

For coming back for me. Or at least saying you are.

He wasn't sure what to say to that, so he elected to say nothing as he turned and walked away.

Walking away from the computer and leaving the library finally broke him from the bubble he'd settled into. What had just happened? Had he really just had a conversation with Julianna? He must have. Most would be able to pull off a trick that named Cassius and Isthim, but no one should know about the Cult being located on Sadurnon. That alone would eliminate any common enemies, and even most clever ones. Only one of the Cult or a mole would know about it.

So there was a dimension between dimensions. It had been speculated about plenty of times over the centuries in the Wheel, but no one had been able to prove it one way or the other. If Time didn't work in that dimension, then even the most advanced races would have difficulty communicating. Isolation and suicide was probably a large factor in the minimal population as well. Only an Akari-bearer would be able to manipulate the Energy, and even then, you would have to have a medium in order to effectively communicate. Playing with light bulbs was good to get someone's attention, but...what if computers hadn't been invented yet? How would Julianna have gotten her message across?

It was all so much to take in at once. He didn't know how to process it. Was this how the others felt when he suddenly returned after a year and a half? How were they going to react now that Julianna had made contact? She'd been expected to be gone a while, and now they'd been thrown a curve ball. Now what?

There seemed to be an odd absence of night life in Fianar, not that Rifun was keen on going to a tavern or other social scene, but he enjoyed seeing people out and about and enjoying life rather than fearing for their lives and futures. This evening seemed rather muted. Oh, people were out and about, but there was a certain urgency among those going home, as if they might be punished for being out past curfew. Was there a curfew? Rifun didn't know.

Regardless, he couldn't return to his family's farm, so he returned to Sadurnon instead.

He decided immediately that he wasn't going to call everyone into an urgent meeting. He had to process things for himself first, before he could hope to explain it to the others. Without Julianna here to explain herself, how did he convince them that her story was true and this was all happening? He didn't fully understand it himself. And assuming they got past that hurdle, what did they do about it? Going after the Book of Abilities was the easy part. How did they rescue someone from a dimension that had had little or no proof of existence up until an hour ago?

He would wait on it, think about it a little. Maybe if he thought about her words, dissected them, mulled them over, then he could come up with a way to rescue her. Rescue her, get that out of the way, go after the Book of Abilities.

She had confirmed one long-held suspicion, that a collapsed portal was the way she got into the dimension. If portal in, why not portal out? Why couldn't she have walked through the portal he had used to leave Fianar? What happened when she tried? Even if Time didn't work, she said the Akari did. The Akari worked on Time, Matter, and Energy. She was able to manipulate the Electricity in the computer to type out her words, so why not the Energy of a portal? What key did she lack?

He wanted to go back to Earth and ask her, but how did he get a hold of her? She could contact him through the computer, or at least get his attention with lights and such, but how did he talk to her? How did he get her attention? Maybe she would still be hanging around the university library; even though it was closed, he could let himself in and they could talk all they wanted. Or maybe she would already be on her way to the cave. Without portals, she would have to travel the slow way, by plane or boat, and that would take time.

They could take the time to brainstorm ideas, then, he decided. That way, in a week, they could all meet at the library or the cave, and try to rescue her before going after the Book of Abilities.

He also had to consider the possibility that they might not be able to rescue her. The dimension only just got confirmation of existence after...how many centuries? Millennia? Suddenly being able to jump in and out didn't seem to be a likely possibility. Or what if there were just factors of physics that meant she couldn't come back? He didn't know what, but it seemed as plausible as anything.

At the same time, he was a Builder now. He should be able to do something. Anything. Opening a more reliable means of communication would be better than nothing. But how? Despite peeling back the curtain to peer at raw reality, he hadn't learned very much. Or maybe his brain was just too small to comprehend everything, so it hadn't retained anything. Or anything of use. How frustrating.

But that was neither here nor there, and it was solving none of his problems.

He sat on his information for two days before concluding that he was getting nothing accomplished. He either needed to contact Julianna somehow or bring the others in on it before going to meet her in five days. As much as he wanted to be the hero and rescue Julianna—and as much as they may have been happy to let him and wash their hands of her fate entirely—there was still the matter of the Book of

Abilities. It was in the same predicament as the Book of Commands.

Finally he got out into the city and started looking for the others. Before he got very far, Isthim met him on the street.

"We need to have a meeting. Finally we got a bit of good news," she said, and then was gone, hopping up the steps into the officers building.

Rifun blinked and shook his head, then turned to follow. Well, it saved him the trouble of looking for them and calling a meeting, and good news wasn't bad to receive. He just hoped it didn't interfere with his bad news.

Cassius was the last to appear, and none of the other Borelians joined them. They still seemed firm in their resolve to detach themselves, at least partially, from the Cult. That was fine with Rifun, actually. They didn't need to get in on the chase for the Book of Abilities.

"A lucky coincidence," Rifun observed. "I was just about to call a meeting myself. But seeing how you beat me to it, why don't you go first? Tell us, what is this good news of yours?"

"We have the Book of Commands," Isthim reported proudly.

"Where is it?" Cassius asked grouchily. "Put it on the table."

"It is currently in the possession of Queen Aronet and Commander Dira. They're on some royal entourage and will deliver it posthaste."

"How did they come to have it?" Rifun wondered. "The Ururian didn't come across as the type to entertain royalty."

"The Ururian didn't have it," Isthim answered. "It came from the Kolkath, giving gifts to the Turitians as a peace offering for their alliance."

"What?!" Cassius spat. "I checked the cargo that was going there! How did it get there?"

She gave him a look. "According to the Turitians, the Kolkath claim it is a journal from an ancient monastery on their world. Commander Dira was able to read it and confirm that it is the journal we are looking for."

"So either the Kolkath don't realize its significance, or they're lying," Cassius growled.

"The Kolkath only just broke into space travel," Rifun said calmly. "They are on the fringes of the Time industry, same as Earth. Their alien contact may be extremely limited. The Ururian could have easily slipped the journal into the bag of gifts, or even just the Kolkath's treasure stores. Maybe the Kolkath have similar journals, maybe not, but they're not going to say so to a royal emissary. So they make up a story about an ancient monastery." He shrugged. "At this point, I'm not holding the

Kolkath liable, and I don't think it matters. The Turitians have the journal, Commander Dira has confirmed it, and it will be in our possession soon enough."

"Can't they just send it here via portal?" Cassius grumbled.

"The Turitians don't want to interrupt their festivities with the Kolkath," Isthim said flatly.

"Understandable," Rifun said. "I believe it will be safe with them for the time being. If anything happens to a Turitian royal emissary, I expect it will garner more attention than a single, small Ururian ship."

"Agreed. I have called off my teams as well." She shifted her stance. "What was the meeting you were intending to call, then?"

Rifun cleared his throat. "Well, I wish I had equally good news. Unfortunately, I think I have inversely bad news." He paused. Then, "The Book of Abilities is missing, and Julianna is trapped."

Dead silence.

It was Cassius who spoke first, in a menacing rumble that did not sound entirely human. "What do you mean it's missing?"

"Have the Akarin taken it and taken her hostage?" Isthim inquired.

Rifun shook his head. "I wish it were that easy. For starters, Julianna is stuck in the Land In-Between, the dimension between dimensions. When she found the bones she supposedly hid the journal in, it was gone and the bones had been scattered. She did some searching, couldn't find it. She didn't want to waste more time actually running out of the cave, so she tried to open a portal instead, and it collapsed on her."

"How do you know this?"

He relayed his adventures around the university and the conversation in the library. He finished with, "I'm convinced that it is her and she is telling the truth." He went on before Cassius could protest. "As for the Book of Abilities, she doesn't know where it is. For all she knows, whoever scooped it up is actually still in the cave and won't appear for some time. But she doesn't know if the Time Trap can still affect her, and she's not keen on finding out. It may be better to wait until that person actually appears in the open, in daylight, away from the cave and the Trap."

"How does she know that some animal didn't get to it?" Cassius asked.

"Agreed," Isthim said. "A human, especially someone who knows what it is and what to look for, would try not to disturb things so as not to tip her off to mischief. An animal will tear things apart."

"Maybe the person was careful and some animal did tear it apart in a separate incident," Rifun said. "I don't know. She doesn't know. Point is, the journal is still missing."

Cassius made a frustrated sound and paced away from the table, angrily whispering, "Find one, lose another." Louder, "Once we get our shit back, can we please do a better job of keeping track of our shit?"

Isthim looked ready to say something, but Rifun beat her to it. "At least we have something. We have two of the journals—"

"I'm not counting the Book of Commands until I have it in my hands," Cassius interrupted. "With the way things have gone, I don't have it until I have it."

"Fair enough, but we still have two of the journals. Now we need to go after the third and figure out a way to rescue Julianna."

Isthim seemed uncertain. "Pretending that everything you've said is true, that she is in this in-between dimension, that Time doesn't work but the Akari does, what do you propose for rescue?"

"I don't know. I was hoping you two might have some ideas to present to her. I'm supposed to meet with her again at the library in Charleston, the city closest to the cave. I can't imagine that she didn't try to go through the portal with me in Fianar. Obviously, she's not here with us, but I would be curious to know what her experience was regardless."

"How much time are we going to devote to this?" Cassius wondered. "We could spend just as much time trying to free her as looking for the journal."

"Agreed," Isthim stated. "We should prioritize the journal. We can publicize proof of the in-between dimension and allow the scientists of more advanced worlds work on that problem, but we can't let the location of the Book of Abilities, or our lack of knowledge thereof, be so public."

"Give people a distraction," Rifun said.

"Exactly."

"Is it wise to publicize that one of our leaders is trapped in this dimension and our great and powerful Akari can't do anything about it?" Cassius threw in. "Or that the Author herself isn't rescuing her?"

Silence.

"You may have a point," Rifun mused, "but we can't just leave her."

"Why not?" Cassius murmured. Rifun couldn't tell if he'd meant to be heard, but probably so.

"Someone has to do the humanitarian work," Rifun answered anyway. "Besides, it's a new discovery, and it may provide some useful information. I don't know what, but we shouldn't pass up the opportunity."

"Your petty projects may have to wait," Isthim told him. "We should prioritize. Book of Abilities first, Julianna second. One we know we can retrieve, the other is questionable at best."

"One we know where it is, the other we don't." He put up a hand. "But I understand your point."

"So what do we do?" Cassius questioned. "Are we going after the journal or Julianna?"

"We—or at least I—will meet with Julianna in a few days. I would like to try a few things and get her out of that dimension."

"And if you can't? What if it's impossible? What if you kill her? At what point do we turn our attention to what matters?"

Rifun shifted his stance and gave him a look. "Then why don't you come with me and we can all talk about this together?"

"Gladly."

He didn't know what it was exactly that apparently put Cassius in such a rotten mood, but he guessed it may have had something to do with the Borelians in the Judgment Wing. Maybe he was no longer head guard or had some other disagreement.

Whatever the case, both Cassius and Isthim—back in her African Disguise she'd used in London—showed up to the library five days later. The two of them got some odd or even hostile glares, though Rifun didn't fare much better. Guilt by association and all that.

"Racist bastards," he hissed.

"You wished to evict all Europeans from your home," Isthim countered. "Is that not the same?"

"Is this Europe?" he countered.

It took some time for them to be able to use a computer. Rifun wondered if it wouldn't have been better to just come back after dark. Maybe they should do so now. They were already being stared at and watched. They couldn't Band, but if they put up a Sound barrier and started speaking with nothing to show for it to onlookers, well, paranoia was a terrible thing. And that wasn't even considering the content of their conversation.

Rifun paused, noting the stares they were getting.

"Maybe we should wait until later," he suggested.

Isthim gave him a look. "You're a Builder who touched the Core, with all the power of the universe," she murmured, just barely loud enough to be heard, "and you're afraid of a few disapproving stares?"

She was right, he had to admit. He had the power to reduce them to atoms, and he wanted to run away because they glared at him? How fragile was he? Where was the power, the triumph, the will of spirit that had compelled him to sacrifice—not just a few chickens, not just a goat, but his own shaman—in order to attain power rarely gifted to a living mortal? Where had his conviction gone? Caught up in the cares of the world, the flight of the living? How cowardly! How...mortal. He had to shake off his mortal self, embrace the spirit, his second nature.

He ignored the stares, erected a Sound barrier, and turned his attention to the computer. For a moment, nothing happened. Then a box appeared and text began appearing on the screen.

I SEE YOU CONVINCED THE OTHERS TO JOIN YOU. THEY DIDN'T BELIEVE IT WAS ME?

"There's some skepticism, yes," Rifun said. "There was also an argument over whether it would be better to free you first or find the journal first. Tell me, why didn't you just walk with me through the portal in Fianar?"

I TRIED. IT WAS LIKE GETTING STRUCK BY LIGHTNING OR HIT BY A BUS. I WAS KNOCKED OUT. WHEN I CAME TO, NOTHING HAD CHANGED.

"So much for the simple solution," Isthim commented.

BELIEVE ME, YOU'RE NOT THE ONLY ONE WHO'S FRUSTRATED.

Again, text left much to be desired by way of intonation or body language, but Rifun could imagine a bit of sarcasm in there.

"What do you think, then?" he wondered. "You're able to move about a little more freely than we are; have you observed anything that might be useful to our search? Or pertinent to your rescue?"

I DON'T HAVE ANY FURTHER INFORMATION ON THE JOURNAL, AND I AM JUST AS STUMPED AS YOU ARE ON MY OWN PREDICAMENT. WE'VE NEVER EVEN HAD PROOF OF THIS DIMENSION UNTIL NOW. I WOULDN'T KNOW WHERE TO BEGIN.

"Maybe that's just it, then," Cassius butted in. "We can start our search for the journal in the cave. In the time we're gone, she can learn more about that dimension, so when we come out, we can save her."

"And who is 'we'?" Rifun wondered. "I'm assuming you mean you. I still don't know what's put you in such a sour mood lately, but I'm guessing that you want to put some temporal distance between you and it. And maybe play the hero while you're at it. And even so, what are we going to do about the Tacagans and the Akarin? Who is going to oversee the daily operations of the Cult?"

"Isthim and I have managed it just fine for the last couple years —"

"Obviously not if we've lost so much ground."

"You and her can run it, then. You can make nice with the politics, and she still has control of the army."

"Or this could be the retreat as a strategy that we discussed," Isthim pointed out. The men looked at her. She continued. "You can both go look for the journal. Two pairs of eyes may find the journal faster, or confirm its disappearance, and you'll be out of the cave that much sooner, cutting down on the time lost. In the meantime, Cult operations can be scaled back out of the Wheel, giving the appearance of disappearance. Keep Misik and my people as the Grandfathers, it will be a standing force ready to attack at a moment's notice."

"We let everything slide back the way it was, back into the Time industry, but how do we keep ties to the Hands and the political side of things?" Rifun wondered.

There was a noise on the computer and Julianna was typing again.

Lily.

"Who's Lily?" Cassius asked, annoyed.

"Your old Apprentice?" Rifun wondered.

Use her. If I'm going to be staying here for a while, presumably, then I won't be needing my turns or other funds (not that they matter much in the present economy, I think). Transfer them to her, get her in touch with some of the more loyal allies. I don't know what her sweet spot is, whether it's money, power, fame, or something else, but I'm sure the right person will know how to find it. When you come out of the cave, the transition should be fairly smooth.

"You want her as part of the Cult, then."

No. She needs to remain solidly Time, which is why her care and grooming should be turned over to others who are Time but also allied to us.

"Why not tie her to the Tacagans?" Isthim suggested. "They have the funds and resources to do whatever it is they expect to do to the Time industry. It will keep everything stable, fill our coffers, and it will make them an obvious, easy target when we do make our move. Their own ego will be their downfall."

"I don't think that would work," Rifun said. "She's human. The Tacagans are...Tacagans. They'll never follow her lead."

"Then leave it to chance," Cassius cut in. "Pure, random chance. Set her up with a lot of money, promise a brand new election cycle, and see where it goes from there. See who comes out of the woodwork, what they're offering, what they're buying, and mold it from there."

Rifun hesitated but nodded. "It could work. If we tell our plans to our allies, they may be able to influence things to hold them in our favor until we get back. The Turitians have the means. The Korin are still in their war dynasty, so we'll have them for a while yet. The Elif may not be bold supporters, but they may have something to give."

"I'm sure I could figure something out in a few years," Isthim told them. "And the Borelians will remain the Grandfathers."

"Yes, but will they remain our allies?"

"To the best that I am able to keep them so, but I cannot overrule the will of Ancrath or the Admirals. And no one would dare defy the Ul Ik Zol without extraordinary reason. I foresee no extraordinary reasons at this time."

"A polite, if long-winded, way of saying, 'I don't know.' "

"I can make no guarantees. There is no good way to know how long you will be gone or what will happen in that time. We may pull the strings, but the marionette dances how it will."

"How philosophical of you." Rifun huffed a breath. "All right, so it looks like Cassius and I will be going into the cave to either look for the journal or confirm that it isn't where it is supposed to be. Is that what we're doing?"

No one seemed to have any objections.

In the meantime, Julianna typed, I WILL BE EITHER LOOKING FOR IT OUT HERE, OR I WILL BE TRYING DIFFERENT WAYS TO ESCAPE THIS DIMENSION.

"Fair enough."

"At what point do we declare the journal gone from the cave?" Cassius wondered. "We can't stay in there forever, and we can't keep going back in every ten years."

"I don't know. It might just be a case of seeing what it is we're presented with in the cave itself. Maybe there are clues there still. Obviously we don't want to linger too long, but, I agree, we can't keep running in and out every ten years."

The conversation came to an awkward pause. Rifun noticed several onlookers outside of the Sound barrier pointing and whispering. He had the power to turn their insides into their outsides, and he was worried about whispers. How frail was he exactly?

"If this is what we're doing, then," Isthim began, "I might suggest making a list of any affairs you need to get in order before you go."

Her comment was directed solely at Rifun. He sighed. "Yes. I have some affairs to get in order. Given the state of things at home, I even have an idea of how I can resolve these affairs more or less peacefully." He let out a breath. "I'm just sorry it had to end like this. On the other hand, I expect that I shall be able to attend my own funeral. Won't that be exciting?"

When do you expect to enter the cave? Julianna typed. How long will these affairs take?

"Faking my death? Not long at all. The funeral preparations, the festivities and everything else? That could take a little while, a few months at most." He went on even though she began typing her protest. "Malagasy know how to party, and we love a good funeral. Give me a break, it's my own funeral and I only get to enjoy it this way once. Besides, it will give me time to plan some of the political goings-on, decide how we're going to use your old Apprentice to bring about the resurrection of the damned Time industry."

"Why are we using your old Apprentice anyway?" Isthim wondered. "Why not use a more loyal soldier as a mole?"

It needs to be believable and utterly pristine, Julianna answered. Neither the Tacagans nor the Akarin should find her at fault, or having anything to do with us, or else they may catch on and attack while three of the four leaders are gone. Besides, I owe her that much. She has talent, for a Harvester. She's had a hard life; she needs a little reprieve, I think. And when we take over, we can offer her the same greatness we have attained.

Rifun nodded. "Sounds like we have some work to do."

30 | Rigi ati Pakute

Rig and Trap

The Caves of Meroian, 1969

kokumbo

Cassius had been rather annoyed by the delay in events, all because Rifun just had to attend his own funeral. He figured that Rifun had tried to make it up to him by helping in the faking of his death. Finding a body hadn't been difficult, and even transferring some of the DNA to make it possibly look like him had barely registered as hard. That was fine. But still. A few months? Of course, Rifun wasn't sure since he didn't know the exact state of things under the Communists, but funeral festivities seemed to be a relatively normal affair. Four weeks, tops, he said.

He thought about just going after the journal himself, get a few months' head start. How would that translate, once Rifun entered the cave? Would they move in slow motion? Would he catch up? Would there be any noticeable difference once they got through the distortion?

That consideration lasted until he spotted Pilory in the city one day, about two weeks or so after the meeting in the library.

"Titik wants to have a word with you," she said, not even bothering with greetings. "Says he's got something to show you."

Cassius nodded once. "All right. I'll find Rifun and—"

"He doesn't want Rifun. Or any of the others. He only wants to talk to you. He likes you."

"I'm deeply flattered, but I'm not into that." At her expression he said, "Never mind. When does he want to meet?"

"In two days." She handed him a piece of paper. "I wasn't sure when I would find you, so he wrote down exactly when. The time is in Wheel calendar notation; you'll have to do the conversions yourself."

Actually, he didn't, because there were plenty of automatic conversion tools available to him in the Wheel.

Things were supposed to start changing in the Wheel soon. Supposedly Isthim and some of the Cult's allies were going to start making changes, making the shift back to the Time industry. He didn't see any of it, and it annoyed him, anyway.

Years of hard work. All the chaos, all the killing, all the bullshit he'd had to put up with from the others, and they were going to let it just slip away. All because someone didn't know how to plan or keep track of their stuff or stay in the correct dimension. Fucking hell.

So the elections would be returning, although they hadn't announced it yet. Part of the way they were rigging it to be in their favor, regardless of how long he and Rifun were gone, was to take his, Cassius' DNA and insert it into the system, just as if he had been elected—to the Zero Hour position, no less. As long as they were able to hold an election within the next decade, his DNA would remain active. Latent, but active. And when he returned, he would still have Zero Hour access to everything.

Or something like that. He never understood how it was all supposed to work. Others had always done it for him.

He'd also backed off on all Wheel activities, which meant he no longer went to the Judgment Wing, no longer worked in the asylum. Not that he'd been able to anyway since he'd had an argument with Misik over it.

After converting the date and time that Pilory had given him, he still had a day and a half until the meeting. He spent that time mostly wondering what it was that Titik wanted to show him.

Soon enough he was walking through Titik's ship, following Pilory. She was a breath of fresh Tibidi air among the less than desirable Psiaco and Urid that made up the majority of the crew. She took him to Titik's quarters, knocked on the door once, and stepped aside. A gruff "Enter" came from inside.

She said nothing as Cassius opened the door, but her expression was enough to make him wonder. Then he turned his attention to Captain Titik.

His quarters hadn't changed any; he still wallowed in wealth like a pig in mud. Cassius still questioned why he'd been so intent on the crown of Srori when it was probably one of the least valuable items in his collection, with exception of sheer challenge to acquire. And the Psiaco pirate himself still sat at his desk, mulling over ship's work.

"Considering you are the one reaching out to me, and that you have something to show me," Cassius began, "I can only assume that something of great significance has happened."

He helped himself to a seat as Titik reclined in his own chair. One set of arms folded comfortably and the other dangled lazily to either side.

"Tell me, Cassius. Do the others respect you?"

"What do you mean?"

"Rifun, Isthim, Julianna, do they respect you?"

Cassius shifted in his seat. "Depends on how you define respect, I suppose."

"Do they fear you?"

"A great deal, I think. Julianna originally hired Rifun to kill me."

"Hm. That goes beyond fear, I believe. Being feared is making people afraid for their security, their comfort. People like comfort and they dislike being uncomfortable. What you describe is avjara."

"I'm sorry, that doesn't translate apparently."

"Making people afraid for themselves. The bestial instinct to survive. Pushing people past mere comfort or discomfort into terror that begets survival."

"Fight or flight."

"Exactly."

Cassius raised a brow. "If you wanted to discuss philosophy, Rifun really is the better choice for conversation."

Titik made a gesture, his lazy arms coming up into a thoughtful pose. "No. He strikes me as a man who has known that kind of fear, has received it. You, however, are a man who has given that kind of fear. You make people afraid."

"Is this a good or bad thing?"

Titik stood and circled back around his chair. He went to a small window and looked out at the stars. "I have given that kind of fear recently."

"If you tell me that you need counseling—"

"Tell me, have you heard from the Turitians lately?"

Cassius blinked, his train of thought derailed. "What? Um, no. But they don't deal much with me. Why? What news from the Turitians? I know they hate you."

"Hate is too strong of a word, or it was. I was merely an annoyance to them. But now, yes, I think it is accurate to say they hate me."

"Can we get to the point?"

"I attacked the Turitians and took their prince hostage."

The train of thought, only just getting back on track, was suddenly halted. Cassius closed his eyes for a moment, then opened them again and said, "What?"

"I think you understood me."

Cassius shifted position. "You have never been inclined to attack the Turitians. And if you took their prince hostage, then you would have had to have gone up against their royal cruisers. Are you insane?"

"Some would say so. Or maybe I wished to do something different, be unpredictable."

"I think you had a different reason, and you're dying to tell me."

Titik moved away from the window. "They could have destroyed me in an instant, but when I took their prince hostage, suddenly they were very willing to talk and negotiate."

"What did they ransom for their prince?"

"A great deal of money, as one might expect." He opened a drawer in his desk and brought out an item. "And this."

It took Cassius half a second to realize that it was the journal, the Book of Commands.

"You do know that the Turitians are our allies? If you were really concerned about us getting the journal, they would have gotten it to us once they were done parading themselves."

Titik laid the journal on the desk and sat down once more. "It was an opportunity I could not pass up. It allowed me to test the capabilities of this Akari of yours. Pilory showed me a few things, though I am hardly proficient. Time was the mastery of my people, and money is the only true pleasure in the world. But again, once I had their prince, it was all negotiation." He choffed a laugh. "It is also why you will not hear of it from the Turitians. As a whole, it is a slight to their pride that I have attacked them, but for the royal family Jalar, it would damage their reputation beyond belief."

Cassius raised a brow and folded his arms. "Why do I feel like you're not going to turn the journal over to me freely?"

"Because I'm not."

"What do you want for it?"

"I want to learn, and I want the Turitians out."

"I can't tell the Turitians what to do. If you want them out, you'll have to force their hand. The only way to do that is by learning and overpowering them."

"Or threatening their already precarious position," Titik mused. "Are you allied with any other families?"

"No, the family Jalar forbade it."

"Ha! They're in no position to do such a thing."

"Your politics and your feuds are your own," Cassius stated irritably. "And as it stands, I don't know how well this arrangement is going to work out."

"Oh really? And why is that?" Titik wondered innocently. "Does it have something to do with your losses in the Wheel?"

"Calculated maneuvers," Cassius informed him. "Ones that we will be forced to continue. Julianna has run into some misfortune, and the only way we can rescue her involves entering a Time Trap."

The pirate's expression turned unreadable. "I see. Then the Cult is to fade into obscurity."

"Absolutely not! We are positioning certain allies to allow for a smooth transition of power once we return. But until then, yes, things will go back to how they were in the Time industry."

"Sounds like surrender to me."

"If that's so, then you'll have no trouble letting me have that worthless little book there. And how do I know it is the real thing? How do I know you didn't just make something up?"

Cassius reached for it, but Titik got to it first. He picked it up, turned it over, studied it, then handed it to him. "Fine. See that it is what you seek."

Cassius snatched it from him and opened it up. At least it didn't appear to have any baking recipes on the inside cover. If it was a fake, it was at least something more true to form.

He read several passages. He didn't remember a lot of the Book of Commands, mostly because he didn't like being told what to do. But for what it did say, it seemed to make sense, like something he might have said and something Richard might have written down.

"All right, let's say this is the real journal. The Turitians acquired it through the Kolkath, and you stole it from the Turitians. You want to learn the Akari, and you want to force the Turitians out of play, is that right?"

"That's right," Titik confirmed, his posture reverting to thoughtful cunning.

"Rifun and I have to rescue Julianna, and we have to go through a Time Trap to do it. There's just no way around it, and we looked for every alternative. We don't know how long we'll be gone. Could be a few months, could be a few years."

"I know how Time Traps work."

"Take the journal to Isthim. Give her your terms."

Titik made a wet sound like he was ready to spit phlegm. "Bah! Never trust a Borelian! I am hard-pressed to go along with this given your alliance with them, but

I want to know what this Akari is."

"Then you'll be waiting until I get back," Cassius told him.

"Then I will wait."

"And the journal? Can you guarantee its safety?"

"If it is the possession of a deity, should the burden of protection not be on the deity?"

Cassius considered this for a moment. Then, "Fine, you may have a point. But know that we will hold you personally responsible for its whereabouts, if it should leave your possession."

"A burden I can handle."

"And another thing. The Turitians are our primary flow of resources: maps, information, supplies, and money. If you want to kick them out, we'll need a new source of goods. You say money is the only pleasure in the world, well, we'll need money. Lots of it. War is an expensive endeavor. Ideology drives some, but money can push the rest. Our treasury will need a starting balance."

"You would trust a pirate to be in charge of your treasury?"

"We can discuss terms later, once we've returned, reoriented ourselves to the new present day, and have had a chance to assess the situation."

Titik studied him for a long moment, four eyes scrutinizing his every move. The Psiaco as a whole were not especially big or strong, not much more than the average human. Titik, though, had some exceptional bulk about his already large frame.

"Considering how desperately you seem to need this book of yours, enough that you have lost control of the Wheel without it, I will agree to these tentative arrangements."

Cassius nodded once. "I am glad we could come to an agreement."

The pirate's expression was unusual, but Cassius thought he could interpret it at least as being related to internal thoughts, imagining life as the treasurer for the Cult. Cassius wasn't sure he wanted to agree to such a thing, but they needed the journal and they would need the money if Titik was serious about ousting the Turitians. Given how fragile the ego and political position of the royal family Jalar, he would take Titik over them. He had no qualms, no morals, no politics to adhere to. Only the love of money, the only pleasure in the world.

Cassius stood. He didn't bother offering a hand. "I suppose I'll see you in a few years."

Titik did not stand, merely regarded him and said, "I suppose so."

Cassius saw himself out, finding Pilory standing just outside the door when he exited the room. He gave her a look.

"So do you eavesdrop or what's your role here?"

"I admit, I'm curious," she said, making a gesture like a shrug.

"Does Titik know you do this?"

"If he does, he doesn't care. I'm his lieutenant. It's my job to know things." She added before he could speak, "But it is not always my place to be part of the discussion."

"Why not?" Cassius wondered. "You're the one who originally wanted to learn, you brought it onto the ship. Why shouldn't you have a say in things?"

"Because I am the lieutenant, not the captain. And you're not the first to tempt my betrayal with such thoughts of disloyalty and personal power. I'm happy where I am."

He shrugged. "Suit yourself."

She turned and led him back through the ship to the cargo hold where portals were permitted.

"So what happened to the spunky, carefree, lively Tibidi who first approached me in the Food Court?" Cassius wondered.

She gave him only a glance and continued walking as she answered, "There is a bird on your home world, I believe it is called a bird of ridicule."

"A mockingbird, but yes."

"It imitates other creatures to get what it wants."

"Given that you just said you have no personal ambition, I'm guessing you're doing this for Titik. What is it that he wants? Obviously not the crown of Srori. If it's the Akari he wants, he could have just asked long ago with no need for this...whatever this is."

Pilory made a sound that might have been a chuckle. "Merely getting what we want is only part of the fun. Most here, at least the Psiaco and myself, we're all Time Agents to some degree. It would be no great feat to use Time to raid the treasuries of lesser worlds. But there is thrill in the chase, the pursuit, the hunt and being hunted. Surely you can appreciate this. You have the power to kill at a touch, even with just your Harvesting abilities. Yet it is the hunt that fulfills you, isn't it?"

"So Titik's goal has always been to become the treasurer of the Cult?"

They reached the cargo hold.

"Captain Titik has many goals. I don't know all of them. I don't understand all of them. But I am able and willing to carry out his plans to achieve them. Seeing how you will be gone for some time, I suggest you don't dwell on it too much. Plans change over the years."

"Plans may change," Cassius said, preparing himself to open a portal, "but according to Titik, the only constant and pleasure in the world is money."

Pilory's expression said she was tired of hearing such nonstop rhetoric from Titik, and she didn't need to hear it from him, too. He did not react to this, merely opened his portal and stepped through.

He returned to the ruins, hoping that maybe Rifun had finally returned to say that his funeral was over and he was ready to leave, but not especially surprised when this did not happen.

"Has Rifun said anything at all?" he complained to Isthim. He found her in her chambers, going over some paperwork. "It's been two weeks and he estimated four. There has to be something."

"I have heard nothing from him," she told him irritably.

He shifted his stance, leaning against the door frame. "You know, I think he's mentioned something about a girl, couldn't tell you her name. He likes her, I think, but he has to masquerade as his own son in order for it to work out. So on the one hand, he can—or he could be himself and share stories of the war and everything. On the other hand, he has to fake his identity, but he finds a woman. But then that leaves you here."

"Are you trying to make a point?"

"Does it bother you that he might be seeing someone else?"

"Why should it bother me?"

Cassius shrugged. "I mean, here you are. A *vodrak*. Capable of pushing all Borelian toxins, including the one for sexual pleasure. Fucking hell, but you jumped him when you went into heat, rode him for four fucking days. There are some men who would kill for that. Some men who would die for that, too. You could give him anything, and he's running off with someone who will only be left with a broken heart."

"Then that is unfortunate for her. She should learn to pick better men."

"Ouch. Should I tell him you said that?"

"A female should choose a good breeding male who will strengthen the people and give her strong children. All other concerns are secondary."

Cassius raised a brow. "So you actually have no issues with him sleeping with another woman?"

She gave him a look. "First of all, you have no proof of this; you are merely trying to annoy me. You are annoying me, but not for the reasons you think. Second, he must deal with me as much as I deal with him. He comes to me knowing that I have had other mates, and I may continue to have other mates since I have been accepted back into my people. I am simply doing as I see fit, for my people and myself. He will do the same."

He stared at her for a moment. "You've been an exile for centuries. You're saying you have children?"

"I had five before my exile, with three different mates. Three of my children are dead now as they never advanced enough in military or political office to learn Time. The other two are still alive but on other assignments. Does this knowledge bother you?"

Truthfully, he wasn't sure. He just couldn't imagine Isthim as a mother. Sure, Borelians were hard-nosed sons of bitches—some just straight bitches—but there had to be some indulgences for children, right? Maybe not.

"No," he decided at last. "It doesn't."

"Good."

"Have you told Rifun?"

"There has never been a reason to disclose such information, and he's never asked."

"What, afraid he would get all bent out of shape and stop seeing you?"

She gave him another look. "The damage to our professional and personal relationship would be noticeable, but it would be entirely on his end. You know this as well as I do, and it would be prudent to refrain from giving him such information."

Cassius shrugged. "People tell me that I should be more personable, more likable. I try, and I end up with information I don't care about and thinly veiled threats about revealing this information. I don't try, and people end up dead. Death may be unfortunate, but it's a lot easier than politics. Actually, I think politics may be a form of slow suicide."

Isthim's expression was bored. "If you are quite done irritating me, then leave. I have work to do."

He sighed dramatically. "Fine. I try to get along with my coworkers, get to know them, and this is how I'm repaid."

He closed the door behind him as he walked away. Once again, he'd ended up with information he didn't want, didn't care about, and nothing to do with it. Given the apparent callous nature of Borelian families, he wasn't going to get any leverage over her by taking her children hostage. And for what? What did he want? He had no idea.

On the other hand, plant a seed. Just a tiny implication. A little veiled threat of his own. Give her a few months or years to mull it over, and see what kind of fruit came from that seed. He wasn't sure that anything would indeed happen, but, like Pilory, sometimes it was just about a suggestion.

It was later in the afternoon when Cassius spotted Rifun walking about the officers building.

"Your funeral is finished, then?" Cassius wondered, intercepting him.

"It has been officially scheduled for three weeks from yesterday," Rifun informed him.

Cassius couldn't stop a sigh, but he did the eye roll on purpose.

"Come now, Cassius, you can't tell me that you have no affairs to get in order before we leave for an unknown length of time."

"None that required over a month of preparation."

"Then I'm sorry that you have so little in your life worth losing."

He didn't seem to have much to look forward to, either, at least for another three weeks. If there was any good news, it was that Rifun didn't expect him or Isthim to show up for the funeral. By his attitude, he didn't want them there at all. This was fine with Cassius, in principle, but he couldn't deny that Rifun talked a good time. Sounded like Malagasy funerals were quite the occasion.

But he was free for the time being.

He went to visit Jora, giving the Ferulian a brief rundown of what was going on. The Ferulian made sounds and gestures of displeasure.

"You know I am a businessman," Jora said, walking around his plush carpet empire. "When you threw things into chaos, that was good for business. That was a boom that I haven't seen since the outbreak of the Dervi-Parkinian war. Naturally, I did not expect it to last long—such booms never do—but profits remained high as your conflict with the Gentleman Killers and the Tacagans continued. Some people wanted to get in on the conflict, or introduce a bit of chaos themselves, and others wanted protection from the conflict, did not want to get dragged in.

"But now, with the Tacagans getting comfortable again, and you telling me that things are going to intentionally slip back into the way they always were with the Time industry..." He made a gesture. "You are going to kill my business."

"You were hardly hurting before the elections," Cassius told him blandly.

"No, but it was you who got me into the business, being the Missing Zero Hour and all the chaos that caused in the wake of your disappearance."

"Hardly a war, or so I heard."

"Chaos nonetheless. Now you're letting it all go to waste."

Cassius grunted. "Believe me, that is not the intention. We won't be gone long."

Jora made a sound that vaguely resembled a laugh. "That's what my third wife said, too, and I haven't seen her in forty years. Shall I wait for you as long?"

"You honestly expect to go out of business?"

"I don't know what to expect. You say that your allies will still hold prominent positions of power, but for how long? Competing interests won't sit idly by, and what happens when your allies have disagreements, hm? Are they really inclined to listen to the Borelians?"

"Didn't you just say that your business thrives on chaos?"

"I did, and it does. But even though I may be an arms dealer, I myself do very little fighting. I will not die for this little spot of ground in the Wheel; I will pack up my business and move it elsewhere. But 'elsewhere' is not the hub of the universe."

Cassius had tired of his complaining several sentences back. "I am not here to tell you what to do with yourself or your business. Actually, I think I'm being rather generous telling you about this at all. What if we had just disappeared, hm? No warning, just gone?"

Jora considered this for half a second and conceded the point. "It is generous." He hesitated. "You really don't expect to be gone for very long?"

"A few months, maybe a couple of years."

"Well, a three years saw you go from parading yourselves through the Wheel as its new masters, to considering this surrender."

"It's not a surrender. It's retreating as a strategy," Cassius defended, quoting Rifun.

Jora did not look convinced. "Well, whatever you're doing, you should do it quickly before you lose even more. Losing ground is one thing. Losing allies is another."

It made Cassius even more displeased with the prospect of waiting for Rifun. He thought he'd done Jora a service by telling him that they would be gone, but he later wondered if it had been the right thing to do. What if Jora told someone else? What if he told the wrong person? What if it got back to the Tacagans? Retreat was met with one plan, but retreat as a maneuver would be met with another plan. The Tacagans could be ready and waiting for them to emerge from the cave. They might act even faster to take the Wheel back and give it to a new Council of Hands.

Any number of things could happen.

He'd also told Titik of their plans. Granted, the leverage at play there was a little more consequential, but what if? Maybe Titik told Pilory and she told someone else. Maybe he told one of his crewmen. Maybe he got to talking at a tavern while at space dock.

Cassius elected not to tell the others what he'd done; he could just imagine the lectures now. He and Rifun wouldn't be gone long. They would be back with plenty of time to spare to clean up any small messes that did erupt from his undiscerning chatter.

Besides, if this plan with Lily did go through, and if the Tacagans and other parties wanted to keep the elections on a regular schedule to match up with the last election cycle—because the secretaries hated discrepancies, no matter how extenuating the circumstances—then they had ten years to spare, maybe a little less. Julianna had been in that cave for hardly three years when she proclaimed the journal missing. He and Rifun wouldn't take much more than that.

Confident in himself again, Cassius pushed everything to the side in his mind and went about his business.

It was another two weeks before he saw Rifun again, and only when the man called a meeting.

"Was your funeral everything you hoped it would be?" Cassius wondered, not bothering to hide his sarcasm and his disdain for this senseless delay.

"My funeral is next week, thank you," Rifun told him. "Judging by the preparations, it's going to be quite the festival. I'm rather touched, actually, and quite moved."

"Does this mean that, going forward, we won't have to worry about you suddenly taking off to deal with family issues?" Isthim asked pointedly. "Burial in your family tombs seems to have been your goal, and few people can accomplish other tasks after death."

"Unless they have the ability to masquerade as fictional children." Rifun went on before Cassius or Isthim could protest. "No, you won't have to worry. Believe me, it is not easy playing my own son. I know far too much, and I can already feel the strain of the disjointed reality I must portray. In a way, I think I shall be happy to leave. I wish the circumstances were better, but, yes, I am achieving a goal I have dreamed of for many decades."

"Good. Can we move on, then?" Cassius asked irritably. "You called this meeting so we can plan exactly what we're doing after you finally return."

Rifun nodded once. "Yes. I was able to sneak off to the university and use one of their computers to talk to Julianna again, and she gave me the exact directions to the bones where the journal was. That alone should shave off some of the time."

He produced a hand-drawn map. "It's a single tunnel from the mouth of the cave until the distortion. Once through the distortion, it stays a single tunnel until this point; she estimates about one hundred feet. Then it branches off to the left and right. It's not a stark contrast, either. It will be very easy to accidentally wander off, so we should stick to the right wall.

"The right tunnel splits again very soon after, and this is where it gets tricky. The tunnel we're following will branch to the left and right, but then another tunnel will meet up with the right branch here, and it will be a large open area. We won't be able to simply rely on the walls at this point to get us out because otherwise we'll walk right into this branch. We'll be heading the right direction, but we won't hit the mouth of the cave."

"Where does that tunnel lead? Is there another exit?" Isthim wondered.

"I don't know, she doesn't know, and we won't have time to find out," he informed her. "Now then, it will certainly be dark by this point, but it won't be total cave darkness."

"We can use Light, then," Cassius commented.

"We should be able to, yes, but I would suggest we wait until after we reach the distortion. On the off chance that someone follows us, we don't need to alert our enemies to our activities, and we don't need any hapless passersby falling into this Trap."

Well, he could concede that little bit, he figured.

"Where this tunnel and this tunnel meet is where the bones are located," Rifun said, "so saith Julianna. If we are able to use Light, we shouldn't have too much of a problem, even if the bones are scattered."

"If they are scattered, we may stumble upon them by accident," Cassius mused.

"Or that could happen, too." Rifun shifted his stance. "Julianna seems to think a wild animal got to the journal. I think the animal went after the bones and the journal was just collateral damage. I don't think it will be too far away."

"Then why couldn't she find it?" Isthim asked.

"Because she's a petty, fretful woman?" Cassius suggested. "She used a flashlight instead of Light from the Akari; that should tell you everything you need to know." He shook his head. "We never should have sent her in the first place."

"Maybe so, but we did, and this is where we are now, in the present moment," Rifun said. "This is what we have to deal with."

Cassius grunted but did not push the issue. It was just like him inviting Isthim and the Borelians into the club. It shouldn't have happened, but it did, and now they had to deal with it. Could they do anything right? The only reason he could come up with for their continued existence was provision from the Author, but even her patience had to be wearing thin. How was it to have to prop up such a weak, sniveling, poorly managed, poorly trained group of suspicious, backstabbing misfits? Exactly what had the Akarin done that made the Cult the better, more righteous option?

"Obviously, once we obtain the journal, we leave as quickly as possible," Rifun was saying. "Per Julianna, we have to walk out of there ourselves; portals are a decidedly bad idea."

"Given the element of time, I would suggest we run out of there," Cassius threw in.

"Only once we're sure of the direction we need to go. I'm not running straight into another Trap or a dead end or anything that will cost us even more time."

Cassius shrugged. "Suit yourself." He shifted his stance. "But I think it's worth asking the question: how long are we going to search? Is there a point where we might have to say that the journal really isn't there?"

"Bold question, coming from you," Rifun mused. "But not unwise to ask."

"Sometimes I have good thoughts."

"Is there an answer?" Isthim wondered. "The longer you take, the more I have to manage."

"I am not unaware of that," Rifun told her. "But considering you ran the Cult for a century while Julianna and Cassius were playing hide-and-seek, I don't think a few more years is going to break your back."

Isthim looked a bit taken aback by his answer. "Am I this group's sitter, then? It would be one thing if I were to manage us in power, but again I find us on the verge of power, taken to the verge of collapse, and here I am—"

"Just don't get us wiped out, I don't care how you manage it. It's only for a few months, maybe a few years if we do have to do some searching. But we will still need to be in a position to put some power back behind our name when we do get the journal."

She looked ready to say more but backed down at the last minute. Cassius merely raised a brow but said nothing.

"As to the question at hand," Rifun said grudgingly, "about whether we would abandon the search. Given the nature of the Time Trap, yes, it would be prudent to not spend our entire lives inside the cave or else we shall outlast the universe. At what point we should give up the search, I don't know exactly. I suppose it depends on what we find when we get in there."

"Julianna couldn't give you any more on that?" Cassius asked. "Couldn't describe the scene, couldn't give us any clues as to what to look for, where, anything?"

"No. She was most unhelpful in that regard."

"Was she helpful in any regard?"

The white-skinned African looked ready with a response, but settled for, "No."

"Then all we have left is to depart for the cave just as soon as you get back from your funeral."

"Do you think we'll need anything for our return?"

Cassius blinked. "Like what? We're not going to be camping, either inside or outside the cave. We go in, we look around, we get the journal or we don't, and we come out. Portals will get us there and back. The only thing that changes is the world around us. And if we're not going to be gone long, then the world shouldn't change so much as to be unrecognizable."

"I am merely trying to give thought to all possibilities."

Sounded more like he was trying to reestablish himself after the little spat with Isthim, but who was Cassius to say?

"And naturally we will have to see where things stand politically before we make any moves when we return," Rifun finished, though whether he was speaking to himself or the group at large was unclear. "Very well then. Now that everything has been established—"

"You're going to return home to Madagascar, enjoy your own funeral, and return when you're quite done and buried," Cassius finished.

Rifun nodded once. "Precisely."

Cassius folded his arms. "If I understand it correctly, your people exhume your dead and make a grand festival of that, too."

"*Famadihana*, yes. Why?"

He shrugged. "No reason."

Rifun raised a brow but did not push the matter.

Actually, Cassius couldn't figure out how Rifun could go to such a funeral or other exhumation festivities, then turn around and chastise him, Cassius, for his sexual preferences. Sure, dig up a body, hand it around, worship it, throw it a party, why not? Have an erection by it and suddenly he's the devil. Hypocritical bastard. And Cassius wasn't the only one who got excited by torture. He might have had better luck with the Borelians if they weren't so high and mighty on themselves.

All this to say that Cassius was rather relieved when Rifun finally departed. Like the Korin and their sense of balance, Rifun's ease of conscience demanded a plan and a justification. Did no one believe in spontaneity anymore? Or was it all just chaos to them?

"I should be the one to go," Isthim grumbled, still standing across from Cassius at the meeting table. "If there is no one to conquer, there is little need for a supreme army commander. I would be the fastest in and out. But no, you don't trust me to bring it back here."

"Trust is a terrible thing, isn't it?" Cassius said casually. "So why don't you go anyway? Rifun's been dealing with funeral preparations for a month. Fastest in and out, you could have done it, couldn't you? It's not as though you value the opinions or orders of a slave species."

If looks could kill, Cassius would be dead as Isthim glared at him. "I have orders from my people, my superiors."

"Ah, so we are still allied."

"By strings, not chains."

"If you were to go after the Book of Abilities and turn it over to Misik, we would still have the Cult and the army, and the fast learning of the Shatai would make them a formidable foe. Send us in, you retain command of the army, and our loyalty to the Cult would bring the Book of Abilities right to you. Even if we didn't hand it over to you for some reason, you have the army, including the Shatai." Cassius shifted his stance. "I smell betrayal."

"Suddenly loyalty means something to you," Isthim stated.

"Call it self-preservation. After all I've done, you couldn't afford to keep me alive, and you know that I will never be anyone's slave again." He went on before she could speak. "And you haven't denied my accusation of betrayal."

"Isn't loyalty to one's own people one of the tenets of the Cult? No loyalty to a business, no swearing fealty to faraway leaders, simply loyalty to one's family and one's people at the discretion of oneself? I am simply doing what I believe is best for my people, holding loyalty to my people first. Despite our interactions and living in close quarters, you may be considered a faraway leader."

"So could you."

"What, then, binds the loyalty of anyone in the army to the Cult? Shall a Shatai be ordered to kill one of his own? Or an Obezod? Or a Kiboz? Or a Fedurian? Or anyone else?"

"It is loyalty to the Author."

"Is she not a faraway leader also?"

"She governs all of us, writes our stories. She dictates even this conversation."

Isthim laughed, which was quite an obnoxious sound coming from her voice assist. "You sound like Rifun but you don't mean it. I read the Book Rifun got. If it is even half-true, you hold no loyalty to the Author. Your loyalty is to yourself, your actions dictated by a dark spirit, maybe even Tujor himself, or one of the six Facets." She shook her head, still grinning. "Do not presume to lecture me on loyalty to the Author." When Cassius did not speak, she continued. "Rifun is the fool here. He is the one who believes in these obscene ideals. He has created for himself a false reality where pieces may fit where they are not supposed to. He claims that this head injury of his clears his mind, cuts through the lies because he cannot see what is not there. In reality, he cannot see because he does not wish to see, and so he plays tricks on himself but doesn't even realize it."

Cassius gave her a hard regard. "And Julianna?"

Isthim shrugged casually. "A useful idiot. Do you think a fool such as she would have gotten anywhere if not for you? And do you think you would have given her any knowledge except for what came from your dark spirit?" She shook her head. "No. This has nothing to do with the Author."

"That's why the Ul Ik Zol were so enthusiastic about this alliance."

"Exactly."

"Why keep Rifun and Julianna, then?"

"As I said, useful idiots. A kind face on a sinister force, to bring the more tenderhearted masses into line."

"Into line for what?"

"Conquest. And death."

He studied her for a long moment. He didn't know what he was looking for, and he actually wasn't sure he wanted to find it. Finally, "The only reason you're telling me this is because you either plan on killing me for it, or you have a proposition to make."

Her expression turned more serious, though amusement was still very much in evidence. "As I said when we first met, you intrigue me. You have qualities that few non-Borelians possess." She shifted position. "There is a movement up for consideration among the Admirals as well as the Council of Ancrath. They wish to establish a new colony. This is nothing new, and it is necessary. What is different about it is that they want to try something a little new. They want it to be overseen and run entirely by the slaves. Naturally, the more loyal slaves are sent to the colonies with less supervision, but there is yet always supervision."

"Why the shift?" Cassius wondered grudgingly.

"Demographics. The death camps are overseen by the Admirals, but the farming colonies are overseen by our elderly. Between wars and an otherwise inhospitable home world, few Borelians make it to such an age. Because of Time, the bulk of our population is yet fit for service, and service must be held. But that growing population means growing needs but shrinking help. There are too few elderly to oversee too few colonies. With the addition of the Akari, our expansion is set to take off in a manner not seen since the first Great Expansion.

"Loyalty is the first requirement. Brutality is the next. Loyalty we can find. Brutality that meets our standards is harder to come by. There may be room for negotiation."

Cassius shifted his stance and raised a brow. "Trust is a terrible thing. Painstaking to build, easy to break, nearly impossible to rebuild. God complex or not, loyalty or not, power or not, I don't believe that you would be entrusted with this kind of information, nor given the power to make such an offer, without something backing it up. Centuries in exile, then suddenly your mentor, your best friend, and your idol all come to your rescue, as well as an Ul Ik Zol priest who suddenly endorses this alliance. Not only that, but you regain your entire commission." He looked her dead in the eye. "Were you ever really in exile?"

"I was in exile before the Cult even existed, remember?"

"I don't think that means much."

Isthim grinned. "You're right. You're also right that I wasn't in exile, not really."

Cassius nodded slowly. "Am I also correct in assuming that you have some connection to the Ul Ik Zol?"

Her expression said more than her words. "I was a priestess in training first. My assignment was military, as eighty percent of them are. As even I have stated, few know the extent of our influence and power.

"When I was only just a lieutenant, I had a vision. I foresaw a brilliant, marvelous, glorious future for our people."

"Don't all Borelians dream of that?" Cassius interrupted.

"Yes, but not to the extent that I saw, and certainly not by the means of a slave. This caused quite a stir among the other priests and I was nearly exiled right there for heresy. But measures were taken, and my vision was confirmed. The exact details were not known, only that it would take an incredible amount of time, patience, and a large swallowing of pride to go to places I did not wish to go, even blasphemies that I must commit, including slandering of the name of the Ul Ik Zol.

"Borelians do not begin to learn of Time at all until they are a lieutenant, and they do not begin training until they are to be considered as a commander. But I began my training at that time, as only a lieutenant. From there, I rose through both Time and military ranks quickly, becoming a rather prominent figure."

"Where does the Akari come in?" Cassius asked.

"Around the time that I first met you, there was some disturbance among the Akarin. This inspired me to know that such was a path I must pursue, but it would not be the Akarin. Blasphemy against the Ul Ik Zol could be forgiven, but to engage the *dijik* could not be. Nor was it the path that I was to take."

"The Akari is not *dijik*, then."

"It is, for it is the power of the Author. I sought the power of Tujor."

"Why were you in that closet in the Wheel?"

"Once my visions were confirmed, it was determined that the best course of action would be for me to continue alone. But few believe that a Borelian acts alone, so I would have to go into exile."

"But not really."

"It was convincing enough; only a few knew the details behind the decision to exile me. I would claim publicly that I sought the Akari, a known *dijik*. The hunters would come after me for a time and then be called off. After all, I was almost a Great

Admiral, I knew everything about them. No need to waste resources on me when I would no doubt perish in the depths of space.

"It was the day before the hunters got called off that I was hiding in the closet. By Tujor's provision, I ran into you. I knew only that you were important, which was why I even spoke to you, tried to spark something by mentioning the Akari."

"That didn't happen," Cassius stated.

"No, but I still knew you were important. Then there was another large stir over in the Akarin. A Book had appeared. A real, true, full, whole Book, written and signed by the Author. At the time, I thought that something must be happening. Something had to happen. There was great tumult in the Akarin as they debated over what it meant, what to do about it. Different leaders had different ideas, cracks began to appear, and then factions started to form. There was civil war among the Akarin. I thought that something must happen. The *dijik* was devouring itself. Something from my vision must come from this."

"The Cult."

"Yes. I watched your fledgling growth, knew that this was the path I had to take. But I was a bit dismayed at how poorly it was run. Of course, how else would such a group accept me except that they had no choice? First you needed my help to get things organized, and then you would hand it over to me for a century as you went and chased down the journals."

"And the whole time, you, in 'exile,' were reporting to your superiors. Misik and Jetindor and the Ul Ik Zol and everyone who was suddenly so eager to come to the table and talk about an alliance."

"Exactly."

"And the only reason you've been going along with this, no matter how messy or political, no matter how much you hated us and wanted to throw us into slavery, is because you need those journals. They're not only sacred to the Cult, they're sacred to you because you believe them spoken by Tujor. Letting us do the dirty work simply keeps you out of suspicion, and if we happen to die on this mission, well, it's easier to explain to the underlings."

He continued before she could speak. "And, if your claim about the new colony is true, my guess is that in the near future you're going to suggest moving the Cult off of Sadurnon. Maybe we're getting too big, maybe someone happens to stumble across our camp. Whatever the case, it's not safe anymore. Everyone gets moved to this new location which is actually your farming colony. I'm put 'in charge' as it were in order to make the transition easier for the grunts, you and your people come back into full alliance again, thereby dampening any suspicion of high-ranking Borelians being around.

"Our other allies will then suddenly decide that they don't like the idea of being allied to us. Some will say they don't like being allied to the Borelians. Others will say they don't like how we take away the Time Capsule markets in favor of the Akari. Resources to the Cult will vanish, leaving us with nothing unless we do the work ourselves, that is, farming, with a majority of the crop going to you. And slowly the rules start changing, cutting off training and the ability to even leave, until you have a fully-functioning farming colony that effectively enslaved itself. And your people have a power that is entirely comparable to the Akari, able to wipe out the *dijik* Akarin."

She grinned and said nothing for a long two minutes, letting everything Cassius just said sink into his brain. Finally, "There it is. You're not as dumb as Rifun thinks you are."

Cassius shifted his stance. "Are your vocal chords truly severed?"

Her expression faltered, and she seemed torn between uncertainty and hostility. "When I went before the Admirals and the Council to give my report, they had to make a show of imprisoning me, for those who did not know I was not truly in exile. Medik, whether she knew or not, still hated me, hated my mission, and sought to silence me. She got to me before Misik did."

"Why tell me all of this now, though? Or why let me work it out? You could have grumbled about the unfairness of not going into the cave all you wanted, stormed out of the room, and we wouldn't be here. Or you could have simply ignored my questions and left. Why this way? Why tell me?"

Her expression was unreadable. "Sometimes people intrigue me. Some people are worth investigating, even if they are a slave species. And we do need someone to run the new colony."

Cassius said nothing as he moved around the table purposefully, closing the gap between him and Isthim in only a few strides. Isthim, apparently sensing his intentions, turned white. By the time he made it to her, she'd removed her clothes and went to work on his.

He did not toy with her mind as he had with Medik, but that did not mean he did not treat her the same otherwise, and he hoped that she found his cruel sexuality just as intriguing as the rest of him. Even when he was finally and completely finished—whether through his exhaustion or hers, he did not know—he kept her pinned for a minute longer, his hands gripping her horns, using Gravity to add strength to the pin.

"So you fuck Rifun in order to manipulate him," he breathed, "but you ignore me. Were you afraid I might be too cruel? Or were you really after the jealousy?"

Isthim may have tried to laugh, but it was little more than a breathy gasp and unintelligible static from her assist. "What is it with you humans and monogamy? He intrigued me just as much, that he could live with his torture so well. I don't deny that I manipulated him with sex, but why should I explain it any further?"

"And ignoring me? Was it somehow in your visions for me to kill your cousin?"

"She deserved it, and she was only a minor casualty. As for you, yes, there may have been a bit of a strategy for jealousy. I had to see just what you would do when just a touch could mean death."

He grinned though she couldn't see, releasing one horn and running his fingers through her hair. "Naughty girl."

He withdrew from her and went to find his clothes. Isthim rolled onto one side, watched him for a moment, then got up and retrieved her garments.

"We have an agreement, then?" he said, tugging his shirt down. "I get to be in charge of this colony, master not slave?"

"Just as soon as you return with the Book of Abilities and the Cult is in control of the Wheel. Then we can start moving people off Sadurnon for their own safety."

"Because someone figured out where we were hiding and is planning to mount an attack," Cassius offered.

"Of course."

"And how do you plan to quell any rebellion? Your people have so far only dealt with Time Agents as slaves, assuming that much. The Akari is a whole different beast."

"Which is how and why the colony governs itself. You can keep them in line in the beginning, help get things started. As the rules change, try to keep up, but also introduce fear. Give a man just a reason to fear, and he will torture himself for you. And men tend to forget how powerful they are when they have no ability to think beyond an immediate need. Change the rules, bring the walls in tighter, cause panic. The grunts will forget the Akari—little though they've learned—and it will not get passed on to future generations. And you will be at the top with all the power."

"I like the sound of that. What about the Shatai, though? They have generational memories."

"They will be dealt with, don't worry."

"And Rifun and Julianna?"

"Rifun is already incredibly susceptible to fear. Keep him alive and he will be the face and the advocate of submission. As for Julianna, well, there is so little known about this in-between dimension, who is going to criticize us for not rescuing her?"

Cassius nodded. "I like how you think. I might even say that I'm intrigued to see where this new partnership goes."

31 | Manomana sy Manatanteraka

Fianarantsoa, 1970

Plan and Execute

Funerals were no small occasion for the Malagasy. In fact, a funeral or a *famadihana* could be ten times as extravagant as a wedding. Preparations took a great deal of time and money, neither of which the Andilan family lacked, in spite of the overall hardships in the country.

Rifun, masquerading as his son Fan, probably had it the easiest out of everyone, if only because he could Band Time.

It was a marvelous thing, not only planning, but also attending one's own funeral. Some people planned their own funerals, and, in a morbid, convoluted way, everyone attended his own funeral, though rarely as a spectator.

The other side of that was getting very little sleep in the days leading up to the actual funeral. Part of this was the preparation itself. The other part was the anxiety over the authorities. Such extravagance was frowned upon, even forbidden to some degree. Volana claimed to know the regional and local authorities very well, and their relationship, combined with a hefty bribe, would allow the family to host this exuberant occasion, but all the promises in the world meant nothing until delivered upon. Until Rifun was safely back on Sadurnon, and not again arrested and in jail, he would never be able to completely enjoy the festivities.

Once more, he felt like a prisoner in his own country.

About a week ago, all the cattle had been moved to a distant paddock for grazing, and Rifun, as Fan, and the rest of the family had gone through the rest of the paddocks and cleaned them. This involved clearing out all manure and filling in any holes that someone might trip in and break an ankle. The grazing kept the grass down so they were able to set up tables, tents, and assorted entertainment areas. The line of tables stretched from the back door of the house, wound through several paddocks, and twisted all the way to the family tombs, almost a mile and a half away, where a magnificent shrine and offering had been set up, dedicated to the spirit and soul of the deceased, ensuring his passage to the ancestors was smooth while asking for a blessing because of it. The body had been laid out before it so the soul would see the shrine and be pleased.

For a time, Rifun had worried about some ill fate befalling him or the family because of the deception. The shrine was intended for him, but the body being buried was not his. Therefore, the soul joining the ancestors did not match. On the other hand, the soul of the man being buried had joined the ancestors long ago with no proper ceremonies whatsoever. Surely the ancestors would be pleased that this offense was being corrected. And if Rifun's destiny was as great as Andrianary had believed it to be, then they would also understand that such a deception was necessary.

He still felt a bit uneasy about it, but he needed the closure. He had to have it before he jumped into the future. Intentions were wonderful things, but what if he did end up further ahead than expected? What if everyone here was dead by the time he returned? Disjointed reality aside, this was his home, his family. He had to fix things while he still could, and those of his generation didn't have much longer to live.

A short newspaper article had been written about him, apparently at Elisette's behest. She knew the printer, she said, and it seemed the right thing to do. It was a simple little blurb, saying that Rifun Ndolo (they had to use his legal name, especially because he was not pureblood Malagasy) had gone missing some time ago under suspicious circumstances. A body believed to have been his had been found in a river. He was a military veteran, known as the Bastard of the VVS, who also fought in the Uprising under Radaoroson and Lehoaha. He had been arrested, tried, convicted, sentenced to death but never executed. He had been released in 1957 and moved to London soon after, only recently returning to Madagascar and living with his family in Fianarantsoa. Then it gave vague details about the funeral arrangements.

Rifun clipped the newspaper article and kept it on his person, if only for his own amusement. He tried not to get overly emotional about some things, and when he did, he simply brushed it off, saying that this wasn't the way he wanted to lose his father.

"Your sister still won't come?" Elisette asked the evening before the funeral. Rifun was standing in the front doorway, looking out into the growing darkness.

Julianna had been the most difficult element to explain, given that she was presently trapped in another dimension. In lieu of that excuse, however, Rifun had elected to go with, "She doesn't want to end up in the same fate, being kidnapped and butchered by Communists."

"And, I think, she despises our customs and traditions."

He nodded. "That, too, but I always thought she loved our father more than she hated where he came from." He shrugged helplessly. "I think she's just trying to wrap her head around it all, and, maybe if she ignores it, she can pretend something, anything else. I just don't want to see her pass this up and later regret it."

"I understand. But we can't control what other people do and think, even our own family. But even if she doesn't come, and even if she ends up regretting her decision later, she is always welcome to visit the tombs, as are you."

"Thank you. I'll be sure to let her know, though I don't hold out much hope."

"People can surprise you. Don't write her off just yet." Elisette turned. "Come back inside. We have an early day tomorrow, and you should get some sleep."

He agreed and stepped away from the door, pulling it shut behind him. The last remnants of after dinner were just being cleaned up as people meandered inside after their customary evening socializing, all turning in early for the same reason.

He caught Lalao's eye, flushed bright red, averted his gaze but unable to hide a small smile. She'd been rather annoyed with him for not writing or calling at all in the last three years. He'd apologized — to everyone — but then it left the two of them in a rather awkward predicament. Did they want to actually confess feelings for one another? For Rifun, he wouldn't have had a problem with such a thing, except he was set to leave her again, and he wouldn't be able to write or call.

He'd toyed with the idea of asking for help from another Akari-bearer. Isthim could write letters, couldn't she? She could stand to write a letter every few months, keep a conversation going, maybe send a generic postcard once or twice a year.

At the same time, though, he would only be stringing her along. And what if he was gone longer than intended? A few months, a year or two, fine. What if he was gone for five years? What about ten? Would she wait for him? Could she? And even if he was out in a year, where would their relationship go? That problem hadn't been solved, just pushed back a little. He still didn't know if he could do that to her.

And, really, bringing her into Time or the Akari would involve revealing himself. He wasn't Fan. He was Rivotra. They weren't second cousins. They were first cousins. First cousin once removed, but still. Cousin marriage wasn't unlawful — that he knew of — but even being second cousins seemed to toe the line of what she seemed comfortable with. And, on top of all of that, he was much, much older than her. He was practically an uncle or even a grandfather figure. In spite of his true appearance, by numbers, he was fairly old.

This conflict kept him awake at night, in spite of any recommendations to get sleep.

He'd gone to the family tombs on a spiritual quest, both seeking answers and seeking closure. He'd come into the family as Fan in order to gather information and spy on himself, in a roundabout sort of way. He'd since made amends with his family, been accepted. With Andrianary's help and sacrifice, he'd attained the power he'd sought for years. Now he was burying his old life, getting that closure, and, as a bonus, helping some poor soul who'd been abandoned with no proper funeral rites.

He couldn't continue as Fan. He couldn't have that life. It wasn't his life, and it would be a complete and utter lie. It was dishonest and unfair to the others. Somehow, he was going to have to make Fan disappear.

Well, if Rifun Ndolo had been captured by the Communists, imprisoned for not being a pure Malagasy in addition to any other crimes they wanted to charge him with, why wouldn't they do the same to his son? Apparently Julianna had the right of things this time. Maybe it was just too dangerous to be in Madagascar right now. Fan found his closure and his unfortunate end.

It was a terrible thing to think about and consider, both that he had to do it and that his country had fallen so far to the wayside of what independence was supposed to have brought, and it did nothing to put him in the appropriate mood for the funeral.

Contrary to European funerals, Malagasy funerals were actually quite joyous occasions, and rarely was there ever just one at a time. Many funerals were used as an excuse for full *famadihana*. With the government restrictions in place, plenty of families were using the Andilan occasion to hold their own funerals and *famadihana* at the same time.

First thing in the morning, with a new shaman presiding over the proceedings, the tombs were emptied, dozens of bodies brought out, unwrapped, and laid out on the warm ground in the fresh air and morning sun. Under cover of darkness, other families had also exhumed their dead and brought them to the festivities for their secret ceremonies. Names written or even embroidered on the silk linens denoted who was who.

The morning was spent giving offerings to the bodies, praying for the guidance of newly deceased into the spirit realm and asking for blessing from those already there.

Rifun went to his mother's body. By now, there was very little flesh left on the bones; her full assimilation into the spirit realm nearly complete, when her individual identity would cease to exist and she would exist only as power and energy within the *razana*, combining with all others who had gone before to give power or punishment to the living.

"This is your grandmother, Lalao," Elisette said, coming up beside him.

"My father talked about her a lot," Rifun said. "He loved her."

"She loved him. He was her firstborn, no matter what Vala said. Now they will be reunited this day in great celebration."

"He's getting what he always hoped for."

He said it pleasantly enough, but it made him feel hollow. This was all for him, because of his supposed death. But the soul that would be meeting his mother and joining the ancestors was not his. And when his time to die did finally come around, assuming it was even noticed and any of this mattered anymore, the celebration would be for someone else. Maybe Fan. Maybe another fictional son or grandson or some other invented relative. But not him.

Would his soul be permitted to join the ancestors? Or would he be condemned as a *sibotra*, a mad ghost separated from the *razana*? If the ancestors had bestowed this grand power upon him, surely they would understand what he was doing here. They would understand his motives. They had to. And besides, he was saving the soul of whoever this man had been, giving him ceremonies when his own family could not. That in itself had to be worth something. Andrianary had sacrificed himself so Rifun could gain the full power of the Akari and become a Builder. Rifun was simply repaying the debt.

"Are any of my father's siblings here?" he wondered before Elisette walked away. "He said he had seven or eight brothers and sisters. Did none of them care for him?"

Elisette frowned. "I never met any of them, so I don't know."

"Weren't they notified?"

"Fan, we don't even know where they are, if they're still alive after the war and the Uprising and everything else. The notice in the newspaper is the most they will likely see outside of the immediate area." At his dismayed expression, she sighed. "I don't know. We didn't see Lalao very much; it was expensive and cumbersome to travel back then. When we did see her, she usually only had Rivotra with her. Vala was a very demanding, controlling person."

"Why did she marry him, then?"

"The shaman proclaimed it a sound match. And some people are snakes in disguise. I wasn't there for the engagement or the arrangements. But I also think part of it had to do with propriety."

"Because she was pregnant."

"That's right."

"Wouldn't the family have taken care of her?"

"Of course, but the engagement happened before that. And everyone took it as a good thing that Vala was still willing to marry her and, by all accounts, accept the child."

"But he didn't."

Elisette sighed. "No, he didn't." She went on before he could speak. "I don't know, Fan. I don't know the reasoning or the methods; that was before my time. Even so, I only married into the family, so I only know what I've been told. Though I can't say that Volana would have much better insight. But whatever it was, however it was, that is how things were meant to be and how they were meant to unfold. One day, when we join the ancestors, then we may see through time and know all things. But as mere mortals, we do not know."

Rifun nodded. "I guess you're right."

She put a hand on his shoulder and grinned. "But enough sorrow. Your father is being buried in the family tomb and joining the ancestors, all as he always wanted. And you are meeting many of the ancestors for the first time. This is a happy day. There will be no European sorrow here, so you best learn to smile."

His sorrow did not come from death—for that he was greatly pleased and even eager—but from his own life. What was he supposed to do with himself now? Europeans saw death as an end. Malagasy saw it as a beginning. And here he was, trapped between the two. He had the power of the dead combined with the physicality of the living. What was his purpose?

With all the ancestors from all the families, the pasture of the Andilan farm was quite the graveyard. Half of Fianarantsoa must have been in attendance. The Andilan bodies were laid out closest to the tomb and the shrine. Related families were next after that, followed by any and all other families desiring to hold ceremonies for their dead. Just looking upon the tables stretching a mile and a half across the land first thing in the morning, Rifun had thought there would be terrible emptiness. Now, looking at things in the daylight, he wasn't sure that a mile and a half was long enough.

At solar noon, the various family shamans said final prayers over the bodies, offering up various rocks, crystals, and other spiritual paraphernalia.

When this was done, it was time to eat. Elisette had been in charge of overseeing all of the food, and feeding upwards of five thousand people was no small feat. Some had cheekily suggested she bring out just a bit of bread and some fish. In reality, a dozen cows had been slaughtered and prepared, as well as multiple sacks of rice, and every family contributed some kind of fruit or vegetable. Some did indeed bring bread or fish or dishes of spices and seasonings or a tray of sweets or whatever they had on hand.

Rifun, being the son of the deceased, had not brought any food for the guests, as he had been tasked with preparing food for the shrine and his "father's" dead body.

Of course, five thousand people did not stretch a mile and a half, but the bodies from the tombs did not merely lie there like lawn ornaments. Once the final prayers had been said and invocations recited, the various family members then took the bodies and seated them at the table with their respective families.

"Here, Rivotra, let's get you situated next to your son, hm?" Jaona said, helping Rifun to maneuver his "father" into the seat next to him. "He may not have been born here, but you raised him well. I am sure he will please you here today."

"Misaotra, Jaona," Rifun told him.

Jaona simply nodded once as he went down and slid between the tables to get to the other side.

Had it actually been a relative's body seated next to Rifun, he would have felt more at ease. As it was, he did not exclude the possibility that some ill fate could befall him because of the false identity.

He situated the plate and utensils in front of the body and looked around at the food spread out before them. To his right was the body, to his left was Lalao. Across from him was another dead relative. With "Rivotra" at the end of the table closest to the shrine and the tomb, the dead relative was placed on his right so they might speak to each other more easily. Next to the second relative, across from Lalao, was Volana and Elisette.

Food was the first order of business. The dead were served first, always their favorite foods. Despite already making up a plate for his dead father earlier, that was a spiritual offering plate. Now, as Rifun scooped out rice and omby onto the plate in front of his dead father, this was intended as a meal plate. It would get thrown out all the same, but the intent behind it was different.

Once the dead had been served, then it was time for the living to take their portions, with the elders being served first. Suffice to say, it was a short wait for Rifun to get any food.

When it did finally make it his way, he scooped out rice and omby and pork and all manner of vegetables. He even got the last piece of fish which he guiltily split with Lalao.

Still they could not eat, not until the elders had taken their first bite. Only when this was done could they touch their utensils, and it was a minute before conversations started popping up.

"You know, we helped Kotomanga and his family get started in pigs," Volana mentioned casually.

"I did not realize cows could birth piglets," Rifun said smartly.

The patriarch laughed. "No, no. We helped him build his shelter, and we knew some pig farmers north of Fianar who had some piglets to sell. Well, give away, anyway. They were surprise piglets, out of season. The government had no idea of their existence."

"How did Kotomanga explain the pigs, then?"

"Orphans," Elisette said, shrugging. "If a pig gets loose and goes wild, no one can catch it. Clearly a wild sow was nearby and had piglets, but she, for whatever reason, was dead."

"And here we are, four years later, enjoying the fruits of labor," Volana finished.

Rifun reached for a pitcher of juice, pouring a glass for his dead father and then himself.

"What will you do now?" Elisette asked him. "Will you return to London?"

"I don't have much of a choice," Rifun said resignedly.

"Of course you do," Lalao said beside him. "Stay here, with us. You are among family here. Clearly your London family doesn't care about you."

"Lalao!" Volana snapped.

She flinched at the rebuke but did not apologize.

"I think what she is trying to say," Elisette said calmly, "is that she is wondering at what point you expect to approach her family with gifts."

Rifun hated his lighter skin because it always gave him away, such as now when he burned bright red. He swallowed nervously. "I've barely been around, and I have a life and a history in London."

"You've had little trouble assimilating here."

"I wouldn't even know where to begin. With any of it. Immigration, work, school..."

"In case this party didn't clue you in," Volana said, "I have government connections."

"Those government connections murdered my father," Rifun cut in, anger flashing through him. "Why should I expect anything different?"

"Your father had a military and political background the government did not agree with. You do not. You will be welcomed here, I promise you."

"You had to bribe people to even have this party, which should have been as simple as any occasion. If the government outlaws our own customs and traditions, why should they suffer someone who comes from a world of different customs and traditions and is the son of a political prisoner whom they themselves executed?"

No one had a good answer to that.

"I am risking a lot to be here, I think," Rifun said. "I couldn't live like that, and I wouldn't want to put Lalao in danger just by association or marriage."

"Then I will come to you," Lalao decided. "I will come with you and live in London."

He shook his head. "No. You would be terribly alone and homesick. I wouldn't do that to you."

"He does speak the truth," Elisette commented.

"Then what are we supposed to do?" Lalao despaired.

"I know, child. It's not fair. Wait a little longer. The answer may present itself in time."

"I am near thirty years old. How long shall I wait to have children?"

Volana sighed and looked at Rifun. "The world has changed since your father's day."

Rifun nodded slowly. "The very country he fought for, sacrificed his mind and body for, is the same one that killed him for it."

The older man shook his head. "No. The same country on the map, perhaps, but hardly the same in heart. We were once a great kingdom, ruled by kings and queens, with fearsome warriors."

"The Malasay."

"Like the Malasay. And the Andilans. Then the kingdoms were toppled, the warriors killed. There was a time of slavery and then the warriors rose again."

"And when the warriors ran out of enemies, they turned on their own people," Rifun stated.

Volana frowned. "We will emerge from this darkness. We will again be the mighty people we once were. But we must be patient."

"Patience is not a virtue of European life."

"But it is in Malagasy life."

"And which am I?"

Volana leaned back in his seat. "That I cannot tell you. You may have to ask the shaman or pray to the ancestors yourself."

Rifun nodded once and took a bite of food. He didn't know what to think. He didn't know what to do. Maybe leaving was for the best. Give it a few years, maybe the Communists would be gone. Maybe Lalao would grow tired of waiting and marry someone else.

Lunch was not a hurried affair, and food was continuously passed around as the afternoon wore on. Rifun did not take much more than his first plate, though he would not deny indulging a little in some of the desserts that had been brought. As expected, he inquired of his dead father several times. It was a formality, no one expected the corpse to answer, but it pleased the soul and the ancestors.

Children ran around here and there, playing games. Teenage boys competed in races, running up and down the length of the tables, trying to impress the girls who looked on.

"How is Faliarivo doing in *savika*?" Rifun inquired.

"He was not so good in the beginning," Volana said, grinning. "It is one thing to practice at home where the bulls know you. It is quite another to set foot in an arena."

"Was he injured badly?"

"Not so badly, no. He was back at it again in a few months."

"Have any girls taken notice of him?"

"He would like to think so, but he is still very young and new to the sport. He must prove himself in more than a couple tournaments."

Conversation meandered here and there. Eventually, Elisette got up and moved off to speak to friends or other relatives, and Lalao did the same.

"She wishes you would, you know," Volana said once Lalao was gone. "She likes you very much."

"I know, but..." Rifun hesitated, searching for the right words. "I think things are too uncertain. I'm too uncertain."

The elder shifted position. "Fan, anyone here could be fined for being here. I could be arrested, not only for hosting this party, but for bribing the authorities to do it. And I am Malagasy. I am Malasay, and an Andilan. No different than your father. The only thing about your father is that he, yes, he didn't look the part. He was easier to pick out and harass, I'm sure of it. He was also an old man. The torture that he endured when he was a young man, he could not handle as an old man."

"They tortured him, then."

"I don't know. It wouldn't surprise me. The point is, every single person here, all five thousand of us, are at risk. But all of the people here knew exactly what they were doing when they agreed to come, when they went out in the middle of the night to bring their dead. It was something they needed." He shifted in his seat. "Long ago, your father wanted to help the people, help the Malagasy break free of French rule. He always thought that was on the battlefield. But you know what else?"

"What?"

"He inspired the people in a different way. He took our stories — our meager traditions and oral history — and put it on one of the biggest stages in the world. He showed Madagascar to the world, and it ignited a fire in the hearts of the people. His legacy was not on the battlefield, but the stage. And even now, I think that legacy is carrying over to this day. The people are living in bondage again. But this here, this gathering of five thousand people, the grandest *famadihana* I have ever seen in my life, perhaps in the history of Madagascar, it may reignite that flame once again. Even in death, your father helps the people."

Rifun almost confessed everything to his cousin right there, but he bit his tongue at the last second. Instead he opted for, "My father was a playwright in the 30's. Madagascar was not independent until 1960."

Volana waved a hand. "Well, wars can put a damper on things, I admit. Hitler and Hirohito were rather inconvenient on that part, weren't they? Nevertheless, it happened. This, too, shall pass." He went on before Rifun could protest. "And if it's not the Communists, there will be some other danger to contend with. There always will be. Do not wait for the world to stop spinning before you decide to make the leap of faith."

At some point late in the afternoon, the music started up. It had come about in minor starts and short movements, to entertain children or show off one's musical talent to a prospective partner. Now the real festivities began.

Each family had its own musical arrangement, for now came the dance of the dead. Each family went to its ancestors seated at the many tables, and got the bodies out of the seats. Large swaths of silk linens were laid out on the ground, each body to a cloth. The bodies were carefully wrapped in a certain manner. Some already had the name of the dead person stitched on, others were written on after the fact. The cloth was tied and the body hoisted high over the heads of the family members. Rifun was at the head of his "father's" body, and the parade began.

With his father being the newest dead, he lead the way, followed by the rest, from newest to oldest dead, accompanied off to the side by the musicians. It was not merely a walking parade, either, but a dancing parade, each person in their own time, their own step, singing songs to honor the dead and welcome the new souls into the ancestors.

The Andilan family took their dead back to the farmhouse; elsewhere, other families were parading their dead back to their own homes. Then they would all be returned to their respective tombs and laid to rest for another seven years.

There were many dead on parade, but for as exciting the festivities were, it was hard to dance for a mile and a half, especially over uneven terrain. It was also difficult to sing and dance on uneven terrain. By the time they reached the farmhouse, his arms were numb and he was ready to fall over. He deliberately avoided thinking about having to take the body all the way back to the tomb.

But first they had to show the dead around the house, brag about how things had improved, show the result of all the blessings the ancestors had bestowed upon the family, that way they knew the blessings were going to good use and would give more.

Water was given to all family members and used to anoint the dead, a last drink before being put to rest.

Despite his fatigue, Rifun refused to Band himself, even his arms, which again lifted the corpse of his supposed dead father, ready to carry him back to the tombs a mile and a half away. This time, the procession went from oldest to newest dead, meaning he was now in the back of the line. That was fine with him. He let his mind go blank, relying on muscle memory for the dancing and singing, keeping his gaze fixed only on the person in front of him.

When they reached the tombs, the bodies were laid out in ceremony, from oldest to newest. From there, they were taken one-by-one into the tomb for reburial.

Rifun's so-called dead father was last. He was presented before the shrine one last time for prayer and blessing by the new shaman, to ensure his soul reached the ancestors. He also prayed over the family and Rifun specifically, asking for guidance and blessing.

When the prayers were over, Rifun, with the help of Jaona and Sambatra, took the last body into the tomb. It was a fascinating experience, laying himself to rest. It was equal parts amusing, mysterious, humbling, and terrifying, and he could not deny that the hair on his arms and the back of his neck stood up as he laid the body on the cold stone.

By the time they emerged, the sun was sinking below the horizon. The only thing left to do, then, was clean up the tables. The women gathered the utensils while the men broke down the tables and chairs. There were twelve hundred tables in all, and somewhere in the neighborhood of six thousand chairs. Not everything belonged to the family, but since they hosted the event, they were responsible for getting it all cleaned up.

It took well over an hour, and it was past dark by the time they got back to the house. It wasn't even as late as they normally stayed up, but Rifun was exhausted. Maybe keeping his arms over his head for three miles had something to do with it. Or the constant activity from sunup to sundown. Or any number of things which had happened to him or crossed his mind today.

Elisette warmed up some leftover food for them, which they accepted and partook of without much ceremony. They didn't even eat at the table, but wherever they felt comfortable: the sofa, a cushioned chair, one's bed, the floor. Rifun sat on one end of the sofa, his food on the end table next to him. If he closed his eyes, he might have been able to fall asleep, but he willed himself to stay awake just a little longer.

"The greatest *famadihana* in the history of Madagascar," Volana chuckled, sounding not a bit fatigued himself. "Greater than the kings and queens of old, even."

"Now that might be a bit of an exaggeration," Jaona scolded mildly. "But certainly a great one, the best in my lifetime."

"Ah, your lifetime has known little outside of war and pain, but I think things are going to get better. I really do." Volana looked at Rifun as he said it. "And you,

Fan, what did you think? It was your first *famadihana*, no?"

No. "Yes. I don't know what to think, but I can't imagine doing such a thing on a regular basis."

Volana grinned and shook his head. "Normally it is only every five to seven years, or at one's earliest financial ability. But it has been too long since the Communists took over, and this was greatly needed, as we spoke about earlier."

"I'm glad I was here, then," Rifun said sincerely. "And I'm glad my father was honored so greatly."

Soon after dinner, the children were put to bed, and even Volana and Elisette retired early. Rifun put his dishes away and went outside. He walked to the east end of the house near the chicken coop and looked out across the dark pasture where stars dotted the sky.

In the moment, Rifun couldn't have imagined being anywhere else in world, and it had seemed as though the celebration would have gone on for half a lifetime. Now it seemed to have passed too quickly for him to really enjoy it.

And just like that, his time here was over. Rivotra Andilan was dead, buried in the tombs of his ancestors. His life was complete. He had indeed remained on the farm and died young, having never married and no children. Well, according to the others, he had, but for Rifun's part, that part of his life, that part of the prophecy had been fulfilled. All that remained was Rifun Ndolo.

"Not tired yet?"

He turned to see Lalao approaching. She leaned against the wall beside him.

"No, I'm exhausted," he confessed, grinning. "Greatest in all of Madagascar or not, that was a big party."

"I know. It's been a long time since I've seen so many people together like that."

"Yeah." He didn't know what else to say.

She tilted her head onto his shoulder. "Why won't you stay here? With me?"

He took an even breath. "I don't know. Danger aside...it's..." He hesitated, but only because he knew the next words were one hundred percent true and false. "It's not my life." He paused. "My father taught me a lot, yes, but I grew up in London. I would be leaving everything I've ever known."

"I am willing to do that for you, but you will not let me," Lalao pointed out.

"Because it's a hard decision. I don't want you to feel hurt and alone. Here you have family."

"Here you have family. You are family."

He turned and kissed her then, putting one hand on her cheek. She did not resist, but gingerly touched his arm. He broke off the kiss and looked at her, searched her face. Not two feet behind him was the window into the men's bedroom, dark but for the orange glow of the light in the living room, making everything outside just visible.

He startled as the rooster in the coop nearest them crowed. Lalao giggled, and he found himself chuckling nervously. Their hands found each other, and they squeezed tight.

"I wasn't expecting that," he said, grinning dumbly.

"Neither was I," she laughed, and this time she kissed him.

He had enough sense to Band the two of them, but not enough sense to stop things from happening in the first place. He moved his hands out of hers, slipping them around her waist to grab her and pull her hips close against him while she put her arms around him. She moved her head, resting her forehead against his chest.

For a long moment, he thought she was going to suggest they not continue. He felt her arms unhook from behind his back. He let his arms go loose around her, and he moved his hands from her butt to each other. Then he felt her push his shirt up and fiddle with the waist of his pants. He slid his hands under the waistband of her skirt, feeling her smooth skin and warm legs. He moved her skirt down so that he only had to remove his hands and it would fall.

She pushed his pants down and he let her skirt fall from his fingers. Once he did that, she lifted one leg around him, and he picked her up, pushing her against the wall of the house.

He kissed her lips, her neck. She ran her fingers through his hair. He lifted his head and looked her in the eyes. He shifted position, teased her just a little, just enough to ask. When she did not refuse, he thrust up and let her slide down onto him. She gasped in delight, and it was all he needed.

She did not know about the Band, did not know that silence was unnecessary. And in a way, Rifun was happy to go along with the charade, the mystique.

Banding helped him to last as long as she did, and afterwards, they sat together, naked from the waist-down, her sitting between his legs, his arms around her, staring through the chicken pen to the horizon beyond.

They said nothing for a long time, and he was fine with that. It would have ruined the moment. Still, he couldn't help but feel tragically guilty. If he could have stayed, he would have married her.

And why shouldn't he? He had the power to choose, to shape his own destiny. Building would not be taken from him. Why not live a life with Lalao? The Cult could live without him. What if some tragedy befell him otherwise? Was it really so dependent upon him? At the very least, Cassius could go into the cave after the Book of Abilities. That would buy him a few years, wouldn't it?

"Your father never talked about his time in the war or in prison, did he?" Lalao murmured.

"Hm? No, he didn't. Not really," Rifun answered.

"But I'm sure he told you that he was blind at one time."

"Yes, and the spirits restored his sight. He was quite fond of that story."

"Did he ever tell you how he went blind?"

"In prison was all he said."

Facing away from him, he could not see her expression. Slowly she reached over her shoulder, touched his shoulder, his neck, his ear, saying, "A pickax to the back of the head." She paused. "Right here."

She jabbed a finger in the back of his head, right into his head wound. He snarled in pain, jerked his head back, hit the wall, tried to go to one side or the other, fell over awkwardly, Lalao going to her side as well. By the time he got situated again, Lalao was between his feet facing him. Her expression was entirely unreadable.

"You're Rivotra Andilan," she stated. "I don't know how, but you are Rivotra."

He did not reply, just moved his hand slowly from the back of his head down to his lap.

"Is Fan even real?"

Rifun sighed and grabbed his clothes. As he stood to dress himself, Lalao slowly following suit, he answered, "No. Fan doesn't exist. And you are right that I am Rivotra."

He hesitated, then pulled off his shirt and dropped his Disguise. Healthy skin was replaced by a burned, melted, scarred, twisted, pitted wretch. Lalao put a hand to her mouth. She looked at his body, looked him in the eye, looked at his scars, looked him in the eye. He replaced his shirt.

"I don't expect you to understand, but the ancestors healed my vision and granted me great power." He sighed. "I don't age like you do. I'm going to be leaving for a while, but I couldn't go without making amends to the family. But I couldn't come as I am. I'm too young. To be myself, I had to be old." He showed her his elder Disguise. "I wasn't sure how the family would receive me at first, so I had to be someone removed from myself, and that day you found me at the tombs, I invented Fan." He dropped the elder Disguise and again showed her the Disguise that covered up his scars. Finally he dropped it all.

Lalao simply stared at him, eyes wide, mouth open. After a moment, she remembered herself and her expression turned puzzled. "Wait. Then...who did we just bury?"

Rifun opened his mouth, shrugged, and said, "Quite honestly, I don't know. A victim of the war, of the Communists, who could tell? There are many unclaimed dead to choose from in these lands. As I said, I'm going away for a while, but I couldn't...I had to make amends and close this chapter of my life. Rivotra Andilan had to die as one of the family. I don't know when I'm coming back, but I...I had to do this. For my sake, for the sake of the family."

She stared at him again. Then, "Did you ever really love me, or was that just part of the act? I guess I should have known; Rivotra was a renowned actor after all."

He took a step closer and took her hands. "No, never. I do love you, Lalao. I have since I set eyes on you at the tombs, but...I didn't know how to go about it. I didn't know how this would all work out."

"And you were just going to leave without another word?" A tear escaped her eye and ran down her cheek.

He took her head in his hands and wiped the tear away. "Believe it or not, I was just thinking about not going after all. Finding a way to stay with you."

She sniffed, managed a lopsided smile, and looked away. Then she looked back at him. He lowered his hands and took hers once more.

"I do love you, Lalao. If you believe nothing else, believe that."

She sniffed again and nodded. "I do believe you." She looked down, then back up. "Why can't I come with you? It's more than just homesickness, I think."

He nodded. "Yes, it is. The monsters that I have to face are greater than the physical world, born of evil spirits and demons. I can't let you go into that."

"And the ancestors chose you for this."

"That's right."

She let out a breath, moved close to him, and put her arms around him. He let out a breath, wrapped his arms around her, and rested his chin on her head. "I'm sorry for the deception, but I think you understand."

"Mhm." She looked up. "I do understand." She took a step back and grabbed his hands. "Go, Rivotra."

He blinked. "What?"

"Go. Fight the monsters born of evil spirits and demons. The ancestors did not choose you for this just so you could idle away as a cattle rancher."

"I don't know how long I'll be gone. It could be years, I may even die, and I don't want you to waste your life waiting for me."

"Don't worry about me. You worry about your own destiny. If the ancestors give such power and immortality to one of the living, the threat must be great indeed. Go. Slay the demons. I will tell the family you've gone. And it will be on good terms."

He took a step forward and kissed her again passionately.

"I will come back for you," he whispered. "I promise."

She grinned and gave him a small kiss. "I know."

He held her for a moment longer before turning and stalking off into the darkness. When he dared to look back, she was gone.

Seeing no one else around, he opened a portal and returned to the tunnels.

Only when he got to the mouth of the cave that opened up into the great Caves of Meroian did he stop and lean against the wall. He felt wretched for leaving her, but there was also a great sense of relief. She'd figured out his identity, learned of the power, and she still loved him.

Damn it all, but if he didn't have to go into the cave and jump into the future, he might have actually brought her here and trained her himself. Or he might have just trained her at home, kept her out of sight of Isthim and Cassius. Point was, if not for having to clean up everyone else's messes, he might have gotten a happy fucking ending.

He waited for the tide of emotions to pass before making his way into the city, though he was still in a less than stellar mood. Twice now he'd been given the chance to have everything he ever wanted. Twice he'd had to give it up on account of prophecies and disturbances among the spirits that the ancestors seemed to think only he could solve.

Well, at least Rivotra Andilan was buried and in good standing in the family. That was all that he'd really set out to accomplish; that was all that mattered.

It was hollow comfort.

"Well, well, look what the cat dragged in," Cassius mocked as he made his way through the officers building toward his chambers. "Funeral go as you always dreamed? Was everyone crying appropriately?"

"Funerals are rather joyous affairs among my people, thank you," Rifun informed him. "And yes, everything went splendidly. My cousin was calling it the greatest *famadihana* the island has ever seen, at least in his lifetime."

"Glad to hear it. Are we ready to go, then? Or is there some afterlife ritual you need to do first?"

Rifun clenched his jaw and focused on sealing up his chambers; no telling how long they would actually be gone, and he didn't really want anyone snooping. Finally he answered, "Nothing else needs to be done on Earth or anything like that. I'm just checking on a few things and sealing up my chambers. Are you ready? Is there anything else you need to do?"

"I've been ready for the last month," Cassius informed him. "And I sealed my chambers five hours ago."

"Well, five hours ago, I was parading a dead body over my head for three miles."

Cassius' expression turned intrigued, and he was mercifully silent on the matter. Still, he followed Rifun around the officers building like a disapproving parent.

"Where's Isthim?" Rifun asked.

"She went ahead to the cave, just in case anyone else somehow got wind of our plans and decided to try something."

Rifun nodded and left the building. "Sensible move. Do you have the map?"

"In my pocket."

They stopped in the middle of the street. "Is there anything that we need to do now while we're here? We might be gone for months or years, I just want to make sure."

"For the last time, no," Cassius said irritably. "You aren't the only one who knows how to plan and get things done. Now let's go."

He didn't want to go to the cave. He wanted to go back home, to Lalao. He wanted to hold her and kiss her and make love to her. He wanted to marry her and have a life.

But what kind of life would it be if the demon within Cassius were permitted to live? Rifun still had not received any enlightenment as to how to kill the evil spirit. Merely killing the body of Cassius would not be enough. But he had a sneaking suspicion that the answer would be made clear in the very near future.

They reached the cave and made their way into the tunnels where Cassius opened the series that got them to the cave where Isthim was waiting. She was in her physical human disguise with black skin, a large wig and hat to cover her horns, and mittens to conceal her extra fingers. Given the snow blanketing the ground, it didn't seem like a bad idea. Having just come from a rather toasty environment, Rifun was unable to suppress a shiver.

"All is in order then?" she asked, looking more at him than Cassius.

"It appears to be," Cassius replied casually, also looking at Rifun.

"The more you look at me and give me accusatory stares, the slower we will be to find the journal," Rifun said defensively. "Cassius said you were making sure that no one had discerned our plans. I take it all has been quiet? You haven't seen anyone, you weren't followed?"

Isthim shook her head. "Nothing. Nor have I seen anyone exit the cave."

Rifun folded his arms, using Thermodynamics to keep himself warm. The snow around him melted. "Well, I don't expect you to camp here for the next few months or years, but maybe come back every so often to check things out. If this Time Trap is as extreme as everyone says, then anyone emerging from this place may be newsworthy material, claiming to have jumped so many years into the future and whatnot. Keep an eye out for things like that."

"Agreed. I have found several such individuals already, but nothing about the journal."

"Well, keep an eye out. I expect the Turitians will turn over the Book of Commands soon, if they haven't already." He put up a hand. "I don't want to hear anything about it, good or bad. I want to focus on what is going on in the present moment, that is, walking into this cave."

Isthim dipped her head once. "Fair enough. Is there anything else before you go?"

Her tone and expression suggested that she and Cassius had been planning this for some time—at least the last few weeks while he'd been away planning his funeral. Rifun cleared his throat. "No, I don't think so."

"You didn't bring a torch?"

"If the bones aren't in total cave darkness, then Light will still be somewhat usable, I think. And if a wild animal did make off with the journal for whatever reason, I can't imagine why it would go deeper into the cave. Either way, Light will be useful for a while, at least long enough for our expedition."

"And at what point are we turning around?" Cassius wondered.

"Once we've determined that there is no possible way the journal is still in the cave. But that will be decided based on what we find inside. Now then, are there any more questions, or are we quite ready to proceed?"

"Don't leave me stranded for another century," Isthim told them.

"If that's your way of wishing us good luck, then thank you," Rifun said.

"No, it's me telling you not to leave me stranded for another century."

"Yeah, good luck to you, too. Don't completely blow our political cover while we're away."

He could feel her glare boring into his back as he and Cassius climbed over the rotting trees and squeezed past the boulder. Once inside, he struggled to comprehend the Bands twisting and threading their way through the cave, distorting Time in such a terrible way. While he hesitated, Cassius took the lead, heading deeper into the cave, a shadow being welcomed back into the darkness.

After a moment, Rifun followed.

The two of them walked right up to the distortion but did not immediately impress upon it. They glanced back where Isthim was struggling to look inside the cave, her horns too big to get past the boulder.

Cassius brought out the map and Rifun used Light to amplify the natural light and show the map.

"So then, we should stick to the right wall until it runs out. When it does, there should be an alcove where the miner's bones are tucked away," Rifun said, pointing on the map. "That's where we'll start, short of any miraculous discoveries between here and there."

"I should hope that Julianna isn't that dense," Cassius growled, refolding the map and putting it back in his pocket. "Insufferable, a bit dim at times, but I hope she isn't that stupid."

"She threw her lot in with you, didn't she?" Rifun said. At Cassius' look, he sighed. "Honestly, Cassius, have a sense of humor."

They walked into the distortion together. It didn't hurt, as Rifun had feared, but it had a similar feeling to that of tar. Heavy, with great resistance, but manageable. Now where had he felt this sensation before? It felt important.

The Core. Yes. On his way to the Core. There was a wretched feeling of tar and fear and loneliness and doubt. Just thinking about it made him want to turn tail and run, but he pressed on. Unlike the Core, this temporal distortion held none of the psychological aspects, save whatever a victim brought in with him. Rifun would not deny his anxiety, but it was hardly crippling fear as he had known before.

Then they were through, emerging on the other side of the distortion completely in tact. Rifun glanced back at it.

"How does it work, I wonder?" he mused aloud. "Does the distortion depend on how long you spend in the network of tunnels, or in the distortion itself? If it is the tunnels, how does it extend beyond this point?"

"I don't know, but do you really want to waste decades on this side of it trying to figure it out?" Cassius asked irritably, already moving away.

"I know you don't have a sense of humor," Rifun said, hurrying to catch up with him. He put his right hand out and felt along the wall. "But have you lost your sense of curiosity, too?"

"Maybe I never had one."

"I highly doubt that, not if you got into Time and the Akari."

Cassius did not respond to that, and the two of them descended, silently, into the blackness of the earth.

32 | Imularada ati Iṣalaye
West Virginia, 1970

Recovery and Orientation

kokumbo

Cassius was not what one might call an expert on caves, but after a good distance, both he and Rifun agreed on two things. First, Julianna was terrible at estimating distances, and possibly also geography. Second, the light from the distortion provided a secondary, albeit weaker, light source which extended the available light beyond what would normally be total cave darkness.

They tried to move quickly, to minimize the time they were gone. Cassius strode confidently through the tunnel, hand brushing the wall, waiting for the moment when it slipped away from his fingers.

"Do you think we'll run into anyone in here?" Rifun wondered, breaking the silence. "The city outside has gotten bigger and will no doubt continue to do so, and it looked like there may be some development in the land around the cave."

"I don't know," Cassius said.

"Obviously you caught up to Julianna in here, so any theories about parallel times while inside are shaky at best."

He didn't want to ask, but he did anyway. "What do you mean?"

"I mean the theory that people entering at different times would be running parallel to each other in their own times and couldn't see each other even though they were standing right next to one another." Rifun paused. "On the other hand, you weren't far behind Julianna. You may have been in the distortion at the same time when you entered, and maybe that makes the difference. She ran out before you did, thus the difference in your exit times. Maybe the theory isn't so far-fetched. Maybe the Time Trap is as much dimensional as temporal, and that's why Julianna couldn't escape via portal. Maybe that's why she couldn't find the journal, because she can't see it."

"All right, what happened?" Cassius interrupted.

"What do you mean?"

"You enjoy hearing yourself talk, but you're too nervous, and you're talking too much bullshit, even for you. What happened at your funeral?"

"Do you care or do you want me to stop talking?"

"Mostly I want you to stop talking, but if I ask now, then I won't have to hear about it later."

For a long moment, Rifun said nothing, and Cassius dared to hope the man had decided to just be quiet. Then he answered, "I had to leave someone behind."

"Someone. A woman?"

"Yes."

"You can go back to her after this."

"She knows who I am. She knows what I'm doing."

"Then what's the problem?"

"I didn't want to leave her."

Cassius raised a brow though Rifun couldn't see. "You didn't have to, you know. I know how to read a map by myself. I can walk on my own two feet in this cave. Or do you not trust me?"

"The thought had crossed my mind," Rifun confessed. "About staying and letting you go alone, that is. It was sorely tempting. But she wouldn't let me. Once she worked out who I was and I explained things to her, she told me to go, and she would be there when I got back."

"Then you are planning on returning. For good this time?"

"I don't know."

"If it's age you're worried about, well, you just said she worked things out. Why not train her, too? Why didn't you bring her along on this expedition; that distortion is powerful enough to expose anyone to Time, enough to make them a potential Timekeeper. Short jump to the Akari."

"I wanted to keep her safe. I didn't know what would happen in here."

"What could happen in here? I don't buy Julianna's story. The only wild animal in here is me. Unless that's what you're afraid of."

"That thought crossed my mind, too."

Cassius chuckled. "Well, just wait until you hear what's waiting for us out there when we get back."

Rifun was silent for a moment, then, "What are you talking about?"

Cassius stopped and turned to face Rifun who just stopped himself from running into him. "Isthim and I had a discussion the other day after you left."

"What kind of discussion?"

So he told Rifun about Isthim, her connection to the Ul Ik Zol, her non-exile, the

Borelian plan to get the Cult to turn over the journals, the Akari, and effectively enslave themselves on a farming colony over which Cassius would preside.

"My guess is that you don't believe her, or else you wouldn't be telling me," Rifun said after a minute of silence.

"I'm not stupid," Cassius stated flatly. "A slave in the house is still a slave. He's just a little luckier than the ones in the field."

Rifun made a motion to keep moving; they were wasting months, if not years, by stalling. Of course, being gone a little longer than expected might throw a wrench into the Borelians' plans, too.

"What do you suggest, then?" Rifun asked, sounding a tad annoyed. "We've just left the Borelians in charge of the Cult and the Wheel; the Turitians are going to hand them the Book of Commands, and we're going after the Book of Abilities. Why didn't you say something before we walked in here?"

"Because he who holds the Book of Abilities holds the future and the power of the Akari," Cassius said. "As long as we have it, we have the leverage."

"How so? The Book of Abilities holds the key to the greater advanced abilities, true, but even the halfway stuff won us the Wheel. If the Borelians are looking to phase out Akari abilities among the Cult, they don't need much more than that. Conquest will be easier for them no matter what. The Shatai will be their biggest obstacle."

"All she said about them was that they had it handled."

They stopped suddenly as they heard a scream followed by sniffling and crying. Cassius immediately used Light, not to illuminate, but to hide, pulling the light and shadows around both himself and Rifun to conceal them. Nothing happened for a long minute. Then, just as Cassius was ready to let go and keep moving, there was a second cry and footsteps in the darkness.

They waited. Someone had to come running by them at any moment. They heard and saw nothing.

Rifun sighed. "Well now, this just keeps getting better and better."

Cassius dropped his use of Light and they continued. Only a dozen steps later, the wall of the cave suddenly disappeared from Cassius' fingers. He walked a few more steps and stopped.

"All right, we're here," he said.

It wasn't total cave darkness, but it was pretty close. Cassius could only just make out the vague shape of Rifun, shadow on shadow, as he, too, found the end of the cave wall and the open area where several tunnels came together.

Rifun took a few steps back and reached out for the wall. Then he slid down until he was on his knees.

"I'm going to use Light," Cassius announced.

"Not yet," Rifun cut in. "Not yet."

"Why? You can't see."

"Have you forgotten? I'm already blind. Besides, we still don't know what that scream was."

It was impossible to make out the details, but Cassius could see that Rifun began a methodical sweep of the wall, looking for the alcove, the bones, and the journal.

"All right," he murmured. "The alcove is here, only reaches about four feet high. Lots of moss and lichen growing. The ground is damp, so I'm guessing there's a small underground stream coming from the other tunnel."

"Are the bones there at least?" Cassius asked.

"I've got a skull, I think. Yes, here's the eye sockets, the nasal passages, the teeth...the jaw is broken on one side." He paused, continuing to feel. Then, "Whoever it was, why he was here, and however he died, it was a long time ago. I would guess even before the distortion was created. The moss and lichen itself is holding the upper body upright against the wall."

"Can moss and lichen do that?"

"Likely it grew on the body while it was still fresh and then retained its shape as the body began to decay," Rifun explained. "The neck is there somewhere; I can feel it under the moss. The arms are completely covered, the outside of the ribs." He cut himself short.

"What is it?" Cassius demanded.

"I can feel the spot where the journal should be. The moss has been ripped away, but then put back. My guess is, she took it out, put the journal in its place, then placed the moss over it again to hide it from prying eyes and fingers."

"But it's not there anymore. You're absolutely sure?"

"I'm sure, but there's something else, too. The lower legs have been disturbed."

"How do you mean?"

"They've been broken apart, scattered."

Cassius sighed and used Light, then, to illuminate their surroundings. Rifun gasped and grunted in surprise, turning away and squeezing his eyes shut.

"Thought you said you were blind?" Cassius said smartly.

The Light, not bright like the middle of the day, but more like a few good lanterns, illuminated everything Rifun just described. Moss and lichen held the upper body of a long-dead man against the wall. Some of the moss in the lower abdomen had been disturbed, ripped up and then put back. The pelvis appeared to be mostly in tact, if disappeared under heavy moss, but the legs were indeed scattered. A femur was several feet away, a knee joint over there, a broken lower leg over that way, and all the small bones of the foot scattered every which way.

"See?" Cassius said. "We really could have saved ourselves two minutes and possibly two weeks just by using Light."

Rifun gave him a look but did not respond.

Instead he walked a few feet down each tunnel, finally returning and saying, "If a wild animal were after something, I would expect it to be the bones. Yes, they're scattered and broken, but they're still here and they don't look ravaged. And besides, unless the animal were absolutely starving, why come in after these moss-covered bones when there is plenty of game outside? It doesn't make sense."

"Then someone stole it," Cassius stated.

"We heard the screams and the footsteps. Think they're related?" Rifun wondered. "I don't understand the relationship between the people who enter and exit at different times, but at the very least, sound seems to carry."

"But we didn't see anyone run out past us."

"They could have accidentally run deeper into the tunnels, taken the wrong tunnel. The sound could have come from an adjacent tunnel and is entirely unrelated."

"You're not suggesting that we go and explore every single tunnel."

Rifun shook his head. "No, not at all. But I think we should have a good look around here before we leave."

Other than the exit tunnel, there were only three tunnels to choose from. Cassius picked one and meandered his way along, listening for any more screaming, crying, running, or just breathing. He used Light part of the way, but saw nothing. After a moment, he extinguished the Light. He gave a moment for his eyes to adjust, or attempt to as he seemed to have finally gone far enough that his eyes did not register any further light.

He turned his attention to Sound, just as he had with Julianna. He heard the wind through the tunnels, the tiniest movements from the smallest insects, the eeking of a bat, the slither of a snake. He could even hear Rifun's footsteps as he explored another tunnel.

Then he heard a second set of footsteps. It was faint, growing fainter, and finally it vanished. Running away, obviously, but in which direction? The echoes of the tunnels made it too hard to tell, and the steps had disappeared.

He returned to the open area and used Light to investigate the bones once more. Nothing appeared to have changed. He kicked at a bone on the floor and was momentarily distracted by something.

The stream did not create what one might consider mud, but it softened the ground enough that he was able to see the impression of a shoe. It appeared to be a very tiny shoe, hardly more than a child's shoe. When Rifun returned from his own exploration, Cassius pointed out this discovery.

"A child?" Rifun wondered, then sighed and shook his head. "Poor thing. He — or she — is going to run out of this cave into a whole new year and not have any clue what's happened."

"But do you think he could have taken the journal?" Cassius asked.

Rifun shifted his stance. "I suppose it's possible. A child, curious and eager to explore, comes into the cave looking for adventure, stumbles upon these old bones, gets excited, starts looking around, finds a journal." He frowned. "On the other hand, Westerners tend to see the dead as *fady*, taboo. It's bad luck to disturb the dead, and it's terribly unclean to touch them and go rooting around in a corpse."

"And you're happy to share a meal with them and carry them three miles."

He ignored Rifun's look. "The point is, I don't think it's terribly likely. But we shouldn't discount the possibility. At the very least, I would be willing to bet that the child was the source of the screams, the crying, and the footsteps."

"Once again, we didn't pass anyone, and no one passed us."

Rifun got down and looked at the print. "The direction of the print points that way, into the adjacent tunnel. Unless there is a child-sized passage between that tunnel and the main tunnel, or a second exit, he's only going to get himself lost."

Cassius thought Rifun seemed genuinely distressed over the prospect. Grudgingly he asked, "Do you intend to go after him?"

For a full minute, Rifun did not speak, seeming to weigh the options. Cassius was afraid that he would actually suggest going after the child. Problem was, what if that lost child really did have their journal? Well, he could go if he wanted to; Cassius was going to leave no matter what. Make up a story of Rifun's fate, let

Isthim and the Borelians sweat a little more about the Book of Abilities, see what he could do to undermine their plans and get rid of them.

Cassius looked around a bit, bored, and when he looked back, he noticed Rifun appeared to be praying to the bones. Was he asking for guidance? Trying to send the old soul to the afterlife? What the hell was he doing? Dammit but this spiritual stuff took up way too much of Rifun's time.

Rifun finished praying, sat up on his heels, then stood. Cassius followed.

"No," Rifun decided. "We should leave this place, go down to the city, figure out when we are, and get back to the Cult."

"What about Isthim and the Borelians?"

"They can't move the Cult until we have the Book of Abilities. We don't have the Book of Abilities presently. And when we do, we're going to move into the Wheel." He went on before Cassius could speak. "I don't know the details. I don't know how much time has passed or what politics have transpired. But first we need to get out of here."

Cassius did not argue. He wouldn't admit it out loud, but he was feeling a bit uneasy himself about how much time they'd spent in the cave. A few months was out of the question. A few years seemed to be too conservative. Was it possible they'd been gone a decade? He tried to think back to when he'd chased Julianna. That hadn't seemed like a very long time at all, yet over a century had passed. This time, they'd tried to move quickly, keep extraneous conversation and movement to a minimum, but how successful had they been?

Once the light got bright enough to confirm that they were on the right track, they quickened their pace from a careful walk, hands on the wall, to something that was almost a jog. Rifun hesitated only a second before pressing through the distortion, but Cassius barreled right through it. Cassius didn't have any problems; it posed virtually no resistance for him. Did Rifun have a different experience? Did Cassius care? It was difficult to tell whether the man was slowed by some demon that existed only in his mind, or if it was the distortion itself. After a moment, Cassius decided to Slow Band. Rifun passed through the distortion, and Cassius dropped the Band.

"Wait long?" Rifun wondered, his expression honest.

"Only an hour," Cassius told him. "I Banded on this side of the distortion."

"I see. Well, with the number of times we've passed through this distortion, including your experience from before and both of Julianna's experiences, we should have plenty of data to consider regarding this cave."

"Great. Are you ready?"

Rifun nodded and made a motion to lead the way.

The first difference they noticed was that a chain had been put up over the opening. The trees had well rotted away by now, but the boulder remained. The two of them ducked under the chain and turned to read the sign.

"Warning: Dangerous Gases," Rifun read, smirking. He shook his head and looked at the boulder. "That's the best they could do? Has no one thought to simply roll the boulder into place?"

Cassius turned to head down the hill, but Rifun paused. "Now what's this?"

Cassius told himself not to go back, but he did.

"Forbes Cave, dedicated April 6, 2005, by the Forbes Family of Charleston, West Virginia." Rifun read from a plaque near the cave's entrance. "On April 6, 1855, 8 year old Tommen Forbes, a well-known explorer in his day, entered this cave and was never seen again. This cave was a legend even among its settler residents as people went in the cave and did not reappear for months or even years, claiming they had been gone only a few minutes. Eventually the cave was sealed off, but that did not stop young Tommen from exploring. He was the youngest person to vanish into the cave. This cave is dedicated by the Forbes family who are the descendants of Tommen's older brother Teo."

"Well, that explains the small shoe print," Cassius mused.

Rifun gave him a look. "Dedicated in April 2005. That's thirty-five years. At least."

It took a second for the realization to sink in, and Cassius blinked. "We couldn't have been gone that long. By that token, Julianna would have had to have been absolutely sprinting into the cave, and she's not a sprinter."

Rifun stumbled back a few steps from the plaque, one hand on his head. "Thirty-five years. At a minimum." He turned and started running.

"Where are you going?!" Cassius called.

Without looking back, Rifun yelled, "Home!"

Thereby leaving Cassius alone near the cave. He stared after the spot where Rifun disappeared, trying to figure out what had just happened. Then he recalled that Rifun apparently had a woman waiting for him. Well, if she'd waited this long, Rifun could probably stand to take a year or two and care for her in her final years. He smirked at the thought.

But it left him free for a while, at least, and how often, just today, had he wished for Rifun to be gone so he could do his own searching?

He looked around the cave a bit, outside and inside, being careful not to touch the distortion. He looked for anything that might point him in the right direction. The journal itself, a note, even another shoe print. Maybe in thirty-five years, Julianna had escaped or else figured out a way to leave them clues, some better form of communication.

But the journal was nowhere to be found. The only paper he found was an empty chip bag and the receipt from the convenience store it had been purchased from. Cassius nearly disregarded this until he actually looked at the information on the receipt.

Purchase date: April 19, 2013.

They hadn't been gone thirty-five years. They'd been gone forty-five years. Forty-three, to be exact.

Forty-three years. Half the time of the last time Cassius had run into that cave, but no less startling. He shook his head. There was no way—no way—that they had been in there that long. It wasn't possible. Julianna said she had gone directly to the bones, found the journal missing, done a quick search, and attempted to leave immediately. That was, what, two years? The two of them hadn't run into the cave, but they'd moved with some amount of purpose. Cassius stopped and told Rifun of Isthim's plans, but that hadn't taken up too much time, had it? Rifun's blind search of the bones was hardly anything to be concerned with, and they hadn't done extensive searching in the tunnels. Had they? Certainly they'd spent no more than a minute or two examining the shoe print and deciding whether to go after a lost child that may or may not have had the journal they were after. Had all those extra minutes really added up that much?

He went back to the cave and peered at the distortion. It was hard to tell because of how dazzling the Bands were, but the strength appeared to be something like half an hour to half a century.

He shook his head and studied the Bands further. That wasn't right. Oh, Cassius could believe that they'd been in there half an hour, but for half a century? No, that couldn't be right. Of course, his estimation of the distortion's strength could be off by, oh, an hour or a decade on either end. But still, it seemed absurd. And who had twisted this distortion together so that it was not only impossibly strong, but it maintained its strength throughout the ages?

More to the point, what the hell did they do now? What had happened since they left? How many allies did they have? What was the state of the Wheel? What were they going to return to in the Cult? What was Isthim's disposition going to be? What about the rest of the Borelians? What would they do when Cassius and Rifun returned without the Book of Abilities?

Cassius wasn't much for politics, but when enslavement was a very real possibility, he suddenly became very concerned.

He decided it best, then, to not return to the Cult right away. Maybe he would acclimate himself to a new world in a new age, see what the latest news was, the latest gossip. Hell, maybe Earth had become Engaged since they were gone, who knew?

After the chain and the plaque and the ridiculous time difference, the next surprise for Cassius was discovering that the trail up to the cave—if that was what it could be called—had been effectively cut off. At a certain point, where it met another trail, the main trail had been cut out a good six to eight feet down, with only a smooth rock face for a good hundred feet in either direction in order to deter the curious. Of course, the curious could still bypass the stone wall on either side, where it tapered off and rejoined the earth on the side of the trail; rules were only for the honest.

It was no tremendous feat to use Gravity to see him safely to the trail below, and soon he was on his way, hiking down the mountain. It was clear that the area had been improved, and he soon broke into a large park that hadn't been there before. Pavilions and picnic tables littered the area, occupied by families and groups of teenagers and a jogging team. A couple of children played on a playground. Cars were parked in a lot just a hundred feet away in a dirt lot.

Overall, nothing appeared to have changed that much. The hair and clothes were different, the vehicles were different, but nothing looked so out of the ordinary as to be alien in nature.

No one gave him a second glance as he walked through the communal area. No dirty looks, no name-calling, nothing. He said nothing about it and passed through unharmed. He made for the dirt lot, glancing at the new cars. Different shapes, different design, but still appearing to function the same.

He went to the road and looked north. The city had certainly done some growing up in forty years; everything looked shiny and new. Even the road looked freshly paved as he began walking. Power poles criss-crossed the countryside, weaving a web through neighborhood after neighborhood, all of it new in the last forty years. Traffic was steady, an endless tide of people going a thousand different places in their personal vehicles, like a bunch of ants.

What he found interesting, though, was that some of the vehicles appeared to drive themselves. They must have been, he reasoned, for some drivers did not have their hands on the steering wheel, nor did they look at the road. Instead, they were looking down at something clearly far more interesting. A book was all he could come up with that they would be looking at. Some still looked up to see where they were going, but many, for the half a second that he observed them, just had their heads down quietly.

What fascinating technology. Perhaps Earth was Engaged now, even if only Limited Engaged. At the very least, there had to be a robust space program going on. Forty-five years ago, a man walked on the moon. How far had they made it since? Mars? Jupiter? Farther? How did this affect humans in the Time industry? How did it affect the Time industry at large? What did the Tacagans think about it?

A car slowed down to roll alongside him, and the passenger window went down.

"Need a lift?" the driver, a middle-aged white man, asked. "I'm just heading into town."

Cassius was ready to refuse, then thought better of it and agreed. The man pulled over onto the shoulder. Cassius went up to the passenger side where the man was stuffing a jacket and other miscellany in the backseat.

"Don't mind the mess," the man said. "Go ahead and hop in."

Cassius did so. He was amazed that this white man was offering him a ride and speaking to him normally. He was amazed that this white man was offering to let him ride in the front seat. He was amazed at how different the interior of a vehicle appeared. He'd seen space ships that didn't look so nice, and here this was just a personal vehicle. Earth had to have a massive space program, and they had to be involved in Time in some way. They just had to.

"Name's Stan," the driver said, peeking in his mirror before pulling back into traffic.

"Cassius."

"Well, Cassius, where you from, if you don't mind my asking?"

"Africa."

"Yeah? Whereabouts?"

"Yoruba land."

The man nodded, though his expression said he had no idea what Cassius was talking about. "All right, sounds good. Can't say that I've ever heard of it or been there, but if I may say so, you speak very good English. I don't even notice an accent. What brings you hear?"

"A Time portal."

Stan grinned and chuckled. "Okay." He nodded. "Okay, that's an answer I don't think I've heard before."

"You pick up many strangers on the side of the road?" Cassius wondered.

"I know it's dangerous. Illegal in some places. But I just couldn't live with myself if I just passed right on by, ignoring someone on what could be the worst day of their life, and I didn't at least offer to help. Or even if it's not the worst day, well, it's just common decency, you know. We need more of it in our society. Where did the decency go? I mean, when I was a kid..."

Cassius tuned him out and looked out the window. The mountains and highways still looked very much the same. Even the city was still recognizable; it just got a bit of a face lift. A new coat of paint, a new style of storefront, some new advertising, but all very much the same.

Suddenly a robotic voice came out of nowhere.

"Incoming call from: Pumpkin."

Cassius jumped, but then Stan started speaking. "Hey, sweetie."

"Hi, Dad," a female voice said. If Cassius was right, she was speaking through the radio. A communication system, then, like on most space ships. He stared at the screen on the panel, but all it said was, "Phone Call: Pumpkin" and a timer.

"What time are we going out this weekend?" the female, evidently the man's daughter, asked.

"We're meeting at three," Stan replied, talking just as if she were in the car with them. "Is that going to work for you?"

"Yeah, I just wanted to make sure. I'm going out with some girlfriends in the morning to go shopping."

"Oh, come on, sweetie, you know you're beautiful."

"Thanks, Daddy. I'll see you Saturday."

"Love you, hon."

"Love you, Daddy. Mwah!"

"Call ended," the robotic voice announced.

"What was that?" Cassius asked.

Stan gave him a brief sideways glance. "Hm? Oh, that's my daughter, Karlie. It's my wife's birthday this weekend, so we're going out to dinner on Saturday, but we're going to meet up a little early and go do some other things, too. You got any kids?"

Cassius blinked, momentarily stunned by the question. Finally, "No. No kids."

"Oh, okay. I'm just asking."

They started across the bridge into the city.

"So I'm going to the grocery store in the East Plaza," Stan said. "There's a bus stop there, just in case you didn't know."

"How many people live here?" Cassius wondered, looking out the window.

Stan chuckled. "A lot more than there used to, that's for sure. You know, my dad used to tell me stories about..."

Cassius never did find out what stories Stan's dad used to tell him, and he didn't care. He was too busy absorbing the sights, trying to reconcile everything. Even when Stan finally parked the car and wished him well, Cassius didn't give much by way of gratitude.

He couldn't figure out just what it was that stunned him so, made him so unsure of himself. He'd met alien species, strode through alien cities like a king, flown through space in numerous types of space ships, handled technology that made Earth-side technology look little better than the Stone Age. He manipulated the physics of the universe for goodness' sake. It wasn't as though he should be a stranger to anything that he saw.

Maybe it was the fact that this was his home planet. Radical changes had come to his home planet. Radical changes had come to his home planet the last time he jumped into the future, but he'd gotten so wrapped up in wars and chasing Julianna that he didn't think much about it, just accepted what he saw and moved on. This time around, he had a little more time and room to think about what he was seeing.

Everyone had these little rectangles, little electronic gadgets with bright screens. A good majority of the people he saw walked around staring at these little screens, tapping away, completely lost in whatever they were looking at. So it wasn't books that people were holding in the autonomous cars, but these little gadgets.

It wasn't until he saw a couple people hold the things to their ears and speak into them that he realized they were some kind of high-tech phone. But it was far more than just a phone. A couple of teenagers were busy showing each other their screens. One would show off his screen, and the group would laugh. Then another would show off his screen, and the group would laugh. A third would read something on the screen, and the group would make faces.

Almost all of the advanced alien technology Cassius had interacted with had been purely practical. A space ship needed to work well more than it needed to look good. A weapon needed to reach its target and do its job. He had no doubt that there were more frivolous uses of technology, and he thought he might recall some of it from his time with the Burid; he'd just never used it. For him, he had a task, and he needed a tool to accomplish said task. Looking around, it seemed that while the portable phone had functional capabilities, the majority of its usage was done in frivolity.

He spent a good two hours simply watching people, trying to get a feel for the new surroundings, debating whether he should return to the Cult or track down Rifun. But if Earth had become Engaged, that would be good information to know. There was a quick and easy way to find out whether this was the case, but he was too fascinated by everything around him. He could pick out the rich men, the working men, the poor families; these things never changed. But there seemed to be an equality between the blacks and whites that hadn't been there before. There was no angry shouting, no threats, no fights, and no apparent segregation of any form. A couple of workers from the same place, one white and one black, stood outside the back door of the business, one casually bumming a cigarette off the other.

That was what confounded him the most. How could they be so casual about it? Didn't they understand the blood that had been spilled? Didn't they understand the lives that had been lost? Didn't they know history? Was there no desire for revenge, to make things right? Did they really expect to just...move on? Where was the happy ending?

Cassius watched a police car light up at the intersection, and a guilty red station wagon pulled into the plaza parking lot, parking off to one side, near Cassius, out of the way of the main flow of traffic through the lot. The police car parked behind it and the officer got out. He was white, maybe fifty or so, brown hair, bushy blond mustache, and, if Cassius saw right, blue eyes.

He shifted his stance. He knew a man like that once. He'd been a prisoner in the gaol long ago, the one who'd escaped. The only reason he remembered that was because of the Book and because he thought the man looked ridiculous with his brown head hair, blond facial hair, and blue eyes. Could it be...? No. Maybe. Hardly.

There was no way. Absolutely none.

But the man had escaped. He'd never actually been apprehended. They'd assumed he'd perished over the winter, but what if?

Cassius pretended to be absorbed in something else. He suddenly found himself wishing for one of the little phone gadgets so he might have something to stare at while keeping an ear on everything else. Nevertheless, he deliberately did not look at the officer, but he manipulated Sound to catch the conversation.

"Do you know why I pulled you over?" the officer was asking.

"Not really," the driver of the guilty car, a man, said. His tone said that he knew he was lying.

"You blew a red light." The officer's tone said he knew the man knew that he was lying.

"The guy in front of me had that huge horse trailer! I couldn't see!"

"You want me to write you a ticket for following too closely, too?"

"No."

"Then keep your mouth shut."

"Come on, man, that's a bullshit light. You get, like, two cars through and it changes. Why didn't you pull over the horse trailer?"

"The horse trailer didn't blow the light; you did. Can I see your license, registration, and proof of insurance?"

The driver handed them over and the officer went back to his car. Cassius waited. He could hear the man was grumbling, but couldn't make out anything distinct. Then the officer returned to the car.

"Here's your stuff back, and here's your ticket. This is the offense, the date, and this is where to take it to pay the fine."

"Aw, come on," the man sighed. "Really?"

"If you want, you can write a letter to the court explaining your position."

"How about this? How about I see you in court? What's your name?"

"Captain Forbes."

"Captain ain't your first name."

"Walter."

"Well, Captain Walter Forbes, I guess I will see you in court."

The officer graciously tipped his hat and sent the man on his way.

Walter Forbes. Well, Cassius couldn't exactly remember the name of the prisoner who'd escaped, but Forbes did sound plausible. Of course, this officer also looked well-fed and well-groomed, a radical change from a starving murderer on death's door. And how convenient that he should now be an enforcer of the law. How ironic, even.

Unable to resist the temptation, Cassius found the closest alley and opened a portal to the Wheel.

It was as busy and as bustling as ever. It was almost suffocating, and Cassius was not given to claustrophobia. When he finally got out of the portal room, he discovered that the interior had changed as well.

He saw no signs of the Cult, or the Akarin for that matter. He saw no signs of the Tacagans or any Gentleman Killers, though they had been pretty well stamped out by the time he and Rifun had entered the cave. He saw no signs of anything except the Time industry. The symbolic notation that the Time industry used as its informal universal language included all the standard symbols, including those for the Hands, the Seat, Time Capsules, and Money. Everything was, indeed, exactly as it was before the Cult got involved.

He didn't know whether this was a good or bad sign, but first he had to clarify a few things.

Two portals in, and he caught a glimpse of black. He paused and watched as three black-clad figures swept silently through the marketplace he was in, the intensely thick crowds parting for them as though they were cursed with leprosy. He could not tell from his distance or vantage point whether they were Borelians, but he had a sneaking suspicion they might be. He might have to take a trip to the Judgment Wing later.

His first stop was the Archives. There he was pleased to see that his DNA was still valid, at least for a little while, and he got unrestricted access to everything.

Earth was not Engaged, as he had assumed. It was not Openly Engaged or even Limited Engaged. Earth remained entirely Unengaged. Scientifically Advancing and Unengaged. There were multiple space programs from multiple countries, hence the Scientifically Advancing, but they would not be considered Advanced until they had sustained, long-term, manned programs.

He did learn that racial equality had indeed come about while he was away, and he wasn't sure how to feel about that, so he skipped to the next thing. Plenty of wars, plenty of chaos, nothing really new. He skimmed for the major things, figuring Rifun was going to be the one to do all the detailed research, if it became necessary.

The only thing he was really interested in for details was the roster of Time Agents for Earth. North America was Region Four, and an interactive map showed him that the east coast, including West Virginia, was District Four.

"Well, well, well," Cassius said, grinning.

He couldn't help but laugh. There it was in black and white. Captain of District Four: Owain Fforidd (current alias: Walter Forbes). As soon as Cassius saw the name, he knew. Owain Fforidd, his escaped prisoner from Beaumaris Gaol. A century and a half later, they finally ran into each other again.

Small world, eh, Walter? Cassius thought. *And how you play the hero. Oh no. No, justice is coming for you.*

He laughed again, garnering a bit of attention from those nearby.

"Oh, and what's this?" he wondered, looking at the roster again. "Probationary Timekeepers: Tommen Forbes." He shook his head. "Finally found a woman who would have you. Finally got domesticated and started an honest life. Heh heh, I don't think so. No, I don't think so at all."

He replaced the tablet but was too giddy to move otherwise. Oh, this was just too good. Too perfect. He couldn't believe the odds or his luck. Author or not, he couldn't pass up this opportunity.

His next stop was the Judgment Wing. The hamster secretary called the Hutch remained in charge of things. If it recognized Cassius, it gave no indication of it, though his evasive answers as to why he needed to go back to the prison clearly made it uneasy.

Eventually he did get let in, a two-way stamp ensuring his smooth entry and exit, though it was hardly necessary. Although, while impossible for normal Time Agents to get past the dampening field, it was no picnic for Akari-bearers to try. Possible, but not easy, even for one skilled like Cassius.

He went to the end of the tunnel, passing through both electrical fields, and stood in the room with the three doors. He elected to bypass the prison momentarily, instead opting for the holding cells and courtrooms. The Borelians were brutal, yes, but the administrators and overseers were more likely to be in the offices.

Current fashion apparently dictated that all Grandfathers wore black shrouds, as he walked into a room full of black-clad monks. None of them appeared to recognize him, instead asking the same old boring desk question, why was he here?

"I need to speak to Commander Misik," he told the receiver.

He immediately decided that he didn't like the shrouds because he couldn't see the reaction of the Grandfather. He knew it was a female, but he didn't know her name, toxin, rank, any of it. And he certainly didn't know what she thought of his request until she answered.

"General Misik," she corrected self-righteously, "is indisposed at the moment. And anyway, he's not here."

"Oh, good," Cassius said, turning it around. "Then he won't mind if I help myself to my old post in the asylum. After all, it's been over forty years since I've doled out a good torture on someone. Given all the activity here in the Wheel, I imagine that there have to be a few more prisoners here than when I left."

The Grandfather stood, apparently trying to find words for some kind of objection, but Cassius merely put up a hand. "No, it's all right. I'll see myself down there; I know the way." He paused at the door. "Oh, but if you do happen to see Misik out and about, do tell him that Cassius Hand wants to speak with him at his earliest convenience."

"Cassius Hand?" the woman echoed.

He grinned at her, then turned and left the room.

It wasn't even half an hour before Misik showed up in the asylum, walking in on the torture session which Cassius was just about to begin. His prisoner didn't look any kind of relieved when Misik walked in the door, at least until the now-general ordered everyone out of the room and the prisoner returned to his cell.

Only when the room was empty did Misik speak.

"Finally you show up," he said.

"Honey, I'm home," Cassius retorted smartly.

"Rifun with you?"

"He actually went home. Unfinished business, apparently, but that's no matter. He'll be back soon enough, if he isn't already."

Misik did not look amused.

"When did you get promoted to general?" Cassius asked conversationally.

"Eight years ago," Misik answered.

"And what does being general get you?"

"Full command of all ground forces on Brelix."

"Sounds serious. Given your concern over me and Rifun, I'm guessing you still have an interest in the Cult."

"Great Admiral Makijor has named me head of the Cult army as well."

"Oh, so she did finally get her promotion." Cassius nodded. "Well, if it's as much of an inconvenience as your tone says it is, I'll be happy to take over for you."

Misik's expression was unimpressed. "You were gone for forty years. We were told a few months, a few years, five years at the most. Yet here we are."

"There were complications as we attempted to avoid Julianna's unfortunate fate. Unless, of course, she has been freed since we've been away."

"No."

"Then you will understand our caution."

The general obviously wasn't buying his story. And why not? He sounded more like Rifun than himself. But Cassius wasn't good at politics, and he knew that there would have to be a little politics involved if he wanted to avoid Borelian slavery and live. He would die to avoid enslavement, but he wasn't keen on giving the Borelians that satisfaction.

"Obviously, we haven't been idle since your disappearance," Misik said, changing topic. "I have business to attend to, both in the Wheel and in Ancrath. And you have stated that Rifun is off on his own business presently. Nevertheless, we should have a meeting soon to bring you both up to speed on the state of things. I'm sure you want to return to the ruins, if you haven't already, and ensure that everything is tidied to your liking."

It was a dismissal, almost a threat. Cassius looked around. The room did appear empty, and it was an asylum so it wasn't as though screams and hollers would be anything out of the ordinary, nothing that would really attract the attention of any guards. But, because of the dampening field and the electrical fields, there was little need for more than a few guards, just what was necessary to get prisoners to and from court, maybe break up a fight if they could be bothered.

Cassius decided to let Misik live. He did need to be brought up to speed on the state of things, and that included the disposition of the Borelians as it related to the Cult. Maybe in forty years, Ancrath had decided to abandon their ideas of a slave-run farming colony. Maybe they grew tired of waiting for a fabled Book of Abilities and wrote off the Cult completely, with exception of Isthim and Misik. Or maybe, seeing how this was a plan a couple centuries in the making according to Isthim, they were poised for total control, total takeover, and Cassius' and Rifun's return was the last piece of the puzzle. All they needed were the leaders, the faces of the Cult, and then cinch the noose around their necks.

Now he really did sound like Rifun, he thought as he left the Judgment Wing. Fretting, worrying, conjuring up ghosts as if the visible enemies weren't bad enough.

He left the asylum, the Judgment Wing entirely, paying no mind to any looks he garnered. Did the Time Agents running around here even know who he was? Did they understand the significance of his presence? Did they know anything about what happened forty-three years ago? Or were they entirely oblivious to the danger and the power that lurked among them?

From everything that he could see and discern, everything about the Wheel had reverted back to the Time industry. Harvesters taking Time, selling it to Merchants who sold it to the public, Timekeepers who kept the peace, secretaries who kept the Wheel itself in working order, and the Hands who presided over all of it.

Had anything gone according to plan? Had anything stayed according to plan? He still couldn't figure out where they'd gone wrong in the cave. They couldn't have been in there that long. They just couldn't have.

He again replayed everything in his mind as he made his way to the portal room, unwilling to believe that their little excursion had been forty years, while Julianna's mission had been only a couple years. Maybe something about the distortion itself had changed, but he didn't think so. Of course, he never really paid attention to it other than to be aware of its existence and stay away from it if possible.

With the Wheel returning to the Time industry, he figured that all security measures for the ruins would still be in place, and he dutifully opened a series of portals before finally traveling to the dark reaches of the tunnels that connected to the Caves of Meroian.

When he emerged from the tunnel, he found the ruins exactly as he had left them: in ruins. He could only hope that the shield or Disguise was still in place and things hadn't reverted back to its ancient, dusty form. Looking down, he saw a few shapes moving in and out of the city. So there was a good chance that things were still the same around here.

He made his way to the city, keeping an eye and an ear out for any form of treachery or other foul play. As he approached one of the gates, he found the shield and pushed through effortlessly.

When the Cult had first moved into the Caves of Meroian, it had been nothing but ruins. Ancient, worn structures eaten by moths and worms and populated by ghosts and skeletons. When he and Rifun had left, forty years ago, most parts of the ancient city had been cleaned up, somewhat rebuilt, the dust and spiders swept out, the streets alive with regular activity.

To look upon the city now was to look upon history as it may have been hundreds or thousands of years ago. Structures had not only been saved and cleaned up, but completely restored, even rebuilt from the ground up. Technology replaced some of the lighting features, and various streets were decorated according to the customs of the residents who lived there, but the city was truly alive. It was no longer a project or a camp for mismatched thugs, but a war camp, a city populated by soldiers and even those who could not fight but wished to help the cause. It was an impressive sight to behold, and even Cassius would admit to being impressed and thinking Isthim had done well to manage the Cult in the last forty years.

She was going to be mad, he thought, walking toward the officers building. She hadn't wanted to be left behind for decades or centuries again, being a babysitter. Both he and Rifun had assured her, had promised, that they wouldn't be gone long. A couple years at most. Well, multiply that by twenty and they weren't lying.

He might have expected that word of his return would have spread quickly, but he hadn't quite expected Isthim to be waiting for him in front of the door to his chambers.

Her expression confirmed his suspicions that she wasn't happy.

"I understand that Earth and Brelix have different lengths of day and year," she began. "I understand that both are different from Sadurnon, and all are different from what the Wheel and the Time industry considers a Base Day or a Base Year. But perhaps you can explain where in the universe you have discovered that two years and forty years are the same amount of time." She went on before he could speak. "At the very least, you should tell me that you have something to show for your efforts and long absence and produce the Book of Abilities."

Cassius made a sound, opened his mouth, and finally said, "No."

Isthim blinked, and he didn't miss how her whole body went rigid. "What do you mean, no? No, you're not going to produce it, or no, you don't have it?"

"It wasn't in the cave. Just as Julianna said."

For a long moment, Isthim just stared at him. Only a sixth sense alerted him to her sudden attack, the Imprint that attempted to distract him while a Band hid her until the last moment when she came at him. He dodged the blow and grabbed hold of her Band, pulling himself inside and using Time Anchors to keep them together.

She struck at him, but he grabbed her arms, covered by her sleeves, and tried to hold her. With a strong, snappy move, she wrenched her arms free and used Force to blow them apart. Cassius stumbled back, tried to regain his balance, while Isthim landed cleanly and came at him again.

He wasn't entirely certain whether her aim was to actually kill him or simply vent a sudden explosion of frustration, but given that she remained pink instead of turning a somewhat safer orange, he guessed that even if she didn't mean to kill him, his death would be incidental anyway.

This time he was more prepared for her, blocking her blows and getting in a couple of his own. This time when he caught her wrist, he used a tiny bit of Force to jar her concentration and Gravity to keep her in place. From there it was simple enough to maneuver her so her back was against the wall. He felt himself grow hard and he made sure she knew it, too, pinning her hips with his.

"General Misik mentioned that you finally got your Great Admiral promotion," he said lowly. "Somehow, this doesn't strike me as acceptable conduct for one of Brelix's most prestigious military commanders."

She heaved a sigh, still glaring at him, but did not deny it. He pressed his hips harder against hers for just a moment.

"I think the more appropriate course of action would be to have a meeting so we can actually talk about things and explain what happened," he told her.

"You want a meeting?" she growled. "Did you turn into Rifun in that cave?"

"Hardly. Did you turn into me while I was gone?"

Another sigh, the continuing glare, but she forced her body to relax.

"Fine," she said at last. "Given that you know of Misik's promotion as well, I'm assuming you spoke to him first. Word will spread. We will have a meeting and figure out our next course of action."

"Perfect."

Cassius let her go and stepped back. She released the Band and looked around.

"Where is Rifun?"

"He had to run home to take care of some business."

"So he could be a while."

"Given his track record, he could be a long while."

She did not look pleased, and Cassius didn't blame her.

"Well then, I suppose that until he returns, we will have to make up for lost time. A day for you has been forty years for me, and few males even feel adequate enough to attempt to approach a female Great Admiral."

Initially Cassius wasn't sure what she was talking about, but when he understood, he was ready. Her disposition was difficult to read, whether this was based purely on biological need, or if she truly wanted him. But, when he gave it two seconds of thought, he decided it didn't matter.

Fianarantsoa, 2013

Communism had been overthrown in the mid-nineties, Rifun learned. Since then, modern Westernization had moved into the cities. It was quite prevalent in Antananarivo, but Fianarantsoa had always been more eager to embrace outside ideas and ideals.

He'd gone to the old farmhouse first. Volana and Elisette were long dead, Jaona, Sambatra, and their wives more recently so. Faliarivo had inherited the farm.

The lanky, athletic teenager had done a lot of growing up. He had a wife—whom he'd wooed via the savika tournaments—and five children, and appeared to be a rather comfortable fifty-something year old cattle rancher who also produced rice, vanilla, and wine grapes on the side. When he'd first opened the door, Rifun thought the poor man was going to collapse; he'd gone white, as though he'd seen a ghost. Rifun could understand his feelings. He wasn't sure what to make of Fan Andilan standing on his doorstep, looking exactly as he had the day he had left forty-three years prior.

Rifun hadn't even bothered to try and invent a new identity for himself, instead simply asking to see Lalao.

"She lives in Fianar now," Faliarivo told him. "She moved there with her husband some twenty years ago or so."

So she had married. Likely had children. Rifun could not blame her. He could afford to wait forty years for someone; he had the years in his life to spare. She did not. But how long had she waited?

He got the address and made his way to Fianar, ignoring the carts, cars, and public transport. He did not marvel at the state of the city, praise or lament its progress over the years. His thoughts remained fixed on finding Lalao.

Her husband had died the previous year, Faliarivo had told him, and she was not in the best health either, although she denied it. Her older brothers were also gone now, though they died fighting the Communists; all she had left close by were her three sons.

Business was booming and traffic was terrible, but Rifun found the street he needed. It was part of the old city that had been heavily damaged during the Uprising. There had been some restoration done during the honeymoon period after independence, but it was largely abandoned during communism. Any work that had been done during that time had simply been demolition and only the promise of new, better housing.

Only recently had that promise come to fruition as dainty, townhouse-type homes lined a freshly-paved street, each house a different color. A few cars were parked on either side, narrowing the road considerably by themselves but dangerously so if two cars happened to be directly across from each other. Lizards were everywhere, sunning themselves on the warm sidewalk, and they barely moved as Rifun walked by.

He came to a particular townhouse, this one painted a rather bright, bold, sunny yellow. The townhouse to the left was a startling powder blue, and the one to the right was an eye-grabbing red. A tabby cat lay on the stone step outside the red townhouse. As Rifun knocked on the left door of the yellow house, it looked up, glanced at him, yawned, stretched, and resituated itself.

He heard some movement inside, and a moment later the door opened.

It was a young man, early twenties, bearing distinct Betsileo features.

"Does Lalao—" Dammit, he forgot to get her married name. "—Andilan live here? Just tell her it's Rivotra."

The man blinked. "She hasn't been an Andilan in almost forty years." His expression grew suspicious. "Let me see if she's up to it."

Rifun didn't like the sound of that, about her health, but he politely agreed to remain on the porch. It was true that Rivotra was a Malagasy word, but hardly a common, or even uncommon, name, and it would be strange to tell someone that the wind had come calling.

But she had waited, at least for a little while. A few years. She had waited for him. She had counted on him. And he'd left her for forty years.

The door opened again and the young man motioned him in.

"Back bedroom," he said. "I don't know who you are, but she lit up when she heard 'Rivotra.'"

The young man didn't know it, but that put Rifun's mind much at ease, and he found the back bedroom with little issue.

If he had been afraid to find Lalao completely bedridden, even upon her deathbed, when he arrived, his fears were alleviated when he saw her.

She was older, yes. By now she would be in her late sixties or early seventies. Her hair had begun to turn gray, and her skin was not as tight and youthful as it was. She bore the weight of childbearing and child rearing and the stress of years of marriage and the recent end of that marriage. But she remained beautifully and faithfully Lalao.

She sat at a large table a few feet from her bed, hunched over a quilt, busy picking up stray needles and either putting them in a tin or sticking them in a pin cushion. He gently knocked on the open door. When she looked up and smiled, all the years melted away.

Well, they only melted away in metaphor. As she went to stand, she struggled, and he was right there by her side to help her up. Her arms went around him, and he hugged her as tight as he dared. When she let him go, he helped her back into her chair, and he sat on the end of the bed.

"I knew you would come back," she said. "I always knew."

"And you got married anyway," he teased. He immediately regretted the comment, and sputtered an apology. "No, that wasn't fair. I'm sorry. Faliarivo told me that your husband passed away last year."

Lalao nodded sadly. "Yes. We had thirty-eight wonderful years." She sighed. "I did wait for you. For a while. I thought to myself, a year, maybe two. He'll be back."

"I had every intention," Rifun offered lamely.

"Oh..." She waved a hand. "Evil does not care about our petty plans. And I knew, deep down, that you were doing great work, even if you doubted yourself. I won't say that I never felt a bit of anger toward you, for not returning when it was wanted or convenient, or for taking me and then running off into the night, even if I was the one who told you to go. Sometimes I wondered if you had perished, if evil had overcome you, or, more romantically, if you had sacrificed yourself so that evil would not prevail. And it made me love you more. For a long time, I simply held onto that love, no matter what I was going through. It was like my little secret."

"I'm guessing a certain young man changed that."

"Young man? Please, Rivotra, I was thirty-two when I met my husband, and he was thirty-five. But you are right. At first it was fun, but eventually I got to a point where I had to choose whether I was going to wait for you, or move on with my life. I told him about you, of course."

Rifun raised a brow. "How much did you tell him?"

Lalao got a familiar Andilan smirk on her face. "I only told him that you had been my first true love and that we'd been together. When he asked why you'd left, I told him that you had been called away by the spirits to fulfill another destiny."

"And the rest of the family?"

"I told them that you had gone back to the shrine to pray and had a vision that called you away immediately. Some protested, some wanted to know where, but I didn't know. You hadn't told me anything other than you would be back as soon as you could."

He sighed. "I really did try. I intended only a year, maybe two. Certainly no more than five. Even five sounded preposterous. And here it is, forty years later."

"You did what the spirits called you to do."

He almost told her that no, he hadn't. He hadn't accomplished anything. But how did he explain that he'd been gone all of a day, sneaking around some dark cave, while years and decades passed out here? In the end, he decided to keep his mouth shut and let her believe him the hero. She was sixty- or seventy-something and in reportedly poor health. Let her have the fond memories.

"What was your husband's name?" he asked instead.

Her expression turned thoughtful, if grim. "His name was Jaona, like my uncle Jaona. He was a professor at the university."

"During communism?"

"Oh, he walked a fine line. He knew it, and he made sure I knew it. Some of the things he had to say and teach, some of the lessons he had to give, some of the lessons he wasn't supposed to give but sneaked in anyway. There were some sleepless nights, when either one of us could have been arrested because of something he'd said in class that day." She grinned and chuckled humorlessly. "I think my love for you was what attracted me to him."

"What do you mean?"

"I always envisioned you fighting evil, commanding the evil spirits to dance at will and destroying them with only a word. With Jaona being a professor under the communists, it seemed as though he did the same thing, except I could talk to him and hug him, and he came home at night. So I guess I have you to thank for my getting married."

"You're welcome, I think."

"After the fall of communism, Jaona, who was known to be no lover of the communists, was made dean of the university."

"Congratulations."

"Yes, life changed very rapidly for us. Suddenly we went from the uncertainty of our days and nights to relative comfort and ease. We no longer had to worry about our boys but could let them run and speak freely and give them the life we never had." She let out a breath and her gaze grew distant. "Jaona would have worked until the day he died, but..." She shook her head. "By the time he was diagnosed with cancer, it was too late to do anything about it. We had money, so we looked for the best doctors, the leading surgeons from a dozen countries. Only one agreed to even look at him. So we spent some time in Germany. He underwent so many tests and tried so many different drugs. It bought him a little time, but it only made him miserable. He decided that it was no way to live, and he confronted the doctor. He said either attempt the surgery, or he was going to stop all treatments and all medication and return home to die in his own bed."

Rifun could only listen sympathetically.

"The doctor removed as much of the tumor as he could, but to go farther would be to risk hemorrhage or permanent disability. And at his age, there was no significant benefit or deficit to either option. So we packed up our things and returned home. Jaona lived another three weeks before his brain hemorrhaged anyway."

"I'm so sorry."

Lalao sighed. "We had a good life." She shrugged. "Of course, I'm not in much better shape."

"You have cancer?"

She nodded. "Diagnosed not even a month after his death."

"What are you doing for it?"

She shook her head. "Not much. Prescription drugs, some home remedies. But mostly I'm just biding my time." She went on before he could protest. "It's my life, and I am of sound mind. Like I had to tell my boys, respect my decision. I'm an old woman who's lived a good, long life, raised a family I'm proud of. I spent too many years under the threat of communists who would gladly kill me for not falling in line, so if this is how I choose to go, this is how I'm going to go!"

Rifun couldn't help but laugh. "Yes, ma'am."

He spent the better part of the afternoon talking to her, about her life, her husband, her marriage, her kids, everything that had happened since he'd left that fateful evening. But as the day wore on and the sun started going down, he could see the growing fatigue.

Her youngest son, Tomas, named for her brother who had been killed by communists, made dinner and got Lalao her pills to go with it. Rifun stayed for dinner, but got the sense that she would be going to bed soon after.

"Thank you so much for coming," Lalao told him, putting her hand on his as he stood from the table. She had not the strength to see him to the door, and he knelt in front of her.

"I told you I would come back," he said. "And I meant it."

She smiled, but it was sad. "I don't think we'll be seeing each other again. If that's the case, I have something for you." She motioned for her son. "Tomas, go in my bedroom. In the closet, in my big chest. Open it. At the bottom on the left side is a smaller chest. Bring it here."

Her son hurried off to fulfill her request.

"He's a good boy," she said, not for the first time that day. "I'm just sorry I won't be around to see the grandchildren he'll give me."

"I'm sure they'll be as wonderful as the rest of them," Rifun told her.

"Oh, I'm sure they will be, too. Ah, that's it." Tomas appeared and handed her the box. "Thank you, Tomas."

It was bigger than a sheet of paper and about six inches deep. Lalao set it on the table before her and opened it up to reveal stacks of yellowed papers and old photos.

"You weren't around when your mother died," she said, carefully picking up each paper and setting it aside. "You didn't take much with you, either, when you left home. After she died and chose to be buried at the family tomb in Fianar, your stepfather, Vala, shipped all her things to the farm. Well, when the French took over, they destroyed a lot of things, but some things they did save, for whatever reason. My suspicion is, the wife got to them and, seeing that these were heirlooms and pieces of family history, wanted to rescue them."

Lalao handed Rifun an envelope. "When my father, your cousin, Volana, took possession of the farm again, my mother, Elisette, found a lot of these old papers and photos hidden in the barn. After they died and we all went through their things, I offered to take them."

Rifun opened the envelope and brought out several photos as well as an official document.

"This one is your mother when she was about eight years old," Lalao said, taking one of the pictures. "She had just started school, under tutelage of the Jesuits." She took another picture. "And this one is when she turned sixteen. She went up to Tana with a bunch of her friends."

The third picture made Rifun's heart stop. It was his mother, sitting up in bed, looking a bit disheveled as she held a newborn baby. But the newborn baby had light skin.

"And this one is right after you were born. When she finally got you to stop 'wailing like the wind' like it says on the back."

Rifun turned the picture over. There, in black ink, "Lalao with newborn son. He wouldn't stop wailing like the wind, so she named him Rivotra."

"From what I understand, your grandmother wrote that."

Slowly, deliberately, he set the pictures aside and unfolded the paper. It was his official birth certificate, issued by the French. Everything was in French, and his legal name was listed as Rifun Felix Ndolo. But there, in big, bold, black marker, in his mother's handwriting, right across the top of the page, "Rivotra Felix Andilan."

He took a breath and carefully put everything back in the envelope, determined to let no one know of its existence.

"Why didn't Elisette give this to me years ago?" he asked.

"She probably forgot she had it. There was a lot to go through in the aftermath of the war and the Uprising, and heirlooms had to take second place to reestablishing the farm and feeding a family. This was tucked in the back of her closet, just like it was in the bottom of mine."

He could think of no words to say as he embraced her.

"I'm sorry I didn't come back," he said, letting her go and settling for taking her weathered hands in his. "I'm sorry I didn't stay."

Her expression was gentle. "Oh, my dear Rivotra. You did exactly what you were supposed to do. Exactly what you were meant to do. And if you want to know something, I don't think you're done quite yet. I think there is more to be done. Something only you can do. And then you can find rest and happiness."

He didn't know how to respond, but as he held her hands, he Banded, stopping time, and Felt her. A year with cancer had ravaged her body, and he could see that she wouldn't have much time left, maybe a few months. Except she had someone who not only cared deeply for her, but could actually do something about it.

It took several hours, but once he got going, he couldn't stop. He found every cancerous cell in her body and destroyed it. But doing that alone would cause toxic buildup in her body, and she would be dead of renal failure within days. So rather than let the dead toxins linger where they could not stay and were not wanted, he turned them into nutrients for her body, performing true alchemy to rearrange the molecular and even atomic structure of the old cancer cells. Now, instead of killing her body, they would restore it, and she would have many good years left in her life.

The effort of the alchemy alone made him dizzy and even nauseous, and still he was holding his Fast Band. He paused and focused on himself for a short span, tried to collect himself so he would not suddenly appear winded and ill once he dropped the Band.

He studied her face. A few more lines and wrinkles, a few more spots, but the eyes were still hers, and he was transported back to that night—hardly a day for him, but forty years for her—when they gazed into each other's eyes, when they crossed that relational line and didn't look back. These were those same eyes, and he loved her still.

He just wished he could have spent the last forty years with her instead of a dark cave rooting around in old bones.

Finally he dropped the Band. If she noticed any change in her body, she did not show it beyond a small gasp and a shift in her seat.

"Mom, you're tired," Tomas said gently. "Do you want to watch some TV or work on your quilt or maybe just go to bed?"

She hesitated. He could see that she knew something had changed, but she didn't know how to articulate it.

Rifun stood, but bent over to kiss her on the cheek, still holding her hands. "Maybe I'll see you again soon."

She smiled. "I would like that very much."

Her words were kind, but her tone was hollow, as if she said them only to be polite. Well, maybe when she went to her doctor next and found that she was cancer free, then she would have a different attitude.

Besides, Rifun had no plans to return to that infernal cave. He didn't need to come and stay for weeks at a time, but maybe they could have lunch together. He could relieve her son for an afternoon, give him a break.

To her son's dismay and surprise, Lalao was able to get up and see him to the door where he hugged her and again kissed her on the cheek, promising to return. He also shook Tomas' hand.

"Your mother is a remarkable woman," Rifun told him seriously. "Your father was lucky to have her."

Tomas didn't seem to know how to respond, but he politely wished Rifun good day and closed the door once he'd gotten down the steps.

He could feel the envelope in his pocket as surely as he could feel a thirty pound weight. The face of his mother had faded some from his memory over the years, except in moments where a memory appeared as a stark relief. But the photos brought everything back, made everything real again, as if he could almost see them.

He could not allow Cassius or Isthim to know of the existence of the envelope under any circumstances. Absolutely none. He could already conjure up a thousand ways to use those photos as leverage. No. He had to do as had been done for seventy years. Bury them in the bottom of his closet, don't bring them out until Cassius and Isthim were dead.

He headed back to Fianar, found an alley, and opened a portal back to the cave. After the alchemy he'd just done, in addition to the portals and the Time Trap and everything else, he would admit to being a tad worried about the portal collapsing and him joining Julianna in the Land In-Between. As it was, he had to sit down for a minute to rest and collect himself. His head hurt, his eyes hurt, and he was emotionally drained.

He may have slept. He wasn't sure. Between the time change from the Trap and the different timezones and spending time with Lalao, he barely knew what day it was, or even where the sun was supposed to be.

When he did finally come back to full consciousness, it was somewhere around midday. He stood, stretched, stretched again, and looked around.

Cassius was nowhere to be seen, but that was to be expected. He'd probably gone to the Wheel or back to the ruins and was impatiently waiting for Rifun to return.

Rifun might have gone, but he wanted to explore a little, get a feel for the new world forty years later, maybe run into Julianna at the library again. They hadn't exactly made plans on when and how they were going to meet after they got out of the cave, but there was still that forty years bit that they hadn't really planned for at all.

The wilderness around the cave had been tamed into something of a community park, trails cut through the trees and an open space providing a welcome area for visitors. From the main pavilion, Rifun could see the city of

Charleston, bright and gleaming in the spring sunshine. A spring breeze buffeted him in the face, reminding him that he was not in tropical Madagascar anymore.

He started walking. Plenty of cars passed him on the road, but none stopped for him. That was fine. He was used to walking. It was good exercise, and it helped to organize his thoughts, process recent events.

He noted the changes in architecture first, and he studied the buildings from afar as he made his way ever closer to the city.

Fianar had enthusiastically embraced Western ideas after the fall of communism, and their new construction was all very modern, but still limited by the resources of a developing nation. Buildings were sometimes slow to be completed, and sometimes concessions had to be made. Sometimes the people wanted the old style of architecture; the communists had taken away what they claimed to have preserved, and now it had to be restored. Other people, while condemning communism, also condemned Westernism. Let the Malagasy return to their roots, their heritage. Let the *razana* breathe again and don't stifle it with Western innovation and Western problems.

Charleston did not appear to have this kind of conflict. Old buildings might be restored, and the downtown shopping district may have had old roots, but even from this, Rifun saw very little identity. He saw plenty of ethnic restaurants and a few museums, but what made this place different from any other place? The colors of the rainbow had blended so much that there was nothing distinct. He recalled the fear and the culture shock that had come from his departure from Madagascar and his time in France. New people, new customs, new identity. Even London had been a bit jarring. Here, he felt nothing. Was the Western world the same the world around?

Perhaps he was so engulfed by the forest, he couldn't see the trees. Or this was what he told himself, unwilling to accept that the whole world had gone gray while he'd been away. Fianar was different from Charleston. Fianar had tropical weather, tropical trees, lizards running every which way, and prestigious universities. At the same time, the townhouses he passed in a suburban neighborhood, while less bold in their choice of paint, looked very much like the ones on the street where Lalao lived.

This was not to say he was overlooked. He knew his clothes were a bit out of date; he hadn't bothered catching up on the latest fashions while in Fianar. But in Charleston, his clothes were a tad bit out of culture as well. That was fine, he decided. He would be the color amid the gray. If anyone had a problem with him walking the streets, well, he wasn't black and he wasn't white, and both appeared to be about their business freely.

The one thing he found most curious about this new age, however, something he saw in both Fianar and Charleston, was the ubiquity of little, pocket-sized tablets. They appeared a bit like the Glass tablets found in the Archives in the Wheel, except they were small, able to fit in a pocket, not clear, and virtually everyone seemed to have one. People looked at the screens while smoking, while sitting, even while walking, looking up every so often in order to correct one's course. Hell, people seemed to be looking at them even while behind the wheel of a vehicle, which seemed exceptionally dangerous. People, especially young people, stood around in groups, not saying a word to each other but staring at the screens, oblivious to the world around them.

Just from observation, Rifun concluded that these things were not limited only to static, librarian information, like the tablets were. Rather, they were multifunctional. The primary function seemed to be communication, as everyone around him called the things phones, yet almost no one did any talking. He heard mentions of "texting" which he concluded was sending electronic text from one phone to another.

Another function of these devices included portable music, if that's what it could be called. There seemed to be some attempt at a beat, but he knew children who could rap a better drumbeat, toddlers, even. And were those supposed to be lyrics? Rifun had spent time in Britain, where language was generally much looser, but even they would have balked at what was being said. And those were just the words he understood; there was plenty that left him wondering if the rest was even supposed to be words, or if it was even English. People around him seemed to be speaking English, but maybe he'd been too quick to assume.

They also seemed to function as cameras, though Rifun couldn't see where the film was placed, nor could he imagine that there were many photographs to be taken because the devices were so slim. And was there a camera on both sides? He watched as a group of girls—dressed in clothing that might have made them prostitutes forty years ago—smiled at the devices from both sides.

He suspected that these "phone" devices did more, judging by the way they captured the attention of everyone using them. It seemed to be very convenient, having multiple devices combined into a single portable unit, but he could also see how it might be very time-consuming, even dangerous. Just watching someone try to navigate a parking lot and tap the screen of their device was a bit like getting distracted at a savika tournament and putting yourself at risk of being gored, to say nothing of the safety of parking lot pedestrians.

He made his way through the city to the public library. Unlike before, other than a brief glance to acknowledge the presence of a newcomer, there was no hostility toward him. No one stared, no one glared, no one whispered. He knew that civil rights had been won in the United States, even back in the sixties, before he left, but had they really, finally reached a state of racial harmony?

"Can I help you?" the librarian behind the desk inquired.

She had a screen on her desk, with another one beside an empty chair a few feet away.

"Um, I need to find a computer," he said awkwardly.

"Sure. Are you just looking for a book, or do you need to use the Internet?"

"Internet?"

Apparently his question was mistaken for an answer as the librarian gave him directions to a computer lab, telling him that the lab attendant could assist him.

The only laboratory Rifun had ever dealt with had been science laboratories at the university. Nevertheless, trying not to seem to be an outsider, he thanked her and went on his way, following her directions to the "computer lab."

He got distracted more than once by books as he walked by them. The covers were glossy, the bindings perfect, the color photographs simply exquisite. Spying a plush couch pushed against a wall, Rifun grabbed a stack of books and sat down to read. The topics ranged from architecture to archaeology to history to animal husbandry to politics to religion. These last two topics helped to shape some of his understanding of current events and the state of things in the world.

In a word: not good. Not that things were ever "good" among the affairs of humanity, but as he followed the rabbit trail into modern military and warfare, there seemed to be a new layer of "not good" heaped on top of these current affairs.

It was a good three hours before he peeled himself away from the books and went looking for the computer lab, whose importance felt like so long ago. Considering, however, that there were numerous mentions of the "Internet" and "cybersecurity" in multiple books across all topics, he decided it might be useful to know what this novelty actually was. He'd read plenty about it, knew well how it worked, from a theoretical standpoint. He knew what electronic mail, or "e-mail," was. He understood search engines and internet protocol and domains. He couldn't make heads or tails of the "programming languages" but he knew that they were what made the websites work. But it was all words on a page at this point; he had yet to actually utilize this marvel.

Time to figure it out, he mused, opening the door to the computer lab.

It had been an absolute, unprecedented novelty that the university in Fianar had had not one, but two computers. And they had been big and bulky, a bit inconvenient, and severely limited in their use. How they acquired them had been a matter of some debate and no conclusions. Nevertheless, it had earned them not a little attention, that a "third-world" communist country was on the cutting edge of technology and had computers in their universities.

They may as well have been boasting about can openers, Rifun thought, looking around the room. Not one. Not two. Not even five. But fifteen computers. Or that was what he assumed they were. A large table huddled in the center of the room, six flat screens resting on top. Watching the people who occupied certain spaces, he saw that there were rolling shelves under the desk that hid a keyboard and the mouse. The tower was tucked away in another compartment. He knew these things only by association, what he'd read in the books.

"Can I help you, sir?" someone asked.

On one side of the room was a row of tables where seven more computers sat, a few of them occupied. On the other side of the room was a desk with a computer and an attendant.

"I...need to use a computer," Rifun answered awkwardly.

"Sure, you can pick any one you want. Login information is taped to the screen."

He picked a computer in the corner. Before him was a wall, to his left an empty chair, and to his right a window with a view of the street.

Someone in the room was busy typing away on a keyboard, their speed most impressive. These people had probably grown up with computers in some fashion. He'd only ever seen one once before in his life, and he hadn't even done anything to it; Julianna had done everything. By that token, even she knew more about computers than he did.

Suddenly Rifun felt very old. He knew how to wire a telegram, how to use old radios, how to send and receive Morse code. Did these people even know what Morse code was? The average age in the room seemed to be about twenty, maybe twenty-five.

He was able to log in without any issues, which helped to relieve some of his anxiety, but then he was presented with a whole network of navigation that he was entirely unfamiliar with.

He tried Banding, but for all his skill as an Akari-bearer, a Builder, even just a Warden Timekeeper, he couldn't make the Band stick to the computer. It was like trying to use a fine sieve to hold water. After multiple unsuccessful attempts, he gave up. No one seemed to be paying attention to him anyway. He could fumble along just fine. Mostly he was just here to see if Julianna might be around. But if computers could no longer be Banded, did that mean she could no longer manipulate them?

He opened a web browser, automatically being directed to a search engine. According to everything he'd read, all he had to do was press the keys on the keyboard, type in whatever it was he was looking for, and it would show him.

"News" proved to be too broad of a search term, and he found himself terribly overwhelmed with literally thousands of different news outlets ranging from world news to local news in other countries.

After about an hour, he was able to more confidently use the Internet, and he brought himself more up to speed on the affairs of the world. A lot had changed in forty years, some for the better and some not so much. But he now knew the latest street gossip people might be talking about, the latest trends among the younger generation, the rise of social media, and he learned all about the marvel that was the smartphone.

It was a lot to absorb, and pretty soon there was an announcement over the PA system that the library would be closing in one hour. Rifun wished he could Band so he could sit and read and learn for at least another day or so.

He decided that the reason he could not Band the computer was because it was no longer a truly self-contained unit. There were physical pieces to it, but it was so interconnected to the other computers in the building and the Internet itself that it couldn't be singled out so easily. He could probably physically do it, in the same way that he could Band someone's nervous system, prevent it from sending signals to the rest of the body, but it would, like paralysis, cut the function of that computer, that single unit, down to only the basic functions contained within the physical pieces which would not help him in his quest for knowledge. The modern computer was more than the sum of its parts, but only because of the power of the Internet, and it had to stay connected.

The PA system chirped again, this time telling patrons that the library was closing in half an hour, please finish up their business and proceed to the front desk to check out their items. The attendant in the computer lab announced that the lab closed fifteen minutes early, so be prepared and please log off as soon as possible.

Rifun finished the article he was currently reading, then took the out, logged off, and left the computer lab feeling a little more oriented to the present day.

He passed by a large rack of newspapers and couldn't help but stop and take a look. At least these he could Band and read.

His curiosity over the state of race relations in the United States had been thoroughly shocked to learn that there was a black president. Although opinions over him were hotly divided, it made him feel a little better about walking down the street. If a black man could be elected president, then a black man on the street could do whatever a white man could. Seeing how Rifun wasn't really either one, he felt even better about it; at least his mixed parentage wouldn't be anything out of the ordinary.

He read world news. He read political news. He read trending and entertainment news. He read trivial and humorous news. He read local news. Although much of it he already knew from looking on the Internet, there was comfort in the black and white, the feel of ink and paper in his hands.

Julianna had not shown up at all, either to his computer or to mess with the lights to get his attention. He dropped the Band and finished his article just as the PA announced that the library was closing in fifteen minutes, all patrons please get in line at the front desk to check out.

Rifun had no books to check out, but that was fine. He left the library, moderately surprised to see the sun was almost down. Sure, he'd sat by the window all afternoon, but it still shocked him just a little.

He was caught up on the ways of the world and had seen and heard nothing from Julianna. He wasn't sure how worried he should be about that. Well, forty years, what did he expect her to do, sit outside the cave all day every day? Sit at the library all day every day? Was there any way that he could contact her? Or was it just a waiting game, hope to cross paths at some point?

Whatever the case, it seemed the only thing left to do was return to the ruins, except he wasn't quite ready for that yet. Maybe he would do that in the morning once he'd slept everything off. This was still only his first day in the twenty-first century after all.

He meandered a bit around town, watching the night life. It wasn't a bad night, a little cloudy, a little breezy, but with the promise of warmer weather to come. On the nicer side of town, teenagers went out to movies, young adults went to bars, and every so often there was a drug deal in the shadows.

The more things change, the more things stay the same, Rifun thought, rather comforted by the thought.

There were several plazas and strip malls in his travels. Some were closing up for the night and others were coming alive.

One store in particular, Rifun was ready to pass by, until he caught a glimpse of one of the workers. He stopped for a moment and waited, just to be sure.

The store was a bakery called Bakery na hÉireann. The sign on the door indicated that they were closing in the next ten minutes. Activity within the store suggested as much as pans were removed from the case and a bucket of map water sat in the middle of the dining room. A worker came from the kitchen to the front counter.

Could it be? No. It definitely looked like— Far too coincidental. But if there was a chance— What were the odds?

Yes. It was. A second worker came up front, and he looked damn near identical to the first.

It was none other than Micaiah Durvin and his twin brother Micah.

What were the odds? Any other person might have called it impossible, or nearly so. Rifun called it providence. But why were they here?

Rifun passed by the store quickly, looked around, then donned a Disguise as an average white male with brown hair and green eyes. After forty years, they wouldn't be expecting him, would they?

He walked into the store.

"Oh, hi," the cleanshaven twin, Micah, greeted, sounding a bit harried and a little disappointed that a customer just walked in.

"Is there anything left?" Rifun asked.

"Um...just this pan of cookies and—"

He was cut off by a sudden clatter of metal objects in the kitchen followed by a curse.

"We talked about this, Tommen," Micaiah said in the back. "Stop cursing when there are customers in the dining room. It's unprofessional and not very chivalrous besides."

"Because that's stopped you when you're in the office," came an accented retort.

"Don't talk back to me."

"One of your kids?" Rifun inquired politely.

"Oh, no. He works here, just started high school," Micah answered. "You know kids."

"Oh, I thought maybe... the accent and all."

Micah grinned and shook his head. "No, actually he's not Irish."

"But he thinks he is, apparently."

"No, the accent's real, but he's from Wales. Well, his family is. He was born here, but, you know, picked up the accent from his parents."

Rifun nodded thoughtfully. "I see. And what did your brother call him? Chivalrous?"

Micah grinned shyly, face turning bright red. "Yeah, it's sort of a nickname. The Chivalrous Welshman. The kids at school use it to make fun of him. We're trying to make it something positive and teach him a bit about chivalry."

"Well, your brother is right that cursing isn't very professional. Nor, I suppose, is it especially chivalrous. But, you know, I spent several years in London."

Micah laughed. "So one little curse is pretty small potatoes. Aye, I know it well."

"Funny how morals can be so different when you're only separated by an ocean," Rifun added.

"Aye, that they can. So, did you want the cookies? We're just about to lock up."

"Ah..."

Rifun didn't have any money. Not that it would matter, since he could Band and take what he needed, but he really wasn't interested in the cookies. In the space it took him to consider this, Micah had already bagged them up and was busy stuffing napkins in the bag.

"Don't tell my brother, but I'll just give them to you and lock up behind you."

He thrust the bag of cookies—chocolate chip, he thought—into Rifun's hands, then moved around the counter. Rifun took the hint, and the out, and went to the door.

"Thanks for the cookies," he said, opening the door and hearing the jingle of the bell overhead.

"No problem," Micah told him amiably. "As long as you promise to come back."

He winked and locked the door behind Rifun, turning the open sign and walking away.

Rifun left the store, dropping his Disguise as soon as he could and digging out a cookie.

Micaiah and Micah in the same city as the cave which no longer held the Book of Abilities. That was the first inexplicable coincidence. He gnawed on the cookie. But then there was the matter of there being a teenager in the same store whom they had called the Chivalrous Welshman. When he'd read the Authored Books in the Akarin Archives, there had been the promise of an as-yet unreleased series called *The Chivalrous Welshman*. Now what were the odds of that? What had Micaiah called the kid? Tommen? Was Tommen also an Akari-bearer? A Time Agent at the very least?

Any fatigue and uncertainty quickly melted away, and Rifun made a trip to the Wheel. Everything appeared to have returned to the Time industry, and no one seemed to know who he was as he went to the Archives completely unhindered. He would think about that later. First he had to figure out this mystery.

It wasn't hard to find the roster of Time Agents, organized by universal coordinates: Quadrant, Parsec, Sector, System, Planet, Region, and District.

Well, fancy that. Tommen Teo Forbes, probationary Timekeeper. And, what do you know, there was also a Walter Forbes listed as the Captain of Region Four, District Four. His registered name was Owain Fforidd, but his current alias was Walter Forbes.

Rifun shifted his stance. The plaque near the Time Trap cave had said that the cave was called Forbes Cave, dedicated to Tommen Forbes, a small child who had vanished into the cave a century and a half prior.

Could it be? By now, the coincidences had ceased to be coincidental and were now fully in the realm of divine providence. Only the Author could have devised this, bringing everyone together at this place at this time.

Lalao was right. There was more that he had to do, and only he could do it. Somehow, this would lead to his salvation, when he would finally be free of this burden and he would finally find everything he had ever wanted. It made him giddy and excited and dizzy and terrified all at the same time. Everything was coming together as he never could have imagined. And with any luck, it would also end with the slaying of the dragon spirit and freedom from the threat of the Borelians, too. Oh, this was absolutely brilliant. He loved it.

He returned to the ruins, briefly stunned at how, in forty years, it had shed the last traces of its ruinous appearance and now stood as a tall, proud, lively city. It lifted his mood even more until he thought his soul might spontaneously ascend. But he had more to do among the realm of mortal men. Only then would his mission be accomplished.

His intent was to go to the officers building and call a meeting, but he was intercepted on the street by Isthim.

"Where have you been?" she demanded.

"Is there some matter of urgency that requires my attention?" he wondered. Slowly he recalled that there were still other politics at play, and some allies might not have enjoyed being abandoned for forty years, left to be reabsorbed into the corrupt Time industry.

"You've been gone for forty years, and the next elections in the Wheel are less than a year away. We have work to do if we want to take over and make some of our allies happy," Isthim informed him.

"Well then, why not call a meeting? Providence has been most kind to me today, and I think we will have more answers and more options than we know what to do with."

She didn't look convinced, but she seemed satisfied that he was ready to get rolling.

All the important people in one place at one time, the Book of Abilities within reach, the elections less than a year away. Things were about the get very exciting very fast. It was a nice change of pace, he thought as he hurried to the officers building and set the cookies in the middle of the table in the meeting room.

Isthim and Cassius joined him in only a few minutes.

"What's this?" Cassius demanded, eyeing the bag suspiciously.

"Cookies," Rifun told him flatly. "Have one. They're actually very good."

"We've been busting our asses and you're out buying cookies?"

"Why, yes, and I got them from the one and only Micaiah Durvin. Apparently, he and his brother own a bakery in Charleston."

"Good to know," Isthim observed. "Do they have the Book of Abilities?"

"It was a chance encounter. I wore a Disguise to check it out, just to be sure it was them. And yes, it is them."

"Any sign of the girlfriend?" Cassius inquired.

Rifun shook his head. "None. However, what I did find was far more intriguing. They have an employee by the name of Tommen Forbes, whom they call the Chivalrous Welshman."

Isthim shrugged. "So?"

"In the Authored Books, there is mention of a series which, forty years ago, did not yet exist. It was titled *The Chivalrous Welshman*, and it had the most Books of any series by the Author. Furthermore, the cave which we have been exploring was dedicated to one Tommen Forbes, a child who disappeared into the cave a century and a half ago."

"The child's footprints we found," Cassius stated. "But he went down the other tunnel."

"Which could have had an exit or led back to the main tunnel, we don't know. But I'd be willing to bet that he knows where the journal is. At the very least, he's a starting point."

"And what do you make of there being a series about him, allegedly?" Isthim wondered.

Rifun shifted his stance. "It means he's important. If he is being trained by Micaiah, it could very well make him one of the greatest Akari-bearers ever. I'm going to follow him a bit, try to discern his abilities, see if I can't find a way to get him on our side. An Akari-bearer like that shouldn't be wasted on bumbling pacifists like the Akarin."

"How do you figure he's that great?" Cassius asked, clearly annoyed by the idea.

"Why else would the Author dedicate so much time and so many Books to his existence? And if he does possess the Book of Abilities, and if he's learning from it, even in secret, it would be a boon to us and a dagger to the Akarin."

"If he has or had the journal, and if he is being trained by Micaiah, there's a greater chance that the Akarin has the journal, if they didn't immediately destroy it."

"All the better reason to infiltrate and take command of the Akarin, wouldn't you say?"

Cassius gave him a look. "Doug? Really?"

"Who better?"

The dark-skinned man sighed. "Well, to add fuel to your savior's fire, the Captain of Region Four, District Four is one Walter Forbes."

"Yes, I saw that," Rifun said. "He appears to be Tommen's 'father' though I doubt his biological one. We should investigate him for Akari-bearing talent also."

"His given name is Owain Fforidd," Cassius went on. "He was once a murderer condemned to death at Beaumaris Gaol."

"The one who escaped?" Rifun was fairly certain that it was in their Authored Book.

"The very same."

"And with all these coincidences, you don't think it might be a tad important?"

"What do you suggest?" Isthim wondered. "We still have political issues to take care of, not the least of which is one Lily Guile who, after forty years of impossible wealth and influence, has apparently decided to stop playing nice with her handlers. And there is the matter of dealing with the Akarin."

"Have they come out of their hole to fight, or to yell and complain?"

"Depends on whether they have the Book of Abilities."

"Something that can be discovered through infiltration." Rifun looked at Cassius who gave him a hard stare.

"And there are a few other loose ends to tie up," Isthim told him. "The most pressing one dealing with the Turitians and a certain Psiaco space pirate known as Captain Morain leRou Titik."

Rifun nodded. "I'll talk to them. In the meantime, has any progress been made on the part of Julianna?"

"Some, yes," Isthim answered.

"Good, because I waited for her for a little while, sitting at a computer, but she never showed up."

"I'll introduce you to our intermediary next week."

"Lovely." Rifun broke out in a yawn. "Well, all this excitement is good and all, but I think the adrenaline is starting to wear off."

"If you would have been here earlier, we could have had a longer meeting," Cassius said sarcastically.

"But then I would not be informed of the state of the world."

"It's shit."

"Yes, it is, but it is highly technological shit. And we're going to be in the middle of it for the next few months, I think. It might be worth knowing what we may be up against. Technology will always be used against the people first in order to exert control and figure out its weaknesses before they become a problem for those in control. Look around and there are security cameras everywhere, always someone watching. But Earth is not yet Engaged. Our actions may have to be clandestine for the time being. Keep that in mind." He paused. "And since no one apparently enjoys a good cookie every now and again—" He snatched the untouched bag of cookies from the table. "—I will take them for myself."

He left the meeting room and headed for his chambers. Everything appeared undisturbed, if a bit dusty, just like last time. He set the cookies aside and went about building a fire in the hearth to drive away the chill that had settled in. When that was good and roaring, he turned his attention to his shrine.

He carefully picked up each piece, cleaned it off, and replaced it. With that accomplished, he prepared a meal and set it down reverently before bowing to pray.

This was more than destiny. This was fate. All of this had been dictated by the Author, planned years in advance. Lifetimes, even. Perhaps even before she put pen to paper she knew all that was to happen. It was as his ancestors had always known, that fate was fixed. Even his choices seemed illusory because it was all predetermined. But that was all right. He was happy to be used as a tool of the Author. Those who fought tended to get hurt. Those who agreed were often the ones who hurt them.

Rifun would be that way now. He would be the weapon that the Author wielded, bringing justice and correction to an errant universe, destroying the Time industry and bringing down the hammer on the wayward, pathetic Akarin. He would free the universe from the fear and tyranny of the Borelians. Above all, he was going to slay the dragon spirit that resided within Cassius.

And somehow, Tommen Forbes was going to help him pull it off.

Author's Note
Michigan, 2021

I think the thing that surprised me the most about this particular book is that I never, in any stage of outlining or thinking or fooling around, did I intend or expect to sneak in a love story. Not once did it cross my mind to give anyone a genuine love interest. Certainly it didn't fit with either Cassius' or Isthim's disposition, and Julianna had her own path to walk. And yet, when I found myself staring at Lalao on the page, I knew exactly what had to happen, that it could not happen any other way.

There are many instances in the journey of a book where something will stun even the author, and this was certainly one of them. It pained me to have to end it the way it did. This does not mean, however, that Lalao is completely out of the picture. Rifun still cares very deeply for her, to the point where he completely healed her of her ailments. This will not go unnoticed, and she will not simply retire to a pleasant memory. In fact, Lalao is set to make an appearance in another series that I haven't even formally announced at this time.

So there you go. There's the official teaser announcement.

I think the second thing that stunned me was that this book ended up being significantly shorter, by page count, than *In the Hands of the Enemy*, although they are almost of equal word count. I think that owes to having more passages of introspection and reflection. I expected it might be about equal, maybe a tad shorter, but I was not prepared for a discrepancy of sixty or seventy pages!

And if there is anything that I have to lament, in the present day, it's that the third book, *The Hand Holding the Knife*, will have to be put off a year, swapped with another single novel, one that has been referenced several times, *Chasing the White Bear*.

The simple reason for this is that I try to release the books in a specific order (although you, Reader, may choose in what order you read, and the surprise only works once while the books are being freshly released). *The Hand Holding the Knife* is going to parallel *The Chivalrous Welshman*, except the final book that it parallels will not actually be released until 2023! This is a bit of a problem, one I had not anticipated. Instead, I decided to swap *The Hand Holding the Knife* with *Chasing the White Bear*, Kayla's novel which may whet the appetite for Micaiah's series coming out after *The Hands of Time* is finished.

If you're staring at the words on this page and getting all discombobulated because you're still trying to figure out the mysteries of the Books and everything else, please, persevere, and follow the rabbit hole to the end. Think things through and consider the implications on more than a fictional entertainment level.

I love you all, and I'm excited to start tying up some of these loose ends and bringing it all together.